It Was A Century In Which
The Hunting Ground of Manhattan
Became A Bustling City . . .
and The Dutch DeKuyper Family
Became An American Dynasty.

JACOB ADAM DE KUYPER, bastard son of a
first Dutch settler, mixed his blood with an English beauty and left their son James with a proud
name and a family fortune.

But young JAMES DE KUYPER turned his back
on riches for high-seas adventure with the infamous Captain Kidd, whose gold fell into the
keeping of James' son Jan.

JAN DE KUYPER, with his passionately courageous wife, was forced to embroil the family in a
dangerous rebellion that soon would flame into
Revolution.

ON MAIDEN LANE

*The Continuing Saga
of New York City*

Other Avon Books by
Bruce Nicolaysen

FROM DISTANT SHORES

BRUCE NICOLAYSEN

THE NOVEL OF NEW YORK 1682-1761

ON MAIDEN LANE

AVON
PUBLISHERS OF BARD, CAMELOT, DISCUS AND FLARE BOOKS

ON MAIDEN LANE is an original publication of Avon Books. This work has never before appeared in book form.

AVON BOOKS
A division of
The Hearst Corporation
959 Eighth Avenue
New York, New York 10019

First Avon Printing, August, 1981

AVON TRADEMARK REG. U.S. PAT. OFF. AND IN OTHER COUNTRIES, MARCA REGISTRADA, HECHO EN U.S.A.

Printed in the U.S.A.

10 9 8 7 6 5 4 3 2 1

For
Frederick Martin Nicolaysen
A gentle man.

ACKNOWLEDGMENTS

Jerry Goldberg/Gerard C. Mooney—who did excellent work on the maps.

Julie Garriott—whose superb editing enriched the text.

Peter Miranda—his friendly enthusiasm has always encouraged me.

Deirdre Hanssen—her creative advice during the writing was a big help.

Barbara Cohen—who might possibly know New York as well as I.

Kjirsti and Inger—my daughters, whose love enriches my life.

AUTHOR'S NOTE

This is book two of *The Novel of New York*. The years it spans—1682 to 1761—were a time of great expansion, uncertainty, and crisis. No one alive today would recognize the New York of these eight decades.

For a number of years the city was the pirate capital of the world. Captain William Kidd owned a fine house on Crown Street, renamed Liberty Street after the Revolution. His fellow brigands, with their jewel-encrusted daggers and heavy rings of Damascus gold, not only walked freely through the streets of the town, but often were entertained as house guests by the leaders of society.

Not that pirates were the only colorful New Yorkers of these years. As the eighteenth century began, citizens were treated to the sight of a royal governor who was also a transvestite: Edward, Lord Cornbury, enjoyed nothing more than attending his own parties dressed in his wife's clothing, flirting outrageously with male guests.

As in the first book of this series, the background of people and events has a basis in historical fact. George Washington appears, as do John Peter Zenger, Andrew Hamilton, and the Viscount Howe. But although such family names as de Witt, de Kuyper, Seixas, and Goelet were common in the New York of this time, the characters bearing them in this romance are inventions of the author.

Alice Livingston is also invented, but her point of view about women and their rights and freedoms was advocated by a good number of well-educated women of the time.

If these years were turbulent, they were also exciting, as the men and women of New York worked to develop the wealth of the new land. Their power and self-assuredness increased—and led inevitably to conflict with the mother country. Londoners thought of the colonies as profit-makers for themselves; the merchants of New York were beginning to think this was a lot of selfish rubbish. It would be these diverging economic views that, more than anything else, would lead to the American Revolution.

But that is another story.

CONTENTS

OUR STORY TO 1761

ENGLISH MONARCHS

Charles II	1660–1685
James II	1685–1688 (deposed; d. 1701)
William & Mary	1689–1702 (Mary d. 1694)
Anne	1702–1714
George I	1714–1727
George II	1727–1760
George III	1760–

ROYAL GOVERNORS OF NEW YORK

Major Edmund Andros	1674–1683
Colonel Brockholls	1683
Colonel Thomas Dongan	1683–1691
Henry Sloughter	1691–1692
Benjamin Fletcher	1692–1698
Richard Coote, Earl of Bellomont	1698–1701

Edward Hyde, Lord Cornbury	1702–1708
John, Lord Lovelace	1708–1710
Robert Hunter	1710–1720
William Burnet	1720–1728
Sir John Montgomerie	1728–1732
Colonel William Cosby	1732–1736
George Clarke	1736–1743
George Clinton	1743–1753
Sir Danvers Osborn	1753–1755
Sir Charles Hedley	1755–

to 1761

The de Kuyper family (omiting members not prominent in our story)

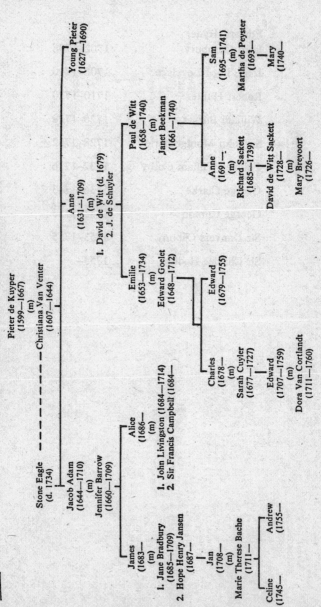

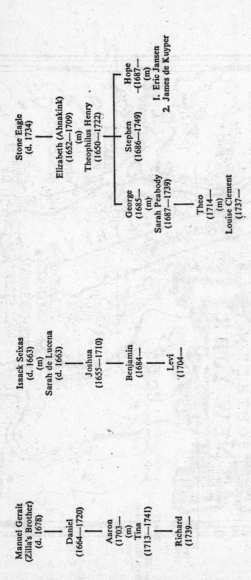

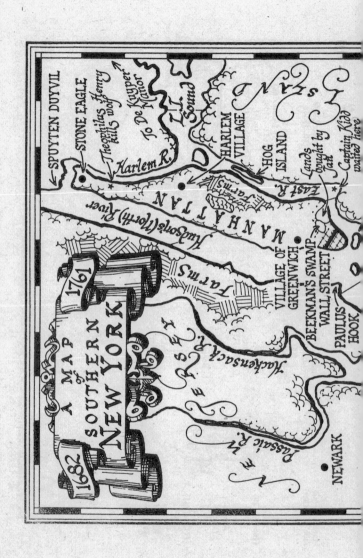

A MAP
of
SOUTHERN
NEW YORK
1682
1761

SPUYTEN DUYVIL
STONE EAGLE
Theophilus Henry
Kills wolf here
To De Kuyper
Manor
L.I.
Sound
Harlem R.
HARLEM
VILLAGE
HOG
ISLAND
Land's
bought by
Jan
Captain Kidd
waited here
MANHATTAN
East R.
Farms
Farms
Hudson's (North) River
Farms
Farms
VILLAGE OF
GREENWICH
BEEKMAN'S SWAMP
WALL STREET
PAULUS HOOK
Hackensack R.
N E W   J E R S E Y
Passaic R.
NEWARK
LONG ISLAND

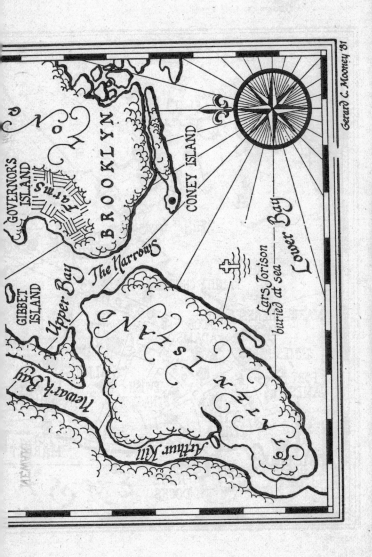

Gerard C. Mooney '81

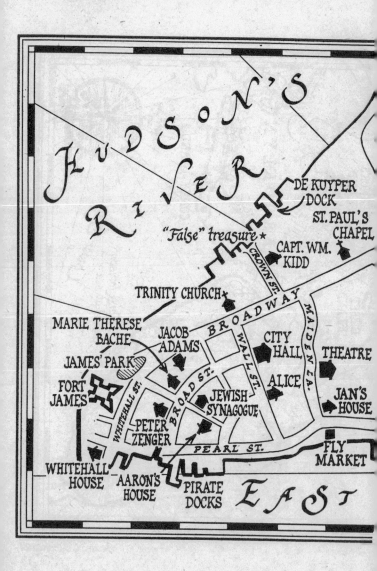

HUDSON'S RIVER

DE KUYPER DOCK

ST. PAUL'S CHAPEL

"False" treasure ★

CAPT. WM. KIDD

CROWN ST.

TRINITY CHURCH ★

BROADWAY

MARIE THERESE BACHE

JACOB ADAMS

WALL ST.

CITY HALL

MAIDEN LA.

THEATRE

JAMES' PARK

WHITEHALL ST.

ALICE

FORT JAMES

BROAD ST.

JEWISH SYNAGOGUE

JAN'S HOUSE

PETER ZENGER

PEARL ST.

FLY MARKET

WHITEHALL HOUSE

AARON'S HOUSE

PIRATE DOCKS

EAST

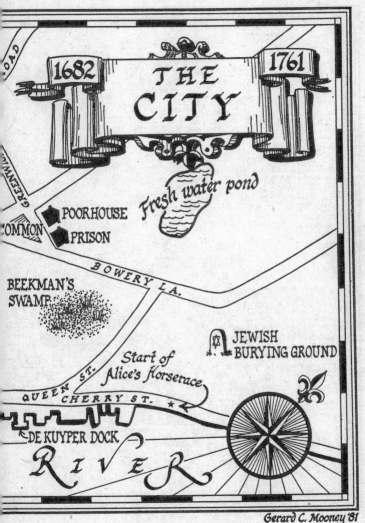

THE
CITY

1682   1761

GREENWICH ROAD

Fresh water pond

POORHOUSE
COMMON
PRISON

BOWERY LA.

BEEKMAN'S
SWAMP

JEWISH
BURYING GROUND

Start of
Alice's Horserace

QUEEN ST.
CHERRY ST.

DE KUYPER DOCK

RIVER

Gerard C. Mooney '81

1

De Kuyper Manor

1682–1688

JENNIFER DE KUYPER WAS TWENTY YEARS old and terrified.

She hurried the few blocks from the splendid de Kuyper mansion on Broad Way to the more modest home of her mother on Stone Street. Once she dared to glance up at the sky over New York, and the sight of the shooting star sent a chill through her body.

Her mother, Elizabeth Barrow, had ordered they spend the day in church along with many of the other women of the province. The good Dominie Nieuwenhuysen, three hundred pounds of righteousness, had assured the members of his flock in his self-satisfied way that a day of prayer would appease the Almighty and cause Him to recall the heavenly visitor. There were few in New York who had the education—or the bulk—to marshal arguments that might challenge the dominie's conclusions.

Jennifer lowered her eyes to keep from seeing the tail of the fiery comet and let herself into her mother's house through the servants' entrance at the back. Elizabeth Barrow, dressed all in black, was puttering around the kitchen, somber and cranky. She dispensed with any greeting for her daughter. "I don't suppose that husband of yours is going to church, is he?"

"No. He has . . . some business."

"Business!" Elizabeth said in contempt, deepening her frown. Her mouth was small and tight and the deeply etched lines in her cheeks gave them the appearance of a plowed field. The bitterness in her heart had made its

1

way to her face. "Jacob Adam and his business. Goddamn him."

Jennifer was a beautiful young woman with smooth, creamy flesh and rosy cheeks. She was slender, elegant; a doe. Her step was sprightly, yet there was an air of innocent sexuality about her. She had been shy as a child, a shoe-scuffer, and even to this day her hand would fly to her mouth when she was shocked—as now, when her own mother cursed her husband.

Elizabeth, not yet forty, was an angry ruin. She scuttled about as if she carried half again as many years, her once pretty features marred by a perpetual scowl. She was a widow, and no matter what she wore—her best green silk, rose-dyed cotton, or loom-woven wool—her clothes always looked like widow's weeds.

Her husband, Captain Barrow, the master of a slave ship killed in a mutiny, had died many years ago, leaving a young, pregnant widow who had desired much. But nothing had worked out the way she had hoped, the wishes and desires piling up like branches on a beaver's dam. The only bright spot had been her daughter, but even that joy had turned to dust when Jennifer married Jacob Adam de Kuyper, the man she loathed above all other men.

"You never give me any reasons why you don't like my husband," Jennifer said. It was a question that had been asked a hundred times.

"He's a devil," Elizabeth snapped. "I'm sorry you married him, but Franklin insisted on it. He *is* the head of the family," she added, and the look on her face told of her contempt for her older brother.

"You never tried to stop it."

Elizabeth looked angry. "What could *I* do? Franklin ordered me to keep quiet. He threatened to cut off my allowance from the family income if I didn't do what I was told."

"He couldn't do that!"

"When you're as old as I am you'll understand there isn't anything a man can't do to a woman. Who makes the laws and enforces them? Men, and they're all bastards. They take care of one another, and woe to any woman who tries to change things."

"But why do you so especially dislike Jacob Adam?" Jennifer persisted.

For a moment Elizabeth seemed about to speak, but she checked her tongue. "He's your husband and you might as well make the best of it. I won't be dragging out old stories. Now, let's get going to church."

The two women pulled dark-colored shawls about their shoulders and walked out through the front door. They avoided looking up at the celestial threat, and they did not talk. Both were lost in their thoughts about the virulent animosity that existed within the family.

Not that Jennifer didn't have her own problems with Jacob Adam. She was thoroughly intimidated by him. He was almost twice her age, more of her mother's generation. At one time, few people in the province would have raised an eyebrow if Jacob Adam had married Elizabeth instead of herself. But Jennifer knew there had never been the slightest possibility of that happening.

During the days when Jacob Adam was courting Jennifer, Elizabeth always managed to have something else to do when he called at their house. The actual details of the marriage had been worked out by Jennifer's uncle, Franklin Riverton.

Even in those days she had been intimidated by Jacob Adam, but he had not seemed as cold and distant as he became after the wedding. She had thought her fears would vanish once she was married. To her dismay, they had only grown worse.

"Serves you right for marrying a man so much older," Elizabeth had said.

The wedding had been arranged by Uncle Franklin, and there had been nothing Jennifer could do about it. In these times most marriages were arranged by the male elders, and the female participants had little to say about their own destinies.

She tried to analyze her fears, but they seemed to have no real basis; and when she thought about them one by one, they seemed almost silly. Her husband was not cruel or abusive; rather the opposite, keeping himself politely aloof. But she thought he used her as a convenience. She was *there*. She performed the duties appropriate to her high station as Mrs. Jacob Adam de Kuyper. And she served a function for his body. She hated the times they were in bed together and his hands touched her naked flesh. She did not resist or struggle, because that would not have been proper for a wife. Against her own will, there were times she actually enjoyed their union, and her own inconsistency confused and upset her. Afterward, while he slept, she would lie awake, staring at the ceiling, adrift from herself, a wounded animal.

Jennifer and her mother entered the church. Dozens of other women hurried in from the streets and alleys, many in tears, all prepared to spend the day in prayer. Jennifer forgot her family problems and joined the others in the common fear.

Many hours later she was still in the church, alternately on her knees and seated on the hard bench, listening to Dominie Nieuwenhuysen explain the workings of the universe. He spoke in English, although Dutch was still a common language among most of the people in his flock. In the past few years, however, as more English people arrived in the province, the dominie found it prudent to preach in the tongue of the reigning monarch.

"The shooting star is a sign of God's displeasure!" the dominie cried for the hundredth time. "It has been sent by God Himself to point out our errors!"

A collective shiver passed among the women, jammed one against another. Fear was transmitted from shoulder to shoulder, mind to mind. Jennifer could almost *smell* the terror wafting up from the woman on her left, and she crowded closer to her mother. Elizabeth was too much involved in the service to notice, her concentration devoted to the dominie's words.

"God demands atonement," the dominie said, his voice hoarse and cracking from the long hours of exhortation. "Atonement! And each one of you *knows* which of *your* sins is personally dragging us all down to hell!"

A low moan rose from the congregation, and scores of lips moved as the women mumbled out their pathetic confessions in a dirge of self-recrimination and scorn. "Look out the window," the dominie urged, flinging his hand upward toward the pale sky. "Look up at the message of the Lord." All eyes followed his direction, and the murmur increased as the women looked at the shooting star, the sign of the coming Armageddon.

As Nieuwenhuysen paced back and forth, Jennifer suddenly realized the man was enjoying all this. Actually enjoying it! What right did he have to frighten all these women half to death? How did he have special access to the wishes of God? And what did he really know about the shooting star? Jennifer was aware that men like her husband looked up at the shooting star, shrugged, and went back to their business. If Jacob Adam wasn't worried, why should *she* care? What *was* she doing in this place?

She had had enough of it all—the shouting, the moaning, the hard slats of the bench cutting into her flesh. She stood up and edged past her startled mother. Walking to the back of the church, she stopped for a last look at the dominie and his sickening performance. Her eyes met the minister's, and they locked briefly. She tried to be courageous, tried to stare him down, but the baleful look of the man was too much for her, and she turned and fled into the street.

She felt a moment's panic when she glanced up at the sky and saw the blazing tail of the shooting star framed against it, but then her nerve returned and she walked away from the church. She pulled the woolen shawl tight around her shoulders to ward off the crisp late afternoon air and decided, since it was close to supper time, to walk to her husband's office on Whitehall Street. They could return home together.

Jennifer passed the parsonage and admired the flowers in the freshly painted wooden box. It was very late in the year for such flowers, and she wondered if God gave a special dispensation to plants belonging to His spokesmen. A chilling thought came to her. If that fool Nieuwenhuysen was His spokesman, then she would be better off in believing as her husband did—in nothing at all. Not believing in God, of course, could have serious consequences, even deadly ones. But Jennifer knew that Jacob Adam had often ventured his opinions in public, and no man had been rash enough to bring him to task for it. Men like Dominie Nieuwenhuysen, it seemed, had the power to suppress only those who did not have the force to resist him.

After the parsonage there was a warehouse and a bakery, both of which were closed at this hour, and Jennifer quickened her steps as she made her way down the dirt road. The silent buildings and the empty street did little for her peace of mind on this dismal and gloomy day. Three old houses were next, leftovers from the earlier Dutch period, their weathercocks, small-paned dormer windows, and Holland-made bricks cemented together with a local lime mixture. Each of the houses had the traditional stoop that was built to protect it from the rising waters of the sea and the canals during flood times—useful enough in the lowlands of Holland but superfluous here in New York. Most of the windows on the houses were tightly shuttered, as if the inhabitants were trying to lock out the fiery visitor that could be seen in the sky.

At the end of the last house there was a narrow alley, and as Jennifer was crossing it, a sinister apparition suddenly lurched from the shadows. She was startled and jumped back, for the moment too terrified even to scream.

"What has we here?" the man growled. He staggered into the street and attempted to focus his bleary eyes on the woman. "And just where do you think you're going?"

After her initial fright, Jennifer commanded enough of her senses to realize the apparition was only a man—a small one at that—and drunk, so much so that he could barely remain on his feet. An overpowering smell of alcohol and other odors reached out from his body and assaulted her senses. Without a word she attempted to pass around him, but the drunk placed himself squarely in her path again. "I asked you a question, missus," he said.

"Please step aside," she said in a calm voice, fighting to keep it from quivering. This wasn't the first time she had been accosted in this manner. There were always a good number of ships in the harbor, and at times—at least so it seemed to the women of the town—the streets were filled with drunken sailors working off the tensions of weeks and months at sea. It had become such a problem that the governor had added several men to the watch and, in theory, the city below was patrolled twenty-four hours a day.

From his speech and dress Jennifer took the man for an English sailor. He was probably harmless most of the time; but still, when a man had too much to drink . . .

"If you don't get out of my way this second I'll cry out for the watch," she said in a surprisingly strong voice.

"The watch, is it?" the man said, and then he giggled. "Oh me bleedin' arse, call the watch on me, would you?" He giggled again and reached out and touched her arm.

The palm of her hand made a resounding "splat" as it connected with the sailor's face. The stubble of his beard hurt her skin; she could feel the tingling all the way to her elbow. The most dramatic effect of the blow, however, was that it knocked the man off his unsteady feet. He lay on his back in the dirt of the road, looking up at her with disbelief. "Call the watch on *me?* No, no, you bloody tart, it's me who's to call the watch on *you!*"

He propped himself up on one elbow and began to shout. "The watch! The watch! Bloody murder here! Help! Help! The watch!"

An answering cry echoed off the buildings, and Jennifer heard the sound of running feet, pounding hard on the dirt and coming fast. In moments two members of the governor's watch came huffing and puffing around the corner. One carried a musket and the other a wicked-looking six-foot wooden stave.

"Hold! Hold for the watch!" the man with the stave cried, hoping to prevent any further violence. He stopped when he came to the man on the ground. He looked at Jennifer, who was standing over the fellow, and his stern look as an enforcer of the law was replaced by bewilderment.

"What's going on here?" he asked.

"Ask him," Jennifer said. "He's a troublemaker."

"She struck me, she did," the sailor said, sounding grieved. "There I was minding my own business, and along she comes and knocks me down."

The confused watchman looked at Jennifer, noted her fine clothes, and then recognition came into his eyes. "It's Mrs. de Kuyper, isn't it?" Jennifer nodded, and the watchman turned back to the man on the ground and scowled. "Here, you foolish sot, just what are you trying to pull?"

"A dangerous woman that is," the man said as he lay on the ground, his accusing finger pointing up at the slender figure above him. "Do your duty, watchman, put her in the lockup."

The big watchman sighed. He reached down, grabbed

the tiny sailor by the collar, and yanked him to his feet. The man began to complain, but the watchman pushed him toward his companion. The second guard shoved his musket into the sailor's chest, causing his breath to come out with a whoosh and effectively ending his string of complaints.

The big watchman touched his hand to his cap. "Sorry about this, Mrs. de Kuyper, but we'll take care of him, don't you worry about that."

A smile crept across Jennifer's face. "I wouldn't be too rough on him if I were you," she said. "After all, I did knock him down."

The humor of the situation escaped the burly guard. " 'Tis a dreadful state of affairs when a lady like yourself can't be safe when she walks the streets of her own town." He shook his head. "These times, what are they coming to, that's what I want to know."

Jennifer nodded politely and continued on her way down the street. It was only after she had gone twenty paces that she realized she had completely forgotten about the shooting star. If it was that easy to forget, how bad could it really be?

She came at last to a three-story dwelling that housed Jacob Adam's multiple business interests. She paused, because she never felt quite at home in this place of commerce. Finally she took a deep breath and opened the door.

There was no one in the outer office. She went to the door at the rear and opened it. This room also was empty. But a door leading to another room was ajar, and she could hear voices coming from the other side. She crossed the room and was about to open the door when a loud laugh and a rough, unpleasant voice made her hesitate.

"Damn! That be most genrous of you, sor. Genrous! A bonus on top all t'other swag."

"I find that loyalty grows stronger as the reward increases," another voice said dryly, and Jennifer recognized it as her husband's.

"For this kind o' money I be chasin' every packet from Cape May to Curaçao," the gravelly voice said. " 'Tis a fortune we be discussin'."

"You won't forget part of that fortune is mine, will you?"

"But, sor," the gravelly voice protested in a tone of injured honor. " 'Tis now third voyage twixt you 'n' me. Dinna I beed fair 'n' square so far?"

"Perhaps," Jacob Adam said calmly. "But I see no accounting of jewels taken from the last ship."

"I know o' no jewels," Gravel Voice protested.

"A string of pearls. Three emerald rings. A diamond brooch. Taken from a lady passenger. Does this refresh your memory?"

There was a short silence. Finally Gravel Voice spoke again, this time in a subdued tone. "How'd ye be knowin' about them, not that I says they'd *be,* but just how'd ye be knowin'?"

"Don't play games, Hodges. I know. Don't do it again."

The gravelly voice was abject and penitent. " 'T'were a mistake, sor, all a mistake. They be such trinkets they slipped my mind. But no man can say John Hodges holds back on his mates, no indeed, sor, I be puttin' things to rights."

Jennifer de Kuyper had stood frozen throughout the conversation, and now she was afraid she'd heard things not meant for her ears. She was about to leave the house, but the sound of footsteps coming toward the door decided the issue for her. Rather than be caught behind the door, she quickly pushed it open and stepped into the next room. The two men were startled, and their expressions were far from friendly.

Jacob Adam relaxed when he recognized his wife. Then his mouth tightened in annoyance. He turned to the other man. "Captain Hodges, this is my wife."

Hodges was a large man with a bristling red beard that did not quite manage to cover coarse features that had been marked by knife and alcohol. But his eyes were alive and penetrating. The black spheres stared unblinkingly and made the girl shiver.

"Pleased to meet you, mum, a great honor indeed," the captain said. His mouth spread into a generous smile, but Jennifer was conscious only of the eyes that continued to bore into her very soul.

Jacob Adam too was staring at her in a curious fashion,

but did not speak. Jennifer became nervous. "I'm s-sorry if I . . . I interrupted you," she stammered.

"The captain was just leaving," Jacob Adam said.

Captain Hodges reacted as if he had been stuck by a pin. He stepped toward the door. "Aye, 'tis best I get aboard *Carib Isle* afore those thievin' gallows-bait gets too drunk to handle ship." He stopped in front of Jennifer and took off his hat, bending forward in an unexpected, courtly bow. "Best o' the day to you, mum."

"A pleasure," Jennifer mumbled, her cheeks turning red. She was very much aware of her husband's stare.

The captain left the room, his heavy boots thudding on the floorboards, the sound diminishing until the outside door was slammed. The room was plunged into silence.

Jennifer forced herself to look at her husband. "I didn't mean to . . . to overhear."

"And exactly what did you overhear?" Jacob Adam asked.

A long pause. "Nothing."

A slight smile came to his lips. "Then what are you apologizing for?"

She stood mute, her eyes lowered.

"What brings you here?" he asked, allowing a measure of softness to enter his voice.

"I've been in church most of the day—"

"Ah, yes, the day of prayer."

"Do you think the dominie could be right about the shooting star? Is it a sign of God's wrath?"

"Do you believe that?"

"I'm not sure," she said tentatively.

"It's not a sign of anything," he reassured her. "You don't get upset when you see the moon, why should a shooting star bother you?"

She stepped closer to him. "I feel safer when you're near me."

Jacob Adam was an imposing looking man, black haired and dark complexioned, slightly taller than average, as taut-skinned and spare at thirty-nine as he had been at twenty. The leanness of his face, punctuated by eyes that missed nothing, gave him a hawklike presence. The eyes, piercing yet opaque, were the feature no man or woman could forget about him. Most of the time his face was impassive, and it was impossible to read his thoughts.

His hands were strong and hairless. His face always looked freshly shaved, for despite his coloring, his beard was slight. He walked with a purposeful stride, his head erect; his manner was the sort that made other men step aside when they met him on the street. He dressed simply and wore no jewelry, but one might have thought he had just come from his tailor. He wasn't in the habit of smiling, but when he did, his face was unusually pleasant.

He took his wife's hand in his, and they walked outside, to Fort James. They passed the somber walls and stopped at the land's end. The Upper Bay stretched before them. In the weak last light of the day they could see the Narrows—two hulking masses, the shoulders of a headless giant rising from the waters.

The shooting star could be seen in the darkening sky, a bright speck of light followed by a lengthy tail. It was racing away from the sun, passing the earth, returning to its birthplace in the hidden depths of the cosmos.

The pair watched the spectacular show in the sky until Jacob Adam's attention was diverted by a heavily laden merchantman sailing up the bay toward the tip of the island.

"That would be *Sussex Light*," he said. "Overdue from Curaçao."

"What is she carrying?"

"Sugar and rum, most likely."

"It amazes me how such tiny things are able to sail on the ocean," she said.

"*Sussex Light* is one of the biggest ships afloat," he said. "About three times larger than the one that brought my father to Manhattan."

"I remember your father. He was a kind man," Jennifer said. "Once he gave me candy. After that I used to wait for him in the street. But I hardly ever saw him again. He was one of the first white men to see Manhatan, wasn't he?"

"One of the first to *live* here," Jacob Adam said, "but there were others who saw it before him."

Jennifer had been raised in the proper fashion of the day. She knew how to cook and sew, cater to a husband and children, and take care of a household. She had been taught to sing and knew the services of the Reformed Church by heart. Any further education was considered useless for a female. Therefore the extent of her husband's knowledge always amazed her. "Who was here before your father?" she asked.

Jacob Adam was not a scholar, nor did he care to be. He was a shrewd trader, a merchant, and a creator of profit. But since Manhatan was the source of his profit, he was interested in everything about it. "The first white man who came to New York was a Florentine named Giovanni da Verrazzano. He sailed for the king of France and searched for an inland passage to the Indies. In 1524 he sailed through the Narrows and anchored off the tip of Manhatan."

"Why didn't he claim the land for France?" Jennifer asked.

"He did, but the French king wasn't interested in anything but the inland passage, and the claim was never taken seriously."

"And then the Dutch came?"

His wife's ignorance did not surprise Jacob Adam. Even the most astute traders he dealt with rarely knew the details of the white men's earliest years on Manhatan, which they considered useless information.

"Estevan Gomez arrived in 1525. He was a Portuguese in the service of the king of Spain, a man who had been with Magellan on the first circumnavigation of the globe. He was a Negro."

"A Negro!" Jennifer said, astounded. "The second man to come to New York had black skin?"

Jacob Adam nodded. "That surprises everyone. Gomez wasn't too impressed by our island, so he sailed down to Brazil, where he was captured by cannibals and eaten."

Jennifer shuddered. Such things happened, of course, but did one have to speak of them?

"After Gomez there were others," Jacob Adam continued. "Jean Allefonsce in 1542, and Jehan Cossin of Dieppe in 1570. Finally, in 1609, Henry Hudson arrived and claimed the land for the Dutch East India Company."

"And the river is named after him," Jennifer said, relieved at finally recognizing a name.

"Yes, although it was originally named after Prince Maurice of the Netherlands. When the English took this place away from the Dutch, they renamed the river. Hudson, although he was sailing for the Dutch at the time, was an Englishman."

Jennifer looked out at the dark hulk of the ship making its way toward the quay. "Was Hudson's ship as big as that one?"

Jacob Adam shook his head. "That ship weighs two hundred tons. Hudson's ship, the *Half Moon*, was an eighty-ton galliot. He was looking for the mysterious inland passage, just like the earlier explorers. The difference was, the Dutch recognized the value of this land, the others didn't. The merchants back in Amsterdam created the Dutch *West* India Company to begin trading for our rich furs."

Jennifer looked around at the comfortable little settlement that was New York and shook her head. "It must have been awful here when there was nothing. No buildings, no people, just . . . Indians."

"I don't know," Jacob Adam said. "The early explorers were pursuing a dream. They went out into the unknown to find what no other man had found before them. What's wrong with that?"

Jennifer looked at her husband to see if he was making fun of her, but she could see he was not. "Nothing, I suppose," she said uncertainly.

"They came looking for riches—mountains of gold and silver. But most of them didn't have the sense to recognize the real riches they had found. They wasted their time on things of less value." Then, after a long pause, he added, "Things that are a waste of time, like your coming down to my office to spy on me."

Jennifer's hand flew to her mouth. "No! I didn't. I would never do such a thing."

"Then why were you skulking about in the outer office?"

"I came to walk home with you."

"If you want to know anything about my work, I'll be happy to explain it to you," he said.

Jennifer came close to tears. It was so unfair. To be accused of *this;* and after spending the entire day in church with that dreadful dominie. "I came to your office because I was afraid of the shooting star and I wanted to be near you."

"We must be honest with each other," he said, trying to

inject warmth into his voice. He put his arm around her shoulder. "And let's not have any tears. We should be able to speak what's on our minds. After all, we *are* man and wife."

They continued walking in silence, and Jennifer felt herself torn between several emotions. Having his arm around her made her feel, for the first time today, safe from the shooting star. But it didn't make her feel any closer to him. They walked together, yet apart. They were strangers. It was odd, she thought, for such a couple to be married.

How could he think she had been spying on him? Didn't he know her at all? Didn't he even try to understand how her mind worked?

Jennifer had many questions, but few answers.

The house on Broad Way had been repainted and given a new roof, but it was still much the same as it had been in Pieter's day. When the old man had died, the house had passed to his son Jacob Adam, who now lived in it with his bride.

As they entered the house, Jennifer gave a last suspicious glance at the comet in the sky, and then the roof sheltered her from the annoying presence. They entered the keeping room, with its cheerful fire and the smells of the good supper being prepared there by Zilla. Two servants worked quietly in the background.

"I was worried you wouldn't be home in time," Zilla said. "Supper's just about ready."

As Jacob Adam sat down, Jennifer excused herself and left the room.

"Aren't you worried about the shooting star?" Jacob Adam asked.

"No. I figure the Lord put it there, so it must be good. It's bothering Jennifer, though. She spoke about it this morning."

"She should have your sense," he said.

"Now don't you always be picking on that girl," Zilla said sharply. "She's young and got a lot to learn. You have to be more patient."

Jacob Adam accepted the rebuke. The seventy-year-old black woman was the only person who could tell him what to do.

The back door opened and Zilla's nephew, Daniel Gerait, came in. He looked startled to see the man at the table. "Mister de Kuyper! Didn't know you were home, sir."

"Hello, Daniel," Jacob Adam said.

"I was just looking over your horses in the stable."

"And?"

"They look fine."

"As good as most of the ones you see at the track?"

Daniel smiled. "Well, we have some pretty nice horse-flesh out there, sir, but your horses stack up pretty good."

"Which means you're not impressed."

"Well, now," Daniel said, becoming uncomfortable. "I didn't say that."

"Will you stop teasing Daniel," Zilla said. "If he sees better horses at the track, it's all your fault. You got him the job."

Daniel was the groundskeeper of the Newmarket Race Course on Long Island, where the local farmers and merchants gathered on race days during the summer, discussing the horses and wagering large sums of money among themselves. As commissioner of the park, Jacob Adam received a share of all the proceeds. It had proved to be a tidy investment in its own right; and its success had increased the worth of the surrounding land, which he owned.

Daniel had taken over the job from his father, Manuel, who had died several years ago. After building the racecourse for Jacob Adam, Manuel had stayed on as head groundskeeper. He developed a love for riding and spent many hours exercising the horses. He would have liked to participate in the races, but a horse would have been too severely handicapped with Manuel's two hundred and fifty pounds on his back.

Jacob Adam had been at the track the day the old man met his end. A young boy was exercising a half-wild two-year-old. The colt ran out of control and bounded over the fence. The exercise boy, holding on for dear life, began screaming as the horse crossed the pen area toward the fence on the other side.

Without a moment's hesitation, Manuel jumped forward into the runaway's path, grabbed the bridle straps, and forced the horse's head down into a position where the animal could no longer see ahead of himself. But the forward lunge of the beast swept Manuel off his feet, and he was dragged along the ground, the flashing hooves cutting into his chest and groin. Despite the punishment, the man held on until the horse finally stopped. But mortal damage had been done. Manuel's body was torn in a score of places, the blood turning his clothes and the ground red.

The doctors patched him up as best as they could, but Manuel was over seventy years old and no longer had the reserves to recover from such wounds. He lingered for several days. In his last moments of consciousness he spoke to Jacob Adam.

"I was your daddy's man, and I was your man," he said. "I want to thank you for everything. Especially what you've done for Zilla."

"No matter what I do for Zilla, it will never be enough," Jacob Adam said.

The old man reached out and touched the other's hand. Then his eyes closed, and he slipped into a coma that would hold him until the last breath had passed from his lips.

His place at the track, at the insistence of Jacob Adam, who knew it would please Zilla, had been taken by his son.

They were very different men. While Manuel had been a giant contemptuous of danger, Daniel was slightly built, introspective, and usually careful about putting himself in jeopardy. He was very shy, and Jacob Adam was certain he was uncomfortable around white men.

"Well, I have to get going," Daniel said. "Good seeing you, Mister de Kuyper."

He kissed Zilla, smiled again at Jacob Adam and left through the rear door.

"He's looking well fed and sassy," Jacob Adam said.

"Sassy!" Zilla waved her hand. "There's not a sassy bone in that man's body. Too bad he's not more like his father."

"He gets along pretty well as he is."

"Of course he does," Zilla said, not believing it. "So what have *you* been up to?" she asked.

Jacob Adam realized she wanted to change the subject. "I'm thinking of building a new house," he said.

"What's wrong with this one?"

"Nothing. But I saw the de Schuylers' new house on upper Pearl. If they can afford a place like that, so can we."

"Since when do you care about that sort of thing?"

He shrugged. "I don't. But a certain amount of show is good for business. People think you must know what you're doing if you appear prosperous."

Zilla dipped a wooden spoon into a pot containing deer meat in a thick brown sauce. Satisfied with the taste, she took the pot from the fire and began to place the meat on a heavy pewter platter. Most families ate from wooden trenchers—wooden slabs with depressions for the food. They were of a substantial size, and two people ate from the same trencher. The de Kuypers ate from pewter plates and used silver spoons and knives. Jacob Adam had also recently acquired a set of the latest fashion in cutlery— forks. There were probably no more than several dozen on the entire island of Manhatan. Jacob Adam's forks were of sterling silver and had been made in London. Everyone who sat at his table was forced to use these new-fangled things—everyone except Zilla. She refused, commenting that a spoon had been good enough during her seventy years of life and she wasn't going to change now. Jacob Adam, as usual, deferred to Zilla.

"I had a visitor today," she said.

"And who was that?"

"Your sister. She was nosing about, trying to find out what it is her son is doing these days."

"Paul works for me. Anne knows that. He was also appointed secretary to Governor Andros. She knows that, too."

"Yes, but she wants to know what he *does*." Zilla stopped and smiled at the man she considered her son. "That boy is just like you. Knows how to keep things secret. Must be in his blood."

Paul de Witt was, indeed, much like himself, Jacob Adam thought with satisfaction—intelligent, and eager to exploit any situation to his own advantage. His own father, David de Witt, had been an astute man of business, but David had died years ago during the Dutch reoccupation of the town, leaving a void in the young man's life. Anne had remarried. Her new husband was Jacob de

Schuyler, but he was hardly a model for a bright young boy. Jacob de Schuyler was a pleasant chap who managed some of his father's properties, but much preferred to spend his time at the racecourse or in a cozy tavern.

Jacob Adam had arranged Paul's appointment as secretary to the governor. It suited his purpose to have a pair of eyes close to the source of English power. The English had come back, this time for good, it seemed. When war had erupted between Holland and England in 1673, a strong Dutch flotilla under Admiral Evertsen entered the Upper Bay and took possession of the city without the firing of a single cannon. The English governor, Francis Lovelace, was in much the same position as Peter Stuyvesant had found himself ten years before: without enough troops or weapons to successfully mount a defense. Anthony Colvé was named the new Dutch governor, and he proceeded to change all the names back. New York reverted to New Amsterdam, Albany was renamed New Orange, Hudson's River was again called the Mauritius.

All this was met with apathy on the part of men like Jacob Adam, to whom the wars of Europe evoked little more than a yawn. The next year, when the Dutch and English signed a peace treaty and New Amsterdam once again was handed over to the English, the names were changed back to the ones honoring the Duke of York.

"I'll drop by to see Anne tomorrow," Jacob Adam said. "If she has any questions she should come to me rather than pester you."

"Oh, I don't mind her pestering. It reminds me of old Mister Pieter. He used to try and get me to tell him what you were up to."

"Did you tell him?"

"How could I tell him? I never knew myself what you were up to most of the time," she said, and smiled. "I can understand what's going through Anne's mind. She just worries that her son is up to no good."

"If making money is up to no good, then that's what he's doing."

Jennifer came back into the room, and the three sat down at the table. The de Kuypers' two servants brought the food; there was little talking as Jacob Adam, Jennifer and Zilla devoured enormous helpings from the pewter plates.

After dinner Jacob Adam left the house for a tavern where he was to meet two men on business. Zilla retired to her room for the night, and Jennifer was left alone in the parlor, a handsome room with fine, substantial pieces of furniture including a tall, pendulum-driven, wood-cased clock; a cupboard displaying pieces of pewter and silver; an oak sideboard filled with forks, knives, and spoons. An oil painting of Jacob Adam hung on the wall. But for all this wealth, Jennifer was not a happy bride.

She sat in the room listening to the gentle ticking of the clock. After a time it seemed to be speaking directly to her. "Wait . . . wait . . . wait . . . wait . . ." Wait? For what? What should she be waiting for? And then she knew what she really wanted—a child. When a child entered the house, everything would change. She would change. Her mother would change. Jacob Adam would change. Yes, a child was the answer, she thought, and hopefully felt her belly. It was as flat as ever.

She sighed. Well, it would only be a matter of time. At least there would be some reward for the many nights she let herself be used by her husband.

Jacob Adam left his house and walked across town toward the dock area on the East River. A fine, misting rain had begun to fall, and while other men turned up their collars and hunched their heads, Jacob Adam strode along as if the drizzle did not exist.

A group of men had started a fire in an empty lot off Broad Street, and they huddled around the yellow flames to chase the chill from their bones. New York was beginning to have a fair number of homeless men, and they existed as best they could with whatever they could find. At least once a week the body of a pauper was found in an alleyway, or under someone's stoop.

Jacob Adam came to Coenties Alley and turned down the narrow, poorly lit street. His destination was the Dark Ship tavern in the middle of the block. There was an altercation going on in front of the building next to the tavern. It was the commonest sort of lodging house, where, for a pence or two, a man could obtain a straw bed for the night and a chance to warm himself in front of a fire. The smell of frying bacon wafted up from the cellar kitchen. A man was singing a sea chantey.

Jacob Adam paused to see what was happening.

An old man, clothed in an indescribable collection of rags, had just been forcibly ejected from the building. The lodging house keeper, a burly fellow whose immense arms hung loosely from a hoglike torso, had a self-satisfied look on his face.

"Don't try to sneak in again," he said, slapping his hands together as if to cleanse them of the dirt from the other's clothing.

The unfortunate old man picked himself out of the mud. "I'll have the money tomorrow, Harry, by Jesus I promise!"

"By Jesus, then you can stay here tomorrow night," the man said, with an admiring laugh at his own wit.

The old man's head drooped. He turned away and shuffled down the alley until he found a doorway. He stepped into it out of the rain and stood there, shivering and mumbling to himself.

Jacob Adam continued past the lodging house and came to the door of the Dark Ship tavern.

It was dim and dingy inside. Men spoke in low voices and the chink of mugs and bottles on wooden tables came from all sides. A haze of tobacco smoke hung in the air and mingled with the odor of unwashed bodies.

The owner spotted Jacob Adam the moment he came through the door. He pointed toward a small booth at the back, and Jacob Adam made his way across the room, scarcely glancing at the men who lounged at the tables. They were sailors and laborers, robbers and footpads, the dregs of their world, and they pretended not to notice the well-dressed man as he passed by. The Dark Ship tavern was a den of thieves, and Jacob Adam often used it for such purposes as tonight's meeting. The men at the tables were well aware of who he was, and also aware it was best to pretend ignorance.

The man who waited in the booth was an English sea captain named Barrent. He had a hard face, and his eyebrows consisted of a single tuft of grayish hair over each lid. His neck was heavily muscled, creating the illusion that his bald, bullet-shaped head came up directly from his shoulders. There were knobby lumps of flesh on his neck, and one on his right cheek. His hands were red and gnarled, and the knuckles had the appearance of having been broken many times.

"Mister de Kuyper," he said politely in a voice that was too high pitched to go with his fierce body.

Jacob Adam nodded, and they sat in silence until Robert de Pauw came into the tavern, saw them, and made his way to the booth. Like Jacob Adam, de Pauw looked out of place here.

"A drink, eh?" he said as he dropped his considerable bulk into a rough-hewn chair. De Pauw's face was blotchy and puffed, and he had developed a wheeze.

A blowsy waitress came over, her ample bosom half falling out of the top of her dress, her eyes openly appraising these finely dressed men. She was in her late twenties, but her lined and knowing face was that of a forty-year-old.

The men ordered beer, and the waitress was about to go and fill their request when her gaze strayed to the fireplace along the left side of the room. "Damme!" she said. "That pest again."

Jacob Adam realized she was looking at the man he had seen thrown out of the lodging house. The old fellow had sneaked into the tavern and was now trying to warm himself by the fire. He was crouching to make himself as small as possible, and he stared straight ahead as if contemplating the horror of his life.

The waitress started toward him, obviously with the intention of chasing him out into the night.

"Wait!" Jacob Adam commanded sharply. The waitress stopped and looked back quizzically.

"Give him this," Jacob Adam said, handing her a shilling. "Let him buy himself a drink or two." The waitress looked at the coin, shrugged and dropped it in the old man's lap as she passed him. The old fellow was startled at first, but then his mouth spread into a wide, toothless grin as he understood this unexpected windfall of good fortune.

"Who's he?" de Pauw asked.

"Let's get on with our business," Jacob Adam said.

They talked for twenty minutes. De Pauw downed mug after mug of the fragrant, heady beer. Captain Barrent finished a pair, while Jacob Adam sipped from a single mug, half of which remained untouched as their business was coming to a close.

"Then it's agreed," Jacob Adam said. "We'll buy the ship and pay the cost of outfitting and supplying her. Half the profits will be returned to us for our investment. The other half will be for you and the crew."

"To be divided as I see fit," Captain Barrent said.

"That is your concern."

"Then it be a bargain," the captain said, reaching across the table and shaking hands with Jacob Adam.

"Be sure to take only French ships," de Pauw said, wagging his finger like a crone. "There would be hell to pay if you bothered an Englishman."

"Who is to know what happens on the seas?" the captain asked.

Jacob Adam gave his head an impatient shake; he didn't want to pursue this line of conversation. The captain understood. "If that be the way you want it, that be the way," he said.

Robert de Pauw downed another half mug of beer. "I still don't know why the ship must be registered in my name," he complained to Jacob Adam. "Dammit, you're putting up half the money."

"I've already explained that," Jacob Adam said mildly. "Half a dozen ships are already registered in my name. I plan to use them in the flour trade. If my competition thinks I own too many ships, they might cause trouble with the governor. The ship has to be in your name."

"Can't say that I'd like to be known as a pirate," de Pauw grumbled.

"*I'm* not a pirate," Captain Barrent said indignantly. "As we've agreed, our prey will only be bloody French ships. 'Tis a service to His Majesty I'll be doing by helpin' drive the Frenchies off the seas."

"Exactly," Jacob Adam said. "And now, if we have no more business, I'd like to get home to bed."

Robert de Pauw's flabby features broke out in an enormous grin. "And that pretty new bride of yours, eh?"

Jacob Adam became annoyed. "I don't think that's a fit subject of conversation."

"Come now, de Kuyper. Jennifer Barrow is one of the prettiest girls in New York. I mean no offense. You're a lucky man."

Jacob Adam pretended to soften. "I'm sorry I took offense. I dislike that sort of talk."

He rose from his chair and started for the door. The English captain walked beside him. "A word in private, if you please."

They stood outside the tavern. Barrent looked about to satisfy himself they spoke in privacy. "Twixt you 'n' me, does it matter what flag a ship flies?"

"No."

"Then all this talk of Frenchies is just for de Pauw?"

"Your job is to capture ships. I don't want to know who they are or where they come from."

"And the flags they carry?"

"Are of no interest to me."

"And to no man on the bottom of the sea."

"We understand one another."

"Aye, it be settled proper."

"I wouldn't want de Pauw to know about this. Now and then he has pangs of conscience."

"Aye, he seems an honorable gent."

"Honorable men die broke," Jacob Adam said, parting from the captain and walking toward his house. He was pleased with the work of the past few months. Piracy was becoming a curse in the new world. Rather than be one of its victims, he had decided to share in the profits. Three ships now sailed the seas as pirates on funds secretly provided by him. The English government, of course, loudly denounced piracy, but as long as the victims were French or Spanish, the English really didn't care. In fact Governor Andros had let it be known that ships attacking French vessels were not to be considered pirates at all, but rather as privateers in the service of His Britannic Majesty. Jacob Adam took this as a mandate to enter the business.

He insisted that the ships be registered in the name of his 'partner,' Robert de Pauw, in case the government later changed its position. He was certain a time would come when pirates would no longer be looked upon with such tolerance. When that day came, he would be able to stand with the innocent.

De Pauw, as always, was a useful man to have around.

Paul de Witt was courting Janet Beekman. The pair

were enjoying an early morning walk before Paul went to work. It was obvious the young man was in love from the way he looked at her, the way he held her hand as he helped her cross the dirt streets, the attentiveness he showed to her every need.

Paul was twenty-two, and physically almost another edition of his late father; but the model for his life was his uncle, Jacob Adam de Kuyper.

Paul's skin was fair, and his hair was the lightest of browns, almost blond. He wasn't particularly handsome, but there was an intelligence to his face, a shrewdness in his inquisitive eyes. His shoulders were broad and his body was somewhat thick, promising a man of considerable girth in his later years. When he became angry his neck would swell and a dark flush would spread over his face, warning of the formidable temper about to erupt.

Janet's height matched her escort's. Her eyes were as green as emeralds, and Paul adored the way the skin around them crinkled when she laughed. When someone told her a story she didn't believe, she would cock her head to the side and saucily close one eye. Her pretty face was a bit too long to admit of classic beauty, but the length only enhanced her lively arch charm. She was very fine-boned, with slender arms and ankles and a twenty-inch waist. Janet would probably always remain thin, even as Paul seemed destined to add weight.

She smiled and allowed him to help her. Holding the hem of her dress daintily, Janet stepped across the tiny puddle in the middle of Beekman Street. It had only recently been named in honor of her father, William, who had arrived in the province with Peter Stuyvesant. Only a few days ago she had been ·jumping over fences with several other girls to see who could leap the highest, but now she was too delicate to negotiate a small puddle.

They walked to the water's edge and stood together. As the mighty waters of the Hudson rolled past, he slowly moved his hand until it was holding hers. She thrilled him by rewarding the hand with a squeeze.

They looked across the bay toward the New Jersey shore, and Paul said, "See that island over there?"

"Oyster Island."

Paul shook his head. "The governor gave it a new name

yesterday—Gibbet Island," he said, proud at being able to impart news to this wonderful creature.

She frowned. "Why?"

"Because condemned men will be sent there to be hanged. The governor thought it more civilized to hang men out of sight of the people. The new name will be announced next week."

"I guess it's better to do it away from all the children," she said, and paused. "But I still think it's a sin to hang men."

Slipping away her hand, she turned and walked back toward the city. Paul followed, filled with regret that he had tried to show off knowledge he'd gained as secretary to the governor. "I . . . I'm sorry if it bothers you."

Janet walked briskly, her eyes straight ahead, and he hurried to stay at her side. They had gone fifty feet when he saw a shiny object on the ground. "Look, a coin!"

He reached down and picked up the dust-covered metal. He rubbed it on his sleeve. It was a sixpence.

The obverse showed Queen Elizabeth facing to the left, with a Tudor rose in the field behind her head.

"Doesn't that mean good luck?" Janet asked.

He handed the coin to her. "Yes. And when two people find a coin together, it means good luck for both of them."

"Together?"

He looked at her beautiful features and his heart skipped a beat. "I think so."

She looked crossly at the coin, and then her face broke into a wondrous smile. "I hope it's true. At least I want it to be true."

The world suddenly seemed a lovelier place, and Paul bravely held out his hand. She took it without hesitation and they resumed their walk.

"I'm sorry about—I mean I didn't realize things like that island would offend you."

"In time, Mister de Witt, I'm sure you will learn what pleases me and what offends me," she said playfully.

He held her hand tighter, and his head was spinning with joy. He did not speak, because he did not wish to interrupt the delirious thoughts racing through his mind. He was young, alive, and in love.

Janet Beekman, regarding him out of the corner of her eye, was pleased by the rapturous expression on his face. She wanted to tell him she loved him, but decided it would be better to make him wait a little longer.

But not too much longer, she promised herself.

Arriving at the government offices, Paul stepped through the door and was greeted by several men anxious to curry favor with the governor's secretary. He answered brusquely, and his fantasies of Janet Beekman disappeared as he realized it was time to get down to the business of the day. He passed through an antechamber and quietly entered the private quarters of the king's appointed representative in New York.

Within moments he was standing at the elbow of Governor Edmund Andros as the Englishman read the final version of the new Bolting Act that was to be placed before the council. Most of the wording was Paul's, although he had drawn it up under careful instructions from his uncle. It was a piece of legislation Jacob Adam dearly wished to be passed.

Andros read the final paragraph and looked up at his secretary. "Very good. We'll place it before the council at this morning's session."

The young secretary allowed himself the slightest of smiles.

"Do you think there will be much opposition?"

Paul de Witt hesitated. The governor was well aware there would be opposition to the law, not so much from the city council, but from the representatives of areas outside the city.

The rich wheat fields of the Hudson River Valley were turning out the best flour in the world. It was becoming as highly regarded a commodity as beaver pelts had been in the last generation. The demand for New York flour was increasing in all colonies of the New World, with requests coming from as far away as the West Indies and Europe itself. But the rapid expansion of the export trade was creating a problem. The individual farmers either did their own milling or brought it to a local mill to be ground and sorted—but to maintain prices it was necessary for all export flour to be of a standard quality. Under the traditional setup this was clearly impossible. The future sale of flour was threatened by a lack of uniformity.

One of the first to perceive this problem had been Jacob

Adam de Kuyper. He reasoned that if the trade were to increase, a greater control had to be exercised over all flour shipped out of the port. With this in mind he bought several houses on lower Pearl Street, adjoining the two he had inherited from his father. He converted these houses into a large grain processing plant, which remained empty and unused.

Next he inspected the old farm in mid-Manhatan that had once been worked by his father, but had been abandoned for years. On this land there was a stream beginning at the large lake in the center of the island and wending in a southeasterly direction toward the East River. Jacob Adam sent men to the farm to build a grist mill on the stream. The new mill stood waiting and ready to process wheat into flour.

Jacob Adam's plan was to get the city council to pass a law that would prohibit all flour from being exported until it had first been sent to New York, where it would be screened and graded—the process known in the trade as bolting. With a bolting law on the books the farmers could no longer do their own milling, but would be forced to hire a government-approved third party. Jacob Adam was ready. He would receive the grain, process it at the grist mill on the farm, bring it to the Pearl Street warehouse, and then sell it to the shippers, keeping a tidy profit for his efforts.

The farmers, naturally, were incensed by the imminent passage of a law that would cut their profits and create a monopoly controlled by the city slickers. But they were unorganized and could not agree on a clear-cut course of action.

"There will be opposition," Paul de Witt said, "but we must set standards for flour to be exported."

"I agree," the governor said, rising from his chair. "Shall we go to the arena to see how the Lions will fare against the Christians?"

Paul de Witt liked this Englishman. Edmund Andros had become governor when the English and Dutch had signed the peace treaty of 1674. He presided over the trial of the former governor, Francis Lovelace, who was accused of cowardice for not resisting the Dutch. Andros had no choice but to follow the directives of the Crown. Lovelace's sword was broken over his head and he was

sent from the court in disgrace. Rather than endure the
sneers of his fellow Englishmen, he retired to Hog Island
—a long, slender bit of land in the middle of the East
River. He lived there with his wife and daughter and had
few visitors. Governor Andros occasionally made trips to
the island to convince his predecessor that people's memories were short and that he could return to Manhatan.
Lovelace always refused. He lived on, a broken man.

The governor and Paul passed through the antechamber and entered the chamber of the city council. It was a
simple room furnished with carved wooden chairs and
tables. A picture of Charles II hung at one end, a
painting of St. George slaying the dragon at the other.
The floor was of polished wood and uncarpeted. Unlit oil
lamps hung from the walls. It was a bright, sunny day,
and the tall windows let in more than enough light.

Andros took his chair at the head of the long table and
waited for the twelve council members to arrive. Men
representing the interests of Albany and the northern settlements along the Hudson River would also attend, as
would men from Long Island. It was from these last two
groups that the loudest protests would come about the
proposed Bolting Act.

Governor Andros watched the faces of the men as they
filed into the room and took their places. Some were
friendly, others not so friendly, but they all showed respect toward the governor. Andros had proved to be a
reasonable man, but they knew he could be tough when it
was required.

He wasted no time in overriding protesting citizens
when the good of the community was at stake. For years
the people had been accustomed to throwing garbage into
the canal that ran down Broad Street. When there had
been only a few hundred people on the island, it made
little difference. But now the canal had become a stinking
pestilence. Andros simply covered the canal and turned it
into an underground sewer. He then passed a law forbidding the dumping of garbage into the bay—another common practice. He hired men to collect garbage, and soon
again the city smelled more of nature than of the wastes
of man.

Another problem had been the stinking odors created
by the tanners. The making of leather might be necessary

for society, Andros said, but there was no need for it to be done in the center of town. The tanners were banned from doing business anywhere but on the other side of Wall Street at the outskirts of the town.

It was Jacob Adam who had urged the governor to widen the streets and extend Broad Way beyond the dilapidated palisade at Wall Street. At the wall the street had narrowed instantly to an old Indian trail; now it was a proper thoroughfare, a great aid to the farmers bringing their goods to town.

It was also Jacob Adam who suggested the building of a stone dock from the Whitehall Slip to Coenties Slip. The long dock greatly speeded the loading and unloading of ships, and all citizens benefited. Jacob Adam, as one of the largest ship owners, benefited more than most.

The governor called the meeting to order. The first, and only, piece of business of the day was the Bolting Act.

Paul de Witt rose and read the articles of the proposed law to the members of the council: ". . . and although the governor is aware there is no law which pleases everyone, he believes this act to be best for the general welfare."

James Wilkington, an English farmer who had arrived with a charter for a manor from the Duke of York, was instantly on his feet. Wilkington was not a member of the council, but the representative of the settlers who lived north of the manors of Fordham and Pelham, and south and east of Cortlandt Manor. His estate ranged over twelve thousand acres north of the settlement of Westchester.

Wilkington was a fiery man, short, slender, nervous as a cat. His manor was one of the great wheat producers north of Manhatan. "The best!" he cried in a loud voice. "The best for *whom?* The merchants of New York? Those bloodsuckers who live by the toil of others?"

The governor slammed his fist on the table. "We will not tolerate outbursts like this! We are willing to listen to arguments against this proposal, but they must be presented in a calm and rational manner."

Wilkington was wise enough to change tactics. "Beg pardon, my Lord Governor, but I was carried away by my sense of justice."

"See to it, sir, that your sense of justice follows parliamentary procedure in the chambers of this council."

"May I speak, sir?" Wilkington asked politely.

"Since you seem to have regained your senses, yes."

Wilkington looked around slowly at the members of the city council and representatives from other areas. He knew he would get little support from those men whose interests were identified with the city. Schermerhorn was a ship's chandler. Brevoort and Goelet were ironmongers. The de Peyster brothers were traders and shippers. The de Schuylers specialized in trade to the West Indies. William Beekman dealt in soft goods. The Van Cortlandts and Rhinelanders were in the sugar and brewery businesses. Franklin Riverton traded in sugar, rum, and slaves. Paul de Witt, the governor's secretary—well, he was the nephew of Jacob Adam de Kuyper, the very personification of city interests.

In short, Wilkington was forced to conclude, all were men with a personal interest in seeing the trade and commerce of New York increased. They would be sure to favor the Bolting Act.

The representatives from Long Island and the Hudson Valley were another story: the Bolting Act could only mean a loss of their profits. They would be sure to support him.

But Wilkington was a realist. The only men in the room who could vote were the members of the city council. It was going to be an uphill battle, but he determined to do his best.

"In whose interests are we passing this odious law?" he asked rhetorically. "It is said the flour must be standardized to a certain quality. Excellent, I say! Who wishes to argue with that?"

He paused and looked around again, allowing his words to be digested. "However, this act means all wheat must be brought to New York to be ground into flour. It specifies the contracts for this work will be issued by the government. Since the bolting must be done within the area of the city, I assume the contracts will be given to men who live here. In other words, sir," he said sarcastically, "this will bring profit to men of the city at the expense of the farmers who grow the wheat."

Governor Andros was a man of great control, but he was forced to grip the edge of the table as he listened to Wilkington's insulting tone.

Paul de Witt managed to stifle a smile. Although Jacob Adam had been invited to attend this session of the council, he had declined. "Let the farmers and manor owners start attacking the city people, and the law will be passed," he had said. "Why should I fight my case when others will fight it for me?"

The prediction was coming true.

Stephen Van Cortlandt came to his feet. Although he was the owner of a great manor to the north, his primary income was from his commercial interests in the city. "I take exception to the remarks of this man," he complained to the governor. "He implies the merchants of the city are nothing but greedy bandits!"

Franklin Riverton also jumped to his feet. "We must have a Bolting Act or we will lose our foreign markets! All flour *must* be brought to a standard quality before it is shipped."

"But why must it be done in New York?" Wilkington asked. "What's wrong with setting standards and allowing each farmer and mill owner to grind his wheat to those specifications?"

"That has been tried, sir," Paul de Witt said. "It has not worked in the past and there is no reason to believe it will work in the future."

"I agree with young de Witt," Schermerhorn said. "It's absurd to ask a hundred farmers in a hundred different places to grind wheat into flour and expect to have it all come out the same."

"Who is to get the contracts for the bolting?" Wilkington asked, seeking another avenue of attack.

"That has not been decided," the governor said.

"Surely you must have a hint of who'll get them," Wilkington persisted.

"Several proposals have already been made," the governor said.

"May I ask by whom?"

"That is not the question before the council. The question is whether we accept or reject the Bolting Act as law."

"I say we must reject it!" Wilkington shouted.

Applause and cries of approval came from the Upper Hudson men. One of them, more intemperate than the others, jumped to his feet. "I say it is all part of a dirty plot to steal our lands!"

This was too much even for James Wilkington. He turned on his supposed ally. "That's rubbish! Such talk gets us nowhere." He turned back to the governor. "But more to the point, sir. Why is it we hear no mention of the names of the men who will profit if this tragedy is passed into law?"

"What are you suggesting?" the governor said in a low, menacing tone, his face beginning to flush.

"Suggest? Why nothing. But doesn't it seem odd that what is common knowledge on the street is not a fit topic of conversation for this council?"

Paul de Witt waited for the explosion. But the governor kept his temper under control. "And exactly what is this common knowledge you hear on the street?"

"Perhaps m'Lord Governor would do better to spend more of his time on the street, that he might hear for himself."

"These . . . *farmers*," de Schuyler said, making the word sound like something contaminated, "are saying the contracts will be given only to men who please Your Excellency—perhaps for a share in the profits."

The governor's eyes became daggers. He turned back to James Wilkington. "Are these your own sentiments, sir?"

"I have never spoken such things myself," the diminutive farmer said unflinchingly. "But I have heard them from others, and I have heard nothing to prove them untrue."

Andros jumped from his chair. "Are you saying this is all a plot to line my own pockets?"

"I say only there will be great profits made, and no man here is willing to name who will make them!"

The governor reached forward and held the table with his trembling hands. "The discussion of the Bolting Act is over. We will now ask the council to vote."

Paul de Witt left the chambers after the vote had been taken. The outcome had been quite predictable. Of the twelve members on the council, eleven had voted to pass the new law. James Wilkington had stormed out of the chamber, followed by the other farmers and estate holders. They were muttering and talking rebellion among themselves. Their anger was so strong that Paul wondered if the city men hadn't gone too far.

"Nonsense," Jacob Adam said when his nephew expressed his fears. "They'll grumble and complain, but in the end what can they do? The governor's agents will be watching all wheat shipments closely. All ships will be loaded at the city dock. Don't worry about it," he told the worried young man.

With the Bolting Act in force, things happened as predicted by Jacob Adam.

The first contract to grind and sort the flour was given to Stephen Van Cortlandt, whose brewery was easily converted to the new business.

The second contract went to Jacob Adam, whose facilities on Pearl Street were ready and waiting. For the first two weeks he supervised the operation himself, but he knew he had too many other interests to remain tied down in the bolting trade. He considered giving the job to his nephew, but decided Paul would be of more use to the family interests by remaining in his post as secretary to Governor Andros.

Jacob Adam was in the tiny office at the factory on Pearl Street when Paul arrived with a good-looking, bright-eyed young man about the same age as himself. His name was Nicholas Roosevelt.

"Roosevelt?" Jacob Adam said, his left eyebrow arching upward.

"My father is Claes Martenszen van Rosenvelt," the young man said. "I thought it best to change my name now that we are an English province."

Jacob Adam nodded. He knew Claes, an industrious farmer who had been in the colony for over thirty years and who owned a successful bouwerie, or farm, north of Wall Street.

"Did you think the English would object to your old name?" he asked suspiciously.

Young Roosevelt smiled. "I'm not ashamed of being Dutch, sir, if that's what you mean. I just can't get the English to pronounce it correctly."

It was a good answer, and Jacob Adam returned the smile. He suspected there was more to the name change than the boy was admitting, but he let it pass. With Holland's recent decline as a sea power, there wasn't the remotest possibility that New York would not remain English. The enterprising young Roosevelt was accepting

the situation and making the best of it. Clever, Jacob
Adam thought: all the more reason to hire him.

"Could you run a bolting factory?"

"I have never done it, but I have been in trade. I think
I could learn."

Jacob Adam spent the next few days with Nicholas and
quickly determined he had found an able man. He was
officially made manager, freeing Jacob Adam to pursue
his other interests.

The bolting factory went into full production. Despite
the grumblings of the wheat farmers, they sent their grain
to New York, where it was milled into flour. The merchantmen tied up at the dock and loaded their holds. The
flour was of the finest quality, and shrewd traders like
Jacob Adam de Kuyper exacted top prices from the ship's
captains and factors. Because they began to be paid much
more than the farmers had been able to bargain for, the
farmers were paid as much as before the Bolting Act went
into effect. Their grumblings lessened. Most weren't
even aware of the great profits being made by Jacob
Adam and the other middlemen.

Late in the fall of '82 Theophilus Henry showed up in
New York. An Englishman who had lived in the wilds of
New England as a trapper and hunter, Henry had adapted
to the wilderness as easily as the courageous and half-wild
Frenchmen known as *coureurs des bois*. The French
woodsmen seemed able to adapt to a wild life, but few
Englishmen had done it; Theophilus Henry was one of the
exceptions. But he had grown to hate the Indians with an
intense passion. Perhaps he had spent one day too many
being pursued by warriors seeking his scalp. Or perhaps
it was one night too many spent under a fallen tree
while the rain seeped beneath his collar and he was
afraid of lighting a fire lest he be discovered by a hostile
Indian. Whatever the reason, his hatred of the red man
had grown to monumental proportions.

Theophilus Henry arrived in New York with no prospects and for no particular reason. He was simply tired of
the north woods and the straitlaced morals of the New
England settlers. New York, with its busy docks, its colorful collection of freebooters, privateers, and pirates,
seemed a more attractive place.

It was by accident he came to Jacob Adam's office on Whitehall Street. Henry knew a man in Plymouth who had done business with Franklin Riverton. Henry decided to look him up, but the first man he asked did not know where Riverton could be found. "He's some sort of relative of de Kuyper," the man volunteered, and directed this strange, buckskin-clad white man toward the office on Whitehall.

Jacob Adam at first thought an Indian had wandered into his office. A second glance assured him he had been mistaken. Henry's skin was dark, but it was white. He was tall, broad shouldered and powerful. Years in the woods had given him the graceful movements of a cat. Jacob Adam became interested when he learned the man was looking for a job.

"It would be safe to assume you know the woods."

"None know them better."

"I have a position that might suit you, if you're interested."

Theophilus Henry nodded. "I would be open to almost anything."

"I've been granted a small manor north of Fordham Manor because I've agreed to become part of the mail service to Boston. I'd like to establish a substantial farm."

The Englishman seemed mildly interested as Jacob Adam explained that by the new service, mail was delivered to one place and held there until it could be passed on. The route started at Fort James, on the tip of Manhatan, and followed the Indian trails north to Spuyten Duyvil. The mail carrier crossed the water and made his way north to Fordham Manor and Pelham Manor. From there he followed the Pequot trails along the north shores of Long Island Sound until he came to New Haven. He then went north to Hartford and Springfield, turning east onto the Connecticut Trail, passing through Worcester and arriving in Boston. The round trip was supposed to be done by the carrier within a month, but it usually took longer. In the beginning the trails were faint, having been used only by Indians, who wore soft moccasins. But as time went on and the service became more regular, the trails became easier to follow as they were pounded and hardened by the heavier boots of the white man, by the hooves of horses and the wheels of carts and wagons. It was the beginning of the Boston Post Road.

"I need a man to help build the manor and run it."

"Seems there'd be other men more suited to that sort of life than myself," Henry said honestly.

"There's been some Indian trouble around there," Jacob Adam said bluntly.

A light seemed to dawn in Henry's eyes. "Then you couldn't find a better man for the task."

"Once the place was running on a steady basis, and you had done a good job," Jacob Adam said, "it could be possible to find other work for you. I have many interests— and there are many Indians."

They shook hands on the deal.

Jacob Adam arranged his affairs, and three days later the two men, accompanied by two others, left New York and went north to survey Jacob Adam's latest holdings.

To save the trouble of an overland journey through Manhatan, they sailed a flyboat up the East River. The land looked nearly as primitive as it had about seventy years ago, when Pieter de Kuyper had first made the trip up the river.

The boat slipped past Hog Island, where ex-Governor Lovelace lived in disgrace. And then it came to the part of the river where the waters flowed eastward into Long Island Sound, while the western waters became the Harlem River. The boat pulled into a cove on the north shore, and Jacob Adam and his party disembarked. From where they stood they could look back across the river and see the small settlement at New Harlem, consisting of five or six families with their houses and barns.

The sun was dipping over the horizon, and Jacob Adam ordered camp made for the night. The men made their provisions for sleeping and cooked a meal of bear meat in a pot over an open fire.

After eating their fill, the men smoked their pipes and sat around the fire. Jacob Adam was seated next to Theophilus Henry, who looked very much at home in the wild setting.

"What sort of trouble are the Indians causing?" Henry asked.

"Stealing. They must learn de Kuyper Manor is not a healthy place to steal from."

"Are there many of them?"

"Enough to cause trouble. They must be taught their place," Jacob Adam said.

"They must be destroyed," Henry said quietly. His voice was calm, but the deadly seriousness caused Jacob Adam to look at the man more closely.

"Why?"

"Because they exist. They take up space we need."

Jacob Adam was hardly a man of universal compassion, but the cold flintiness of the other surprised even him. "I don't think they need to be exterminated. They must only be taught to fit into our society."

"That they will never do. The Indian is incapable of fitting in. By his nature, he is incapable of doing the right thing. He will always steal and cheat. The only way to deal with him is to kill him."

"We have to be a little careful about that," Jacob Adam warned his new employee. "Technically we're at peace with the tribes in these parts."

"At peace until one of them sneaks into your house at night and cuts your throat."

"I want you to keep peace at the manor, not start an Indian war."

"I won't have to start one. *They* will," Henry assured him. "And maybe this time we'll finish it. Properly."

Jacob Adam did not entirely disagree with the woodsman. Society was built on the observance of certain rules. When a man did not conform, he was faced with the whip or the gallows. The white man, no matter how poor or wretched, understood this necessity. The red man, no matter how intelligent, or how much exposure he had to the white man's culture, never seemed to understand; it was almost as if he didn't want to. He had his own ways and his own ideas.

But Jacob Adam did not want to be the cause of another Indian war. "You must promise me not to take the killing of Indians into your own hands."

Theophilus Henry smiled. "Of course. The Indian will be the cause of his own destruction."

The fire burned lower, and the men covered themselves with their coats. They twisted and turned as they tried to find a comfortable spot on the hard, level ground.

Jacob Adam glanced at Theophilus Henry, scarcely a
foot away, and saw the Indian fighter placing a thick log
as a pillow behind him. Almost as his head touched the
wood, his eyes closed and his breathing changed to the
rhythms of sleep. Jacob Adam lowered his own head onto
a canvas sack. At least it was softer than a log, he
thought, and then he too fell asleep.

He awoke when a musket exploded, so it seemed, next
to his ear. A loud scream instantly followed the explosion.

Jacob Adam came to his knees as he grabbed his pistol. It was still night, pitch black, and the dull glow from
the dying fire was too feeble to alleviate the darkness for
more than a few feet. Then he saw the figure of a man
standing on the opposite side of the glowing embers. The
man pitched forward and lay motionless.

Jacob Adam assumed it was the man who had
screamed and that he was one of their own party. He
started toward the still form and stopped when he saw
two other men struggling out of their sleeping gear. "What
the hell's happenin'!" one of them shouted.

Jacob Adam looked at the body and realized it was a
man he had never seen before. Before he could say anything to his two men, who were now on their feet with
weapons in their hands, a short, strangled cry came from
the woods to their left, and then a crash as a heavy object fell into the brush. The three men looked toward
the disturbance, their eyes darting back and forth, their
fingers nervously touching the triggers of their weapons.
Silence.

Finally one of Jacob Adam's men whispered. "Where's
Mister Henry?"

For the first time Jacob Adam realized the Indian fighter
was not in the camp. "Henry, where are you?" he called
out. Something whizzed by his ear, and he knew it was an
arrow. He threw himself to the ground, and his companions needed no urging to do the same.

A second shot rang out, this time the lesser explosion
of a pistol. There was a grunt of pain, and Jacob Adam
watched in fascination as a wounded Indian staggered
into the camp. He stood upright for a moment, his hands
grabbing at his back. Suddenly he dropped to the ground,

twitched, and then lay still. There was a blood-soaked hole in the middle of his back.

The calm voice of Theophilus Henry came out of the dark woods. "It's all over. You can relax."

As the three men stared at the spot where the voice had come from, the Indian fighter noiselessly stepped from the cover of the trees. He came over and looked down at the fallen Indian. Using the toe of his moccasin, he lifted the chin of the man to get a better look at his face. "Huron," he said. "He's a long way from home."

"Who are these two men?" Jacob Adam asked.

"*Four* of them," Henry said. "Two Indians and two white men. If the Indians are Hurons, then the white men are probably French."

"So they aren't local Indians?"

Theophilus Henry smiled. "Too bad, isn't it? If they were, it would have proved the point I was making earlier."

Jacob Adam bent down and turned the white man over until he was on his back. The man's face was coarse, heavily lined, tufted with bits of a scraggly beard, and marked now with the agony of death. "There are two others, you say?"

"Were," Henry replied. "Out in the woods."

"What happened?" one of the other two men asked.

Henry went to the fire and rubbed his hands over the embers. "A noise woke me and I slipped out of camp. I took the first Indian with my knife." He pointed toward the body of the white man. "That one was sneaking into camp, and I shot him with my musket. I got the other white with my knife. And, well, you saw what happened to him," he added, with a shrug of his head toward the Indian on the ground.

Jacob Adam shuddered. "All of us might have been murdered as we slept. And for what? We have nothing of value with us."

Theophilus Henry was going through the pockets of the white man's coat. "These renegades will kill you for the boots on your feet." He found something in one of the pockets and brought it out into the feeble light of the embers. Jacob Adam could see it was a French coin.

"They came a long way to die," he said quietly. "I suppose we'll have to bury them."

Theophilus Henry shook his head. "Leave them be. There's enough critters in these woods to take care of them. By the next nightfall they'll be bones."

There was no more sleep that night. When the first rays of the new sun lessened the darkness on the horizon, the men shouldered their weapons and packs and started on the faint trail.

They arrived at the virgin lands of the new de Kuyper Manor and spent over a week laying out sites for the house and farm buildings. A neighboring farmer, a nephew of Jonas Bronck, came by and offered his suggestions. He claimed that the local Indians were peaceful, that all they asked was to be left alone. Jacob Adam arched his brow and looked at Henry, who received this news stoically.

During the week he spent on his new land Jacob Adam spent hours wandering through the grassy plains. He could envision a great house attended by a host of servants. He could see the neat, whitewashed fences blocking off gardens that would be filled with flowers. And after he envisioned it all, he realized he would never be content to live in this place. Only a few days out of Manhatan, and he missed its excitement and commerce. He missed the give-and-take as deals were made in the taverns and along the wharfs. No walk in the country, no smell of a flower, no sight of a bush in bloom could equal the smells and excitement found near the docks, where men haggled over the price of cargoes to and from the far corners of the globe. This trading and haggling was the blood of his life.

Theophilus Henry, despite his interest in slaughtering Indians, seemed a good choice as manager. There wasn't a thing about the woods he didn't understand. He knew which trees to cut down for whatever purpose needed. His skill at procuring fresh game amazed them all, and his knowledge of roots and herbs would have made an Indian medicine man proud. If his hatred of the red man could be kept in check, Jacob Adam did not doubt that his new manager would create a thriving establishment in the middle of the forest.

In the spring of '83 Jennifer Barrow de Kuyper gave birth to a son. Jacob Adam said it was only fitting that

this first 'English' de Kuyper be named after the city's
patron, James, Duke of York.

The family gathered at the house on Broad Way in
honor of the occasion.

Jacob Adam greeted them all, reserving true affection
for his nephew, Paul. The others he accepted as relatives
of one sort or another, to be tolerated only because they
were exactly that.

Paul was accompanied by Janet Beekman. Jacob Adam
took pleasure in looking at her pretty face and admiring
her creamy skin and bright young features. His own wife
wasn't much older, he reflected, and he was amused by
the idea of his nephew and himself having wives who
were contemporaries.

"And how long will we have to wait," he said to the
girl, "before there's a gathering like this for your baby?"

Janet Beekman pretended to be shocked. "Mister de
Kuyper!" she exclaimed, and then turned her head
aside and giggled. Paul's face reddened, and his look of
helplessness seemed to say that he was sorry, but he had
no control over his uncle's tongue.

"It shouldn't be too long," Jacob Adam persisted con-
fidently. "I've noticed the way you look at one another."

Paul cleared his throat. His voice took on its manliest
inflection. "But, uncle, I haven't even brought up the subject with Mister Beekman."

Janet patted his arm and smiled. She looked Jacob Adam
straight in the eye. "He hasn't even brought up 'the subject' with me yet." Paul turned an even darker shade of
crimson.

"Well, I've been meaning to. That is," he started to
say, and then gave up. Janet took his arm and gave it an
affectionate squeeze.

Jacob Adam walked away. He was pleased with the
girl Paul had chosen. She came from a good family and
was obviously a young woman of spirit. He wasn't sure
that an early marriage was a particularly good thing for a
man; he himself had waited until he had been in his
thirties. A man could waste too much of his juices on a
woman, especially if he was young and inexperienced.
He had seen it happen to may young men with seemingly
bright futures. All too often they spent their vital years
womanizing and drinking, and when they came to the

prime of their life, when it was time for them to build on
what they had already established, they discovered they
had established nothing, and everything they tried to
build was on a foundation of shifting sand. The stronger
men, however, seemed to withstand the handicap of an
early marriage, and he had no doubt his nephew
would prove to be such a man. He silently gave his blessing to the forthcoming marriage and went about the business of seeing to his other guests.

His sister, Anne, came with her husband.

"So, at last, my little brother is now a father," Anne
said with a smile. "About time."

Jacob Adam kissed her cheek. "And I approve of your
son's girl. She'll make a nice addition to the family."

Anne looked across the room and saw Paul and Janet,
their heads together, happy with one another in the se-
cretive way of lovers. She sighed. "It would have been
nice if his father had lived to see him married," she said,
and Jacob Adam heard the trace of loss in her voice.

"I'm sure Paul will become everything David would
have wished for his son," he said, his eyes going across
the room and stopping on Anne's second husband, who
was helping himself to a large drink.

"You don't think I should have gotten married again,
do you?"

"It wasn't for me to say."

Anne shook her head. "Well, maybe you should've
said something. I might have listened."

"I think the problem is that no one will ever live up to
David de Witt's memory—at least not in your mind."

The smile returned to her lips. "And in yours, you
fraud. You know as well as myself what sort of a man
Jacob de Schuyler is. Oh, he's kind, and there's plenty of
money. Thank God for that—he spends more on drink
in a week than most men make in a month."

"Do you want me to speak to him?"

"About what? The relative virtues of gin or rum? He
spends every evening at Kock's tavern."

The mention of the old tavern suddenly caused them
both to smile. It had been their father's favorite drinking
place. Old Frans Kock had died, but the place was now
run by a son who could have passed as his father's twin.

"Maybe we could go down and blow the roof off with a cannon," Jacob Adam suggested.

They both laughed at the old family joke. On the day of Anne's wedding to David de Witt, a number of soused revelers, led by Young Pieter de Kuyper—their own brother—had accidentally blown the roof off the tavern with a small cannon.

Anne squeezed her brother's arm. "You're not going to believe this, but I think I prefer my second marriage to be this way. There's nothing to detract from my memories of David."

Jacob Adam nodded his head. He didn't think it strange at all. His sister had had her share of love and was now willing to settle for comfort. He did not think the less of her.

Anne's daughter, Emilie, came with her husband, Edward Goelet. Emilie was twenty-nine years old and had two children of her own. She was also expecting a third. Like her mother, she had high cheekbones, a strong jaw, and a very fair complexion. Her lower lip was a bit too heavy, and it gave her a slightly pouty look. But she was quick to smile, her eyes were large and blue, and the frame of soft, blonde hair created an effect of striking loveliness. She was beginning to develop the same look of maturity as her mother, and one had only to glance at Anne to know how Emilie would look at fifty. Emilie's sons were named Charles and Edward Junior. Charles was seven years old, and Edward six. They were well-behaved children, always aware of the stern eye of their father, who ran the biggest and most prosperous ironmonger works in New York. Edward Junior was shy, but Charles had enormous self-assurance for a child of his age.

"Young Charles Goelet," Jacob Adam said with great seriousness. "Will you be an admiral or a general when you grow up?"

"A man of business, sir."

Jacob Adam was startled. "Isn't that a tame ambition for a young man?"

Young Charles was quite serious. "My mother says you're the greatest man in New York, sir. I want to be like you."

Jacob Adam patted the lad on the head and silently

wondered how Emilie had ever come to such a conclusion. She was his niece, but the difference in Anne's age and his own was considerable, and Emilie could easily have been his own sister. He had never realized his niece had such a high regard for him.

He looked at young Charles. "I have a feeling you'll get your wish, Charlie Goelet, and you have my blessing."

He attended to his other guests.

There were assorted de Witts, who were relatives of a sort, since the family was related to the de Kuypers through Anne.

Franklin Riverton came with his wife, who had arrived in New York many years ago and had never stopped sniveling about how badly she wanted to return to England.

Zilla presided over the entire affair as if she were the grande dame of the de Kuyper clan, which in Jacob Adam's eye she was. There was not a man in the province who would challenge him about the seeming impropriety of her authority, although they were not above discussing it in private when Jacob Adam could not overhear. Zilla's nephew, Daniel, came and paid his respects to the newborn child; but the color of Daniel's skin made him feel out of place, and he quickly found a reason to excuse himself.

Captain Lars Jorisen came to honor the new grandson of his long-dead friend.

"You look as fit as ever," Jacob Adam said, although he silently recognized the old captain was finally showing his age.

"Don't lie to an old sea dog," Jorisen growled. "My ship *William*'s got rot in her bilges and so do I. Maybe it's time we both raised anchor and left for a new harbor. I've no regrets. I've lived a life that's pleased me. I leave little behind, but then I've no one to leave it to. Most of the men of my day are gone and I think it's time I joined them. 'T'will be good to see your father again."

"I'll miss you," Jacog Adam said quietly.

"Ah, but not very much, I suspect. We all seem to make do when others pass along. It wouldn't be proper any other way. As much as I loved your father I found life went on much the same without him."

The two were about to part when the captain suddenly remembered something. "Do you still have the knife your father gave you?"

"The one that was supposed to belong to Henry Hudson?"

"Yes."

"I have it still. I suppose one of these days I'll pass it along to my own son. Why do you ask?"

"Something your father said to me one time. That the knife and his family were among the first to arrive here from Europe. That knife was like a symbol of his own life."

"I keep it in a safe place," Jacob Adam said. "It will be passed on."

Lars Jorisen walked away, stooped with age, but for all his years a vital man. He wound up in the corner of the kitchen talking to Zilla, the only one present who could share his own memories. Jacob Adam saw them together—the last living links with his father—and was suddenly aware that it couldn't be much longer that he would have Zilla. It seemed impossible that she would die. She had always been there, from the very first moment he could remember. His own mother had died as he was born; of her he had no memories, but of Zilla he had thousands.

Baby James awakened, ignored the guests who were gathered in his honor, and screamed, demanding to be fed. Jennifer took him into a side room, and within minutes the content infant was burping and ready to go back to sleep.

Elizabeth Riverton Barrow arrived and spent a few minutes with her grandchild. She took a glass of thick, cloudy rum and walked into the garden. She wandered about, enjoying the budding flowers, and accidentally came upon Jacob Adam.

"Congratulations," she said.

The old resentment and hostility at the way she had treated him years ago returned instantly. He would have preferred that she had not come to his house, but it would have been too cruel to deny a grandmother a glimpse of her new grandchild. He looked at her coldly. "Welcome to my house."

"It's the first time I've ever been here."

"I know."

"My father spent his whole lifetime waiting for an invitation. Your father never offered one."

"My father could not forgive your father for being a slave trader."

"And you?"

"I have nothing against slave traders."

"Then what do you have against me?"

He looked at her, remembering the way she had looked many years ago and that he had desired her; desired to take her and marry her and give her everything. She had rejected him. And life had not been good to her.

"I always questioned your judgment," he said coldly.

"What are you talking about?"

He stared at her and realized she was truly puzzled. "There was a time when I wanted you," he explained. "A pity you chose another road."

She suddenly realized what he was saying. "You can't be serious! You're saying you resented the fact I married Robert Barrow instead of you?"

"You knew that."

"But, my God," she protested, "you weren't much more than a child!"

"Even a child has feelings, and you hurt mine."

"That was so many years ago," she said, and then her head tilted to the side as she peered more closely at him. "As mad as it seems, do you still resent what happened?"

"No, because now I would be married to an old woman," he said, taking no enjoyment from his own cruel words. "Instead I have a much younger and prettier copy."

Elizabeth's face turned ashen. "I can forgive the insult to myself. I only pray to God you didn't marry my daughter simply to get back at me."

He was silent for a moment, and then his words seemed to reach her from some dark, cold void. "It was one of the reasons. Why do you think your brother and I planned the wedding without letting you have anything to say about it?"

"Yes," she said bitterly, "I've never forgiven my brother for giving away my only daughter against my will."

"He had a choice of giving me his niece, or seeing his entire fortune wiped out. I don't know if he told you about that. But it's true. He'd lost several ships and was heavily in debt. Without me he would have gone under."

"And so he repaid you by giving you my daughter. What a pair of bastards!"

"I don't know about that. I've given Jennifer a good home. And now a son. What more do you want?"

She pulled back in revulsion. "It would kill her if she knew why you married her."

Jacob Adam looked at the drawn features and the tiny lines formed about the enraged mouth. He had finally taken his revenge on this woman, but somehow it didn't please him. "You are welcome to visit your grandson in this house whenever you wish," he said, and walked back into the house, leaving the woman alone in the garden.

Trembling with rage, Elizabeth Barrow sat on a garden bench to collect her strength.

He is a monster, she thought, a cold-hearted, unfeeling monster. And her own daughter was in his clutches. She had several wild thoughts about revenge, and then realized how powerless she was. Certainly there was no recourse to law. In New York a woman was a second-class citizen and had almost no rights against a man. Especially a man as powerful and influential as Jacob Adam de Kuyper.

Elizabeth's temper had been a problem. It had always been a fight to keep it under control, and with each passing year it was a fight she lost more and more often. And now her anger increased and the blood seemed to rush to her head. She lost control of herself and could think of nothing but doing harm to Jacob Adam. And suddenly it came to her in a flash. She must kill him! Yes, that was the answer. She would go into the house . . . find a knife. She would ease her way to his side, and when his head was turned the other way . . . she would raise the knife and plunge it into his back!

She went back into the house. After a short search in the kitchen she found a long, sharp knife with a black wooden handle. She picked it up and walked purposefully back into the parlor. She saw Jacob Adam standing on the other side of the room.

She stood still for a moment, her hand clutching the knife beneath her cloak; and then she began to walk toward him, her eyes blazing, her mind silently chuckling over the fate about to overcome this hated man. And then she froze as Jennifer entered the room and went to her husband's side. Jacob Adam smiled and took her hand in his. Jennifer returned the smile and whispered something in his ear. The two of them began to laugh. Jennifer looked radiant and happy, warm and protected at the side of her husband.

Elizabeth's resolve shattered.

What was she thinking about? What was she doing with a knife in her hand? Was she crazy? About to murder the husband of her own daughter? About to kill the father of her new grandson?

A sense of self-revulsion came over her, and she walked back to the kitchen and replaced the knife where she had found it. She looked at it a last time and shuddered. How insane, she thought as she slipped out the back door and made her way to her own house.

She breathed heavily as she walked, and the air helped clear her thoughts. By the time she reached her own home she knew the truth about herself; she knew why she had been so angry.

She hadn't wished to kill Jacob Adam in defense of her daughter. *It had been for herself.* When her husband, Robert, died, she had been pregnant. For the first two years after Jennifer's birth, she had had no wish to marry again. But then she had conceived the idea that it would be proper to find another husband, and that husband would be none other than Jacob Adam de Kuyper. She was a very attractive woman and did her best to be noticed by the man she had set her cap for. He was turning into a very handsome and successful young man, and she was certain they would make a good match. But no matter what she did, no matter how hard she tried, she failed even in capturing the young man's momentary attention. Still her single-minded desire had persisted, and it prevented her from seeing the worth of any other man who might have been willing to marry her.

She realized that a good deal of the bitterness of her life could be laid at the doorstep of Jacob Adam. The man who had once desired her utterly rejected her. And he had the heart of a devil.

But even as she seethed, she realized the eternal truth of it all. Jennifer was young and fresh and she was not.

She did not want to be old. She said it over and over, hoping somehow that if one said a thing enough times, it would become true.

She arrived at her house. "I do not want to be old," she said aloud. No answer. "I do not want to be old," she said again, in a louder voice. Still no answer.

There was no one in the house—or anywhere else—to answer, and she knew it. She went to bed and cried herself to sleep.

The last guest had long ago gone home. Everyone in the house was in bed and asleep, except Zilla. She sat near the dying embers of the fire with baby James in her arms. One of his tiny hands was curled tightly around her bony thumb. She rocked gently back and forth, the softest crooning coming from her lips. Her eyes were filled with love as she looked at the infant.

Even in the feeble light, the contrast of the color of their skins was great. Baby James was smooth and creamy white. Zilla was wrinkled, and the darkness of her skin made it appear as the bark of an ancient and revered tree.

They say I got no baby, she crooned. *They say I had no chile. They think I been unlucky, they think I should be sad.* . . . A smile came across her face, and she glowed with happiness.

Jacob Adam had been her baby. And a fine son he was. And now she had a grandson. And he would be a fine man, as fine and strong as his daddy. *James, my grandson James.*

New York slept and Zilla sat and rocked her grandson on her lap. She thought herself the happiest woman in the city.

There was no one who could dispute her.

The next week Jacob Adam fired Nicholas Roosevelt from his job as manager of the bolting factory.

Making one of his infrequent visits to the building on

lower Pearl Street, he arrived at the same time as a farmer was delivering a heavy wagonload of wheat.

The main part of the building was a two-story shed, half of which was below the level of the street. Jacob Adam had been surprised to find a makeshift ramp leading to the bottom, and he was standing at its base when the farmer led his team onto the steep ramp. Halfway down one of the horses slipped, jerking the harness of the second horse, which panicked. The farmer jumped clear as both horses charged down the ramp, the wagon bouncing and teetering behind them. Jacob Adam just managed to get out of the way, but even so the side of the wagon hit his shoulder, tearing his coat and sending him sprawling against the wall. The men on the floor scattered, but one unfortunate wasn't swift enough, and the heavy wagon whipped around and pinned him against the wall. A single excruciating shriek could be heard above all the other noise.

A large man with red hair boldly leaped in front of the horses, grabbed the reins, and succeeded in bringing them to a halt.

Nicholas Roosevelt came running across the floor, but his steps slowed as the wagon was moved away from the wall to reveal the crushed pulp that had been a man. He looked away.

"What the hell is this ramp doing here?" Jacob Adam asked angrily. "There's supposed to be a chute so the grain can be unloaded at street level."

"The chute collapsed," Roosevelt confessed. "I . . . was using this as a temporary measure."

"When did the chute break?"

"Two weeks ago, sir," the young man said miserably.

"Two weeks. And now there's a man dead. You're through here," Jacob Adam said, and turned his back on the man. "Who's next in charge?"

"I am, sir," said the redheaded man who had stopped the horses. "John Lesley's my name."

Jacob Adam considered him for a moment. Lesley was a clean-shaven young man, about twenty-five, with a brawny build and an uncomplicated look. "Do you think you can handle the job of manager?"

"Yes, sir," Lesley said, looking uneasily at the back of the departing Nicholas Roosevelt.

"It's yours as of now," Jacob Adam said. "First thing to do is to take care of the dead man."

He started walking up the ramp, then paused and leaned against the wall.

"Best you take a rest, sir," Lesley said, coming to his side and taking hold of his arm. "That was a nasty bump you took."

"I'll be all right," Jacob Adam said impatiently, but he allowed the other man to hold his arm until they came to the top of the ramp.

"If it's all right with you, sir, I'll walk with you," Lesley said. Jacob Adam did not object, because he felt a bit dizzy.

"That's a shame about Mister Roosevelt," Lesley said as they walked. "He's a good man."

"That was a foolish thing to do," Jacob Adam snapped. "He needed a swift kick in the pants."

They arrived at the intersection of Duke Alley, and Lesley jerked his thumb up the street. "That's where I live, sir. You wouldn't care for a spot of rum, would you? You still look a bit shaky."

Jacob Adam decided it might be better to regain his composure before returning to his office. "All right, a small drink," he said.

John Lesley's house was the back half of the bottom floor of an old building that looked as if it had been one of the original structures in the alley. The floorboards sagged and showed old water stains. The low ceilings were blackened from the soot of a thousand fires that had burned in the fireplace.

Lesley's wife was a pale, thin woman who was visibly nervous in the presence of so important a guest. She kept flicking invisible wisps of hair from her face as she helped her husband prepare two goblets of rum from the makeshift piece of furniture they used as a sideboard— several unfinished planks that were nailed to the wall.

Jacob Adam sat in the chair offered by his host; it was the only good one in the room. The other chairs were as battered and worn as the table, and an uncomfortable looking bed fit into the alcove next to the single window.

"Doesn't look like much yet, sir," Lesley said proudly. "But we have plans to fix it up right. Sure is better than the dump we were living in until only a few weeks ago."

Jacob Adam smiled pleasantly and took a stiff swallow of the burning rum. This room, he reflected, was not unlike the rooms of many people in New York. It was, in fact, better than a good many of them. A man of lesser convictions might have felt uncomfortable when he compared it to the far grander style of his own life, but Jacob Adam's philosophy was that a man lived as well as he was willing to work hard.

"We'll pay you what we paid Roosevelt," he said. "You'll be able to do even better."

Far from being offended, Lesley smiled and nodded in appreciation; he was in full agreement with his employer's assessment of the economic facts of life.

Jacob Adam finished his rum, left the house, and refused Lesley's offer to accompany him the rest of the way. "You get back and get rid of that ramp," he said.

He returned to his office, and his chief clerk noticed the rip in his coat. "Mister de Kuyper! What happened?" the little man said, clasping his hands before him in his fussy manner.

"Nothing," Jacob Adam said, sitting down in his chair and picking up a stack of correspondence.

It was midmorning, late in the summer. The crew of the *William* was mystified. Captain Lars Jorisen had yet to make an appearance on deck. Usually he was up before dawn.

Finally the mate knocked on the captain's door. No answer. He turned the handle and opened the door, entering the cabin without permission for the first time ever.

The Danish captain was dressed and seated in his chair behind the long table that served as his desk. A pile of charts was before him, and he held a long string of wampum in his hand. The left sleeve of his coat— the empty one—was pinned neatly to the shoulder. He wore his cap.

"Sor?" the mate asked, but there was no reaction.

He stood in front of his captain, whose eyes were closed. "Sor?" he said again. Finally he reached out and touched Jorisen's shoulder. The slight push was enough to send the captain back into the chair. His head lolled to one side, and the mate knew Lars Jórisen was dead.

Jacob Adam de Kuyper was informed, and plans were made for the *William* to slip anchor the next morning for a burial at sea.

When Zilla heard of the captain's death, she insisted she would sail on the ship for the burial. Jacob Adam tried to talk her out of it, citing the breezes as being bad for someone her age. She wouldn't listen and, of course, had her own way.

They stood on the deck of the *William* as Dominie Nieuwenhuysen read the service. Although Jorisen had never attended services, it was assumed he had a preference for the Dutch Reformed Church. Jacob Adam knew the only church recognized by the captain was the Church of Lost Seamen, but he kept his knowledge to himself.

The body slid into the water just beyond the Narrows, and Zilla wept as the last traces of the good Danish captain slipped to the bottom of the sea. She stood at Jacob Adam's side, holding tightly to his arm.

The *William* returned to the dock, and Jacob Adam made inquiries about the legal ownership of the vessel. The captain had left no heirs, and there was no one who claimed ownership.

He went to the city hall and looked up the records. The *William*, it seemed, belonged to him. Lars Jorisen had made out a will that carefully specified the division of his property, mostly among his crew.

Jacob Adam was puzzled why Jorisen had left the ship to him, but then he remembered his own father had given the ship to the captain when he died. Now the captain was returning the favor.

He thought about it for a time, and then made a decision for the *William*. It didn't occur to him that it might not have been the captain's first wish as a fate for his ship.

A bright songbird warbled his happiness at the splendor of the beautiful spring day. A slight touch of early morning crispness brought a flush to Janet Beekman's cheeks, and she took Paul de Witt's arm as they walked toward the Water Gate.

"How do you like being a betrothed man?" she asked.

"It's really terrible." He managed to keep a straight

face, but his hand couldn't resist patting the slender fingers gently gripping his arm.

The people of the town were already bustling about their business, for this was market day. Horse-drawn carts filled with firewood creaked their way through the narrow streets as wisps of smoke from many chimneys gave testimony of the great demand for this commodity. Women were out sweeping their stoops, washing windows, and polishing their brass door knockers.

Farmers from the northern parts of Manhatan, Westchester, Long Island, and even New Jersey had set up their stalls. A large variety of fresh vegetables and succulent fruits, sparkling and gleaming from a recent washing, could be had for a few pence a peck. Dozens of different kinds of meat and fish hung on hooks under shading eaves or behind the windows of a merchant's store. Live sheep and pigs were in pens waiting for buyers. Tethered goats scrounged for scraps to eat while cattle contentedly chewed the hay that had been set before them. Coopers and tinsmiths made a racket as they banged their wares, loudly and visibly proclaiming their sturdiness and value. There were trappers with furs, tanners with leather goods, and blacksmiths with nails, shackles, bolts, and other tools fashioned of iron.

Many of the townspeople dressed up on market day —inspired no doubt, by a desire to distinguish themselves from the farmers, drovers, and "hayseeds" who were drawn to town on this day. The men wore hats with wide brims, long coats with rows of polished silver buckles, velvet waistcoats and silk breeches. The women's hair showed signs of a recent frizzing, their skirts were new and colorful, and their jackets had leg-o'-mutton sleeves. Most of the women also used market day as a time to display their best jewelry, including girdle chains of silver or, if they could afford it, gold.

Greetings were being exchanged, for it was still not a very big town, and most of the people who lived here permanently knew one another. Even at this hour men could be seen entering the dark taverns to have a few fast eye-openers before beginning the work of the day. For some there was no work, and these men would either stay inside the tavern or right outside the door, talking and drinking, meeting their friends and buying them drinks—all providing grist for the mills of the preachers, who never stopped complaining about the enormous amount of spirits consumed in the province.

The Water Gate gave access beyond Pearl Street through the tall palisade that stretched along Wall Street from one side of the island to the other. A battery of a dozen guns frowned down on the river. On this fine spring morning, however, there wasn't even the suspicion of trouble, and the four soldiers on duty drowsed in the warmth of the early sun.

Paul and Janet often enjoyed early Sunday morning walks. They passed beyond the wall and the several slaughterhouses that had been banished from town and stood near the bank of the East River. Janet tried to pretend these places, with their smells and mournful sounds, did not exist.

They walked through the small, marshy area drained by a brook and dubbed "Maiden Lane" because it had been customary for the young girls of the town to bring their soiled clothes to the sparkling water. The arrival of the slaughterhouses was causing many of the girls to take their washing elsewhere—to the dismay of the loafers who enjoyed ogling so many fair young maidens in one place.

Paul stopped at Peck Slip and pointed to the horn hanging from a tree. "Should we take a boat ride across the river?"

Janet shook her head. "I'd prefer to keep walking. Besides, it's too early for the boatman to be up."

Paul nodded in understanding. Klaus was one of the most undependable men in the province. He charged only a few pennies to row customers to Brooklyn; but he bestirred himself only when the mood was upon him, and if he didn't like your looks, nothing would persuade him to cross the river.

As they walked, Janet kept sneaking sidelong glances at her husband-to-be. Paul had an intense manner that never failed to stir her heart. He approached everything with a burning desire to do it well. She felt sure he would make the best husband in New York. From what she had heard, Paul had the business acumen of his uncle, but it was tempered by a gentleness lacking in the older man. Good. She never felt completely at ease around Jacob Adam. There was something cold and distant about him, something almost inhuman. The thought made her feel guilty, because Jacob Adam had never treated her with anything but friendly consideration. Caught up in her own thoughts, she suddenly realized Paul had been talking and she hadn't heard a single word. She listened carefully to pick up the thread of his conversation.

". . . so it seems advisable for me to continue as the governor's secretary at least for a bit longer. Uncle Jacob feels it will stand me in good stead when I finally devote all my time to the family business. My own belief is that as bankers we must tie ourselves to the real estate interests. People can do without many things if they must, but they will always need land—land to live on and work on. Without the land there's nothing."

"Yes, that makes sense," Janet said, not quite sure what he was talking about, but hardly willing to admit it.

"You're very unusual, you know," Paul said seriously. "Most women don't understand a thing about business. They don't seem to have any interest in it."

"Most women don't understand it because men exclude them from it," Janet said, and Paul nodded his head in agreement, missing the barb in her seemingly innocuous remark.

They passed the edge of Stuyvesant's bouwerie, where the crusty old ex-governor had moved after he had been expelled from power by the English, and walked through the area known as the Flats or the Common. It was a pleasant, open place filled with colorful flowers and bright, green grass; a place where cows grazed and pigs roamed freely.

And now they came to the greatest landmark outside the town, the Collect—*Kolch Hoeck,* or shell point—a large lake where shellfish had been taken by the Indians. It was just north of the marshy area of salt flats known as Beekman's swamp.

"How does it feel to have a swamp named after you?" Paul asked playfully.

"It's named after my father," she said indignantly. "And I wish he'd never bought it. What does he want with a swamp? I could murder the scoundrel who sold it to him."

"Hm," Paul said, feigning disinterest.

"You know very well who sold it to him."

"I do?"

"Your uncle's sometime partner."

"Really?" Paul said, failing this time to appear innocent.

"Yes, it was that fat Robert de Pauw. As if you didn't know."

Paul pointed toward a flight of birds landing on the lake. Their wings churned the air and raised spray as their bodies settled on top of the water. "Look at that."

Janet immediately became involved with the beauty of the birds, forgetting their discussion.

Paul breathed a sigh of relief. It was true Robert de Pauw had sold the swampy land to Janet's father, but what Janet and her father didn't know was that de Pauw had acted only as agent for the real owner—Jacob Adam. His uncle often bought and sold land through the offices of other men. No sense letting everyone know what a man was about, was Jacob Adam's reasoning. This was one land transaction Paul hoped would always remain a secret.

They stood at the edge of the Collect, holding hands as they peered into the deep waters which marked the divide of the watershed between Hudson's and the East rivers. Suddenly, Paul had an idea. Without a word he took Janet by the arm and started toward the Old Kill. A small wooden bridge had been built over it—the Kissing Bridge. The custom of the day decreed that a man walking or driving with his lady over the bridge had the right to stop there and kiss her.

They came to the top of a small knoll, and Janet immediately understood where he was taking her. She pretended ignorance and chattered about the birds and the sky and the flowers.

They arrived at the kill, and Paul led the way onto the bridge. As soon as Janet stepped on the first wooden plank, he stopped and faced her.

"Why, Mister de Witt. Surely you don't intend . . ." she said in mock horror, and then found herself crushed against his body as their lips met. They had kissed before, light, affectionate pecks, but this was different. She could feel the hunger in his lips, and something deep within her responded. Her soft mouth opened wider, and her arm slipped around him, pulling them even closer together. She closed her eyes and felt the warmth of his body. It was as if they were blending into one person.

A sudden shout brought them back to earth and to themselves.

They looked across the meadow to the plain stretching below the small hill that was crowned by Webber's Tavern. Men were shouting and a fracas was breaking out.

The field had been given to the Jewish community, the congregation of Shearith Israel, as a permanent site for their cemetery. Members of the congregation were gathered around an open grave in what appeared to be a burial ceremony. They had been set upon by a dozen men—sailors, from the looks of their clothing. The seamen had charged into the mourning Jews, and fists and feet began to fly. Suddenly the glint of a knife caught the sun as one of the sailors stabbed an elderly man who was trying to back away. Several women screamed.

One of the Jewish men grabbed the sailor with the knife and began fighting with him, the two of them rolling over and over on the ground for control of the knife.

"That's Joshua Seixas!" Paul said. "And—good God! —there's my uncle!"

And, indeed, standing at the rear of the mourners was Jacob Adam, dressed in a dark suit as if he had come to pay his respects to the deceased.

"Paul, what can we do?"

But Paul hardly heard Janet's question. He was already running toward the melee. "Paul," Janet shouted, "you'll get hurt!"

"Stay there!" he shouted over his shoulder as he ran. "I'll be all right."

He paused only to pick up a fallen tree branch on the side of the path. He cracked it over the top of a boulder to break it in half. He now had a hardwood stave about six feet long and two inches in diameter, a formidable weapon weighing six pounds.

Joshua Seixas was fighting like a lion, pitting his slender hundred and forty pounds against the might of a two-hundred-pound ruffian.

The sheer bulk of the sailor was overcoming the fierce defense of the smaller man when Paul arrived on the scene. He raised the stave and crashed it down on the neck and back of the unsuspecting sailor. There was a loud crack. The sailor fell to the ground and crawled away, holding his back and screaming.

"De Witt!" Joshua said in astonishment.

"What the devil's happening?"

"We were burying old Mordecai . . . these men attacked. I never saw them before . . ."

There was no more time for talk. The sailors were wading into the Jews, flailing indiscriminately at men and women, scattering them like leaves.

But by now the Jewish men had recovered from their initial shock, and they were picking up rocks and sticks and fighting back. One of them grabbed a sailor who had just knocked down a woman, and flattened him with a looping roundhouse punch. What had started as a rout was now turning into a pitched battle.

Paul glanced toward the perimeter of the group and saw his uncle standing there, observing what was going on, but making no move to participate. So far none of the sailors had gotten near him. If he was calm, he was also wary, and his eyes kept darting from man to man.

Paul's attention was diverted as two sailors charged down on him. They were met with swift ferociousness. One had his teeth knocked out by Joshua's rock; the other's arm snapped like a dry twig as he tried to fend off Paul's heavy stave. A third sailor bore down on Paul with a sword in his hand.

Janet Beekman, watching in horror as the flashing blade threatened her future husband, began running toward the field.

Paul's attacker lunged forward, the razor point of his sword aimed at the heart. The heavy stave knocked the blade aside; and now Paul attacked. He swung the heavy piece of wood in an arc and almost caught the sailor. It missed, but only barely, causing the man to stumble backward and fall. The stave whipped through the air again and pounded the earth—the barest instant after the intended victim had managed to roll aside. He jumped back onto his feet. Paul and the sailor began circling, a look of wariness and respect on both faces.

Meanwhile Joshua Seixas had armed himself with a gravedigger's discarded shovel. Other young men of the congregation came to his side, weapons in their hands, a desire for revenge in their eyes. Older men picked up rocks. Now there were over twenty facing the sailors; the combatants had become evenly matched.

The leader of the sailors looked at the angry men and took out a pistol. It was the first firearm exposed. He raised the weapon and pointed it at Paul de Witt.

There was an explosion, and a look of surprise came over Paul's face. The sailor with the pistol took a single staggering step forward. Then the weapon fell from his hands and he dropped to the ground. All eyes swung to the man who had shot him. Jacob Adam de Kuyper looked calm even with a smoking pistol in his hand.

Everyone seemed frozen for a moment—the sailors, who looked dumbly at their fallen leader; the Jews, who were surprised by this help from an unexpected quarter; Janet, who had stopped running and who had watched in horror as the sailor aimed his weapon at Paul; even the people who had come out of Webber's tavern to watch the excitement from the safety of the hill.

The first person to come out of his momentary trance was a sailor who cursed loudly and tugged at the pistol held in place by his belt. He never managed to draw the weapon. Once again the loud explosion of a gun shattered the scene.

A black man holding a musket was moving toward the combatants. Behind him were a dozen more black men, all armed with muskets. The black who had already fired dropped his useless weapon and pulled a pistol from his belt. He aimed it at the sailors. The other blacks followed the signal and raised their muskets. The sailors found themselves facing death.

There was a moment of hesitation. Two of the sailors broke and ran; the others saw, hesitated, then followed until all were gone, leaving behind three wounded on the field of battle.

Paul de Witt's eyes widened as he saw an unarmed black man come from behind his companions and address his uncle. It was Daniel Gerait. "Well, Mister de Kuyper, we were here just like you told us."

"Uncle—" Paul began, but his thoughts came too swiftly for words.

Jacob Adam put his pistol away. "Thank you, Daniel."

"For a moment there I thought we was going to be too late. Yessir, too late."

"You were quite on time," Jacob Adam said. He turned to the other black men who were coming closer. "Thank you all for doing me this service. I'll not forget it."

Several of them smiled and a few assured him it was their pleasure.

"What's going on?" Paul finally managed to say.

"You know Daniel," Jacob Adam said blandly. "He was simply doing me a favor."

"Who are the others?"

"Free black men. They live here near the Collect. They're friends of Daniel," Jacob Adam said. He did not add that he was amused by Daniel's usual cautiousness in making sure that it was other men who stood in the front ranks with weapons. Daniel had fulfilled Jacob Adam's request, but he had done it in his own way. How unlike his father he was. Old Manuel would have stuck a knife between his teeth, taken a cutlass in each hand and bodily thrown himself at the entire contingent of Portuguese sailors. Yet, in his way, Daniel was probably just as effective.

Daniel joined Jacob Adam, Paul, and Joshua as they walked to where a sailor had fallen. Paul examined the man and announced he was dead.

They went to the weedy patch of grass where the other two sailors were lying. The one who had been cracked in the face by Joshua's rock was still unconscious, but the other was awake, moaning from the pain in the arm that had been shattered by Paul's stave.

"Why did you attack these people?" Paul asked.

The sailor looked up in fear, his eyes darting back and forth among the menacing figures above him.

Joshua shoved the edge of his shovel against the man's neck just below his right ear. "Talk!"

A garble of unintelligible Portuguese sprinkled with a few English words came from the man's mouth.

"I count to three," Joshua said, adding a little pressure to the shovel. "One . . ."

"Yes! Yes! Please! Yes!" the sailor sputtered in a desperate attempt to make himself understood.

"Why did you attack these people?" Paul repeated.

Hesitation. The shovel was shoved forward. Some blood appeared, and the man winced.

"I talk. We paid silver."

"Who paid you?"

"English. Englishman."

"An Englishman told you to attack the Jews?" Paul asked.

The sailor nodded. A hand suddenly grabbed his collar and pulled him up about a foot. Jacob Adam was very matter-of-fact as he spoke.

"But I was the one you were supposed to kill, wasn't I?"

The sailor tried to hold the steady gaze of the other, and failed. A little line of spittle came from his mouth as he looked away. Jacob Adam let go of the collar and the man slumped back to the ground.

Paul looked questioningly at his uncle. "They were trying to kill you?"

Jacob Adam nodded.

"But why? And how did they even know you'd be here at the funeral of a Jew?"

"Mordecai used to work for me," Jacob Adam said curtly, and he turned to Daniel Gerait. "Would you take care of burying the dead one, and seeing that these other two are taken to the jail?"

"Yes, Mister de Kuyper," Daniel said. "And I'm sure glad we could do this for you." He turned to the other black men and began issuing orders.

Paul was about to persist in questioning his uncle when Janet came running up and threw her arms about him. "You might have been killed," she cried, and held on with all the strength in her arms.

After a few moments the stares of the others made Paul uncomfortable. He loosened her grip, and then put his arm about Janet's waist and began to walk her away from the bloodied field. He held her not so much out of tenderness as out of an instinctive desire to protect her from the ugliness she had seen. It was strange, but the fighting and blood had brought them close together in a more meaningful way than had the kiss on the bridge. The kiss had been something between them, and no one else. The attack had brought an evil side of the world into their lives —an evil that had threatened to separate them from one another forever.

The burial of Mordecai was postponed to the next day.

The mournful relatives had the unenviable task of leaving the cemetery with the corpse in the cart. They were accompanied by the other members of the congregation, including the wounded.

Joshua stood at Jacob Adam's side. "What makes you think the attack was meant for you?" he asked.

"I keep informed."

"You could be wrong," Joshua said with a shrug. "Some people just like to attack Jews."

"Or maybe some people would like us to believe it was just an attack on the Jews."

Joshua's left eyebrow arched up. "Then this was no surprise?"

"No."

"Can I help?"

"Thank you, but I'll take care of myself," Jacob Adam said, and he walked off.

A strange man, Joshua thought. He watched him walk across the meadow, a stern, lonely figure making his way toward the bridge that led to town.

From a distant knoll another eye followed Jacob Adam through a spyglass until he reached the bridge. James Wilkington lowered the spyglass and snapped it shut. "Dammit! Those stupid Portagees bungled the job!"

His companion made a sour face. "Too bad, it was a good plan. If de Kuyper and a few Jews had been killed together it would have been an accident—very sad, but an accident nonetheless."

Wilkington shoved the spyglass into his pocket and started back for town. "Those damned Nigras! They had to come and spoil everything before—" A thought struck him, and he grabbed his companion by the arm. "You don't suppose de Kuyper knew—and had those Nigras planted here?"

"How could he have known?" the other man protested. "The only ones who knew were ourselves and the Portagees."

Wilkington released his hold on the other and resumed his rapid pace. "If that bastard de Kuyper even suspects what really happened, there'll be holy hell to pay!"

The activity of the traders was far greater now than it had been twenty or thirty years before.

Furs were still in great demand in Europe, but in their voraciousness the trappers had depleted the supply of fur-bearing animals along the coasts. They simply could not reproduce themselves at the rate they were being killed. Some furs continued to come down the Hudson River, but the French blocked the way to the rich northern lands of fur-bearing animals. The traders knew the vast lands stretching westward held great animal populations; but they were mostly uncharted lands peopled by hostile Indians, and most men figured their lives were worth more than a load or two of furs.

But as the fur trade slowed, others came forward to fill its place. There were many fish and there were foodstuffs and timber products that could find a ready market. Because of the English Navigation Acts, which forbade sending to England products that would compete with the home markets, the traders turned to the Catholic countries of Europe and their possessions. France, Spain, the islands of the Azores, Madeira, and the Canaries bought almost all the fish that could be shipped. The West Indies bought timber, horses, cattle, and fish to feed their growing slave population. Because the fish sent to the Indies was the lowest grade possible, unwanted in Europe or at home, "Jamaica fish" quickly became the popular term for food unfit for anyone but a slave.

Tobacco was another product that sold wherever it was delivered; and, as Jacob Adam had noted profitably, New York flour was welcome in any port in the world, being preferred above any other kind.

With this great increase of merchantmen on the seas came a new pestilence—pirates, hundreds of them. The combined navies of the English, Dutch, French, and Spanish were unable to police the vast bodies of water around the world. Moreover, each nation encouraged its own privateers to scour the oceans and capture prizes flying foreign flags. Many ships started as privateers, but soon turned into outright pirates, looting ships and cargoes without regard to the flag flown at the mast.

Jacob Adam de Kuyper had been one of the first New Yorkers to engage in this shady business. His privately financed ships were technically privateers helping clear the waters of hostile ships, but actually they attacked almost any ship that contained worthwhile booty. There were few witnesses to tell the truth, since the ships were captured at sea, looted, and sunk, and the crew left to drown or be eaten by sharks.

In the event a privateer should lose a battle and its crew be captured, there was little chance of finding out the names of the real owners. Usually only the captain knew the names of his patrons, and he had been well paid to keep his mouth closed. Besides, even if a captain did talk after he had been captured under such circumstances, he would still be hanged. Jacob Adam took the trouble to insure their silence in a more inventive way. He only worked with men who had families somewhere—and there weren't many of these, he had to hunt around for them. If one of these men were captured he knew, if he kept his mouth shut as he went to the gallows, Jacob Adam would make a generous settlement with his relatives.

There were other ways that proved Jacob Adam to be a far-seeing man. Very often a pirate would capture a rich cargo and then be at a loss where to take it. If it was a cargo of a simple commodity like timber or flour, it could usually be disposed in the Indies. But as the pirates captured ship after ship, they also began to accumulate a treasure of other objects—jewels, fine silks, coins of the world, and precious stones. These could be sold in various markets, but usually for a price far below their worth. Jewels that had been taken from a New York merchantman would not find a ready market in New York or neighboring towns, because a purchaser would not wish to take the chance of being discovered with stolen property, even though he had not stolen it himself but bought it from a pirate.

The two pirate ships financed by Jacob Adam and captained by Hodges and Barrent had been accumulating a good deal of this awkward treasure. Jacob Adam decided he would use the noble *William* to transport the accumulated pelf to the pirate market at Madagascar.

A few years later the Madagascar market would be the premier illegal market of the world. But when Jacob Adam decided to send the *William,* it was still a novel idea.

He stood on the deck of the *William* when she met the other two ships on the coast halfway between Sandy Hook and Cape May. The two pirates—*Carib Isle* and *Lord Blackton*—gave up chest after chest of valuable jewels, gold, and silver that disappeared quickly into the cavernous holds of the new transport ship.

Jacob Adam had no illusions about the trustworthiness of his partners Hodges and Barrent. They were pirates, scoundrels who would cut their own brother's throat for profit. But he knew they needed him because he gave them valuable information about prospective "prizes" and was able to dispose of the loot. Furthermore, he had important connections in New York, and these might prove to be of value if there was trouble. It was an uneasy alliance, but an alliance all the same.

The chests were secured aboard the *William*. The old ship's decks once again bristled with cannon. The crew that had sailed with Lars Jorisen was gone, having been replaced by a band of thieves, escaped convicts, and men wanted for crimes in other provinces.

Captain Barrent, master of the *Lord Blackton,* approached Jacob Adam. "She's all loaded, sor."

Jacob Adam nodded and beckoned toward Captain Morrison, the new master of the *William*. "You may sail at any time."

Morrison grunted. He was an Englishman who had been in the slave trade, but had turned to piracy as a more exciting and profitable way of making a living. It was rumored his father had been a clergyman. Whether it was true or not was something no man could say, but Captain Morrison never went anywhere without a worn Bible in his pocket. He now took it out, opened to a marked page. "A short prayer, if you will," he said, looking at Jacob Adam.

Jacob Adam gestured in agreement. Captain Hodges exchanged a cynical look with Captain Barrent.

" 'The wolf also shall dwell with the lamb, and the leopard shall lie down with the kid,' " Captain Morrison intoned. He closed the book and looked piously at the other men. "Isaiah, twelve, six. Amen."

"Amen," Jacob Adam replied.

"And now I'll be off to Madagascar."

The two other captains looked with suspicion at this man who was taking away their hard-won treasure. If they had found the slightest evidence to suggest he might not return, they would have cut his throat. But they had agreed to this plan, and now all they could do was trust in Jacob Adam's wisdom and hope for the best.

"Fair wind at your back," Jacob Adam said.

"And fair wind on your return," Captain Hodges said meaningfully.

Morrison smiled. "Hopefully within the year," he said.

Jacob Adam, Barrent, and Hodges left the *William*. Barrent returned to the *Lord Blackton* as the other two men went aboard the *Carib Isle*. They watched as the *William* raised sail and headed away from the coast toward the open ocean. The moon shone brightly and tiny waves slapped on the slats of the wooden hull. It was difficult to remember that these peaceful waters were the most pirate-infested of the North American coast.

"D'ye trust him?" Hodges asked.

"No. But he'll be back," Jacob Adam said. "He is a man of greed. He'll come back because he knows we'll have more treasure for him."

" 'Tis an easy job 'e 'as," Hodges said. "A good profit with no risk."

"He's sailing into the waters of Madagascar on a ship laden with treasure," Jacob Adam said. "Don't you think there'll be men there who would like to take it from him?"

Captain Hodges laughed—a deep, mirthless laugh. "True enough. I beed to Madagascar. They's men who would slit your throat for a farthing. I guess Morrison be earnin' 'is pay."

The *Carib Isle* set sail and slipped back to Manhatan under cover of darkness. Jacob Adam was put ashore in a longboat, and the *Carib Isle* turned and headed back through the Narrows. She was on her way north in search of French packets. If ships flying other flags strayed into her path, that would be all right, too.

It was an hour after dawn when Jacob Adam returned home. He was tired and about to retire to his bedroom when he heard noises in the front room. He walked to the half-opened door and peered inside. Shafts of sunlight poured through the east windows, brightening the room, filling it with a golden glow.

His son, James, now more than two years old, was playing a game with a woman half hidden behind a chair.

Her back was toward the door, and Jacob Adam assumed it was Jennifer. The woman tossed a ball of yarn and little James scampered after it, emitting a tiny cry of glee.

Jacob Adam stepped through the doorway and silently watched as James picked up the ball and threw it back toward the woman. But his intentions were bigger than his arm, and the yarn bounced on the floor, falling far short of its destination.

"Very good," the woman said, crawling forward on her hands and knees, stopping when she came to the yarn. "Now I'll throw it over . . . *there!*" she said, turning sideways as she sent the ball flying across the room. At the same instant she looked up and saw Jacob Adam in the doorway.

It wasn't Jennifer. It was her mother, Elizabeth Barrow.

Jacob Adam wished he had not entered the room. He would have preferred not to meet his mother-in-law. But it was too late for that; and besides, his son had a smile on his face and was toddling toward him. He disliked Elizabeth, but decided he would be pleasant for the sake of his son.

Elizabeth, however, did not choose to be pleasant. "Out all night again?"

Jacob Adam considered turning his back and leaving without a word, but the malicious look on Elizabeth's face annoyed him. "What I do is none of your business," he said coldly.

"A beautiful young wife at home and he spends the night carousing, drinking, and God knows what else," Elizabeth said, keeping her tone as mild as if she were speaking to little James.

"Keep your poison away from my son. I warn you. If you don't, you'll not be welcome in this house."

Elizabeth stood up and smoothed the front of her long dress. Her face was twitching, and lines of age and anger made her look far older than she was; even evil, ugly. "Welcome? I've never been welcome in this house, never! What kind of man are you? Keeping a woman from her own daughter and grandson?"

Jacob Adam became angry. All this was untrue. Despite his own feelings, he had never spoken a word to Jennifer about her mother. He had never forbidden her to come to the house to see her grandson. In fact, to keep the peace, he had gone out of his way to have as little as possible to do with Elizabeth. So when he spoke, his words were meant to be cruel. "I thought it best for the boy to grow up without knowing his grandmother was a human wreck."

Elizabeth's attempts at restraint ceased at Jacob Adam's stinging words. "You bastard!" she fairly screeched. "You unfeeling, selfish bastard!" The years of sorrow filled her mind; the rejection by Jacob Adam consumed her and made her righteous. "You'll destroy my daughter as you've been destroying me! You'll destroy your son! You'll destroy everything you touch because you're an evil man, Jacob Adam de Kuyper! You'll burn in hell when you die!"

The little boy looked at his grandmother in alarm. He looked back to his father and saw only smoldering anger. He began to cry.

"Please leave this house," Jacob Adam said, fighting to retain control of his temper.

"Why, tell me why," Elizabeth said. "Are you afraid I'll tell your wife the truth about you? That you wanted to marry me years ago? That I was your first choice?"

He knew it was pointless to get into an argument with this half-crazed woman; but he couldn't help himself. "As you yourself have been good enough to remind me, I was only a boy. When I was a man and you wanted me, I turned you down."

"But you wanted me! You wanted *me!*"

"The dream of your life, woman, was to sleep in my bed," he said scornfully. "You never made it."

Elizabeth felt herself ready to snap. Her eyes widened and glinted; moisture beaded on her upper lip. She was about to scream and shout. But she held back.

The vivid memory of the time she had a knife and was going to stab him was imprinted on her mind. Her anger and hatred could be pushed too far, and she knew it. Ever since the knife incident, she had constantly warned herself she must retain her senses during any further encounters with her son-in-law. She was allowed to feel anger toward him—yes, hatred even. But to commit murder? No, a thousand times no!

She held herself rigid for a few seconds and allowed the

red haze to clear in front of her eyes. She looked at Jacob Adam and forced herself to speak calmly. "No, I never made it. I was lucky."

"Get out of my house," he said, equally calmly, but there was a deadly edge to his voice. Young James began to cry again as he tottered toward the door, but he moved too quickly for his chubby legs and fell down in a heap, tears bubbling from his eyes as he wailed his unhappiness.

Jennifer burst into the room upon this scene. Her eyes went from her husband to her mother to her son. She leaped to James and scooped him from the floor, hugging him to her breast. She looked angrily at the other two. "You can hate each other as much as you want," she said in a deep animal voice that was not her own. "But you are to leave my son alone!" She clasped the child closer and kissed his cheeks. James stopped crying and turned his head to look fearfully at his grandmother and his father. One look was enough for him, and he buried his face against his mother, escaping the angry scene as best he could.

Jennifer gave a last glance toward the other two and then left the room, clutching her son tightly, reassuring him, protecting him from these people of his own blood.

Her departure drained the anger from Jacob Adam. He looked at Elizabeth and saw a foolish old woman. He was as bad as she for allowing himself to be drawn into such a stupid scene. His features tightened, and he left the room without a word.

Elizabeth too seemed deflated, emptied of hate. Her shoulders hunched forward, and the lines on her face deepened. She went to the front door and left the house. She didn't bother getting her wrap or her canvas bag of overnight things.

Jennifer sat in the kitchen, moving back and forth on the rocker with James in her arms. The boy's tears dried and his heaving breast subsided. He stared over his mother's shoulder, and his bright mind tried to understand what had happened. But he was only two years old, and nothing like this had ever before happened. All he knew was that he had been terrified of this big man who had been so fearsome. He hoped he would never see him again. That would be nice, he thought—to be with his mother alone—just the two of them—forever and ever. He fell asleep as Jennifer rocked back and forth.

A few months later, some thirty miles off the tip of Cape May, the *Carib Isle* attacked a merchantman flying the English flag. Unfortunately for Captain Hodges, the merchantman turned out to be heavily armed. The battle raged for over two hours. By the time the pirate was able to close with the merchant, half the crew had been killed by cannon fire. The remaining men swarmed aboard the other ship only to be met by a withering fire from sailors armed with flintlocks. The tide of battle turned, and the sailors of the merchant came aboard the *Carib Isle*. Captain Hodges died on his own quarterdeck, his pistol empty, his cutlass red with blood. The slaughter continued until only six pirates remained alive, and these surrendered rather than join their shipmates who lay lifeless on the decks.

The *Carib Isle* was brought to New York, where the surviving pirates were thrown into prison. The victorious merchantman belonged to a consortium of Hudson Valley men headed by James Wilkington. When this firebrand learned that the *Carib Isle* was registered in the name of Robert de Pauw, he immediately filed a lawsuit accusing the Dutchman of being a pirate. Wilkington saw this as his big chance of discrediting the "city slickers" who were taking profits from the bolting of upstate flour.

De Pauw, a weak man in the best of times, fell apart completely. Jacob Adam called at his home and came away convinced that if the case ever came to court, de Pauw would crack. Under the slightest pressure he would name Jacob Adam as his partner in the pirate activities. He could also be made to agree that the entire merchant community was involved in "pirate" activities of one sort or another. Jacob Adam knew that if he allowed this to happen, it could seriously affect the standing and credibility of the merchants with their overseas English masters—and he would bear the brunt of the abuse from the other merchants as being the cause of the trouble.

The solution, therefore, was obvious. The case must never be permitted to come to public trial.

Jacob Adam went to see the newly arrived governor, Colonel Thomas Dongan, an Irishman who had accepted his appointment from the Crown with the understanding that if he did an acceptable job, he would return to his homeland as the Earl of Limerick.

Andros had been tough, but also intelligent and fair. His replacement by Dongan had not been viewed with favor by the men of New York. But the Crown appointed the governor, and the whims of the Crown were many. The turnover had been very high.

Thomas Dongan was a dull-witted man and vain; he thought little of the colonists and universally treated them as inferiors. He had retained Paul de Witt as his secretary on the counsel of ex-Governor Andros. "After all," Andros had said, "having a man around who knows the province will save you time and trouble." Dongan agreed, and within a week he had learned not to act without first seeking the advice of de Witt. He was pleased when the young man informed him of the visit of his uncle. Colonel Dongan knew that Jacob Adam de Kuyper was one of the province's wealthiest and most influential citizens. In short, he was a man well worth cultivation, even for a governor.

Dongan warmly welcomed Jacob Adam into his office, and the two men sat in comfortable chairs with silver goblets and the finest brandy placed before them.

They indulged in some small talk, as befitted two men of position, wealth, and ease. Jacob Adam chatted of matters of commerce, while the governor spoke grandly of his plans for expanding the happiness, health, and prosperity of the province. He boasted of his closeness to the king and spoke of the Crown's own desire to see New York thrive and prosper.

"I'm glad His Majesty is interested in our prosperity. That is the reason for my visit. A certain matter has come up which threatens this prosperity."

"And what is that?" the governor asked in alarm. He had only set foot on these shores and a dark cloud was beginning to form.

"One of the major reasons for the recall of Governor Andros, as I'm sure you are aware," Jacob Adam said smoothly, "is that he raised taxes to confiscatory levels. This caused many businesses to fail and brought him a great deal of criticism at the court."

"Yes, yes, of course I know all that," Governor Dongan

lied. He knew of the king's unhappiness with Andros, but
had thought it was because the governor had not collected
what the Crown thought were sufficient taxes.

Dongan's understanding happened to be closer to the
truth but Jacob Adam chose to interpret matters in his
own way. "The popular belief is that Andros did not gen-
erate enough income, and that is true enough. But the
reason for this was the many business failures. Men simply closed their doors rather than pay ruinous taxes. It is
a sad state of affairs, but one that is easily corrected."

"Yes?" the governor said hopefully.

"It would seem to me," Jacob Adam said, "that fair
taxes spread over a great many businesses would produce
far more income than high taxes from a few. The idea is
to encourage more men to get into trade."

"I cannot disagree with that."

"Which brings me to an issue presently coming to the
dock before Your Lordship that could, at one stroke, drive
more merchants out of business in a few months than
were driven out during all the years under Andros."

Dongan was horrified. If Andros had been recalled for
economic incompetence that had taken years to evidence
itself, what would happen to *him* if, in only a few months,
he presided over the financial disintegration of New
York's business community? He saw his vision of wearing
the ermine collar of an earl disappearing.

"Go on, please, go on," he said.

Jacob Adam knew he had hooked his fish. "A lawsuit
has been filed against Robert de Pauw. If it comes to trial,
it will ruin half the merchants of the city."

"De Pauw," the governor said, trying to recall the case.
"Ah, yes. But isn't that a case of piracy?"

"That's what the accusation states, but it is only a ruse.
The Hudson Valley farmers are attempting to have the
Bolting Act repealed. Do you know why?"

The governor did not know, but was most interested in
finding out.

"They wish to see the city shrivel and die. They are
jealous of our prosperity. But look at what will happen if
the life of the city is stifled. Three quarters of all taxes in
the province now comes from the city. If the Hudson Valley men have their way, you will be deprived of the greatest source of your Crown revenues."

The governor was Irish and had a vivid imagination. If he lost three quarters of Crown revenues, he would never become Earl of Limerick. He would be lucky if he escaped imprisonment in the Tower.

"But this is monstrous, sir," he said, coming to his feet. "I had no idea there were men vile enough to take advantage of me simply because I am new in the province!"

Jacob Adam assured the governor such men existed.

"Robert de Pauw is no pirate," he said. "He owned a privateer and was unlucky because his captain turned pirate. But de Pauw is innocent. If he is convicted, it will mean disaster."

The governor struggled to see the reason, but was having difficulty.

Jacob Adam supplied the answer. "All the other merchants who support privateers, myself included, will not wish to take the chance of being named a pirate because of an errant captain. We will sell our ships and take our losses. But think of the loss to the Crown. Our privateers are one of your major sources of revenue."

The governor was aghast. If Jacob Adam had not come forth, he might have committed a blunder that would have ruined his career.

"If there's ever anything I can do for you, de Kuyper, anything at all, please don't hesitate to ask. I am your servant."

"And I, sir, am yours," Jacob Adam replied.

The very next day, assisted by his provincial secretary, Paul de Witt, the governor examined James Wilkington's complaint and the evidence gathered against Robert de Pauw. De Witt pointed out a certain paragraph in the complaint:

"Forasmuch as this singularly bold act of piracy is but an outstanding example of all sorts of piracies which the self styled Lords of Commerce residing in the City of New York are wont to practice regularly on their hard working fellowman, it can be considered that their practices are but the common manner of their doing business."

"Your uncle is absolutely correct," the governor said.

"These fellows want to destroy the entire commerce of the port."

"And its Crown revenues," Paul added.

The governor was now thoroughly convinced of the correct course of action. The case of Robert de Pauw was privately reviewed and summarily dismissed.

James Wilkington and his supporters complained loudly, but to no avail. The governor, as legal representative of the Crown, was the final voice on any issue in the province, and in this instance no man's judgment could have been more final.

James Wilkington seethed; once again he had lost.

Business kept him in New York for a few days; and he was having lunch at the Lion's Head Inn on Pearl Street, which Governor Andros had renamed Queen Street but which everyone still called Pearl, when he noticed Robert de Pauw seated at a table on the other side of the room.

He continued to eat his 'brace of birds' and drink his ale, but found his meal hard to digest in the presence of the man who had made him look like a fool in the eyes of his peers. He had assured the other Long Island and Hudson Valley farmers that the piracy case was their chance to quash the "downriver scoundrels."

Finally he threw his knife on the table, creating a loud clatter that caused his neighbors to pause in their conversations and stare at this short, red-faced man.

Wilkington stood up and strode across the room.

"Well, de Pauw, I suppose you'll go right on with your bloody piracy?" he said by way of greeting when he arrived at the other's table.

Robert de Pauw, who had been thoroughly enjoying his stew of deer meat, looked up, startled.

"Don't try to fool me, you overstuffed Dutchman," Wilkington said. "I wouldn't be surprised if you've more than one ship at sea doing your dirty work."

"Of course I have ships at sea," de Pauw protested, the words muffled as he tried to choke down his mouthful of venison.

"All pirates, are they?" the pugnacious Wilkington insisted.

"Damn you, sir," de Pauw said as the food passed to his gullet. "Our ships are not pirates. They are privateers on king's business."

James Wilkington's anger evaporated as a new thought flashed across his mind. *Our? Our* ships? And then he looked at the man sitting on the other side of the table.

It was de Kuyper.

It took only a second for everything to become clear. A man had to be more than a fool like de Pauw to be caught as a pirate and still get away with it.

"So it is really *you*, de Kuyper," he said.

Jacob Adam was annoyed with de Pauw's indiscretion, but his face was impassive and his voice showed not the slightest concern. "Think what you wish, sir, but remember when you attack one of us, you attack us all."

"No, no," Wilkington said, waving his hands in the air, "don't try that on me! I might have known you had something to do with this. One of these days you'll get caught out. When that happens, I'd be one of the first to applaud as they lead you to the gallows!"

"To follow, no doubt, in your footsteps, sir," Jacob Adam said, returning to the enjoyment of his lunch.

Afraid of looking weak by pardoning de Pauw, Governor Dongan took to excess. He prepared a spectacle to prove how merciless he could be in pursuit of the king's justice.

He sentenced the pirates from the *Carib Isle* to be hanged on the gallows. The six men were paraded about the town with signs hanging from their necks: "So die all pirates!" "I broke the Law, I pay the Penalty." "Because I stole, I now belong to the worms." And then they were executed.

Two men convicted of minor crimes, the usual punishment for which was a few days labor on public works, were thoroughly flogged in the stocks at the Battery. The beatings were so savage that one man died and the other did not fully recover for months.

"A very tough and formidable man, this Governor Dongan," Robert de Pauw said to a group of merchants gathered at the bridge at Stone and Broad streets, a traditional meeting place for men of trade. Although the reason for the bridge had disappeared when Governor Andros had removed the canal, the structure remained and the meetings continued.

"No one is going to put anything over on *him*," a trader said. "Don't you agree, de Kuyper?"

"But of course," Jacob Adam answered blandly.

It rained lightly as Zilla was working in the garden. She didn't pay any attention to the mist that soaked her head; it felt pleasant. But the next day she woke with a terrible cough, and an ache in her bones. As usual she went to the kitchen and began preparing breakfast, but started coughing and became so weak she had to sit down. She tried to go back to work, but the coughing started again and she allowed the two servant girls to put her back to bed.

The next day the cough was worse, her forehead hot and clammy. The doctor was summoned. He announced she had a severe case of lung fever and gave her syrup to drink; but by the next day the fever was even higher, and nothing could be done for it. At some moments Zilla would be lucid, but most of the time she mumbled and babbled incoherently.

Jacob Adam never left her side. He sat in a chair by the bed, and when his eyelids became too heavy he would doze off to sleep for minutes or even an hour. No one could convince him to go to his bed for a proper rest. He stayed at the old woman's side, holding her hand and helping her to drink cooling liquids when she was awake.

The bout with pneumonia lasted five days, and then her spirit passed from her body and she was dead. Hours earlier there had been a period of consciousness, and she had looked out through her rheumy eyes and smiled when she saw the loyal Jacob Adam in his chair.

"I've been lucky," she said very weakly.

"You're going to get well."

"What difference does it make?" she said dreamily. "I've led a full life and I have a fine son." She patted his hand. "Take care of my family. I won't be here to do it."

He wanted to protest, but could not, and sat at her side as the tears flowed unashamedly down his cheeks.

Jennifer was amazed when she came into the room and saw her husband crying. It was unthinkable that he was capable of such emotion. She knew he cared a great deal about Zilla, but she had been unaware of the depth of his feelings. And it confused her even more. How could he be so tender with the old black woman, and not with her? What was she doing wrong?

She became even more nervous than before, and in her struggle to make things better, made them worse.

Jacob Adam knew the members of the Reformed Church would object to the burial of the black woman in their cemetery, even as they had objected when he had wanted to bury Manuel there. Rather than enter into a futile argument, he took Zilla's body to the farm, where the grist mill was operating at full tilt and where she had spent many happy days years ago when old Pieter de Kuyper was still alive.

Zilla was buried. It was not a big ceremony: Jacob Adam, Jennifer, Anne de Witt and her son Paul, Daniel Gerait, and the servants.

Jacob Adam himself put the tombstone in its place.

What need'st thou snatch at noon
What will be thine at night?

Paul de Witt turned to his uncle. "That is an inscription for a child."

Jacob Adam did not disagree. "She had the faith and love of a child. She was open and simple and good. And as far as I'm concerned, her time came too soon. It is a fitting inscription."

The people left the graveside and returned to New York, where most of them soon forgot about the old black woman whose body rested in a sunlit grave to the north.

But Jacob Adam remembered. He vowed that once a year until he died he would visit the farm and place fresh flowers on Zilla's grave.

Governor Dongan summoned the appointed representatives from everywhere in the province; Jacob Adam allowed himself to be nominated as a delegate from the city. The assembled body of men voted for a charter of liberties and privileges.

The new city charter contained many guarantees for the colonists that would form the nucleus for all future charters. Among them was that every freeman had the right to vote for representatives; that a man had the privilege of being tried by his peers, composed of twelve in number; that taxes could be levied only by direction of the council; that standing armies could not be kept among the people against their will; that martial law should not exist; and that writs of habeas corpus be recognized and enforced. The charter also directed that no person should be discriminated against because of his religion.

This provision led to an unusual scheduling of services at the church in the fort on Sunday mornings. The Reformed Church held the first service in Dutch; it was followed by a Church of England service in English, which was followed in turn by one in French for the Huguenots. Dongan himself was a Catholic, but since his was an unpopular persuasion, he contented himself with holding services in a chapel within his own house. For this purpose an English Jesuit was imported, and he spent most of his time within the walls of the fort, rarely daring to venture outside: half the town believed that if the priest took off his boots, he would reveal cloven hooves.

Even the Quakers, Baptists and Jews—although not invited to the fort's church to hold services—were permitted to gather in peace.

Dongan's charter also divided the city into six wards. Jacob Adam became Leader of the first ward, a position he desired not for the honor, but for the extra leverage it would give in dealing with other men of business.

He was the prime mover in the council's creation of counties—Kings, Queens, Suffolk, Dutchess, Richmond, Orange, Ulster, Albany, Westchester, Dukes, Cornwall, and New York. Each county was allowed to form its own government, which reported to the Crown.

Although this appeared to help the men from the rural counties, the key effect was to free the city dwellers from outside interference. Jacob Adam had correctly foreseen that the merchants of the city would be able to act more swiftly if they did not have to deal with the farmers of Long Island and the Hudson Valley. As leader of the first ward, he became, after the provincial governor, the most influential man in the city.

In 1685 two events of diverse significance occurred.

Charles of England died, and the Duke of York, his brother, was crowned as James II. With his ascension the status of New York was changed to a Crown colony—a possession of the king's. James was ambitious. He conceived the idea of uniting the colonies of New York, Massachusetts, and Virginia into a single Royal Dominion. This was looked upon with horror by the men of all three colonies. Acting as separate entities, they had a certain amount of freedom and could press issues that were in their own interests. If the king had his way, however, their individuality would cease and they would all be governed from a single seat of authority. Any way the colonists looked at it, a dominion meant more control by the Crown and a subsequent loss of freedom by James's subjects in America.

The second event was much more personal. Jennifer de Kuyper gave birth to a girl, who was named Alice.

It was a difficult birth, almost a month premature, and for several long weeks the baby's life hung in the balance. But Alice proved to be a tough little soul, and she accepted nourishment and gathered strength until the crisis was passed. After six weeks the doctor pronounced her sound and, barring the usual threat of childhood diseases, predicted she would grow up to be perfectly normal and healthy.

The arrival of Alice brought a change in Jacob Adam. Perhaps it was because there had been a void in his life since Zilla's death, or perhaps it was simply that his heart went out to this infant who had come into the world with the odds heavily against survival.

He would go to the child's room every morning before he left for his office. If Alice was asleep, he would stand at the side of her crib and look at her, the trace of a smile on his lips. If she was awake, he would softly stroke her chin and let her tiny fingers twine themselves around one of his.

As the child grew older, Jacob Adam remained as attentive as ever, rejoicing in her every attainment.

He came home early one June day and, after refreshing himself with a glass of beer in the kitchen, went to the nursery. Alice was awake and standing in her crib, holding on to the top of the chin-high railing.

"Good afternoon, young lady," he said in the tone he used when speaking to adults; his daughter was only nine months old, but Jacob Adam had never addressed her in baby-talk. Alice's face broke out into a wide smile, and she chortled in reply.

She was a pretty baby, with deep-blue eyes and silky flaxen hair. Her cheeks were rosy and full, and she seemed to have an extra zest for life.

"Let's get out of that prison," Jacob Adam said. He picked Alice up and carried her to the center of the thick-woven carpet, setting her down gently while she swung her arms and made cooing sounds.

Now he held out his hands, and the baby took hold of both thumbs. He raised his arms slowly. She held on and came to a standing position. Very carefully he worked his thumbs out of the little grip, and Alice was standing on her own, without support. Her father moved back a pace, waited a moment, and then held out both arms in a signal for her to come to him.

Alice looked from side to side in momentary confusion, but then timorously moved her right foot forward. Her own movement seemed to startle her, and a look of unhappiness crossed her face. Jacob Adam spoke soothingly and encouraged her. She took three more wavering steps until she was close enough to grab his arm. And then she sat down suddenly and laughed. She realized what she had accomplished and was proud of it.

Jacob Adam went out of the room, called Jennifer, and brought her back for a repeat performance.

"I don't believe it," Jennifer said as she watched the infant take half a dozen steps, growing more sure of herself with each one. "Most babies don't walk until they're at least a year old."

"Alice is a very unusual child," Jacob Adam said, and the look on his face told Jennifer that he was quite serious.

She watched as her husband played with their daughter, and then she became aware of a small figure standing beside her, tugging at the edge of her dress. It was James. The little boy was staring at his father and sister, his eyes wide with attention.

Jennifer knew Jacob Adam never played with the boy in this way. "Maybe James would like to join the game," she said.

The man looked at his son. "A boy should learn there are other things in life than games," he said. "The sooner he learns, the better." He went back to coaxing Alice to her feet.

"He's still little."

"But one day he'll be a man."

Jennifer shook her head and took her son's hand. She knew her husband well enough to realize this was a fixed idea and there was no use in trying to talk him out of it. Girls could play, but boys must get on with the business of the world. Even if they were only three years old.

As she led James into the garden to find a ball to play with, they were accompanied by the sounds of Alice's delight.

"I hope you don't really understand all of this," she said as she found the ball and bounced it toward her son.

James grabbed the ball. He smiled and was about to throw it back when an especially loud and joyous squeal issued from the house. He stopped and the ball dropped to the ground. His smile was gone.

Anne de Kuyper sat alone in her kitchen and stared at the letter in her hand. It was from her older brother, Pieter, who had returned to Amsterdam many years before. This was the first word she had heard from him since, so long ago, he had fought with their father and left the house for good.

Anne had tears in her eyes. The letter informed her that he was dying.

She was now fifty-four years old, which meant her brother was almost sixty. The last time she had seen him, he had been thirty years younger. Jacob Adam had been only a child. She wondered if she would even recognize Pieter if she were to meet him on the street. And would he recognize her?

She reread the letter. Pieter had married and had three children and eight grandchildren. He had led a happy, successful life. His one regret was that he had not maintained his ties with his family in New York. Many years ago their aged father had made a trip to Amsterdam, and the two of them had patched up their differences. Young Pieter had planned on coming to America, but then he had heard his father had died, and the urgency of a trip passed. He had not written, because he always planned on coming in person. But the years had slipped away, and now it was too late. He was to blame for what had happened, he said, but he hoped his brother and sister would forgive him. Their father had understood it was better to make peace and reconciliation in this world, rather than to wait to make them in the next. He hoped his dear brother and sister felt the same way.

Anne decided to take the letter to Jacob Adam. She fussed with her cloak and bonnet, sighed when she looked at herself in the pier glass near the door, and left the house to walk the short distance to Whitehall Street.

The walk left her short of breath, and she envied the young girls she passed, their slender figures an insult to her own stoutish form. She realized that weight was a sign of prosperity, but wondered it it might be better to look less wealthy and perhaps feel more energetic.

Jacob Adam read the letter and placed it back on his desk.

"Do you intend to write to him?" he asked.

"Yes. I only hope it isn't too late," Anne said, dabbing at her eyes with a handkerchief. "Will you write to him as well?"

Jacob Adam looked out the window. "He is a stranger to me. I wouldn't know what to say."

"He is your brother!"

"My brother walked out thirty years ago. I have no brother."

Anne stood up, pushing the chair back angrily. "Isn't it hard enough for him that he fought with our father? Isn't it enough that he's dying? He'd like to hear from his only brother at least once before he goes to his reward."

"If he wanted to hear from me, he would have written to me. Obviously it's you he wishes to hear from."

Anne walked toward the door. "What kind of a family are we? Father against son. Brother against brother. Will there be no peace until all of us are dead?"

Jacob Adam moved from behind his desk and came to the side of his sister. "I have no quarrel with Pieter. But this is the home our father chose for us. Pieter left and went his own way. That was his choice. I am doing nothing but accepting his wishes. If he had wanted us in his life, he knew where to find us. Now that he's dying, he wants to cleanse his conscience. I'm sorry, but I can do nothing for him. Years ago he made peace with Father—

only because Father went to him. That is something I will never do."

Anne left the office in a fury. Both of her brothers were crazy. One had run away, and the other was a cold-blooded monster.

The early morning fog was thick. The sun had risen an hour ago, but had made little penetration through the heavy mist that shouldered its way through the Narrows and spread out across the Upper Bay. It rolled over the island, a dense cloud burying the land from sight. Buildings were huddled ghosts. The bodies of men were gray shapes whose legs disappeared before they touched the ground.

"Be ye sure your man will be along?" Captain Barrent asked Jacob Adam, who stood beside him. Even at a distance of a few feet it was difficult to make out a man's features with certainty.

Jacob Adam pointed down toward lower Pearl Street. "He will come from there," he said. Then he nodded in the direction of the Red Lion Tavern, whose sign was scarcely visible. "And he'll head for the door of the tavern."

"Be sure it be him," the captain said in his startling, high-pitched voice. "It be poor business to make mistakes in a matter like this."

Jacob Adam did not take kindly to cautions. He stared at the other man until he became uncomfortable and suddenly took a great interest in the lapel of his coat. The two passed the next few minutes in silence.

Their vigil was for the man who had caused trouble over the Bolting Act and the piracy charges. But it was for neither of these reasons the men waited for James Wilkington this morning.

Jacob Adam had placed a few bribes in the right hands and had learned that the estate holder from Westchester was the man responsible for the attack of the Portuguese sailors at the Jewish cemetery. It was the sort of threat that could not go unanswered.

As he stood silently in the fog, Jacob Adam knew that what he was about to do hadn't the slightest hint of revenge about it. It was an act designed to give men pause before they tried to upset the business of the colony. Wilkington had transgressed and had to accept the consequences.

Captain Barrent wrinkled his brow and peered into the gray wall of fog that was Pearl Street. "Listen!" he whispered. They cocked their ears and heard the faint sound of footsteps.

The footsteps came closer, and then the dim outline of a man could be seen. Captain Barrent stepped forward and blocked the man's way to the tavern. "Beggin' your pardon, sir," he said, slurring the words to make himself sound like a drunk.

"Get out of my way," Wilkington said, "or I'll have the watch on you."

Jacob Adam stepped forward. He peered closely at the man's face to make certain they had not made a mistake. They had not.

James Wilkington noticed the movement behind the man blocking his path. He peered into the fog, and the half-seen face of the second man was familiar. "De Kuyper!" Wilkington said breathlessly, taking a step backward.

"Now!" Captain Barrent said.

Two burly sailors stepped from an alley leading off Pearl Street. The first grabbed Wilkington from behind; the other stepped in front of him. The sharp knife made a single incision. Wilkington's throat was slit from ear to ear, and his corpse was allowed to fall to the ground.

Jacob Adam nodded at Captain Barrent and walked down lower Pearl without a word. The captain and his two cutthroats turned back into the alley, and the heavy fog muffled their steps until they could be heard no more.

A nasty business, Jacob Adam thought as he walked toward his Whitehall Street office. It wasn't exactly the kind of work he liked, but it was something that had to be done.

There would be a minor commotion. Accusations would be made and fingers pointed. Nothing would come of it, of course, because nothing would ever be proved. But a few men would know why James Wilkington had his throat slit; they would be Wilkington's friends and other men with complaints about the businessmen of the town.

In the future, Jacob Adam hoped, they would keep their complaints to themselves.

It was the last day of the year 1687.

Theophilus Henry was on his way down from de Kuyper Manor to the city to give his yearly accounting. Jacob Adam's hunch about the man had proved correct: the manor had prospered from the day he became its manager.

The snow had been falling heavily, and Henry moved silently through the ghostly landscape, avoiding the heavier drifts and picking his way beneath the whitened trees. The deep snow muffled all sound, and the man moved as if in a dream. Having crossed the Harlem River in a canoe he had hidden beneath the heavy branches of a fallen tree, he was now passing within a half mile of the settlement of Harlem when his sharp eyes spotted fresh tracks on the snow. He stopped and inspected them. Within the past few minutes a wolf had passed this way.

The beast had never enjoyed a large population on the island of Manhatan. And for the past fifty years every farmer, trapper, and trader in the island had hunted wolves without mercy. It was not surprising they were becoming quite rare.

In no hurry to reach his destination, Henry decided to follow the tracks. They led to the north, and he paced after them as they wound between the trees, emerging into an open plain and continuing across it in a straight line until they entered a stand of dense trees.

He followed the tracks for over an hour. Finally he spotted his prey in a small patch of open ground. It was an old gray-muzzled male, his winter coat dense. The wolf had stopped to rest at the base of a large tree and gave no evidence that he was aware of the man pursuing him.

Theophilus Henry was a good hunter. He carefully kept a line of trees between himself and the wolf. Having determined the direction of the wind, he moved, slowly and silently, to keep downwind of the animal. He advanced with great caution, a foot at a time, sometimes mere inches.

And now he was close enough to attempt a shot. His musket was ready, having been loaded and primed when he began following the wolf. He raised the weapon to his shoulder and edged the barrel around the side of the slender tree that concealed him.

The old gray-muzzle was still unaware of the danger. He was seated on the ground, his hind feet drawn beneath him and his front paws spread out before him. His mouth was open and his tongue hung from one side.

Theophilus Henry was about to make a noise that would startle the wolf and bring him to his feet. In that instant he would have a shot at his heart.

But it was a loud sound to his left that brought the wolf to his feet.

"Whoop! Whoop! Whoop!!"

A bone-tipped arrow flashed across the open space and sank into the wolf's heart. The beast was dead as he stumbled to the ground.

Henry whirled about, his musket ready, his eyes wide with the anger he felt at being cheated of his kill. But he was also wary. An arrow meant an Indian, and an Indian meant an enemy.

A figure emerged from behind a snow-covered thicket. As Henry suspected, it was an Indian. He sighted down the barrel of his weapon and prepared to pull the trigger.

"Do you always shoot women?"

The clear voice stopped him, and he raised his head to get a better look. To his surprise, he was looking into the unwavering eyes of a young Indian woman.

"Only a coward would shoot a woman," she said, and, without a second glance at the man, walked to the dead wolf. While the man watched, his jaw slightly agape, she proceeded to turn the carcass over, inspect the jaws and tail, and retrieve the arrow. Then she looked up at Henry.

"He was an old warrior who would have died soon anyway," she said. "His fur is thick and good."

Theophilus Henry, the incurable Indian-hater, was at a loss for words. He had long ago decided Indians were nothing more than cunning animals themselves, but now he found himself admiring the cool courage of this girl who seemed to fear neither beast nor man.

She stood up. She was slender, and her skin glistened with the oils she used to preserve and beautify it. "He is very heavy. Will you help me carry him to my village?"

Henry still could not find his voice. The girl misinterpreted his silence. "It is not very far," she said.

"It isn't that," he managed to say. "Did you know I was trying to kill the wolf?"

"Of course."

"And you took him from me?"

"You would have taken him from me," she said, her voice firm and her eyes looking straight into his. "I have more use for him."

Maybe she was an Indian, but she certainly was a brave one. "I'll help you carry the wolf," he said.

She nodded and then entered the woods, returning with a stout branch. With quick, sure movements, she broke it into a pole of suitable length. Using long pieces of deer sinew, she tied the wolf's feet together and then passed the pole between the feet and the body. They each took an end of the pole and picked up the wolf. With the woman leading the way, they went through the woods until they came to her village, not far from the south shore of the Spuyten Duyvil.

Several women came and took the wolf away. The girl raised a flap on the side of a longhouse and gestured for Henry to enter. Once inside, she pointed to a place near the fire. While the man warmed himself, she went about the business of providing him with food and drink. When this was all arranged, she sat down nearby and began to eat strips of dried meat.

"Where did you learn to speak English?" he asked.

"From the man who owns a farm on the other side of the river. Ever since I was a little girl I would go there and play with his daughter. I grew up speaking English as well as the language of my own people. The man's name is John Archer, and his daughter is Sarah."

Henry nodded. He knew Archer—a good farmer and a man quite capable of defending his own interests, either in a court of law or with a gun. It surprised him that a man like Archer would have allowed an Indian girl to be the playmate of his own daughter.

"What is your name?" he asked.

"My Indian name or my English one?"

"Both."

"Ahnakink. In our language it means 'in the earth.'

John Archer gave me the name of Elizabeth. He said it was in honor of a great queen of his people."

"Elizabeth," he said softly. It did not seem to be a strange name for the nut-brown maid who sat at his side.

They talked for several hours. Elizabeth, it turned out, was the daughter of the chief Stone Eagle. He was the blood son of a great chief named Senadondo, who had been instrumental in ending the long war of 1643–1645. Elizabeth herself had been given to a warrior, but before they could become man and wife, the warrior had been killed by a white trader who claimed the Indian was trying to steal from his camp.

"Do you hate the white man?" Henry asked.

"No. There are good and bad white men."

"And what am I?"

"If I did not think you were a good white man, you would not be here," she said simply. "The arrow would have been for you instead of the wolf."

Theophilus Henry tarried for a week at the village. He met Stone Eagle. The warrior had been given his name many years ago because, like a stone, he was silent; like an eagle, he missed nothing. Both men held each other in mutual respect for their strength and independence.

Near the end of Henry's stay, Stone Eagle did an unusual thing. He went to the fire pit at the end of the longhouse, where his visitor was warming himself near the hot coals. He sat and offered his pipe to the white man. They smoked in silence for several minutes. It was not unusual for Stone Eagle to share his pipe with a white man, but the chief had always waited for the white man to come to him.

They spoke of the woods and the stars; of the wolf and the bear; of the forest. And then Stone Eagle asked questions about the white men who lived at the tip of the island. After a time Henry realized the chief knew a great deal about the white people, more than he would admit directly.

"So you once met Pieter de Kuyper?" he asked.

The chief nodded.

"And his son, Jacob Adam?"

Another nod. "When he was a boy."

Theophilus Henry spoke of the town and the manor. He spoke a great deal about Jacob Adam. The chief seemed curious about this particular man—for what reason, Henry could only wonder. What possible connection could there be between this forest-dweller and the cold-eyed man of commerce? Theophilus Henry could think of none and dismissed the matter from his mind as he continued to answer the old chief's questions.

Stone Eagle sat alone before his own fire that night. He watched the flames die to flickers, the logs to embers. His thoughts went back many years—first to the time during the wars, when he had disgraced himself by taking a devil-possessed woman.

In the solitude of his conscience a man must face his own deeds. By an act of dishonor he had, perhaps, given the woman a child. And then his thoughts bridged a dozen years afterward, to the moment he met the son of Pieter de Kuyper. This young man, Jacob Adam, had caused his soul to stir. There was something about him that . . . If a child had been born of that woman he had taken, he would be the same age. The eyes of the boy, and the way he looked at others . . . looking a great deal but saying little . . . It was far-fetched, and yet Stone Eagle had sharp intuitions and insights that came from being a creature of the forest. These instincts had not been blunted and softened by civilization, not weakened by European ways. His body had not been corrupted by their putrid food, nor his brain by their alcohol. Through the night he sat. The sun rose and his fire had turned to dead ash, but his thoughts were alive. The boy he had seen years ago, this Jacob Adam de Kuyper, could be his own son. He rose and walked into the crispness of the dawn. He filled his lungs and started to trot toward the place where the waters came together. It was a good place to clear one's thoughts.

Theophilus Henry was also awake, and he watched the chief passing through the village with his easy, mile-devouring stride. Stone Eagle was not a young man, but, Henry knew, he could maintain that pace for hours at a time. There wasn't a white man in America, including himself, who could duplicate the feat. For the first time in his life he began to see the majesty and value of the Indian. He almost began to think of Stone Eagle as a friend. As for Elizabeth, his admiration was fast increasing to devotion. He went to sleep at night with visions of her beautiful face and strong, lithe body. She wore her black hair tied in braids that bounced on her shoulders as she walked. Her eyes were set a shade too far apart, perhaps, but the effect was to make her face seem triangular, even more exotic and exciting. Her nose was a trifle smaller than most Indians', emphasizing the pert quality in her bearing.

During the day they hunted deer together. This was not the normal way of life among the Indians, but in some ways Elizabeth had become almost as much white as Indian.

Finally Henry continued his journey to make his report to Jacob Adam de Kuyper. But on the return trip he stopped again at the village by Spuyten Duyvil, and this time stayed almost a month. When he finally did return home, he amazed everyone at de Kuyper Manor by presenting Elizabeth as his wife.

Elizabeth moved into the manager's house as if accustomed to such surroundings from birth. She took over the household the moment she arrived. At first the men of the manor saw docility in her soft-eyed beauty, but her quick, biting tongue soon put an end to this idea.

Theophilus Henry became a devoted family man, especially when Elizabeth gave birth to a son.

The wolf she had killed had been made into a fur coat, which she gave to her husband as a wedding present. It became his proudest possession, and he wore it from early fall almost through spring.

There was one important thing about this coat that he did not know: the wolf had been the last to be killed in a wild state on the island of Manhatan.

An era had passed and no one was even aware of it.

2

The Pirates of Madagascar

1696–1710

JAMES DE KUYPER, ALMOST FIFTEEN YEARS old, stood at the open door of the main house at de Kuyper Manor and watched his breath come out as great clouds of steam. In another moment the first light of dawn would pierce the blackness of the sky and the stars would fade into the blue of another day. It was the middle of November, and the first serious frost had set in, bringing winter upon the land. It signaled a big event in the life of the manor.

Today was hog-killing time, and four old tuskers were destined to be turned into food for the winter.

Theophilus Henry, along with James and several other men, had already been at work for two hours. They had set a huge iron kettle filled with water over a roaring fire. As a man kept fueling the fire, the water grew hotter and hotter, and now approached the boiling point. The pot would be ready at sunrise.

George Henry had the sturdy build of his father and the intense eyes and copper skin of his mother. He came to the door and stood at James's side. The two had been friends throughout the nine years of George's life, and they thought of each other as brothers. It never entered James's mind to look down on the boy he thought of as his brother simply because one of his parents was a full-blooded Indian.

"Finally got up, did you?" James said sarcastically to the yawning boy.

"No one woke me," George said.

"Get something hot to drink."

"Later. I want to watch."

The manager's house stood across from the manor, and a small figure darted through the door. It was Stephen, George's seven-year-old brother. His eyes were wide; he feared he had missed the magic moment. When he saw two men leading a large hog out of the pen, his anxiety disappeared and his pace slowed. It was not too late. He walked on toward the kettles as he stuffed the tail of his shirt inside his trousers.

Theophilus Henry, holding a long, razor-sharp knife, approached the first hog, who was now outside the pen. Two men took firm hold of the animal. While Henry stood to one side, another man approached with a sixteen-pound iron-headed sledge. He brought the hammer down on the head of the pig with the full force of his body. The tusker grunted and his front legs buckled, sending him to the ground. Henry stepped forward. With one quick motion of his wrist, he inserted the knife and slit the animal's throat.

Although the blow of the hammer had left him almost unconscious, the pig squealed loudly and thrashed in the leather traces. The two strapping men holding him were almost dragged off their feet by the struggling beast. The high, unearthly squeals continued. Finally the pig was finished. He fell to the ground as a stream of warm red fluid turned the frost crimson and steamed as it touched the cold ground.

Before the squeals of the first pig had ended, the process was begun on the second animal, followed in turn by the third and fourth. It was a hellish cacophony, but the men moved matter-of-factly about their business while the eyes of the three boys shone with excitement and anticipation of the rest of the drama.

The women of the manor had stayed indoors during this time, and they held their hands over their ears, not wishing to hear the terror of the dying hogs—trusting animals who had regarded the men as their friends and providers. Even so, the shrill screams penetrated, and most of the women wept for the animals they had cared for from the time they were born.

One exception was Elizabeth Henry. She continued to work in the kitchen, preparing for the moment the men would start bringing in the meat. To Elizabeth, the killing of an animal bred and raised to be killed seemed the most natural thing in the world. Besides, there was much to do, and she had no time to waste in covering her ears or wishing things that could not be.

Her daughter, Hope, worked at her side for as long as she could stand it. "If Mother can do it, so can I," Hope thought. But after a time the squeals became too much for the girl, and she returned to her room and covered her head with a heavy feather quilt.

Now James took his place with the men and worked at their side. Theophilus Henry had promised that next year he could be the actual slaughterer. Even though the knife had been honed to a sharpness that could split a hair, it took strength to cut through the tough skin of a full-grown hog's throat. By next winter James de Kuyper would be able to do it.

The men grunted and strained as they pushed the carcasses onto sleds and dragged them next to the kettle, whose water was bubbling and steaming into the air. The sun was now rising, and the heavy oil lamps were extinguished. A heavy block and tackle was raised on a stout tripod hewn from young hickory trees, and this was used to draw the carcass of the first hog into the air. It was raised high and positioned over the top of the kettle, then lowered until it was covered with boiling water. Fuel was added to the fire to keep it at a roaring blaze. After about ten minutes, Theophilus Henry ordered the men to use the block and tackle to lift the hog clear of the kettle.

It was now placed on a wooden rack, where the men set about it with bell-shaped utensils, scraping off skin and hair. While this was being done, other men raised the second carcass with the tackle and dropped it into the kettle for its time of scalding.

The first carcass was emptied of intestines and beheaded. When all the hair and skin were gone, the men dragged it to the kitchen. There the women began to process it into the winter's meat.

Under the direction of Elizabeth Henry, the kitchen became a scene of great activity. The women cut the fat away from the carcass and began rendering it into lard.

The back meat was chopped up for sausage, then seasoned and stuffed into the intestinal skins, which had been cleaned and washed. Most of this meat would be smoked, but some of it was placed aside to be eaten fresh by the people of the manor and the neighbors, who, by tradition, would drop in for a visit the day after hog killing.

Bacon and ham shoulders, to be smoked, first went into barrels of brine for cooking.

The hog's head and feet were cooked at once, and this meat was mixed with vinegar and spices and made into head cheese and souse. As the cooking pots filled and bubbled, the entire manor air took on the wonderful smells of the feast to come. The livers were cooked and chopped into very fine pieces that would be stirred into a mush, usually of corn meal; the mixture would be cooked in pans and allowed to cool. The result, scrapple, was considered a delicacy. Women guarded their spicing recipes with great jealousy, because it was one of the finest accolades to be called a master scrapple maker.

As the lard kettle bubbled and made delicious noises, bits and pieces of the rendered lard broke away and floated to the top. They were carefully removed, and everyone—men, women and children—vied to get a piece of these cracklings, a prime reward on hog killing day.

By the end of the day nearly two thousand pounds of meat had been prepared in one way or another. With this much in the provision larders, everyone breathed a sigh of relief and looked ahead with less trepidation toward the rigors of winter.

Throughout the day James did his share of work as a man, and George and Stephen dogged his steps, helping as they could and learning more as every hour passed.

"Are you ready for next year?" Theophilus asked James.

"I think so. I've practiced using the wrist the way you taught me. If I lean my body behind the knife, I can bring more strength into the thrust."

The manager patted the son of the manor's owner on the shoulder. "Good boy. Now let's get into the kitchen, because it's time for dinner."

They sat around several tables—the manager and his wife and family, the other workers and their wives and children, and James de Kuyper. The tables were heaped high with fresh backmeat and hams that remained from hogs slaughtered the previous year. Jealously guarded sausages and pans of scrapple, also from last year, were brought from their hiding places and passed around. But the feast was not limited to hog meat. There were great platters of venison and bowls of bear meat smothered in brown sauce. Sideboards groaned under steaming bowls of succotash, beans, and squash, baskets filled with steaming fresh rolls and great slabs of bread, tins of hot, delicious meat pies, fish pies, berry pies—all brought forth and devoured by the hungry crew, who quaffed buckets of cold beer as they ate. The men added rum and brandy to their beer, and the very room seemed aglow with happiness.

"I can't eat another bite," James said, placing both hands over his full belly.

"You've hardly begun," Theophilus Henry said. "Open another notch in your belt, lad. And then help yourself to more venison pie."

"If he's had enough, he's had enough," Elizabeth said, her own plate empty. "Too much food is as bad as not enough."

Theophilus Henry laughed. "Don't listen to this old squaw," he said. "The Indian is out to kill us even if starving to death is the only way he can find."

"We don't have to starve the white man to get rid of him," Elizabeth responded. "You'll die from overeating."

James laughed, and found the effort caused him to feel sick to his stomach.

Theophilus proposed a toast to the Indians for having produced such a wonderful woman. The men all raised their mugs and drank the toast, but most of them drank to Elizabeth rather than to Indians in general.

James ate but one more mouthful of the meat pie before he dropped his spoon in surrender. He did manage, however, to drink more beer, and this, on top of all the food, made him sleepy. It was many hours after dark when he finally left the cheery kitchen of the manager's house and returned to his bedroom at the manor. It was cold there, and he snuggled under the heavy covers, shivering until his body warmth filled the cavity.

These were the happiest times in James de Kuyper's life —when he lived as part of the family of Theophilus and Elizabeth Henry at the manor. Life here was simple and

open, and a boy was not afraid to act the way he wanted
to act. In the city, in the house on upper Pearl Street, he
always felt his father's eyes watching him, questioning him
mutely, ready to accuse him for the smallest breach of
conduct.

He was afraid of his father, as were most other people
he knew. But the others only had to deal with Jacob
Adam from time to time, and then they could retreat to
their own homes and lives. As Jacob Adam's son, James
had no place to go—nowhere but here.

James would be at the manor another week before he
had to return to New York and once again waste his time
at that damned school his father insisted he attend.

He truly hated to study Latin and Greek. What good
were such things? To kill a hog was a skill a man could
use all through his life; but to be able to say "the farmer
stands in the field" in Latin seemed a total waste of time.

A smile came to his lips when he remembered the full
week at the manor, and James de Kuyper, heir to a fortune he knew nothing about, fell asleep.

Theophilus and Elizabeth Henry lay naked, flattened
against one another under the blankets.

As the urge of nature became strong, the man entered
the body of the woman, and the two become one with an
intensity that electrified them both.

When it was over, he tossed the blankets from their
panting, sweating bodies. Although the air was frigid, it
had seemed warm in the room, and the sudden coldness
was a relief.

For the ten-thousandth time in his life, Theophilus
Henry thanked Providence that his finger had hesitated
on the trigger of his gun that day long ago in the woods
near the settlement of Harlem. He knew he had found
the woman for his life; he would never be content with
another.

On the day James was occupied with pig killing at the
manor, his sister was challenging one of the Livingston
boys to a horse race.

The child who had been the apple of her father's eye
had turned into a high-spirited, strong-willed young girl.
Now thirteen, Alice had a high, intelligent forehead, long

blond hair that she wore tied behind her head, sparkling eyes, and the quick temper of a mule driver. She was pretty, but not beautiful, yet the boys of her age were more in awe of her than of any other female of their acquaintance.

"My mare can outrace that overstuffed, spindly-legged creature of yours," she said angrily to the boy on horseback.

John Livingston, fifteen years old and already possessing the body and strength of a man, looked down at the tiny girl who stood with her hands spread defiantly on her hips. He had just galloped his horse past the corner of Wall and William, where a group of girls had been having a pet cat show. He had done it to impress them with his manliness and courage, but the result had been a disaster, as the terrified felines, hissing and meowing, scattered to escape the terror. As the other girls were scrambling about to retrieve their pets from under stoops and entice them down from roofs and rafters, Alice had elected to tell off the cause of all the trouble in no uncertain terms.

"Racing around like a fool on that horse, you big boob!" she shouted. "Somebody ought to crack you over the head!"

"I was just having fun."

"You think you're so wonderful, I'd like to see you in a *real* race. I could beat you myself."

"Name the time and place," John said, showing bravado, but feeling foolish about arguing with a girl in this manner.

"Right now!" Alice said.

"You mean .... *now?*"

"Unless you know another meaning of the word," she said. "Wait here. I'll get Sugar ready. And don't try to run away and hide." She strode off.

"I'll be here," the boy called after her.

But his thoughts were depressed. *Sugar,* he thought. What a sissy name! And what if his friends found out he was racing a girl?

He decided he might get away with it if they took the horses into the country. They would hold the race where no one would see them. It wasn't that he was afraid of losing; no, it was impossible that he would lose to a girl.

But even when he won, what was the point? So he beat a girl, big deal.

He sat in the street on his horse, feeling stupid.

Jennifer was coming home from a shopping trip, and she saw her daughter as she passed the stable. "Going riding, my dear?"

"Yes," Alice said. "I'm having a race with that snotty John Livingston."

"A race? Isn't that dangerous?"

"Not if you know what you're doing," Alice said, and she slipped the bit into Sugar's mouth and arranged the cheek strap and brow band on her mount's long head.

"Well . . ." Jennifer paused, puzzled; then she just sighed and said, "Good luck." She left the stable area and went into the house. She had given up trying to manage her daughter. Alice was just like Jacob Adam, and the only thing you could do with the two of them, together or separately, was give them their head and let them go about their business as they saw fit.

Alice came riding around the corner from the stable at a trot. Her bay mare was four years old and a high step- per. Sugar had been a present from Jacob Adam on her tenth birthday. Jennifer had objected, pointing out that a pony might have been a better choice, but Jacob Adam had insisted on a full-sized horse. "I don't want my daughter looking up at everyone when she goes riding," he had said.

"Shall we go out beyond the Commons?" John Livin- ston asked when the girl reined up beside him. "There's good open country and flat ground out there."

"Afraid someone might see you lose?" Alice knew she had hit home when the boy turned red.

She spurred Sugar and trotted to the head of William Street. "We'll go up to Cherry Street where it goes past Beekman's Swamp," she said, in a manner that clearly stated she had thought it all out. "Then we'll race down Queen Street, past the Slip, the Old Slip, down Dock Street, over the bridge at Broad, and finish where White- hall crosses Pearl."

The boy caught his breath and looked at her as if she had pulled a gun on him. "That's right through the busiest part of town!"

"So what?"

"But there'll be a lot of people around. Somebody could get hurt . . . carts and wagons . . . it's dangerous," he protested, groping for any reason that might prevent this looming disaster.

"Are you afraid?"

"Of course not," he said quickly. Too quickly, because in truth the idea of galloping a horse down the length of the city was not the most intelligent thing to do. In fact it was quite mad. He could just hear what people would say —worse, what his *father* would say when he heard about it.

"Then it's decided," Alice said emphatically. "We go right through town." She brushed the reins against Sugar's neck, and the horse started north on William Street.

The other girls had gathered their cats and taken them home. They had come back and were cheering Alice now as she rode up the street, the miserable boy trailing her by a few paces.

On the way to Cherry Street they met several other boys on horseback, and Alice took great glee in informing them about the race while John sat sulkily on his horse, mutely accepting the sneers of his friends. They were joined by this group and soon met several others who hastened to get in on the fun. By the time they reached Beekman's Swamp, they numbered twenty horses and riders—nineteen boys and Alice de Kuyper.

She stopped her horse in the middle of Cherry Street— a dirt lane that derived its name from the new cherry orchard next to it. "I'm ready," she announced.

"Look, we don't have to go through with this if you don't want to," John said, in a tone of voice he hoped was humorous.

"But I want to," Alice insisted. She looked over at the group of boys on their mounts. "Somebody get over here and start this thing."

One of the de Peyster boys came over. "Why certainly, Miss de Kuyper. And may the better man win. Ready, Livingston?"

"Hm," John replied.

"Wait a minute," Alice said. "What's the wager?"

"Wager?"

"The bet," she said impatiently. "How much? Ten pounds?"

The boy gulped. "Ten? I don't want to take you—"

"Too much, huh? All right, make it five." She turned back to de Peyster. "Start the race."

De Peyster made sure the two horses were on a line. "All right . . . ready . . . *go!*"

Alice dug her heels into Sugar's sides and the little mare jumped forward as if she had been shot from a catapult. The boy was a shade slower in reacting, and by the time he had his horse at a full gallop, the girl was two lengths in front and racing for the head of Queen Street as if she was going to a fire.

Alice bent low in the saddle, keeping down to cut wind resistance, all the while talking a steady stream of encouragement to her mount. John was close behind, digging his heels into the horse and using the whip to spur him on to greater speed.

Meanwhile, the eighteen other horsemen followed at a frantic pace, all of them shouting and whooping it up.

As they raced down Queen Street, they began to enter the more populated area of the city, and people stopped in their tasks to watch this strange sight.

"Crazy kids," muttered a farmer, who was bringing a small flock of sheep down to town. The horses flew by the sheep, scattering them and causing them to bellow their protests. Just as all began to calm down, the young horsemen who were following the race came by, and the sheep scattered again.

John Livingston's horse was bigger and stronger than Alice's mare, and on the straightaway to Wall Street, with only a slight bend at Golden Street, he overtook the girl. They raced neck-and-neck.

"We ought to stop," he shouted over to his opponent. "The streets ahead will be too crowded."

Alice's answer was to use her crop on Sugar's haunches, prompting an extra burst of speed.

They picked up their first dog. A mongrel saw the horses and, no doubt thinking this would be great sport, sped along in their wake, barking his enthusiasm.

As they approached Wall Street, the racers could see a large group of people waiting and cheering them on. Alice's friends had gone through the neighborhood telling everybody they saw about the race, and people were now out in the streets in force. The two horses and their crouching riders crossed Wall Street at an all-out gallop, and the cheers of the crowd could be heard for blocks around.

Jennifer was in her parlor when she heard the muffled shouts and cries. "I wonder what that's all about?" she asked the maid, who was polishing a silver bowl.

"Supposed to be some sort of horse race, ma'am."

A horse race? Alice had spoken of a horse race. She wondered if—but no, not even Alice would be crazy enough to race a horse right through New York.

The cheers continued as horses, riders, and dogs came down the street at a breakneck pace. The noncompeting youngsters on their horses cheered the crowds as they passed.

The road narrowed and became crooked when it changed from Queen to Dock Street.

A cartman was pulling his wagon toward an alley on the west side of the street when the two galloping horses came straight at him. He looked up in alarm; and then they were upon him. One horse veered to the right, giving ground to avoid hitting the wagon, but the other—and the cartman couldn't believe his eyes, because it looked like the rider was a girl—leaped right over the wagon and sped on in a straight line down the middle of the street. The cartman raised his fist and was about to shout his protest when he was surrounded by a pack of yelping dogs, who tore past as if he didn't exist. He took a deep breath, turned to his cart—and saw another horde of riders swooping down on him. The cartman dove into the alley, where he crouched on the ground with his hands over his head.

Alice had regained the lead because of the hurdle over the cart, and she rode down Dock Street, flashing past shops and people. The workers and the loafers alike blinked and jumped back out of the way to save their skins.

Two hefty Dutch traders, having just concluded a deal, were pausing to light their pipes at the bridge on Broad Street. One suddenly shouted to the other and pointed to the horses that were thundering down on them. The two fat men almost knocked each other over in their haste to get off the narrow bridge. The slower of the two barely made it intact. Alice's horse struck him a glancing blow as he tried to lunge off the bridge. The impact knocked him a dozen feet, and he landed against a cart that was hauling fish from the docks. The cart tipped over and dumped its load on top of the Dutchman.

And now the two riders were in the home stretch—the last bit of Dock Street before it ended at Whitehall. This was one of the most crowded areas of the city, and the activity at the wharfs and in the shops was at the high point of the day. Men and women jumped aside to avoid being ground beneath the flashing hoofs. Boys hooted and whistled from the sidelines. The pack of dogs had grown to over a dozen, and all continued to contribute their barks and bayings to the bedlam.

John had drawn even again, and he could see the end of the street, where the imaginary finish line was set. At this point on Dock Street the east side of the street was a forest of masts, spars and booms, the latter jutting out over the land and threatening to decapitate the riders if they came too close. Piles of freshly unloaded cargo were piled in the street, and the two horses were forced to maneuver around and between them. When they were forced near the booms, Alice and John had to get their heads down as close to the horses as possible.

Toward the end of the street was a large stack of crates; it was obvious the space between the crates and the booms was too small to permit the passage of two horses side by side. The race became a question of who could get to that space first.

The boy would have done it, except he was forced to guide his horse around a pile of small barrels. As he did this, Alice took her life in her hands and hurdled the barrels in the same way she had hurdled the cartman's wagon. When they came to the opening by the crates, she was clearly in the lead, and John passed through the crates and the booms behind her.

The horses remained in this position as Alice flashed across Whitehall Street and won the race. She went halfway up the next block of Pearl Street, almost bowling over two drunken sailors, before she was able to bring the mare to a halt. She turned and started back toward Whitehall as John Livingston brought his horse alongside.

The two mounts were panting and wheezing from the exertion, and their hides were slathered with white foam and sweat. The riders seemed almost as much out of breath, as the other horsemen who had been following reined up and began cheering the victor.

When the horses stopped, the dog pack also came to a halt; but the animals were so excited they began to snarl and fight among themselves. Several men jumped into their midst in an attempt to separate them, and a new bedlam was created.

"Look there, de Kuyper!" said the French merchant from Martinique as the two men came walking down Whitehall Street toward Jacob Adam's office. "Do your citizens race horses in the streets?"

Jacob Adam's eyes narrowed when he saw that one of the riders was his own daughter. He walked to the corner and waited until she spotted him.

"Hello, Father," she said, breaking into a big smile. "You know John Livingston, don't you?"

Jacob Adam nodded curtly at the boy and tried to ignore the chaos of dogs, riders, and angry shopkeepers that swirled about them in the street. "What's this all about?"

"John and I had a race," Alice said brightly. "I won."

Jacob Adam looked at her and realized she was probably the cause of all the commotion.

"You aren't going to be peeved with me, are you?" she asked.

"So you won," Jacob Adam said. "Was there a prize?"

"Yes, five pounds," Alice said, looking derisively at John Livingston. "I wanted to make it ten, but he didn't want to take that much money from me."

Jacob Adam smiled as he watched Alice ride away and through the gesticulating crowd of well-wishers and detractors.

"Your daughter?" the French merchant asked.

"Yes."

"Quite a girl."

"She is."

"But all this for five pounds?" the Frenchman said, surveying the scene.

Jacob Adam arched an eyebrow. "Anybody can use an extra five pounds," he said.

Paul de Witt was having breakfast with his wife, Janet, and their three children in his comfortable house off

Moore Street, which had received its name from the ships that customarily moored at the bay end.

He was thirty-eight years old and quite proud of himself. In between mouthfuls of food and swallows of Brazilian coffee, he couldn't keep from smiling.

"Something special happening today?" Janet asked.

"Oh, nothing unusual."

"I don't believe it."

"I'll tell you about it tonight," he promised, and then rose from the table, touching his mouth with a napkin.

Janet walked to the front door and watched as he put on his heavy coat. "You're up to something," she said.

He took her in his arms and kissed her, a loving kiss that hinted of the passion they shared. "Tonight I'll tell you all about it."

"What has Uncle Jacob Adam put you up to?" she asked, well aware of the older man's influence on her husband.

"He has absolutely nothing to do with what I'm up to. I'll tell you that much," Paul said. He opened the door, smiled at his wife, and went out into the street.

He walked briskly to his office on Whitehall in the building he shared with his partner, Nicholas Roosevelt, and his uncle. The morning frost was still on the ground, although the sun had made an appearance almost two hours before.

He nodded to a few acquaintances, spoke a few words with his brother-in-law, Edward Goelet, and finally arrived at his destination. He remained only a few minutes, gathering some papers and stuffing them into a leather case. He left the office and went to city hall, where he met Roosevelt.

"Do you have the letters of agreement?" Roosevelt asked.

"Yes. And the survey papers. And the letter of credit."

Roosevelt smiled. He patted his partner on the arm. "Then we're ready to do it."

"Yes."

The two men walked toward the land clerk's office. Paul was thin and athletic looking, but Roosevelt had begun putting on the weight characteristic of prosperous burghers approaching middle age. Apart from physical appearance, however, there were few differences between them. They had been successful in their business dealings and had done well for themselves. Jacob Adam's friendship and guidance had hardly hurt their careers.

After he had been fired by Jacob Adam thirteen years earlier, Roosevelt had become a much more serious man. He had quietly provided for the family of the man who had been killed in the accident at the bolting factory. And he had gone on to be one of the most diligent and hardworking young businessmen in the city. Jacob Adam had carefully watched his progress, and finally forgave him for the accidental death of the man on the floor of the factory. Although he had never said so, he had been pleased when his own nephew became involved with Roosevelt in various business ventures.

The land clerk greeted the two men by name when they entered his office. He had been expecting them, and papers were quickly signed and exchanged. The letter of credit was turned over, and the men shook hands at the conclusion of the deal.

Paul and Nicholas went back to Whitehall Street, their eyes bright.

"Will you tell your uncle?" Nicholas asked.

"We'll do it together," Paul said.

The partners entered Jacob Adam's office and exchanged self-satisfied glances. Jacob Adam looked up from a legal document to see who it was, and went back to his reading. "And why am I so honored by this visit from two princes of trade?"

"We just concluded a marvelous deal," Paul said. "We waited to tell you until it was all done."

Jacob Adam put down the papers and regarded his nephew. There was the slightest hint of a smile on his face. "A marvelous deal? And you did it without me?"

Paul couldn't help but feel smug. "We didn't do it behind your back. We just wanted to do it without your help." He looked over at his partner. "Nicholas and I wanted to prove we could pull it off."

Jacob Adam nodded with understanding. "Very commendable. I understand completely. Now, if you please, tell me what the two of you have done."

"Shall I?" Paul said, looking at Nicholas.

"Of course," Roosevelt said.

"You know the big parcel of land that starts north of the creek on Maiden Lane?"

"Yes."

"We just bought it," Paul said proudly. "Eleven acres of prime land. More and more people are moving to New York. The city is moving beyond the wall. We intend to build a dock just north of the creek. Think how much more valuable our land will be in a few years. Prime land with easy access to a dock."

Jacob Adam looked impressed. "You realize the city will retain rights over the waterway?"

"Naturally. But that doesn't affect us."

"The city also owns an easement along the river's edge."

Paul smiled and looked back at Nicholas. "We know that, but the city has always been willing to lease the rights to an easement."

"Maybe somebody already has a lease on the easement."

Paul's smile diminished slightly. "I doubt it. Why would anyone bother to have a lease on useless land?"

"*You* don't think it useless."

"Not in the future. But how many men look ten or twenty years ahead?"

Jacob Adam shrugged. "If it doesn't bother you, it doesn't bother me," he said, picking up his papers. "But if it was my deal, I'd have made sure the lease was available before I bought all that land."

"We ought to check on that," Roosevelt said with concern.

"If another man was the leaseholder, he could make the pair of you pay a great deal for that lease," Jacob Adam said. "After all, you can't build your dock without it."

Paul started toward the door. "We'll get it right away." His smile returned. "But don't worry for our sake, uncle. Who would have taken a lease on apparently worthless land?"

The two younger men left, and Jacob Adam returned to the business on his desk.

Paul and Nicholas hurried back to city hall. They went to the city engineer's office and inquired about the lease on the easement.

The engineer's clerk looked up the record and said, "I'm sorry, but that lease has already been taken."

The partners were stunned. They looked at one another and then back at the clerk. "You can't be serious," Paul said.

The clerk pointed at the document on the desk. "It's right here in black and white. The lease was taken out only last week."

"Last week!" Roosevelt said. "Then somebody must have known about our plans!"

"Who owns the lease?" Paul demanded, his face turning dark with anger.

The clerk squinted at the document. "Jacob Adam de Kuyper."

The partners were speechless. They looked at one another and then at the clerk. The old man shrugged. "Mister de Kuyper comes in here just about every week, just to check up on who's doing what," he said.

Paul began to laugh. "The old bandit! He knew all along what we were planning to do. He found a loophole in the scheme and plugged it up."

"What are we going to do?" Nicholas Roosevelt asked.

"There's only one thing we can do. Go back and find out his price."

That night Paul told his wife the story as they lay side by side in bed.

"Did your uncle sell you the lease?" Janet asked.

"Yes. For a profit. He told me it was the price of learning a good lesson: don't think you've made a deal until you know all the facts."

"Was it worth the price?"

"Every penny. Now come here, woman, and do your duty."

Her hand reached out and gently touched his chest. "Think of how much more I'd love you if you were as smart as your uncle," she said teasingly.

He grabbed her and smothered her mouth with kisses, and his hands explored the smooth skin of her body. There was no more talking in bed this night.

It was a clear, wintry day in February 1697, the crisp coldness tempered by a brilliant sun. Snow was piled on the ground, but the sky was blue and James and several of his friends were enjoying the excitements offered at the tip of Manhatan. They made snowballs and held mock battles, each boy fighting to become king of a tall drift that had built up at one end of the dock.

Suddenly a strange sight caught their eyes. A dark-skinned man with a turban wrapped around his head emerged from a ship and made his way across the dock toward the head of Pearl Street.

James looked at one of his mates. "Shall we?" he asked.

The other boy, Albert Livingston, John's younger brother, thought for a moment, and then a mischievous smile appeared. "Why not," he said.

James packed a heavy snowball, allowing the warmth of his bare hands to melt the outer snow, squeezing it into a formidable projectile. Albert Livingston and three other boys did the same.

The turbaned man reached the end of the dock and stepped into the street. At a signal from James the boys threw the snowballs. Two of them hit the turbaned man, a sailor from the faraway port of Goa, on the western coast of India. One caught him in the back of the neck, the icy snow almost knocking the windings of cloths from the top of his head. He whirled; another snowball caught him full in the face, obliterating the savage expression that had been visible for the briefest moment.

"We got him!" James shouted as he wound up and pitched another snowball. The other boys cheered and joined in the barrage.

The Goanese was a big man with a scanty sense of humor. The back of his head ached, and his face hurt— and the source of this pain was the pack of screaming boys at the end of the dock. He shouted and started to run toward them.

The chase was on! The boys fled from the dock and dashed past a group of stout, swaggering men emerging from the Chest o' Gold, one of the many waterfront taverns. One of the men wore a rich blue coat trimmed with gold, another a green coat with pearl buttons, white knee breeches, and embroidered hose. All carried daggers with jeweled hilts stuck in their belts. At first they were startled by the shouting boys, but they relaxed and began to laugh when they saw the huge Goanese lumbering after them, his head and shoulders still carrying bits of the snowballs. They shouted and urged the boys on.

The men were pirates, and everyone knew it. New York had become the buccaneer capital of the world. Hoar, Evans, Thwaite, Wade, Coates, and other famous pirates of the world's seas came to New York and berthed their ships with impunity along the docks at Pearl Street. They drank and took their meals at places like the Chest, the Dark Ship, the Barnacle, and the Prince Inn.

Benjamin Fletcher, the governor since '92, made threats now and again, but he was easily quieted by bribes from these sea rovers who brought the plunder of the world to Manhatan. And even if the governor had been serious in his attempts to rid the city of pirates, he would have been dissuaded by men who had great stakes in this new source of wealth—powerful men like Robert Livingston, Frederick Phillipse, Franklin Riverton, and Jacob Adam de Kuyper. These men argued that only a few years ago the major currency of Manhatan had been *wampum;* but now the city had seven thousand inhabitants, and the pirates were bringing wealth to all. Men traded in gold and silver instead of the bead money of the Indians. Now goods were bought with Greek byzants, Arabian dinars, Hindustani mohurs, and Spanish doubloons as well as pounds sterling, Dutch guilders, German thalers, and French Louis d'ors. The source of this wealth was the pirate trade, and even an honest governor would have had trouble keeping it out.

The boys, led by James, fled down Whitehall toward Pine Street, which had been King Street until the fall of James II. The Goanese, still shouting curses in his native tongue, followed through the twisting streets and alleys. The boys ran past shops piled high with goods brought by the pirates; the staggering array of wealth would have been at home in the Levantine or in a Teheran bazaar. Everything from everywhere was for sale—tables of intricately carved teakwood, rugs from Anatolia and Dagestan, vases of hammered brass and silver, portières from Baghdad, rubies, diamonds, emeralds, fans of ivory, jade from the land of the khan, boxes of sandalwood, rich silks, shawls edged with gold thread, even statues of heathen gods.

"This way!" James shouted at his friends and led the way toward the towering steeple of the newly built Trinity Church—the English answer to the steeple on the older St. Nicholas, the Dutch church within the walls of the fort. Even as the English had conquered the Dutch, now the steeple of their church towered over the church of the former owners of Manhatan.

The boys darted down an alley behind a tavern, where another group of pirates was gathered. These men saw what was happening and shouted encouragement. One of them jumped up and pounded on a wooden plaque commemorating the hanging of Jacob Leisler and his son-in-law John Milbourne, who led a rebellion in 1691 when James II had been dethroned in England. It had been a short-lived rebellion, but Leisler continued to be a symbol of the city's defiance of authority. Such plaques as the one on the tavern were forbidden by law, but again the bribe had been sufficient and the corrupt Fletcher had looked the other way.

James's breath was now coming in great gulps, and he began to question the wisdom of picking on such a tough customer as the Goanese seaman. He looked around to see how close the man was and slipped on a bit of ice. Landing heavily, he tore the knee of his trousers. As he came to his feet, the Goanese was upon him. But the boy was quick: he dropped down and slipped out of the grasp of those huge hands. The sailor's momentum carried him forward, and he tripped over an icy mound and went sprawling to the ground.

The pirates at the door of the tavern cheered, further enraging the Goanese. He forgot the other boys and turned all his wrath on this one who had made him look so foolish. James realized he was now the sole target. He doubled back, again passing the tavern. While the Goanese took after him, the other boys scattered in all directions, quickly losing themselves in the rabbit-warren of alleys behind the streets.

As the Goanese passed the men at the tavern, one of them stuck out his foot, and the sailor again went crashing to the ground. James heard the noise and paused to look back.

The man shook his head as he picked himself up, looking for the cause of his newest discomfort. He saw the laughing men at the tavern door and realized they had come to the aid of the boy. But these were men, not boys, and he decided to deal with them accordingly. He took a long curved knife from his belt and attacked the group. Their laughter stopped, and the pirates acted as one. The Goanese was grabbed by a half dozen pair of hands, the knife ripped from his grasp and tossed harmlessly onto a pile of snow. He was thrown backward and dumped unceremoniously on his backside. There was a tense moment, and then one of the pirates began to laugh again. He pointed down the street toward James, who was collecting his breath in case the pursuit should resume. He was a pathetic sight in his torn trousers, looking terrified, gasping for breath.

The Goanese also looked at James, then at the laughing pirates—and then at himself. His anger vanished, and he too began to laugh at the ridiculousness of the situation. One of the pirates walked over and helped him to his feet. The Goanese turned toward James and waved his hand. The chase was over.

James smiled and began walking back to his home on upper Pearl Street.

Jacob Adam was in the parlor when he heard the door open and saw his son enter.

Jacob Adam was in a good mood. He had just calculated his profits from his ship *William*, which had sailed the previous year from New York with a cargo of Jamaican rum, Madeira wine, and gunpowder. The ship had taken this haul to the island of Madagascar, in the western Indian Ocean. The rum that had cost two shillings a gallon in New York sold for three pounds sterling in Madagascar. The wine had cost nineteen pounds a pipe and sold for three hundred. The gunpowder had returned a one thousand percent profit on its investment. For her return voyage *William* had loaded up with goods, stolen from East India merchantmen, that would be sold for enormous profits in New York. In addition to the cargo, the *William* carried twenty-five paying passengers whose fares added four hundred pounds sterling to the coffers. Moreover, twenty slaves had been shoved into the hold —each bought for one pound sterling in Madagascar and sold at the going rate of twenty pounds in New York.

The net profit from this single voyage was slightly

more than ten thousand pounds sterling. Even considering that the *William*'s master, the Bible-toting Captain Morrison, had stolen as much as he dared, it was an extremely profitable return, and Jacob Adam had much reason to be happy. However, he scowled when he saw his ragamuffin son standing in the doorway.

"Come here," Jacob Adam said.

James came across the room, his happiness vanishing.

"Playing again?" the father accused. "When are you going to stop playing and act like a man?"

James stood silently and let his eyes drop to the floor.

"Look at me when I'm talking to you!" Jacob Adam said, annoyed by his son's weakness. The boy refused to take life seriously. When he had been his son's age, he was already involved in land schemes with David de Witt and old Michael de Pauw. "I want you to remember you are a de Kuyper. Men will expect you to act in certain ways. How will you know what to do if you spend all your time at play with rowdies and children?"

"I spent the earlier part of the morning at the office," James said in his own defense. "I've been learning to keep the ledgers for the affairs of the manor."

"Ledgers," Jacob Adam said, allowing a sneer to color his voice. "What are you going to become? A bookkeeper at a brewery?"

"May I go to my room, Father?" James asked, his anger growing. He was afraid if he stayed any longer, he would say something he would regret.

James was a good-looking lad with strong, square features, dark hair, deep-blue eyes, and an easy smile. He was tall for his age, but large-boned, promising a formidable presence in manhood. He was thoughtful and usually took his time when he spoke. This mannerism gave his words something of a drawl, lacking the normal New York inflections and harsh accents. When he became angry, as he was now, his face would redden and his eyelids would droop down, half covering the brooding eyes.

"Give your trousers to the servants. A de Kuyper doesn't walk around with torn trousers."

"Yes, Father," James said. He turned to leave the room.

"I haven't dismissed you yet."

James turned back to face his father. His anger overcame his fear. "Dammit! You were the one who told me to learn to keep the ledgers!"

"I told you to learn to use them, not to make them your life's work."

"Why do you always pick on me? Is it your way of getting back at my mother?"

This startled Jacob Adam. "What are you talking about?"

"You've always hated her, and now you're taking it out on me!"

"That's absurd. I love your mother."

"No, you don't! I know!" James said, his voice turning into a loud, shrill cry. "You hated her and you married her to punish her! I know, because Grandmother Barrow told me!"

Jacob Adam had barely spoken to Elizabeth Barrow during the past fifteen years. He was well aware of her intense hatred for him, but he had somehow hoped she would have enough sense not to pass this along to his children. It had been a vain hope, he now knew, and he had been wrong to ignore the problem. It would have been far better to bring it out into the open and deal with it; but it was a bit late for that.

"I'm sorry you choose to believe nonsense," he said.

"It's true!"

"You grandmother is a twisted, bitter woman. She's a liar."

"She's not the liar, you are," James said, his anger and resentment taking complete control. All the years he had been afraid, all the years he had dreaded talking to his father, all the years he had lain in bed and waited until his father had left the house: a lifetime of resentment had built up, and it now spilled out in a torrent.

"You hate me! You're always picking on me! No matter what I do it's wrong. Well, I hate you as much as you hate me. I hate you even more, because you're trying to kill my mother. You want her to die; you—"

The solid smack of Jacob Adam's hand resounded in the room, and the skin about James' mouth began to redden. He looked at his father in surprise and pain.

Jacob Adam had never before struck his son. He looked at his own hand as if it belonged to someone else, as if it were not a part of his own body.

James's anger vanished. Tears welled into his eyes. He walked from the room, wishing to cry but refusing to show more weakness in front of his father.

Jacob Adam sat down in his chair and stared out the window. His thoughts focused quickly, even though he was upset at himself for having lost his temper with the boy. Was history repeating itself? Was he doomed to repeat the tragedy that had been played between his own father and his brother? Would he, like his father before him, drive away his eldest son?

He shook his head, and for one of the few times in his life, he was at a loss for answers. In almost everything he had done, he had been more than competent. But in this situation he felt helpless. His own son, a boy of fifteen, hated him and had just accused him of wanting to kill his own wife. Surely the boy knew it was nonsense, but the hatred that prompted such a statement was there.

Alice had heard the commotion, and she came into the room where her father sat brooding, his eyes dark as he looked out the window.

"I heard all that," the thirteen-year-old girl said.

"It would be better if you hadn't."

"It would be better if you tried to be more understanding."

"The idea that I hate your mother is absurd."

"I know. But James thinks you don't love him. He said that about Mother because he was angry and getting back at you."

"He has no cause to be angry."

"But he *thinks* he does, and that's what counts to him."

Jacob Adam looked at his daughter. "Why is it that you can understand these things, and he can't?"

Alice went over to a chair and sat down. There was a long pause before she spoke, and then it was in an uncharacteristically gentle voice. "I don't know, Father. Maybe that's a question you should be asking yourself instead of me."

And was she right? he thought. Is my son the way he is because of me? As the twig is bent, so grows the tree.

"If you could only prove to James that you loved him as much as you do me," Alice said, "the problem might be solved."

Ah! And perhaps this was the deepest and darkest root

of the problem. Did he truly love his son as much as he loved his daughter? It was not a new question; he had asked it many times before.

And he had yet to give himself a satisfactory answer.

James went to his room and closed the door. And then he let the tears flow. He was desolate, destroyed, without hope. His father was a hated creature who hadn't the slightest idea his son was a human being, with a life that he must try to satisfy in his own way.

There was only one answer, he decided. He would run away. He would leave New York and find happiness and peace in some other part of the world.

He thought about it a long time. The first questions were how to run away and where to go.

He decided he would find a berth on a ship. It would be risky, because his father was well known to men in the shipping trade. But if he used a false name and kept out of sight until the ship sailed, he had a chance of getting away with it. Finding a berth wouldn't be that difficult, because ships always needed new sailors to replace the ones who had decided they were ready to leave the sea and try their hand at something on solid ground.

He would go to the docks in the morning. Now that he had made up his mind, he went to sleep in a peaceful mood.

As James planned to run away, it chanced that a very special ship was in New York. It was the fruit of a scheme by two men of wealth who planned to make themselves far wealthier.

The first was the Earl of Bellomont, an old-time aristocrat, a favorite of the king and a man of great influence at the Court of St. James. The other was Robert Livingston of New York, an uncle of John and Albert, the contemporaries of the de Kuyper children. Robert Livingston was a Scot who had migrated to Albany, where he had become town clerk. He had married Alida, sister of Peter de Schuyler and widow of Nicholas Van Rensselaer. With these excellent family connections he had managed to obtain a grant for a vast estate on the river in the Hudson Valley.

These two men conceived the idea of financing a heavily armed frigate to fight against the scourge of pirates. Or so they said in public. The real mission would be to capture French ships and stragglers of other nations—in fact, to capture anything that floated. The idea was presented to King William, who blessed the mission, provided he receive ten percent of the spoils. This was most acceptable to Bellomont and Livingston.

Now the two men began looking for a third partner, who would share the cost of the ship and also sail as her master. They finally chose the son of a Scots Presbyterian minister, a man of modest wealth who had retired from the sea to enjoy the pleasures of his new house on Crown Street in New York. He was a pillar of respectability, having recently been one of the men given the honor of laying the cornerstone of Trinity Church. This last fact was important to give an aura of solid believability to the entire scheme.

The man's name was William Kidd—*Captain* William Kidd.

At first he was less than enthusiastic about the thought of sailing the seas looking for cutthroats. But he changed his mind when the others spoke of the great profits to be made, and revealed that their venture had the approval of the king himself. Kidd finally agreed and became a full partner. He put up a third of the required six thousand pounds sterling to buy a ship and to provision and outfit her. The three partners were to share equally in the profits —half to them and half to the crew (with a silent ten percent to His Majesty).

He bought a handsome frigate, the two-hundred-and-eighty-seven-ton *Adventure*, outfitted her with thirty-six guns, and set sail from England in May 1696. The ship arrived in Plymouth and added more crew. Captain Kidd sailed it through the Narrows, and the *Adventure* was now docked at Pearl Street, where the final complement of ninety men was to be signed aboard.

It was to this ship that James de Kuyper presented himself as an apprentice seaman seeking a berth.

The first mate was Charles Lewis, a tough, sea-hardened man who had been in hundreds of ports and on every ocean known to man. He took one look at this stripling and knew he was not the sort to take aboard a privateer.

"What's your name?" he asked.

"James . . . King."

"James King, eh?" the first mate said, knowing the boy was lying. "Have you been to sea before?"

"Yes."

"What ship?"

"The *William*," James said, aware his father's ship was not in port at the present time.

Charles Lewis knew the *William*. And he knew what work she did. The lad standing before him was not the sort of sailor they wanted on *that* ship, either. "I'm afraid we're in for a rough voyage, lad," he said. " 'Tis best you go home and forget this ship."

To the mate's surprise the boy produced a handful of gold coins.

"These are yours in return for a berth on this ship."

Charles Lewis looked more closely at this boy. It was hardly common practice for a sailor to buy his way aboard a ship, nor was it usual for a young boy to have so much money. "Best be putting away that money, lad," he said in a kindly tone. "There be those who'd put a dirk in your back for the likes of that."

James pocketed the coins. "It's important that I get a berth."

The mate was again about to tell the boy to go home, but he hesitated. He studied his face and saw an intense desire that bordered on panic. There was an unspoken plea here that he found difficult to refuse.

"Make your mark," he finally said, indicating a clean line in the log on the table.

James signed his name with a flourish. "I can write, sir," he said timidly.

The mate scowled. "That may be so, but you still don't have any sense. Don't let me catch you flashing gold around like that again."

"No, sir," James said quietly.

"Be aboard in two days. We sail with the morning tide on the third."

"Yes, sir!"

James left the ship feeling free and deliriously happy. At last he was going to get away from his father! At last he was going to be an adventurer! At last he was going to lead his own life!

For the next two days he did nothing to attract attention to himself. He spent some time composing a letter to his mother. He would have preferred to tell her face to face, but she would only try to stop him and he didn't want that to happen.

He crept from the house before dawn, leaving the note on his bed. He was in the habit of sleeping late (another thing that angered his father), and he knew his absence would not be discovered until after the *Adventure* had cleared the harbor. By then it would be too late for anyone to stop him.

He reported aboard the ship and was given a berth in the fo'c'sle along with the other men. Shortly before dawn the crew was mustered on deck and divided into watches. Captain Kidd gave a brief speech about their mission and promised full shares of the expected booty to all hands.

The tide was favorable, and the *Adventure* raised canvas, slipped her moorings, and departed silently down the seaway toward the Narrows. James scampered happily about, learning the duties of his new life under the tutelage of Charles Lewis.

The ship passed through the shoulders of the Narrows, changed course to a more southeasterly direction, and started on the long voyage down the side of the continent. It would continue south until it reached a point where the currents would be favorable for a passage toward the tip of Africa and the Cape of Good Hope.

It was almost noon when Jennifer realized she had not seen her son all morning. She looked in his room and saw the note on the bed. She knew, even before she read it, that her son had gone. Her fingers trembled as she opened the folded paper, and tears came to her eyes as she read the two brief paragraphs. And then, abruptly, the tears stopped. She took the letter to her husband's office on Whitehall. Without a word she handed him the paper and waited silently as he read it.

"So my son chooses to avoid his responsibilities and run away," Jacob Adam said. "I'm disappointed, but hardly surprised."

"We must get him back."

"He says he shipped on Kidd's frigate. She sailed with the dawn tide."

"You have ships. Take one and bring back our son!" Jennifer said angrily.

"If I thought it the right thing to do, I'd do it," Jacob Adam said. "But the boy is determined to run away. Who are we to stop him?"

"You drove him away."

"It's time he became a man. Maybe this will do what I've been unable to accomplish," Jacob Adam said, trying not to reveal his pride in this son who showed courage in his defiance.

Jennifer could not understand. She pleaded and begged and cried, but all to no avail. Jacob Adam would not lift a finger to retrieve his son. She left the office and returned home. She told her daughter what had happened; Alice, to Jennifer's surprise, agreed with her father and was proud of her brother.

Jennifer could not and would not understand. She became moody and sulked about the house for many days, convinced her son was in terrible danger. She blamed his supposed plight on her husband and was no longer afraid of him, her fear having been replaced by anger. The house was in a constant turmoil.

"Oh for pity's sake," Alice said one day in the middle of one of her mother's tirades. "Nothing is going to happen to James. He's gone to sea. Lots of boys do it and they come back men."

"You can say that because he's not your son."

"He's my brother, and I love him as much as you do."

"He'll be frightened on that ship."

"He's not a little boy any more. Let him grow up."

Jennifer shook her head. "He needs me," she said, certain that without her protective presence the boy would spend his days in wide-eyed terror.

"Sometimes I think he ran away from you as much as from Father," Alice said.

But Jennifer knew only that her son was gone—the person closest to her in the world. And her husband and daughter refused to understand how much it meant to her.

The *Adventure* had a long, uneventful sail down the coast of Brazil, finally going out into the open ocean on a course that would allow her to round the Cape of Good Hope.

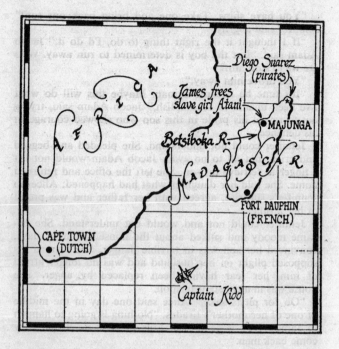

By the time they neared the African cape, James de Kuyper had become a passable seaman. Charles Lewis taught him to do his work properly and not get hurt in the process. He learned to scamper like a monkey through the shrouds, tie knots, stand watches, read the stars, and move easily amid the maze of spars, booms, and riggings.

James turned brown under constant exposure to the sun, and his young muscles hardened. He had an easy nature, and his mates in the fo'c'sle took a liking to him as he adapted to their rough ways and language. On his off hours he sat in the crew's quarters and listened to the tales of the other men. He hardly had time for regrets, since the work of the ship kept him busy during most of his waking hours; but at unexpected moments he would picture the face of his mother and feel melancholic.

As they rounded the cape, James stood at the railing. He could hardly believe that the distant shore, a vast greenness shimmering in the haze, was actually the coast of Africa. Africa! A huge, unknown land that—the sailors assured him—held great treasures of gold and jewels, all untouched because no white man dared venture very far into the interior of the continent, which was filled with savage beasts five and six times bigger than horses, and even more savage men. Africa, James had learned, was the most dangerous land on earth, with black men who were ten feet tall, had four arms, and lived on the flesh of other human beings. As the boy recalled the stories he had been told, the beautiful shoreline began to look sinister, and he imagined what terrible deeds must be taking place at this moment, just out of his vision.

The ship remained at Capetown only long enough to take on fresh supplies and for Captain Kidd to hear the latest rumors about pirate activities from the authorities. Two men who had grown sick on the voyage were put ashore, to recover or to be buried in nameless graves in a strange land thousands of miles from their places of birth.

Charles Lewis took James ashore, partly to enjoy Capetown through the boy's fresh eyes and partly to keep an eye on him. This was no place for a naïve youngster to wander about by himself.

"Africa," James said in awe, staring down at the ground beneath his feet at the base of the Adventure's gangplank.

"Aye," Lewis said, and he pointed to the north. "And if you started walking in that direction, you might reach the other end of it in a year or two."

He paused as James squinted and peered into the distance. "That is if you weren't killed and eaten by wild animals or wilder men," the mate added.

"I think I'll take my chances with the ship," James said, and the mate laughed.

Charles Lewis was about average height, but his barrel chest and solid arms made him appear large. He had green eyes, red hair, and a full, bushy beard that contributed to his look of rugged strength. When he laughed, his wide shoulders hunched forward and his entire body seemed to join in the enjoyment. He usually had a pipe—lit or unlit—stuck between his teeth, and he rarely took it out when he talked. It was his habit to stroke the front of his beard when he was thinking or enjoying himself—as he was now.

The ship berthed next to the *Adventure* was a whaler recently come into port with a hold full of blubber. James watched as the sailors and dockmen brought up the barrels stuffed with flensed meat and then lowered them to the dock, where other men rolled them away. It was a scene he had witnessed many times in New York. Somehow the sight of something he knew so well made Capetown begin to seem ordinary. This idea quickly evaporated when they passed the whaler: there on the dock was a wooden cage with a ferocious-looking beast penned inside.

Keeping a prudent distance from the cage, James watched as the animal twitched its tail and glared through amber eyes at the dockworkers, who walked by without giving it a second glance.

"What in the world is that?" James asked, almost in a whisper.

"I take it you've never seen a lion before, eh?" the mate replied with a chuckle. "They're pretty common here in Africa."

"Why, it looks like a big cat."

"That's exactly what he is, a big cat. Now how would you like to take that fellow on your lap and pet him?" the mate said.

The lion chose this moment to let out a deafening roar, and James jumped straight up in the air. The mate shook with laughter, and tears came to his eyes. "Aye, what a picture you make, lad. Now what's to be afraid of? That's a stout cage he's in."

"I'm sure of that," James said, trying to undo his lapse of courage by acting blasé. But then his curiosity got the better of him, and awe crept back into his voice. "What are they going to do with the lion?"

"God knows," the mate replied. "Probably being sent to some place where a king will keep him on a golden leash."

"But why?"

" 'Tis strange tastes kings have," the mate answered.

They continued on down the dock, and James saw another sight that startled him. A huge man, weighing well over three hundred pounds, with blotchy yellow skin, bare-chested and barefooted, came walking past. He carried a curved sword in his cloth belt and wore a large golden earring.

The mate noticed the boy's interest. "A Chinee, that one is. Best you stay clear of those heathen sods. They'd as like to cut your heart out as look at you."

James turned and watched the yellow man as he waddled down the dock in his strange, rolling gait. He silently vowed to abide by the mate's warning.

A trim bark with a hull of reddish wood was tied up at the end of the dock. The sails were carefully furled, and the deck was tidy. A man dressed in white stood near the bowsprit. He was smoking a pipe and staring out over the town. As they passed, Lewis swore beneath his breath.

"What's the matter?" James asked.

"I know that ship. She's a slaver," Lewis said. "That sort gives me the creeps."

James nodded his head in understanding. Slave ships were not common in New York, but he had seen a few and knew exactly what the mate was talking about. There *was* something evil about a ship whose sole purpose was to transport the bodies of damned men and women. As he and Lewis walked past, James imagined he could hear the chains rattling below and the crack of a whip on naked flesh.

They spoke no more until they were clear of the dock and into the town itself.

James was surprised at the many similarities between Capetown and New York. Then several men walked by, talking rapidly in Dutch, and the boy realized both towns had been settled first by people from the Netherlands. He understood every word as the men argued about the cost of grain; it was as if he had been transported back to Broad Street and was overhearing New York merchants as they haggled over prices.

"I could never make out a word of that bloody language," the mate said.

James smiled. "We speak English at home, but Dutch is more or less a second language to us."

The mate's eyebrow went up. "I thought your name was King. Doesn't sound very Dutch to me."

James's heart skipped a beat, and he felt like jamming a rag into his mouth.

"Almost everyone in New York speaks Dutch," he said, keeping his eyes averted from the man who walked at his side. Charles Lewis wasn't fooled, but, having no intention of spoiling the lad's day, he let it pass.

"Look at those buildings," he said. "Don't they look just like the ones off Dock Street in New York."

James looked down the street and recognized the familiar gables, windows, and stoops. As in New York, many of the houses had the year they were built imprinted on their fronts, and if they had been picked up and dropped on Pearl Street, no one would have given them a second glance. The Dutch, it seemed, had consistent ideas about architecture and, wherever they went in the world, built solid, comfortable houses that made them feel at home.

The two men from the *Adventure* walked a bit more until they came to a street filled with vendors who displayed their wares on trays in front of their stalls. A throng of people—every man among them carrying some sort of weapon—went from stall to stall, filling the air with the babble of a dozen languages.

James's attention was diverted by a beautiful silk shawl hanging from a wooden peg. The shawl was a deep, rich blue. A bird was painted in the middle, and there were threads of silver around the hem.

"How much?" he asked the man leaning against a wall behind the tray.

The man took a gold toothpick from his mouth and regarded the lad. "You want to buy it?" he finally said.

"Yes. What kind of money do you take?"

The man smiled, and James could see gaping holes where teeth had been. "Any kind. We're not particular here."

James reached into his pocket and brought out a Spanish coin of gold. The man's eyes brightened. "That is enough," he said quickly.

Lewis reached out and took hold of James's arm. "That's too much. Get something else."

The vendor's eyes narrowed, and the fingers of his left hand strayed to the hilt of the knife in his belt. The mate grasped the shaft of his own knife, and the gesture was not lost on the vendor. "Yes, of course, too much. What other money do you have?"

James took out a large silver coin of Portuguese inscription. The vendor took it, and the smile returned to his face. "The shawl is yours," he said, with a sweep of his hand.

James took the garment down from the peg and carefully rolled it into a bundle.

"What lucky girl is going to get that?" the mate asked as they continued down the street.

"Oh, just a friend," James said, not wanting to admit that he didn't really know any girl well enough to give her such a gift; that it was for his mother.

After several hours Charles Lewis had had his fill of walking. He took James by the arm and led him into a tavern, where they sat down at a table and a slatternly barmaid brought them two huge mugs of beer.

It was unlike any other tavern James had seen. The place had a central courtyard with no roof, only a trellis of latticework that held hundreds of creeping vines and flowers. It would have been unsuited to New York's more rugged climate; but how pleasant it was to sit here, in the middle of a Capetown day, drinking beer as the warm rays of the sun filtered through the fragrant trellis.

James felt drowsy as he finished his beer and the mate ordered two more mugs. He leaned back against one of the posts that held up the trellis and started to doze. For a moment he thought his half-closed eyes were playing tricks on him—but no, the rolled-up shawl that he had placed on the bench next to him was starting to move away. His eyes popped open, and he found himself staring into the face of a boy who was pulling the shawl toward himself.

James jumped up, and the boy fled with the shawl in his hand.

The mate didn't know what had happened. One moment his companion was sitting quietly; the next he was running out the door at top speed. "What the hell!" he exclaimed as he slammed down his mug and headed for the door.

The boy sped down an alley, with James right on his heels. They ran across a street, then down another alley. The boy was obviously at home in these twisting byways. But he was not as fast as James, who finally caught him and hurled him to the ground.

"That shawl is mine," James cried.

"Come and get it," the boy snarled in Dutch, and came to his feet with a knife in his hand.

James hesitated. The knife glinted in the sunlight, and its owner held it in a way that said he knew how to use it. "Why do you steal from a fellow countryman?" he asked, also using the Dutch tongue.

The boy was startled. "You speak Dutch."

"My name is de Kuyper."

The boy laughed. He put away the knife and handed over the shawl. "You were speaking English in the tavern, so I thought you were one of that lot. I'm sorry."

James took a good look at the other boy. He was a year or two younger than himself, but thinner. His trousers had many holes, his boots were falling apart, and his shirt was beyond repair.

James reached into his pocket and took out a small gold coin. He handed it to the other boy, who was astonished: he looked at the bit of gold in his palm as if it weren't really there.

"Don't steal from your own people," James said. He tucked the shawl under his arm and walked out of the alley.

Charles Lewis was in the main street, looking about in concern, and he heaved a sigh of relief when he saw James walking toward him. "Bloody hell, lad, you gave me a scare. What happened?"

James related the incident, and by way of response the mate took him to a nearby shop. He picked out a very sturdy, very evil-looking knife from an array of weapons and handed it to James.

"It's time you carried one of these, lad. You'll feel undressed without it in most of the places we'll be going."

The *Adventure* slipped anchor the next morning and made her way into the Mozambique Channel, at the western edge of the Indian Ocean. She sailed north until the island of Madagascar came within sight, and now James felt the true excitement of the voyage. Madagascar was the most infamous pirate retreat in the world, a place where buccaneers could rest in safety and sell or trade their loot to customers from the far corners of the earth.

The ship came around Cap d'Ambre and dropped anchor in the harbor of Diégo-Suarez, a free-spirited, wide-open town at the northern end of the island. The longboats brought the men ashore, and James found himself in a world he had only half believed existed.

The Arabs had sailed here since the ninth century, but the first European to visit the island had been the Portuguese navigator Diogo Dias in 1500. Soon afterward the English had attempted to plant a colony and failed. The French now owned Fort Dauphine, at the southeast tip, and several European settlements could be found on the coasts, but no nation pretended to own the island. It was a meeting place for pirates and freebooters from all over the world. Dutch and English pirates walked the same streets as the Lascars and Goanese pirates from the other side of the Indian Ocean. The Chinese were here, and dark East Indians. It was as cosmopolitan a place as existed in the world, and all the men here had one thing in common—they were not about to let mere laws stand in the way of their quest for riches.

James went ashore with Charles Lewis and several other men. They walked the streets of the bazaar and the riches of the world were laid out before them. Gold, silver, and precious stones abounded in the shops and in the hands of the sharp-eyed traders. There were slave markets, and James blushed when he saw naked white women being paraded before the eyes of their potential buyers. White flesh, black flesh, yellow flesh, brown flesh —it was all here for the taking.

They stopped for refreshment at what the boy took to be an inn, but it turned out to be a pleasure house with every delight for the flesh. The men gorged themselves on fresh meat, vegetables, and fruit, all washed down with prodigious amounts of frothy ale.

"Have ye ever had a woman, lad?" Charles Lewis asked.

James knew it was unmanly to admit to such a deficiency in his education, so he was nonchalant. "Of course, many times."

Charles Lewis looked at him and knew he was lying. "I think we deserve to have a good time," he said.

The mate found the proprietor, and a deal was made. "Pick a gentle one for my friend. He's not much more than a boy."

"The gentle ones don't last long around here," the proprietor said in the patois that was the common language of the island. A mixture of a dozen tongues, it was accompanied by a great amount of gesturing. It was, however, a passable form of communication, and the men of Madagascar made their wishes known to one another. The wishes were usually basic ones, concerning the price of an object or a woman, or the cost of fitting out a ship. Philosophers and lawyers would not have found the island a good place to exercise their subtler talents.

"This will be his first woman," Lewis insisted. "It must be a good experience."

The proprietor of the pleasure house was a fat man, part Portuguese, part Malagasy, mostly Indian Ocean polyglot. He looked across the room at the innocent face of James de Kuyper and sighed.

"Very well," he said, "I have a young girl who will be most suitable."

When the proprietor told James to follow him, the boy had no idea of what was in store. They went through a series of rooms until they were in a courtyard. It was a gigantic flower garden, and paths among the bushes and trees led to many small buildings. James was sent down a path and told to enter the cottage at the end.

He stepped into the darkened room, and his nose began to twitch from the strong odor of incense burning in a brass bowl. He suddenly became aware of another person in the room. He moved closer and saw a brown-skinned girl who had large slanted eyes and wore a red jewel on her forehead. She smiled and stood up; and even though James was not yet grown to his full height, he was at least a half foot taller than the girl.

It took him a few more moments to realize what was happening. Then his face flushed, and he could feel his skin burst out in goose bumps. He became awkward. His feet and hands seemed clumsy, too big for the rest of his body.

The girl moved with a natural grace. She guided him to a soft cushion and helped loosen his collar and remove his coat. Neither knew the other's language, but there was no need for words. If James hadn't the slightest idea how to act, the girl was mistress of her art. She gave him a metal goblet, and the fiery liquid that burned his throat also helped him relax.

She took one of his hands and placed it on her bare

breast. The tingling in his fingers passed up his arm and made his brain whirl. The small, practiced fingers moved about his body, becoming more daring and curious, causing him to lose his breath and feel the manhood between his legs begin to rise.

She removed his clothes piece by piece until he was naked, and then she straddled him, a knee on either side, caressing and exciting him. Her body came lower and lower until it was gently brushing against his, the hard nipples of her breasts tracing tingling little paths across his chest and belly. Her head came down, and her tongue flicked out to lick the lobe of his ear, then to explore deep into the passage.

James had been passive, but now sensations aroused by the girl's insistent attentions made his hands raise up—almost against his will—and he began to stroke her soft flesh. The fingers of his hands seemed to be burning as they traced the smooth line of her hip and rounded the splendid firmness of her buttocks. She inched her knees to the sides until the tip of his penis met the soft part of her body that was covered with a fine, downlike hair.

James thought he felt every hair on his own body rise as one of the girl's small hands wrapped itself around his rigid penis and slowly guided it inside her. The opening in her body felt all warm and tight and liquid. His penis went deeper until it had disappeared, and James felt a pressure threatening to erupt within himself. With a gentle persistence the girl began to slide her body up and down, using a subtle sideways motion at the same time—very slowly at first, then faster, faster, and faster—and the eruption mounting within could no longer be contained and his sperm exploded into her.

He was whimpering and crying out—such a mixture of delight and pain could not be! All the while his hands were digging into the girl's flesh, but she didn't notice. She had become excited when she realized the boy was a virgin; now she matched his orgasm with her own.

They lay on the soft cushions, side by side, panting and covered with sweat. James felt sated with pleasure.

It was only the beginning.

After a few minutes passed and their breathing had resumed its normal rhythm, the girl's hand again encircled his penis and began to stroke and touch it in such a magical way that his erection came back as hard and stiff as before. And then she shifted her body so she was seated on the lower part of his legs, and he watched in wonder as his erect flesh slowly disappeared into her mouth. First the tip, then more, until it was gone. *This* was something he had not even heard about.

Soft lips and darting tongue worked expertly until his body was on fire. All the while the small hands were moving about his flesh, finding crevices and places that had always been there, but never in his wildest dreams had he thought they could be put to such uses.

His second orgasm took place in her mouth. This wonder was followed by many others that night, during which James learned half a dozen different ways of making love.

And when he was finally spent, the girl was sophisticated enough to realize it. She handed him another glass of the strong drink and proceeded to rub every inch of his flesh with a cool, wet cloth. This proved to be almost as pleasurable to James as what had gone before.

By the time he left the cottage and walked wobbly-legged back to the main building, James had crossed a threshold in his life, one that could never be crossed again.

"Did you have a good time?" Lewis asked when he came aboard the ship.

The glow on his face told the whole story. "It was all right," he said, embarrassed.

"Think you'll be wanting to do it again?"

"Oh, yes," James replied with such earnestness that Lewis roared with laughter.

"I'll bet you do, now that you've discovered the best part of your body!"

The next day Captain Kidd paid a visit to the man who represented what little law there was in Diégo-Suarez. The man was a former pirate universally known as the Falcon. He lived in a large villa that stood on a hill overlooking the harbor. The room where he received visitors looked more like the seraglio of a Turkestani prince than a room in a house owned by a European.

That the Falcon was European could be seen from his features, but the rich silks on his body and the jewels on his fingers and around his neck were from the eastern cultures. Together with other powerful pirates, the Falcon kept peace in the port, helped negotiate trade among the captains, and lived a life of hedonistic luxury.

Slaves, mostly black, were everywhere in the house catering to the slightest whim of the master. A half dozen of them served drinks in silver goblets to Captain Kidd and the members of his group. The Falcon was polite: he patiently waited for Kidd to state the reason for his journey to Madagascar.

It all seemed strange to James. The stated mission of the *Adventure* was to capture pirates. If that was so, why were they here, sitting down and enjoying the hospitality of a pirate? And what was more, how come they had not taken one pirate ship in the long journey? They had sighted several that might have been pirates, but had avoided them at all times. James concluded there was more to this voyage than anyone was talking about.

"Are there many French ships in these waters?" Kidd asked the Falcon.

The man shrugged. "Ships in these waters rarely fly the flag of any country. It is hard to tell which are French and which are not." The Falcon's eyes narrowed. "But why do you ask?"

"French ships have been bothering vessels sailing under the protection of His Britannic Majesty. I would like to make sure they do not bother the ships coming from India."

"I thought you were a privateer."

"I am," Kidd replied. "But I will have nothing to do with ships that sail for His Majesty."

"If you want *Frenchies*," the Falcon said, "look around Fort Dauphine. But don't be surprised if the *Frenchies* come out looking for you."

"Thank you," Kidd said. "I will heed your advice."

"Have you treasure to be disposed of here in Madagascar?"

"No, we stopped only for supplies."

"When you have treasure to sell, come back to see me," the Falcon said. "I will give you the best prices in the world."

"I'll remember," Kidd said smoothly. "But I thought the richest markets were those of the New World."

"For some things that is true," the pirate said, "but for others, Madagascar is your place. If you have wine to sell, or weapons, the market here is ten times better than all your American ports. On the other hand, there are so many rubies and emeralds and pearls here, you are better off carting them across the ocean. And, of course, unless you enjoy the protection of one of the monarchs, Europe is a good place to avoid. Too many patrol ships in those waters."

Even James knew the wisdom of this. He had heard other men talking about the constant patrols sent out by the East India Company, and also of the ships of William of Orange that scurried up and down the French coast looking for prey. It was not wise for an ordinary pirate like the Falcon to compete with the bigger pirates who sat on the thrones of Europe.

The Falcon reached for a tidbit at the same time as James, and their hands touched. The pirate looked at his guest and realized he was not much more than a boy.

"What is your name?"

"James King."

"May there be a long life ahead of you," the Falcon said in a kindly voice. "Have you been long at sea?"

James blushed. "This is my first voyage."

"Do you have a father?"

"No," James lied. "That's why I went to sea. There was nothing for me back home."

The Falcon nodded his head in understanding. "So it was for me. When a man has nothing, he takes to the sea and the waters of the ocean become his home. May she be kind to you."

"Thank you," James said self-consciously.

"May your first voyage bring you happiness," the Falcon said. "And may you live to have many more. Perhaps someday you will tire of the sea and make your home here. It is a good place. There is nowhere else in the world that men like us call home. Everywhere else they spit on us. But here no one curses us or tries to drive us away, because this is our own."

Captain Kidd seemed embarrassed at this speech, and it also confused James. The Falcon was obviously a pirate, and he was talking to Kidd as if to one of his own kind. James had heard the captain speak of this voyage as a "high mission on a noble purpose," and what did that have to do with what the Falcon was talking about? His earlier suspicions about the strange nature of this voyage were being substantiated by the emerging facts. But what *was* going on?

"Enough of business," the Falcon was saying. "You are my guests and you must let me entertain you." He clapped his hands, and more slaves appeared with great platters of food. A group of musicians began playing, and rum flowed. Other pirates arrived, and the evening turned into a raucous affair as the men grew drunk and began devoting their attentions to the many slave girls of the house.

At first James thought the wild behavior of the men would anger the host, but the Falcon proceeded to get as drunk as the rest and behave as badly. James relaxed, drank, and found himself chasing the slave girls with the other men. This time, when he placed his hand on a black girl's thigh, he knew the answer to his lust. He took her behind a curtain in an alcove, a nicety most of the pirates didn't bother with, and proceeded to enter a woman's body for the second time in his life. The mystery was gone, but the pleasure remained. He would have had a totally enjoyable evening, except he drank so much rum he vomited all over a pillow and could hardly make his way back to the ship. He awoke the next day, his head pounding as if he was being hit with a hammer, a sickening feeling in the pit of his stomach.

They remained at Diégo-Suarez for the better part of week, and James found ample opportunity to go ashore with shipmates, exploring the shore and surrounding area.

The thing that continually amazed him was the diversity of the people on the streets. He had thought of himself as cosmopolitan because his home had been New York, but that city had never seen the polyglot his eyes feasted on in this place. Especially exotic to him were the many Moslems—men who stopped what they were doing several times a day, knelt down on the ground, and offered their prayers to a god they called Allah. It was easy to recognize these Moslems, swarthy men who wore strange robes and a type of loose burnoose on their heads. But he was very surprised to see that not a few men who practiced this odd religion were black. *"Ah salakium salaam,"* could be heard from black men's lips at all times of day.

There were women, too. Black ones who went half-naked through the streets. White ones who lived with their pirate husbands, and shopped in the markets, haggling and arguing over prices with the merchants much the way it was in New York or any other place in the world. There were Moslem women, of course, but James never got a good look at any of them, hidden as they were behind their head-to-toe *chadors*.

"Don't trust anybody here," was the mate's warning. "Black, white, yellow, brown, or pea-green, if they're in this place they have something crooked about them. Watch your step."

James tried to follow the mate's advice, but he found himself going into strange places with his shipmates simply because he was too curious not to.

He went to his first cockfight and won a handful of silver coins with a series of lucky bets. At first he was appalled by the savagery of the fights and cringed when the feathered creatures began tearing each other apart with the razor-sharp blades that had been attached to their legs.

But after he had been persuaded to place a bet by his fo'c'sle mates—and won—he became caught up in the excitement over the bloodletting in the pit.

One of his companions was a vicious and evil-smelling sailor named William Moore. " 'Ere, King," Moore said, poking him in the ribs. "What made you bet on that bird? What do you know that I don't?"

And James was thrilled as he watched his bird, one with silver-streaked feathers, strike his opponent in the chest with a flashing blade and then, emitting a great row of squawks, end the fight with a slash to the throat.

"Beginner's luck," Moore mumbled. He had bet on the other bird and lost a fair amount of money. "Who do you like in the next match?"

"The red," James said.

Moore shook his head. "Not a chance. The other bloke will take him apart."

James didn't argue the point. He left Moore and went over to the fat bet-making Turk to collect his winnings and place a wager on the next contest.

The red won the next match, and James collected as much as Moore lost. And so it went for the next three matches, with James winning and Moore losing. The sailor's dislike for his young shipmate hardened.

William Moore was a London gutter urchin who had never had a thing in his life that he hadn't stolen or cheated from someone else. He was shorter than most men, but broad, his body lean and hard from years of scrabbling on the streets and docks. He was a bully in the fo'c'sle, abusing men who were weaker or less violent than himself. His face and arms bore the healed wounds of knife fights, and his back was crisscrossed with the scars of past lashings received when his masters had chosen to point out the error of his nasty ways. His nose had been broken and had not set properly; it was permanently squashed into the middle of his face so that he looked like an angry gorilla. He had scraggly brown hair and a mouth that seemed set in an eternal sneer. He never had a good word to say about anyone. When he visited the brothels in Diégo-Suarez or any other place, his first choice for a playmate was a young boy.

That was part of his resentment of James. He had made advances and the boy had brushed them aside. At first Moore thought the boy hadn't understood, but after the third time he realized James King was perfectly aware of what he wanted and had chosen to reject him.

The other part of his hardening dislike stemmed from the fact that James obviously came from a better background than his own. To Moore, the boy *reeked* of an easy life.

And now he was winning money while Moore was losing. It was like rubbing salt in a raw wound.

"Goddammit!" he shouted when another of his choices lost his match.

"I told you not to pick that one," James said.

"Who gives fuck-off what you think!" Moore said, reaching into his pocket for more money to bet on the next fight. "Keep your mouth shut!"

James shrugged and hastened to get his next bet down on the yellow-feathered bird that was being brought to the edge of the pit.

He watched his choice set loose and joined the rest of the mob as they came to their feet and howled. He failed to notice that William Moore was watching him and not the birds; and his expression revealed the blackness in his heart.

There were many diversions in Diégo-Suarez other than cockfights, and James seemed determined to see them all. The variety of animals fascinated him.

"Remember how scared you were of the lion in Capetown?" Charles Lewis reminded him, and James laughed at the memory. He no longer became concerned when he saw strange beasts, either caged or uncaged, because the town was filled with them. He saw crocodiles and camels, wild gazelles, ferocious pigs, a dozen varieties of apes and monkeys, endless species of birds—big birds, small birds, birds with dull plumage and birds with brilliant feathers, birds that walked erect on two legs and were taller than any man.

"There's something for you," Charles Lewis said, pointing to a vast gray animal who was placidly standing next to a tall tree.

"What in the world is it?" James gasped. If he was becoming casual about the great cats and apes, he had never seen anything like this before. The animal was as big as a house!

"An elephant, it is, lad," the mate explained. "Weighs thousands of pounds and as strong as a hundred men."

James watched in fascination as the animal used its long nose to pluck a tasty morsel of straw and poke it in its mouth.

"Care to go for a ride on his back?" the mate asked.

James gulped. "People can do that?"

"Yes."

"I mean, is it safe?"

"I've done it many times myself," the mate said.

"Well . . . if you say so."

In moments they located the elephant's owner, a Hindu mahout dressed in a turban and a filthy loincloth. He readily agreed to let James take a ride for the silver coin the mate offered him.

James was terrified as the mahout placed a block of steps next to the great beast and instructed him to climb up. It was like mounting a whale with legs. When he got to the top, he saw there was a small seat behind the beast's head. He sat down, and as he looked about him, the whites of his eyes could be seen clearly by those below.

"Hai!" the mahout cried, and he poked the elephant below the ear with a metal-shod drover's stick. The elephant moved forward with a rolling gait that sickened James and made him positive he had made a great mistake.

They paraded down the streets of Diégo-Suarez, and some of James's assurance returned as he realized this wasn't all that different from riding a horse—a gigantic, ungainly horse, to be sure, but the principle was the same.

He was feeling like an old hand at this sort of travel when they came to the end of town and the elephant decided he had had enough of this nonsense. The beast lumbered forward at increased speed, and the mahout began shouting and waving his drover's stick. But he was wasting his time. The elephant easily outdistanced him and Charles Lewis, who also began to run.

The elephant pounded down the road, and James held on for his life. He kept looking back, but the figures of the mahout and the mate kept getting smaller.

The elephant came to the beginnings of a patch of jungle. As he plunged into the wild brush, James was swatted and belted by leaves and branches until he was sure he would be beaten to death. Finally the elephant passed under a tree with a thick, low-lying branch, and James was swept off the back of the pachyderm. He fell heavily to the ground, moaned a few times, then gingerly inspected his arms and legs. Nothing seemed to be broken, so he got to his feet.

The mahout came running by. He paused to shout a few curses at James, who was dusting off his clothes; but as the boy didn't understand a word of what the Hindu was saying, he could hardly take offense. The mahout ran into the jungle after his elephant as Charles Lewis arrived, panting and breathless.

"That was a hell of a thing to do," he gasped.

"You told me there was nothing to it," James said accusingly.

"Well, I was wrong," the mate said, and then admitted he had never in his life been on the back of an elephant.

"So why did you lie?"

"Ah, lad, you might not have gone through with it had I told the truth. Look at the wonderful experience you would have missed."

"Almost getting killed is a wonderful experience?"

It was only after the fifth rum-spiked ale that James found it in his heart to forgive his friend and mentor.

But youth recovers quickly, and James was back in Diégo-Suarez the next day with several other sailors from the *Adventure,* including William Moore. They were making their way to a brothel where the size of the rum drinks was exceedingly generous.

"Set your eyes on that bunch, will you," one of the sailors said, and James's attention was directed toward a group of black men advancing down the street.

There were a half dozen, and not a man among them appeared to be less than seven feet tall. They were jet black and wore feathered ornaments braided into their long hair. At ankles, wrists, and neck of each were other elaborate ornaments fashioned from bone. From his bearing and ornaments, it was obvious one man was the leader. The others carried long, slender spears, but he was without any weapons. The stately leader carried a long staff and looked neither right nor left as he walked. People in the street seemed to melt from his path. His companions walked a few paces behind and kept their eyes on him.

William Moore stood next to James in a crowd of men who had stopped to watch the tall black men. "He's one of those big chiefs from the mainland," Moore said. "Wonder what he's doing here."

"I wouldn't want to tangle with him," James admitted as he eyed the man's imposing frame.

A smirk came over Moore's face. "If you did, his friends would slit your gizzard. A chief is supposed to be sacred. Uppity nigras."

It occurred to James that he had never seen any black slaves in New York that looked like these warriors. Small wonder. What slave catcher would dare lay his hands on such men? It would be suicide.

The procession of warriors came closer, and to get a better view he leaned forward against a wooden box that came up to his knees. When the chief was almost abreast of his position, James felt a heavy hand shoved into the small of his back. He pitched forward over the box and landed in a heap on the very spot where the chief was about to place his foot. The giant paused, and instantly two of his warriors were beside him, their spears raised over their heads, ready to plunge the deadly shafts into the body of the creature that had offended the dignity of their leader.

The chief looked down at the shocked white face below him and saw that James was only a lad. He gestured with one hand, and the spears paused. Another gesture and they were lowered.

The chief and James looked into each other's eyes for a long moment, and then the imposing figure stepped around the boy and continued his regal passage down the street.

James came to his feet and angrily looked at the place where he had been standing. William Moore was nowhere to be seen. But it didn't matter. James knew who had shoved him, and why. He also knew there would have to be a day of reckoning.

That evening, when all hands were back aboard the *Adventure,* Captain Kidd announced the ship would depart the following morning to cruise the waters off the Malabar Coast in pursuit of pirates.

James wondered why they would hunt through the ocean wastes for pirates when they had discovered an entire island crawling with them. He mentioned this to Charles Lewis.

"The pirates here outnumber us forty to one," the mate said. "Them's odds Kidd would not like to take. But the real reason, lad, is that we've probably not come for pirates in the first place."

"What do you mean?"

"I think the captain would like to keep things on the safe side and take only French merchantmen, not some pirate who's armed to the teeth. But since we haven't seen any Frenchmen, I wonder how long he can keep the crew in check."

"What will they do?"

"They receive no pay other than a share in the booty. If there be no booty, there be no shares. I've already heard complaining. There's men aboard that would be taking any ship, and to hell with the flag she carries."

"But that would make *us . . . pirates,*" James said, his eyes widening with the thought that his suspicions were proving true.

"There's men aboard that wouldn't have come if they hadn't thought such were the case," the mate admitted.

James had spent a goodly amount of his gold on the girls of the pleasure houses. He had learned something new and had been happily perfecting the art. It was only on the last day ashore that he heard of the pox, and it frightened him half to death. His luck had held through a dozen brothels but he spent the next week inspecting his penis and waiting for the worst to happen. By the time his fears ended, the clean air and salt spray had also cleared the cobwebs from his mind.

For four months the *Adventure* sailed the Indian Ocean. Several times they sighted other ships, and they stopped some of these—always ponderous merchantmen who obviously could not put up much of a battle. But every one proved to be in the service of the East India Company, and Captain Kidd let them go unmolested. Each time, the complaints of the crew grew louder.

The mood of the men aboard the *Adventure* was aggravated as supplies of fresh food began to run out and signs of scurvy appeared among the sailors. They would gather in knots, and when they looked toward the quarterdeck and the captain's cabin, their faces were dark and angry.

Captain Kidd had ordered James to repair a locker at the rear of his cabin, and he was so employed when the door opened and the captain entered, followed by the mate.

"There be mutiny in the air, Cap'n," said Lewis. "The men are hungry and thirsty. Unless something is done right soon, I don't know how we'll avoid trouble."

William Kidd was not the bravest of men. He was a trader with a sharp eye for business and had done well, but his success had never depended on personal bravery. Now his mettle was being tested, and he was worried.

"It won't do much good to return to Diégo-Suarez for supplies. There's hardly any money left. The prices they charge are ruinous."

"Well, we can't go back to New York," the mate said. "We'd all starve to death before we got halfway there."

"What am I supposed to do? The idea was to capture French ships and use the booty to support ourselves. We haven't even *seen* any French ships."

"Then there's nothing to do but capture some other kind of ship," Lewis said. "It's that or take our chances with mutiny."

"I suppose . . ." Kidd said absently. "I suppose that's what Bellomont and Livingston had in mind all the time. I mean, who is to know what happens on the Indian Ocean?"

The mate nodded. "Exactly. With your permission I'll pass the word that we'll take the next ship we meet."

"Yes," the captain said in a small voice. The mate left the cabin.

James had been fascinated, forgetting the two men might not like having been overheard. But it was too late to do anything about it. He stood up from where he had been kneeling and coughed.

The captain looked at him, startled. "I forgot about you, boy. So you know the truth, do you?"

"Yes, sir."

"Do you agree with my decision?"

"That's not for me to say, sir. You're the captain."

"Aye, that I am, and damned if I don't wish I had never left my snug shore berth. But there's no use wishing what can't be."

He eased his bulk into a chair. "You heard what was said. We take the next ship."

James returned to the deck and watched as the mate passed among the men, informing them of the captain's decision.

Unfortunately, the next ship sighted was a merchant-man flying the flag of the East India Company. The men watched the captain for the signal that would turn the *Adventure* into a pirate.

Kidd stood on his quarterdeck, looking at the merchant through his glass. He paced back and forth, but no signal was forthcoming. Grumbling began among the men as the merchantman passed the *Adventure* and sailed on its way. Several of the sailors went to the deck area below the quarterdeck and looked up at the captain. There was an angry murmuring among them, like the buzzing of bees after the honey has been stolen. Charles Lewis, along with the second and third mates, edged closer to the ladder. The captain was reneging on his promise, but they were officers and knew their duty was with the master.

William Moore stepped forward. "Well, Cap'n, and why hain't we gettin' ready to board yon ship?"

The captain looked at the ship and then back at Moore. "We take the first ship that doesn't fly that flag," he said.

"Liar!" Moore shouted, and an electric tension spread among the men. "By God, we be takin' yon ship or we be feedin' our cap'n to the sharks!"

James was standing near the ladder to the quarterdeck, and he felt himself thrust aside as Moore grabbed a belaying pin and started up toward Kidd.

"Avast!" Lewis shouted, but he was on the other side of the ship; a throng of fifty men stood between him and the captain.

Moore made it to the top of the ladder and raised the belaying pin over his head, but William Kidd showed a speed and agility that surprised everyone. He leaped forward and wrestled with Moore, tightly grasping the arm that held the belaying pin, fighting desperately to keep the heavy hunk of wood from crashing into his skull.

James rushed up the ladder and grabbed Moore from behind. The man turned his head to see who was on his back, and the scarred face crinkled in rage when he saw his assailant.

"You . . . you whore's bastard!" he yelled, and turned his attentions away from the captain. He struggled free from James's grasp and raised the heavy belaying pin to crush his skull.

But James was quicker. He buried the top of his head in Moore's stomach, forcing out a great whoosh of air. The sailor was driven back, but not before he had taken a vicious swipe with the club. James blocked the blow with his shoulder; but it numbed his arm and side, and he slumped to the deck, a half-cripple, as the enraged man stood over him, preparing to deliver the killing blow.

Captain Kidd had recovered from his initial surprise, and now he saw that his would-be savior was about to become a victim. A heavy oaken bucket was on the deck near his feet; he picked it up and swung it in a deadly arc aimed at Moore's head. The sailor's attention was completely fixed on the boy, and the bucket cracked into the side of his skull. The belaying pin fell from Moore's hand as his lifeless corpse crashed to the planking.

James was panting from exertion and terror. He looked up, and his eyes met those of the captain. Even in his pain, James could see the captain was as terrified as he.

Charles Lewis sprang to the quarterdeck with a pistol in his hand. "There'll be no mutiny!" he shouted to the crowd of men. He pointed the vicious-looking muzzle of his weapon at the top of the ladder. "The first man up arrives with no head."

The other mates came to the quarterdeck, and the men became restless and worried. If Moore had succeeded in killing the captain, that would have been one thing. But the captain was alive and Moore was dead, and many of the sailors instinctively despised men who would mutiny against their captain. The training of the sea fosters a deep sense of obedience.

The captain was still breathing heavily, but he had the presence of mind to realize the next move was up to him.

"We take the next ship that does not fly that flag," he said loudly. "That is my promise and I will keep it."

There was a short silence. A man at the back of the crowd shouted, "And we're with you all the way! A cheer for Cap'n Kidd!"

The ugly mood was broken. The men, cheering, were again shipmates under their captain, the tension among them dissolved.

Kidd turned to James and touched his shoulder. The young man winced from the pain and pulled back.

"Easy, lad, easy," the captain said. He turned to the mate. "Get him below to my cabin. And bring the doctor."

Lewis and the second mate carried James below and put him on a long padded bench. The "doctor" arrived and made his examination. Never having seen the inside of a medical school, he was simply a sailor who had picked up enough medicine to be of use in a situation where some knowledge was better than none.

He determined no bones had been broken; the muscles had been bruised and would be painful for a few days.

"We can offer thanks to God for that," Captain Kidd said. He broke out a jug of rum, filled a mug to the brim, and handed it to James. "For the pain."

The rum brought a general euphoria to his body. He rested back against the pillow and felt quite pleased with his quick display of courage and action.

"I'm going topside," the mate said, "to throw Moore's body overboard."

"We first must have a proper service," Captain Kidd said.

'But he was a mutineer," the mate protested. "Why waste prayers over scum?"

"The man is dead," Kidd said. "Whatever his sins, he is now in the hands of God."

The service was held, and Kidd read prayers from his Bible. The men stood with their caps off at the side of their captain and watched in silence as the body of Moore slipped over the side to become a tidbit for the sharp-toothed wolves of the sea.

James spent the rest of the day in the captain's cabin, where Lewis saw to his comfort. As the big man busied himself with the lad's food, James finally asked a question that had been on his mind for some time. "Why do you always go to so much trouble for me? What do you want?"

Lewis smiled. "The truth is I want nothing," he said. "I had a brother once. He was a lad like you and I cared a great deal for him. He shipped out on a packet. When the ship returned, the lad was gone. His body had been given to the sharks."

"How did he die?"

"Scurvy. He just wasted away and died. I wasn't there, but I've seen enough scurvy in my day. 'Tisn't pleasant."

"I'm sorry," James said.

"It happened long ago and I most forgot it. But that day you came to me and offered gold to buy your way onto the ship, I guess I sort of adopted you as my new younger brother."

James was embarrassed and touched. He could think

of nothing to say to this strong, hard man who had revealed so much feeling in so few words.

The next day a sail was sighted on the horizon, and this time Captain Kidd left no doubt in the minds of the crew. He ordered the ship readied for battle and changed course to bring the *Adventure* across the path of the other.

As the minutes passed, the other ship grew larger, and now it was possible to make out some of her details. She was a modest-sized packet, obviously a merchant and not a frigate of war. The crew of the *Adventure* lined the rails as they finished priming the cannons and checking the weapons that the mates had passed out from the arms store. There was no complaining, no grumbling. There was only the anticipation that after months of boredom the mission of the ship was about to be fulfilled.

James was hardly ready for a fight, his right arm being cradled in a sling of cloth, but his eyes were as bright as those of the rest of the men as he looked forward to the approaching action.

The merchantman had perceived the danger and was trying to escape, but she was a beamy old scow and could not match the speed of the pursuing frigate.

Captain Kidd took his glass and inspected the flag flying from the ship's mast. "We're in luck," he said to the mate and James, who stood at his shoulder. "She flies the flag of the Great Moghul. They're only a bunch of heathens."

The word was spread among the men that their prey belonged to a heathen king and, the *Adventure* would be acting in the service of the Christian God by attacking the ship. Not that it mattered to most of the men. In their present frame of mind they would have attacked a seventy-two-gun frigate carrying William of Orange himself.

Captain Kidd was relieved. He knew that an attack on any ship of the Great Moghul would be shrugged away in London and New York. To the rulers of white Christendom, there were enough woes in life without worrying about godless savages.

As the frigate closed on the packet, Kidd knew they had picked a good victim. The ship of the Great Moghul was poorly armed, yet she wallowed low in the water; it was obvious her holds were filled with cargo.

The *Adventure* came up on the packet and steered to port to give her cannons a chance to batter the decks before the men boarded. The cannons began to fire, and the heavy shot tore through the packet's riggings, crashing into the side planking, stoving in the timbers. Death and gore accompanied the flying iron balls. The packet offered a feeble defense with its own four guns, the port ones being put out of commission within minutes. The *Adventure* maneuvered to this defenseless side, and her guns ripped the packet at will.

Now the ships closed, and grappling hooks were thrown across the water. When the ships were a few feet apart, the wild and anxious sailors of the *Adventure* jumped across the open space or used ropes to swing across, and they engaged the enemy with a ferocity born of months of frustration.

The crew of the Great Moghul's ship were men of Goa. They were good sailors, but not known for their ferocity in battle. Besides, they were outnumbered four to one. The battle was never in doubt. The Goanese fought bravely, but they were cut down without mercy. As they turned to defend against one shouting attacker, they were dismembered from another direction. Within minutes not a Goanese was alive on the deck.

Several men were found below decks; but the crew of the *Adventure* was mad with a blood-lust, and soon these men too were as dead as their fellows above.

The battle was over. The men lolled on the deck, panting, sweat coming from every pore on their bodies —but their faces shone. They were happy for the first time in months.

James had stood at Captain Kidd's side on the quarterdeck of the *Adventure*, and although he had watched the slaughter, he did not feel they had been in a battle. It had been over so quickly.

And now it was time for the men to see what they had captured. They went below decks to feast their eyes on the loot. William Kidd and James boarded the ship to inspect the plunder.

They found barrels of pungent peppercorns, filling the nostrils with their delicate sharpness. There were chests crammed with precious saffron leaves, and barrels of roots, dried fruits, and blossoms—the trading goods of the Great Moghul.

The men scoured the ships for chests of gold and jewels, but they were to be disappointed. The only store of such riches was found in the captain's cabin, and it was pitifully small to men who had imagined entire holds filled with gold coins and bullion.

Even so it was a rich haul and a source of sorely needed money. Captain Kidd set a course for Majunga, where they could sell their cargo as quickly as possible. They sailed into the harbor, at the mouth of the Betsiboka River on the western coast of Madagascar. Many traders frequented Majunga, seeking cargo to bring back to Europe or the New World. That anything at Majunga was certain to be stolen goods did not bother these men, who had no stomach for piracy themselves but were not above profiting from the piracy of others.

The cargo of spices was sold, along with the hundreds of bolts of rich cloth taken from the ship of the Great Moghul. Part of the money was used to buy a full load of supplies, and the rest was distributed among the men to extend the lease on their loyalty. Once ashore, the crew spent a great deal of their share on the pleasures offered at Majunga—rum, brandy, and slave girls. As the inland kings used the Betsiboka River to send their slaves to the coast to be sold, the slave market in the port was always glutted, and the prices were so low it was cheaper to buy a slave than to frequent a brothel. A man could buy a female, make use of her body, and then simply abandon her when his ship left the harbor. The owners of the brothels tried to discourage this practice, and often a sailor who had bought a slave would be found in a ditch, his eyes gouged out and his genitals stuffed in his mouth. But the practice continued, and soon a new trade sprang up: the recapture of slaves who had been bought and abandoned. These were dragged back to the flesh pits of Majunga and sold again, some of them into exactly the same sort of situation, thus setting up a cycle of slaves being sold, freed, captured and sold, only to be freed again to provide more employment for the professional slave catchers.

Several sailors from the *Adventure* bought slaves in this manner and passed them freely from one to another.

Because of his fear of the pox, James resolved to have nothing to do with these girls, but he indulged in rum—and woke up one morning with a naked girl at his side. He reasoned she had already given him pox, or else she was clean. Using this logic, he stayed with the girl for three days.

She was tall, very black, and wore her hair in tight braids that came down to her shoulders. Her face was pretty, and her nose and ears were delicate. Atani was sixteen years old, and she had been drifting from one man to another for over two years. This didn't seem to disturb her, but as he got to know her, it bothered James. What kind of a life was this for anyone?

They sat on faded mats in a small hut, having eaten a dinner she had cooked of strange green vegetables and a bit of lamb. The domestic tranquility of the moment made James feel like talking, and they spoke of Majunga and the ships. Finally he asked her where she was from.

"My people live at the base of the high hills farther in the island," Atani said in surprisingly good English, learned during a six-month period spent with the sailors from a ship out of Liverpool.

"Why don't you go back to them?"

She looked at him in amazement. "I was the fourth girl-child, and my father sold me because he could not afford to keep me."

"Your own father sold you into slavery?" James said, hardly able to believe his own ears.

Atani shrugged. "My people are poor. There was nothing else to do."

At his urging the girl told of her life in the village, and there was a wistful, lonely quality to her voice. She said it was a common practice for fathers to sell their daughters. Also, the king who lived in the middle of the island sometimes demanded slaves for himself. Very often the king would turn around and sell them to the Arab slavers, who took them back to their own country or to India.

"But you weren't sold by the king," James said, his mind still reeling with the thought. "You were sold by your own father."

"What's the difference who sells you?" she replied. "In the end it is the same thing."

"But don't you ever wish you could go back?"

Atani sighed. "I think about it sometimes. But I am a slave, and I will never have enough wealth."

"What do you mean? What would you need money for?"

"Among my people it is impossible for a woman to win a man unless she is able to bring him enough wealth to make it worth his while. My father was poor, and he used his few possessions to get men for my older sisters. There was nothing left for me."

"But you could do something if you had enough money —isn't that what you're saying?" he persisted.

"If I could buy six goats I could go back to my people and find a man who would have me."

"And you wouldn't have to be a slave anymore?"

Atani's voice was very deep—deeper than any woman's he had ever heard—and now when she laughed it seemed to come from the very depths of her body. "The easiest thing in the world is to buy yourself out of slavery," she said. "All you need is money. And then with more money you get a man. When a woman has a man to protect her, the slavers leave her alone."

James thought about it for a time, and a plan began to form in his mind. "How much would six goats cost?" he asked.

She looked closely at him, understanding what was in his thoughts. The idea made her catch her breath. "One gold coin for each," she said.

Six gold coins, James thought; better make it seven just to be on the safe side. Why not? Would he ever find a better use for his money than to buy freedom for someone who had been kind and tender to him?

"In the morning we'll get the goats," he said. "And since I'm your present owner, I'll set you free and you can go home to your people."

Her eyes opened wider, and she reached out and touched his arm. Her hand was trembling. "You would do this for me? A slave? You would give me back my life?"

"Yes," he said quietly, feeling self-conscious in possessing this strange power to buy and sell other human beings.

"Oh," she uttered. "Oh, oh, oh."

Her face was flushed as she pushed him down on the mat. She began to make love to him. When he was fully aroused she rolled over on her back and pulled him on top of her.

He entered her body, and it was amazingly liquid and slippery. Her long, taut legs wrapped around him, and for a moment he thought she would squeeze him to death. Then his lust took over, and again and again he plunged deep into her while those long legs snaked about him with ferocious energy. He finally erupted in what seemed an endless orgasm. He tried to rest; but she refused to let him go, and they kept thrashing about until he eventually collapsed on top of her body, the two of them panting, gasping, soaking wet.

The last thing he remembered was drifting into sleep while Atani held his head on her lap, stroking his brow and singing softly in a strange language.

The next morning they went to a livestock dealer and bought the six goats. As Atani had predicted, the cost was six gold coins.

They walked inland together for several miles, herding the goats as they walked. Finally they stood on a ridge and the girl pointed to a distant hill. "My people live there," she said. "It is not necessary for you to go farther."

James reached into his pocket and took out the seventh gold coin. Without a word he handed it to her.

The coin reflected the sun as she held it in the palm of her hand and studied it. "What is this for?"

"For luck."

She put her arms about him and hugged him to her bare breasts. "I will never forget you, James."

He watched as she made her way across the plain, a tall, handsome figure carefully herding a half dozen goats. And then she disappeared into the taller grasses and was gone.

James went back to the ship. After supper he stood at the railing and told Charles Lewis the story of Atani.

"Seven bits of gold, eh?" the mate said.

"It meant everything to her."

" 'Twas a good thing you did, a good thing."

"It didn't seem right she should go on being a slave," James said quietly.

"Will you ever be able to live again in New York?" the mate asked suddenly. "You're taking some pretty big bites of a different way of living."

"Why would I want to live in New York?"

"To be with your family."

"I have no family," James said, looking out to sea.

Lewis smiled. "I never did believe that story about not having a father. You lie badly, lad, but if you wish to stick with the story, that's your business. I'll abide by that."

"Thank you," James said. "Perhaps someday I'll tell you. But not yet."

"As you wish," Charles Lewis said. "I be on your side no matter what."

The mate's words comforted James; he had made a friend for life.

The *Adventure* went back to sea, this time with a satisfied crew and no pretensions about the nature of their voyage.

Captain Kidd accepted his fate. He knew he could not stop the crew without causing them to mutiny. For the next several months the *Adventure* plundered many ships and, in the practice of the day, rarely left survivors. The holds filled with the treasures of the Indian Ocean, and Kidd waited until the ship had a full cargo before returning to Majunga or Diégo-Suarez. The ship became a well-known trader in these ports, and the other pirates never gave her a second thought.

Not all merchantmen proved as easy to capture as the first. The battles caused losses of life aboard Kidd's ship, and replacements were recruited from Madagascar. These seamen were among the most savage cutthroats who sailed the oceans. Their only bond to captain and ship was the promise of riches that would enable them to settle in Madagascar and live like pashas and rajahs among the pirate "nobility." The odds were not on their side. There were thousands of pirates on the seas, but not more than two dozen had managed to retire in style on the island. But these were men who had begun with nothing. A life of piracy at least gave men a chance of satisfying their dreams. And if it did not work out, it was better to die with a cutlass in one's hand than to starve to death in a London, Marseille, or Lisbon slum.

The turnover brought new mates to the fo'c'sle, and James learned to hold his own with the worst of them. He had grown several inches and added many pounds—all of it muscle—and was no stranger to razor-sharp dirks and cutlasses. He had fought in battles and had the scars to prove it.

But the biggest change that had come over him was not physical. He had boarded Kidd's ship as a boy with little experience and almost no worldly knowledge. Now he was no longer a boy, but a battle-hardened young man who had killed with pistol and blade, who had watched as his fellow crew members murdered prisoners in revenge after an especially bloody fight. And this murdering was unlike the ritualistic hangings he had seen in New York. Terrified prisoners were made to walk the plank with their arms tied behind their backs. The doomed men were poked with swords until they reached the end of the plank and fell into the water to be eaten by sharks, sometimes before they drowned. Others were shot in the face, their brains spraying anyone unlucky enough to be standing behind them.

One time he even witnessed the keelhauling of the captain of a merchantman who had put up an unusually strong defense and had foolishly allowed himself to be captured alive. Ropes were tied to the captain's hands and feet, and he was dragged from fore to aft along the keel of the moving ship. The motion of the ship pinned him against the bottom planking, and the doomed man was dragged across the barnacle-encrusted wood. The sharp, rough edges of the barnacles wreaked havoc on the captain. By the time his body emerged at the stern, most of his clothing and upper layers of skin had been torn off and the man no longer resembled a man, only a piece of butchered meat. And yet he was still alive—although only barely, having nearly drowned while his skin was being flayed. He was sent back for a second trip along the keel, and what remained of him thereafter was of interest only to a shark.

James had watched this savage killing without the slightest twinge of conscience. It was all part of a way of life he had come to accept.

But now a new problem arose. After many battles the *Adventure* herself was badly battered. It was possible to have her repaired at Diégo-Suarez, but the facilities were primitive and the process would probably take the better part of six months. This suited neither the crew nor Captain Kidd.

The captain also had become hardened to the new way of life, but he was an older man, and, unlike James de Kuyper, he remembered his other life fondly and sorely regretted that it had passed. He now lived with one thought in mind: to gather enough treasure to satisfy the crew and return to New York to give an accounting of his voyages. Half the money, after the king had taken his ten percent, would belong to Kidd and his two partners.

But Captain Kidd's desire to hurry the voyage proved to be his undoing.

A large ship was sighted—the *Quedagh Merchant,* flying the flag of the East India Company and heading directly across the path of the *Adventure.* Kidd's instruction was to let her pass, but the sailors argued against it. Who was to know what happened in the middle of the Indian Ocean? Finally Kidd allowed himself to be persuaded. The other ship was large, and from the looks of her gunwales, riding low in the water, she was laden heavily with cargo.

The *Adventure* came down on the merchantman and opened the battle with several rounds of shot. To Kidd's surprise the other ship did not fight back, but immediately raised a white flag of surrender.

"Mister Lewis," the captain said, "what do you make of this?"

"She must have almost no defenses."

"And she hopes to gain our mercy by surrendering."

"Aye."

The battle was over even as it began.

Kidd and his men cautiously went aboard the other ship, half expecting some sort of trick. None was forthcoming. The captain turned out to be an Englishman. He calmly surrendered his ship and waited for the pirates to make the next move.

Kidd consulted with his mates. A group of men, including James, gathered close as their leaders talked.

"This ship is twice as big as *Adventure,*" the second

mate complained. "She's filled with cargo, and it won't fit aboard our own ship."

That was one problem. Charles Lewis brought up another: "The crew is alive, every one. What are we to do with them?"

"We cannot kill them," Kidd said firmly. "I absolutely refuse to slaughter so many men. Besides, the captain and many others are English. It's one thing to feed bloody heathens to the sharks, but I draw the line at Englishmen."

A few men, unusually bloodthirsty even for pirates, voiced objections, but they were shouted down. The consensus was that it would be wrong to commit such slaughter.

"Why not take their ship and give them ours?" James suggested.

Captain Kidd looked at the young man and smiled. "You have given us the answer," he said. "We will simply put them aboard our ship—"

"After we've moved our cannons to their ship," the mate said.

"Yes, of course. We'll take our cannons and exchange ships," Kidd said.

The captain of the *Quedagh Merchant* calmly accepted his fate—unsurprisingly, since it was better than the one he had expected.

The cannons were removed from the *Adventure*, a back-breaking task that took the better part of a day. The crew of the merchant were put aboard and ordered on their way. The English captain lost no time in raising all possible canvas, and the ship retreated from the *Quedagh Merchant*, which now was a heavily armed pirate ship.

"Shall we inspect the cargo, Captain?" Charles Lewis asked as they watched their former ship depart.

"Aye," Kidd said, without interest. Even the greediest of the pirates had so far shown little curiosity about the cargo, expecting it to be no different from the other cargoes they had taken—spices, china plate, bolts of rich cloth. They weren't disinterested in the money such goods would bring, but they were in no hurry to poke their noses into barrels of peppercorns.

Spices there were, in great quantity, in the first and second holds, and the men were satisfied this booty would add more than a little to their purses. But the third hold was filled with heavy chests bound in brass and iron. The first chest was opened, and the men stood with their mouths agape as they gazed into a treasure store of Chinese jade. Another chest was opened: the glint of gold coins was reflected even in the murky light of the hold. More chests were opened, and the men realized that, at last, they had captured their dream—a true treasure ship, its holds filled with a fortune in precious stones and metals.

"My God!" James said softly as he looked into chest after chest of an immense fortune.

"I never thought I'd live to see this day," Lewis said.

"That door leads to another hold," James said, "but I'm almost afraid to open it."

The mate opened the door, and they moved into a section filled with silver plate, coins, and other objects—all made of the finest silver.

They came on deck, their eyes glazed from the riches they had seen. One man stated that such a treasure must surely belong to a great maharajah, or perhaps even the Great Moghul himself.

Kidd ordered the ship on a course that would take them to the harbor at Diégo-Suarez.

In a world of thieves, the safest place for the *Quedagh Merchant* was the very den of thieves itself: no pirate would dare to attack another buccaneer at Diégo-Suarez, because the hand of every other man would instantly be turned against him. The value of the port was that it be kept wide open; this meant no stealing from your fellow thieves. There was no exception to this rule, and no mercy shown to an offender. Occasionally some pirate would be overcome by greed, but the others would hunt him down and bring him back to Diégo-Suarez to suffer a hideous death. The offender was tossed naked into a pit crawling with lice, roaches, and other vermin. At first a man would fight against the thousands of attackers, but then his strength would ebb. He would sink to his knees, and finally his vermin-encrusted body would fall to the ground and all but disappear beneath a sea of hungry insects. By this time he could no longer make any sounds, having screamed himself hoarse within the first half hour. Even the most jaded and ruthless of men would wince inwardly at the thought of leaving this world in such agony.

The *Quedagh Merchant* found a safe anchorage, and Kidd took no chances. Guards were posted along the railings during the day and night.

When Kidd and Charles Lewis went ashore to negotiate the sale of the spices and the hoard of silver, James de Kuyper went with them, walking two paces behind to guard their backs.

They met once again with the Falcon. After contributing his part to the small talk that was the Falcon's ritual, Kidd came to the point. "I have more spices to sell. I offer them first to you, as you have been fair in the past."

"Ah, yes, spices. I will be most happy to buy them." He smiled, then arched his brows as if in confusion. "But is it not true you have other items to sell?"

"Other items?"

"I hear rumors you have a great treasure aboard your ship."

Kidd was ready with an answer. "I also have a fine collection of silver—plate, statues, and the like. I will sell these to you if you wish."

"And nothing else?"

"Nothing else is for sale."

The Falcon stroked the sides of his face and tried to act in a casual manner. "But the rumors speak of a vast treasure. Perhaps you are telling me this is no more than a rumor?"

"No doubt," Charles Lewis answered. "These waters are filled with rumors."

The Falcon's eyes darted to James. "What do you say, young man, are there rich treasures aboard your ship?"

"The spices are unusually fine," James said blandly, trying to look as innocent as possible.

"And the other treasure?"

"There is the silver the captain spoke of," James replied. "Other than that we have nothing for sale."

The Falcon's face broke out in a smile. He turned back to Captain Kidd. "This one has aged well at sea, Captain. You should be proud of him."

"I am."

There was more talk, but the Falcon made no more attempts to learn of the treasure. He was a clever man and already possessed fabulous wealth—more than most men would dream of having. He was convinced there was a fabulous treasure aboard the *Quedagh Merchant*, but he also knew it could not be worth upsetting his present life or the peace at Diégo-Suarez. He agreed to buy the spices and the silver. After Kidd left, he ordered two ships to anchor near the *Quedagh Merchant* to act as guards. There would be no trouble.

The spices and silver brought over sixty-four thousand pounds sterling to the crew of the ship. It was a sizable fortune: one could buy a house for fifty pounds and a healthy slave for twenty. When the men heard of their incredible wealth, many insisted on receiving their share at once. Rather than risk another attempt at mutiny, Kidd distributed some of the gold coins he had received from the Falcon. About half the men immediately left the ship to begin an orgy of drinking and wenching.

Kidd was on deck with Charles Lewis. "Now would be a good time to take the ship back to New York," he said.

"But many of the men are ashore," Lewis said in surprise. "They'll be wild if you leave them behind."

Kidd shrugged. "They're cutthroats and pirates. They'll find another ship. Unless I leave now, I'm afraid I'll never leave. I'll end my days as a pirate living at Diégo-Suarez."

"And is that so bad a fate?"

"For me, yes."

"Who knows what is waiting for you back in New York?"

"There's only one way to find out," Kidd said, and he gave the order to get the ship under way. Some men aboard complained, not because they cared about deserting many of their shipmates, but because they too had been anxious to enjoy the pleasures of Diégo-Suarez. These men were quickly silenced by others, who realized their own portion of the treasure would be that much greater if there were fewer men to share it.

The *Quedagh Merchant* slipped anchor and sailed back around Cap d'Ambre, headed down the Madagascar Strait until she came to Capetown, and then began the long voyage across the Atlantic to New York.

The cannons were kept primed, and flintlocks were always within reach. They were a treasure ship, and none knew better how to be prepared against pirates than pirates themselves.

However, it had been two months since they had captured the *Quedagh Merchant*. In that time the *Adventure* had returned to England, where the English captain reported the loss to the owners, a consortium of English and Armenian merchants who had been shipping the cargo to the Levantine for the Great Moghul. Several of these men were English peers, and they immediately registered a complaint with the king. William of Orange was horrified. He declared Kidd a pirate "without recourse to mercy." This meant Kidd could never be granted a pardon under any circumstances and was, in fact, a man condemned without a trial.

His Majesty also sent a secret letter to Lord Bellomont, who was now Royal Governor in the New World. The king wished to have his own involvement in the Kidd affair buried as quickly as possible. He was a subscriber of the adage that dark secrets were best kept by men in their graves.

William Kidd, of course, was at sea and knew nothing of all this. The *Quedagh Merchant* sailed ploddingly across the Atlantic. Twice she was sighted by pirates, but the presence of the *Quedagh Merchant*'s fifty guns was enough to send them off to hunt for weaker prey.

James was helping the captain go through the papers in the master's cabin, and they came across a document that explained why such a rich treasure ship had been so vulnerable to attack.

The *Quedagh Merchant* had been loaded at Madras. A frigate of the East India Company had been ordered to join her; but the frigates of the company were spread few and far between, and the escort had never arrived. As the news of the great treasure on the ship spread through Madras, the English captain decided it would be safer to take his chances at sea rather than remain at anchor under the eyes of every cutthroat and thief in the Indian town. If he remained, it would only be a matter of time before an attempt was made to take the ship; but he could hope to hide in the empty wastes of the ocean. He had gambled and lost, but even though he had lost his ship, his quick surrender to the pirates had saved his own life and the lives of his crew.

Now that James was about to return home, he spent a great deal of time thinking about the city and his family. He wondered if his mother would be in good health, and hoped she had forgiven him for running away.

His sister, Alice, would be sixteen years old now. He imagined her all dressed up, her hair neatly combed beneath a bonnet, her dress starched, her hands white and slender. He felt a lump in his throat at the thought of seeing her again.

His emotions were mixed when the stern image of his father passed through his mind. Jacob Adam, he was sure, would not have changed a bit; nothing could change him. But the son had changed a great deal. James was not sure how he would react to Jacob Adam, but he did know he was no longer the frightened boy of three years ago.

"Are you looking forward to seeing New York?" Charles Lewis asked.

"I suppose I am."

"What you ran away from is probably still there."

"I never told you I was running away."

The mate lit his pipe. "Yes, but I never believed you. I also never believed that your father was dead. What will you say when you see him?"

"I don't know," James said, dropping the lie. "But I know I'm not afraid of him anymore."

The mate looked down at the dark waters as the heavy timbers of the ship plowed through them. "Is he an important man?"

"I guess so. I *should* be afraid of him. But I'm not," James said, looking straight into the other man's eyes.

The mate nodded. "After what you've seen, I doubt if you'd be afraid of the Devil himself."

The Devil, James thought; isn't that exactly the way I've always thought of my father? A devil who stood lurking in the shadows, waiting to find my every mistake.

He wondered, finally, if he wasn't being too harsh with the memory of his father. After all, Jacob Adam had been a strong man, and he a boy who had adopted the timid ways of his mother. He loved her no less, but he was now more aware of her weaknesses and her insecurity —and of how such behavior would not be acceptable to a man like his father.

It was with such a new perspective that James was returning home, and he tried to visualize how he would fit back into the life of the family. He would come back to them with the slate wiped clean. How they chose to react to him would determine the future.

Captain Kidd was nervous about his reception in New York. He didn't know if he would be greeted as a returning hero or a wanted pirate. He decided to take steps that would give him some protection if the need arose.

The ship stopped in the West Indies and put in at the port of Santo Domingo. Kidd used a portion of the loot to buy another ship—a small, fast schooner named the *Antonio*. He told the crew he was leaving the *Quedagh Merchant* in the islands and taking only a small portion of the treasure to New York. The bulk of the treasure, he said, and most of the men would remain with the *Quedagh Merchant*.

Meanwhile Charles Lewis chose thirty of his most trustworthy sailors and formed a crew for the schooner. At a time when most of the men were ashore, sodden with rum and bedded down in brothels, Lewis and his men transferred the treasure to the *Antonio*. They left a few of the bulkier items behind as payment for the betrayed sailors. When the transfer was completed, the schooner shipped anchor and headed north to New York.

Captain Kidd brought the schooner through the Narrows and anchored off the Brooklyn shore at Wallabout Bay.

The *Antonio* was a small, nondescript ship and attracted no attention. A longboat with six men under Lewis's command was sent to the city with orders to go to the taverns and snoop about for the latest news. The captain wanted to know what he was walking into before he set foot on land.

As the longboat approached Coenties Slip, James was enraptured by the familiar sights of his homeland.

The stone government house built by Stuyvesant—the Whitehall—looked neat and trim and was surrounded by shrubs and lawns. Fort James, its guns bristling in the fading light of the day, dominated the southern tip of the island. It now boasted a second battery of guns, installed by the British against the day there would be trouble with the French. The streets were old friends—South, Broad, Pearl, Stone, Whitehall, Broad Way.

They tied the longboat at the head of the slip, and James was surprised that the British flag no longer flew over the state house on Pearl. He later learned a new city hall had been completed on Wall Street; the city was moving its boundaries and places of business north.

The men split into two groups, James and another seaman remaining with Lewis. They walked down Whitehall Street, and James's heart was pounding as they passed his father's office building. He saw a shadowy figure moving behind a window and imagined it to be Jacob Adam, pacing back and forth as he pondered a business deal.

Lewis decided to stop at the Dark Ship tavern. James and the other sailor drank beer as the mate engaged a gnarled old man in small talk. At first the conversation consisted of general questions asked by a man who had spent the past few years at sea, but finally Lewis steered the conversation to pirates.

"Aye, we've still got a bloody lot of 'em around," the old man said guardedly, knowing that in these streets every man was a potential pirate. "But Bellomont swears 'e'll clean 'em up."

"Is Bellomont now governor of New York?"

"Ye been away. New York is part of a Royal dominion, she is. Bellomont be guv'nor and lives in Boston."

"It's been three years since I've been here," Lewis said. He tried to be nonchalant about the next question. "Tell me, whatever happened to William Kidd?"

Another man, a sea captain, by his looks, had been listening to the conversation. He slammed his hand down on the table. "Kidd, d'ye say? Now there be a man with the finger of fate pointed at his black heart."

Lewis turned to get a better look at this man. James recognized him instantly. It was the bald-headed Captain Barrent who had some connection with his own father.

"The last I heard of Kidd," Lewis said, "was he went off to rid the sea of pirates."

The captain roared with laughter. He poked James on the arm, and for a moment the young man thought he had been recognized; but there was no way for the captain to know this tough-looking eighteen-year-old was the boy he had met several years before, and then only in the most casual manner.

"The bloody scut turned pirate himself! And did *that* make Bellomont mad! The king hisself wants Kidd's head, or puttin' it more proper, he wants the bloody bastard's head at the end of a rope!"

Lewis acted as if this news meant nothing to him. "Does anyone know where Kidd is?"

Barrent became suspicious. "I don't recall seein' your face 'round these parts afore," he said menacingly. "You b'ain't one of these piss-faced bounty hunters, be you?"

"No. Only a sailor who's been to sea for a long time."

" 'Tain't healthy to be askin' certain questions."

"Of course," Lewis said, and smiled. "I mean no trouble."

"Yes, I can see that," Barrent said, and his sudden disinterest seemed patently false. He stood up and walked to the door. "I can see you mean no trouble."

Several men nearby also got up and left the tavern. James turned to the mate. "Will there be trouble?" he asked.

"None that we'll make," Lewis said calmly, but James noticed his hand strayed down to the hilt of the knife stuck in his belt.

"What should we do?" the third sailor asked nervously.

"Finish our beer and go back to the longboat."

When the trio left the dank interior of the tavern, they were aware that every pair of eyes followed them.

They made it back to Pearl Street without trouble, and James was congratulating himself when several men materialized out of the pitch-black alleys and surrounded them. One lunged at Lewis with a knife in his hand, but the mate stepped aside and knocked the man to the ground.

The other seaman from the *Antonio* was not as lucky. Before he was aware of what was happening, two men grabbed him and slit his throat. James had been bringing up the rear, and he heard the tread of a heavy body almost upon him. He whirled about and grabbed the man's arm just as he was about to strike with his knife. For the briefest instant the two were face to face, and James could smell the man's sour breath.

With a single swift motion James wrenched the arm down. He twisted it behind the man's back until the knife fell to the ground, and then he kicked his opponent squarely in the middle of the back, sending him sprawling on his face.

His own knife was out in a flash, and he faced the other shadows coming from the alleys. Lewis was at his back, facing the other way, and they were determined to sell their lives dearly. But there were over a dozen men around them.

"You be a right sharp lad for a bounty hunter."

James turned to the owner of the high-pitched voice.

"But soon you be a right sharp *dead* lad."

"This is all a mistake, Captain Barrent."

The captain was startled. He stopped, and the other men, who had begun closing in, now hesitated. "How d'you know my name?"

"A word in private, if you please."

The captain looked suspicious, and his eyes darted to the dirk in James's hand.

James let the knife fall to the ground. If these men wanted to kill him, one knife wouldn't be of much use.

"No tricks," the captain said.

"No tricks."

The captain took a pistol from his belt and trained it at James's heart. "Come over here."

They stopped a few paces away from the other men. "Now what d'ye want?" the captain said.

"It would be a mistake to kill me."

"Why?"

"My name is James de Kuyper. Jacob Adam is my father."

The captain was startled, and he allowed the muzzle of his pistol to drop. "Jacob Adam's son? He be a runty lad."

"When was the last time you saw him?"

The captain squinted as memory came to his aid. "Come to think of it, there was a story that he went with William Kidd."

"It's the truth. I have been with Kidd."

Barrent stuck his pistol back in his belt and moved closer for a better look. "You really be who you say you be?"

"If I wasn't, would I know it was my father's money that bought your ship, *Lord Blackton*?"

The captain grabbed James's arm. "I believe you, lad, but is Kidd here on Manhatan?"

"Aboard a ship across the river at Wallabout Bay."

"Best he stay there. The news is bad. He's to be hanged along with t'others who shipped with him."

"That includes me," James said glumly.

The captain put both hands on James's shoulders. "Sorry I took you for a bounty hunter, lad, but just look at yourself. You be a man, and that's for sure." He turned to the other men. "These men be all right. Leave 'em alone."

The men disappeared as silently as they had come, leaving Captain Barrent alone with James and Charles Lewis.

The mate inspected the seaman from the *Antonio* whose throat had been cut. The man was very dead.

"Beggin' your pardon about that," Captain Barrent said. "It be a mistake."

"I knew the man," Lewis said. "If his throat hadn't been cut here, it would have happened somewhere else. He was a rascal."

Barrent sighed. "Best be leavin' the body. It be nothin' unusual around here. There be nobody t'ask questions."

"It's time to be on our way," Lewis said, with a final glance at his dead shipmate.

The captain walked back to the slip with them.

"How is my father?" James asked.

"As fit as ever. And as tough to deal with."

"I don't want him to know I'm here."

"If that be your wish," the captain said. "But if I might offer some advice, you be in trouble and he be a good man to know."

"When the time comes," James said.

"It be comin' quick, to my way of thinkin'."

They found the other three sailors waiting at the long-boat. They quickly went aboard. "Take care, laddie," Captain Barrent said as he untied the mooring line. "Take care, all of you. You be in mortal danger."

As they rowed across the river, Lewis looked at James. "Who is your father?"

"He's one of the richest men in the city. And he has some connection with Captain Barrent."

The mate arched his brows.

"My father is a businessman. He's not a pirate, if that's what you're thinking."

"I was thinking nothing, just listening."

"The bad news," James continued, "is that we've all appointments at the wrong end of a rope."

"A bad business," the mate said. "Kidd will take it hard."

"No harder than myself."

The mate was thoughtful. "If your father is rich, then he is also powerful."

"Remember it was my father who made me run away. He might want nothing to do with me."

The mate shook his head. "He may be a hard man, lad, but he's still your father. I doubt he'll turn his back on you."

The longboat returned to the *Antonio*, and Lewis related the news to the captain.

Kidd tossed off a goblet of rum. He finally looked at the mate. "What would you do if you were in my place?"

"Return to Madagascar."

"And be branded a pirate the rest of my days."

"Better that than to swing on the end of a rope."

"But they haven't heard my side of the story."

"I think they've heard all they care to hear."

They talked for hours, and finally the captain made up his mind. They would sail to Boston, where Kidd would make a direct appeal to Lord Bellomont. After all, wasn't the man one of the partners in the venture? Surely he would listen to reason.

The *Antonio* weighed anchor and sailed up the East River, passing through the turbulence of the Hell Gate and out into the calm waters of Long Island Sound.

During this voyage the captain decided it would be a mistake to sail into Boston harbor aboard a ship filled with treasure. Too many people might misunderstand.

The *Antonio* was anchored off a deserted shore on Gardiner's Island, and the chests of treasure were taken to the land on two longboats. A large hole was dug, and then Kidd sent all but four men back to the ship. Remaining were the captain, Charles Lewis, James de Kuyper, and a seaman named Ian Kyle, whom Kidd trusted because he had known him for twenty years.

One chest was placed in the hole and covered with dirt. The remaining treasure was stored, covered over, inside a cave. Now the true hiding place of the bulk of the treasure was known only by four men. If any of the others attempted to retrieve the fortune, they would find only a single chest of the nine that had been brought ashore.

The *Antonio* continued her voyage to Boston and anchored in the roads. Captain Kidd went ashore, bringing an expensive diamond necklace as a present for Lord Bellomont's wife. The governor was delighted to see William Kidd. He accepted the necklace, declared it evidence of Kidd's perfidy, and ordered him clapped into irons.

"But you haven't heard my side of the story," Kidd protested.

"We will hear it at your trial," Bellomont said. "Which will take place just before the hanging."

"What if I'm found innocent?"

The governor smiled. "I don't think there's much chance of that."

"Why don't you take me out and shoot me now? It would save everyone a lot of trouble."

"We must do things properly," the governor said. "After all, we are civilized men."

"I thought we were partners."

A mystified look came over the governor's face. "My dear Kidd, whatever are you talking about?"

"It's all a cover-up, that's what it is," Kidd said angrily. "You're afraid. Even the king is afraid. Well, I'm not going to let you get away with it. I'm going to—"

Bellomont signaled the guards; Kidd was thrown to the floor, and a heavy stick was placed in his mouth and tied with rope. Kidd tried to talk, but the stick caused him to choke. His hands were bound behind his back.

"I don't think you're going to do much talking," Lord Bellomont said, and ordered Kidd placed in his private dungeon.

Within an hour a squadron of Royal Marines went aboard the *Antonio* and took the crew ashore, where they were thrown into prison.

The next day Kidd was sent to London aboard a frigate, his arms manacled in chains and his mouth still gagged.

The governor offered a full pardon to any man who would reveal the hiding place of Kidd's treasure. One man told of the hiding place on Gardiner's Island, but only one chest of treasure was found. None of the three remaining men who knew the real hiding place would talk. The governor conveniently forgot his promise of a pardon for the one man from the *Antonio* who had revealed what he knew; he was thrown back into jail with the others. The next morning he was found in a corner of the cell with his throat slit from ear to ear.

The men of the *Antonio* were boarded on a ship and sent to New York. They went in chains, and the guards harassed them brutally. Several men died from the treatment, including Ian Kyle. Now there were only three men in the world who knew the hiding place of the treasure: James de Kuyper, Charles Lewis, and William Kidd, who was on his way to Europe.

They arrived in New York half starved, smeared with their own excrement, their clothes in tatters, their bodies bruised and clotted with dried blood where the guards had beaten them with whips, cudgels, and musket butts.

A quick trial was arranged, and it was obvious the presiding judge had orders to find them guilty and hang them without delay.

The men were crammed into a dungeon too small to hold them, and their smell caused the guards to hold their noses as they brought food and water to the prisoners. Charles Lewis and James sat on the floor at one corner, their eyes hollow.

A guard appeared at the iron door and said he wanted "a James de Kuyper."

James went to the small opening in the door.

"I'm de Kuyper," he said through the narrow iron bars.

The guard unlocked the door. "You have a visitor."

James followed the guard down the stone corridor, whose musty smell reeked of human misery. As they walked up the steps, James blinked from the unaccustomed bright light. He was taken to a room and the door closed behind him, For the first time in over three years he looked upon the face of his father.

The two stood studying each other in silence. James waited for the other man to step forward; he wanted to touch him. But Jacob Adam did not move.

James felt self-conscious about his miserable condition, then suddenly realized he no longer hated this man.

"Did you miss me?" he asked, breaking the silence.

"Yes," Jacob Adam said without hesitation.

"And I missed you, Father," James said honestly.

"There's talk of hanging you," Jacob Adam said. "Captain Barrent came to me with the whole story."

"We were pirates," James admitted. "But we didn't have any choice."

"If we can save you from the hangman," Jacob Adam said, "the experience might have done you some good."

James dreaded asking the next question, and his lip quivered as he spoke. "How is my mother?"

"At first she blamed it all on me. After a time she began to blame you as well. Now that you're back she'll get over it."

"And my sister?"

"Alice is in good health. She has a mind of her own. As, it seems, do you," Jacob Adam added, not without pride.

"I want to see them. And the rest of the family, too."

"All in good time."

"I . . . I wouldn't want them to see me like this."

"I can understand that," Jacob Adam said dryly. He became brisk and businesslike, and James recognized the father he had known. "A man is waiting outside to see you. He's a lawyer from Philadelphia, and we've had dealings in the past. He's agreed to present your case to Lord Bellomont."

Jacob Adam spoke to the guard, and moments later he introduced his son to Andrew Hamilton, a handsome and dignified middle-aged man.

"Tell me how it happened," Hamilton said, and listened as James sketched an outline of his adventures with Kidd. When he was finished, the lawyer nodded his head.

"A young boy runs away to sea, finds himself unwittingly on a pirate ship. He has no choice but to remain aboard . . . Yes; yes, I think I can present the argument to Bellomont in a proper manner."

"Then you believe you can get my son released?" Jacob Adam asked.

"I've already spoken to His Lordship," Hamilton replied, smiling slightly as he spoke. "He would be pleased to do a favor for you and your son. Paul de Witt has spoken to him as well, and you know how highly the governor values him."

"You mean . . ." James said, hardly able to believe his good fortune. "The matter is already settled?"

"There are a few formalities, but yes, the matter is settled."

The smile on James's face didn't last long. "What of the others?" he asked. "Will they be sent to trial?"

Hamilton shook his head. "There will be no public trial, only a brief private hearing. The governor has decided to treat them as men already convicted. They are to be sent back to England and hanged as a public spectacle."

"All of them?"

"Yes."

James looked away, thinking of the man who had been the most influential person in his life for the past three years. He realized it was now his turn to do something for the mate. "I must ask a favor of you," he said, looking at his father and then at the lawyer.

Jacob Adam regarded his son. There was none of the little boy in his voice; no begging, inferior of superior. James was asking a favor as one man to another.

"What is it?"

"There's a man named Charles Lewis among the prisoners. A good man who helped me learn the craft of the sea. He deserves to live."

Charles Lewis was brought to the room and scrutinized by Andrew Hamilton. After a half hour of questioning, the lawyer turned to Jacob Adam. "I believe I can make a case for this man as well. The question is, are you willing to exert your influence with the governor? Beyond what he has already agreed to, I doubt he'll consider anything involved in this matter on facts alone."

Jacob Adam looked at his son. Knowing that the fate of Charles Lewis was important to James, he waited for

him to plead for his friend. No plea was forthcoming;
James's expression was hard and unchanging. Jacob
Adam was pleased by this show of inner strength.

"I'll do everything I can," he said, and was rewarded by
the smile that returned to James's face.

The appeal was made to the governor, and, in a
week's time, Hamilton returned with pardons for the two
men.

"How can I ever thank you?" James asked the man
from Philadelphia.

Andrew Hamilton was thoughtful. "Life has a way of
working these things out."

James de Kuyper and Charles Lewis left the jail as free
men. Jacob Adam had sent over new clothes, and as the
two of them made their way to the de Kuyper house on
upper Pearl, or, as it was sometimes called, Queen Street,
they looked a world apart from their wretched condition
of a few days ago.

James was welcomed by his father and sister as he entered the house he had run away from, so very long ago
it seemed. His Aunt Anne was there, and his cousin Emilie Goelet with her husband and children. Paul de Witt
clapped him on the shoulders, and Janet wiped a few tears
from her eyes.

"Look at you," Emilie said in wonder. "I don't think
I'd recognize you if I met you on the street."

"Nonsense," Anne said. "He's got the same face, only
now it's on a different body."

"We must hear of your adventures," Paul said.

"Give him a chance to relax, will you," Janet protested, then looked at the other man. "You must be the
Mister Lewis we've heard so much about."

James introduced his friend. In the beginning the mate
was uncomfortable, but Alice broke down his reserve by
handing him a goblet of rum and by treating him as one
of the family.

James looked nervously about for a missing face.

"Your mother is in her room," Jacob Adam said. "Waiting for you."

As James knocked on the door, his hand felt like a
fifty-pound weight.

"Come in." His mother's voice was cold and distant.

She was standing at the far side of the room, framed in the light coming through the window. She looked older, thinner; there was no smile.

He stood stiffly inside the door, wanting to go to her, but realizing it would be a mistake. "How are you, Mother?" he asked formally.

"Does it matter to you?"

"It . . . yes, it matters to me."

Jennifer regarded this handsome young stranger. She had never pondered what changes might have happened in her son: for three years she had pictured him as a boy, helpless, alone in the world. At first all her anger had been directed toward her husband. As time went on, she began to transfer some of her anger toward this son who had been too selfish to understand she needed him at her side.

But now as she looked upon this son, this *grown* son, she realized how much she loved him and had missed him.

"I'm supposed to be angry," she said. "But looking at you, and seeing how you've changed . . . is it possible it's all been for the best?"

"I'll try not to hurt you again," he said, and his voice was hoarse with emotion. "I never stopped thinking about you, Mother. I bought you a present, but it got lost in all the excitement and I don't—"

Suddenly he realized he was rambling in his nervousness. Jennifer de Kuyper was smiling.

"It was a beautiful shawl," he finished lamely.

"If it's not out of keeping with your new character, could you give your mother a kiss?"

James strode across the room and took her in his arms. He was much taller now than his mother, and she had to bend her head back to look into his eyes. "I'm very proud," she said with a sudden fierceness.

"It's wonderful to be home," he said, and felt his eyes mist over.

A huge dinner followed this reunion, and they washed it down with copious amounts of beer and good wine. James was so stuffed he decided to slip out of the house and go for a walk. Alice spotted him as he was opening the door.

"Want some company?" she asked.

"Sure."

They walked to Wall Street and headed west toward the Hudson River. There were many new trees planted along the street, and the window boxes bloomed with flowers, their perfume suspended over the setting. Some windows were filled with a golden light, and the houses themselves looked solid, monied, and respectable. The chirpings of crickets filled the air with night music, and in the distance an owl hooted.

"This is the loveliest street in town," Alice said. "Someday I'm going to have a house here. I'll give great parties, and when all the guests have arrived I'll sweep down the staircase and make a grand entrance."

James was amused. "How do you plan on talking Father out of the money to buy such a house?"

"I'll have my own money," she snapped. "And my husband will have some, too."

"A husband, eh? Any particular boy in mind?"

"No, not yet, but that won't be any problem. Most boys are like puppies you can lead around on a leash."

As if to prove her point, two boys a bit older than Alice came walking toward them. They looked vaguely familiar to James, but he couldn't place them.

One moment the boys were engaging in horseplay, cheerfully shoving and insulting one another, but when they saw Alice, they were suddenly serious. One smiled shyly, tipped his cap, and greeted her.

She nodded curtly and lifted her nose a bit higher as she walked past the boy without further acknowledgment.

James smiled. "You really cut that kid down. I guess he's not on your list of marriageables."

"You could be wrong. That was John Livingston and I like him a lot."

"*That* was John Livingston? I *have* been away for a long time. I never would have recognized him. The last time I saw him he was just a little kid."

"So were you," Alice reminded him.

They passed the new city hall, at the head of Broad Street, within sight of the newly constructed Nassau Street. They crossed the rutted tracks of wheels in the dirt of New Street, and came to Broad Way. From there they could see the waters of the river shimmering silver under the incandescence of the full moon.

"Now, big brother, I have a question for you."

"Yes?"

"Those places you were describing at dinner sounded pretty wild. I guess you could do almost anything you wanted. Correct?"

"I suppose, but you had to be careful, otherwise you'd wind up in an alley with a knife in your back."

There was a devilish look on her face as they passed the freshly planted yard at Trinity Church. James realized she was leading up to something. "What's on your mind?"

"I was wondering how many women you've had."

"Wha—" His voice was choked off in a fit of coughing. His face was red with outrage. He finally managed to clear his throat, and Alice broke out in a merry laugh.

"Well, are you going to answer me?"

"What kind of talk is this for a girl? You come from a respectable family."

"So do you, but it probably didn't keep you from intimate knowledge of exotic women," she said with a wicked relish, and continued walking toward the sandy shore and scattered docks at the river. He hurried after her.

"There are some things a girl shouldn't talk about," he said stiffly.

"My, my, have we grown up only to become a prude?"

"Alice," he said, grasping her arm. "You wouldn't talk like this in front of Mother."

"Of course not. She'd be too embarrassed. But I'd do it with Father."

"You wouldn't!"

"Why not? The mating process wouldn't be news to him. How do you think we got here?"

They came to the river and looked out over the endlessly flowing waters to the distant Jersey shore. There was a small, dark ship in the middle of the river, slowly drifting south toward the Upper Bay; a punctuation mark in an endless watery dialogue.

"Well, how many did you sleep with?"

He looked away. "Enough," he said in a small voice.

"Well, well."

"Does it make you happy to know?"

"I knew it anyway, I just wanted to hear you admit it,"

Alice said blithely. "Honestly, I don't think there's anything wrong with it. In fact, I'd worry about you if you
were still a virgin."

The too-casual use of the last word came as another
shock. He shook his head and muttered beneath his
breath. This annoyed Alice.

"I suppose you never talked about these things when
you sneaked off with the other boys," she said.

"That was different."

"Different! One set of rules for boys, and another for
girls, is that it? Well, I think it's stupid."

Her chin was thrust out, and there was a stubborn set
to her finely chiseled features. "I believe you actually
would talk to Father about these things," he said in awe.

"Certainly. But it's more fun talking about them with
someone I can shock. Like my brother."

And then she giggled and took his arm. Her glee over
her own wickedness was contagious, and they both
laughed as they walked home with their arms locked together.

Theophilus Henry raised his weapon, sighted down the
barrel, and slowly squeezed the trigger. The explosion
seemed all the louder because of the deep silence that
had preceded it. The heavy lead bullet struck the buck in
the chest and entered his heart.

The wounded animal bounded forward in instinctive
reaction to the noise, but after a few yards he stumbled
to his knees, and his body crashed to the ground. Death
came swiftly.

James de Kuyper and Charles Lewis followed Theophilus as he left the woods to inspect his prize where it
lay in the clearing.

"I'd hate to have him tracking me," Lewis muttered to
James. "First he *smelled* the deer, and then tracked him
down without making a sound."

"Well, lads," the woodsman said as they looked down
on the body of the deer, "now we can celebrate your
visit with fresh venison on the table. Here, give me a
hand with him."

They cut a long pole from a branch and tied the deer's
feet together with strips of rawhide. The pole was passed

between the bound legs, and the deer carried upside down as they returned to de Kuyper Manor.

For the first few days of their freedom James and the mate had stayed in New York, making the rounds of taverns and soon finding themselves bored with the constant retelling of their adventures with Captain Kidd. James had suggested that they spend some time at the manor to get away from all the well-wishers.

They had arrived at midday, and Theophilus took them out to track down a deer for supper. What they didn't realize was that Theophilus had brought them along simply to carry back the deer.

By the time they had covered the two-mile distance to the manor, the heavy animal hanging from the pole that was cutting into their shoulders, they found themselves wishing they had gone rabbit hunting instead.

In the slaughter house Theophilus gave orders that the choicest parts were to be cut out for the evening meal; then the three men went to the kitchen for a much-needed drink.

"Eight-pointer," Theophilus announced to Elizabeth, greeting her with a kiss. "Good set of antlers for the wall."

"I hope he's tasty," she said skeptically.

"I could eat anything right now," James said. "Even a horse."

"I've eaten horsemeat," the mate said. "Matter of fact, I've eaten worse."

"You may be eating it again tonight," Elizabeth said. "Eight-pointers are better trophies than they are eating."

James was suddenly aware of a figure seated near the fire. It was Stone Eagle, paying a visit to his daughter. The Indian looked as strong of body as ever, even though he was an old, old man now—how old, no one could say.

Charles Lewis was introduced to the chief and the men sat drinking beer while Elizabeth left to inspect the meat.

"These two have been far across the waters," Theophilus said to the old chief. "Seen many lands and wonderful sights."

Stone Eagle's face was impassive. "But it is good for a man to have a home," he said, and James thought he detected an ironic note in his voice.

"Do you still live in the village at Spuyten Duyvil?" he asked the Indian.

"Yes, the same place."

"And nothing has changed?"

"More farms with white men," the chief said without bitterness, but James knew that more farms meant less unrestricted land, and that meant a further encroachment on the Indian's way of life.

"But there is peace," Stone Eagle added, as if he understood what was going through the young man's mind.

They drank more beer from the keg and spoke of many things, and all the while Charles Lewis kept staring at the chief. This was the first time he had ever been involved in conversation with an Indian. Born in Dublin, he had spent his early years in the British Isles, and had been at sea for the rest of them.

Stone Eagle was aware of the man's interest, and he understood the reason; other men had stared at him in this manner, as if they half expected him to let out a war whoop and go for his tomahawk.

"You have been in many strange places?" he asked.

"I still don't believe half of what I've seen with my own eyes," James admitted.

The chief fixed Charles Lewis with his steady stare. "These strange places, how are they different?"

"Well, that's hard to say, there's been so many," the mate said, scratching his head. "India is certainly strange. And Java, that's really different."

"Yes, but in what way?" the chief persisted.

"The people wrap themselves in strange dresses—men and women alike, and they don't have a stitch above their waists. Wear rings on their toes, too." He paused, and thought for a moment before he continued. "But I guess the strangest place was an island called Borneo. There was a kind of people there called Dyaks who used to shrink human heads. I don't know how they did it, but they could shrink a head down to the size of an apple. I bought one and brought it back to the ship, but the captain I was shipping with was superstitious. Said he wouldn't sail with any shrunken head on *his* ship. Made me throw it overboard, he did."

"A place like that must really be something to see," Theophilus said dreamily, and for a moment he thought of the freedom of his former life. Then Elizabeth returned to the kitchen with a stack of venison steaks, and he knew he was content.

"And what is the strangest place you've ever seen?" James inquired of the chief.

Stone Eagle did not hesitate. "New York."

Theophilus burst into laughter, and James and the mate joined him. Stone Eagle did not, but James was certain the crinkles around his eyes contracted for a moment.

Just before dinner Hope Henry came into the kitchen. A few years younger than James, the small, dark-skinned girl with the quiet ways had always been one of his favorites. She was a part of his memories almost as far back as they went.

"You've become famous," she said, looking up at him with clear, unwavering eyes. She reached out and touched his arm. "Now I can say I've touched a famous man."

"You have the same sense of humor as your grandfather."

"I met Mrs. de Peyster earlier today," Jennifer said as she brought coffee to her husband's study. "Annette's mother," she added, placing the cup and saucer on the desk near his elbow.

"Annette's mother," Jacob Adam repeated blankly, looking up from his papers.

"The de Peysters would like James to marry her. . . . Remember James? Your son."

"Oh. Annette, yes; dark-haired girl, as I recall."

"I'm sure James still thinks of her as she was several years ago, but she's blossomed into a beautiful young woman."

"Has he talked to you about getting married?"

"No."

"I should think not. He should be deciding what he wants to do with his life."

"Choosing a wife would seem to fit into that category. Besides, every woman in New York with a marriageable daughter has her eye on him."

"Why not? He's a de Kuyper," Jacob Adam said flatly.

"Speaking of his future, have you talked with him about it?" she asked.

Jacob Adam picked up his cup and sipped the hot

brew. "I promised myself—and you, madam—that I wouldn't interfere with his plans. That's assuming, of course, that he has some."

A few years ago Jennifer would have been afraid to comment on this last statement. But the problems with James had made it clear that Jacob Adam, like other mortals, was not above mistakes, and she had resolved to speak up when she disagreed with her husband.

"Give him a little time," she said. "And don't try to jump in and make his decisions for him."

"I wasn't planning on 'jumping in,'" he said in annoyance. "But I see nothing wrong with a father offering counsel to his son."

"Exactly, *counsel.*"

Jacob Adam scowled. "I'll be the soul of discretion and tact," he said. He picked up the sheaf of papers and rustled them. "And now, if it's permitted, I'd like to get back to work."

"Oh, by all means," she replied airily. "A day without financial profit is a day wasted."

The remark startled him. He looked sharply up at her, then relaxed, and a shy smile crossed his lips. "We've come a long way together, haven't we?"

"Everything works itself out in time," she said as she walked toward the door.

And Jacob Adam kept his word.

Over breakfast three days after James's return from the manor, Jacob Adam suggested his son walk with him to his office.

An old woman stood on a corner, hawking her flowers to the passersby. She recognized Jacob Adam and dismissed him as a possible customer; he had passed her by for ten years without ever buying anything. But James stopped and picked out a red boutonniere for his coat lapel.

"And one for you, Father."

Jacob Adam shook his head. "Waste of money to buy a flower that's already dead."

Ignoring this argument, James picked out another flower and inserted it on his father's coat. He stepped back and cocked his head to one side, admiring his handiwork. "It gives you a more dashing look," he said.

Jacob Adam shrugged. "If it pleases you that I look like a dandy."

"Oh, no, sir, no," the flower-woman protested. She was toothless, and her gums seemed to flap against one another. "Makes you out right 'andsome and dashing, it does."

James laughed. "See, it's already doing something for you." He reached into his pocket, drew out several small coins, and handed them to the woman.

"Thankee, sir," she said, delighted at this windfall. "Thankee."

The two men resumed walking, and Jacob Adam brought up what was on his mind. "I've been wondering if you've made any plans for yourself," he said.

James looked warily at the older man. "I've given it some thought."

"Care to talk about it?"

"You might not agree with my conclusions."

Jacob Adam waved his hand in dismissal of the idea. "Let's get one thing straight. You're a man now, and a man must make up his own mind about things. If I don't agree with you, I'll say so. But I won't carry it any further."

James nodded. It seemed a fair enough proposition. "I'm aware you'd like me to come into the business with you," he said. "And I've given that idea reasonable consideration."

"Sounds like you've decided against it."

"I have. In the first place I don't think I'd be very good in business. And I'd be living in your shadow again. It wouldn't work," he said bluntly.

"I won't say I'm not disappointed," Jacob Adam responded, choosing his words carefully. "But I won't give you any argument, either. Work is a large piece of a man's life, and he must be happy with his choice."

James was surprised by his father's mildness. It made it easier for him to broach his idea. "What I'd like to do is move permanently to the manor. Theophilus would stay on as manager, but I'd take an active role in expansion. I have ideas about new kinds of crops, and there's much to be done to improve the breeds of our horses. What do you say to this?"

"We've had farmers in the family before," Jacob Adam

replied thoughtfully. "Your own grandfather tried his hand at it. I suppose he must have found it satisfying."

"I can tell from your voice that *you* wouldn't find it satisfying; but we're different people, you and I. It's my decision to give it a try."

Jacob Adam had already accepted his son's decision, and was at work on its future. "The breed that could stand the most improvement is the workhorse," he said, rapidly sifting through the information in his mind. "Some of the European strains are bigger and stronger. Now if you could breed a horse that could be worked more productively, you'd stand to make a fortune."

James didn't try to hide his smile. Some things would never change, he thought.

The trial of William Kidd was held in England, and the reports that came back proved it had been a farce. Kidd was tried on several charges of piracy and also for the murder of William Moore.

"The murder of Moore!" James said in disbelief when his father told him. "Moore was a mutineer, and Captain Kidd killed him to save his own life."

"Nevertheless, he was charged with murder and the court found him guilty," Jacob Adam said. "He was hanged at Wapping, and his body stayed in chains until the birds made it too hideous to look at."

"There was no justice in that court," James said.

"Nor was there meant to be. Too many highly placed people were connected with Kidd. From their point of view the man had to be put out of the way."

James and Charles Lewis were now the only two men alive who knew the true resting place of the buried treasure. James wanted to get it, but the older man advised caution. "Leave it where it is for a few years. By then people will have forgotten about Kidd. But if a man showed up now with that sort of wealth—especially either of us—he'd be a prime suspect."

James agreed, and the treasure of Captain Kidd remained untouched on Gardiner's Island.

It quickly became clear the matrons of New York regarded James as a good match for their daughters. During the course of the year many women called on Jennifer, and most brought along a blushing daughter to be inspected. Jennifer took this business seriously, and every time James came to the city from the manor, she subjected him to a stream of dinners and parties. Girls seemed to be lurking around every corner in the house. To James, they all blended into one another, and he was forever calling Miss Schermerhorn Miss Schuyler, or Miss Livingston Miss Brevoort.

He managed to avoid entanglement, and was content now and then to spend a few days in the city with his family before returning to the hard, clean life of the manor.

He was in the city when a great ball was given to honor the new governor, Lord Cornbury. Jacob Adam, of course, was invited, and Jennifer made sure an invitation was extended to her son. The ball was to be one of the largest ever held in the province, and every eligible young lady was sure to be there.

The new governor was a cousin of Queen Anne, the daughter of James II, who had succeeded to the throne at the death of William of Orange. What the people of New York did not know was that the new governor had been sent across the ocean because Anne couldn't stand to have him in the same country as herself. But on this eve of the great ball, the members of New York society were a-twitter at their first meeting with a blood relative of the monarch.

James arrived with his mother and father and sister, and they were impressed by the aura of the great hall of the governor's house. The rooms were ablaze with candles, and freshly cut flowers perfumed the air.

Jennifer busied herself with a group of ladies, and Jacob Adam was soon discussing business with several merchants and men of affairs. The orchestra started playing and the dancing began, but everyone was puzzled that their host had not put in an appearance.

James managed to avoid the first few dances and was sipping at his third glass of wine when he happened to glance up at the balcony that ran around one side of the room. A large, rather portly woman was standing near the railing, an ivory fan covering the lower half of her face. The fan would twitch every now and then, and

James could see the woman was wearing extreme make-up.

He became curious over her identity and wondered what she was doing on the balcony of the governor's private quarters. He continued to stare at her; she saw him and smiled back. Then she hid coquettishly behind the fan, allowing one eye to peek over the top.

James became amused with the game. He would pretend to look away, then snap his eyes back on the woman and wave. Each time she waved back, and then affected embarrassment as she hid behind the fan again.

James suddenly became aware of a tinkling, melodic laugh at his shoulder. He spun around to face the most beautiful girl he had ever seen. He realized he was acting like a fool and the girl had caught him at it. His face turned red, and she laughed again.

"I'm sorry," she said, "but I can't help myself."

"I do look foolish, don't I?" he said, and joined in her laughter.

"Who *is* she?" the girl asked.

He looked back at the woman, who now was miming annoyance that James was paying attention to someone else. "I don't know," he said. "I've never seen her before in my life."

"The way she's acting, I think you're really her lover and you're jilting her."

"My—" he said, half speechless. Most girls of New York wouldn't dare to use such a word. And especially not at a fancy ball at the governor's house.

"She doesn't really look like your type," the girl said seriously, but the edge of her mouth curled up and gave her away.

"Oh, I don't know," James said. "She has her good points."

They both looked up again, and the woman fanned herself rapidly, theatrical in her pique. She looked down at James, then haughtily turned her head and proceeded toward the staircase at the end of the balcony. She walked with her head in the air, the fan still moving rapidly. She came to the top of the staircase and descended regally.

As the tableau with James had progressed, other people had begun watching; and now a lull came over the room as more and more heads turned and watched this strange woman make her entrance into the ballroom.

She came to the bottom step and walked across the floor toward James, who had begun to feel self-conscious. He tugged nervously at the edge of his collar, much to the delight of the pretty girl at his side. He became more self-conscious as he realized the woman was heading straight for him.

Every head in the room was now turned toward the woman, and every pair of eyes followed her as she stopped in front of James. She peered over the top of the ivory fan and then lowered it.

"Well, my sweet, you certainly were quick to throw me over for this bit of fluff," she said, flicking her fan in the direction of James's companion.

James looked at her and realized, to his horror, that the woman had the stubble of a closely shaved beard and was in fact, not a woman but a man!

He looked at the pretty girl; she, too, was beginning to understand, her features reflecting her distaste.

The transvestite tapped James on the chest with the fan. "Is this any way to welcome your new governor, you naughty boy!" And then, flaunting his silk velvet cape and low-cut bodice of the dress beneath, Governor Cornbury traipsed away, greeting people and welcoming them to his house.

James was stunned. He turned and shook his head as the new governor made his way across the crowded room, smiling and flirting with the men—all to the horror of the gentry, who were beginning to comprehend what sort of a joke the Crown had played on the province.

James was now laughing so hard that tears were running from his eyes. "The governor! I can't believe it. I was flirting with the governor!"

He wiped his eyes and looked at the girl again. She had the most wonderful smile, he thought. And her eyes sparkled with laughter. "Forgive me," he said, "but no one has taken the trouble to introduce us. My name is James de Kuyper."

"So you're the one."

"The one?"

"The one everyone's talking about." And then she added playfully, "You're supposed to be the most eligible bachelor in New York. Don't tell me you didn't know that?"

"I've heard something to that effect," he said sourly. "But tell me, what's your name?"

"Jane Bradford."

"Have you been here long?"

"Four years."

"You arrived just about the time I went away."

"Yes. To be a pirate."

He shook his head. "No, I didn't go away to be a pirate. It just worked out that way."

She slipped her arm about his. "I'd like to hear all about it."

James felt his heartbeat quicken. When she spoke, the words came out all soft and silky.

Jane Bradford was a tall girl, but her feline movements tended to modify her height. Her auburn hair shone as it reflected the lights. She had an aristocratic nose, a generous mouth that seemed perpetually curved in the beginnings of a smile, and a chin with the faintest trace of a dimple. Her creamy, slender arms ended in long, tapering fingers that had an artistic look. She had a habit of clapping her hands together when she laughed or became excited, which was often.

"I'll be most happy to tell you what happened," James said, and for the first time in months he looked forward to talking about his days with Kidd and the pirates. Regretting that he didn't have even more stories, he decided to make up new ones when he ran out.

For the remainder of the evening they danced, talked, and never left one another's side. This did not go unnoticed by Jennifer de Kuyper. She had a passing knowledge of the girl's family, and approved. She informed Jacob Adam of what was happening.

"Bradford? Yes, I've dealt with the father in business," he said.

"Oh? What is he like?"

"One of those people who thinks he's cleverer than he really is. I wouldn't mind doing business with him again," he admitted.

This wasn't exactly what Jennifer wanted to hear. "They're very respectable people," she insisted.

"You can be respectable, and dumb too," he said, watching as his son escorted the girl to the dance floor.

"They make a handsome couple," Jennifer said, her eyes bright with pleasure.

"We're not supposed to make any choices for him, remember?" Jacob Adam said dryly.

"He seems to be making this one for himself."

The big topic of conversation at the ball, however, was not the budding romance of James de Kuyper and Jane Bradford. It was Lord Cornbury. By the end of the evening the prancing, posturing figure was thoroughly detested by the leading citizens of the province. The council met the next day, and thunderous denunciations were heard. But in the end the council members admitted there was nothing to be done. Lord Cornbury was a cousin of the queen, had been lawfully appointed, and would remain governor until he died or was removed by the Crown.

Cornbury wasn't always playing the part of the fool. There was another side to this well-born Englishman, and that was his determination to amass wealth. It soon became possible to buy almost any political favor.

Jacob Adam found the man thoroughly outrageous, but he was happy enough to do business with him. He owned a large tract of land, known as the Queen's Farm, on the west side of Broad Way extending to the banks of the Hudson. Trinity Church wanted it, but was unwilling to pay Jacob Adam the asking price. He sought an audience with the governor to explain a complicated scheme, which, he reasoned, would make everyone happy.

"I'll give half the land desired by Trinity to Your Lordship," he said. "In return the Crown will grant me the land patents on several hundred acres around Spuyten Duyvil. As the Crown requires, these lands will be developed into farms that will produce tax revenue."

"What's on the lands?" the governor asked, not playing the fool now.

"Almost nothing. An Indian village. And a sawmill near the confluence of the Hudson and Harlem rivers."

"Why would you give away valuable land in the city for a tract of wilderness?"

"A day will come when it will no longer be wilderness."

"The lands in the city are worth more."

"Now. But I'll receive five times more land near Spuyten Duyvil. I'm willing to take the risk."

"I see no value to the Crown in this transaction."

Jacob Adam knew the man was only pretending to miss the point. "The lands I want belong to the Crown, but since they produce no revenue they're worthless at the moment. The lands I give you are yours personally, to sell to Trinity and keep the profit."

Lord Cornbury examined the proposal. He would receive the money from Trinity. Trinity would get Queen's Farm at a price less than that asked by de Kuyper, and de Kuyper would get the lands along the Harlem. The only "loser" in the scheme would be the Crown. But the Crown would possibly earn revenues at a later date, so even the Crown was not a loser.

"I like this plan," the governor said.

"Done?"

"Done."

And so, after many years, the lands that had been given by the Indian Senadondo to Pieter de Kuyper, only to be taken away by the government, returned to the family. The difference was that it had been Pieter's intention to keep the lands as they were—a wilderness— with the understanding that the people of Senadondo could remain there as long as they wished. This noble idea hardly suited the plans of his son Jacob Adam.

The first thing he did was hire a surveyor to detail his new lands with the intention of dividing them into farms. He also planned a new settlement at the confluence of the two rivers.

Jacob Adam's newest purchase seemed odd to some New Yorkers when they heard of it. The man was now in his sixties, and this sort of ambition seemed more appropriate to someone younger, who might expect to live to see his plans fulfilled. But Jacob Adam was not one to worry that he wouldn't be around to finish what he started. If he died before he accomplished his tasks, it would be up to his family to carry on.

For once, James seemed interested in the continuity of the de Kuyper dynasty. Three months after he met

Jane Bradford, they were married at Trinity Chruch, where her father was on the board of trustees.

When Governor Cornbury heard about the forthcoming nuptials, he decided his dealings with Jacob Adam had been so profitable it would be a nice gesture to give the de Kuypers and the Bradfords the pleasure of his company. He sent word that he accepted the wedding invitation, although he had never received one.

"Can't you talk him out of it?" James asked his father.

"The man's the governor, and if he wants to come, he comes."

"He might be amusing," Jane said.

"Yes, and so would a hurricane," James replied.

"Don't worry about disasters that haven't happened," was Jacob Adam's final word on the subject. But everyone else was nervous about the impending visit of the unpredictable governor.

Only a short time ago he had arrived in a woman's dress to take his place at the head of the troops marching in honor of the queen's birthday. The parade had started out at the gates of Fort James, and had continued only a few blocks when Cornbury fell down and began giggling. The enraged captain of the guard had several burly soldiers carry the governor back to his house, where he was put in a locked room. He wanted no part of this treatment, of course, and began shouting and pounding on the door. Finally two soldiers took turns sitting on him to keep him quiet. Later, when he sobered up, Cornbury took the whole affair quite good naturedly, and invited the captain and his men into the house for a drink.

So, on the day of the wedding, James breathed a sigh of relief when the governor arrived at the church sober and in normal clothes. During the ceremony he sat quietly and inconspicuously, smiling pleasantly at those about him. At the end of the service he filed out with the other guests.

"See, he was a lamb," Jane said.

"The day's not over," James said, hoping his fears would prove unjustified.

They weren't.

About an hour later the governor made his appearance at the reception, in Jacob Adam's house, and his

breath announced he had already got a start on the
drinking at the party.

"You're a lucky young man," he said to James as his
eyes surveyed the bride from head to toe.

"I know it, sir," James said.

"And you're a lucky young woman," the governor said,
wagging his finger at Jane while giving the groom an admiring glance.

"Ah, youth, *youth!*" he exclaimed, and turned to Jacob
Adam, who was standing nearby. "If only it could be
combined with the experience of men of our age. Isn't
that so, sir?"

"I expect my son has had enough experience," Jacob
Adam said laconically.

The governor became more interested in James. "Is
this true? Have we been up to naughty things?" he said,
poking his elbow into the other's ribs.

James was nonplussed. "No more than other men,
Your Excellency."

A leer came to Cornbury's face. "Then the lovely bride
is in for a pleasant surprise tonight, isn't she?"

James gulped and grabbed a goblet of rum from the
table. "Cheers," he said. The governor took another goblet, drank most of it in several swallows, and moved on
to another room, ready to find new playmates.

"He's mad," James muttered to his father.

"Except when it comes to pounds and shillings," Jacob
Adam answered. "Then he's saner than most."

"How can you stand making deals with someone who's
crazy?"

"What does that have to do with business?"

The party warmed up as the guests consumed vast
quantities of food and drank the endless flow of rum, gin,
brandy, wine, beer, and ale brought out by the servants.

Jacob Adam was enjoying a plate of sweetmeats when
the father of the bride approached him. "Now that we're
in-laws I suppose we'll be seeing a great deal of one another," the elder Bradford said.

Jacob Adam, hardly entranced with this prospect,
nodded almost imperceptibly. Bradford was one of those
men who thought he was one up on the world simply because an accident of birth had made him English. He was
loud, overbearing and opinionated. But he had money

and the right social contacts, and so was widely regarded as a pillar of the community.

"Great pair of kids we've got, de Kuyper," Bradford boomed.

Jacob Adam made another miserly gesture.

"And maybe we can do a little more business one of these days," Bradford said with a chuckle, patting himself on the stomach as he spoke.

"Indeed," Jacob Adam said, thawing slightly at this prospect.

"Well, it's time to feed the inner man," Bradford said. "Good talking with you, de Kuyper."

Jennifer had been standing nearby, listening to the exchange with ever-narrowing eyes. "You were rude," she whispered near her husband's ear.

"He doesn't know it."

"In the future you must be nice to him," she insisted. "For James's sake."

"All right, I promise not to notice that he's a buffoon."

Sometime later James was in the garden talking with the Henrys when a distraught servant came running toward him, grabbed his arm, and led him inside the house.

James was appalled when he saw the governor dressed in a ragtag collection of his mother's clothes. Nothing fit, of course, but he had patched together a ridiculous outfit of petticoats, shifts, scarves, and a beaver wrap. He was taunting an angry Charles Goelet.

"What do you mean I have some nerve," the governor said coyly. He reached out to touch the other's arm, and Goelet pulled it away as if he had seen a snake.

"Keep your filthy hands to yourself!"

"My, my, temper, temper," Cornbury chanted, taking another goblet of rum from the tray of a passing servant.

"If it's temper you want, I'll use my stick," Goelet said.

He was a few years older than James, a florid-faced man with an air of self-importance. He was tall, fleshily handsome, and quite a dandy, with gold buttons on his coat and strands of silver thread in his breeches. He worked for Jacob Adam, who thought quite highly of his brains.

"What's going on?" James asked his mother, who was standing in the parlor doorway, wringing her hands.

"Well, he, I mean the governor—for Godsakes, James, you can see what's going on for yourself!"

"Where's Father? He'll know how to handle it."

"He went to his office," she said, and, seeing the surprised look on her son's face, added, "I know it's your wedding day, but you know how your father is."

"I'll see what I can do," James said, grimly accepting the burden that had fallen to him.

"Can I be of any help?" he asked as he sauntered over to the men having the altercation.

Charles Goelet's face was beet-red, and his lips twitched. "This . . . this *poltroon*—"

"Don't let him call me that!" the governor screeched, grabbing James's arm and pretending to hide behind him.

"Listen . . ." Goelet began, and stopped as his rage seemed to choke his tongue.

"Anyway, why would I bother with the likes of you," the governor said petulantly. He gave James's arm a squeeze.

James winced, partly from the squeeze and partly from the stench of rum from Cornbury's mouth.

"Why don't we go into another room?" he suggested.

"Yes, yes, let's get away from this beast," the governor said quickly, allowing James to lead him into the dining room—where, unfortunately, the bride was chatting with a group of her friends.

"You lucky, lucky girl!" the governor called loudly when he saw her, giving James's arm another painful squeeze. "What muscles! I don't suppose you'd lend him to me sometime? I promise to return him in one piece."

His own remark struck him as the height of hilarity. He doubled over in a series of guffaws and slapped his knees with his hand.

James gestured that he needed help, but Jane smiled and mouthed the words, "He's your friend."

"Music!" the governor cried, and several musicians, who had been watching with open mouths, snatched up their instruments and began to play.

"Something more lively!" the governor demanded, and the players switched to a fast-tempo reel.

Cornbury, delighted, began to dance in a circle around James, singing gibberish in a high falsetto.

"La-la, la-la, tarumpa tarumpa, bibbety-bop, tarumpa-la, la-la."

None of the guests could believe their ears or their eyes, especially when Cornbury jumped on top of a table and danced from one end to the other, knocking crystal, chinaware, goblets of pewter and silver, roasts of ham and beef, turkey legs, pickles, and bowls of creamed corn into one big, gooey mess on the floor.

"La-la, la-la, bibbety-bop, tarumpa-la, la-la."

James had had enough and was about to forcibly restrain this madman when the governor's wife entered the room.

"Pinky, get down from that table and stop making an ass of yourself! Do you hear me, Pinky!"

When Cornbury heard the hated nickname, he stopped dancing, looked down at his wife, and scowled. "I've told you not to call me that."

"I'll stand here calling you Pinky until we leave this house."

It was obvious the governor's behavior was nothing new to his wife, and equally obvious this no-nonsense woman had learned how to deal with it. He climbed down from the table and glared at her.

"Come along, Pinky," she called over her shoulder as she walked toward the door. The governor was muttering with rage, but he followed after her and left the house, trailing Jennifer's petticoats.

James sighed with relief, and then noticed his hands were trembling. "I need a drink," he announced, and took a tankard of beer that had survived intact amid the shambles on the table.

"Be sure you don't drink too much, Pinky," his brand-new wife said.

"At last you're a grandfather," James said as the two men stood together, looking down at the infant boy in his crib.

"It took you long enough," Jacob Adam said. Several years had passed since James's wedding day.

"Not for lack of trying," James replied with a smile.

Jacob Adam's eyebrow arched, thinking his son was being too casual about a delicate subject, but he forbore to comment on this lapse.

"At last there's a healthy Jan de Kuyper in the New World," he said, acknowledging that the baby was named after his own brother who had died in childbirth many years ago.

"We thought it fitting," Jane said. "The last Jan never had his chance at life."

"Should you be walking around like this?" James asked with concern. "So soon afterward?"

"Having a baby doesn't make a woman an invalid," she replied. "We've been at it for a long time."

"But—"

"Besides, it's been a whole week now. It's time I got back to my normal life."

She went into the manor's kitchen to help prepare the meal, but Jennifer and Elizabeth shooed her into the garden and made her sit in a comfortable chair under a shade tree. James came out and lay on the grass beside her, looking up through the branches of the tree at the fragments of clear-blue sky.

"What do you think Jan will be when he grows up? A sea captain? A man of commerce? Or will he stay on the manor with us?"

"Aren't you rushing him a bit?" Jane asked.

"A lad's got to get started early, as Father always said. Otherwise he'll turn out to be a ne'er-do-well like me."

She clapped her hands together and poked his ribs with her foot.

Giving birth had taken a lot out of Jane. She was pale, and her features seemed gaunt. In contrast to her face, her body retained some of the puffiness incurred while she was carrying the baby. But to James she was as lovely as she had been on the night he had met her.

"I'm the happiest man alive," he said. "I have absolutely everything I want in this world. The perfect place to live, a perfect wife, and now a son."

"A *perfect* son, you mean."

"Of course, what other kind could we have," he said, and his hand reached out and touched her foot. "Maybe next time, we'll have a girl."

"Let's have several of each kind."

"That might mean more visits from the governor," he complained. "Maybe we'd better forget the whole thing."

She looked at him and laughed, meanwhile kicking off

her shoe so she could feel the touch of his hand on her naked skin.

Lord Cornbury had invited himself to the manor to pay his respects to the child, but much to his parents' relief, the day passed and the governor had not arrived.

They heard later that he had actually started the journey, but had stopped at every tavern he passed on the King's Road. By the fifth one, the Pig and Whistle, he had become roaring drunk and organized a swimming party. He led a merry group of fellow drinkers to the river at Kip's Bay, where they went splashing into the water wearing all their clothes. Luckily several fishing boats were in the bay, and the laughing drunks were rescued with boathooks and hauled to shore, safe from the peril of the fast-moving water.

The governor returned to the Pig and Whistle with his new friends, forgot why he was on the road, and drank himself into a stupor. His long-suffering guards dumped him into a horse cart and took him home.

While James and his wife lolled in the garden, Jacob Adam and Jennifer were in the nursery, looking at their new grandson. Not that it seemed to matter to little Jan, who slept through all the fuss made about him.

Jacob Adam stood quietly, lost in his thoughts, wondering if Jan would be the de Kuyper who would carry on the family tradition. He had learned to accept James for what he was, but that didn't mean he had to surrender his dreams for the future. Perhaps Jan . . .

"I used to be afraid of you," Jennifer said, intruding on his thoughts with a totally unexpected subject. "Do you remember?"

"You were young," Jacob Adam said.

"It all seems silly now," she said easily. "Look at it this way. If I'm this child's grandmother, then you're his grandfather, and how can anyone be afraid of a grandfather?"

"Are you planning on buying me a cane?"

"There were times when I wanted to hit you over the head with one."

"I might have hit you back," he said, and there was something in his voice that said he meant it. "But not very hard."

"I've had a lot of time to think about what was wrong with us," Jennifer said softly.

"We've just learned over the years to get along very well," he said testily.

"Yes, but it wasn't always that way. I was always waiting for you to come to me, but that isn't your nature. You couldn't reach out. So I swallowed my pride and went to you. I felt like a fool, and I was sure you'd reject me, but you didn't. That was quite a few years ago. Do you remember the night?"

The sharp lines of his face seemed to soften. "Yes. "Yes. And I remember how pleased I was, and touched."

"What would we change if we had it to do all over again?"

"Nothing that matters," he said in a tender whisper.

She leaned her shoulder against him, and clasped his hand in hers. In this moment they were one, and she understood a great truth; to love means to give all and ask nothing.

It was a clear fall day. The last canvas sail of the packet *Peter Minuit* was tied down, and the handsome ship moved slowly under bare poles over the last few yards of water to its berth at the Old Slip dock. The place was alive with activity.

Paul de Witt, standing by the port rail with his fifteen-year-old son, Sam, waved to the people waiting on shore. Jacob Adam was there with Alice, and Paul's wife, Janet. The three smiled and waved back. Janet began to cry. It was the first time she had seen her husband and son since they had left for Amsterdam over four months ago.

"This is no time for that," Alice said, taking a clean cloth and handing it to her cousin's wife. "You'll make your eyes red."

The packet drew alongside the wharf. Sailors scampered. Thick hawsers were thrown and wrapped around posts. Spring lines were set out. A gangplank was lowered to shore, and Paul de Witt was the first man off the ship. He had been married for years, but he swept his wife into his arms as if they were newlyweds.

Jacob Adam stood a discreet distance away, waiting for his nephew to finish greeting his wife. Alice did not stand on such ceremony. She put her arms about them and kissed them both, even though Janet had not been anywhere.

"Uncle," Paul finally said, disengaging himself from his wife and shaking the older man's hand. "Good to see you."

"Our negotiations with the Twining Brothers?" Jacob Adam said in greeting.

"The House of Twining is now our official banking representative in Europe," Paul said. "They'll honor all letters of credit and arrange payment for cargoes in our name."

Jacob Adam was pleased. "They will act as our agent in all matters?"

Paul nodded. "More than that," he said with a satisfied smile. "They feel the need for someone to represent them here in New York. They want us as *their* agent."

This was more than Jacob Adam had expected. To be agent for one of the largest banking houses in Europe was quite a feather in their caps. "I assume you turned them down," he said dryly.

"Of course," Paul answered. "For about two seconds." He reached into his coat pocket and drew out a packet of documents. "Here are the signed agreements."

"I'll look at them later," Jacob Adam said, glancing over at Sam, who was still being crushed in the embraces of his female relatives. "Did the boy do well?"

A sour expression crept across Paul's face. "He tries his best, I suppose, but he doesn't seem to have the imagination for this sort of thing."

The two men regarded the youngster, who was grinning and babbling of his adventures to the women. Sam was a rather average lad, but Jacob Adam knew Paul was damning his son when he spoke of his lack of imagination.

Sam had always been a disappointment. He was short, with a round face and ears that stuck out too far from the sides of his head. His waspish temper would have been better suited to a woman than a man, Jacob Adam thought. Curious business, this diversity within the same family. His own son, James, had ability, all right, but no interest in matters of import.

Jacob Adam's sober thoughts were interrupted when Paul tapped him on the shoulder and pointed toward the gangplank. An old man of great authority was striding down the heavy planks. "Stone Eagle."

"Yes," Paul said. "He was one of the chiefs invited to England as guests of the queen. He told me he's met you."

"Come," Jacob Adam said, walking toward the end of the gangplank. "I would meet him again."

Stone Eagle's face was deeply lined, and his skin had taken on the gray pallor of a mummy; but the years had done little to dim his eyes or alter the quickness of his mind. He stood still, his back as straight as a newly formed arrow, waiting for the two men to approach.

"I have met your son," Stone Eagle said to Jacob Adam.

Jacob Adam nodded. "He lives as one family with your daughter and her sons."

"Even as we have been friends."

And then the chief did something that was so out of character it startled Paul. He put his hands on Jacob Adam's shoulders and looked into his eyes. "The spirits of the woods decide the fate of men. Ours was decided long ago."

Jacob Adam held the other's stare, mesmerized by the limitless depths of his eyes. Paul was utterly confused. He looked back and forth at the two men, but neither seemed interested in giving him an explanation.

The mood was broken as Janet, Alice and Sam joined them. They pressed questions on the chief about his impressions of London, and Stone Eagle became almost loquacious.

"Too many people. Too much dirt." He looked around at the activity on the dock. Several other ships had recently arrived, and the street was jammed with carts and horses. Men were unloading tons of cargo from the ship's holds. A few berths down the quay stood a dark-hulled slave ship. It had been in port for a day, and now the first coffle of slaves, chained neck to neck, were being prodded down the gangplank. They had been washed and scrubbed for the event, but the removal of filth and dirt had only made it easier to see the sores and whip marks that covered their thin bodies.

"It has taken London a thousand years to get so crowded and dirty," Paul said in defense of his home. "It will never happen in New York; there's so much land beyond us."

The chief was skeptical. "In my own time I have seen many changes. Soon the number of your people will be as great as the leaves on the trees. My people dwindle away with the wolf and the bear."

Jacob Adam knew there was truth in the chief's words, but wished to soothe his feelings. "There is room for all."

"Your people have been in England for many years," the chief said. "I saw none of my people there."

"But Indians were never there!" Sam protested.

"Queen Anne told me there once were forest-dwellers in England who painted their faces blue like the Mohawk. Now the English Mohawk are gone."

Sam's face took on a superior smile. He looked at the old Indian as if he were a child, and tittered at his statement. But Jacob Adam wondered just how far the old Indian was from the truth.

Stone Eagle looked out on the river. Jacob Adam followed the old man's gaze and saw a large war canoe, paddled by a half dozen braves, cutting smoothly through the water toward them.

"Your people?"

"My people."

The canoe pulled silently alongside the quay. There was no waving of hands, no greeting. The braves waited quietly as their chief boarded the sleek craft.

"The Manitou who guides my life wished us to meet a final time," Stone Eagle said. "Now it is done."

Jacob Adam knew he would never see Stone Eagle again. He was strangely touched, but did not know why. After all, what was this man to him? An Indian he had seen only twice in his life. Two passing ships . . . nothing. And yet he could not deny the odd feeling of a bond between them. Perhaps it was because both were able to see the world as it really was, clearly, without indulging in vain hopes and irrelevancies.

The canoe moved swiftly upriver, rounded the bend, and disappeared behind the jutting promontory. Stone Eagle was gone.

As Jacob Adam and the others were leaving the quay, they passed a black man who was hurrying to meet the ship. It was Daniel Gerait.

"Good morning, Mister de Kuyper," Daniel said, tipping his hat politely.

"Morning, Daniel," Jacob Adam said. "Getting something from the ship?"

"Yes, sir, some tin. At least I hope there's some for me."

"It's been a long time since we've seen you," Jacob Adam said. "You must stop by the house."

"Yes, sir, Mister de Kuyper, one of these days I'll do just that."

He tipped his hat again, smiled at the others, and hurried toward the ship. Daniel liked Jacob Adam, but knew he would never pay that visit. The truth was, he did not feel comfortable or safe down here, in the heart of the white man's Manhatan. He came here only when he had business, and then left quickly.

Gerait was in his forties. He was married and had fathered three children. With the lands he had inherited from his aunt, Zilla, Daniel was one of the wealthiest black men in New York. A prudent man, he lived north of the town in a simple house he had built himself. He had remained living in it long after he could afford a better home. His reasoning was that white people regarded all blacks as slaves and would not look kindly on one who seemed unaware of his place.

Daniel had learned the craft of a pewterer and had a shop at the back of his house. Here he kept his supplies of lead, copper, and tin. The last item was extremely difficult to get, and Daniel, along with other pewterers, generally had to work with tin from discarded pieces that had been fashioned in Europe. He picked up his shipment of the precious material from the *Peter Minuit* and hurried home.

He was working at his forge when nine-year-old Aaron entered the room.

Daniel put his hammer down on the edge of the forge and smiled at his son, a husky young boy.

"Come to watch me work?"

"Yes," the boy said, but he looked nervous and bothered. This was not lost on Daniel, but he said nothing, waiting patiently for his son to speak his mind.

Aaron was a quiet and deliberate lad. After a long time, during which Daniel worked on a mug he was fashioning, the boy finally spoke. "Why are most black people slaves?"

Daniel looked up. "The white men came here to find a new life. Our people were captured and brought here against their will."

"But why only black people? Why don't the white people capture other white people?"

"Many white people don't think we have souls, so it's all right to make us slaves."

"How do they know we don't have souls?"

Daniel looked at his son, and his heart went out to this boy who thought about such matters at so young an age. Life would not be easy for a man who asked certain questions. "It is convenient for them to believe that."

"I met a white boy, and he asked why I wasn't a slave. I didn't know."

Daniel patted the boy's arm and set down the awl he was using to tool the rim of the mug. He told Aaron the history of his family as best he knew it. He spoke of his father, Manuel, who had come to America from Brazil as a slave, and he told of the great-grandfather who had gone from Africa to Brazil in chains. The boy listened intently and then asked another question.

"Is is possible for them to make us slaves again?"

"Yes, it's possible. But we have one thing that all white men respect—money," Daniel said.

This seemed to satisfy the boy, and he left the workroom and went back outside. Daniel thought about the last question and knew he had given only half an answer. If the white government wished to enslave all the free blacks, it would not be difficult to do. Daniel was aware the traffic here was not as great as in the provinces to the south, but he also knew this was not due to any philosophical reason. The way of life in the northern colonies did not call for gangs of slaves to work in vast fields. More often than not, New York slaves were used for domestic work; and often they were given a chance to buy their freedom. But even so, the black man could not attend the white churches, was not invited to white houses, and did not get elected to office or have any say in the government. The poorest white looked down on the black, even on a man like Daniel, whose worth was not unsubstantial.

Daniel Gerait suspected there would be trouble one of these years. The black population on Manhatan was growing, and the whites resented their dusky neighbors. When something was stolen or a fire started, it was usually blamed on the blacks. It was one of the reasons Daniel preferred to live in rustic isolation. As long as there was but one black man in the area, the white farmers didn't feel threatened. Daniel determined to move if other blacks ever settled near by. It wasn't that he didn't feel compassion for his fellow Africans, but only that he was, above all else, a prudent man.

He had a premonition that his son would not be such a man and hoped this would not cause the boy trouble when he grew to manhood. He also had a premonition that his hopes would be in vain because his son would be one who asked many questions. Daniel had done well by not asking too many questions.

The island was white with snow as Alice and John Livingston rode in his carriage-sled along the frozen shore of the Hudson. The sun shone bright, but the air was crisp and cold, and people were bundled in heavy fur coats. The horse's breath came out in long ribbons of steam.

Alice was now twenty-four years old, and the strong features that had distinguished her as a girl had attained a maturity that heightened her prettiness. As usual John was trying to talk her into marrying him, and as always she was thinking up ways to fend him off. She wasn't quite sure why, except that she enjoyed her independence and was chary of relinquishing it. Unfortunately, she also had to deal with her own growing suspicion that she actually loved this John Livingston.

"I still don't understand why we can't get married this spring," he insisted. "You've been putting me off forever."

"I'm not ready."

"Come on, it's time you took life more seriously."

"You sound like my mother."

"She feels the same as I do. She told me she's in favor of our marriage."

Fire came into Alice's blue eyes. "I'm not an old-country hausfrau. I make my own decisions. I'll marry when I choose, and whom I choose," she said testily. "I suppose you've already discussed this with my father, too?"

"Yes. I thought I should assure him I'm capable of assuming responsibility for you."

"I'm sure he already knows your worth down to the last farthing."

"The worth of the Livingston family is well known," he admitted.

"Don't worry about assuming responsibility for me, *Mister* Livingston. I have a good deal of property of my own."

"When you get angry," he said with a smile, "your little nose flares like a horse's. I want to kiss it."

She absent-mindedly put her mittened hand to her nose. She suddenly realized what she was doing, and her anger evaporated into laughter. "Maybe you *deserve* someone who looks like a horse."

"That's when I first became interested in you," he admitted. "That time you raced me through town and beat me."

"I knew I could do it. You never were much good on a horse."

"I forbid you to ever speak to me like that when we're married."

"Forbid me! And what's this about *when* we're married? Who says we're going to get married at all?"

"We are, you know. Why don't you just accept your fate?"

"Maybe I will, just to shut you up."

He grabbed her hand and squeezed it. "That's the best idea you've had all day."

Still following the Hudson, they were now over a mile north of the city, and there were few signs of human habitation. They drove on in silence.

Alice's thoughts were interrupted when John stopped the sled. They had come to a creek that snaked its way across the land to empty into the river. The creek was frozen over, but Livingston was too prudent to risk taking the heavy sled over the ice.

They got out and walked down to the ragged crust of ice at the shoreline of the river. They stood gazing out at the mesmerizing waters, and he put his arm about her waist. She snuggled closer.

A deer walked out of the woods, looking for forage in the world of white. He saw the two people and stopped, wary.

"Isn't he beautiful," Alice said.

"Not half so beautiful as you," he said, pulling her tight against his side. Through the thicknesses of two fur coats, she felt the strength of his body.

The deer decided the people were not a threat, and he ambled across the frozen creek, looking for greenery and not finding it. He finally disappeared in a thick grove of trees.

"He looked so proud and free," Alice said. "I want to be like that."

"You are."

She looked into his eyes and her expression was very serious. "Do you promise I'll always be as free as that deer?"

"I'd die before I'd do anything to make you unhappy," he said huskily, and she knew he spoke the truth.

"Then we shall get married," she said. "But not in the spring. I want us to marry in the fall, when the leaves are turning and the world is at its most beautiful."

He took her in his arms, and they stood together as one for a long, long time.

Both families were delighted to hear the news, and the marriage was planned for the fall.

Winter passed, and spring, and now summer had arrived. Not a person alive could have predicted the coming disaster. It was to change many lives and alter many plans.

Including the forthcoming marriage of John Livingston and Alice de Kuyper.

Plague!

The dread cry was heard, and terror spread through the city.

It had been a long, hot summer, and New Yorkers had sweltered under the sun, staying indoors as much as possible. Ships had come and gone almost daily, loading wheat, flour, skins, fashioned goods of all kinds, and stout trees to be taken back to England and hewn into masts for the growing fleet of the Royal Navy.

The tragedy began unfolding when a slave ship docked

near Coenties Slip and the human cargo came ashore in dreadful condition. Arriving slaves always looked half-starved and sickly, but these wretches could barely walk. They were taken to one of the buildings used to house new slaves to be fattened and brought to some semblance of health before being sold. But these men did not fatten; they began to die.

The people of New York learned plague had descended on their city. The slave ship was set afire and put adrift in the harbor, and the slave house was burned to the ground. Many citizens fled into the countryside.

But it was too late for precautions.

A few of the sleek black rats that carried the diseased fleas had escaped to shore. Companionable with man, they took refuge in his dwellings and barns and brought their parasites with them.

Plague gripped New York by the throat and began to choke the life from her.

Jennifer de Kuyper fell ill and could not rise from her bed. Three days passed, and her condition worsened.

Jacob Adam sat on a chair outside her bedroom door. His customary aloofness was replaced by an air of anguish. James had come to the city to gather the children of the various family branches—de Kuypers, de Witts, Goelets, and de Schuylers—and take them north to the relative safety of the manor. Now he approached his father to take his leave.

"Can I go in and see her?" he asked, looking at his mother's door.

Jacob Adam shook his head. "You'll be with all those children. You can't risk it. Besides, she's delirious and won't recognize you."

"She'll get well," James said with as much optimism as he could muster.

"Of course," Jacob Adam said, his voice hollow.

James stood silent, shifting awkwardly from foot to foot, debating with himself whether he should speak his thoughts. "When I was a boy, I thought you hated her," he finally said. "How wrong I was, Father."

"It's in the past."

"I feel so helpless. Isn't there anything we can do?"

"If there was I'd be doing it," Jacob Adam snapped,

and then regretted his anger. He reached out and
squeezed his son's hand.

There was nothing more to say. Their hands held in the
tight grip for over a minute, their eyes on the bedroom
door. James managed a weak smile, and left the house to
take the children to the manor. Alice went with him, all
but kicking and screaming her reluctance to leave; but
leaving, at last, at Jacob Adam's insistence.

Jacob Adam sat motionless for over an hour, until he
heard noises from behind the door. He went into the bedroom.

When he saw his wife, his body lurched as if someone
had stabbed him in the back.

Over the last few days he had watched in horror as the
pestilence spread through her body; as she was wracked
by maddening headaches and bone-twisting backaches;
as chills gripped her and made her teeth chatter; as the
chills were replaced by fevers that bathed her in her own
sweat. The high fevers reached into her brain and
brought delirium. She had remained in that state for the
past six hours.

But now this delirium had ended, and Jacob Adam
watched helplessly as his wife vomited blood over herself and her bed.

He turned away. Strong as he was, it was beyond him
to watch this dreadful sight. He staggered from the room
and stood outside, clenching his fists, releasing and
clenching them again, and again, and again. The doctor
was sent for, and for the twentieth time that day he
shrugged his tired shoulders and said there was nothing
he could do for the patient.

It ended. Jennifer passed into a final delirium and was
dead in minutes.

Jacob Adam watched as her shrouded body was placed
in one of the governor's death carts to be taken to the
Collect and burned with the bodies of other plague victims. Jennifer was to be denied the dignity of a decent
burial. It was a hard rule, but her husband understood.
The only sure method of preventing contamination was
annihilation by fire.

Jacob Adam wept.

He stood alone in front of his house, oblivious of the
scurrying passersby, oblivious of the servants who peered

at him through the windows, oblivious of everything. When his tears were used up and gone, his shoulders continued to heave in dry sobs that shook his entire body.

Finally he drew a deep breath of air into his lungs and walked stiffly but steadily to his office on Whitehall Street. There wasn't another soul in the building, but he didn't notice. Jacob Adam went to his desk and worked.

The city turned into a charnel house.

Stricken people staggered down the streets, weaving from side to side, crying out in agony until they fell to the ground spewing vomit and blood; until delirium brought them a respite from their suffering—a respite that, for most, lasted for eternity.

Men with painfully enlarged groins or necks, their bodies caked in filth, their throats hoarse from screaming, dropped in the streets and died. Their fly-swarmed corpses were avoided by everyone, left to putrefy under the sun until they were picked up by the death-cart men, soldiers of the garrison who had been pressed into this vile service by the governor who had replaced Cornbury— John, Lord Lovelace, Baron of Hurley. They wore heavy cloth masks over their faces and looked for all the world like the ferryman, Charon, come to take lost souls across the River Styx to the infernal fires of hell.

A pall hung over the earth. Men seemed afraid to speak lest they attract the finger of pestilence, dealing out destruction where it pointed, sparing few it touched. The deathly silence was broken only by the feverish rantings of the afflicted and the lamentations of those who mourned them.

Elizabeth Barrow was wracked with fever, and except for the red-veined, greenish lump that grew at her throat, the flesh seemed to melt from her body. In the final moments of her life, alone and abandoned in her drenched bed, the mother of Jennifer de Kuyper pulled herself to a sitting position. "The bastard, oh, the bastard!" she croaked, and then fell back, passing into a delirium from which there was no awakening.

Robert de Pauw, overweight and suffering from gout, staggered about his house in a drunken state until he came upon a servant girl.

"The plague is going to get us," he said.

"Yes, yes," the terrified girl agreed, and her eyes rolled in their sockets.

Ordinarily de Pauw was a quiet, polite gentleman, but now something snapped in his mind. He tore the clothes off the girl and copulated with her on the rug in his dining room. Rather than resist, the girl shared his frenzy, and they savaged one another until his heart gave out. De Pauw wheezed; a cry stuck in his throat, and he rolled off her and died. The panting girl was so excited she scarcely noticed.

Men and women throughout the city became crazed to perform the act of procreation. Respectable churchgoing men, suddenly demented, threw themselves on any woman they could find. Women who had been paragons of virtue tore off their clothes and gave themselves to strangers.

It happened in the houses and the barns and the stables, and even in the dust of the street. People took carnal knowledge of one another in the gutters as the death carts rolled by, unheeding of the curious stares of the cartmen.

Perhaps it was an instinctive desire to perpetuate what seemed to be a dying race; a frantic, primeval attempt to replace the lost ones, to affirm life in the very face of death. Whatever the reasons, a mad choreography of copulation and death was danced from one end of the city to the other, accompanied by a dirge of wails and moans.

The plague took Anne de Kuyper de Schuyler. She was one of the few victims granted dignity in death. She was an old woman and had been ill for several years. When the first breath of pestilence entered her body, it found no resistance, and she died within the hour. There had been no pain and no suffering. Since her death occurred at the very beginning of the epidemic, before the governor had ordered the mass burning at the Collect, her husband and her brother, Jacob Adam, had buried her in her own backyard, quickly and quietly. Few would be as fortunate.

For most it was the ignominious death cart, winding its mournful way up the dirt road to the Collect. Once there, the bodies were dumped into roaring bonfires tended by soot-covered men who worked at a frantic pace in this living hell. The stench of burning flesh filled the air, and the winds caught the acrid smell and carried it across the surrounding rivers to Long Island, Westchester, and New Jersey.

The demon finger of plague snaked up the island, reached into the hinterland, and found the tribe of Stone Eagle at Spuyten Duyvil. The red men had even less resistance than the whites, and they dropped like flies.

Elizabeth Henry prepared to leave the manor to go to the aid of her father's people.

Theophilus attempted to talk his wife out of it. "What will you be able to do for them?"

"I will be there. That is something."

"But you might contract the disease."

She shrugged. "If it is meant to be."

"I will go with you."

"No," she said firmly. "They are suffering and would not want you to see them that way."

"But you'll see them."

"I am of their blood."

The woodsman's face was wan. "I would be lost without you, you know."

She brushed her hand across his cheek. "You must take care of things here."

She mounted a horse and rode off into the forest to the southwest of the manor. Her hair still swung in braids behind her head, only now the black was streaked with gray.

She was stunned when she arrived at the Indian village. The fields and nearby woods were littered with the bodies of her people. Only a few remained alive in the longhouses. One of these was her father.

Stone Eagle was lying on his sleeping furs, already passed into delirium. He came out of it only once, to see his daughter bathing his overheated body with a damp cloth.

"Ahnakink," he whispered.

"I am here. Your spirit will find its way," she said, continuing to soothe his body with the cloth.

He closed his eyes, and they never opened again.

Elizabeth did her best to help the dying Indians, but it was not enough. They passed away, some in agony and chattering like monkeys, others quietly and silently, as if lost in their dreams.

On her fourth day at the village Elizabeth felt horrible

pains in her head, and an ache in her back that took her off her feet. Her temperature rose. The powerful disease took hold of her body, and as she passed from one stage of the illness to the next, there was no one to comfort her or cool her brow. The few Indians who had been spared had fled, and Elizabeth was the last person alive in the village.

She died alone as darkness crept over the land, and the only sounds were the mournful notes of crickets and the hushed lapping of water in the river.

Just when it seemed the people of the manor would be spared the pestilence, James fell ill. His face red and covered with beads of sweat, he returned from the fields, hardly able to stand on his feet.

Fearing he would contaminate the children if he was in the house, Jane made a bed of straw for him in the barn. He had chills and fevers and almost went mad from thirst, although Jane poured enormous quantities of water down his throat.

For three days he hovered at death's door. Then, suddenly, he began to recover; it was something that happened to fewer than one in a hundred people. The fever left his body, and the swelling disappeared. He was able to eat. In two days he was sitting up, and in three he was able to walk to the door of the barn and feel the warmth of the sun on his chalky face.

And then fate played one of her strange tricks.

Even as James was returning to the land of the living, Jane crossed over to the realm of the dead. She lay on the pallet of straw while the chills and fevers grasped her body and shook it until the life in it gave up and wafted into the air. Three days after she had been stricken, her desolate husband knelt at her side and wept for his loss.

James and Theophilus buried her in a grave on a little hill where she had liked to pick flowers. Neither man could speak, because by this time Theophilus had learned of Elizabeth's fate. They patted the last bit of earth on the grave and returned to the manor, where they burned the barn.

The cloud of death that hung over New York was finally washed away by a summer squall that drenched the land. For three days the waters beat down, lashing the houses and fields, soaking the people, cleansing them, ridding them of pestilence that had taken a third of their number.

And now they began to pick up the broken pieces of their lives. There had been almost seven thousand people in the city when the plague descended on it. A third of these were gone. Things would never be the same, of course; too much had been lost for that. But New York could not stand still. Nor could its people.

Jacob Adam arrived at the manor. With James at his side, he stood in silence at his daughter-in-law's grave.

After a few minutes they walked back to the manor. Little Jan was on the porch, playing with a yellow cat under the watchful eyes of a black servant. He smiled when he saw his father and chortled in the language of the nine-month-old.

"I hope you have as much luck with your son as I've had with mine," Jacob Adam said.

James was touched. "I haven't exactly fulfilled your plans," he said.

"That's true," Jacob Adam admitted. He reached down and picked his grandson off the wooden slats. The child squealed in delight. "But what a man does with his life is his own business."

"Are you giving me some advice for him?" James asked, poking little Jan in the ribs with his finger.

"Why not? Let him grow up to be his own man."

"Maybe he'll grow up to be the son I never was."

Jacob Adam shook his head. "Ten years ago I couldn't really understand why you wanted to stay up here. Now there's no doubt in my mind that this is what you should have done. But then maybe I'm just getting soft in my old age."

James couldn't help but smile at the thought. Besides, when a man admitted to a weakness, it was usually one he didn't have. "I've been giving some thought to little Jan," he said. "Would you like to take him back to the city with you?"

"For a visit?"

"Yes and no. With his mother and Elizabeth gone,

there's no one to take care of him but the servants. Let him live in your house for a while. It would be good for you, and Alice, too."

"Why would you do that?" Jacob Adam asked.

"I'd like him to grow up knowing your kind of life as well as mine. Give him some perspective. Then when he's old enough, he'll have a better idea of what he wants."

Jacob Adam considered the proposal for a time as he jiggled the child on his knee. Trust James to come up with the unusual, he thought.

"Very well," he said. "I'll take him home with me. But don't blame me if he turns out to be a city boy and wants to go into the family business."

James nodded.

Jacob Adam put the child back onto the porch, and he immediately crawled after the cat.

"Where's Theophilus?"

James jerked his thumb toward the manor's kitchen. "He spends all his time there."

Jacob Adam entered the kitchen and saw Theophilus Henry staring into space. "Well, old friend," he said gently, "we have both lost a great deal."

Henry looked up, his face expressionless. He turned his head away.

Jacob Adam had been expecting this. Tales of the woodsman's behavior had reached the city. He walked over and grabbed the man by his shoulders.

"You've lost your wife. So have I. They're dead, gone forever. Nothing you or I can do will bring them back. But others still live. Your sons, my son and grandson. They go on, and we must help them. Death takes whom he wishes. The living must care for one another."

For the first time since the death of his wife, Theophilus Henry spoke. "I do not want to live."

"I do not want to live," Jacob Adam said in a mocking tone. "Fine. Then die and be done with it!"

Jacob Adam was smaller than Henry, and older, now in his sixty-seventh year, but he dragged the other man to his feet. "Go ahead, feel sorry for yourself!" he said angrily. "Go ahead and die! The best part of you went with your wife. I only wish she had lived. Do you think she'd give up? Do you think she'd be a self-pitying coward?"

Henry's face twisted, and he began to cry. They were long, drawn-out sobs of anguish, the sobs of a man not accustomed to crying. Jacob Adam held him in his arms. They stood locked for several minutes before Henry looked his friend in the eye.

"Thank you. You were right to say what you did," he said haltingly. "I have no right to die. I must do what Elizabeth would do if she had lived."

The two men spent the next day together, and Henry ate food for the first time in over a week. He began to plan for the future: he would continue to manage the manor; his sons and daughter would help.

Jacob Adam left the manor and returned to his home in the city with his grandson.

On the anniversary of Jennifer's death, Jacob Adam went to the Collect and placed a large wreath of flowers near the waters of the pond in tribute to her memory. Then he walked down to the fort and watched the ships as they crossed the bay. He had been here as a boy, shipping on a whaler and learning the trade of the sea from the long-dead Lars Jorisen. He had been here with his father, learning his first lessons of business. He had been here in times before he could remember: he had been here with his mother, who died when she gave him life inside the fort during the Indian Wars.

And now he was an old man, still sparse and lean, still quick-minded and alert; but there were lines about his eyes, deep streaks of gray in his hair, and less briskness in his step.

He watched as a group of men raised sail on a small schooner, a new boat that was being given its first taste of the sea. The side planking was freshly painted. The spars and rigging sparkled in the sun. The brass shone, and the sails were stiff and brisk, their whiteness telling of their virginity. New ships are launched and old ones put to rest, Jacob Adam thought.

He returned to his office and busied himself with the affairs of the day.

Just before three o'clock an angry man burst into his office, brushing aside the chief clerk, and strode to the edge of his desk.

"You can't—I tried to stop him, Mister de Kuyper—"

Jacob Adam's raised hand stopped the clerk. "He's here now, so leave us."

The embarrassed clerk shot an evil glance at the intruder and closed the door behind him as he left the office.

Jacob Adam knew the man, a Portuguese trader named Rodriques. They had been involved together in an illegal shipment of gunpowder to the Dutch Indies. Rodriques and another partner in the venture had conspired to cheat Jacob Adam. Learning of the double cross, Jacob Adam made a deal with the Dutch authorities, who impounded the ship and cargo as contraband. The grateful Dutch rewarded Jacob Adam with his full share, but his erstwhile partners lost theirs.

"You cheated the wrong man, de Kuyper," Rodriques shouted, his swarthy skin red with rage. Jacob Adam regarded the man's threatening fist and noted idly that he still looked overfed and still wore gaudy rings on his fingers, although the word around New York was that the Portuguese was ruined.

"You made a play for it all, Rodriques," he said calmly. "And you lost. Be a man."

"I'll show you what kind of a man I am," his visitor said, pulling a pistol from under his coat.

"Don't make a fool of yourself."

Rodriques raised the pistol and fired point-blank. The lead slug ripped into Jacob Adam's chest, and he staggered backward to the wall. He had a quizzical look on his face as, slowly, he slumped to a sitting position on the floor. He looked at the front of his shirt and touched it. When he drew his hand away, the fingertips were red with his own blood.

The door flew open and several men ran into the room. Crying out, they pounced on Rodriques. One disarmed him, and two others pinned him to the floor to prevent his escape.

The chief clerk was down on one knee at his employer's side. He attempted to inspect the wound, but Jacob Adam pushed his hand away.

"You know that shipment of furs we bought from de Peyster yesterday?"

The clerk nodded.

"Make sure he delivers," Jacob Adam said. In another minute he was dead.

No one was surprised to learn he had left his affairs in tidy shape.

There was a will. There were notes to James and Alice. There was a sealed letter to his grandson, Jan, to be opened on his sixteenth birthday.

"Make sure he delivers," Jacob Adam said. In another minute he was dead.

No one was surprised to learn he had left his affairs in tidy shape.

There was a will. There were notes to James and Alice. There was a sealed letter to his grandson Ian, to be opened on his sixteenth birthday.

3

Jan and Marie Therese

1730–1731

JAN DE KUYPER PEERED OVER THE RIM OF his tankard and knew he was in for a fight.

Until a few minutes ago he had been enjoying his dinner at a public house in the settlement of Montreal. But two large Frenchmen now sat at a nearby table, and the scene was becoming ugly. They were woodsmen and trappers, men who universally hated the English. Over the past few decades English trappers had been moving in on their territory, and the pelts had been going south to Albany. The Frenchmen considered each pelt lost as their livelihood stolen.

"Eh, Jacques," the first trapper said to his friend in a whisper that carried across the room, just as it had been intended to do. "You 'ear about this King George, you know, the one whose mother she not marry 'is father?"

The second trapper smiled, and there were snickers from other men in the room.

" 'S'true," the trapper continued. "This King George, 'e one fine bastard!"

Jan took another sip of beer and looked resignedly at his two companions—his twenty-three-year-old cousin, Edward Goelet, and fifteen-year-old Theo Henry. Jan was only twenty-one, but he was the acknowledged leader of this trio embarked on the greatest adventure of their lives.

It had begun the previous fall as a wild idea of Jan's after he had seen a sketchy map shown in a tavern by a

217

Flemish fur trader. The trader claimed he had come from Montreal to New York by canoe.

"It's impossible," Edward Goelet had said. "The man's mad."

Jan was not so convinced. "Let's hear him out," he had said, tossing a few coins onto the table. His eyes reflected the pleasure his imagination was having with the outlandish idea.

Several hours and many drinks later, Jan and his cousin had left the tavern, their heads filled with excitement as they walked toward Jan's home on Wall Street. "Damned if I don't think he was telling the truth," Jan said.

"Maybe it can be done," Edward admitted. "But Good God! Think of what's involved. Lakes and rivers . . . unmapped forests . . . storms . . . Indians. The man's damned lucky to be alive."

"Then you agree the Frenchman made the trip just the way he claimed?"

Edward was silent for a moment, his attention diverted by two pretty girls walking toward them. He doffed his hat and smiled. Pretending to be annoyed, the girls looked the other way. But Edward continued to smile; he knew he and his cousin had made a favorable impression. They were both young, handsome, and smartly dressed.

Jan was the taller of the two, with deep-blue eyes, brown hair, and teeth that seemed even whiter than they were because of his tanned skin. His chin was slightly squared, and when he became angry or stubborn, he would pull it back toward his neck, accentuating its straight line. Edward was more slightly built, but his devilish grin and jaunty walk proclaimed his cheerful self-confidence.

Only after the girls had stepped around the corner did Jan's insistent stare bring Edward back to the matter at hand. "Yes, I think he actually did it," he said.

"Then we can do it too."

"You can't be serious!"

Jan was perfectly serious. They were young and free, he said. It was the best time in their lives to try something like this.

"Most of the journey would be through French territory," Edward pointed out. "That won't help *us*. And the route also takes you right through Mohawk country. There's a good chance your scalp would end up dangling from a deerskin belt."

They argued, but in the end it was Jan who prevailed. For every argument raised by Edward, he had an answer.

Young Theo Henry was included in the adventure because of his skill in the woods. People said his ability was inherited from his grandmother, Elizabeth, an Indian, but Theo knew that his white grandfather, Theophilus, had been as good a woodsman as any Indian. It was in his blood on both sides.

The older members of the families all tried to talk them out of their "fool's errand," as Paul de Witt characterized the venture. Charles Goelet refused even to speak to his son about it. George Henry said that if the other two were foolish enough to try such a journey, he was hardly foolish enough to allow his son to accompany them.

But there was another voice to be heard.

"I think we ought to let the young fellows do what they want," James de Kuyper said. James didn't often interfere in family affairs, but when he did, his mildly spoken words carried a great deal of authority. "A little adventure never hurt a young man," he added, remembering his own days with Captain Kidd.

The others grumbled to themselves, but backed off, and in the early spring the three young men sailed through the Narrows.

The first ship took them to Boston, and after a few days' delay they found berths on a Portuguese packet bound for the French provinces to the north. The packet foundered off the desolate Newfoundland coast in the Channel Port aux Basques, and the young men lived in the wilds until they found a coastal trader willing to take them down the great river past Quebec City to Montreal.

After their sea voyages and days in the wilderness, the settlement of Montreal seemed large and cosmopolitan to the three. It was not as big as New York, or seemingly as prosperous, but the customs were different and the French language was exotic to their ears. For the first few days, exuberance and youth kept them from accepting that young Englishmen were not welcome among the sharp-eyed merchants and tough woodsmen of this frontier of New France.

But the hostility was brought home to them now, as they sat at the table in the public house and listened to the two men at the next table.

"Eh, English," the larger of the two called out. "'Ow come you 'ave bastard sitting on your throne, eh?"

"Pay no attention," Edward Goelet said between clenched teeth.

Young Theo Henry, who possessed the face of a boy but the arms and strength of a man, tensed in his chair, his legs pressing down on the floor to gain traction for a fast move if it were needed.

"English all like that," the first Frenchman said. "Bastards and cowards."

"Like King George," the second agreed.

"And Louis Philippe," Jan said pleasantly. Even as he spoke, his hand wrapped around the arm of the chair at his side.

The two Frenchmen were pleased they had finally provoked the Englishmen. The first one had a smile on his face as he started to rise from his chair, but Jan was too quick. He lashed out with the chair, and the heavy wood knocked the man backward into his own table; food and drink crashed to the floor. The second Frenchman was on his feet and coming toward Jan, but a blur hit him from the side, knocking him on top of his companion. Theo Henry seemed to bounce off the man after he hit him, landing on his feet like a cat, his knife in his hand.

"Let's get out of here," Jan said. The Frenchmen were still on the floor, scrambling about in puddles of wine, curses pouring from their lips.

The three young men dashed out the door, disappearing around the corner and down an alley before the two Frenchmen emerged from the tavern. They rushed through the doors, cursing and shouting, accompanied by the owner of the inn, who demanded to know who was going to pay for all the food and the damage to his establishment.

While they argued, their antagonists made good their escape.

"You shouldn't have said that about Louis Philippe,"

Edward said, panting, as he resumed a normal walking pace. "Trying to get us killed?"

"If I hadn't started the fight, they would have found another excuse," Jan said. He turned to Theo Henry. "I didn't catch you by surprise."

Theo smiled. "When you fight wolves, come prepared."

They avoided any more trouble by pretending to be Dutch Huguenots who had come to settle in New France. Since they all spoke Dutch fluently, no one questioned them. But the intensity of French hatred for the British was clear.

"There will be war someday," Jan said. "The French hate us because of what our privateers have been doing to them."

Edward nodded in agreement. "As soon as a privateer puts out to sea, it becomes a pirate."

"Our laws encourage them."

"French laws are no different."

"You'd think this land would be big enough for both of us," Jan said grimly. But he was young and carefree, and the sobering thought did not long remain with him. The adventure of going south through these wild lands became paramount and soon commanded all his interest.

They met a group of Huron Indians camped on the banks of the Richelieu River and traded a string of black-shell wampum for a birchbark canoe. Following their map, they paddled south along the river, past the Isle aux Noix and down into the shimmering beauty of Lake Champlain.

It was a journey through a paradise of wild fowl. The big geese and ducks of a dozen varieties were all succulent and easily caught; they made a nightly banquet.

As they followed the west bank of the lake for the fifth day, the skies erupted in a great storm.

The thunderclouds had been scudding over their heads for over an hour. They knew the storm was coming, but expected it would start, as usual, with an increase of wind and light rain, giving them warning to head for the shore and safety. This storm, however, swooped down upon them with no preliminaries, immediately turning the lake to froth. The wind tore at the canoe, snatched at their clothing and hair, fought against their paddles, and blew water into spray that soaked them instantly, almost blinding them. They started paddling toward land, but the wind was coming off the western shore, forcing them to struggle directly against its might.

Edward tried to shift his weight, and the movement almost overturned the craft.

"Stay down low, Ned, dammit!" Jan shouted, trying to be heard over the howling winds.

"Afraid of going for a swim?" Edward shouted back, grinning evilly. But he hunkered down with the other two, and they all drove the canoe forward with their paddles, slowly closing the gap between themselves and the shore. Another sixty feet . . . fifty . . . forty . . . and suddenly the canoe was almost thrown over on its side as a heavy object slammed into its bow.

It was a tree, its branches clawing at the canoe and its inhabitants, threatening to punch holes in the birchbark and topple the men into the water.

"Back-paddle, back-paddle!" Jan shouted, and they were forced to extricate themselves from the branches by moving farther from the shore. They gained a distance of twenty feet, paddled past the tree, and once again flung themselves straight at the storm. This time they were lucky; there were no more floating trees. It seemed to take forever, but they finally felt the bow of the canoe bump into the mud of the bank. They jumped out into the shallow water and scrambled ashore, dragging the frail craft with them.

They were exhausted and sought the easiest shelter—a space under a fallen tree a few feet from the lake. "And you worried we weren't going to make it," said Goelet, all airy reproach, and won dirty looks from his companions.

Everything was too wet to make a fire, and the three spent a miserable night, shivering in their wet clothes while the gale whipped the waters to a frenzy a few feet from their primitive camp.

Their journey took them down to the tip of the lake, where they made portage to Lake George. They paddled by day and slept by night until they came to the southern tip of the long lake. This time portage was made through a boggy swamp. Even Theo's feet betrayed him repeatedly on the slippery ground, and once Edward disappeared below the waters of a pond whose surface had been hidden by lily pads. Finally, after a twelve-mile portage that had taken them two days, they stood on the banks of a quick-moving stream, aware this was the beginnings of the same mighty Hudson River they knew in the south. They were too exhausted to care, and spent three days and nights resting and readying themselves for the final part of the journey.

On the third day they broke camp after dawn and set out on the waters that would eventually sweep past Manhatan. The journey to the head of the Mohawk River was uneventful. They camped a mile north of the place where the two rivers joined, and there spent the night.

Early the next morning, as Jan was placing his bedroll in the canoe, he looked downriver and saw something that sent his hand involuntarily to the pistol in his belt. Five Indians were paddling toward shore in two canoes.

Edward came up to their own canoe with more gear and stopped when he saw what was holding his cousin's attention. He watched the Indians pull their canoes ashore. They looked at the white men and started toward them.

"Mohawk?" Edward whispered to Jan.

"I'm not sure."

"They're Mohawk," said a quiet voice behind them. It was Theo.

"Do you think we'll have to fight?" Edward asked, rubbing his chin nervously.

Jan shrugged. "Let's see what they want."

As the Indians came closer, the whites could see that three were carrying flintlocks of French origin. Jan shifted his own musket so it was in plain sight.

The Indians stopped and regarded the whites. The bronze men were tall, with impressive physiques. Despite the chill of the morning air, no clothing encumbered their arms.

Jan held up his hand. "We are friends," he said, speaking slowly and distinctly in English.

"You are not *Française?*" the first Indian asked.

"No. *Anglaise.*"

"But you come from the land of the long stream," the Indian said, pointing upriver toward the north.

"To return to our home," Jan said, pointing with equal dignity toward the south. "New York."

The Indian spoke in his own tongue to the brave at his side, who then started to reach into a pouch. Jan thought the man was going for a weapon. He raised the muzzle of his own flintlock.

"No," the first Mohawk said. "No trouble with English. Friends." He raised his hands skyward, palms up, then lowered them and pointed at the man who had reached into his pouch. "He give present. For King George."

With his eyes fastened on Jan, the brave pulled a small object from his pouch and held it out. Jan took it and turned it over in his hand. It was a piece of bone, delicately carved to resemble an eagle; whether or not it was human bone was impossible to tell.

"King George will be pleased," he said.

The Indian nodded solemnly. "Our people are friends of King George. The *Française* are our enemy. Come to steal. Kill."

Edward moved closer to his cousin's side. "Did you think we were French?"

"We did not know."

"And if we had been French?"

The Indian looked blankly at Edward for a moment and then turned and led his men back to the shore. They pushed their canoes into the water, climbing aboard with practiced grace, and paddled off to the south.

"What do you make of that?" Edward asked.

"That the stories we've heard are true. The Mohawk hate the French. If it ever comes to war, they'll be on our side."

"Never trust the Mohawk," Theo Henry said, remembering the stories told him by his father, who had heard them from his mother.

Jan smiled. "That's the Algonkian in you coming out."

Theo shook his head. "No, it's the truth. You may think the Mohawk is your friend, but the moment you turn your back you'll find a knife in it."

Jan did not argue. He thought Theo was simply carrying on the tradition of hatred that existed between the Mohawk and the people of his grandmother; but there was a nagging doubt: those Mohawk warriors had a chilling deadliness about them.

The trio continued their journey, passing by the growing community of Albany without stopping. The summer was fleeing and the air turning cooler, and they were in a hurry to return home to their families and friends. Visions of reunions to come passed through their minds, and they pictured themselves being treated as heroes for the daring of their exploits. Pretty girls played a prominent part in the visions, especially for ladies' man Edward Goelet.

They paddled down the southern reaches of the Hudson at a rapid pace, but even three eager young men could not help but marvel at the natural beauties of the river and its coastline. Rolling hills, turning from green to the rainbow of autumn—gold, silver, blue, vermilion, orange—lined both sides of their wide waterway. Occasionally the banks of the shoreline would close in on the river and become forbidding, craggy cliffs that dropped sheerly from a great height to disappear beneath the surface of the waters.

They paddled south, straight as an arrow down the middle of the river, ignoring the gentle bendings and swayings of the land on each side: in the morning the river sparkled, reflecting the sun as if in greeting; at noon it was frivolous and active; and in the peace and stillness of the last light of day, it settled into repose. And then the moon would emerge and the darkened waters would mirror its passage across the night sky. They paddled through it all, day and night, resting at odd hours; and although they never spoke of it, each one was touched in his own way by the beauty of this land.

Here and there the vast wilderness was punctuated by the hand of man. They saw the roofs of the manors of the great Hudson River estates—the homes of Van Rensselaers, Livingstons, Morrises, Van Wycks, Van Cortlandts, Phillipses, and the other landgraves who had used Dutch law to win themselves an empire—an empire perpetuated by the English, who honored the Dutch patents, thus succoring this vestige of feudalism in the New World.

They arrived at the southern reaches of the river. The frothing, angry waters to their left marked Spuyten Duyvil and the entrance to the Harlem River. They increased their efforts, for they knew the shoreline now on their left was Manhatan—home! It had been a journey of twenty-five hundred miles—by ship, by foot, by canoe and portage—and now, finally, they were reaching the end!

It was early in the afternoon when they came within sight of the buildings of New York. It was a fair-sized town now. The governor reported to His Britannic Majesty that 8,622 people lived in the colony—over seven thousand of them freemen, the others slaves or indentured servants.

Jan guided their canoe toward the dock that stood at the end of Pine Street. They were a block north of Wall Street, and the imposing tower of Trinity Church was a welcome sight.

"We've done it," Edward said, somewhat in awe of his own achievement.

"I was sure we would," Jan said quietly.

The men near the dock stopped working and watched as the three buckskin clad travelers, tanned to the point that some mistook them for Indians, hauled their canoe ashore. They were dirty and tired; but their muscles were hard and strong, their eyes had the look of eagles, and they walked with an air of independence.

After paying a shilling to a loafer to look after their canoe and equipment, they proceeded down to Wall Street. A few homes were in the Dutch style, with ornamental dates inscribed over doorways set into yellow tile exteriors; but most of the houses of the wealthy were in the new Georgian style that featured low, pitched roofs. The white stoops were clean and swept; the brass doorknobs were polished; the windows sparkled—all a world away from the simple beauty and peace of the wilderness the young men had traversed. The people they met on their way stared at them as if they did not belong here.

The Goelets lived farther south on Broad Street, and Theo's home was at the manor in Westchester. So the three made their first stop at Jan's house, which really belonged to his Aunt Alice.

Jan led the way through the front door, sweeping past the black servant who stood with his mouth open at the sight of them, and descended on the closed doors of the large front parlor. He threw the doors open, let out a war whoop, and shouted, "Alice de Kuyper Livingston, you old fraud, your bad penny has returned!"

He stopped dead in his tracks, his horrified eyes wandering over a room filled with well-dressed women.

They returned his stare with emotions ranging from borderline terror to frank amusement.

Among the amused was Alice de Kuyper Livingston. "This is my nephew," she said in a matter-of-fact voice. "Announcing his return, I believe."

A few of the women began to titter, and one laughed loudly.

"I'm . . . sorry," Jan said, trying to master his confusion.

Alice came over and kissed him gingerly on the cheek, mindful of the dirt and grime. "Welcome home. We can all use surprises from time to time."

"But what's—I mean . . ." Jan had turned red under the continuing scrutiny of thirty pairs of eyes. Edward and Theo, meanwhile, began edging away from the open doorway.

"It's a new women's organization I've started," Alice explained. "We discuss politics."

"Politics? But—"

"Not a fit subject for women?" Alice interrupted sharply. "That's what the city fathers thought when we badgered them into building the new poorhouse. We stood outside City Hall and sang at them until they gave in. Took us about a week."

Jan looked at Edward in embarrassment. His aunt had always been outspoken, but he was never quite sure that others realized she meant no harm. Alice noticed the look and turned her gaze on the other young man.

"I know what your father would say. Charles Goelet has been stuffy ever since I can remember—which goes back to when he was about fourteen. I remember him saying that he didn't approve of the way I rode a horse like a man. He told me he was going to tell his mother. Imagine! As if a woman like Emilie would care! What a fussbudget he was, even then."

"I think we'd better clean up, Aunt Alice," Jan said, nudging his cousin with his elbow.

"Not a bad idea," she said, elevating her nose as if she smelled something unpleasant. "All three of you," she said, raising her voice as she included Theo and Edward in her dismissal.

"I think I'll go home," Edward said. "Mother and Father will want to know I'm back."

"Give my best to your mother," Alice said. "Your father will be at his office, no doubt. The curse of this family is work, and our successful men."

Edward managed a weak smile before he trotted out the front door, almost knocking down the servant who had scurried to open it.

Jan hurried toward the staircase, which led to the upper floors and his bedroom. Theo lost no time in following him. They passed through the entryway and walked into the large foyer containing the staircase. In his haste Jan bumped into a young woman coming from the other direction. He reached out to keep her from falling, apologies tumbling from his mouth. "Forgive me. I didn't see you—" And he stopped, confronted by the face of a most beautiful girl.

She took a step backward, smoothed the sleeve of her dress, smiled prettily, and walked toward the front parlor. Dumbstruck, Jan watched her go.

"What's the matter with you?" Theo asked.

"Who *is* she?"

"I don't know. She doesn't live at the manor, that's for sure."

The entrancing vision was just disappearing into the parlor, her long strides accenting her shapely slenderness and grace. Jan started to follow after her, and then remembered his grimy face and shabby clothes. This was hardly the time for romance.

"I must find out who she is," he muttered under his breath, turning and heading up the staircase.

That night at dinner, after he had spent hours telling Alice about his journey, with elaborate nonchalance he inquired about the young woman.

"What did she look like?" Alice asked.

"Oh, pretty, I suppose. Long blond hair, blue eyes, I think. A short straight nose, high cheekbones."

"Good set of legs?"

"Oh, yes, indeed."

"You didn't get much of a look at her, did you?" Alice asked innocently.

"Not much."

"How much did she weigh?"

"I'd say about—" Jan saw the look on his aunt's

face and knew he was caught. "You do know who I mean, don't you?"

"You're going to have to stand in line to get near her."

"Who is she?"

"The daughter of Whitby Bache. They arrived in New York only a month ago. Her mother is the youngest daughter of Benjamin Fletcher."

"The former governor?"

"The same. Mr. Bache moved here because he wants to be closer to his West Indies business—rum, I think it is."

"And the girl's name?"

"Marie Therese. But I must warn you, since she stepped ashore she's been the most popular girl on Manhatan."

"It doesn't surprise me," Jan said, forgetting his earlier pretense. "She's the most beautiful thing I've ever seen."

"Kind of aloof, if you ask me."

"She hasn't gotten to know me yet."

Alice shook her head and laughed. "Good luck. You'll need it. And speaking of luck, Paul de Witt knows you're back. He sent word he wants to see you in his office in the morning."

"For what reason?"

"He thinks it's time you stopped running around the country and began to take your place in the family business."

"Hm."

Alice patted her nephew on the arm. "Everyone seems to think you're exactly like your father, that you don't have a head for business."

"I'm going up to the manor tomorrow to see him."

"He'll be happy to see you."

"At least he won't be like Uncle Paul or the others, trying to push me into the business," Jan said, with a wry smile.

"I think he knows as much about you as I do. Which means he doesn't worry any more about you than I do."

He leaned over and gave her a kiss on the cheek. "The family business. Ah, with Paul de Witt and Sam and Charlie Goelet around, why do they worry about me?"

"Someone has to take care of those musty old books."

"But why me? Especially when there's so much else to do?"

"Like chase after girls named Marie Therese?"

"That too," Jan said honestly.

"So I take it you're not going to see Paul in the morning?"

"Let him wait."

"He won't like that."

Jan looked innocently at her. "That's too bad, isn't it?"

Alice laughed delightedly. "I'm sure it will make him furious, but I'll bet you can handle that when the time comes."

Jan smiled.

After dinner, exhausted, he fell asleep in a leather chair by the fireplace. A cup of coffee cooled on the mahogany table, untouched, unwanted. Alice tucked a blanket about him and warned the servants to make no noise. He was her favorite—the son she'd never had. In a way, he *was* her son: his mother had died of plague, and she had raised him. James had agreed it was best for his child to be brought up in town by a woman. Alice sighed as she looked at the sleeping young man.

She had been married years ago to John Livingston, but he had been killed in an accident. She still wore a mourning ring on her finger. There had been other men who had wanted her, but to each she gave a firm refusal. The popular belief was that she had been so devoted to Livingston, she could never marry again. But deep in her heart she knew there was another reason. It was this young man who slept. Jan de Kuyper. In her diligence to raise him well, she had allowed nothing else to interfere.

The men who ran the de Kuyper family business— Goelet and de Witt—were always complaining about Jan's lackadaisical attitude. They kept insisting she use her influence to make him settle down to work. But she had never found it in her heart to do it. Jan would come to grips with himself when the time demanded, she was sure. He had the brains of his grandfather and the resolute independence of his father.

She thought of the Bache girl and wondered just how long it would take the young woman to learn what she was up against. Alice wouldn't like to place a bet that her nephew couldn't get anything, or anyone, he wanted.

My son, she thought again, as she looked down on the sleeping form. There were men who were cursed with the running of the world, and she believed Jan was one of them. She breathed a silent prayer he would be up to the demands that would be put upon him.

The first signs of de Kuyper Manor appeared, and Jan became excited as he rode his horse down the road. The stone markers . . . vistas of cleared fields . . . great stands of virgin oak and pine . . . a well-tended dirt road winding its way toward the cluster of farm buildings . . . the imposing manor house itself.

He had come up the Boston Post Road from Manhatan, paid the tuppence fee at the ferry, and continued upland into Westchester, past the manor of the Morris family and the bucolic Fordham Manor. Many years ago Jacob Adam had considered buying the latter before he settled on land farther to the north. It was finally acquired by John Archer, who paid an annual quit-rent of twenty bushels of peas for all twelve hundred and fifty acres. Fordham Manor was one of the few bargains old Jacob Adam had ever passed up.

And now Jan urged his horse to canter. They crossed a little stream, and then the sight of a split-rail fence told him he was on the lands of his father's manor.

The sun was dipping down toward the horizon, but several men were still in the fields, preparing for the final corn harvest of the year. Now the days were growing shorter, and all the work must be done—and done quickly, before the frosts put an end to the crop.

Smoke curled from the chimney of the large kitchen that stood next to the manor house, but detached from it. The kitchen served not only the inhabitants of the manor but also its workers, who lived in separate dwellings on the property. The manager's house stood on the other side of the kitchen building, and the farmhands' houses were settled about fifty yards away, in clusters surrounded by well-kept hedges. The farm buildings were set back, behind a stand of trees, giving the manor some privacy from these working parts of the operation.

Jan took his horse to the barn. Will Masters was there alone, working his enormous deerhide bellows. From the blacksmith's forge came the horseshoes, latches, hinges, andirons, nails, tools, and cob-irons of the manor.

"Mister Jan," the man said with a smile, letting go of the bellows handle and walking toward the son of the manor's owner. "Let me take your horse."

"Hello, Will. Quiet in here today."

"Good. That way I get more work done."

Jan patted the dust of the road from his sleeves and then looked at his hands. "I'd better wash up before I let anyone else see me."

The smith nodded and pointed toward the trough used to water the horses. "Best I can offer you."

Jan took off his coat and rolled up his sleeves. He washed his hands and face and dried them with a heavy cloth held out by the other man. "Thanks, Will," he said. The huge blacksmith smiled again and playfully pinched Jan's shoulder until he winced. The man had known Jan since he was a toddler and had a proprietary interest in him. Jan only wished Will would remember his own strength.

He walked over to the kitchen. Several women were preparing a thick soup in an immense pot and cooking chunks of meat with roasting forks. George Henry spotted him as he entered the large room.

"Welcome home!" the manager boomed. He strode to clap Jan on the back, trailing several farmhands who wore wide grins of welcome. "Theo's been telling us all about your adventures."

Jan looked about for his father.

"He's down toward the creek," George said, reading his thoughts. "Theo's with him. They're clearing rocks off a new field there."

Jan slipped out of the house and walked toward the stream. It was dusk now, but he could hear the sounds of men and animals at work. The manor was not the sort of place where you sat and grew fat.

Jan stood at the edge of a clearing and watched the men as they pulled a boulder from the ground. Using shovels, they dug around the huge stone until most of it was clear of the earth. Then a workhorse was brought up, and his traces were placed around the boulder.

"Hey-up!"

The massive horse leaned forward, straining against the heavy leather traces, stretching them with the tremendous pressure. The men positioned themselves on the other side of the stone and, as they wielded stout timbers as levers, shouted encouragement to the horse and to one another. Slowly the great rock moved an inch, then two inches; and finally it rolled up from the spot where it had lain for hundreds of years. Then it was dragged to the side, where other men immediately set about breaking it into the smaller pieces that would be added to the stone walls lining the fields and paths of the manor.

A large man who had been working a timber at the very bottom of the hole stepped up into view; it was Jan's father. And the man who had directed the horse, working side by side with James de Kuyper, was Theo Henry.

Jan felt a twinge of guilt. Theo was more like a son to the man than was Jan himself.

For a moment Jan had the urge to walk over and knock Theo on the side of the head for stealing his birthright.

And then, recognizing the newcomer, Theo waved.

Jan waved back and felt himself blush at his irrational jealousy.

James stood back, wiping the sweat from his brow, and admired the size of the rock they had taken from the earth. It was at least four tons, enough to build a sizable bit of wall. He walked over and patted the sweating horse on the shoulder. He nodded to Theo and suddenly was aware of the man walking toward him. He squinted his eyes in the failing light and recognized his son.

They shook hands warmly. There was no embrace or other sign of special affection. James had always treated Jan more as a friend and equal, rather than a boy and his son.

"Your journey went as planned," James said. "Or so Theo tells me."

"As planned, Father."

"Even the fight with the Frenchmen in Montreal?"

"Even that," Jan said with a laugh. "I see Theo didn't leave out much."

"But I haven't got *your* point of view yet, have I?" James said and gave the horse a final pat.

It was a magnificent animal, broad through the chest,

the shoulder muscles bunched and rippling with sweat from their recent exertion. Jan measured its height with his eye.

"Almost sixteen and a half hands," James said. "Most of it pure muscle."

There was a pride in the older man's voice, and Jan understood why. Ever since he could remember, the stock at de Kuyper Manor had been improving.

"He's mostly Flemish," James explained, "but I've introduced English Shire blood into the line. Look at the result—a more solid horse. Heavier, with greater power. In two or three generations the height will be up to seventeen hands. I sold a pair to a Virginia planter a few months ago. Maybe in a hundred years all the work-horses of the colonies will trace their beginnings to the stock I'm breeding here."

It was said half in jest, but Jan knew his father hoped there was some truth in his words.

James told his workers the day's labors were over. He turned to his son. "Let's walk down to the creek and smoke a pipe."

As the workmen gathered up their tools and Theo led the horse back toward the barn, James and his son walked down to the banks of the creek. It was a narrow stream, shallow in parts, making its way sluggishly toward the waters of Long Island Sound. They found a comfortable bank of earth, still warm from the sun's heat, and sat down. James filled his pipe and lit it. The bluish smoke curled about his head as it rose, adding its perfume to the hundreds of other scents carried through the moving air.

They sat in peace for a few minutes, enjoying one another's presence. The last light of the day was creeping from the land, leaving a grayish world punctuated by objects of solid black.

"What are your plans now?" James asked.

"Paul de Witt thinks I should take my place in the business," Jan said, falling into the measured, easy-going speech pattern set by his father.

"But you don't want to do it?"

"Not on his terms."

"Then set your own."

Jan looked at his father and could almost detect a

smile on the darkened features. "Maybe I don't want to do it at all."

James shook his head. "Of course you do."

Jan sat in silence for a moment.

"You wouldn't think me a traitor if I went ahead and plunged into commerce? I mean, wouldn't you prefer it if I came here to the manor?"

"But you don't want to do that, do you?"

It was a simple question, asked without guile. Jan realized he must be as candid as his father. "No. I like it here on the manor. But it isn't what excites me."

James puffed his pipe, and now the darkness was complete. Jan plunged ahead.

"I want to go into business. The idea of owning ships and sending them around the world seems grand."

"I've known that since you were five years old," James said. "You were always playing with money, and swapping and trading. That's why I never reversed my decision about having you brought up in the city. Especially when you were seven or eight years old, it bothered me that you didn't live here. But I knew that even if I brought you back to the manor, you would eventually leave it."

"I knew how you felt," Jan said, almost whispering. "Aunt Alice told me that it was a secret, but you really wanted me out here with you. She said the decision was up to me. I chose to stay. I prefer that life to this."

"Are you prepared to handle Paul de Witt?"

Jan smiled. "I think so."

"Then you'll be entering a charmed circle of people he can't shout down or intimidate. His wife is one. Alice is another. I guess I'm a third, because he's never quite known what to make of me. And now you'll have to try to be the fourth."

There was a long silence. Finally, without turning his head, James spoke. "Sitting here in the darkness I can almost imagine you're really my father and not my son. I imagine when he was the same age, he was much the way you are now. With one difference—I think you've more heart. Alice thinks the same."

The silence dropped again, and Jan was left with thoughts of this strange father. The merchants of New York, almost to a man, were envious of James. Here was a man with everything they wanted—wealth, power, land —and he chose to live quietly, without taking advantage of anyone or anything. The men who knew him well— and there were precious few of these—realized that if, by their lights, his tastes were strange, they were not born of weakness or lack of character. They knew he was a man not to cross, and left him to his own devices.

Father and son sat in the darkness by the waters of the little creek until the older man knocked his pipe against a rock. He used his boot to grind the ashes into the soft earth. "Let's see what they have to eat," he said, rising to his feet.

Jan stood up, and his eyes were at the level of his father's. In the dim light the two men seemed identical— large, with broad shoulders and straight carriage; strong men, yet gentle. Both seemed to sense this sameness, and it made them friends, but also embarrassed them.

They walked in silence, and James thought how proud his own father would have been of this young man. Jan was the son Jacob Adam had always wanted. Too bad it had taken an extra generation for him to be born.

"By the way," he said, as they reached the door of the manor kitchen, "I had Alice buy three lots for me on Wall Street. Down past Broad Street. Near—what is it called now—William Street."

Jan was surprised. His father was usually unconcerned with property in the city.

"Perhaps you can help me with my plan," James said with a slight smile. "What I had in mind was building a small park."

Later that evening Jan sat thinking. He could just hear what Charlie Goelet would say if asked to donate a park for the welfare of the populace. The air would be blue for half a mile in all directions.

He opened the bottom drawer of his desk and reached into the back for a weathered paper.

It was the letter written to Jan by his grandfather, on whose instructions Alice had withheld it from her nephew until the day of his sixteenth birthday.

"Grandson," it began; nothing more. No "dear," no name, nothing but the single salutation.

Jan reread Jacob Adam's words for the hundredth time, dwelling on his favorite parts.

Some would call it unfortunate that we never knew one another, but perhaps that is just as well and you will think kinder of a memory than of the actual presence you might have confronted. Reality is rarely as kind as our idea of it.

There is no way for me to know what sort of man you will turn out to be, but as I am a firm believer in bloodlines, I think I am able to make an educated guess. My hope is you will be a man who will work to increase the fortune and influence of the de Kuyper family. You hold in your hands the fruits of the labors of your forebears. It is not yours to squander.

The old man certainly didn't mince words, Jan thought; you almost had the feeling that if you didn't do as he said, he would rise up out of his grave and come back to chastise you.

There was more. Jan skimmed over it, knowing almost every word without having to glance at the paper. And then he came to the end.

Do not waste today what you will need tomorrow. Do not expect good times to last. Do not attempt to win the good will of your fellow men by being as foolish as they are.

Jacob Adam de Kuyper

That was all. No good-byes. No words of affection for the grandson he had known only as an infant. A few terse and practical admonitions. And, abruptly, but with a flourish, his signature.

Jan put the letter back in the drawer. Quite a family I seem to have, he thought. He closed the drawer and left the room to join his father for dinner.

Sam de Witt hurried out of his house on Water Street. His wife waved good-bye, but he didn't see her. He was on his way to the building on Whitehall Street that housed the family enterprises.

Sam was thirty-seven years old and third in command,

after his uncle Charles Goelet. His father, Paul, who headed the business, treated him with the same cavalier attitude he displayed toward other men. Sam often felt the pain of a tongue-lashing from one or the other of these two tycoons. Easy enough for them to scoff at his efforts, he thought: how much could *they* accomplish if they had to do it today? Good God, in their day half the trading was done in wampum; and hard money in gold or silver was difficult to come by. Yes, compared to Sam, the old men had had it easy.

But today, for a change, it was with delight that he pondered his father's irascible disposition and acid tongue. Jan de Kuyper was due in the office this morning, and Paul de Witt was going to rake him over the coals. The prospect was more than pleasant from Sam's point of view.

It wasn't that he particularly disliked his cousin. It just seemed to him that Jan had too many advantages over him.

Sam de Witt was short, nearsighted and overweight. He wasn't stupid, but neither was he lightning-fast. He had inherited none of the better traits of his father or his mother. He was a hard worker and hoped someday to inherit control of the family businesses. His greatest fear was that Jan would bypass him and become head of the de Kuyper enterprises. That had to be prevented.

The clerks were already at work when Sam came through the front door of the Whitehall office. He checked to make sure his father had not arrived. He wanted to be at the door to greet him with a piece of good news.

Ten minutes later the imperial figure of Charles Goelet, silver buttons shining in the sun, the ever-present silver-headed cane swinging boldly at his side, appeared and entered the building.

Charles Goelet was a tyrant and, like most men of the sort, quite despised those who knuckled under to him. His dislike of Sam was only faintly disguised. "You want me with you when you talk to Paul this morning?" he asked curtly, ignoring his nephew's respectful greeting.

"It's what we discussed," Sam said, the trace of a whine in his voice.

Goelet grunted and went inside. Damn ninny, he

thought; can't even talk to his own father without someone there to hold his hand.

Sam waited patiently until the second stout figure came through the door.

"Good morning, Father," he said. "May Uncle Charles and I have a word with you?"

Paul de Witt nodded and walked briskly to his private office as Sam scurried after him, almost forced into a trot to keep pace. Even at the age of seventy, Paul de Witt displayed evidence of the strength and determination that had made him one of the city's leading businessmen.

A clerk hurried into the office with black, steaming coffee in a cup of fine bone china. He set it down on the oak desk, bowed, and disappeared as rapidly as possible.

The office told the range and interests of the de Kuyper empire. There were little wooden models of ships they owned, and several paintings of ships on the walls. There were also paintings of buildings, docks, warehouses, and scenic landholdings. A map of Manhatan, marked in red, catalogued their real estate holdings on the island. There was a chart listing the number of barrels of wheat, flour, and timber sent across the ocean. There was a picture of the office building, which housed the de Kuyper bank, both symbol of and key to the other enterprises.

Charles Goelet had been apprised of Paul's arrival. He entered the office, walked to a chair at the side of the room, and sat down. Paul nodded toward him, then looked at his son and arched an eyebrow, a signal, borrowed unconsciously from Jacob Adam, to get to the business at hand.

"With your permission I've been selling real estate in the city," Sam began. "Lots totaling more than twenty acres in the past week."

Paul scowled. It was Sam's idea to turn real estate into cash—cash they would use to invest in other ventures. In his heart he was against the plan. Most of the landholdings went back to the days of Jacob Adam, but some went back further, to Pieter, the founder of the de Kuyper family in the New World.

"You really think this is the wise thing to do?" he asked.

"We've been through all this before," Charles Goelet

said impatiently. "If we agreed it was the right thing to do last week, then it's right for this week."

"We can't keep so much money tied up in land," Sam persisted. "Investing in the triangular trade would bring us triple and quadruple profits."

Paul didn't approve of this trade, not for any moral reason, but because he felt there were too many risks involved. A ship would leave New York with rum for Europe, then sail down to Africa to take on a load of slaves for the West Indies. The slaves would be sold to the plantation owners in the Indies, and a cargo of sugar and molasses would head north—most of it intended for the manufacturing of more rum. And so the cycle would start once again.

The hazards were many. Pirates infested the coasts of Africa and the Indies, although, Paul had to admit, they were becoming less of a problem in the North American waters. This was due entirely to the growing size and ability of the British Navy and its ferocity in dealing with these wolves of the sea. Any pirate who allowed himself to be captured these days was as good as dead.

Also, shipping slaves was always a nuisance: there was constant fear of plagues or mutinies. The company could well do without such worries, Paul thought.

Another risk was the undependable price of sugar. The damned plantation owners were so greedy there was a danger they would glut the market and drive down the price.

"I'm not saying we shouldn't profit from trade, but must we sell land?"

"Most of our land just sits there," Charles Goelet said. "Earns nothing."

"Land values in New York are always rising," Paul argued.

"Only if you sell, Paul," Goelet said disagreeably. "And they don't rise as fast as the profits we could take from good cargoes."

"Uncle Charles is right, Father. Owning land is costing us money."

"You sold twenty acres, you say?"

"Yes."

Paul glanced at the map with its red markings. "Soon we won't own any of the island."

Sam forced a little chuckle. "I hardly think that will happen. Besides, we sell a great deal of the land by making loans from our bank. If the buyers can't pay," he said, indulging in another chuckle, "why, we'll simply foreclose and take back the land."

"Wonderful business," Paul said belligerently. "Selling land in the hope we can steal it back."

Sam knew it was time to drop the subject.

"Are we finished?" Charles Goelet asked. "If we are, I'd like to get back to my office. And do some *real* work," he added, with an unkind glance toward Sam. It was his rebuke to the other man for being too weak to argue his own case without an ally.

"Sorry to interrupt your busy day," Paul said blandly as Goelet exited without another word. Sam closed the door and waited.

Paul started to look at some papers that were neatly piled in the middle of the desk. He suddenly realized his son had not left the room. "Well? What else?"

"I . . . this is the morning you have . . ." Sam stammered, but his nerve failed him.

"Say it, man, dammit, say it!"

"Jan de Kuyper is due here this morning."

"Where is that scoundrel?" Paul said, pulling out a large watch from his waistcoat. The gold chain clanked against the desk. "Eight o'clock already. Doesn't he know the hours of the office?"

"He isn't very disciplined," Sam said piously. "I suppose he's been spoiled."

"I'll spoil him," Paul grumbled.

Sam fought to keep back a smile. "It's about time someone brought him into line. His own father certainly won't do it."

Paul de Witt looked with suspicion at his son. He was enjoying himself too much. And he was a fool to underestimate James de Kuyper.

"Why are you still here?" he asked. "The *Lightning Arrow* arrived last evening. I want a full report on her cargo by the end of the day."

Sam's heart skipped a beat. The *Lightning Arrow* was a large packet. A thorough investigation of her cargo would take all day, and then some. "Don't you think—I mean, shouldn't I be here when you talk to de Kuyper?"

"What the hell for?"

"Well, I am third in command. My position—"

"Mind your own business," Paul said testily, and watched without satisfaction as his son slunk out of his office, carefully closing the door so it wouldn't make the slightest sound. He shook his head and picked up the papers on his desk. He looked at them without comprehension for several seconds and then threw them down in disgust.

Third in command, he thought, third in command. Good God! He looked around the office. It had once belonged to Jacob Adam—a man of iron. And for years now it had been his own. Well, he hadn't done badly by it. At least he had tried to live up to the standards set by the old man. But the future?

Charles Goelet was capable enough, but so arrogant he made enemies unnecessarily. And pigheaded! The sort of man who would cut off his nose to spite his face. Paul wasn't quite sure how the family fortunes would fare with such a man at the helm.

As for Sam—well, no surprise there. He had known it from the beginning. Turning the business over to Sam would be a disaster. The man was almost forty years old, and he still acted like a puppy, standing around slavering, waiting for you to throw him a bone. Paul was sure the world was run by order and justice: something in his own past had angered God and caused him to curse him with such a son. He thought about it, but could not figure out which particular deed had so offended the Almighty. What difference did it make? The deed was done.

Two hours later, Jan de Kuyper strolled into Paul de Witt's office. He was dressed in a handsome linen coat, a jaunty hat, and silver-buckled shoes. "Good morning, Uncle," he said brightly. "I've been told you want to see me."

Paul looked up from his work. "Good *afternoon*, Mister de Kuyper. I trust we haven't interrupted your beauty sleep."

"As a matter of fact, no. I went for a ride in the country at dawn."

"While men of business added profit to their purses."

Jan sat down and crossed his legs. "I actually had some business of my own to conduct."

"And what was that?"

"I bought a few lots on the East River. I wanted to see them in the early light." Jan walked over to the map hanging on the wall. "Here's the very land, Uncle. On your map and marked in red."

"What?"

Paul de Witt was out of his chair and at his nephew's side. Jan used his forefinger to trace the location of his new lots.

"Dammit man, you're buying land that Sam's selling!"

Jan returned to his chair. "Yes, I know."

"Do you mean to say Sam didn't know who was buying it?"

"I was . . . ah, discreet, and used a third party."

"Where did you get the money?" Paul asked suspiciously.

"The timber rights on some land given me by Aunt Alice. England is starving for proper ship's masts. The price they'll pay is quite out of line."

"And how would a man of leisure know about the shipping boom?" Paul said. His voice was tinged with sarcasm, but there was a wariness in his eyes.

"Come, Uncle, did you ask me here to quiz me about my knowledge of affairs?"

"No," the older man snapped. "But it's time you began a serious day's work here in this office, six days a week."

Jan's lips drew into two tight lines. He smiled, but with a pronounced lack of humor. "I have no intention of hunching over ledger books in this dingy place."

Paul de Witt almost choked. "How dare you, sir! This *dingy place* is responsible for the handsome coat you wear. And the house you live in. And everything else you have."

"Not this office, Uncle, but the brains of men like my grandfather and yourself," Jan said quietly. "About getting down to work—I agree with you. But I plan on doing it in my own way."

"And what way is that?"

Jan glanced again at the map of real estate tracts. "It may not be in line with your own recent policies."

"Come, come, man, don't play with words. What do you plan on doing?"

Jan walked over to the map and placed his hand on it. "I intend to buy land in the city, not sell it. I also intend to buy ships."

"We already have ships," Paul snapped.

"Not as many as we should. The de Kuyper family should own ten or fifteen."

Paul slammed his hand down on the desk. "Fifteen ships? And where do you plan on getting the money?"

"We own vast tracts of Hudson Valley land between here and Albany. I want to sell the timber."

"Those lands are to be used by tenant farmers."

Jan was mild, but firm. "Times are changing, Uncle. The days of vast estates with tenant farmers are numbered. Men don't immigrate to America to become serfs to other men."

Paul de Witt slouched back in his chair and regarded this self-assured young man. "Let's say you're proven correct. What happens then?"

"Then I run the company."

Paul turned purple. His first reaction was to bluster and threaten in answer to this audacity. But his astonishment was so great it kept him at a loss for words for a long moment. When he finally spoke it was in a very low voice.

"What about Charlie Goelet? Or my own son?"

Jan smiled again. "Now you're playing with words, uncle. I'll make a deal with you. Step down today and appoint either one of them to run the company. I promise to go along with it."

Angry as he was, Paul de Witt could not suppress his smile. Damn! This young bugger had trapped him! "Very funny."

"You do see my point, don't you?"

"All right, all right," Paul said, sweeping his hand over the top of the desk as if to clear it of the thought. "How do you suggest we proceed?"

Jan shrugged. "I'll start coming here, to do work of my own choosing. You back me. In a small way at first; but as I prove successful, I'll expect to be in control of more and more of the company's activities."

The older man knew he was trapped. A fight with

Jan could start a feud that would rip the company apart. James de Kuyper and Alice Livingston—large shareholders in the business—had always gone along with his own judgment. But if it came to war, they might well back the younger man. It was unthinkable to risk a confrontation.

"Very well," he said. "I'll arrange a suitable office for you."

"Thank you, Uncle," Jan said, rising to his feet. He reached across the desk and held out his hand. Paul took it gingerly. "And now if you'll excuse me, there's a most important matter I must attend to."

"More city land?"

"No. A lady named Marie Therese Bache."

The older man's eyes narrowed. This was more the sort of talk he was used to hearing from his nephew. "Chasing women will never get you anywhere."

"I don't intend to chase her, sir, I intend to marry her."

"Good luck," Paul growled, and waved his hand in dismissal.

"And good day to you, Uncle," Jan said cheerfully as he opened the door and stepped outside.

Paul de Witt sat quietly at his desk for a long time.

It suddenly seemed quite possible he was dealing with the true spiritual descendant of Jacob Adam.

He suddenly felt the full weight of his years.

Perhaps he would have been willing to take on Jan fifteen or twenty years ago, but not anymore. He was too old to pick a fight with someone who would probably beat him anyway. While he was stomping and fuming, Jan de Kuyper would help him destroy himself. He had watched old Jacob Adam do it to many men. Well, it wasn't going to happen to him.

He would give Jan his head and watch his star rise— all the way to the top, probably. In the meantime he would remove himself from the everyday running of the business. That would be handed over to Charles Goelet.

Paul de Witt smiled at this idea. Charlie could never see the worth of any man but himself. Let *him* pick fights with young de Kuyper, let *him* wear himself out in vain. *Serve Charlie right*. Trying to stop Jan might very well be like trying to stem the tide of the Hudson with a twig.

He called in his chief clerk and ordered him to find a suitable office for Jan. "In a different part of the building," he instructed. It was one thing to know you had found your successor, he thought, but quite another to have the man in the next room.

After he left his uncle's office, Jan sought out Sam de Witt. The chubby man greeted his cousin and waited for him to pour out his tale of woe. Sam wanted to hear all the details: what the old man had said; how he had shouted and raved; how he had ordered Jan to fall into line. He wanted to smell the blood and see the guts on the floor. He was astonished by the other's opening words.

"How do I meet Marie Therese Bache?"

"What?" Sam said, trying to focus his thoughts. "The Bache girl?"

"An angel. She has the face of Hera and the body of Athena," Jan said, drawing on the knowledge that had been pounded into him years earlier by a classical tutor. "Marie Therese. Do you know her?"

"We've met. But what about Father?"

"We had a nice chat. I'm to have an office here. But enough of business. Tell me about the girl."

"She's friendly with my wife," Sam managed to say.

Jan nodded. "Could you arrange a meeting?"

"I think so . . . but—"

"Good. A garden party next Saturday. Nothing fancy. Just be sure Marie Therese Bache is there."

Sam de Witt nodded. "Yes, of course. I'll see to it. But what about Father?"

"By all means invite him too."

That same week a servant appeared before Alice and announced she had a visitor—Captain Charles Lewis.

For a moment she couldn't place the name. Then, remembering, she got up quickly from her chair and went to the parlor.

Charles Lewis's hair was gray now, and his face showed his sixty-five years. But he was still a large man, and he held himself erect. The mark of the seaman was unmistakably on him.

"Charles Lewis!" Alice cried as she swept into the room. "My God, I thought you must have died years ago."

Lewis smiled. "Because you haven't heard from me? Aye, and maybe that was a mistake, but I never thought I was the sort to mix with the likes of the de Kuypers. James and I have stayed in touch, though."

"Not a word for thirty years! Shame on you! Now sit down and bring me up to date."

He told her of his life. He was captain and owner of a Hudson River packet. He had settled down in Albany and married a widow with no children; nor had any children come to them. "I guess it's the one regret I have," he said, "but it's a small one. My wife's a wonderful woman and we have a handsome house on the river. 'Tis but a short walk to the docks and my packet. I have the best of two worlds—a ship that takes me over the waters, and yet I'm never far from a good wife and a good home."

"I know why you've never brought your wife here," Alice teased. "You're afraid I'll tell her about the days when you and my brother were pirates with Kidd."

"She knows all about that," he said. "Oh, I might've left out a bit here and there—to spare her some of the more painful truths."

She laughed. "I'll bet you have, you old rogue!"

They chatted for a time of the old days, enjoying coffee and cake. Finally Captain Lewis came to the purpose of his visit. "Tell me about Jan de Kuyper."

"He's a bit wild and wooly," Alice said, "but he's got a good head on his shoulders."

As he sat in Alice's parlor, the captain was acutely conscious of the wealth it represented. "He'll come into a good deal of money someday. A man needs a proper mind to know how to handle it."

"My nephew will bring no disgrace to the name de Kuyper."

"Your brother thinks the same. I was with him yesterday. James and I came to a decision about something we've had on our minds for many years."

Alice sat back as Captain Lewis told her of the buried

treasure in the cave on Gardiner's Island; of how he, Kidd, James, and a sailor had hidden the treasure so that not even the other members of Kidd's crew knew where it was. It had remained a secret all these years and was, no doubt, still waiting in the cave for someone to come along and take it.

"Kidd's treasure," Alice said in wonderment. "And James has known about it all these years."

"Aye. The other sailor and Kidd are dead, so now there's only James and myself. And you."

"But why me? Surely I've no right to it."

" 'Tis the lad, Jan, we have in mind."

"In mind for what? And why isn't James here himself if this is so important?"

The captain shrugged. "He said to tell you his best mare is due to foal any day now, and he didn't want to leave her."

"I have a feeling he didn't want to get into an argument if I don't agree with whatever it is you're about to propose," she said testily.

"He said you might say that."

"Well, go on. What is this plot you've cooked up?"

"James and I have asked ourselves—what do we do with all that money? I'm getting along in years, and only the good Lord knows how much time is left for me. I have everything I want in life. And anyway, what would a man of my age—and with no children—do with a treasure?"

"And James?"

"Well, you know how James is. He and I are of the same mind about the bloody thing. We really don't need it or want it."

Alice had forgotten the cup of coffee in her hand. She took a sip and made a face. It was cold. "You still haven't told me how you and James think I fit into all this."

"As I said, we've given it a lot of thought. A fortune like this should be put to a good use, and Jan might be the right man to figure out what to do with it. James thought I should hear your opinion."

Alice's back stiffened. "I couldn't think of a better person to entrust with a fortune."

Captain Lewis smiled and reached into his coat. He

took out a well-handled piece of oilskin, opened it, and unfolded the map inside. "Gardiner's Island," he said, and tapped a finger against a spot marked on the map.

"I've seen that part of the coast," she said. "It was uninhabited when I visited the Gardiner family on the island a few years ago."

The capain nodded. "Still is. As late as last year I took my ship there to make certain. 'Tis the same as it was years ago. The treasure rests undisturbed."

Alice called a servant and ordered more coffee. She turned back to the captain. "I still don't understand what you and my brother have in mind. If you both want to give Jan the treasure, why not do it? Why talk to me?"

The captain smiled. "This was James's idea."

"Idea? What idea?"

"You're the one who'll decide when Jan is to be told of the treasure."

Alice contained her impatience as the servant returned and poured the coffee. When he was out of the room she leaned forward. "I *still* don't understand. Why me? And how will I know when it's the right time?"

"James thinks you can be objective about the lad. He's passing his decision to you. My situation is a wee bit different."

"How so?"

"I'm an old man," Lewis said with a sigh. "But you're a young woman, you'll still be here when the time comes."

Alice laughed. "I haven't been called a young woman in a long time. I'm forty-six years old and fast going the way of all flesh. But as you've come out of your way to flatter me so outrageously, the least I can do, I suppose, is say yes."

"What a bunch of fops," Jan muttered.

Edward Goelet looked down self-consciously at his own splendid clothes and couldn't see much difference between himself and the others, Jan included, at Sam de Witt's garden party.

"Look at that one," Jan said, pointing to the scion of the Van Dam family. "See the handkerchief dangling out of his sleeve."

After peeking to make sure his own handkerchief was hidden, Edward said, "Damned silly way to act."

"There you are!" a voice called out. Jan and Edward turned to see Janet Beekman de Witt, Sam's mother. Her voice dropped almost to a whisper. "My son tells me you have an interest in Marie Therese Bache."

"Correct," Jan said.

"Well? What have you done about it?"

Jan smiled. "Do you have any ideas?"

She cocked her head and looked at him for a moment. "Leave it to me," she said, and moved purposefully toward the other end of the garden.

Marie Therese Bache was standing beneath a large tree with Dora Van Cortlandt. Dora was quite a bit shorter than her friend, but she had a petite figure and arrestingly wide, intense eyes. Her fawnlike attitude of shy, often startled helplessness was not without its attractions for the opposite sex.

Janet smiled as she stepped amid the group of young men surrounding the two belles. She whispered in Marie Therese's ear and led her back to Jan.

"This is Marie Therese Bache," she announced. "And these two rascals—Jan de Kuyper, Edward Goelet—fit into my family somewhere."

Jan bent low as he kissed the outstretched hand. "A pleasure to meet you again," he said.

"Oh? Have we met before?"

"Yes," he answered, puzzled. "The other day in my Aunt Alice's house. We . . . uh, we bumped into one another."

"Was that you? I thought it was an Indian."

Janet de Witt was watching closely; it was time to leave the young couple to their own devices. She coughed. "You must excuse me. Sam always expects me to play the part of second hostess at his parties. Ned, come with me," she said, taking him in tow. "I want you to meet some friends of mine."

Edward followed reluctantly, unhappy at being taken away from this marvelous creature only seconds after having met her.

"I might have looked like an Indian at that," Jan said, turning his full attention to Marie Therese. "We had just returned after months in the north country."

"So I've heard," she said coolly. "Tell me, Mister de Kuyper, do you always spend your summers paddling up and down the Hudson?"

"No, Miss Bache, I've spent many summers whiling away my time with certain empty-headed young girls of New York."

"And which do you prefer?"

"The river," Jan said solemnly. "Definitely the river."

Marie Therese smiled and replied sweetly. "Coincidentally, I find New York full of empty-headed, self-important young men. But then you wouldn't know about that, would you? You seem to spend all your time with Indians."

"And wild women," he said, purposely forgetting his manners. "They have an unusual virtue as far as I'm concerned."

"Which is?"

"They don't talk. There are times women look prettier with their mouths closed."

Marie Therese kept her lips firmly together as she walked back to rejoin Dora.

Jan found a table where he could treat himself to rum punch. Edward joined him.

"Why aren't you still with that wonderful girl?"

"Beneath that face of an angel beats the heart of a devil. But don't worry, Ned, she'll still make a fine wife."

Two days later Jan called on Whitby Bache at home. The older man welcomed him to his house, and they sat in an anteroom enjoying an afternoon beer. After a few minutes of polite conversation, Jan came to the pretended subject of his visit.

"I understand, sir, you own a bit of land next to Beekman's swamp."

"Yes," Bache agreed. "Damned stupid of me to buy it. Worthless property. Full of mosquitoes."

"I'd like to buy it from you."

Bache peered more closely at his visitor. "Is this some sort of game?"

"No. If we can agree on a price, sir, I'll buy it."

"Only last week, your cousin Sam was trying to *sell* me an adjacent pair of lots."

Jan shrugged. "That's his affair," he said, making a mental note to find out the price of Sam's land.

"Your family has a strange way of doing business," Bache said, shaking his head. "But if you're serious . . ."

"I am."

"It's a total of six acres. I'll sell for thirty pounds an acre."

"Done." He held out his hand.

There was a moment's pause. Finally the Englishman took the proffered hand. He smiled and invited Jan to stay for afternoon tea. They walked to the parlor, joining Mrs. Bache and several older women. Jan nodded toward the women, and, recognizing him, they tittered and whispered among themselves. Jan saw no sign of Marie Therese. He accepted a cup of tea and some tiny cakes. He planned on eating as quickly as politely possible and then departing. He gulped down the last of his tea and was about to take leave of his hostess when Marie Therese walked into the room.

"More tea?" Mrs. Bache asked him.

"How could I say no?" Jan said, taking up a position near the large silver pot. He pretended not to see the figure walking toward them, concentrating instead on Mrs. Bache. "Extraordinary tea, a new type, isn't it?" he asked her.

"I'm not sure," Mrs. Bache said. "Oh, have you met my daughter, Marie Therese?"

Jan turned and smiled.

"We've already met," Marie Therese said, "at least twice."

"Actually only one and a half times," Jan said to the mother. "I believe Miss Bache mistook me for an Indian the first time."

Mrs. Bache looked at the patrician face and the handsomely tailored clothes. She was shocked. "How could you do that?" she asked her daughter. "He looks no more like an Indian than I do."

"We all make mistakes at one time or another," Jan said patronizingly. "That's why one should always be willing to apologize."

"What a lovely philosophy," Marie Therese said, a frost heavy in her voice, but unnoticed by her mother who was moving away to see to her guests.

"Ah, so you've met my daughter," Whitby Bache said, arriving at Jan's side and resting his hand on the young man's shoulder.

"Yes," Jan answered, without taking his eyes off the girl. "May I make a suggestion, sir? With your permission I'd like to show your daughter around the city."

"An excellent idea," Bache said. "Don't you agree, my dear?"

Marie Therese's eyes flashed. "I wouldn't dream of imposing on Mister de Kuyper."

"It would be my pleasure."

"Then she accepts," Bache said, oblivious of the undercurrent between the two young people.

"Will tomorrow at eleven be convenient?"

Bache looked at his daughter and became uncomfortable as she hesitated. "Come, come. The gentleman is waiting for your answer."

"Eleven will be most convenient," she said.

A few moments later Marie Therese invented an excuse to leave the room. Five minutes after her departure Jan claimed that the press of business required his presence elsewhere.

Whitby Bache was alone with his wife for a moment. "Quite a nice young chap, that de Kuyper. Good family, too."

"What are you thinking of?"

"Soon, my dear, our Marie Therese must get married. Why not someone like young de Kuyper?"

Why not indeed, she thought. If only he has the strength of will to control her. It was difficult enough to have been blessed with a beautiful daughter; worse still that she had a mind of her own.

It was a beautiful fall day, the air hinting of the past summer's warmth, but crisp with the expectation of winter.

At exactly eleven o'clock Jan arrived at the Broad Street home of Marie Therese Bache. As he waited in the parlor, Mrs. Bache fluttered in and out, and Jan was well aware he was being inspected. When ten minutes had passed, she made her appearance. Her coat, hat, and muff were trimmed with beaver, and her long blonde hair was tied in a knot behind her head, her green eyes sparkled.

She looked so fetching that Jan almost forgave her for keeping him waiting.

They drove around the town in his calash. A jaunty, one-horse, two-wheeled coach, it boasted a covered top, which was now folded back out of the way. Jan played to the hilt his role of guide.

He pointed out the printing shop of William Bradford and explained that it was the home of the *Gazette,* the city's first newspaper, which had begun printing only a few years earlier, in 1725.

And over there, at the corner of Wall and Water Streets, was the Merchant's Coffee House, where the traders and shippers bought and sold shiploads of goods as they sipped Brazilian coffee and munched at lusciously overstuffed fruit pies.

There was the Fly Market; the Bear Market; the market at the Old Slip. Much of the produce sold at these markets had been brought in small boats by farmers and unloaded that very morning. The end of the day always turned into a contest between the farmers, who were anxious to sell the last of their goods and go home, and the housewives, who knew this and waited for the prices to be lowered. The last sales were always the best bargains of the day.

They passed De Peyster Street, named after Abraham de Peyster. "Our mayor from 1691 to 1695. That used to be his father's house," Jan said, pointing toward an impressive building.

"City Hall?" Marie Therese asked in surprise.

"Well, City Hall is a newer building," Jan admitted. "But that's the site where old Johannes de Peyster lived. They wanted to make him mayor of the city, too, but he refused because he couldn't speak English."

"Imagine a mayor of New York not speaking English."

"A ruler should, I suppose, speak the language of his people."

"Of course."

"That's the way they do it in England? Not like here in the provinces?"

"Certainly."

"William of Orange couldn't speak English when he was king of England," he said. They drove in silence for a few moments, Marie Therese's cheeks flushing a shade redder.

They paused in front of the Dutch Reformed church, and Jan pointed out the graceful cast-iron bell donated by his father in the name of Jan's grandfather, Jacob Adam. "Cast in Holland by German ironmongers working with French ore," Jan said, "but installed by English workmen. Our family is internationally minded."

They came to the new temple of Shearith Israel, on Mill Street. Built in 1729, it was the first permanent home of the Jewish community since the arrival of the first Jew, Jacob Barsimon, three quarters of a century ago. A husky man, bearded and dressed in gray clothes, was pruning back a tree outside the building in preparation for winter. Jan reined in the horse.

"Doing your own gardening, Ben?" Jan called out.

The bearded man looked up and smiled. He put down his shears and came over. "You know how it is, Jan, if you don't do it yourself, it doesn't get done."

The two men shook hands. "Marie Therese Bache," Jan said, introducing his companion. "This is Rabbi Benjamin Seixas."

"A pleasure," the rabbi said, taking the girl's hand in his own and holding on to it for a moment. "I see the de Kuypers still have the best eyes in town when it comes to the ladies."

Marie Therese blushed and self-consciously withdrew her hand.

"And on that note we bid you good-bye," Jan said with a smile, and started up the horse. As they drove on, he explained that Ben's grandfather had worked for his great-grandfather and the two families had become friends. He noticed Marie Therese was silent. "You have Jews in England, haven't you?"

"They . . . well, they more or less keep to themselves," she replied.

"I guess we're a bit more tolerant in America," Jan said, unable to keep an edge of superiority from his voice. "You'll find it works better that way."

He next pointed out Cherry Street. The site was formerly the cherry orchard of Richard Sackett, who was now married to Anne de Witt, daughter of Janet and sister of Sam. At a nominal price, Sackett had sold part of the property to the city for the street.

"Actually it was all part of a family deal," Jan explained. "Charlie Goelet was mayor that year, and he asked Sackett to sell it because a street would make it easier to get to our family's docks. I'm sure Sackett received something in return."

"Your family is used to getting its own way around New York, isn't it?"

"Why not? We were here first."

They drove in silence until they came to the end of Wall Street. Near Nicholas Bayard's sugar house, where hundreds of tons of the sweet substance was warehoused, stood a flourishing slave market.

Marie Therese's eyes narrowed as she watched a group of chained black men being led around the block for exercise.

"When did your family drag those men from their homes in Africa?" she asked.

"Those men probably never saw Africa," he replied nonchalantly. "Most slaves in New York come from the West Indies. Ships come up with rum, limes, and coffee. If there's extra space, they cram on a few Negroes."

"How convenient," she said, making no attempt to hide her contempt.

"For other people, perhaps," Jan said seriously, "but not for the de Kuypers. Our family has never engaged in the slave trade."

"Not enough profit in it?"

"On the contrary, there's great profit. But we don't traffic in slaves. It was the unwritten rule of my great-grandfather, the first de Kuyper in America."

The look in her eyes changed, and the hard line of her mouth softened. Satisfied, Jan was about to drive on when he saw a tall, muscular black man standing near the dock. The man was also watching the slaves, and the expression on his face was not pleasant to see.

"Morning, Aaron," Jan called out.

Aaron Gerait forced himself to lose his scowl. "Good morning, Mister Jan."

"How are things with you?"

"Passable."

"It's been a while since I've seen you. Are you married?"

A flash of hostility crossed the black man's face. "I have a woman, but we're not married. Why get married if we don't have souls?"

Jan sighed. Unlike his father, Daniel, whose ambition was to live in peace, Aaron Gerait was a rebel. He was tolerated in New York because he was a third-generation freeman, and also because of his long-standing association with the de Kuyper family. But the white merchants and officials distrusted him and were always expecting trouble.

"Not all white men believe black men don't have souls," Jan said in a conciliatory tone.

"Not enough of them. Otherwise we wouldn't see sights like that," Aaron said, jerking his thumb toward the line of chained men.

"Aaron, this is Miss Bache," Jan said, switching topics. "She arrived from England only this year."

"Welcome to New York, Miss Bache," Aaron said. "And may I offer a word of caution?"

"Caution?"

"This young man is the most notorious rogue in New York," Aaron said in mock seriousness. "He deals in the slave trade himself . . . the *white slave* trade."

It was a light jest and eased the tension. "Troublemaker," Jan said with a laugh. "If you weren't as big as a house I'd give you a hiding."

"Yes, *baas,*" Aaron said, using the Dutch term the English were already corrupting to "boss." He reached out and swatted Jan's horse with his palm. The animal snorted, reared, and took off as if he had been stung by a bee. Aaron roared with laughter as the other man fought to regain control of his coach.

Jan finally slowed the horse. As he and Marie Therese rode on, he explained Aaron's connection with the de Kuypers. "I worry about him. He's smart, but stubborn as a mule. He has a good life. I don't know why he worries about every slave that comes from Africa."

"Perhaps he feels for the suffering of others."

"Yes, and so do I," Jan said quietly. "But being angry all the time serves no useful purpose. I'm afraid he'll suffer for it one day."

They returned to the Bache home. Jan helped Marie

Therese out of the calash and walked her to the front door. "Well, did you enjoy your tour?" he asked. She stepped inside the house and closed the door in his face without so much as a word.

Jan looked at the door, scratched his head, and then walked back to the coach. He stopped and looked again at the house. The blind eyes of the curtained windows stared back at him.

"I'll be damned . . . I'll be damned. . . ." He repeated the words over and over to himself as he drove away.

Aaron Gerait returned to his small house off River Street. He closed the door behind him and accustomed his eyes to the darkness within.

"Aaron?" The voice was anxious.

"Yes, it's me."

A woman came from the back room. Her skin was a silky brown and her long hair covered her shoulders. "When you aren't here, I'm afraid," she said.

He took her in his arms and kissed her on the mouth and cheeks. "I told you there's nothing to worry about. Nobody knows who you are. Nobody even knows you're here."

"They'll find out," she said. "They always find out."

"If they do, they better not try to do anything about it," he said with a sudden ferocity. "Or I'll make them sorry."

She snuggled into the protection of his great arms and body—two hundred and forty pounds of muscle, sinew, and bone—and felt safe and content for a moment. And then the fears returned.

Tina was a runaway slave who had fled her master in Philadelphia after he raped her. She probably would have died in the wilds if a friendly Indian hadn't helped her and brought her halfway to New York. A black freeman living in New Jersey had brought her across the river with the idea of selling her back into slavery, but he'd had the bad luck to reveal his scheme to Aaron. The freeman wound up in the river with a broken neck, and Aaron brought the girl to his home. At first his plan was to set her free somewhere on Long Island; but she was so beautiful, and her skin was so soft, and . . .

Now she was his woman, and he would die before he gave her up.

But he knew what would happen if she was caught. She would be sent back to Philadelphia, where she would be put under the whip. And himself? There was only one penalty for men who helped runaway slaves. And it was never tempered with mercy.

Later that afternoon Marie Therese was walking along Wall Street with Dora. They had just attended a lecture on the arrangement of flowers—an activity that had only recently become popular among well-to-do girls and women of the city. The common folk had no time for such frivolity: flowers had a small place in the lives of people whose workday of twelve or fourteen hours paid a wage of about fifty cents.

Suddenly a horse came cantering down the street. The approaching rider was dressed in tan buckskin—trousers, jacket, and soft moccasins. And a buckskin mask. The horse came alongside the young women, and both screamed as the rider reached down and scooped up Marie Therese.

She was dumped unceremoniously over the front of the saddle, and the rider urged his horse to greater speed as they cantered toward the Hudson River. The girl struggled, but the powerful grip of the rider held her helpless.

Dora stopped screaming and stood in the middle of the street in a state of shock.

"Don't worry, Miss Van Cortlandt," Edward Goelet said as he came toward her from the other side of the street. "It's only a prank."

Dora was too astonished to hear what he was saying. "You must stop him. He's mad . . . he's—"

"No, please listen," Edward said. "Nothing's going to happen. It's all a joke."

The girl looked at him with wide eyes. "But who would do such a thing?"

"A man in love."

A light seemed to go on in her mind. "Jan de Kuyper?"

"Of course."

Her attitude changed. "I told Marie Therese she was asking for trouble," she said, looking after the cantering horse, which by now was almost to the river. "It *is* romantic, isn't it?"

Edward Goelet had seen Dora Van Cortlandt many

times in the past. They had, in fact, grown up together. But her fragile beauty had never captured his imagination until now.

"Since your companion seems to be occupied, may I escort you home?" he said gallantly.

"That would be nice," she replied, and forgot Marie Therese.

Marie Therese, however, could hardly forget her position. The horse stopped, and the rider let her slip to the ground, holding her arm to prevent her from toppling.

She shook her head angrily and wiped away the hair that had fallen over her eyes. "What do you—"

"Miss Bache, you have just been swept off your feet," Jan said, turning his horse and galloping away.

"Why *you* . . ." Marie Therese began angrily. Then she realized she was addressing the fast-disappearing figure of a horseback rider.

Two hours later Jan, now dressed in a handsome wool coat, silk waistcoat, silk breeches, tricornered hat, and his finest silver-buckled shoes, called at the Bache house.

"Might I see your daughter?" he inquired politely of Whitby Bache.

"See here, de Kuyper," Bache thundered, his face reddening. "I heard what happened, and—"

"It's all right, Father," a voice from behind him said. "I'd be delighted to see Mister de Kuyper."

Whitby Bache turned and looked on the radiant face of his daughter, then back again at Jan.

"I assure you my intentions are most honorable," the younger man said.

Bache shook his head and walked from the room. Marie Therese closed the door after him and turned to Jan. "You certainly know how to get a girl's attention, don't you?"

Sam de Witt was on the East dock going over the cargo manifest of the de Kuyper packet that had berthed before dawn. The sheets of paper went on and on, listing the quantities of goods that had come down from New England.

"Dry goods," Sam mumbled to himself. *And today of all days!*

Other ships on the docks of the Old Slip were loading or unloading far more interesting cargoes. A sleek, rake-masted schooner was disgorging rum, molasses, and sugar. A sweet smell hung in the air; and if a man walked too close, the bottom of his boots became tacky from a film of spilled molasses. The sound of braying could be heard as mules from the Spanish Main awaited their turn to disembark. Another ship was loading flax, to be re-turned one day from Ireland as linen. A ship bound for the West Indies was boarding wheat, peas, rye meal, In-dian corn, apples, and onions. Still another was filling its holds with beef, pork, pickled oysters, boards, and staves. Wine casks came ashore from Spain and Madeira. Cord-age and tea were being unshipped from Hamburg and Holland. The trade goods of the world met in passing on the docks of New York.

It was not quite ten-thirty that morning when Sam completed his work on the manifest. He placed his signa-ture on the last sheet and hurriedly made his way to the Whitehall offices. He went straightaway to Charles Goe-let. That imperious old gentleman was waiting for him. Together they marched down to Paul de Witt's office.

Paul was surprised when the two men came into his chamber with determination on their faces. "What can I do for you?"

"This idea of Sam's that you've been against," Charles Goelet said. "I've deferred to you because of your posi-tion. Until now."

"And the idea?"

"The triangular trade, Father," responded Sam, trying to speak bravely. "We stand idly by while others are mak-ing fortunes."

"I let you sell land."

"But you've not allowed us to buy shares in the cargoes of ships in the African trade."

"It's a filthy business."

"We're losing a great deal of money," Sam whined.

"*That's* got to stop," Charles Goelet said, pounding his fist on Paul's desk for emphasis.

"I see," de Witt said dryly, pointedly regarding the spot where Goelet had hit the desk.

"We won't take no for an answer this time," Goelet said, holding de Witt's eyes with his own.

"So you mean business, Sam, do you?"

Sam straightened his back. "We must think of the good of the company."

"Yes, I agree with that," Paul drawled. "Excuse me for a moment."

He walked out of the room, leaving the puzzled men alone. Sam shifted his weight from one foot to the other and then back again. He had expected almost anything but this. His father might argue, yes; and shout, perhaps —that was to be understood. But to take their demands calmly and leave his office? The perspiration began to sprout on his forehead and upper lip.

Goelet didn't make things easier. He stood as motionless as a rock, his bushy eyebrows pushed down close to his eyes, glaring across the room.

Paul returned in two minutes. Jan was with him, as well as a clerk with an armful of what looked like leases.

"Perhaps you would repeat what you said for Jan's sake," Paul said.

"What's he got to do with this?" Goelet asked angrily.

Paul smiled mildly and nodded at his son. Sam repeated his request.

Jan and Paul exchanged glances. "So this scheme is sure to make us a fortune, is it?" Jan asked.

"Yes," Sam said quickly. "I've worked out the details."

"You'll need a great deal of money."

"We'll use the money we've been getting from the sale of land," Sam said eagerly. "We've been unloading all winter long."

Jan walked to a mahogany chest of drawers that stood against the wall. He started to pull out the top drawer and paused, looking at his uncle. "May I?"

Paul nodded. Jan opened the drawer and took out a soft deerskin. He unfolded it, and the four men looked at the gleaming blade of a knife.

"This knife was given to my great-grandfather, Pieter, when he was a boy, on his first voyage to America. The legend is that it once belonged to Christopher Columbus himself."

"What does that have to do with anything?" Goelet said brusquely.

"This knife is a symbol of my great-grandfather's attachment and commitment to this New World. It is the finest heirloom he passed on to us. He also passed down a hatred of the slave trade. If we trade in human flesh, we might as well break the knife," Jan said, moving as if to snap the slender blade against the chest.

"Don't!" Sam cried in alarm. "Pieter was my great-grandfather too."

"I'm glad you remember," Jan said.

"A lot of damned rubbish," Charles Goelet said.

"Is it?" Jan said quietly. His look made Goelet uncomfortable. Almost against his will, his eyes disengaged from Jan de Kuyper's.

Sam suddenly saw his case going up in smoke. No, he thought, he couldn't let it happen. This was his chance to prove his worth, to prove how much money he could make for the company, to prove he should one day run it —to sit in the chair now occupied by his father.

"But the profits! How can we ignore anything with such vast profits?"

Until this moment Paul had been mild and soft spoken. Now he erupted. "Profits! Don't talk to me of profits." He took the top paper from the pile in the clerk's hands. "This is a lease," he said, waving it in the air. "And so is this. And this. And this."

"I don't understand—"

"That's right, Sam you *don't* understand! These are leases on lands you've been selling—and Jan has been buying, and leasing them out for profit. It turns out you've been selling at a time when you should be buying!" Paul said, taking lease after lease from the clerk's hands and tossing them into the air. He threw the last one at his son and turned to the clerk. "Pick them up and get out!"

The hireling scurried about on his hands and knees, retrieving the leases. When he held the last one, he stumbled to his feet and headed for the door.

Charles Goelet turned on Sam de Witt. "So you've been doing your best to ruin us, have you? Don't ever again come to me with any more hare-brained schemes!" he shouted in Sam's face.

Charles Goelet stomped from the room, and Sam looked as if he wished the earth would open up and swallow him.

Jan stepped in to his rescue. "It isn't your fault, Sam. Not everyone saw the market for land turning up."

"*You* did," Paul snapped. He turned to his son. "If you get any more wonderful ideas for making money . . . forget them."

Jan had not expected Paul de Witt to humiliate his son before witnesses. Embarrassed, he turned away as his cousin left the office in disgrace. He wanted to take him aside and console him, but no doubt the best course was to leave him alone.

Sam returned to his own office. He slumped into his chair. In a fit of rage he kicked the wall until his foot hurt. Up to now he had resented Jan, had been jealous of his cleverness, his charm, his freedom. But now his cousin had deceived him by not telling him what he was doing in the land market. He had set out to trick him, to make him look foolish. And he had succeeded.

A deeper emotion displaced Sam's negative feelings about his cousin. Hatred.

4

Trials and Riots

1732–1747

COLONEL WILLIAM COSBY STEPPED FROM THE
ship, followed by his wife, two daughters, and a small dog
on a ribbon leash. Most of the leading citizens were on
hand to greet the new representative of the king. Charles
Goelet was there, as well as Paul de Witt, assorted
Brevoorts, Van Cortlandts, Livingstons, Morrises, Beekmans, and the head of the city council, the elderly Rip
Van Dam. He had been acting governor for nine months
in the absence of Sir William Montgomerie, who had returned to England for reasons of health.

Jan stood to the side with Edward Goelet and Marie
Therese Bache. Like many other young people, they
greeted their new governor with a certain cynicism. None
of the other governors in their experience had been above
corruption. Why should this one be any different?

Van Dam began. "Welcome to these shores, your—"

"Speak when you're spoken to," Cosby roared in the
dignified old man's face. He glared about at the others.
"Who's Goelet?"

"I am, your Excellency."

"You've been acting as city treasurer?"

"Yes."

"Good. I want to speak to you about my back pay."

"Back pay?" Goelet replied, mystified. "I assumed
your Excellency's pay would start when you arrived today."

"Well, you assumed wrong," the governor said. "Mont-

265

gomerie's been gone for nine months. My pay starts the day he left."

Cosby turned back to Van Dam. "You acted in Montgomerie's place?"

"Yes, of course, but—"

"Then I hold you responsible for getting me the money," the governor said, and he turned to his wife. "Come, m'dear, let's see what these colonials call a governor's palace."

He walked stiffly away; a short, florid-faced man with an air of grand self-importance. His wife and daughters affected his airs. The beribboned dog trotted pertly after them, his little black nose held high in the air.

"God save us," Jan said in a low voice to Marie Therese.

"The dog seems nice enough," she replied.

"And he'd probably make a better governor than Cosby," Edward said. "At least he didn't ask for any money."

"I believe this Cosby will turn out as badly as some of our other governors. No offense intended," Jan said, deliberately avoiding Marie Therese's eyes.

"Any particular governor in mind?" she asked.

"Yes, of course. Now what was his name," Jan said, looking upward and snapping his fingers. "Benjamin . . . Benjamin . . ."

"Fletcher," Edward said.

Marie Therese pouted. "That's not fair."

"Of course, I forgot," Jan said. "Benjamin Fletcher was your mother's father, which makes him—"

"Your grandfather," Edward said triumphantly.

"Yes, that would be the relationship," Jan concluded.

Marie Therese tried to keep the smile from forming on her lips, but failed. "Old Ben *was* a rascal, wasn't he?"

Jan playfully put his arm about her shoulder. "Let's hope some of his rascality's been passed along to you."

As they walked away from the dock, Jan became serious. "We can laugh about it, but when a governor's first act is extortion, I think the word *bribe* is going to be very popular around here."

The people of New York soon learned the truth of Jan's prophecy. Bribery became a way of life, much as it had been in the old days under the Dutch rule of Willem

Kieft and the English rule of Benjamin Fletcher. But Kieft and Fletcher had been rather modest in their demands; Cosby proved rapacious. Where a hundred pounds would have pleased Fletcher, Cosby demanded two hundred. Kieft had given away hundreds of acres of good land for almost nothing, but Cosby niggled and squeezed every farthing out of a single city lot or zoning ordinance. The men who bribed him moaned and complained. But they still paid, because it was the only way of getting anything done.

And the pettiness: Cosby demanded money for every civic function he performed. If he wore a wig to court, he charged the city a wig rental fee for the day. He insisted that all his food and drink be charged to the city as a business expense. The maids demanded by his wife and daughters were put on the city payroll. If a man came to petition the governor, he was charged a "carpet tax" for the privilege of standing in front of the desk while the representative of the king ridiculed him. If a man failed to pay his property taxes, he was chased from his land by the king's agents and his property sold to the person who offered the largest bribe. If a ship owner complained of the high duty rates, his cargo was impounded and released only after the owner had humbled himself to the governor and paid a sufficient "embargo tax"—a tax that not even the most agile legal minds in the city could find embodied in any law or regulation governing the colony.

Alice de Kuyper sent a dispatch to the London banking house of Twining Brothers, inquiring of the new governor. When the reply arrived aboard a packet, she took it to the de Kuyper offices on Whitehall Street.

"Cosby comes to us from Minorca," she said, "where he was the worst governor they ever had. The people of the island were finally able to get rid of him after he impounded a cargo of snuff worth nine thousand pounds sterling. He pocketed the money without even the pretense of giving a shilling to the Crown. The snuff, unfortunately for him, belonged to a peer who had great influence at the court. King George was forced to recall him. But now, do you think he paid the money back? Oh, no. He took his family on a grand tour of Europe and presumably spent the entire nine thousand pounds."

"And the king sends us a man like this?" Jan asked in surprise. "Is he out of his mind?"

"Careful," Charles Goelet warned. "The king has many ears."

"I don't care if he's got a hundred *heads*," Paul de Witt said angrily. "How could he send a felon to be our governor?"

"His wife is the sister of the Earl of Halifax," Alice said. "Our dear governor is not without influence at court."

"We don't stand for it," Paul said.

"There's not much we can do," Charles Goelet said. "He's the king's man, and if we act against him, we act against the king. That's a hanging offense."

"So we don't act directly against him," Jan said. "But there must be ways to fight back."

"Exactly," Alice said. "Do you have anything specific in mind?"

Jan thought for a moment and then answered, measuring his words. "Cosby has raised duty on all cargo. But if cargo doesn't move through the port, then there's no duty to pay. I suggest we find other places to unload our ships."

"Smuggling again," Charles Goelet blustered. "That may have been all right in your father's day, but it's too damned risky today."

"Nonsense," Alice said blithely. "Our ships should bypass New York if possible. Can we arrange to take our cargo elsewhere?"

"If necessary," Paul de Witt said carefully.

"It is necessary," Alice replied.

Jan shrugged. "Then we'll do it."

"And you wanted us to get even more heavily into trade," Paul de Witt said scathingly to Charles Goelet.

"Times change," Goelet replied condescendingly. "I don't know why that should surprise anyone."

De Witt shook his head. Charles Goelet would probably go to his grave claiming he wasn't dead. "All right, then it's agreed," he said. "Our ships will avoid New York."

Sam de Witt spoke for the first time, belatedly echoing Goelet. "Smuggling? Isn't that too dangerous?"

Paul de Witt was about to explode at his son, but Alice interrupted him. "Sam, don't be an old lady," she said, and Sam's face reddened.

"Now, Charlie," she continued, "I want you to find out how we can avoid paying this despicable man any other bribes besides these so-called duties."

"That might not be so easy, and dammit anyway, woman, sometimes the cheapest way to get something is to pay a bribe."

"Don't you 'woman' me, Charlie Goelet, and don't patronize me by explaining bribes. The very house I live in was obtained through a bribe."

"It was?" Jan said in surprise.

Alice nodded her head. "Nicholas Bayard and Colonel de Peyster owned all of Wall Street at one time. It was called De Peyster's Park. We arranged to obtain several lots through a well-placed series of payments. Isn't that right, Charlie?"

"Yes, I arranged them. And since that's the case, why are we suddenly becoming honorable now?"

"It has nothing to do with honor, Charlie. I simply can't stand this man Cosby. I refuse to give him anything that isn't absolutely necessary."

"Sometimes it *is* absolutely necessary."

"Then pay it—but I hope he chokes on it."

Goelet nodded. "I just hope he doesn't choke us first."

For over a year, Governor Cosby hounded the citizens for every possible shilling. The beginning of real trouble was his stepped-up harassment of the elderly Rip Van Dam.

Van Dam was one of the most distinguished citizens of the community. A man who had made a modest living as a merchant, he had been elected to the city council as a gesture of respect by his peers. He had unwillingly assumed the role of interim governor and had filled the post honorably, if without distinction. But now Governor Cosby was insisting that Van Dam personally make good the nine months' salary he claimed was due him. It amounted to nine hundred pounds sterling, and Van Dam refused to pay it. He was not a wealthy man, he complained, simply an old man with a small income. He wished only to live out the rest of his life in peace.

Cosby was not one to be moved by such appeals, but no amount of hounding and shouting moved Van Dam to capitulate, and the governor finally resorted to skulduggery. A summons was issued demanding Van Dam's appearance in court. Although it was never delivered, two waterfront loafers attested they had handed the summons to him and he had accepted it. Naturally, Van Dam failed to show up in court on the appointed day. Cosby ordered the old man held in contempt and had his property confiscated.

The members of the council and Van Dam's many other friends were outraged. They posted the bail, and the old man went into hiding in his own house.

Alice de Kuyper Livingston decided it was time for the full story to be published in the newspaper, so everyone would know of the governor's perfidy. A published account would also make a suitable document to send back to the right people in London.

Jan and Edward Goelet went to the printing shop of William Bradford, the publisher of the New York *Gazette*. Bradford refused to touch the story. He was afraid of Cosby and wanted no trouble with the authorities. He ordered Jan and Edward out of his shop. And when the young men didn't go quickly enough, he flew into a rage.

"Get out! Get out! You'll not involve me in any treason against the king!"

"We're not talking about the king," Jan said. "We're talking about the governor—"

"This fool Cosby," Edward said angrily.

"No man who calls the king's governor a fool is a loyal citizen," Bradford said, his chin jutting forth. "Perhaps I shall see the governor hears of this."

"You bloody bastard!" Edward shouted. "Do that and I'll wring your chicken neck!"

He started toward the printer, but Jan restrained him. "Fighting isn't the answer," he said, and then turned to Bradford and willed himself to sound as pleasant as possible. "Can you suggest another printer?"

"Not to print lies."

"Maybe you're right," Jan said mildly. "We'll give it more thought."

The printer grumbled and stepped back inside his shop, slamming the door after him.

The cousins walked back to Wall Street, Edward fuming. "Why didn't you let me break his neck?"

"Then Cosby would hang you, and how would that solve the problem? Anyway, I knew we'd get nowhere after his first outburst."

"You acted like a mouse. If I didn't know better, I'd say that you were afraid of him."

"I hope that's what he thinks. I doubt he'll bother reporting us if he thinks we're scared. Why should we give ourselves away before we've even begun?"

Edward looked at his cousin and then shook his head. "I suppose you're right, but I'd love to go back and punch him in the mouth."

"And ruin everything."

"You're missing half the fun of life," Edward complained.

They arrived back at the house on Wall Street and found Alice with a distinguished guest, Lewis Morris, whose family owned the estates of Morrisania, across the Harlem River in Westchester.

Morris was the former chief justice of New York. Cosby had ordered him to confiscate Van Dam's property. Justice Morris had refused and was immediately replaced by one of the governor's cronies, James de Lancey.

"Alice has told me of your plans to publish the story of what Cosby is doing to Van Dam," Morris said. "I came to offer my services to help write the truth."

"Bradford won't print it," Jan said.

"I might have known," Morris said, downing his dram of gin. "He's nothing but a . . ." he said, and faltered.

"Son of a bitch," Alice said. "Don't worry about your language on my account. Sometimes swearing is good for a man. And for a woman too."

Morris laughed. "My dear lady, from this moment on I will cease to mind my tongue for your sake."

"The *Gazette* is the only newspaper in New York," Edward said glumly.

"Maybe it's time we had another one," Jan suggested.

"Exactly," Alice said. "Boston has more than one. So does Philadelphia. Why shouldn't we?"

"There's a printer over on Broad Street," Edward said. "A German, I think. John Peter Zenger."

"Everybody calls him Peter," Jan said.

"How's his English?" Morris asked.

"What difference does that make? We'll write and he'll print," Alice said.

"Print a newspaper?" Peter Zenger asked in surprise as the four visitors surrounded him in the middle of his shop. "But why?"

"Because New York needs a voice of protest against Governor Cosby," Alice said.

"It's our duty to tell the people of all the corruption," Lewis Morris added.

"I certainly must agree with you about the governor. But why me? Why not an Englishman?"

"We can't find one with guts," Jan said. "Or brains."

Zenger scratched his head. "I speak English, but as probably you can tell, perfect it is not."

"We can understand every word you say."

"Talking is one thing, printing another."

As Zenger brought up argument after argument, the visitors answered each one and brought up further reasons why he should print the newspaper.

Zenger was intrigued, but cautious. He had a good life and did not want to disrupt it. Born in Germany, he had lived five years in the United Netherlands and had come to New York in 1710 in the middle of a typhus epidemic. After his first tough, raw years in the New World, he had moved on to easier days—first as an apprentice to William Bradford, and now as owner of his own print shop. Why should he risk throwing all this away? But in the end, the others' enthusiasm sparked his own and wore down his resistance.

"All right, all right," he said, waving his hands and walking about the room. "But you can see my operation is a very small one, and so also the newspaper must be small."

"One sheet, printed on both sides and folded to make four pages. Can you do that?" Jan asked.

"That and no more. All my other printing still I must do," Zenger said, pointing toward a stack of paper. "Mostly in Dutch and German for people who have supported me for years. I cannot forget them."

"No one's asking you to forget your old customers. You'll print the—" Alice stopped and turned to the others. "What's the name of our newspaper?"

"The *Journal*," Edward suggested. "The *Daily Journal?*"

Zenger shook his head. "It is impossible for me to print it every day. Once a week is the most I can perform."

"Then 'Journal' is out," the erudite Morris said. "The word means 'daily' in French."

"Nonsense, who cares about the French," Alice said. "We'll call it the *Weekly Journal.*"

"And if any Frenchman objects," Jan said wryly, "we'll simply shoot him."

The *Weekly Journal* printed its first edition. It consisted of a long, documented attack on Governor Cosby.

The *Weekly Journal* was an instant success. The first day of publication brought hundreds of people to the shop, each with a penny in hand, eager to read of the misdoings of their governor.

Jan brought his uncle to Zenger's shop. After glancing through his copy of the *Journal*, Paul de Witt looked up at his nephew. "I think you're out of your mind."

"It's nothing but the truth."

"You're dealing with a lunatic. There's no telling what he'll do."

"Maybe he'll learn to have better manners."

"Or worse ones," de Witt said quietly.

"The articles are unsigned," Jan said. "Who is the governor going to attack?"

"He can certainly find out where the paper is being printed."

"Let him. Zenger will claim he doesn't know who wrote it. He'll say a stranger came to him with a printing job, so he printed it. It's not his fault what the article says."

De Witt shook his head. "If you believe that, you're as much of a madman as Cosby."

As the *Weekly Journal* continued to print its articles against Governor Cosby, everyone expected a strong reaction. It was not forthcoming.

The reason was simple enough: the governor couldn't read well and chose to leave this profitless activity to others. His wife and daughters couldn't read at all. The governor's men who read the *Journal* hadn't the courage to bring the attacks to Cosby's attention, because he was as irascible and unpredictable as he was greedy, and no one wanted to be the bearer of bad news. The governor remained unaware that New York's second newspaper spent most of its pages attacking him.

But others were not so silent about what was happening.

"This has to stop!" Charles Goelet roared at his nephew. "You're jeopardizing everything we own. I'm surprised you haven't been hauled off to jail."

"Since when is it a crime to print the truth?" Jan asked.

"When you attack the Crown, it's *always* a crime."

"We're not attacking the Crown, only a corrupt governor."

Charles Goelet was furious, but he could get nowhere with Jan. He took his case to Alice Livingston. "You must stop this meddling immediately," he said, attempting to control his temper better than he had with Jan.

"Meddling? Since when have you become a defender of Cosby?"

"I'm not defending Cosby, merely pointing out that if the governor decides to take offense over these attacks, he could ruin our family."

"Nonsense, the *Journal* prints the facts. Let him take us to court if he wishes."

"Take you to court," Charles Goelet said sarcastically. "Yes, and then what happens? Cosby prefers the charges. His stooge James de Lancey sits on the bench. Who do you think will win?"

"The basis of English law is the recognition of truth," Alice said heatedly.

"The basis of English law, my dear cousin, is the recognition of power. And no one in New York has more power than a governor appointed by the Crown."

"I don't believe an Englishman can be tried and found guilty when no crime has been committed."

"A crime has been committed when the governor *says* it has. What must I do to convince you of that?"

"Nothing, because if that's the truth then I'd prefer to go to the gallows."

Goelet started to leave, but Alice stopped him at the door. "Besides, who knows who writes the articles? They're never signed, except with obvious pseudonyms."

"Everyone knows who writes them."

"But no one can prove it," Alice said firmly, and a livid

Charles Goelet left the house without another word, his head lowered like a bull, his silver-headed walking stick flashing at his side, warning all to stay out of his way.

"Why don't you go have a drink, Charlie?" Alice called after him. "You look like you need one."

Jan and Marie Therese had two seats on the aisle in the theater on Maiden Lane at Pearl Street. Tonight was the opening night of a new English play, *The Recruiting Officer*, and the theater—except for the first two rows in the middle—was filled to overflowing.

It was a new building, the first in the colony built especially for the presentation of plays. The seats were benches of hardwood. If you wanted a cushion, you brought your own. A painting of George I hung on the left side, and George II graced the right wall.

"See the empty seats up front," Jan whispered in Marie Therese's ear. She nodded. "For the governor and the city council," Jan explained. "Cosby's ordered all of them to attend this performance. He doesn't want to sit with ordinary folk."

"Who does he think he is, the king?"

"I doubt he'll think that after tonight."

"Why?"

"Wait and see."

There was a commotion outside the building as a carriage pulled up, accompanied by half a dozen mounted soldiers. As the dust settled, a footman jumped down and opened the coach door nearest the theater. Governor Cosby, dressed in a heavy fur-trimmed coat, stepped down and looked disdainfully at his surroundings.

The brook at Maiden Lane had become the site of the city's tanneries; now it was being transformed into a respectable residential neighborhood, even if it was still a bit far out of town. The governor's nose caught evidence of the tanner's art, and he whipped a perfumed handkerchief to his face. With the other hand he assisted his wife from the carriage. His daughters followed, and the foursome swept into the theater without a glance at the people crowded about the entrance.

"Now the real play begins," Jan whispered as the governor strode to the front row and, with a great deal of rustling of his coat, took his seat.

The theater manager stepped in front of the curtain. He bowed to the governor and signaled for the play to begin. Several attendants dimmed the lights at the back and sides of the theater while another brightened the ones on the stage.

The play began.

An actor dressed in a soldier's tunic walked across the stage, looking about as if seeking something. He smiled when his eyes rested on a sign that confirmed he had reached "The Thrush." The actor went to the wooden bench and table in front of the inn, sat down, and began opening the saddlebag he had been carrying.

There was a loud rustle from the front row, followed by an audible grumble of complaint.

The actor looked down and saw that the source of the commotion was Governor Cosby. He became confused and stared offstage as if appealing for guidance. There was an awkward period of silence, then Cosby began grumbling again, this time louder and more persistently.

This brought the manager back on stage. "Something wrong, m'lord?" he asked.

The governor waved his arm at the empty seats that surrounded the four Cosbys. "Why do you start the play before everyone arrives?"

"My orders were to start when you arrived, m'lord."

Cosby looked at the manager, at the empty seats, and then back toward the manager. He blinked. "Continue," he growled.

The manager smiled and bowed again. He snapped his fingers at the actor and walked into the wings.

The play began again. The unnerved actor tried to pick up where he had left off, and failed. He went offstage and started at the beginning, repeating his entrance and his search for the inn's sign. He was looking in his saddlebag as a second actor came onstage. The latter inquired if it was possible to get a good meal at the inn. The first actor replied that he was a stranger in the area. On business? the other asked. On king's business, the first actor answered smugly, whereupon the second became suitably impressed.

While the play was progressing, the governor was grumbling and fidgeting in his seat, his heavy coat rustling against the wooden bench. Everyone in the audience was

watching the governor and ignoring the play. Finally
Cosby stood up. The actors had been nervously watching
him from the corners of their eyes, and the one who was
speaking now stopped in midsentence.

"Dammit," Cosby shouted. "Where are the members
of the city council? I commanded them to attend this performance!"

There was a long, long silence, and then someone in
the darkened theater laughed.

"Who's laughing?" the governor demanded. "Dammit!
Who's laughing at me? Who?"

Someone else chuckled and was quickly echoed by
another, then laughter erupted in various parts of the theater.

"Lights! Lights!" the governor ranted as he strode the
few feet to the stage.

The frantic manager dispatched attendants to light the
lamps. As the theater brightened, the laughter subsided.
The governor stood in front of the stage, his face purple
with rage. There was another long silence, and then the
governor spoke. He was so angry it was difficult to understand what he was saying.

"I know who was laughing! I know the damned council
did this to make a fool of me. I know who my enemies
are. . . ." He sputtered until he couldn't speak at all, and
finally he stomped toward the door, followed by his wife
and daughters and the anguished theater manager.

Jan laughed until his eyes watered. "You knew this was
going to happen!" Marie Therese said accusingly.

"Of course," he replied. "The council members are fed
up with Cosby. They all agreed not to attend this command performance. I can't wait to read about this in the
Journal."

"And you'll be the one to write the story, won't you?"

Jan smiled at her, and then his attention was diverted as
the manager returned to the stage. He stammered his apologies and ordered the lights dimmed and the play continued. The comic scene with the governor had put the
theatergoers in an excellent mood, and their responsive-
ness brought joy to the actors' hearts.

Afterward, Jan took Marie Therese home. They stood
on the small porch at the entrance, and he put his arms

about her. "Since I can't keep any secrets from you, I might as well marry you."

"That seems as good a reason as any," she said playfully. "Do you have any others?"

"Well, yes, but it's unimportant."

"Tell me."

"I've wanted to marry you ever since the first time I set eyes on you."

"When you were my Indian?"

"Yes."

"I suppose that's when I knew too."

"You wanted nothing to do with me until . . . I swept you off your feet," he said, with a smile of remembrance.

"No, it was the first time, at your aunt's house. I knew who you were the moment I saw you."

"You did?"

"Of course, I had heard all about you and had decided that you might be the husband I was looking for."

"Then why did you act so snooty?"

"I'm glad you know so little about women," she said, placing her hands on the back of his neck. "I won't have to worry about you when you're not home."

"Hey-*up!*"

The wedding guests in the garden behind Whitby Bache's house lost no time in getting out of the way as a drover brought his team through the open gate. They were large, spirited workhorses—three of them, two chestnuts and a roan—and the driver had to struggle to keep them under control. He reached the center of the lawn and halted the team. They stood impatiently, snorting, tossing their heads, and pounding the ground with their forefeet.

James de Kuyper was standing next to his host. Both were dressed in soft, expensive coats, silk shirts with ruffles, and velvet knee breeches. Only an hour ago they had witnessed the joining in marriage of Jan and Marie Therese.

Charles Goelet swaggered up. "Well, where's *your* team?" he asked James.

"On their way," he replied, signaling a man who waited outside the fence. "All set to pay up, Charlie?"

Goelet snorted. "You don't stand a chance."

A murmur of approval swept through the crowd as a pair of matched black horses trotted into the garden. They were magnificent animals, their nostrils flaring as they tossed their heads, their feet stepping high and their bunched muscles rolling easily under sleek hides that shone in the sun. They were taller than the other horses, and heavier, but still it was two against three. The guests began to make wagers, and the odds heavily favored Goelet's team.

James took off his long coat and waistcoat. He untied the silk ruffle around his collar, and undid the top buttons on his shirt. He handed the garments to Goelet. "Hold these, will you, Charlie?"

Goelet mumbled something inarticulate, but took the clothes and stuffed them under his arm.

"Good luck," Bache said.

"Luck!" Goelet exclaimed. "When a man makes a wager as foolish as this he needs more than luck to win!"

A few days earlier he and James had gotten into an argument about horses. Goelet insisted the other was wasting his time trying to breed better horses. "The ones we have are good enough," he said.

"I've bred mine to the point where two of them are probably as strong as just about any three others," James said.

"Ha! Easy enough to say."

"You pick any three you want," James said coldly. "We'll pit them against two of mine."

"That's dumb!"

"You asked me to prove something, Charlie. Are you backing down?" James's voice was as sharp as the edge of a knife.

Goelet recognized the tone and agreed to the contest. "But let's make it interesting," he said. "Let's do it for five hundred pounds."

"All right. The purse goes to Jan and Marie Therese as a wedding present."

And now the contest was about to commence. The excited guests watched from a safe distance as the two teams were backed toward each other and the heavy leather harness traces attached to points opposite one another on a stout iron ring. When either team pulled forward, it would be pulling directly against the other.

James took control of his own team. He looked to see that the boundary stakes were in place and the traces of both teams taut. The first team to pull the other horses a distance of twenty yards would be declared the victor. James looked at Whitby Bache and nodded.

Bache, on whom had been bestowed the dubious honor of being the starter, cleared his throat.

"Get ready . . . *begin!*"

Twenty hooves dug into the ground and five huge bodies heaved against their traces as both drivers shouted their commands. The earth seemed to rumble beneath their feet. Within seconds the team of three began to move forward, dragging the black horses after them.

But James shouted encouragement, and his horses managed to halt their retreat. They struggled and strained, their hooves tearing up the turf and sending showers of dirt toward the cheering spectators. The five animals were locked in a standstill.

As he stood next to Alice Livingston and Charles Goelet, Whitby Bache sourly watched the destruction of his lawn. It had been the pride of his garden—the finest lawn in all New York, as he had been accustomed to bragging—and now it was being churned along their plows. Why, they might as well have brought it along their plows. He shook his head. This entire celebration was beyond him. Being English, he had a sense of restraint, something lacking in his new in-laws. All that damned Dutch blood, he thought. They drank too much, danced too much, spoke in loud voices, and, in general, behaved quite unlike a proper Englishman.

His thoughts were interrupted by Alice. "Too bad about your lawn," she said. At that moment a large clod of grass and dirt flew through the air and landed at Bache's feet.

"Quite all right," he lied.

"If it was my lawn I wouldn't be as calm as you," she said. But then her attention was riveted on James, who was leaning his back against the rear of one of his horses, joining his strength with that of the team. Encouraged, his pair lunged against the traces and began to win ground. The other drover began using his whip, but the blacks continued to move forward. One yard . . . two . . .

three, and then the sweating, straining animals were once again locked in a quivering standstill.

"You're going to lose, Charlie," Alice said.

"The hell I am!"

"Care to bet another five hundred?"

Goelet grimaced. "You're as crazy as your goddamn brother."

"It runs in the family, but what the hell, you're in the family, too. Don't you get a nice warm feeling?" she said turning to Whitby Bache, whose mouth had dropped open at all this profanity. "After all, you're part of our family now, too."

"Yes, Mrs. Livingston . . ."

"Then do you want to bet?"

"Madam, I never bet," he replied stiffly.

"You'll get over it, don't worry," she snapped.

The blacks were straining in their traces, their grunts and groans carrying across the garden, rivers of sweat turning white on their ebony hides. The immense strength that James had bred into them began to tell. While the other horses were beginning to weaken, they were not.

The two people who were the cause of all this celebrating watched the contest from the gazebo at the far end of the garden. Although it was their day, at the moment they were being utterly ignored. Jan took advantage of the situation. He reached over and grabbed a piece of Marie Therese's right buttock.

"Ouch! Stop that!"

"You're my wife now. I can do anything I want."

Her stern look disappeared, and she giggled. "Later."

Theo Henry sidled up to the groom. "I saw that," he whispered in Jan's ear, delighted at catching him in embarrassment. Theo had not yet forgiven Jan for deserting the ranks of free, unencumbered bachelors.

"Saw what?" Jan asked blandly, not bothering to lower his voice.

"What you did."

"Oh?" Jan turned to Marie Therese. "Theo says he saw what I did."

"What did you see, Theo?" she asked innocently.

Theo was flustered. How had he fallen prey to the very embarrassment he had hoped to cause Jan? "Oh, n-nothing."

"You must have seen *something*," Marie Therese persisted, giving Jan a gentle poke in the ribs.

Theo pretended a sudden overwhelming interest in the contest between the horses.

As a matter of fact, the only people at the reception, guests and servants alike, who weren't interested in the contest were Edward Goelet and Dora Van Cortlandt. They were hidden behind the rosebushes, plastered against one another and kissing passionately. His hands began to explore her body. She responded to his touch, her body snuggling tighter against his, her hands stroking the back of his neck, her lips locked with his. Edward's hands became bolder, more exploratory. A soft moan came from his throat. Suddenly she pulled away.

"What's the matter?" he asked in bewilderment.

There was a frightened look in Dora's eyes. "We . . . we don't know what might happen."

"I wouldn't let anything happen to you."

She seemed so tiny and vulnerable, as if lost in a dangerous place. He wanted to protect her, to reassure her that nothing was going to happen. He put his arm about her and hugged her.

"I'm glad you're strong," she said in a tiny voice. "I trust you to keep us from making mistakes."

A sudden surge in the cheering coming from the lawn invaded their privacy. "What's going on out there?" he wondered aloud.

The black team had finally broken the spirit and the strength of the other and was dragging it toward the wooden stakes. The latter could take no more punishment; still in their traces and stumbling over their own legs, the three horses were being dragged by an irresistible force.

It was over, and James controlled his team long enough for his drover to leap in and unlock the harness lines from the iron ring.

The crowd cheered as James patted his horses and then turned them over to the drover, who took them out of the garden.

"Well, Charlie," James said, his face covered with dirt and sweat, the sleeves of his shirt torn, his velvet breeches beyond repair. "It was a fair contest, no?"

Goelet wasn't the most gracious of losers but he tried his best. "Fair, James. Congratulations."

"Look at my lawn," Whitby Bache complained. "I mean, there *isn't* any lawn anymore."

"I'll have a dozen men here in the morning," James said. "They'll resod it with a new type of grass I've been developing. The lawn will be better than ever."

"How long will it take to look good again?"

"The sod will have full-grown grass," James explained. "By tomorrow night you'll never know this happened."

"Yes? Well, indeed," Bache said, suddenly buoyed. "Say, why don't we go have a drink?"

The excitement was over.

Jan climbed on top of a table and called for silence. "I propose a toast," he said, holding up his glass.

"To the *Weekly Journal,* and may it continue to print the truth about Governor Cosby!"

It was an audacious toast to make in front of so many people, and there was a moment of hushed silence; but then someone picked up the cry "To the *Journal!*" and the other guests joined in the brazen affront to their governor.

"Next we'll be hearing toasts for the king of France," Sam de Witt complained.

"Oh, don't be such a grump!"

Sam almost jumped out of his skin as the voice barked in his ear. He whirled to face Alice.

"Sometimes, Sam, I wonder what goes on in that brain of yours. You know our family's committed to supporting the newspaper."

"We can get into trouble—"

"We can get into trouble by breathing. Why don't you relax and have a good time? Get drunk, you might find it interesting."

Passing by, Paul de Witt overheard this last bit of advice. "That's a good idea, why don't you?" he called to his son.

"Why don't I what?"

"Get drunk," Paul said. He looked at Alice. "Occasionally, my dear, you do have a good idea. And on special occasions, even a fine idea."

"See, the whole family's behind you, Sam," Alice said as she turned and walked away.

Sam was seething. The whole family was *against* him, and that was the truth of the matter. Every last one of them—always praising Jan and picking on him. Somehow he'd show them! He'd get revenge!

And then a practical idea of *how* to get revenge occurred to him.

Could the rumor he had heard be true? That Governor Cosby had not reacted to the *Journal*'s attacks because he had never read them and all the people around him were afraid to open their mouths?

It seemed incredible, but it almost had to be the answer. Cosby was not the man to stand idly by and suffer *lèse majesté*.

But what if someone were to tell him?

It had to be done in secret, of course, because if the family ever found out it was him who had told—Christ! what hell there'd be to pay!

But if handled correctly, what could go wrong? It would serve them right if the governor jumped all over the family.

Sam felt a great deal better now that he had a plan of action. He walked over to one of the temporary bars at the end of the garden and got himself a tall glass of beer mixed with rum. He took a deep swallow, and then his eyes met Jan's.

"Health to you, Sam," Jan said, raising his glass mug in a toast.

"And to you, dear cousin," Sam replied silkily. Now he could afford to be generous. "And to your lovely bride."

Marie Therese smiled back, but when Sam had walked out of earshot, she turned and whispered to her new husband. "What's he so happy about?"

"He had a pleasant day yesterday," Jan replied. "He robbed three widows and cheated six orphans out of their property."

"That's an awful thing to say," Marie Therese said, and then giggled. "But probably the truth."

"Sam is the sort of person who keeps a dog so he can kick it," Jan confided.

"I am the same way with husbands."

Jan smiled and allowed his hand to creep lower. He reached out and grabbed his wife's behind again. She let out a little yelp, which startled people near by. Her face turned red as her mother gave her a questioning look. "Someone stepped on my toe," she lied.

"What an interesting place to have a toe," Jan said in a low voice that only she could hear.

Sam de Witt hurried across the grass at Bowling Green. Only two years old, the park had been given to the people of New York through the efforts of James de Kuyper and a few of his friends. They had bought the land, given it to the city, and then arranged to have it rented back as a park for the sum of one peppercorn a year. Sam passed the small bronze plaque attesting to these facts, but did not see it. His mind was on the coming meeting.

He arrived at the governor's residence near Trinity Church, assured himself that he had not been observed, and entered between the columns that stood on either side of the doorway. An officer of the guard recognized him and politely asked his business.

Several minutes later he was ushered into the governor's office. Cosby sat behind his desk. They were not strangers to one another. Sam had been in this room several times before when it had been necessary to buy the governor's assistance on matters of business.

"What is it, de Witt?" the governor asked pleasantly. He had no doubt that Sam was again petitioning for a favor, in which case a bit more gold would be added to his coffers. It was the sort of transaction that made the governor's morning more amiable.

Sam reached into the pocket of his coat and withdrew a recent edition of Zenger's newspaper. "I've come about the articles in the *Weekly Journal,* Your Lordship."

Cosby looked blankly at the newspaper. "Articles? What articles?"

Indeed, Sam thought: the man hadn't the slightest clue about what was being printed. "Have you read them, m'lord?"

Cosby waved his hand. "No, no, I'm much too busy to read these local papers."

Sam placed the newspaper on the desk and smoothed his hand over the sheet. "As a loyal subject, I feel it my duty to point out the unfavorable nature of articles such as this one."

The governor looked down at the newspaper, squinted, and became irritated. "Yes, yes. Ah, what does it say?"

So this too was true, Sam thought: the governor

couldn't read, or, if he could, did it so badly it was too much of an effort. "Shall I summarize it for you, m'lord?"

"Yes, yes, that'll save me the time spent in reading."

"It says, m'lord, that you are extorting money from Rip Van Dam. It says that you are using the power of your office to force Van Dam to pay you money he does not owe."

"What!"

Sam took another edition of the slim *Journal* from his pocket. "This issue claims you accept bribes. It goes on like this week after week, Your Lordship—scurrilous attacks against you and the government."

"Why haven't I been informed of this before?" the governor asked in a voice choked with rage. "Is there no one loyal to the Crown?"

Sam started to speak, but the governor stormed to the door and shouted at the guard to fetch Judge de Lancey. He left the door open and turned back to Sam. "If you think you're going to get away with this . . ."

"But, Your Lordship," Sam protested, "it was I who pointed out what's been happening."

Cosby stopped, and his face twitched as he pondered this fact. He suddenly nodded his head. "Of course, de Witt, of course. I've never questioned your loyalty."

"Perhaps, then, you would grant me a small favor, m'lord?"

"Yes?"

"Many people in the colony would not understand if they learned it was I who brought these articles to your attention."

"What are you asking?"

"That my connection with this matter be . . . forgotten."

An ugly look crossed the governor's face. He finally grunted. "As you wish."

"Thank you, Your Lordship."

James de Lancey came through the open door, breathless from having run from the other end of the building. "Yes, Governor?"

Cosby picked up one of the newspapers and waved it in the air. "I've just learned we have a newspaper publishing treason. Why has no one brought it to my attention?"

De Lancey's face reddened. "We thought it would only disturb Your Lordship," he stammered.

"Disturb Your Lordship," Cosby mimicked. "It disturbs His Lordship a great deal more that the scoundrels who print this trash are still at liberty. What I want to know now is, who is responsible?"

"The printer is a man named John Peter Zenger," de Lancey said.

"He's the printer, you say, but is he also the author?"

"He's a German," de Lancey began cautiously.

"Well?"

"Probably not, m'lord," de Lancey said. "Zenger doesn't have the education to write such pieces. It would seem there are others involved."

"Who are they?"

De Lancey shook his head. "I don't know, sir. The articles are always signed with names like Cato, Brutus . . . Socrates."

"Brutus," the governor mumbled, and then he turned and looked at Sam de Witt. "Do you have any idea who writes this treason?"

Sam could feel the perspiration beading up on his chin. He wanted to blurt out his cousin's name, but knew that would be going too far. "No, m'lord," he said in a very subdued voice. "I have no idea at all."

"Well, we'll see about this," the governor said angrily. "I won't rest until I find out who's behind this plot."

I hope you do, Sam thought silently, I hope you do. Only it won't be on my head; thank God for that. The family will never be able to say I gave you their names.

"Have this Zenger fellow arrested," Cosby said to Justice de Lancey.

"I'll issue the order at once," de Lancey said as he backed away toward the door.

"And find all the issues of this rag," Cosby said, tearing the copy of the *Journal* into shreds. "Burn them."

De Lancey fled from the room as the governor began pacing back and forth, mumbling to himself, threatening mayhem to anyone connected with the newspaper. Sam thought it appropriate to make his exit, and he edged toward the door.

"If you bring me any more bad news like this," Cosby suddenly shouted at him, "I'll throw you in prison, too!"

Sam almost ran from the building. He didn't relax his pace until he reached the park at Bowling Green. There he stopped, he took off his hat, and wiped his brow. Then he smiled, plopped the hat back on his head, and headed for his office on Whitehall Street.

Zenger's arrest did not come quite as easily as the governor wished. When Judge de Lancey issued the order, it became a subject of heated argument in the chamber of the city council. It specified that the public hangman be the one to arrest Zenger, but the council refused to authorize the hangman to carry out the order.

Of all the councilmen, Charles Goelet was the loudest and most argumentative. Although he had been against the *Journal* from the beginning, he also realized members of his own family could be put in jeopardy. Therefore he became one of the governor's stubbornest opponents.

"What right does anyone, even the governor, have to issue orders to someone in the service of the council?" he asked. "This council's rights are guaranteed in a charter signed by the king. Does Governor Cosby wish us to believe he is a higher authority than our sovereign in England?"

Furious debate followed. Cosby's lackeys argued that any order of the governor was also an order of the king, and must be obeyed; but a majority of the members aligned themselves with Charles Goelet. Two days of acrimonious debate followed, during which time, of course, neither was Zenger arrested nor were his newspapers destroyed.

Finally the governor ordered the sheriff to carry out the order. This unhappy man took his black slave to Zenger's shop and informed the printer that his stock of newspapers must be burned.

The sheriff and the printer stood at the door of the shop as the slave started a fire and dumped load after load of newspapers on it.

"I'm sorry to do this, Zenger," the sheriff said. "Mind you, it's none of my doing. I'm only following orders."

Zenger shrugged and watched as the latest edition of his *Journal* went up in flames. When the last paper was on the pyre, he turned to the sheriff. "And now I suppose you must take me to jail?"

"No," the sheriff said in surprise. "I've no authority to do that. If Cosby wants you there, he'll have to find someone else to arrest you."

That night a secret meeting was held at Alice's house. Jan, Marie Therese, Lewis Morris, and Peter Zenger were there.

The practical Lewis Morris opened the discussion. "Let's get right to the point. What do we do now?"

"I say we continue to print the *Journal*," Alice said.

"Won't the sheriff just come back and burn it?" Marie Therese asked.

"Unless we print from a new location," Jan said. "A secret one."

"A good idea," Lewis Morris said. "Do you have any particular place in mind?"

Jan smiled. "Last week I bought the new theater on Maiden Lane. The back part of the cellar would be the perfect place to set up a press. With performances regularly being held in the theater above, who would suspect something else was going on down below?"

"Let's get the press moved there tonight," Zenger said, settling the issue. "We'll need several men who can be trusted to keep a secret."

Jan nodded in agreement. "There's myself, and Lewis," he said. "Ned Goelet can be trusted, and Aaron Gerait."

Alice rapped her knuckles on the table. "That should be enough. Marie Therese and I can act as lookouts. We don't want any of Cosby's spies finding out what we're doing."

The printing press was taken from Zenger's shop in the middle of the night. Placed in a cart and covered with canvas sailcloth, it made the short journey from lower Broad Street to Maiden Lane without incident.

The way was deserted except for a few drunks, either homeless or afraid to go home. The streets were far safer than they had been a dozen years ago, Jan reflected. Recent governors—even Cosby—had increased the number of watchmen, and their orders were to treat offenders roughly. Gradually the numbers of footpads and holdup men had declined, and the streets of New York were now far safer than those of the larger cities of London or Paris.

The cart was unloaded and the press taken below to the cellar of the theater.

"Thanks, Aaron," Jan said to the sweating black man, who had almost single-handedly carried the press to the cellar.

"So you're the one after Cosby," Aaron said with a wide grin. "You sure don't pick easy fights."

"No fun winning the easy ones."

"You be careful now," Aaron said, suddenly becoming serious. "I sometimes do favors for the governor's slaves. They tell me things."

"Things?"

"Things about land sales, trading deals. Sometimes I profit from the information, and part of the money I make goes back to my friends. But—"

Jan whistled in appreciation. "Maybe we can get together on some of these ventures. I've some extra capital to invest."

"Why not," the black man said with a shrug. "But what my friends also tell me is that this man Cosby is crazy and mean."

"I know that," Jan said testily. "Why do you think I've been writing all these newspaper articles?"

"Well, I still think maybe you should be a little more careful. But if there's anything I can do to help, ask."

Jan thought over the offer for a moment, and then he had an idea.

"There is one question I'd like to resolve. How did Cosby finally discover what was being printed in the *Journal?*"

"You think somebody you know told him?"

"If that *is* what happened, we'd be safer knowing about it than not."

Aaron nodded. "I'll ask around."

"I'll pay twenty pounds."

"This one is on me," Aaron said.

They left the theater in pairs to avoid attracting any attention to themselves. Jan and Marie Therese walked home together.

"What happens when they arrest Zenger?" she asked.

"His wife knows how to operate the press."

"Maybe it won't come to that. After all, they haven't arrested him yet."

"A technicality," Jan assured her. "Cosby will be foaming at the mouth until he has Zenger behind bars."

"I'll help his wife," Marie Therese said. "If she can learn to run a press, so can I."

Jan was naked in bed, emptying his mind of thoughts, preparing himself to make love to his wife. He imagined he was on a cloud, floating weightless through a sea of formless white puffs. Beyond the clouds was a deep blue; all was peaceful, quiet. His muscles relaxed, and then his flesh began to tingle. A giddiness swept over him, and he closed his eyes and waited.

As Marie Therese undid her stockings, she imagined the touch of Jan's fingertips on her thighs. She lifted her shift slowly over her breasts and thought of how the nipples would harden when he held them between his fingers and gently squeezed. By the time she was undressed, her body was quivering with anticipation.

But neither was in a hurry; they had learned that the more time they took, the greater their pleasure.

She slipped under the coverlet and was beside him. They felt the heat increase, filling the space between them. His hand crossed this space and touched her leg above the knee. His fingers moved lightly upward until they came to the softer flesh that was the beginning of her belly. He stopped and withdrew his hand.

She reached out and found his chin. Ever so slowly, the fingers moved down his neck, tracing a line across his chest, advancing lower and lower until they came to the beginnings of the thatch of coarse hair. The fingers stopped and rested near the rod of flesh that was becoming harder.

Neither moved for a few moments; and then it was his turn to excite her.

The night had only begun to unfold.

Two days later the governor himself appeared in the chamber of the city council and forced Judge de Lancey's order to a favorable vote by threatening to disband the council. The members could do nothing but go along with the governor. Two soldiers were sent to Zenger's shop to arrest the printer.

Jan visited the dark and dingy jail later in the day. The prisoner and his visitor were forced to talk through a small hole in the middle of the heavy oak door, and Jan never actually saw Zenger.

"We're going to get you two of the best lawyers in the city," he assured the printer. "James Alexander and William Smith. They're both friends of Lewis Morris and have agreed to take the case."

"With James de Lancey as the judge, I think I will not have much of a chance, Jan, no matter who is my lawyer," Zenger said.

"If worst comes to worst, I intend to step forward and identify myself as the writer," Jan said.

"Then there will be two of us in trouble."

"No. The blame is mine. After all, you were only a printer getting paid to do some work."

"In the meantime," Jan said, swiftly changing the subject before Zenger could demur, "we've got another edition of the *Journal* to get to press."

"If my wife has any problems with the machine, send her to me. I think I can explain to her how to keep it working."

"Good man," Jan said. "In the meantime is there anything I can get you? Paper? Books?"

"Send over some good German wurst," Zenger said. "Being in jail makes a man hungry."

The two lawyers retained for Zenger spent weeks sifting through all the material. Every accusation printed in the *Weekly Journal* was painstakingly checked for accuracy. The governor was basing his case on libel; and if it could be proved that nothing libelous had been printed, it didn't seem that the Crown had much of a case. Still, they were dealing with an erratic man and they didn't want to leave anything to chance.

"Even though we're in the right," Alexander said to his partner, "Cosby may win in court no matter what we do."

William Smith shrugged. "I don't see that there's much we can do about it."

"What if there wasn't any court?"

"What do you mean?"

"Hear me out," Alexander said, and during the course

of the next hour the two lawyers devised their strategy for the preliminary hearing.

The bailiff called the court to order, and Judge de Lancey, weighted down by his gown and wig, entered the room and made his way to the bench. The two lesser judges entered and took their places beside the chief justice.

The room was packed, mostly with people who secretly sided with the printer. It didn't pay to be too outspoken against the governor, as several men had already discovered. One of them was Francis Beekman, Janet Beekman de Witt's younger brother and a good friend of Rip Van Dam. He had testified against the governor in the city council chamber. His actions were reported to Cosby, and Beekman suddenly found the doors of his soft-goods shop shuttered. It appeared there was a technicality about his business license. Normally this would have been a routine affair, and a merchant would have had no trouble renewing his license by paying a small fine. In this case, however, the fine was refused, and Beekman's doors remained closed. The man found himself without his normal means of making a living.

The word of such harassments spread, and most men were unwilling to risk sustaining a similar blow.

Judge de Lancey sat down, and the room was filled with the sound of chairs and benches scraping the floor. Peter Zenger was brought in and placed on the dock.

"Oyez! Oyez!" the bailiff intoned, and then read the charges placed against John Peter Zenger by Governor Cosby.

"By Your Lordship's leave," William Smith said, rising to his feet.

"Yes, what is it?" Judge de Lancey asked, a bit peevishly, as he had no great affection for this case. As far as he was concerned, it was already decided. The governor was preferring the charges, and that was enough.

"A point of order about the constitution of this court."

"Yes, yes?"

"It is the contention of the defense that this court is not duly appointed and is therefore unauthorized to dispense the king's justice."

A heavy silence fell over the room. The chief justice

blinked and glanced at his two colleagues behind the
bench. He turned back to William Smith. "What nonsense
is this? What are you talking about?"

Smith held up a piece of paper. He walked forward and
placed it in front of de Lancey. "It is the contention of
the defense that the rightful Chief Justice of New York is
Lewis Morris. We claim he was illegally removed from the
bench by Governor Cosby. The appointment of a chief
justice is made by the king and can be rescinded only by a
new decree from that sovereign lord."

The court was suddenly filled with a hundred voices,
whispering, babbling, discussing this incredible diversion
on the part of the defense.

De Lancey banged his gavel several times before there
was quiet. "Are you telling me I have no right to be
here?" he asked angrily.

Smith bowed politely. "The true Chief Justice of New
York is there," he said, pointing toward Lewis Morris,
who sat in one of the front rows between Alice and Jan.
"If he may be permitted to resume his place on the bench,
the defense will proceed with the matter at hand."

"And if he is not permitted to take the bench?" de Lancey asked in smoldering tones.

Smith picked up another paper from the table at his
side. "Then we would file a petition for the dismissal of
this illegally established court."

He walked back to the judge and handed over the paper. De Lancey scanned it quickly and looked up. "This
is an outrage. I'll hold you in contempt of court."

"What court?" Smith asked blandly. "Until this petition
is ruled upon, there can be no other business discussed
here. Peter Zenger cannot stand trial in a court that is not
a court."

James de Lancey looked toward the other two justices
in confusion. He was a weak man who could stand his
ground only if absolutely certain of his position. But now
his authority was being questioned, and he wavered.

The other two judges had been friends of Lewis Morris, but, for fear of their own positions, had remained silent at his dismissal. They were secretly pleased by this
turn of events.

"What do you think?" de Lancey whispered, and his

head swiveled back and forth between his two associates.

"I'm not sure of the law on this matter," one of them whispered in de Lancey's ear. "But I suspect the man may have a point."

De Lancy looked to the other. "Perhaps our colleague is correct," the judge said, adding to the chief justice's confusion.

De Lancey's mind filled with panic. If he wasn't going to get any help from his associates, then he decided he wasn't going to fight the battle. "This matter will be brought to the governor for a ruling," he announced. He banged his gavel, gathered his robes, and scurried out of the courtroom.

Lewis Morris watched from his hard wooden seat. He turned to Jan and shook his head. "I'm sorry I let Smith take this course of action."

"Why?"

"It's too dangerous. Who knows what Cosby's reaction will be?"

"The worst he can do is to keep de Lancey on the bench."

Lewis Morris remained unconvinced. "I'm afraid you really don't understand how vindictive he can be."

They walked out of the courtroom together. "Well, I must be getting to the theater," Jan said. "This calls for a special edition of the *Journal*."

"That's the last of them, Ned." Jan said, handing a bundle of newspapers to Edward Goelet. They had worked all night to write and print this edition.

"I'll get these distributed near Whitehall Street," Edward said. He pointed toward a bundle of tied-up newspapers on the bench. "What about that lot?"

"I'm taking them to a packet bound for Albany. I'm sure our northern cousins will be interested in what's going on down here."

"Don't get caught."

Jan chuckled. "I could give you the same advice about Dora Van Cortlandt."

Edward attempted a weak smile, and Jan caught the troubled look on his cousin's face. "Of course," he said, "I've been assuming that you *want* to get caught."

"To tell you the truth, I'm beginning to have second thoughts about her."

This was news to Jan. "What's wrong?"

Edward was uncomfortable. "It's hard to put into words; it's more of a feeling. You know how gentle she is, and how you always want to protect her?"

Jan shrugged. "I've never felt exactly that way, but I know what you mean. If you insulted Aunt Alice or Marie Therese, they'd haul off and sock you in the jaw. Dora would cry."

"Yeah—but then again, she's not always like that. When she makes up her mind about some things, she can be harder to deal with than Alice."

Jan whistled. "Dora Van Cortlandt?"

"Crazy, huh? But it's true."

"But what's wrong with that? So the girl turns out to have a mind of her own, why should that bother you?"

"That's the problem. It shouldn't bother me, but it does. I'm confused about her."

"Sounds like a case of love to me. Now I want her, now I don't. Don't worry, you'll get over it," Jan said, picking up the bundle of newspapers.

He came up from the cellar and entered the empty hall of the Maiden Lane theater. He paused at the door before stepping outside. It was the hour after dawn, and a few early risers could be seen beginning the work of the day. No one paid any attention to the young man with the bundle as he walked quickly toward the dock at Coenties Slip.

He hid himself in a doorway as two city guards passed by and continued on their way down the street. All guards were under direct orders from the governor to confiscate and burn all copies of the *Journal*. Several men caught with the paper had already been arrested, but since they had obviously been doing nothing more than reading it, Cosby had let them off with light fines. Jan wasn't certain what would happen to someone caught with an entire bundle, and if he could help it, he wasn't going to be the one to find out.

The guards rounded the corner, and Jan continued on his way. He cautiously approached the packet at the dock, looking for the captain, who had promised to take the newspapers north. The deck of the ship was ominously quiet. An early morning fog rolled across the docks.

"Hey you! Stop!" a voice commanded. Jan whirled about and saw the half-obscured figures of the two city guards coming toward him. He realized they must have doubled back from the other street as they made their rounds of the docks.

If he couldn't see them clearly because of the heavy fog, then they couldn't recognize him, he reasoned. He ran down the quay, away from the guards and toward a large barque that was ready to take on cargo piled on the dock. Jan darted in and out among the boxes, crates, and barrels, hearing the curses of his pursuers as they made their way through the maze.

He knew he couldn't keep going down the dock. He'd eventually come to the end, and capture would be certain. He darted up the gangplank to the barque and found himself in the middle of another jumble of boxes and crates. A few sailors, bundled in heavy blankets, were asleep on the deck. He looked around for an escape route and saw a rope ladder hanging over the railing on the side of the ship away from the dock. He went to it and peered over the side. A small rowboat was tied to the ship at the foot of the ladder.

The two guards were coming up the gangplank, making a great racket as they ran, and the sleeping sailors were beginning to stir. There didn't seem to be any alternative. Jan went down the ladder to the rowboat. As his head disappeared below the railing, the two guards came aboard on the other side.

"Where'd 'e go?"

"Who's makin' all the racket?" complained one of the sailors, who was wiping his bloodshot eyes and trying to quiet his fierce hangover.

"The man with the package," the guard demanded. "Where'd 'e go?"

"What man?"

"The one with the bloody package!" the second guard roared.

"Listen 'ere, mate, shut up or I'll put a belayin' pin aside your ear."

"Threatenin' a member of the king's guard, are you?"

"Shut up!"

While the guards and sailors argued, Jan wondered about his next move. He could sit there in the rowboat and wait until the guards left the ship. Unless, of course, he was discovered. This thought sent him searching in the bottom of the boat until he found a pair of oars. He quietly placed them in the swivel locks and found the line that held the rowboat to the barque. He unslipped the knot and waited. If the guards found him, he would drop the line and row away from the barque. The fog was very thick down here on the waterline, and a man couldn't see more than ten or twelve feet. If discovered, he might be able to row away from his pursuers.

The city guards were searching the deck of the barque for signs of the man they had been chasing. They came closer and closer to the railing above Jan's head. For a moment he thought they were going to pass by, but one of them glanced down. "There 'e is!"

Jan dropped the line to the big ship, picked up the oars, and began rowing with all his might. "Stop!" shouted the guard. "Stop, or I'll shoot!"

A few more pulls on the oars and the rowboat was swallowed up in the fog. The guard fired his musket.

"What the 'ell are you firin' at?" the second guard shouted.

" 'E's out there somewhere."

"Let's get down to the end of the dock. That's where 'e must be 'eadin'."

Once he was hidden in the fog, Jan began to row quietly, and blindly, toward the packet that was bound for Albany. He couldn't see any better than his pursuers, but he knew his intended destination and they didn't. As he approached the ship, he could hear the guards running down the dock on the opposite side. One stumbled over a crate and filled the air with curses.

Since the moment the guard had fired his musket, the entire dock area had been in an uproar. The fog augmented the chaos.

Jan felt the bow of the rowboat bump into the seaward side of the packet. "Captain Moran," he called out softly. "Captain Moran."

A sailor's face poked over the top of the deck railing. "Eh? Who's that?"

"Where's the captain?"

A second head appeared at the top of the railing. "I'm Moran, who's down there?"

"Jan de Kuyper. Here's that package we discussed," Jan said, as he tossed the newspaper over the railing. "Better stow it out of sight."

"Aye," the captain said. "And are you the cause of all this ruckus?"

"I'm afraid I am."

"Best be stowin' yourself away somewhere," Captain Moran said, with a friendly grin.

Jan waved and rowed his boat back toward the river. He passed the end of the slip and rowed north until he came to Peck's Slip, where he eased the rowboat alongside. He tied it up, climbed to the top of the dock, and looked around. Nothing seemed to be moving. He smiled as he listened to the shouting and cursing coming from Coenties Slip, to the south.

He took a last look at the rowboat and felt a twinge of guilt about having stolen it from the barque. But then he saw the name of the mother ship painted on the back of the rowboat, and he had no doubt it would find its way back to its owners before the day was out.

A few sailors were gathered at the shore end of the slip, their ears tuned to the sounds downstream. They looked at Jan as he passed.

"What's all the commotion about?"

"Don't know, but I'm glad it's not me, mates," Jan said blandly. He began to whistle as he walked back to the theater on Maiden Lane.

The governor had purposely absented himself from New York on the day of Peter Zenger's preliminary hearing. He had wanted to show how fair he was by not even being in the city when the charges were presented. He returned three days later and was stunned when Judge de Lancey told him what had happened.

"You did *what?*" he screamed.

"Called a recess until I could ask Your Lordship for a ruling," de Lancey repeated, his lower lip trembling and his hands shaking with fright.

"A ruling? You damn fool! I can fire chief justices and I can hire them. Fire and hire! What's to rule about?"

"Well, sir, I wasn't sure, and Zenger's lawyers—"

"Lawyers, eh? What are the names of these meddling fools?"

"One is William Smith, and the other is James Alexander."

"I know them, troublemakers both."

"Oh, yes indeed, they—"

"Issue an order disbarring them for life. Get it to me immediately for my signature."

"Yes, m'lord."

"They'll never stand before a king's bench again. Unless it's to stand trial for treason."

De Lancey coughed nervously. "Does Your Lordship mean they cannot represent Zenger in the coming trial?"

Cosby looked at the judge in disbelief. "Issue the order *immediately*. Disbarred for *life*, d'you hear? From this *moment*."

"Yes, m'lord," de Lancey said, and hurried to leave the presence of the angry governor.

When he returned to his own office, his clerk was raising a cup of tea to his lips.

"Wasting time while on duty, are you?" de Lancey snarled. "Get over here, there's work to be done."

The startled clerk hurriedly put down his cup and came over to the chief justice's desk. "Yes, Your Honor."

"Draft an order disbarring William Smith and James Alexander for life."

The startled clerk's hand flew to his mouth. "Oh dear, disbarment for life. Is it possible—I mean, do we have the right to do such a thing?"

"The *right?*" de Lancey screamed in his best imitation of Governor Cosby. "You damn fool. I can bar and disbar whom I please. Hire and fire, fire and hire! Now get busy and draft the order. Immediately!"

The clerk scurried to his own desk, selected a quill, and began writing the order that would end the legal careers of two of the finest lawyers in New York.

The news spread through the city in a matter of hours. Everyone was dismayed. Not only was Peter Zenger left without legal counsel, it didn't look as if he was going to get any. What lawyer wanted to risk his career when it was obvious the governor would stop at nothing to win this case? To defend Zenger was to attack the governor.

Jan, Alice, and Lewis Morris were glum as they sat in Alice's parlor trying to think of a solution to their problem.

"I can't really blame any of the younger lawyers for refusing to handle the case," Morris said. "They've got their entire careers before them."

"How about the older ones?" Alice asked.

"Older lawyers don't tend to be heroes," Morris said.

"How about yourself?" Jan asked.

"I'd do it," Morris said with an affirmative nod of his head. "But Cosby wouldn't permit it. Since he recently fired me as chief justice, he'd claim I'd be biased."

"Wouldn't you be?"

"Of course."

"So what are we going to do?" Alice snapped. "We certainly can't let Zenger be punished for something we're really to blame for."

"Well, we've known it might come to this all along," Jan said. "I guess I'll have to give myself up as the writer. The governor will switch his prosecution from Zenger to me."

"That's a terrible solution," Morris said.

"But it might be the only one," Alice said. "I won't let you take the blame by yourself, Jan. I'm as guilty as you are."

Morris threw his hands up in the air. "Wonderful. We'll all go merrily dancing off to jail."

The trial was less than a week away, and if they didn't do something to change the course of events, Zenger didn't stand a chance. Bradford's *Gazette,* in an effort to show its loyalty to the governor, was already proclaiming his certainty of victory over the libelous printer.

They were glum and could think of nothing to do, short of Jan's solution.

The next day James arrived from the manor.

"I've been sort of watching what's been going on. What are you planning on doing?"

Jan explained their intention of giving themselves up if no other solution presented itself.

"Maybe there's something else we could try," James said.

"What's that?"

James ignored the question. "Do we have a fast ship in the harbor?"

Jan nodded. "The *Bristol* lies at anchor at the end of Wall Street. It's a two-masted schooner."

"May I use it?" James asked.

"Of course."

"And will you come with me?" he said to his son.

"Certainly, but where are we going?"

"Philadelphia."

"Philadelphia?" the others parroted in unison.

"What's Philadelphia got to do with this matter?" Morris asked.

"If I'm successful, you'll know," James said. "And if I'm not, well, there's no sense in raising your hopes."

When James and his son had gone, Morris and Alice sat down and relaxed with a pair of stiff drinks.

"Whats he up to?" Morris wondered aloud.

"I've never been successful at reading my brother's mind."

"I guess there's nothing we can do until they return."

Playfulness came into Alice's eyes. "We could enjoy a nice quiet meal together. God knows there's been enough excitement around here. It might do us both good if we relaxed a bit."

Lewis Morris smiled. He looked at Alice and realized there had been a subtle change in their relationship. And what was wrong with that? he asked himself. Alice was an extremely handsome woman, bright and witty, certainly as good a companion as any man he knew. And he was a widower. Aside from his work there was little to his life, and he was, he admitted to himself, rather lonely.

"I think dinner would be splendid," he said.

Alice was also conscious of a shift in their relationship. It pleased her, but she wasn't about to admit that—at least not yet.

"Mister Morris, would you care for a game of backgammon before dinner?" she asked in her semiformal voice.

The *Bristol* slipped its moorings and headed down the bay toward the Narrows. It was a sparkling day. The sky was blue, punctuated by snowy clouds. The hills of Staten Island were crisp and green to starboard as the ship made its way into the open ocean.

James stood on the windward side, enjoying the breeze as the schooner rounded the point at Sandy Hook and headed south for Cape May and the mouth of Delaware Bay. Jan came and stood beside him.

"I'm pleased we're going by ship," he said.

"You've made the overland trip to Philadelphia, haven't you?"

"Once," Jan said with a grimace. "And once was enough."

"It's actually a longer trip by sea," James said. "But the land roads are so bad, I think the sea is quicker."

Jan thought of the commercial coach he had taken several years ago. Eleven passengers and a driver—three to a row and no backrests except on the last bench. The canvas top offered some protection from the elements, but there had been no side curtains, and rain had whipped through the coach, soaking the passengers to the bone. "When I arrived in Philadelphia I couldn't stop shaking for two days," he said. "All we did was bounce up and down for the entire trip."

James nodded. "The sea is the best way. A stiff breeze and a tang of salt in the air. Ah, there's nothing like it."

"The roll of a deck feels good under your feet, too," Jan said. "I can understand how the sea gets into a man's blood."

"And yet you never wanted to go to sea, did you?"

"What boy doesn't toy with the idea? But no, I never really had any great urge to spend my life on the ocean."

"It's just as well. A sailor's life is a hard one," James said. "Weeks, months at sea. The drinking water turns foul and the food rots. And in the end most sailors wind up on the beach without a shilling in their pocket, and nothing to show for their lives."

"You went to sea," Jan pointed out.

"I was a boy. At the time I hated my father, and I ran away to spite him." James laughed softly. "And to think that of all the ships in New York, I picked the one belonging to Captain William Kidd."

"You've never told me about those days," Jan said quickly, hoping his father would speak freely about a topic he rarely mentioned.

"There's not much to tell. Kidd turned pirate and we sailed around the Indian Ocean attacking merchantmen.

It's not something I'm proud of having done. But I can't feel too guilty about it, because I didn't set out to be a pirate; it was an unhappy accident."

"Whatever happened to Kidd's treasure?" Jan asked.

James peered at his son for a long moment. "What do you think happened to it?"

"More or less what everyone else thinks," Jan replied. "That Kidd buried it somewhere, killed anyone else who knew about it, and took the secret with him to the grave."

"The treasure was ill-gotten. Perhaps it's best that it remain hidden."

Jan was suddenly alert. "You know more about it than you're telling."

James smiled. "Perhaps."

"And you won't talk about it?"

"I never talk about it."

"There's many a man in New York who'd slit your throat for even a hundredth part of what's supposed to be in that treasure," Jan said.

"Yes, but no man in New York has the slightest idea that I know anything about it. Except you, of course. And when the time comes, you'll know more."

An hour later they passed a black-hulled brigantine heading in a northerly direction. The brigantine's bow went into the wind, halting her, and the men aboard the *Bristol* knew they were being scrutinized.

"That ship flies no flag," Jan observed.

"A privateer," James said. "One that turns pirate at the right opportunity, no doubt."

"Will they attack us?"

"They would if they thought they had a chance," James said. "But look at her bulk. Our ship could easily outrun her. As soon as they figure that out for themselves, they'll go on their way."

It was as if the captain of the brigantine had been listening. Barely had James spoken when she turned northward again.

The remainder of the journey was uneventful, and two days later the *Bristol* made her way up the Delaware River, past Pea Patch Island, past the new settlement at Chester, arriving finally at the confluence of the Delaware and Schuylkill rivers.

Philadelphia was larger than New York and rivaled it as a center of trade. It was also very much more English. The Dutch heritage of New York had done a great deal to shape the style and character of that city, but there was hardly a trace of the Dutch in William Penn's city. The name of the river that bisected Philadelphia—the Schuyl-kill—was Dutch, but it was not even pronounced in the Dutch fashion. It had been anglicized into "Schoolkill."

"Well, Father," Jan said. "I've managed to restrain my curiosity, but now would it be possible to tell me why we're here?"

"To talk to a man."

"Any particular man?"

"A very particular one."

They embarked from the *Bristol* and made their way through a series of streets and alleys to Letitia Street. James stopped in front of a handsome brick house with an immaculate little garden and a bronze doorplate that reflected the rays of the sun. "Unless I'm mistaken, this is the place."

He knocked at the door. A servant answered, and the two men were ushered into the library and asked to wait. Except for the massive fireplace, and the windows, which gave a view of the garden, the room was lined with book-shelves—and more books than Jan had seen in his life. He looked about in wonder and realized they numbered in the thousands.

"James de Kuyper," a voice said, and Jan turned to see a man standing in the doorway, looking at his father, an impish smile on his face. The man must have been eighty years old, but there was nothing frail or weak about him.

He came forward with a brisk and steady step. "Now what brings one of Kidd's pirates all the way here to a cranky old man's house?"

The *Bristol* arrived back in New York two nights later. James and the man from Philadelphia went to Alice's, and Jan made his way to the house he had recently built on Maiden Lane not far from his theater. He entered through the back door and found Marie Therese dozing near the kitchen fire. She heard the sound of his footsteps and looked up. He leaned over and kissed her on the forehead.

"I thought you'd never get back from Philadelphia," she complained sleepily.

"At least you missed me," he said. "That's a good sign."

"What's it all about?"

"My father decided to spring a little surprise on the good governor."

"What is it?"

"It's a secret," he said teasingly.

"I'll tell you my secret, if you tell me yours."

"Oh?"

She hesitated for a moment, but the desire to tell him her news was too great, and the words came from her lips in a torrent. "It's your Cousin Edward, Edward and Dora Van Cortlandt, you know they've been seeing a great deal of each other, well, that's putting it mildly, they've been seeing more of each other than anyone's suspected, and Dora's expecting a child."

"What?" Jan said in disbelief. But as he digested the news, he began to laugh.

"Sh," Marie Therese cautioned. "You'll wake the servants."

"Why, the little devils. But I'm not that surprised. From things Ned has told me, I suspected they were having fun for themselves."

"You're awful!"

"Well, it is fun, isn't it? Or are you only putting on an act when we're in bed together?"

"That's different," Marie Therese said. "We're married."

"I don't see how that makes any difference. I don't ever remember stopping in the middle and thinking to myself, All right, Jan, you can enjoy this, you're married."

"That's not what I mean, and you know it."

"So what's going to happen?"

"Well, Mister Van Cortlandt exploded, naturally, and he threatened to get his gun and shoot Ned. He went to the Goelets' house, and fortunately Ned wasn't there. But his father was, and so the fathers settled the issue. Ned and Dora are to be married as soon as possible."

"I think that would have happened anyway," Jan said.

"Yes, but now there's scandal attached to it."

"Nonsense. Five years from now no one will remember

what happened. There'll be a couple of children and two smiling grandfathers."

"Somehow I can't imagine Charles Goelet with a happy smile on his face."

"It is a bit farfetched, but stranger things have happened."

"All right, I've told you my news," Marie Therese said happily. "Now tell me your secret."

"I never said I would."

"You did."

He shook his head. "I didn't. You blurted out about Ned and Dora before we made any deal."

"That's not fair."

He put his hand on the side of her cheek and let his fingers play with the tip of her ear. "I'll make a deal with you now, though. Let's go to bed and get in trouble the way Ned did. If you please me, *then* I'll tell you what happened in Philadelphia."

A sudden flash of anger came to her features, and then it dissolved into a smile. "You don't play fair, but you do make the nicest deals," she said, getting to her feet and leading him by the hand toward their bedroom.

The morning of the Zenger trial found half the population of New York with a new *Weekly Journal* in their hands. Jan and Edward had worked most of the night to get out an edition that catalogued their grievances against Cosby, especially in relation to Peter Zenger.

The jury had been sworn, the benches were packed with spectators, and there was excitement in the air.

James and the elderly man from Philadelphia were in the front row. Jan, Alice, and Lewis Morris sat right behind them.

Alice looked about and saw Charles Goelet seated next to Stephen Van Cortlandt. "I don't see your rakish cousin," she whispered to Jan.

"Under the circumstances, he thought it best to lay low," Jan said. "But the older generation seems to be taking it well. At least they're getting along well enough to sit with one another."

Alice sniffed. "Stephen Van Cortlandt has always been just as stuffy as Charlie. They deserve each other."

Judge de Lancey entered the room with his two associate justices. Everyone stood as they took their places on the bench. The bailiff called the courtroom to order, and the prisoner was led to the dock. Everyone sat down. The bailiff read the charges, and then took his place by the side of the bench.

The only person of importance in New York who was absent from the courtroom was William Cosby.

The attorney general came to his feet and addressed himself to the charges against Zenger. "There can be no doubt of this man's libelous actions," he said. "We offer as evidence to the court the various editions of the man's own newspaper, the *Weekly Journal*. Since he has already admitted that he printed these newspapers which contain the libels, he stands convicted by words from his own mouth."

Judge de Lancey nodded his approval of these sentiments and looked toward the table where the defense attorney sat. John Chambers looked untroubled by the prosecutor's words, and for good reason. When no lawyer had stepped forward to defend Zenger, the court had appointed him. Chambers was a mediocre lawyer whose most apparent quality to the defendant and his supporters was a lack of interest in this case. He was a realist who understood his role: go through the motions, observe the niceties of English law, and don't cause any trouble. He would be amiable to the court and the attorney general, and perhaps even to his client. He would ask a few questions—none that would give the prosecution any difficulty—and after the trial he would go home, pleased that he had been able to do a favor for the government. Perhaps one day the governor would remember and be good enough to return the favor. John Chambers was under no illusions that he was here to further the cause of justice.

"If it please the court," James de Kuyper said, rising from his seat.

Judge de Lancey looked at him and frowned. He smelled trouble. "Yes?" he asked, sounding querulous.

"It is no longer necessary for Counselor Chambers to assume the onerous burden of Peter Zenger's defense," James said innocently, with a polite smile directed toward the defense attorney. "We will now spare him any further trouble, as we have procured the services of another attorney."

A titter ran through the courtroom. Everyone was aware of the role Chambers was to have played in this farce.

De Lancey was confused. "Another lawyer? But I've been informed that every lawyer in New York has turned down this case."

"The new lawyer is from Philadelphia," James said, pointing to the elderly man who sat on the bench beside him. "His name is Andrew Hamilton."

A noisy confusion erupted among jury and spectators alike as the elderly man came to his feet. He had a full shock of white hair, an aquiline nose, and eyes that were piercing points of brightness. He moved with the dignity of his years and a lifetime of assurance of his own position.

Andrew Hamilton had become the most famous trial lawyer in America. He had been a King's Councillor, attorney general for the city of Philadelphia, and a barrister who had argued cases before the bar in London. No man in the New World had a greater reputation for knowledge of the law or devotion to justice.

Judge de Lancey blinked his eyes in disbelief, as if he hoped the leonine countenance of the old man would disappear.

"If it please the court," Hamilton said, stepping forward to the defense desk, "I shall begin my argument." His voice was deep and resonant, imbued with the timbre of absolute conviction. He smiled at John Chambers and patted him on the shoulder in dismissal. Chambers shrugged, picked up his papers, and headed for the door. If this was going to a real court case, he wanted no part of it.

"Is this man acceptable to you?" the judge asked the defendant. Zenger quickly nodded his assent.

"You may proceed, Mister Hamilton," de Lancey said warily, after looking for guidance from his associate justices and receiving none.

"How can a man be convicted of libel when there is no libel?" Hamilton began as he faced the jury. "Where is the treason if all a man does is tell the truth? If it be treasonable to tell the truth," he said as he paced in front of the jurors, "then, gentlemen, we should all be proud to proclaim ourselves traitors—each and every one of us, from the most humble to the exalted personage of the Crown itself."

The jurors were, to a man, stout merchants with a substantial stake in New York, and they were all well aware of the character of their governor. In private most of them sympathized with Zenger, but they had been resigned about the outcome of the case. If no lawyer could be found to stand up to the governor, why should they?

But now Andrew Hamilton began changing their minds.

"Take the case of the governor's demand for his back pay," he said. "Look at the evidence." And he brought fact after fact into his argument, proving the demand was not only outrageous and greedy, but also illegal.

"Consider the port duties charged on Charles Goelet's ships—duties above the legal limit, duties above the good conscience of any responsible government. Why are they so high? Because that good man opposed Governor Cosby in the city council," Hamilton said. "The governor is obviously using his public office to gain personal revenge. How would you like that to happen to you? Consider that for a moment."

Hamilton paused dramatically while the jury sat in silence.

The lawyer broke the spell and continued. "The attempt to extort money from Rip Van Dam: now what exactly are the facts in this case, and do they differ from what has been printed in the *Weekly Journal?*"

They did not differ as he proceeded to point out.

Andrew Hamilton kept hammering away at only one thing: did a given something really happen, or did it not?

The facts about the land scandal near the Fresh Pond.

The facts about the bribes paid to obtain better docking facilities.

The facts about the bribes paid to obtain an ordinary business license.

The facts about the contracts awarded in supplying the government troops with provisions, and the facts about the bribes given to receive those contracts.

The facts about dozens of instances of extortion, ranging from tiny sums to small fortunes.

The facts.

By the noon recess, things were looking up for John Peter Zenger.

James de Kuyper and Andrew Hamilton were enjoying a picnic lunch at a bench on the grass outside the courthouse when they noticed Judge de Lancey hastening toward the governor's house.

"That should be an interesting conversation," James observed.

"I knew the judge's father," Hamilton said. "He was a wonderful man, built the finest house in New York. It must have been thirty years ago."

"The judge lives there now, and it's still one of the best houses in the city. Too bad the son isn't the same sort of man as the father."

"It often happens that a strong father will so overshadow his son, the lad will turn out weak," Hamilton said. "I'm happy to see that it didn't happen with your father and yourself."

James laughed. "I found the only way to deal with Jacob Adam was to ignore him. Maybe that's why it all worked out for the best."

"And your own son?"

"He'll take care of himself."

By the time their lunch was finished, a crowd of people had gathered at a respectful distance to gaze upon the great lawyer with their own eyes. For over fifty years he had been considered one of the intellectual giants of the New World. To see him here in the flesh, eating a hard-boiled egg and enjoying a glass of beer, was a treat, the sort of thing a man would tell his grandchildren. "Yes, yes, I was there the day of the Zenger trial, saw Hamilton myself. Not more than ten feet away he was, eating lunch with one of the de Kuypers, a wonderful man, a wonderful man," and they would speak as if they had had something to do with the trial and Hamilton himself, and maybe over the years they would come to believe that it was true.

"You've got the jury convinced," James said.

Hamilton shrugged. "Zenger and your son did most of the work for me. One collected the facts, and the other printed them."

"True, but your presentation of the case is having a strong influence, only you're too modest to admit it."

The lawyer shook his head. "At my age a man has no time for modesty. Any competent lawyer could have presented this case."

"But none of them *would*," James pointed out.

"Another nice thing about being my age," Hamilton said with a smile, "is that there's nothing left to be afraid of. Once I passed seventy-five I considered every day of my life a bonus."

"You would've taken this case if it had been offered to you forty years ago."

"Probably," Hamilton admitted. "I like the uncomfortable ones."

"Like the time you saved me from hanging?"

"Peter Zenger deserves to be punished for libel just about as much as you deserved to hang."

"Do you think we'll win this case?"

"How can we lose?" Hamilton said airily.

The time for the court to return to session approached, and Judge de Lancey returned from the governor's house. He wore an assured smile.

"It sure looks like *he* thinks we can lose," James said.

The court was resumed.

"And now, Your Honor," Hamilton said, "I would like to call witnesses to give further testimony as to the truth of the statements printed in my client's newspaper."

"That will be unnecessary."

"Unnecessary?" Andrew Hamilton repeated, puzzled. "But how else may we expect this court to judge whether or not Peter Zenger published libelous statements?"

"That is not the function of this court," de Lancey said. He turned and addressed himself to the jury. "The court's position in this case is clear. All critics of government are libelers and disturbers of the peace. *Ipso facto* they must be considered men who threaten to overthrow government and society."

An angry murmur swept through the court, and the judge was forced to pound his gavel for silence.

"Therefore," he continued, "the truth of the statements contained in the *Weekly Journal* is not properly the issue before us. The question at issue is whether Peter Zenger did, or did not, print them."

Zenger looked up at Hamilton, who was struggling to contain his anger at de Lancey's preposterous statement.

"Are you truly saying, Your Honor," the lawyer asked in a low, dangerous voice, "that truth is not an issue here? That it is possible for the court to find a man guilty of printing the truth? I find it incomprehensible that we are expected to subscribe to such an interpretation of the law."

De Lancey, fresh from his encouraging session with the governor, answered smugly. "You are expected to believe that traitors have no rights."

Andrew Hamilton's voice dripped acid. "It is true that in times past it was a crime to speak the truth, but that was the practice of wicked and bestial kings, the method used by arrant cowards to cut down and destroy the innocent."

Judge de Lancey's expression was terrible. "Pray, Mister Hamilton, you go too far."

"Do I?"

"Yes indeed," Judge de Lancey said angrily. "We do not intend to sit in this courtroom and hear our beloved sovereign referred to as a wicked and bestial king."

"But surely, Your Honor, you misinterpret my words," Hamilton said mildly. "All men agree that we are presently governed by the wisest and best of kings. I was speaking of other kings, ones dead and buried for many years."

He fixed de Lancey with his stare. "Or are you suggesting that the present king is wicked and bestial?"

"No, no," de Lancey said quickly, startled at finding himself in the position of defendant. "What man in his right mind could think that?"

"And that is exactly my point," Hamilton said, resuming his pacing up and down in front of the jury. "We are governed by a sympathetic monarch, one who is a staunch defender of freedom. What would our sovereign lord, the benevolent George, say if he were here in this courtroom today? Would he not hear this court denying those very freedoms which he himself has either granted us or upheld for us? Would he not be appalled? Would he not be angered? Would he not bring down the sword of his justice—not on the head of my client, but on the heads of those who are making a mockery of his own words, his own cherished beliefs?"

De Lancey looked nervously at the jury, who stared

back at him with hard faces. "This has nothing to do with the issue on trial," he said, his voice quavering. "Did, or did not, the defendant, John Peter Zenger, print the *Weekly Journal?* If you find that he did print it, then he is a traitor, and guilty of libel."

"Are you saying that you define everything he printed as libel?"

"Yes," de Lancey answered recklessly.

"There are two things to consider about your statement," Hamilton said. "Its stupidity and its evil. As for the stupidity, look at this newspaper," he said, holding up one of Zenger's editions. "It has a date on it. By your own admission, that date is libelous."

"And now to the more important question of evil," Hamilton said, dropping the newspaper back on the desk. "If we are to accept your definition of libel, then there is scarce a piece of writing that may not be called libelous. Does not Shakespeare libel Iago? Does not Julius Caesar libel the Gauls and the people of Germania? Plato is a libeler. Socrates as well. And the Bible . . . does not the Bible itself libel the Devil? The word of God is libelous? Are we to conclude the Devil has just cause to bring God to trial?"

The lawyer's voice became even more sonorous. He walked back and forth like an angry lion, and his anger became a contagious thing.

"I am an old man, as you can see, burdened by infirmities of the body; yet old and weak as I am, I believed it my duty to come here today to help quench the flame of persecution.

"Today we are witnessing the arbitrary attempt of men in power to injure and oppress the very people fate has placed in their care. Their abuses provoke these same people, causing them to cry out and rightfully complain. And what happens? These abusers of power point to the people who are arguing for their rights and call them traitors—using the very complaints themselves as the basis for new oppressions.

"But take care!" the lawyer warned, pausing and pointing his finger at the jury. "Each step along this road is one more step down the road of perdition, and who knows when the very next step may be the one that finally makes us slaves.

"For what can slavery be but this: to suffer the greatest injuries and oppressions without the liberty of complaining.

"The loss of liberty, to a generous mind, is worse than death.

" 'You Romans,' said Brutus, 'are assisting Caesar to forge those very chains which one day he will make yourselves wear.'

"The question before the court, and especially you, gentlemen of the jury, is not of small or private concern; it is not the cause of a poor printer, nor of New York alone, which you are trying. No! It may, in its consequences, affect every freeman who lives under the British flag in America!

"It is the best cause; it is the cause of liberty; and I have no doubt that after your decision today, every man who prefers freedom to a life of slavery will bless and honor you as men who have baffled tyranny.

"Slavery? Or freedom? That is the choice; that gentlemen of the jury, is the issue here today. The fate of your children and your children's children is in your hands. May God give you the wisdom and strength to do what you know in your hearts is the only thing for a free man to do."

There was a long silence, and then Andrew Hamilton spoke in a voice that was little more than a whisper, but was heard by every man and woman in the courtroom.

"You must find John Peter Zenger not guilty, else you condemn yourselves."

As the venerable lawyer resumed his seat, the spectators broke out in loud cheers. Zenger reached over and touched the lawyer's arm in affection.

"Quiet! Order in the court!" de Lancey was shouting. He pounded the gavel for a full minute before the last of the cheering stopped.

"No more of that," the judge said, his face distorted and mottled with anger. He turned to the jury. "The facts in this case are clear. Zenger printed the newspaper. He admits it. That is all you are to concern yourselves with. Now retire and return when you come to a decision."

And as the jurors were filing out, he called after them, "I don't see that you have any choice."

Ten minutes later the court reconvened and the jurors

filed back to their places. There was a short, breathless wait.

"Gentlemen of the jury," de Lancey asked. "Have you reached a verdict?"

The foreman stood up. "We have."

"In the matter of John Peter Zenger, how do you find?"

A short pause.

"Not guilty," the foreman said loudly.

Pandemonium swept the room. People cheered and many rushed forward to shake the printer's hand, congratulate him, or slap him on the back.

Judge de Lancey began banging his gavel and then gave up. "Court's adjourned," he growled, although no one was paying any attention. He stomped from the room in a rage.

Governor Cosby had been rejected.

James de Kuyper hosted a party for Andrew Hamilton at the White Horse tavern, at the corner of Pearl and Broad.

Hamilton sat near a window with James and Paul de Witt and looked across the street at the house of James de Lancey. "Here's a bit of irony," he said. "We celebrate our victory while one of the losers sits across the street and watches."

James glanced at the handsome building on the other side of the street, its dormer windows protruding from the slanted roof of the top floor, every shade drawn. "Maybe we should invite him over."

Hamilton laughed. "De Lancey's probably hiding in the cellar, afraid to face the governor."

"It couldn't be worse than facing a Philadelphia lawyer," James said.

"Is that a special breed?" de Witt asked.

"You only call for them in hopeless cases," James said. "They never fail."

"Why is that?"

"Because if they can't do it honestly, they'll find another way."

The three laughed.

A curtain in the window of the house across the street moved back an inch, and James de Lancey looked upon the merrymaking in the White Horse with great hatred in his heart.

It's unfair, he thought. I had the law on my side. I had the governor. I had the might of the Crown. And yet I lost, and now I am sure to be removed as chief justice.

He closed the curtain and poured himself a glass of rum. He blamed his misfortune on the de Kuyper family. They had done this on purpose, of this he was certain. The two families were rivals in business, and this entire affair had been arranged to discredit the de Lanceys. Someday they would outsmart those damned de Kuypers.

But the judge's venom did not cross the street and poison the party.

Several of the city's most prominent men proposed toasts to Hamilton. The lawyer accepted each one graciously, raising his teacup with a smile, sipping while the others downed their glasses of spirits or beer. Charles Goelet made a well-meaning, but pompous statement about Hamilton's "earning the respect of the business community." Peter Zenger mumbled his thanks in a touching way. Rip Van Dam's case had been dropped by the governor, and he too added his praise.

But the statement that touched Hamilton most deeply was made by Alice Livingston, the only woman who dared propose a toast in the midst of so many of the city's leading men.

"To Andrew Hamilton," she said. "To his courage, to his wisdom, and to the freedom he has won for us.

"And I would do more than raise a glass," she said, looking around the room at the solid and prosperous faces. "I am donating a thousand pounds to begin a public library in this city."

Her eyes continued to wander from face to face. "I ask each one of you to join me. Our people must be educated and have access to books if they are to take advantage of, and to keep, what Andrew Hamilton has won for us—a freedom of the press."

There was a short silence, and then the wealthy merchant John Millington stood up. "Freedom of the press, what an excellent way of stating it. Mrs. Livingston, I will join you by adding two hundred pounds to your thousand."

James de Kuyper stood and added a further contribution. Many of the others did the same. New York would have its library, and a more fitting memorial to Andrew Hamilton could not have been found.

The next morning the venerable old lawyer was escorted by over a hundred people as he returned to the *Bristol* to make the trip back to Philadelphia.

"Good-bye," James said, as the two men stood at the foot of the gangplank. "I look forward to seeing you again."

Hamilton shook his head. "That would give me the greatest pleasure, my friend. But consider how much time has passed between our two meetings. Is it likely we will greet each other again?"

"If not in this world, then surely the next," James said.

"Unless God intends to punish you for your piratical youth," Hamilton said, a twinkle in his eye. He patted James on the arm, then turned and walked up the ramp to the deck of the ship.

As the *Bristol* took on sail and made its way down past the tip of the island, more than a dozen ship's captains fired their cannon in tribute to this old man who had contributed so richly to upholding the rights of man.

The *Bristol* sailed down toward the Narrows, growing smaller with each passing minute.

Jan stood at James's shoulder and realized that his father was silently crying. With the tears still coursing down his cheeks, James said, "Don't misunderstand, son. It's not that I'm sad. It's just that I feel privileged to have known one of the greatest men of our times."

In silence they walked back together toward Wall Street.

The following year Governor Cosby died.

His defeat at the hands of Andrew Hamilton had turned him into a near-recluse. Not that he still hadn't insisted on bribes for the granting of favors, nor that he wasn't still greedy and irascible: he had simply lost the heart to press an issue if a man seemed willing to fight.

Now that his intended victim Peter Zenger had had a taste of the newspaper business, he decided to continue the *Journal*. The de Kuyper family played no part in his affairs after the defeat of Cosby. Lewis Morris published an article in the paper from time to time, but Alice and Jan wrote no more.

The city council met and elected one of its members, George Clarke, as acting governor. One of his first official duties was to appoint Peter Zenger as public printer of all government proclamations. The German immigrant had come full cycle, from accused traitor to official of the establishment.

His case was truly closed.

It had been a busy year for Jan de Kuyper.

In addition to the theater and the house, he had bought a good deal of marshland in the Maiden Lane area. Since most men considered this land almost worthless, he paid considerably less than he would have paid for a comparable amount of property farther south on the island. He made his transactions quietly, without attracting attention to himself. Although some of his buying was done through the de Kuyper company, most was done with private funds—his own, or funds supplied by his father and aunt.

But it was on behalf of the company that Jan had made his latest acquisition, and on a crisp fall morning he escorted Paul de Witt to the docks to inspect it.

"A coastal trader," Paul said in mild surprise when he saw the trim two-masted craft tied to the pier. "But our ships have always been in the Atlantic trade."

"Exactly," Jan said. "Come aboard and take a look."

The two men went up the gangplank and walked the decks of the ship. It was a sleek little schooner. The beam was narrower than that of a ship built to cross the ocean. The bottom was also more rounded, making it possible for the ship to enter very shallow waters. Unlike ocean-going vessels, whose sails were square-rigged because they were usually left on the same tack for many hours, or even days on end, the schooner's mizzenmast was equipped with fore and aft sails that gave it more maneuverability in the light and shifting airs off the coasts.

Jan pointed out the large area allotted for cargo. Since the ship had been built for short journeys, little space had been set aside for provisions or comfort. The belowdecks areas were starkly utilitarian.

Paul leaned against the railing and regarded his nephew

with a critical eye. "And why are we going into the coastal trade?"

Jan shrugged. "The colonies are growing every year. More people means more trade, and even right now there aren't enough ships in the American coastal trade. That means people are willing to pay high prices to get their goods moved—say from Virginia to Boston, or from Philadelphia to Georgia. I think the time is right for us to get into this business."

"And what about our oceangoing packets?"

"We'll sell them, or at least most of them. The big profits are going to come from ships like this one," he said, tapping his hand on the smooth mahogany rail.

Paul shook his head. "I guess I'm getting old, because I'd be too conservative to take this step. What's wrong with the profits we make in the European trade?"

"Look at the conditions there," Jan explained. "The French are becoming more powerful and greedy every year. How long do you think it will be before England is at war with her? Spain and England are already at each other's throats. Their ships attack one another and are destroying the Caribbean trade. And we hear reports of a war in Austria."

"But the greatest profits are coming from the tobacco trade to Europe," Paul protested.

"For how long?" Jan asked. "If England goes to war against France, the Atlantic Ocean will become a graveyard for ships. I don't want them to be our ships."

"But surely if this war happens, it will spread to our own shores."

"Yes—and then the British generals will need ships to carry troops and supplies. Up to New France, down to the southern provinces. I want *those* ships to be ours."

"Dangerous work. If what you say is true, our ships will be fair game for every French and Spanish privateer from Quebec to Curaçao."

"Yes, but we'll be ready for them. I intend to buy only the fastest ships, and I intend to arm them with cannon —at the king's expense. Governor Clarke has agreed to give me the money."

"He has! How in the world did you convince him to agree to that?"

"By telling him that our ships—if armed—could be

used for the defense of New York in case of an attack."

Paul de Witt shook his head and laughed. "Damme, but that's the sort of thing your grandfather would have done." He reached out and gave Jan's arm an affectionate pinch. "Well, that convinces me of two things."

Jan waited expectantly.

"It's time you took over the company, and time for me to spend my days in my garden."

Jan said nothing. There was no smile, no gloating. He simply reached out and touched his uncle's arm.

Exactly the way his grandfather would have reacted, Paul thought. "Let's go back to the office and make it official."

The members of the extended de Kuyper family were the first within the company to be informed of the change.

Sam de Witt failed to hide his resentment. His father ignored his behavior, but Jan acted as if Sam had offered his warmest congratulations. That made Sam all the angrier.

Charles Goelet had surprised Paul by taking the news calmly, with no argument and none of his usual bluster. Later Goelet walked into the former chief executive's office.

"Thanks for being such a good sport, Charlie. I hope you understand it had to happen sooner or later."

"A year or two ago I would have gone through the roof," Goelet admitted. "But I've been observing our young kinsman in action. He's good, damn good, and anyway, I'm getting old. There's no sense in trying to fight that."

"I came to that conclusion concerning myself some time ago."

"What the devil am I supposed to do now, Paul? I've been standing in line behind you for so long, I don't know if I could work for somebody else. Besides, Jan may be what this company needs, but Jesus Christ! I still think of him as a little kid."

"How old are you, Charlie? Sixty? Sixty-one?"

"Do I look that old? I'll be fifty-eight next month. So what?"

"Stay on for two years, until you're sixty. Help the lad as much as you can, and then retire like me."

"Who takes my place?"

"I don't think either of us will have a say in the matter," Paul said quietly. "I suspect Jan will have his own ideas."

Goelet nodded. "I guess so. I only hope he doesn't pick my son. Or yours, for that matter."

"Ned's not a bad fellow, Charlie. Anyway, he's got a head on his shoulders. Which is more than I can say for Sam."

"So what are we, Paul, failures?" Goelet said, suddenly angry. "Think of it, the two of us have spent our lives slaving for this company. Meanwhile James sits on his arse up on that farm of his, fooling around with pigs and horses. Then along comes his son, who just walks in and *takes* the business, without even raising a sweat. Our own sons are off in a corner somewhere, picking their noses and getting girls pregnant and fucking up in general. Sweet Jesus! Where's the justice in this world?"

Paul de Witt smiled. "Charlie, when was the last time you and I left the office in the middle of the day to go to the King George and get drunk?"

"I don't think we ever did it."

"Then it's time we learned."

The two men left the de Kuyper building, crossed to the other side of Broad Way, and entered the tavern, feeling better about one another than they had since Paul had been a very young man and Charles only a boy.

During the year since the trial Lewis Morris and Alice Livingston had become good friends. No one was surprised, then, on this sunny fall afternoon to see them walking together down Broad Way and past the park at Bowling Green to the tip of the island.

They paused at the southwestern point near the rocks below the fort. They filled their lungs with the salty sea air, which ruffled their hair and brought color to their cheeks.

Morris was holding Alice's hand. He gave it a gentle squeeze. After a long silence, he said, "I've been thinking about the two of us a great deal."

"And?"

"And I'd like to marry you . . . if you'll have me."

She squeezed back and then took her hand away. "Let's walk some more," she said.

They began to follow the curving street as it passed south of the fort and made its way back toward Whitehall and the beginning of Pearl. They walked in silence for a while, but finally he stopped and faced her. "Well?" he asked.

"I don't know, Lewis, what's wrong with what we have now?"

"Nothing. But I'm in love with you and want to marry you. Don't you feel that way about me?"

"Love you? Yes, I suppose I love you. But marriage? Why do we have to upset our lives? It seems to me we have everything a married couple has, and more."

"But we're together so much of the time," Morris protested. "People see us and they say, 'he's a widower and she's a widow,' and after a while they expect something more to happen."

"Who cares what they think? Neither of us is exactly a spring chicken, and if we can't do what we want by now, well, the hell with it."

Morris smiled. As far as he was concerned, one of Alice's most endearing qualities was her irreverence.

"Maybe what *I* want to do is get married," he said quietly.

"I'll tell you what I'll do. I promise to think about it—think about it, but that's all for the moment. After all, there are times when I breathe a sigh of relief when you go home to your own house. I enjoy the times I'm with you, but I enjoy having time to myself as well."

Morris sighed. "You're a hard, hard woman, Alice Livingston."

"Oh, don't start that. You mean to say there aren't times when you're in your own comfortable house, alone, delighted I'm not getting in your way, pestering you with a lot of nonsense?"

"I can't remember your ever being in my way."

"Rubbish. It would happen all the time if we were under each other's feet. Take that book you're writing about—what *is* it about?"

"Patterns of legal change in the City of New York."

"Yes, well. You see I haven't the slightest idea what it's even about, and aren't there times when you like to be left alone with it? Sometimes I don't see you for three or four days, and I know you've been home cooped up with your book, happy as can be."

"It's my work."

"And I respect you for it; enough so that I don't want to interfere with it."

"There's also a moral issue here," he said stubbornly, using his lawyer's logic to nibble at the problem from all sides.

"Oh, *come* now."

He attempted to look stern, and failed. "All right," he said with a chuckle. "If your virtue doesn't mean a damn to you, I guess I can learn to live with it. Or do I mean without it?"

She smiled and took his hand.

A series of major events—some good, some bad—swept through the assorted branches of the de Kuyper family over the next two years.

Marie Therese gave birth to a baby girl, but the infant was sickly and died the next day. The parents were heartbroken, but took the blow as the will of God and soon resolved to bring another child into the world. For many weeks after she lost her baby, Marie Therese could hardly look at a little child without coming close to tears. Attached to Jan's sorrow was his feeling of urgency to beget an heir.

Especially now, as he took firm control of the family company and built up the largest fleet of coastal packets in the province. His holdings of Manhatan real estate had also grown, and he had a policy of rarely selling land, but holding on to the title and leasing the property.

Jan ran the business fairly much on his own. Charles Goelet had made it plain that he was getting ready to retire and wanted to relinquish all major responsibilities. Sam de Witt, of course, didn't figure at all in Jan's plans. He wasn't clever to begin with, and his jealousy made him a clear detriment to the business. There was another reason Jan disliked Sam, but, out of deference to Paul and Janet de Witt, he had decided not to pursue the matter.

There was Edward Goelet, of course. Jan had planned to bring Ned along in the company until he stood at his side as Charles Goelet had stood beside Paul de Witt.

But now he was of a different mind. Edward was changing into a sort of elegant loafer. His work as a cargo master was performed desultorily, without interest; and when he made mistakes—which was often—he would laugh and shrug them off. He was also turning into a whoremonger, a thing Jan found distasteful. The man had a delightful wife, and shouldn't that be sufficient? Apparently not, because Edward was often to be found in the company of gamblers and women of easy virtue who gathered in the taverns near the docks on the Hudson River. Disappointed in his cousin, Jan decided he was worthy of only minor jobs. Edward, for his part, seemed content with a lackluster future, pleased if he had enough money to satisfy his gambling debts and the demands of the women who bestowed their questionable favors on him.

There were many competent men in New York, of course, and some of them were even now working for the company. But Jan was reluctant to bring any outsider into the top ranks of the firm. From the beginning it had been a family affair, and he had no wish to change this order of things. There were a few younger members who showed promise—especially David de Witt Sackett, Paul's grandson through his daughter Anne—but David was only fourteen, and it was still too early to tell how he would turn out.

So Jan took control of everything; and the only person to whom he confided his fears about the family's future was Alice.

"Don't worry about it," was her advice. "Someone always turns up. Long before Jacob Adam died, he admitted James wasn't the man to take over. But Paul de Witt stepped into the breech and everything was fine. And then everyone looked at Sam and wondered how—well, *wondered*. And then you appeared. When it's your time to step down, there will be someone to take your place."

"I hope so."

"Look at you," Alice said, and laughed. "Not yet thirty and already worried about a successor."

Jan smiled, but the problem was still there.

Of all the family events, the most surprising was James's announcement that he was getting married.

Hope Henry Jansen—the sister of George Henry, manager of de Kuyper Manor—had been widowed for two years. Her children were grown, and she had returned to the manor, where she and James had grown up together. Hope took over the job of supervising the work in the kitchen, and James began taking his meals with her. After a few months spent sharing childhood memories with Hope over dinner, it occurred to him that here were two people who had much in common and who, as they finally admitted to each other, were lonely. It was as simple as that. James asked Hope to marry him, and she accepted.

The wedding was held at the manor. The family gathered in a pastoral setting of great oaks and abundant fields to witness the solemnizing of this late-blooming romance between the grandson of the family founder, Pieter de Kuyper, and the daughter of Theophilus Henry and Elizabeth, whose Indian name had been Ahnakink and who had been the daughter of the legendary Stone Eagle, the last chief of the Indians of northern Manhatan.

Marie Therese was in the barn looking at a handsome bay gelding that James, in his desire to share his newfound happiness, had just given to his daughter-in-law.

The bay delicately ate the grain she cupped in her right hand as she stroked his smooth forehead with her left.

"I don't think it's right when they do that to horses," a voice behind her said. She turned and saw Dora Goelet.

"Do what?"

"You know," Dora said with some embarrassment. "Fix them so they can't have babies."

"I doubt if this one could have *had* babies in any case," Marie Therese teased. "He's a boy."

"Well, he could have been a father. It's wrong," Dora said, coming over to the stall to take a closer look at the horse. "It's unnatural and against the laws of God."

Marie Therese sighed. Ever since Dora had had a miscarriage, she had been acting strangely. At first her pregnancy had terrified her. But when she lost the child, having a baby suddenly became the only apparent goal in her life. She was always going to the park near the Battery and mooning over the small children and babies who were taking the air with their mothers or nannies.

Remembering her own pain when her baby had died at the age of one day, Marie Therese easily sympathized with Dora. But Dora had continued to dwell morbidly on her loss and seemed to see it reflected everywhere.

"They geld certain horses in order to improve the breed," Marie Therese said in a matter-of-fact tone, and gave the animal a pat on the nose.

"That's something that should be left to God. Who are we to decide which animals are better than others?"

"Perhaps you're right," Marie Therese said, wishing to avoid any arguments on this festive day. "Why don't we go back to the manor and see what's happening?"

"God will decide who has babies, and who doesn't," Dora persisted.

Marie Therese put her arm about her friend's shoulders as they walked back to the main house. "Don't worry about having a child. It was unfortunate that you lost your first baby, but it happened to me, too. We'll have others."

"You really think so?" Dora asked. Her head was cocked to one side, and there was an odd, feral look in her eyes.

"Of course."

"But only if it's the will of God," Dora said shrilly.

"It will be."

This seemed to satisfy Dora. Her features relaxed, and the wild look left her eyes.

As they walked back to the house, Marie Therese worried about her friend. She wanted to help her, but didn't know how. The only thing Dora wanted was a child, and there was nothing Marie Therese could do about that.

Several months after James's wedding, Paul de Witt's heart failed him and he was dead. The family mourned the loss of this man who had spent his life building and guarding their collective fortune.

Six days later his wife, Janet, passed away quietly in her sleep. The second family funeral in a week's time was held. Jan stood beside his father as they watched Janet's coffin lowered into the ground beside the freshly covered grave of her husband. "I thought she was in good health," he said.

"She seemed almost happy at Paul's funeral," James said softly. "I think she knew she was going to join him."

"Can people really understand things like that?"

"I think so. When our time on this world is almost over, sometimes we become more curious and knowledgeable about the next. Janet knew she was going to join her husband."

One immediate result of the deaths of Paul and Janet was that Jan moved against Sam de Witt.

It was early in the morning when he called his cousin into his office. Sam was startled by the presence of the black man, Aaron Gerait, who was sitting in a chair by the wall.

"You're through, Sam," Jan said bluntly.

"Wha . . . what do you mean?"

"You're finished here at the company. I want you out today."

"But I own shares—"

"Which the company has the legal right to buy back if it so desires," Jan said, cutting his cousin off in midsentence. "And it so desires."

"You're ruining me!"

"I hardly think so. The price of your shares plus what your father left you should take care of you for the rest of your life."

"You can't do this," Sam protested. "I'm part of the family."

"You went against the family when you told Cosby about Zenger. You endangered the family, Sam, all of us, and now we're throwing you out."

"I never went to Cosby."

Jan looked over at Aaron. "You're a liar," the black man said.

"Dammit, I'm no liar, *you're* the liar!" Sam said, recklessly adding, "And I demand satisfaction."

Aaron rose from his chair, crossed the room, and towered over the short, fat man. "I wouldn't make any threats if I were you."

Sam took a step backward, his courage fading quickly before the undisguised strength of the other man. He turned back to his cousin. "It's my word against his.

What are you going to do? Take sides with a damned nigra against your own cousin?"

"This *nigra*," Jan said coldly, "has more honesty in his finger than you have in your whole body."

"But I'm family."

"So's he. The Geraits have been with us since the time of great-grandfather Pieter."

"You're really going to do this to me?"

"It's done."

Sam looked around wildly, as if there was someone else in the room who would help him; but there was no one, and he realized he was beaten. "I'll get even, you wait and see."

Jan shook his head and sat down in his chair as his cousin stomped across the room. He stopped at the door and glared back. "A damned nigra . . ." he said, and then he was gone.

"I'm sorry I had to do that," Jan said softly, almost as if he was talking to himself. "But he had it coming."

"Would it be too much to ask if this nigra made himself a drink?" Aaron asked.

Jan pointed toward a sideboard next to the window. "Make two," he said.

"Would you like some lunch, Sam?" Martha de Witt asked, peering through the half-opened door of her husband's study.

He looked up, and the smiling face annoyed him. Everything annoyed him these days. "I haven't the time," he snapped.

"It isn't good for you to miss meals," she said. "Besides, I have those potato pancakes you like. And sausages."

"Good God, woman, I'm trying to work, and all you can think about is eating. No wonder we're fat as hogs."

Martha's maiden name had been de Peyster, and she had inherited all the intelligence and spirit that were hallmarks of that family. It was at such times as this that she used that intelligence and that spirit in recognizing that marrying Sam had been the biggest mistake of her life. She looked down at her own trim, slender figure, and then back at Sam. "I don't see that *all* of us are getting as fat as hogs," she said meaningfully.

"Get out!" Sam shouted. "If I want anything to eat I'll let you know!"

"You may let me know, *dearest*, but I'm not sure I'll have anything ready then," she said sweetly, and closed the door.

Sam snorted and tried to force his mind back to plotting against his cousin and the nigra. But nothing came to him. He gave up and went to the kitchen, where he proceeded to stuff himself with potato pancakes and sausages. He ate in silence and brooded on his problem.

The dog came to the table, his head raised as he sniffed the delicious aromas. Sam kicked out with his foot, but the dog was accustomed to the ways of his master and jumped nimbly aside. The activity did not interrupt the flow of Sam's thoughts.

Something would occur to him, and soon. Later today, perhaps, or tomorrow; certainly by next week.

Actually, several months passed before something happened that gave Sam the idea he was looking for.

The fire in Governor Clarke's house, near the fort, started on the roof. A hot spark flew up the chimney and settled on a cedar shingle. The winter of 1741 had been a cold one, without much snow, and the shingle was dry and brittle. In a matter of minutes the fire spread to the surrounding shingles and then found an opening and snaked inside the house. The angry flames licked at the walls and floors; the spark had become a raging blaze.

The alarm was raised. The governor and his servants began carting government records into the street. A bucket brigade of neighboring householders was formed, and the oak containers passed from hand to hand until they reached the man at the end of the line. He optimistically threw the pitifully small amount of water toward the mounting flames, which were now devouring the entire house.

Two horse-drawn carts of the volunteer fire department arrived. The department had been organized only in 1737, and it had been necessary to bring all the firefighting apparatus from England. Each cart contained a large water tank, a long hose, and a four-man pump operated by two handles on either side of the tank. Two men pumping up and down on each handle generated enough power to throw a jet of water almost sixty feet through the air.

But the fire engines did little to halt the progress of the fire, and now the bucket brigade began tossing its water on the nearby houses. These could be spared, but it was agreed that the governor's house was doomed.

When he heard the fire alarm, Sam de Witt had jumped out of bed and dressed hastily. He was about to leave the bedroom when Martha woke.

"Where are you going?"

"There's a fire."

"*Here?*" Martha asked, her thoughts on the two children sleeping down the hall.

"No, not here," Sam growled. "I'm going out to see if I can help."

"Be careful," Martha pleaded. "Don't take any chances."

"I won't."

He left his house and rushed to the scene of the fire. His wife's warnings had been unnecessary, as he had no intention of joining the firefighters. It was simply that he had always enjoyed fires—the shouting, the feverish activity of the men and women in the bucket brigade, the flames shooting to the sky, the general excitement and panic. Sam liked to stand at the back of the crowd and observe the disaster in safety.

The best part was listening to the people as they talked: the old biddies cackling and enjoying the misfortune of another; the businessmen who stood around estimating the size of the loss, pompous in the way they bandied about sums of money, secure because it was not their own money; and the victims themselves. Some would stand nearby in a dazed condition. Some almost philosophically accepted what was happening. Others became hysterical, sometimes even trying to fight their way back into the burning house and being forcibly restrained by the firemen.

As a set of burning timbers fell into the street, he became interested in the conversation of two old women who stood in front of him.

"It's part of a conspiracy," the first one said. "The nigras."

"The nigras?"

"They're plotting to burn down the whole town."

A man standing nearby also overheard and scoffed. "Nonsense. Why would the blacks want to burn New York?"

"To get even with us," the first woman said.

"Everyone knows they can't be trusted," the second one chimed in.

"I could say the same thing about a lot of whites I know," the man replied.

"Could you, now?" the first woman said with a sneer. "You look a bit on the dark side yourself."

"What are you trying to say?" the man asked.

"Who but a nigra would want to stand up for another nigra?"

The man shook his head and walked away. But the exchange had suddenly given Sam the idea he had been looking for.

He walked slowly back to his house. The two old crones were probably not the only people who thought Negroes were responsible for the fire. If this idea could be encouraged, it might offer a way to get revenge on his cousin and that damned nigra Aaron Gerait.

He entered his house and sat in front of the dying embers of the kitchen fire. If there was a sudden rash of fires, it might be possible to blame them on the blacks. The first problem was to get someone to start the fires.

Sam smiled. He knew the perfect man for the job.

The next morning he hurried to a dingy waterfront tavern run by John Hughson. The tavern occupied the ground floor of two adjacent ramshackle buildings whose upper floors were tenanted by transients—navvies, sailors, cartmen, and casual laborers of all sorts. Most of them rented the dark, musty rooms by the week or less.

Sam was the owner of these tenements, but no one except John Hughson and himself was aware of it; he had not wanted it known among the family that he was involved in such a shoddy business. He entered the tavern and found Hughson. The two men sat at a secluded table at the rear of the room.

"I need a job done," Sam said, taking care to keep his voice low. "No questions asked."

Hughson nodded. He was a practical man, and shrewd. A job with no questions usually meant it was illegal, and therefore would pay very well. He managed to suppress his interest. "Well, that might be possible."

"The man who does it must know how to keep his mouth shut."

Hughson waited for the other man to get to the point.

"I want some fires started," Sam continued. "I want it to look like they were set on purpose. By nigras."

"Setting fires is easy," Hughson said. "But I'm not so sure about this other part."

"Fires are no good unless they can be blamed on the nigras."

Hughson scratched his head with fingernails that were caked with dirt. "The only way you'd know it was nigras was if somebody was to catch them at it."

The two men sat in silence for a few moments pondering the problem. Sam finally had an inspiration. He rapped his knuckles on the table. "After we set the fires, why can't we find someone who will swear they had seen it being done by nigras?"

"Nobody would ever believe most of the men I know," Hughson replied.

"There must be somebody."

After a few moments of silence, Hughson nodded. "There's a woman, not much more than a girl, really, Mary Burton, lives upstairs. She's dull-witted, but mean. For a pound or two she'll say anything you want."

"And people will believe her?"

Hughson scratched his head again. "Well, she acts kinda tetched and has a way of getting people to believe her because she begins to believe herself."

"Good," Sam said happily. "When can we get started on the fires?"

"Tonight's as good as any time. How about two a night?"

Sam nodded his assent. He reached into his coat pocket and withdrew a large leather notecase. "How much do you want?"

"Twenty pounds ought to do it for now. Some for me. Some for the other man I have in mind. When I need more, I'll let you know."

Same counted out the money. Hughson counted it again and then shoved it into his pocket.

"There's something else I want," Sam said. "Information about a nigra named Aaron Gerait."

Hughson's eyes widened for the first time. "That big mean buck? What do you want with him?"

"I want you to find out where he lives."

"Don't have to find out. He lives in the alley behind Mill Street."

"You know him?"

"Sure, he comes in here once in a while for a drink. Say, you're not planning on messing with him, are you?"

"What if I am?"

"I seen him in a fight one time," Hughson said. "Right here in this room. He was sittin' over there, drinkin', mindin' his own business, and this great big Dago sailor comes in and sees him. 'I don't drink with no slaves,' he says. I tell the Dago that Gerait ain't no slave, that he's a freeman. 'All nigras is slaves,' the Dago says, and he makes a grab for Gerait.

"Well, I never seen the likes of it, afore or after. Gerait picks the Dago up like he was made of straw, raises him above his head and smashes him down over his knee. The poor son-of-a-bitchin' Dago didn't even have time to scream. Crack! His back broke like a twig and there he was on the floor, deader'n hell.

" 'What do you want me to do with this here?' Gerait asks, all quiet and nonchalant. I tell him to dump the Dago in the river. He picks up the body, easy, like it don't weigh ten pounds, and walks out the door. A few minutes later he's back at the table, actin' like nothin' happened. After the word got around, *Mister* Gerait, he don't have any more trouble in this place. Men see him comin', they look *through* him."

"The alley behind Mill Street," Sam repeated, as if he hadn't heard a word of Hughson's story.

He left the tavern and went to the alley behind Mill. He stood in the shadow of a building and watched the row of small houses. A half hour later he saw a young black woman with a fishnet shopping bag on her arm come out of a doorway. A little boy, about three years old, followed her as she walked down the street. Sam waited another twenty minutes and then stiffened as he saw Aaron Gerait coming down the street. The man walked toward the door where the black woman had come out, opened it, and went inside.

Sam turned and walked away gloating.

That night, in an old house on Beaver Street, the first fire was started. It was an old, dried-out structure, and by the time the carts of the fire department arrived, the building resembled a torch. Several of the adjoining buildings were also damaged.

A house burned on Queen Street.

Two houses went up in flames on the very next night in an alley behind Broad Way.

Every night for over a week there were more fires, and the sound of the fire alarms became commonplace.

A warehouse belonging to Richard Sackett caught on fire, and Sam was at the scene as it burned.

"Damned nuisance, all these fires," Sackett complained as he stood helplessly in the street and watched his property blaze away in the night.

"I heard someone talking about nigras being seen around here a little while ago," Sam lied. His voice was loud enough to be overheard by other men standing near by.

"Nigras?" Sackett said in bewilderment. "But why would they want to burn my warehouse?"

Sam shrugged. "There's talk of a plot."

The group of men began discussing the black people, and Sam managed to keep from smiling as he listened to the rumor being spread among the townspeople. They were angry, and because none of them had any answers, they were ready to believe almost anything.

Sam even paid a cartman to help spread the rumor. The man went to Peter Zenger to get the story printed in his newspaper. Zenger refused to print anything about the Negroes until someone could give him evidence.

Sam got his revenge by having the printer's house burned the very next night.

Zenger was more fortunate than most, because the bucket brigade managed to extinguish the flames before his house was destroyed. It was still a formidable mess, however, with one wall gone and most of the furniture damaged by smoke and water.

"Still feel like defending the nigras?" Sam asked the exhausted printer as he leaned against the side of a building across the street from his ruined house.

"Nobody's shown me any proof," Zenger said stubbornly.

"But who else can it be?" Sam argued.

Zenger shrugged wearily. "Just about anyone, as far as I can tell."

Two weeks passed and forty buildings lay in ruin. The rumor about the "nigra plot" spread, and the greater part of the population wanted to believe there was some truth to it.

Governor Clarke ordered the nightwatch doubled and offered a reward for information leading to the capture of the arsonists.

Sam decided it was time to take the next step in his plan. He visited Hughson, and together they climbed to the third floor of the tenement where Mary Burton had a room.

Sam held his nose in the smelly hallway as Hughson knocked on the girl's door. The hall looked as if it had never been washed, and the stench of over fifty years' urine permeated the place.

The door opened, and the two men stepped into the room. There were a few broken and battered sticks of furniture to be seen, and a large straw mattress filled one corner.

Mary Burton was almost pretty, Sam thought. She had a slight, narrow-waisted body; and he found her face appealing until he noticed the tight, mean mouth. She spoke slowly, as if she pondered every word. But it was all right that she was not too sharp. In fact it was probably an asset.

"What d'you want?" she asked sulkily.

"I have a job for you," Sam said.

"Yeah, what's in it for me?"

Sam proceeded to tell her of the nigras and their plan to burn the city to ashes. He mentioned the governor's offer of a reward and said that if she helped him bring the blacks to justice, he would match the amount out of his own pocket.

She looked suspiciously at Sam. "Give it here."

He coached her carefully in her story. They spent the day going over every word until Sam was satisfied that she could do her part. The next morning he took her and John Hughson to City Hall, on Wall Street.

The de Witt name was well known to Governor Clarke, and the three visitors were quickly ushered into his presence. Sam began to explain the nature of their visit, but he had managed to speak only a few words when he was interrupted.

"You mean to say all these fires are part of a Negro plot?" the governor asked in surprise.

Sam explained that he had learned this from the girl. As he talked, Mary was looking around at the expensively appointed room.

The governor turned his attention to her. "Now tell me, young woman, just how do you know all this?"

Mary Burton wanted to speak—she had memorized every word of what she was supposed to say—but the elegant surroundings and the stern voice of the governor intimidated her, and she couldn't get the words out.

"Don't be afraid," Sam said, stepping to her side. "Just tell Governor Clarke the story exactly the way you told it to me."

"Uh-huh . . ." was all that Mary managed to force from her lips.

The governor looked at her and then at Sam. "See here, de Witt, is this a joke?"

"No, no," Sam said, feeling frantic. And then he had a sudden inspiration. "I think she wants reassurance about the reward money," he said to the governor.

Governor Clarke looked back at the girl. "If you have any information we can use to arrest the guilty parties, you have my personal guarantee you'll get the money."

The mention of money gave Mary the courage she needed. She swallowed, and then the words tumbled from her mouth.

"I was in the tavern. I'd been sleeping on a bench. When I woke up I heard these nigras talking. There were five or six of them sitting at a table. They come in often. They talked about burning down all of New York. They were tired of being treated like slaves, they said, and they wanted to kill every white man and woman they could. I was afraid to move. I was afraid they'd kill me for listening to them, so I pretended to be asleep until they left."

"Are you telling the truth?" the governor asked.

"Oh yes! Yes, sir, indeed, sir," Mary said, and tears began to flow down her cheeks as if she really believed she had spoken the truth and was devastated to think she might not be believed.

The governor turned to Sam. "How did she come to tell you this?"

Sam explained that she had told the story first to John Hughson, who then told it to him.

"Why did you go to Mister de Witt?" the governor said, addressing the hard-looking tavern owner for the first time.

"Well, Your Worship, I know Mary, and I know she's an honest girl. But, being a poor man and all, I wasn't sure I could get anyone of Your Worship's stature to listen. I've had some dealin's with Mister de Witt, and *he* knows *I'm* honest, so I took the story to him. I figured no one would doubt a man of his standin'."

"I questioned the girl at great length, Your Excellency," Sam said. "I'm convinced she's telling the truth."

The governor stroked his chin with his hand. "That's all very well and good, but where does this leave us? Who were the men she overheard in the tavern?"

"She can identify them by their faces," Sam said.

"And I know who one of them is. He lives in a house in the alley behind Mill Street," Mary said quickly, speaking the words Sam had drummed into her brain. "I could bring you right to it."

Within fifteen minutes Mary Burton led Sam, the governor, John Hughson, and a detachment consisting of a sergeant and twenty soldiers to the row of houses behind Mill Street.

The sergeant knocked loudly on the door of Aaron Gerait's house. No one answered. The sergeant put his head against the wood and listened. "I wouldn't swear to it," he said, "but I think I heard someone moving around in there."

"Break down the door," the governor ordered.

The sergeant began battering the door with the butt of his musket. The noise startled the people in the next house, and there was a sudden commotion. One of the soldiers cried out as he spotted a black man trying to climb out the side window of the house.

All activity at Gerait's house ceased as the governor ordered his men to break into the second house. The door was smashed down and the soldiers entered. There was a scuffle, and the sound of a musket echoed from inside.

A black man, blood pouring from his chest, staggered through the door and fell to the dirt of the street. The governor stood above him, looking down with wide eyes as the man died.

There was more shouting from the house, and then the soldiers emerged from inside, kicking and prodding five more black men before them. When the black men tried to protest their innocence, the soldiers only wielded their musket butts more freely.

The shot and the screams brought the surrounding neighborhood to life; people—black and white—came out of their houses and milled about in fear and confusion.

The soldiers shoved the blacks against the side of the house, and there was a lull in the action.

"Do you recognize any of these men?" the governor said to Mary Burton.

She bobbed her head up and down. "Oh, yes, that one over there," she said, pointing at one of the men against the wall. "And that one next to him. Yes, yes, they were both at the tavern."

The governor was pleased. "Good work," he said to the girl. "We'll take good care of this lot, never fear." And he turned back to glare at the terrified Negroes.

Sam was quickly calculating what had happened. The governor could hang these black men or set them free as far as he was concerned. None of this meant a thing unless he got Gerait.

"We can't forget the other house," he said to the governor. "There should be three or four more of them."

The governor ordered the soldiers to smash down the door of Aaron's house. Sam was so anxious to see the black man's face when he was arrested that he followed the soldiers inside. Mary Burton, confused by the turmoil, stayed close at his heels.

Aaron Gerait's woman, Tina, had jumped in fright when the sergeant had first pounded on her door. Her first thought had not been of herself, but of her three-year-old son. But then, after the initial racket, there had been a reprieve as the soldiers had concerned themselves with the house next door. During this time Tina had taken the boy, Richard, and hidden him in a small opening under the floorboards in the back room of the two-room house. It was a place the runaway slave had prepared for herself years ago, when Aaron had first brought her here. But the hiding place was too small for both herself and her son. She put Richard beneath the boards, made him promise to be quiet no matter what happened, and quickly replaced the concealing boards. Then she had gone back to the front room and waited.

Sam regarded her blankly. Where the hell was that bastard Gerait?

Mary Burton, at Sam's elbow, suddenly cried out. "That's her! There was a woman in the tavern that night. That's her!"

The soldiers dragged Tina outside, twisting her arm cruelly and making her cry out. The growing crowd of whites greeted her with loud catcalls and jeers, for by now the word of why the blacks were being arrested had spread.

"Kill the arsonists!" a man shouted, and the cry was taken up by others.

"We'll teach them to burn our homes!"

"Kill them!"

"Everything must be handled in a legal manner," the governor said hurriedly.

But Governor Clarke had misgauged the mood of the crowd. These were people who had been in terror for weeks, afraid to go to sleep lest someone come and burn their house from under them. Some were actual victims, and they wanted revenge, legal or otherwise. As the mob began to close in on the blacks, the governor realized something had to be done, and quickly.

"We will have trials!" he cried out.

"When?" the querulous mob wanted to know.

"Immediately," the governor shouted, realizing these people would brook no delay. "We'll go back to City Hall and try them now!"

The crowd roared its approval, and the governor breathed a sigh of relief. He ordered the sergeant to take the Negroes to City Hall. The soldiers began to goad their frightened charges down the street.

"What about their leader?" Sam asked the harried governor.

"Who?"

"The man who owns this house. We haven't got him yet."

"Dammit, man," the governor replied. "The first thing is to take care of this group. Now, before there's a riot."

Sam became desperate. "Where's the man you live with?" he demanded of Tina.

Tina was a timid person, afraid of almost everyone and everything. But until Richard was born, the one glorious, bright spot in her life had been Aaron Gerait. She looked straight at Sam and was silent.

He realized that time was precious. "Where is Aaron Gerait?" he shouted at the woman, and lashed her across the face with the back of his hand, cutting her lip and raising a welt.

Tina really did not know where Aaron had gone. She knew only that he had left the house early in the morning and would be back by evening. She knew this much, but she also knew that she would die before she told this white man anything at all about her man.

Sam raised his hand to hit her again, but the governor restrained him. "Stop this! We've got to get to City Hall before this mob goes berserk!"

The governor led the way, with Sam and Mary Burton close behind. The soldiers followed with their prisoners, and behind them swirled the mob. As they made their way toward Wall Street, more people joined them, and by the time they came to City Hall, there were over three hundred people in the streets.

"Hold the trial! Hold the trial!"

The governor sent for Judge de Lancey, who somehow had managed to hold on to his position after the Zenger affair, and the trial began at once—right out in the open, on the steps of City Hall and on the spacious green in front of it.

The first Negro was dragged to the stand. The judge banged his gavel. "This man is accused of . . ." he began, and then realized no one had told him what the trial was about.

"He's one of *them!*" Mary Burton cried out to the judge when Sam pinched her elbow.

"One of whom?" de Lancey asked in understandable confusion.

"One of the ones who's burning down the city," Sam cried.

The mob took up this chant. Judge de Lancey looked over at the governor, who nodded his head and pointed his thumb toward the ground in the way the Romans had done when they wanted a gladiator to go for a kill in the arena.

That was enough for de Lancey, whose motto was "Never argue with a superior." He turned to the black man who had been shoved before him. "What is your name?" he asked in his most official voice.

"Nero, sir," the terrified man replied.

"Who do you belong to?"

"Yes, sir, Mastah Roosevelt, sir."

"Well, Nero, do you have anything to say in your defense before this court passes judgment on you?"

The man's eyes widened. His lips parted, but what was there to say? His shoulder ached where the soldier had pounded him with the musket; he didn't understand what he was being accused of; he didn't know what the judge was asking; he hadn't the slightest idea of why the mob had dragged him to this place. So he said nothing.

"Burn him!" a man near the front of the crowd cried out.

"The court finds you guilty, Nero, and your punishment is . . . Your punishment is that you are to be taken from this place and hanged by the neck until you are dead," de Lancey concluded, having glanced again at Governor Clarke.

"*Now!* Hang him *now!*"

The cry was taken up by the crowd, and for the third time the judge looked toward the governor.

Clarke was well aware it wouldn't take much of a spark to ignite a full-scale riot. If he had been a stronger man and more secure in his power, he might have been able to follow his conscience. It might have helped had the judge been someone other than de Lancey, someone who would have questioned his decisions. But ever since Clarke had been appointed acting governor, upon the death of William Cosby, he had worried about being replaced by someone from England. Five years had passed, and his appointment had still not been made permanent. If he didn't act quickly, there would be a violent riot, and he would be held responsible.

He looked at de Lancey and nodded his assent.

The judge turned to the master-at-arms. "Take this man out and hang him now," he said.

A great cheer rose from the people, and many of them followed the soldiers as they dragged the unfortunate Nero toward the gibbet which always stood in front of City Hall. Even as they were putting the rope around the condemned man's neck, the judge ordered the second black brought before the bar.

There was a sudden agitation at the rear of the crowd, which had now swelled to four hundred people, and two burly men came forward, dragging a black man between them. "This one is guilty too," one of the white men shouted. The crowd howled its approval, and the black man was shoved forward until he stood with the others accused of arson. Following this lead, a few other men saw the occasion as a good opportunity to get rid of some poor black they disliked. They would track down the marked wretch, drag him out of house or stable, and bring him to the middle of the crowd. "Here's another arsonist," the white man would cry, and that was enough evidence for the mob.

Jan de Kuyper and Theo Henry arrived on Wall Street and could hardly believe their eyes. A trial was being conducted on the green in front of the government house. Just down the street an angry mob was hanging a Negro.

But now the mob was no longer content with hanging the blacks one by one. It was too slow. They took a condemned man and tied him to a tall stake. They piled wood and brush at his feet and set fire to it. The smoke curled up around the tortured man's face, and he screamed and began choking as it entered his lungs. The soldiers stood idly by and allowed the mob to do as it wished.

"What the hell is going on?" Jan asked in astonishment.

"They must have caught the Negroes who've been setting the fires," Theo said.

Jan shook his head. "Do you believe those rumors?"

"I don't know," Theo admitted. "But it looks as if a lot of other people do."

The activity was everywhere, and Jan and Theo scarcely began looking at one horror when their attention was diverted by another.

"Good God!" Jan said, grasping Theo's arm and pointing toward a woman who was being tied to a stake atop a pile of wooden faggots. "That's Aaron's woman."

"You're sure?"

"Yes. I've only seen her a couple of times, but that's her, all right."

"What can we do?"

"The governor's over there by City Hall," Jan said. "Let's talk to him."

The two men shoved their way determinedly through the mob. No one paid them any attention.

Jan finally managed to fight his way to the governor's side. "Why are they killing that woman?" he demanded, pointing toward the stake where Tina was now firmly bound.

"What's it to you?" the governor snarled, and then he recognized Jan. "She's one of the ringleaders."

"Ringleaders of what?"

"The ones who've been setting all the fires."

"That woman didn't set fire to anything," Jan said. "How did this all start?"

"Ask your cousin," the governor replied, and pointed toward Sam de Witt, who stood apart with Mary Burton, watching intently as a soldier approached the stake with a burning brand.

"What's Sam got to do with all this?"

"He's the one who uncovered the plot."

"Sam?"

"Together with that woman with him."

Jan peered closely at the governor to make sure that the man was serious. Then, convinced that he was, he began making his way toward his cousin. The air was suddenly filled with Tina's shrieks as the flames began lapping at her bare feet and legs. He stopped and watched, paralyzed, as the flames shot higher. The smoke swirled about the slender figure of the woman and, mercifully, brought suffocation and a quick death.

Jan looked back toward his cousin and quickly turned away again, sickened by the satisfaction he saw on Sam's face. He pushed his way back through the mob and walked away from the display of sadism. Theo finally caught up with him at the docks along the bank of the Hudson.

"They're really savages back there," Theo said. "They're dragging corpses to the Fresh Pond and throwing them into the water. And not always in one piece. People are chopping off hands and feet. It's unbelievable, Jan; the water is turning red."

Jan had nothing to say. He drew in large gulps of fresh air to cleanse his body of the awful stench of burning flesh and the sight of bodies dangling from broken necks. The problem of the Negroes had finally exploded. He had seen trouble coming for some time. Over the past few years more and more laws had been passed restricting the blacks' freedom of action. It was forbidden for three of them to gather in any one place. A black man caught with a club in his hands was given fifty lashes. No black slave could leave his owner's property without permission. It was a procession of law after law, indignity after indignity.

But he had never expected to see the people of New York acting like wild animals.

He walked back to his house on Maiden Lane with Theo at his side, but neither man felt any desire to talk. They passed angry gangs on the streets; men hunting down Negroes, chasing them down streets and alleys, cornering them in dead ends and doorways, beating them and then dragging them off to the tender mercies of Judge de Lancey and the mob at City Hall.

Jan and Theo split up. Each of them visited several taverns and liberally dispensed money to anyone who could tell them about the origins of the rioting.

It didn't take Jan long to confirm what he knew in his heart: that the governor had been telling the truth and the accusations of his own cousin, Sam de Witt, had precipitated the murderous madness. He went back to his house on Maiden Lane and downed several stiff drinks while he waited.

The door opened.

"Theo?"

"Yes, Jan," said his friend, entering the room and heading straight for the sideboard with the rum bottles. "What did you learn?"

"That little bastard Sam—it was him."

Theo nodded. "Hear anything else?"

"You mean there's more?"

"I was in a place run by a man named Hughson. Somebody gave me a tip it was him who actually started the fires. I accused him of it," Theo said, taking a big swig of rum and refilling his glass. "It's amazing what you can learn when you put a gun to someone's head."

"You really used a gun?"

Theo nodded. "It was a rough place. Anyway, I found out that Hughson paid men to set the fires. But he wasn't really behind it all, because another man had paid *him.*"

"Did you get that man's name?"

"Yes."

There was a pause and Jan waited, anxious for the news, but dreading to hear it.

"It was Sam."

"Jesus Christ!"

"What are you going to do?" Theo asked.

It was dark when Aaron Gerait came back across the river from New Jersey. He knew something was terribly wrong when he saw the fires burning in the Wall Street area and heard the shouts and screams in the dark. There was also a complete absence of the usual activity along the wharfs. He tied up his sloop and stepped warily ashore, his hand not far from the pistol he had taken the precaution of sticking in his belt.

He made his way toward his house in the alley behind Mill Street and was a block away when he came across an old white man carrying a heavy stick. The old man lived in the neighborhood, and he and Aaron were nodding acquaintants.

"Jesus, man, where you been?"

"Away," Aaron said curtly. "What's going on?"

"You mean you don't know?"

Aaron shook his head and the old man proceeded to tell him about the uncovering of the plot to burn New York. "They came to your house, too," he said. "Took your wife away. Don't know where. God only knows what they did with her."

Aaron eyed the man's stick with suspicion. "And of course you've had no part in any of this?"

The old man realized Aaron was looking at his stick. "Not me. I'm only carrying this to protect myself," he said, gesturing toward the stick with his other hand. "It's gotten completely out of hand. Now people are claiming there were whites involved in the plot. Already hung two or three of them—white men, that is. I guess it's a good time for a man to get even with his enemies. Anyone comes accusing me of anything is going to get this right in his face."

"Thanks," Aaron said softly, and then ran the remaining distance to his house. He stopped when he saw the battered door. He peered inside, saw nothing, and stepped over the threshold. He made his way to the back of the house to see if anyone was in the hiding place under the boards.

Marie Therese had left the house earlier to visit Mary Brevoort at her family's farm a few miles north of town. She was alone in the back of her carriage as it approached Maiden Lane and she saw a group of men chasing a terrified boy. He was white, about sixteen or seventeen years of age, and his pursuers had finally trapped him against an iron fence. He stood there with a smear of blood on his face, his trousers torn, panting like a wounded and exhausted animal.

She ordered her driver to stop, got out of the carriage, and came up behind the men who were moving in to pounce on the boy.

"What do you think you are doing!"

The men whirled about, ready to attack anyone who tried to interfere with them. But the imperious voice and expensive clothing of the woman made them pause. She was the epitome of a class they were accustomed to treating with deference.

"Well?" Marie Therese said.

"This here scum be one of them who's been burning the buildings," said a burly man, whose open mouth revealed a great many missing teeth.

"Nonsense," Marie Therese said. "He's an indentured

boy who works for the saddler in the shop near the theater. He does odd jobs for me as well."

"He be one of the nigra plotters," the man said with a bit less conviction than before.

"That's stupid," Marie Therese said. "Anyone can see he's white." She turned toward the cowering boy, who was trying to clean some of the blood from his cheek. "You come along with me now, and I'll see that you get home safely."

The leader was about to renew his objections, but one of the other ruffians stepped to his side and whispered in his ear. "I work at the docks, mate, and I've seen her before. That's Jan de Kuyper's wife."

"So what?"

"So you touch her and you'll bloody well dance at the end of a rope, that's what."

"Come along," Marie Therese said to the boy. "Nobody's going to harm you."

The boy slowly made his way forward and climbed into the carriage next to Marie Therese. The coachman snapped his whip, and they moved away from the knot of sullen, frustrated men.

"You didn't really have anything to do with the fires, did you?" Marie Therese asked the boy.

"No, ma'am, not a thing."

"That's good to hear."

"You mean, ma'am, you weren't sure about it back there?" the boy asked.

"No, how could I be?"

"Then why did you save me?"

"I don't like mobs," she said. "You'd better come home with me. You can spend the night in the hayloft above the stable."

The boy crouched down as low as possible. "Yes, ma'am," he said gratefully.

Marie Therese had no idea what had been going on, but anything that caused such fear in a simple boy had to be wrong.

Jan came to the back door when he heard the knock. He opened it and took a step back when he saw the shape of a man standing in the shadows.

"It's only me—Aaron," the visitor said, stepping into the weak light coming from the lamp inside the door.

"Come in," Jan said quickly. He stepped outside and held the door for the black man, who was carrying his young son in his arms. Jan looked up and down the alley and was satisfied that nobody had followed Aaron.

The little boy was placed in a bed in an alcove, and he went back to sleep immediately. Jan poured a generous amount of rum into a goblet and handed it to Aaron, who downed it at once and handed it back for a refill.

"Tell me what happened."

Jan related the events of the day as best he knew them, his account not differing greatly from what Aaron had heard from the old man and seen for himself on the streets. Then, finally, Jan had to say it.

"They burned Tina. I saw it myself. There was nothing I could do. The smoke got to her quickly, so it wasn't as bad as it could have been," he added, hating himself for trying to minimize the enormity of a burning at the stake.

Aaron said nothing. He sat in the chair, his hopelessness written on his face. He shook his head when Jan offered to refill his goblet a second time. "It might be best if you took your son and went to my father's manor," Jan suggested.

Aaron shook his head again. "Not me. But I'd be in your debt if you arranged to send Richard there."

"My father will be glad to have him," Jan assured the anguished man. "He'll turn the lad into a farmer."

"Too bad he can't turn him white," Aaron said bitterly.

"What do you plan to do?"

"They came to my house and dragged her away," the black man said, his cold tones suggesting he was in full control of his passions. "Poor Tina. She never hurt anyone in her life. And then to die like . . ." He looked up at Jan. "I'm going to find out who led the mob to my house. I'm going to find out and then . . . he belongs to me."

Jan was wrestling with his conscience. Sam de Witt, after all, no matter what he had done, was still his own cousin. But then he remembered Sam's face as he had watched the woman burn.

"Sam de Witt's the man you want."

Aaron's eyes opened wide.

"More than that," Jan continued in anguish. "He's the one who started the fires that everyone's blaming on the blacks."

"Good God!"

"I think he organized the whole thing just to get at you."

"Me?" And then Aaron understood. "Because of the Cosby thing? I found out about him and told you, is that it?"

"That's what I think."

"But all those other people . . ."

"Sam wanted revenge, and to hell with how many innocent people would get hurt," Jan said bitterly.

Aaron's face was a stone. "You know what I'm going to do, don't you?"

Jan nodded.

"I must do it, you understand that?"

"Yes."

Aaron stood up. He moved toward Jan, and the two men clasped hands. Then Aaron started toward the door.

"You're always welcome here," Jan said.

"After this, how could I have any doubts?"

Sam de Witt was in his cups as he celebrated with other members of the lynch mob at the Squire's tavern. Half a dozen men were sprawled over the benches and on the floor, passed out from drink. Sam mumbled his good-byes and slapped several men on the back as he wove his way unsteadily toward the door. He staggered out to the street, where he tried to collect himself. He straightened his hat, smoothed his coat, and began making his way down the narrow street toward Broad Way. He had gotten halfway down the block when he felt himself grabbed from behind. A heavy hand lashed against the side of his head and he fell into unconsciousness.

When he awoke, he began to shake his head to clear his vision, but was quickly stopped by the intense aching of his head. And then he forgot the pain as he realized Aaron Gerait was only a few feet away, staring at him with unblinking eyes.

Sam looked about wildly. They seemed to be in the bottom of a small boat. A heavy canvas covering was drawn over the top, and the only light was from a flickering candle.

"What do you want?" Sam managed to say through lips that were thick and dry.

"I've thought about making you die the way she did," Aaron said softly. "But I can't do it. I'm not that sort of a man."

"What are you talking about," Sam said nervously, his aching head now completely forgotten. He was alone with this giant black and realized that if the man wanted to kill him, there wasn't a thing he could do about it.

"The woman you killed."

"I didn't kill anybody."

Aaron ignored this. "The only way to do it is the quickest way."

He picked Sam up with one arm, took him to the side of the boat, and threw back the canvas covering. Sam saw that the boat was tied to the end of a pier and the dark waters of the Hudson were directly below him. And then he realized there was a length of heavy anchor chain tied to his legs.

"No—" He started to cry out, but the black man dropped him over the side and the heavy chain pulled him down through the water. His mouth was open, and he started to choke and claw at the cold death about him. The chain struck the bottom. Silt and mud drifted up around Sam as he frantically tried to undo the chain from his legs. But he failed; his tortured lungs ruptured and he died.

Aaron didn't look back after he had thrown his victim into the water. He pulled the canvas over the boat and left the wharf.

He didn't even feel good about what he had done.

The furor over the "Negro plot" ended within a week. In all, over three dozen men and women were known to have died. No one ever learned what had happened to Sam de Witt.

The restrictions against Negroes were made harsher than ever, and the black people of New York walked warily through the streets. They were all aware that even the freemen among them had no rights in the eyes of a mob.

Mary Burton enjoyed a certain notoriety for a few months, but then her body was found behind Hughson's tavern. She had been horribly mutilated. No one knew if a Negro had taken his revenge or if it had been one of her drinking companions. No one seemed to care, and no attempt was made to find her murderer.

John Hughson's assistant arrived for work one morning and found his employer behind his own bar. His back had been broken. Since Hughson had lived a violent life, the manner of his death came as no surprise.

Judge de Lancey was finally removed from the bench. He did not leave with good grace, but kept insisting all his problems had been caused by others and he was nothing more than an unfortunate victim. He began to spend most of his time in taverns, telling all his woes to anyone who would listen. After a time people stopped thinking of him less as the awful judge he had been, and more as the pest he had become.

Aaron Gerait took it upon himself to become Jan de Kuyper's personal bodyguard and companion. At first Jan protested that he had no need for such a thing. But Aaron was not to be dissuaded, and finally Jan put him on a salary with the company. He stayed with Jan, and Richard Gerait began to live the life of a young farm boy on de Kuyper manor.

Aaron had concluded that if he aligned himself more directly with the powerful de Kuyper family, he might be in a better position to help other men of his own color. Surely he could be more effective if he stood with men of influence. He decided he would become a black voice of conscience in the midst of the ruling white class. It was as grand a task as this that he set for himself, and as simple.

Charles Goelet retired from the company, and Theo Henry was moved into his place.

In the spring of 1742 Alice de Kuyper Livingston made her first trip to England. There was nothing particularly unusual about a wealthy woman from the colonies paying a visit to the old country. Alice, however, chose to go in the company of Lewis Morris. Tongues wagged over the scandal, but Alice paid absolutely no attention to any of it. Then, in a surprise move, she and Morris visited Amsterdam. "Most of my family," she said by way of explanation, "still consider the Netherlands as the mother country rather than England." The remark did little to endear her to Lewis Morris's friends in London.

She looked up the Amsterdam de Kuypers and found several cousins, sons and daughters of her father's brother. who introduced her to their own sons and grandsons, daughters and granddaughters. A festive reunion was held to celebrate this mingling of the far-flung branches of the family. Before Alice left Holland, all her cousins promised to visit New York sometime in the future. Alice confided to Lewis Morris her opinion that they made these promises only because they didn't want to hurt her feelings. "What a fat, self-satisfied bunch they are," she said. "It's a good thing Grandfather Pieter came to America, otherwise we'd all be like our smug cousins, content with our beer and sausages."

In 1743 Marie Therese gave birth to Celine de Kuyper, a lively, healthy baby. Jan was pleased, although he would have preferred a boy. The succession of leadership in the company remained to trouble him.

In the same year, George Clinton arrived from England and took up his post as governor of the province. George Clarke, of course, was convinced he had been replaced because of the riots.

In 1744 Henry de Forest started the first afternoon newspaper in New York. Alice Livingston was invited to contribute to the *Evening Post,* but her first three articles were scathing attacks on Governor Clinton's treatment of women as inferiors, and de Forest politely informed her that her services would no longer be required. Still, she succeeded in having the governor blacklisted from several of the more important social events of the season. Henry de Forest also found it difficult to obtain invitations to the better homes in New York.

The years were passing, and the de Kuyper family was enjoying an increase in its fortunes and an absence of tragedy in its ranks.

James de Kuyper was flattered when, in 1745, a touring marquis brought two of his powerful workhorses and shipped them back to England. "They make our stock look like sows," the marquis said of James's horses.

David de Witt Sackett was sent to London for further schooling. Jan instructed him to concentrate on the study of law, as that would be the most valuable skill he could bring back to the family business.

Edward Goelet was still the black sheep of the family. He drank. He gambled. He didn't come home for days on end. His father refused to speak to him and told Edward's wife, Dora, that she should leave him.

Edward got into a brawl one night in 1746 over cheating in a dice game, and his left foot was cut badly by a knife. It was a week before he went to a doctor, but by that time the foot was bloated and discolored and the doctor wanted to cut it off. Edward refused to allow this and almost died; but when the struggle was over, he had kept both his life and his foot. As a reminder of the experience he had a slight limp that would remain with him for the rest of his life. Everyone in the family thought that now, at last, Edward would come to his senses, but nothing of the sort happened. Two weeks later he was back drinking and gambling as before.

Jan was beginning to suspect there was more to his cousin's behavior than anyone knew. He went to see him one morning as Edward was on the docks checking the cargo of one of the company's ships.

"I'd like to find something better in the company for you," Jan said.

Edward smiled. "You can put me in charge of our wastrel department."

"I'm serious," Jan said in annoyance.

"So am I."

"What the hell are you doing to yourself? You ignore your wife and the rest of your family. Your father won't speak to you and he's told you never to enter his house. You spend your time with gamblers and whores and bums. Now I come to you and say I'd like to do something for you, and you won't let me."

"Damn it, leave me alone," Edward said fiercely. "That's all I ask. I'll do my job here, and if I want to get stinking drunk every night, well, that's my own business."

"And the whores?"

"That too."

"But *why*, Ned?" Jan asked. The use of the boyhood nickname and the soft plea in his voice touched Edward's heart and brought him close to tears.

"I can't tell you, Jan. I can't tell anyone. Maybe some-day, but not now."

He walked away, his head bowed and his shoulders pinched forward. His limp seemed more pronounced.

Jan was suddenly sorry he had attacked his cousin. The man carried a sorrowful burden, and Jan was ashamed for not realizing it before now. His sense of shame melted slowly into a mild anger. He and Edward had always been very close, and it seemed that if his cousin had a prob-lem, he should confide in him. Who else would be more understanding?

The useless, debauched existence of Edward Goelet be-came a cankerous sore to Jan. He thought about it, brooded over it, and, in the end, tried to forget about it. If Edward wanted to live his own life, and to share his problems with no one, that was his decision and he would have to live with it.

But the basic question about Edward never really left his mind. What the hell was wrong with the man?

It was during this time that James came down from his manor and badgered the governor into putting a second bridge across the Harlem River.

"The population of Westchester is growing," he argued. "There are many more farmers now than there were a few years ago, and it's often difficult for them to bring their crops and cattle to the city. Goods become scarce and their prices go up. A second bridge would ease the transportation problem and increase our prosperity."

Governor Clinton was indifferent, and the city council voted against the expense. But James refused to give up.

He organized a farmer's boycott of the city and threat-ened to ship all cattle, fresh produce, dairy products, and other goods to Philadelphia or Boston. For two weeks nothing entered the city from the north. The ship owners and warehousemen complained. The merchants who needed fresh produce and meat to maintain their busi-nesses complained. The draymen, who were now spending their days in idleness, complained. Everyone was com-plaining, and finally the merchants held a meeting and a delegation was sent to the governor.

Governor Clinton recognized that the boycott was play-ing havoc with the city's economic life. He ordered the city council members to reconsider their recent decision.

He made it quite plain that he would be peeved unless the council agreed to finance James de Kuyper's new bridge.

The council met and Charles Goelet, still a member and as acid-tongued as ever, suggested that "as long as James de Kuyper comes to this chamber as a bandit to get his way, he might as well go all the way and wear a mask and carry a gun."

Even James couldn't conceal a smile at this gibe, and the council hastened to vote to raise the necessary funds to build the new bridge.

In the fall of 1747 a de Kuyper ship returned from a voyage to the northern Maine coast. The captain filed his report and claimed he had been fired on by a ship flying a French flag. Governor Clinton said the ship must have been a pirate and dismissed the affair, refusing even to make a mild protest to the French government.

"That was no pirate," Jan said to Theo. "Every year the French grow bolder. And every year they move far-ther and farther south."

"It's the same in Europe," Theo said. "The French are out to gobble up the world. The day will come when we won't be able to ignore the French threat."

"So, you think we're heading for war?"

"Don't you?"

Jan was silent for a moment. "Yes," he finally said. "I've always hated the idea of a European war being brought here, but I'm afraid it's going to happen."

"We'd best prepare for it."

"More cannon for our ships would be a good place to start."

5

Buried Treasure
1754–1758

A COLD NOVEMBER WIND SWEPT ACROSS THE
lonely spit of land—a wind grown frigid from grazing Atlantic wavetops for thousands of unhindered miles until
it encountered this rocky island at the edge of the American continent. A full moon bathed the world in silver. A
small sloop rocked at anchor, and a procession of figures
moved inland, their steps guided by two pitch torches as
they made their way through a stand of leafless trees and
came to an outcropping of gray, iron-tinged rocks. They
moved northward along the rockface until the leader held
up his hand and the column stopped. The leader searched
carefully, and found the place he was looking for. He
stepped into a thicket of heavy bracken. When he moved
the brush aside, the dark mouth of a small cave was revealed.

There were five people, four men and a lone woman:
Alice Livingston, James de Kuyper and his son Jan,
Aaron Gerait, and Theo Henry. James entered the murky
cave with a torch in his hand. Jan followed close behind.

The flickering light pierced the gloom, and James looked
about, sifting back through his memory to recall the last
time he had stood in this place. It was several minutes before he moved over to a large, flat chunk of sandstone.
He stood silent for a few moments, then tapped the sandstone with his foot.

"It was here," he said. "I'm certain we buried it right at
this spot."

There was no discussion. They walked out of the cave,

and James lit his pipe while the three younger men took
picks and shovels and went back inside. Alice stood beside her brother as he smoked, both of them listening to
the muted sounds of digging.

"It wasn't wise of you to come," James said.

"Nonsense," Alice replied. "After all these years I
wanted to see what the fuss was all about."

"This is neither a healthy place nor a safe one for a
woman," James insisted, and then playfully added, "especially one who's getting along in years."

"What am I supposed to do? Sit by the fire and knit?
Or pet the cat?"

James reached out and touched his sister's arm. "I wonder how much more you could have done for the family
had you been a man."

She took his hand and held it affectionately. "The men
we have seem to be doing all right."

"We seem to hold up," James admitted. He was seventy years old, but his body was still trim and well kept.
His full shock of hair was now silver heavily flecked with
white, accentuating the perpetual tan of his skin.

The minutes passed slowly. It was as cold as a tomb
inside the cave, but the men were sweating from their
labors. Half an hour later Theo's shovel bit down into the
hard earth and reverberated with a metallic ring. The
men stopped for a brief instant and then doubled their
efforts.

Ten minutes passed; another ten.

James put aside his pipe when he saw Aaron dragging
a chest from the cave. It was ancient and scarred, oak
banded with broad, heavy strips of iron and sealed with
a three-pound lock.

The others gathered about in fascination as Aaron
wedged an iron bar behind the hinge plate of the lock.
The sweat popped from his forehead and his neck muscles stood out as he bent the bar until the lock tore off
with a loud screech. He wiped the dirt and rust away
from the hinges, looked at the others, and then slowly
raised the lid.

There was an audible exhaling as Theo's torch gave a
glimpse of the chest's contents. James gingerly dipped his
fist into the treasure and then brought it back up. A wa-
terfall of coins dripped from his open hand—coins of all

sizes and shapes, their surfaces catching and reflecting the
flickering light of the torch.

Gold.

The lost treasure of Captain Kidd was seen by living
men for the first time in over half a century. It had remained on Gardiner's Island, undetected and unclaimed,
exactly where James had helped bury it when he was little more than a boy.

All of them—except Alice, whose dignity restrained
her—dug their hands into the treasure, feeling, touching,
their disbelief registered on their faces. There were coins
of gold, chains of gold, brooches of gold, pendants and
pins of gold, buckles and clasps of gold, plates and goblets of gold, bits of gold, chunks of gold—gold, gold, gold
—more of it in one place than any of them except James
had ever seen before.

"That's a lot of wampum," Theo Henry said, attempting to sound humorous and unimpressed.

"This is one of the gold chests," James said, and then
explained. "We kept the gold, silver, and jewels in separate chests."

Jan shook his head at his father's matter-of-fact tone.
There was a fortune here, a great fortune, and his father
spoke of it as if it were a cargo of lumber, nails, or tar.

"Hadn't we better get the other chests out of the
ground?" James asked.

There were eight chests in all, and by the time they
were dug out of the ground and dragged to the sloop, it
was dawn and everyone was exhausted. Before they departed, however, James insisted they re-cover the cave
and remove any traces of their presence.

They shipped the sloop's anchor and set the sails, and
the little craft made its way back into Long Island Sound.
When it was out in open water, it turned west and began
the return voyage to New York.

It was a rather shabby looking boat, and that was the
very reason Jan had chosen it. Nothing about the sloop
made her look like a worthwhile target for a pirate or enterprising privateer. On the other hand, despite her looks,
the little sloop was as swift a craft as anything to be
found in these waters. Even if they did encounter a pirate, they could probably outrun him.

For a long time no one spoke. Each was immersed in

his own thoughts, all of which concerned the chests hidden belowdecks in the narrow hold. The wealth of the
Indies rested beneath their feet, protected by a few inches
of wooden hull on a small sailing vessel that carried not a
single cannon. Considering the dangers to be found in
these waters, theirs were sober thoughts indeed.

Jan had known about the treasure for three years. He
had taken his father's advice and left it undisturbed because it seemed the wisest thing to do. The events of the
past year had changed all this.

The English and the French were now at war in the
New World, and their desperate struggle for one another's colonies was becoming known as the French and Indian War. At first it seemed an unequal struggle, because
the English had a million and a half settlers in America
while there were only about sixty thousand Frenchmen.
But the English were spread from Georgia to Maine, and
the French were collected mostly in the Quebec area,
controlled directly from Montreal. Furthermore, the English had been at war for so many years in Europe—with
the Netherlands, with Spain, in the War of the Austrian
Succession—that their resources were stretched and their
forces faltering, while the French were at the zenith of
their power and influence.

The French also had the assistance of the powerful
Hurons and other Indian tribes of the north.

Jan's trading experience had made him well aware of
the vital role the Indians would play in this war. He had
been among the first to press for a pact with the chiefs of
the five tribes of the Iroquois Nation. The delegation sent
to Albany for this purpose was headed by Benjamin
Franklin of Philadelphia and, at Jan's urging, had included Theo Henry.

Theo had reported back that the Iroquois were most
anxious to fight the French and their Huron allies. "But
the chiefs want a great deal in the way of wampum and
weapons. Knowing Indians as I do," he said, "if we don't
keep them happy, we won't keep them fighting."

Jan had agreed, and the two of them went to the governor to ask that he make Theo his liaison to the Iroquois
chiefs in the north.

"You're part Indian yourself, aren't you, Henry?" Governor Clinton asked, looking somewhat dubiously at Theo's darker-than-average features.

"I'm also part Englishman," Theo replied evenly.

"And he knows the capacities of this port," Jan said. "He'll be able to tell what we can deliver and what we can't."

"Promise something to the Indians, and then if you don't deliver, you're in trouble," Theo added.

The governor finally nodded his assent.

"Ironic, isn't it?" Theo said to Jan as they left the governor's office. "Now I'm the man who'll supply the same tribes who used to slaughter my grandfather's people."

"Just do the job and forget ancient history," Jan grumbled, aware that the other man sometimes used his Indian blood to create sympathy for himself. But he had smiled inwardly, because he knew that if their positions were reversed, he would do the same whenever it seemed convenient.

Despite all the obstacles put in his path—by governmental bungling and by the uncooperativeness of men who didn't understand why whites should supply weapons to Indians—Theo had been doing a good job, far better than the governor had thought possible. It had become a full-time task, keeping him from his normal work at the de Kuyper company. But he never complained: it was something that had to be done.

But now, as he stood at the railing and watched James de Kuyper at the helm of the sloop speeding across the cold waters of Long Island Sound, his thoughts were not about the English and the Iroquois. Like the others, he had fixed his mind on the treasure below.

"I don't know," Aaron Gerait said, shaking his head. "I still think it would have been safer back there in the ground."

"Possibly," James admitted. "But when it's in the ground no one can use it. And I think this is going to be a tough war—one we must win. We can't have French privateers skimming the cream of wealth from our ships."

"I'm sure the French feel exactly the same way about us," Jan said.

James was patient. "Yes, but in this case we're right and the French are wrong."

Aaron shrugged. "I don't see that life would be much different if we lived under the French."

"He's probably right," Jan agreed. "Our city started as a Dutch possession and became English. It made no difference to the fortunes of our family."

"We're English and will not live under a French flag," James said with rare anger. "The Dutch came as exploiters, as did the French. The English are different. They came here to live, not to drain wealth from the land."

"Nonsense," Alice said from her cozy position under a heavy blanket. "They've all come to take what they can get." She looked at her brother. "They say Grandfather Pieter died of a broken heart because the English drove out the Dutch. Are you planning to do the same if the French take over?"

"No," James said quietly. "I'm getting to the point where nothing's going to kill me except old age. But don't you think of yourself as an Englishwoman? What does the Netherlands have to do with you?"

"It's where our people came from."

"It's not where we are now," James said stubbornly. "We're in New York. We're English, and we must fight the king's enemies."

Jan was about to speak out, but he changed his mind. He realized for the first time in his life that there was a very basic difference between the way he looked at New York and the way his father did. James thought of himself as an Englishman, and Jan was beginning to have another view. He thought of himself as English, yes; but there was a difference between himself and the London traders and merchants. The latter came to the colonies for profit. If the colonies disappeared, they would seek riches elsewhere. But Jan and his family looked upon New York as home as well as the source of their wealth. And as a trader Jan lived daily with the inequity forced upon the colonists by the British Navigation Acts.

The acts decreed it was against the law for colonials to sell most goods to any buyer except England and her colonies. Naturally, Jan and the other traders did their best to circumvent this law; hence the proliferation of privateers doing business with anyone who would pay a fair price.

But it was unfair, Jan realized, and it set up a barrier between Englishmen living in England and those residing elsewhere.

He also realized that his father was probably right about their most urgent need being the defeat of the French. That had to come first. Then the men of the colonies could go about the business of righting the other wrongs.

The sun came up slowly, not as a bright red disc, but as a dim yellow haze hidden behind the heavy storm clouds. But it was enough to give some visibility and make it easier for the man at the wheel. They took turns at the helm throughout the blustery day, their eyes constantly scanning the horizon for the appearance of other vessels.

By the time they reached Hell Gate and passed down along the lee side of Blackwell's Island in the middle of the East River, it was the middle of the next night.

They welcomed the darkness as they docked at the company pier and transferred the cargo under canvas wraps to the theater on Maiden Lane. It was stored in a hidden vault that had been prepared in the cellar. Before returning to their homes, they allowed themselves the privilege of looking at the contents of several chests. No one else was to know about the precious hoard. Not Marie Therese, or Charlie Goelet. Certainly not Edward Goelet, who at forty-seven looked ten years older and walked around in the perpetual haze of a middle-aged drunk.

James returned to his manor, content that he had properly dispensed with Kidd's treasure. It now rested in the hands of his son and in the will of God.

The first person to greet him as he rode up to the stables was Richard Gerait, Aaron's teenaged son, who was developing into a gifted horse trainer. James did not mention to Richard that he had seen his father. He greeted the young man pleasantly and then went into the house, where Hope waited with a hearty soup and a cold glass of beer. He never mentioned the treasure to her, either.

Jan went back to work, and the cellar on Maiden Lane receded into the back of his mind. The war with the French created a fourfold increase in the activity of the port of New York. Troopships arrived steadily and disgorged their additions to the army being built up on American shores. Cargo ships of all sizes and types came from Europe and the far-flung English colonies. Jan's business prospered and his workday lengthened, especially now that Theo Henry was gone for weeks at a time.

Theo went at least once a month to Albany, and from there into the hinterland to work with the chiefs of the Iroquois. The red men were constantly unhappy with the arms shipments delivered to them, claiming the French were doing a far better job for the Hurons. Theo was aware that many of these complaints were unfair, but it was his task to soothe the chiefs and make them as happy as possible. Let them complain so long as they remain loyal was the official order from the governor.

With Theo gone, Jan realized how valuable he had become to the company. Theo had taken over much of the work connected with their ships, leaving Jan to proceed with his land investments and developments. But now, with Theo almost never around, Jan found himself spending all of his time with the ships and their cargoes. They had to be dealt with immediately; the land deals would have to wait until the war was over.

The war. Things didn't look too bright on *this* front. General Braddock had fought a battle with the French in Virginia. His forces had been soundly beaten, and Braddock himself was mortally wounded in the savage fighting. The leader of his colonial auxiliaries, an obscure young colonel named George Washington, managed to lead the remainder of the troops to the safety of Fort Cumberland.

An army of thirty-five hundred colonials and four hundred Indian allies built Fort William Henry and defeated the French at the battle of Lake George. It was supposed to be the beginning of a great surge to the north, but, to the puzzlement of observers in the city, no such action was taken.

Theo returned to New York and reported what had happened. "Our army was supposed to move north and take Crown Point," Theo told Jan. "But our organization was terrible. Each group of militia considered itself a separate army. Nobody could agree on anything, so nobody moved, and the French still hold Crown Point."

"How about the Indians?" Jan asked. "Did they give you any trouble?"

Theo shook his head. "If the white soldiers had followed orders as well as the Iroquois, we'd have taken Crown Point in a week. The Indians turned out to be the most disciplined force we had."

Nor was this the only bad report that came to New York. The English were faring badly on all fronts. Each new piece of bad news was followed by an outburst of spending by the government. The need for supplies became greater, and the English bought from the colonials at outrageous prices. The merchants and traders of New York were growing rich on the profits of war.

Jan observed the mounting expenditures of the government with apprehension. Someday there would come a reckoning, and all this matériel would have to be paid for. But by whom? he wondered.

"The king will pay for it," James insisted, remaining doggedly loyal to the Crown. "After all, this is his war."

"And what if he tries to get the colonies to pay?"

"We should pay our fair share."

"What if the share demanded isn't fair?"

"That will never happen."

Jan dropped his argument. His father was willfully blind to everyday realities. The English were already demanding that the people of New York house and provision the troops at their own expense. "It's for their own protection," the governor claimed; but one had to wonder why New Yorkers needed several thousand troops quartered in their midst when the fighting was taking place hundreds of miles away.

But even with the increasing demands expressed by the governor, the war continued to bring a windfall of unexpected wealth to many people in the city. The blacksmiths and leather workers had more business than they could handle. The armorers were swamped. Ship's chandlers were demanding fees that were almost extortionist, but they were still being paid every shilling they asked. The provisioners of meat and fresh vegetables and fruit found they had more buyers for their wares than they could supply, and as the clamor for food grew, they raised their prices—sometimes two or three times in a single day. An expecially sharp rise in the price of freshly slaughtered beef at the market near the Fresh Pond triggered a riot in which three men were killed.

Jan's ships left the harbor crammed to the gunwales with provisions for the troops of the English forces. Even though he had foreseen an increased need and had bought more ships, it became clear that he hadn't bought enough. The demand grew, and merchants were willing to pay almost anything to have their goods transported. They knew they could mark their wares up to outlandish prices and still have no trouble selling them. Jan calculated that the average square foot of cargo space on his ships was being sold for five or six times as much as it had just a few months earlier. He sometimes felt guilty about making so much money from a war, but the merchants didn't seem to care what he charged them as long as he shipped their goods.

Colonel Charles Lawrence, the governor of Nova Scotia, personally came to New York and demanded that a fleet of ships be placed at his disposal for "work that takes precedence over everything else."

The newly appointed governor of New York, Sir Charles Hedley, wanted no trouble with his imperious counterpart from the north.

"Mister de Kuyper, I appeal to you," Sir Charles said, standing before Jan's desk with a sad look on his face and his hat in his hand. "Colonel Lawrence needs ships in Nova Scotia, and bless me, if you can't help me I don't where we'll find the ships."

"But what does he want them for?" Jan asked, wary that the Nova Scotian might be planning to commandeer them and turn them into warships.

"He wants to transport some people out of his colony. He plans on sending them to New York, New Jersey, Virginia—anywhere as long as they'll be safe."

"What sort of people?"

"Refugees."

"Who are they?"

"I don't know a thing about them. But look at the situation, man, just look. The French are strong up in that area. They have thousands of Indians at their beck and call, wild men all of them, running around and scalping white people with their bloody tomahawks."

"Refugees, you say," Jan mumbled, weakening in his resolve not to give his ships away, moved by the thought of people in mortal danger.

In the end he relented and added four of his ships to eight other cargo packets that were being sent north. But he decided to accompany them, partly out of curiosity to see firsthand how the war was going in the north and partly because he wanted to be on the spot to protect his ships if the notoriously arbitrary Colonel Lawrence decided to overlook the terms of their agreement. Jan's commitment was to take the refugees from Nova Scotia and deliver them to places designated by the colonel.

The voyage along the coast was uneventful, and for the first time in two years Jan escaped the pressures of running his business. On board ship there simply wasn't any business to conduct. He wasn't the captain; he was simply the owner, along for the ride. At first the sailors were wary of him, but when they saw he enjoyed swapping stories and drinking rum with them in the evenings, they relaxed.

The ship continued to head north, the cold winds swooping down on them, chilling them to the bone. Jan was disappointed that they didn't sail close enough to shore to see Boston harbor, but the captain averred that there were too many French privateers hovering near the coastal town.

During the voyage Jan did not have to speak a word to Colonel Lawrence: by choice they sailed to Nova Scotia on different ships. Jan had no interest in spending time with a man he had come to dislike within ten minutes of their introduction to one another. Lawrence had the face of a shark, and a temperament to match. He was egotistical, pompous, and accustomed to getting his way by shouting everyone else down. During their one meeting together the colonel had tried that, but Jan had stared at him coldly and left the room without a word. He had consented to follow through with his part in the mission only after the colonel had sent over a formal apology. But the two men had not renewed their acquaintance since that time.

Jan was standing at the railing with Aaron Gerait at his side. "Think of how unpleasant this voyage would be if we had to suffer that boorish colonel," he said.

"Men begin voyages together," Aaron said, letting his hand stray menacingly to the hilt of his knife. "But they don't always finish together."

Jan laughed. "So it's dispatching English governors you're turning your hand to these days?"

Aaron shrugged. "One man dies as easily as another."

"Why do you dislike him so much?"

"Any escaped slave caught in Nova Scotia is whipped and returned to his owner. It's the law, I guess, to ship him back, but the whipping is the colonel's own idea of justice."

Jan was impressed that Aaron had come by this bit of intelligence; it was something he had not known himself. But then he remembered Aaron always made it a point to know what was happening to other black men. Jan's own company hired a greater percentage of free blacks than other companies, and paid them higher wages. It was something that Aaron had accomplished quietly, and Jan had let the practice become policy.

The next morning the ship entered the wide jaws of the Bay of Fundy, sailing close enough so they could see the eastern shore of Grand Manan Island through the purplish haze. The flotilla continued up the bay, entered the Minas Channel, rounded Cape Split, and anchored in a deepwater cove far off shore. A small town could be seen in the distance.

"Mister de Kuyper!" Colonel Lawrence called from a longboat resting alongside Jan's ship. "I'm going ashore to see about moving the people aboard the ships. I wish you to accompany me."

"Is that an order, or a request?"

"A request, if you wish," the colonel replied stiffly.

"I'll be right there," Jan called down, motioning for Aaron to follow as he began his descent down the rope ladder toward the slender longboat.

As the longboat pulled toward shore, Colonel Lawrence looked with discomfort at Aaron. In addition to his dirk, the black man now carried a matching pair of silver-handled pistols.

"Do you always permit your servant to go armed?"

"Aaron is not my servant, Colonel, but a business associate."

Lawrence wrinkled his nose. "My experience has taught me you can trust these people only to a point. For no reason at all they'll turn on you."

"Really? And why is that?"

"It must be because they're not long out of the jungle," the colonel said.

Jan was aware that Aaron had heard every word, but from the black man's expression, one might assume he was deaf.

"Perhaps you're right," Jan said blandly.

"Yes, I know I'm right."

"Aaron's grandfather worked for my own great-grandfather for forty years, but I guess there's no telling when they'll turn on us."

The colonel's face reddened at Jan's sarcasm. He turned away and faced the land as the sailors bent their backs into the oars, struggling against the heavy undertow.

They came ashore, and it was on the inspection tour of the refugees that Jan learned the awful truth of this voyage. The people were confined in pens—pens that had been built for pigs and smaller livestock—and they weren't refugees under protection. They were Acadians, people who had made their home on Nova Scotia for several generations. Colonel Lawrence had questioned their loyalty, demanding that every Acadian take an oath of allegiance to the English king. Since the Acadians considered themselves French, they refused the oath. They promised they would cause no trouble and would take no sides in the war, but the colonel refused to believe them. Every Acadian who had refused to swear the oath—which meant most Acadians—was now locked up in these pens, waiting transfer to places unknown to them.

Colonel Lawrence handed Jan a stack of documents. They were manifests for this human cargo, papers calling for each ship to dump small groups of the "refugees" in different places; in other words, they were to be dispersed. Jan was appalled.

"This is wrong, Lawrence. It makes no sense to scatter these people like seeds in the wind. What do we gain by it?"

"They all have French names, and they refuse to swear allegiance to King George. And yet they expect us to believe they'll be neutral in this war," the colonel scoffed. "Would you coddle traitors, de Kuyper?"

"They aren't traitors, Colonel, and you know it. They're simple farmers and fishermen who happen to be French. Why won't you take their word?"

Colonel Lawrence was frostily proper. "These people became English when the Peace of Utrecht was signed over forty years ago. They refuse to accept that fact, and therefore they must pay the penalty." He turned to a man wearing the insignia of a captain. "Proceed with the embarkation."

The captain saluted, and on his command the soldiers herded the people out of the filthy, foul-smelling pens. Long lines formed as the Acadians began the forced exile from their homeland.

Jan walked up and down the lines and looked at the faces of the people. They stared back—open, honest faces, faces that reflected lives of hard work and simple pleasures. But now there was confusion and fear in these faces. The children, like children everywhere, adapted to this new adventure, scampering about at their play, stopping only when the anxious hand of an elder pulled them back into line.

The ships were finally loaded, and Jan realized he had slightly more than fifteen hundred unwilling passengers, one quarter of the total being transported. He signed the forms presented him by Colonel Lawrence. "This is an evil thing you're doing," he said as the colonel dried the signatures with fine-grained sand.

"You took the contract to transport these people," the colonel said. "Don't blame me."

"I didn't know what I was signing," Jan said, pushing his jaw closer to Lawrence's face. "You lied to me."

A flush of anger crossed the colonel's face. "Under different circumstances, sir, I would demand satisfaction for that remark. As it stands, however, we are involved in king's business during time of war. If we fail to attend to our duties, sir, the gallows awaits us."

Jan knew the colonel was correct. There was absolutely nothing he could do about the situation. He had accepted the king's contract, and if he didn't fulfill it, he might well wind up at the end of a rope. Any form of treasonable conduct during wartime was punishable by death.

"Perhaps, sir, I will have the pleasure of meeting you at another time, one that will not be as inconvenient as this one," Jan said, and there was no doubt in either man's mind about what he meant.

The colonel nodded curtly. Jan turned his back and walked toward the longboat that was waiting to take him to his ship.

It was low tide, and now Jan realized why the ships had anchored so far from shore. In this area of the Minas basin the tides were spectacular, as great as any on earth, rising and falling over fifty feet at a time. Improperly moored ships were left stranded in mud when the waters swept out toward the ocean. As the flotilla of ships made its way back toward the Bay of Fundy, it seemed to Jan that they passed through only half as much navigable water as they had when they entered at high tide.

The ships headed down the bay, and as the land mass of Nova Scotia disappeared in the afternoon mist, Jan found himself standing next to an Acadian. The man appeared to be about his own age, in his early forties. The Frenchman glanced at Jan and then looked away again in anger, as if he blamed him for the predicament of his people.

"I don't like this any more than you do," Jan said softly. "But in times of war one has no choice but to carry out orders."

The expression on the other man's face changed. "I suppose you are right," he said in halting English. "But it is hard, because my people love this land. We wanted nothing more than to remain here in peace."

The Acadian's name was Labiche. He told Jan of his people's history: how their land had been claimed for France in 1604 by De Morts; how they had been living on this peninsula for over one hundred and fifty years. Labiche called the land by its French name—Acadie— even though in 1713 the English had renamed it Nova Scotia—New Scotland. Labiche explained that when the land had become English, the Acadians had accepted the event. They remained at their work, paid the duties required, and went about the business of caring for their families.

"But we do not want to swear allegiance to the English king," he said. "Maybe we are foolish. But we think of ourselves as French, and it is a point of honor."

"You've acted nobly," Jan said.

A rueful smile came over Labiche's face. "And now we are paying the price for our pride."

The Acadians were separated into groups and dropped off at various points from the rugged New England coastline to the shimmering rain forests of Georgia and Louisiana. Most of them had heard of a wonderful French city to the south, and large numbers of the Acadians continued their journey to New Orleans after they were put off the ships. Some went by sea, but most made the hazardous journey overland via Maryland and Virginia.

The Acadians who made their way to New Orleans settled as a community, just as they had done in Acadie. In time the community fanned out to the rivers that fed into the Mississippi, and they built houses and farms in the bayous and swamps. They continued to speak French, but over the years the language became different from the one spoken at the court in Paris. As time passed, the Acadian people became part of the Louisiana scene, but they always maintained a separate identity. They became known as *Cajuns* and were important participants in the development and economy of the area.

Jan returned from Georgia to New York understanding that he had been a part of a filthy bit of business, a cog in the wheel that dragged six thousand people from their homes and set them adrift on a hostile continent.

He returned to his de Kuyper company affairs and never spoke of his part in the shameful uprooting of a peaceful people.

Jan de Kuyper had become, on the one hand, a prime supplier of the troops of the British king; and on the other, a lawbreaker circumventing the British Navigation Acts. The law was quite specific: English colonies could trade only with England; only England itself could trade with other nations. But supplies were in desperate need, and often there was no place to turn but to the Spanish and Portuguese colonies to the south.

While negotiating a deal with a Dutch trader from Curaçao, Jan attended a dinner at which one of the guests was a hero of the war, Colonel George Washington. He found himself in conversation with the colonel over brandies served after the heavy meal. It was the colonel's first visit to New York, and he spoke of the impression the city's commerce and activity made on him. "In my opinion," he said, "New York has everything necessary to become the commercial capital of the Americas—a fine deepwater port, a lively population, and magnificent rivers that afford an easy access to the interior."

Intrigued by this young man, Jan became curious to know where his sympathies lay. He found his opportunity as their talk turned to the war and the shortage of supplies.

"How can a New York businessman, loyal in every other respect, afford to stay within the bounds of the Navigation Acts?" he asked Washington.

The colonel gestured toward his uniform. "As a servant of the king, I can hardly support the breaking of the law."

"But if we're not careful, these laws will break the colonies," Jan said boldly.

"There is a war going on," Washington said stiffly. "All of us must be prepared to make sacrifices."

"The acts came before the war, and they will continue after the war is over. They were passed to give an unfair advantage to the English traders."

"Aren't you an English trader, Mister de Kuyper?"

"In all matters but this, yes. In this instance I am decidedly a second-class citizen."

Colonel Washington sighed and looked closely at Jan. "I hear many men of business talking as you do, sir, and I fear you make a strong point. May I make a prediction?"

"Of course."

"When the war ends—and we will be the victors, naturally—the king and his advisors must come to grips with this issue. If they do not, I believe our people—and by this I mean we colonials—must protest vigorously. I don't wish to sound disloyal, but I think we would have justice on our side."

Jan nodded, and his respect increased for this Virginia colonel. He was young, but shrewd. His language was polite; still, it skirted the treasonous.

Marie Therese had spent an hour playing with her son, Andrew, who would be three years old in a few months. Thirty-seven had not been the best age to bear children, but there had been no complications, and Drew was a healthy, spunky, mischievous little boy.

"It's time for his nap," Marie Therese said to the Scots nanny, Lorna, who was half dozing in a chair on the other side of the room. Lorna stirred from the comfort of the chair, yawned, and came over to the little boy.

"Don't want a nap," Drew said, looking toward his mother with as much appeal as he could muster.

Marie Therese pretended to think it over, and finally snapped her fingers. "All right, you don't have to take a nap," she said. "But any little boy who doesn't take his nap doesn't get a piece of chocolate cake."

"Don't want any cake."

"That's fine with me," Marie Therese said as the nanny shifted from foot to foot behind the boy. "I guess you just don't like cake."

Drew put his thumb in his mouth and looked up at his mother, his expression defiant. But when another ten seconds had passed, he reached up for her. "I'm going to take my nap now."

Marie Therese bent low for the kiss.

"Lorna will take you," she said, and the heavyset woman came forward and picked the child up.

"I guess I know one little boy who's going to get some cake," Lorna said.

Drew smiled. "It's *me*," he announced proudly.

"Who's me?" Marie Therese teased.

"Andrew Pieter de Kuyper," the little boy said, pronouncing every syllable carefully and getting the entire mouthful out without error.

After Lorna took Andrew up to bed, Marie Therese went to the ornate escritoire that stood next to the window. The tall upper portion was enclosed by glass-paned doors. There were three drawers beneath the writing surface, which she folded down to its working position. She sat down to do her correspondence for the city library. For years the task had been done by Alice, but now the older woman claimed her eyes were failing and she could no longer do such close work.

Marie Therese smiled at the thought. There was nothing wrong with Alice's eyes. It was only that the correspondence was a boring task and she had decided it was time for someone else to take a turn. Marie Therese had sighed and volunteered, and her offer was immediately accepted by the library's board of governors. She now found herself writing an endless succession of queries to publishers about the availability of new books, and new editions of older ones.

She sat straight in the chair and moved her quill stead ily and precisely over the paper. At forty she was still one of the most striking women in New York. Her high cheek-bones and almond-shaped eyes were the envy of many a twenty-year-old who aspired to be the most sought-after beauty in the city. It was especially galling for these younger women to know they could only hope to run second best to a woman who wasn't even sought after, for the simple reason she wasn't available.

Marie Therese signed the letter with a flourish. It was to a London publisher requesting a copy of a new edition of Ben Jonson's plays, Jonson's comedies being favored by most literate New Yorkers. Marie Therese believed it was because Jonson was irreverent and poked fun at stuff-iness, a quality that gave him a greater affinity with the colonials than with his kinsmen back in England.

It occurred to her it was a bit nonsensical to be ordering books when there was a war raging in America. And yet the war, at least to her, seemed unreal. No fighting had reached the city. There had been no battles, and no men killed here. True, the port was the scene of a great deal of activity, and Fort George was crammed almost to the bursting point with soldiers from across the ocean; but it all seemed more a part of a great pageant than a war.

She sealed the letter with hot wax and reached for the next piece of correspondence on the desk. She looked up as she wiped a wisp of hair from in front of her face, and her eyes rested on the gold-framed oil painting on the wall. It was a portrait of a proud Jan de Kuyper holding Andrew, painted not long after the child had been born. She smiled. How happy she was that Jan finally had the son he had so desired. Time had almost run out on them. Their child Celine was now thirteen. Jan had begun to despair of having a son, and then, when it almost seemed too late, little Andrew had come along and Jan had his heir.

Marie Therese felt a chill run up her spine as she looked at the amazing likeness of her husband. How well she knew that face. The eyes. The nose. The mouth. She shivered again as she closed her eyes and thought of the thousands of times those lips had touched her own, kissed her neck and breasts, hungrily nibbled her flesh until she could barely hold back the screams of pleasure. How delicious it always had been, and, as a matter of fact, still was. How lucky she was.

She opened her eyes and smiled again at the images of her husband and son.

There was a soft knock at the door. A servant entered and announced a visitor, Jan's cousin, Edward Goelet. She was surprised: Edward hadn't been inside this house for several years. He had been invited, but it had been his own choice to cut himself off from his family.

Edward came into the room and stopped as Marie Therese moved to greet him. He blinked. "God, you're as beautiful as ever," he said. "If I didn't know better, I'd swear you've made a pact with the Devil."

Marie Therese laughed. "I don't see you for ages and the first thing you do is insult me."

Edward looked about the room. He put his finger between his neck and shirt collar, and the small gesture betrayed his discomfort. The parlor of Jan de Kuyper's Maiden Lane house was a beautiful and orderly room— leather chairs, mahogany tables, an unusual japanned chest of drawers, oil paintings, a bookcase filled with leather-bound volumes, a fireplace surrounded by rich oak paneling, candlesticks of polished silver, a Chippendale secretary. It was a room that spoke of quiet and expensive taste.

Edward was dressed in a shabby coat several sizes too large. His boots were dusty and the buckles chipped and tarnished. He had a two-day growth of beard, and his eyes were red from gin and rum. His hand trembled as he took the cup of tea that Marie Therese offered him.

Marie Therese tried to make her guest feel at ease. She chatted amiably for several minutes and was now telling Edward about the president of King's College, the city's first institution of higher learning. It was only several years old, having been founded in 1754.

"The president's name is Samuel Johnson, *Doctor* Samuel Johnson, from Stratford, Connecticut. Jan and I had dinner at his house recently—part of his program to get people to donate money, I suppose, but the man is such a pompous bore."

Edward nodded. "Most men are boring when they're trying to get money from you."

Marie Therese continued. "He claims he'll make King's College another Harvard. Can you imagine! And he said it with a straight face. By the way, your father was at the same dinner. He seemed to get along very well with the doctor."

"He would," Edward said sourly, fidgeting in his chair, and Marie Therese realized he was anxious to get to the reason for his visit.

"Now, tell me," she said, as casually as she could, "is this a social visit, or do you have something specific on your mind?"

"Now that I'm here I feel like saying it's only a social visit, but that would be a lie," Edward said quietly. "I really came because I want to ask you about Jan."

She cocked her head to the side. "Yes?"

Edward leaned forward to place his cup on the table, and the trembling in his hand caused the china to rattle. "I really shouldn't be bothering you at all, but I can't seem to get up enough courage to go straight to Jan. It's about this war. Everyone is rushing about, keeping busy. Everyone seems to have a purpose, Marie Therese. Everyone but me."

He paused and looked at her in stark hopelessness. "I can't live with myself if this goes on much longer."

"What do you want to ask me about Jan?" she said softly, fully appreciating the difficulty Edward was experiencing.

"If I asked him to give me a job, something useful, something that might help us win this war, would he give it to me? Or do you think he'd take one look and throw me out of his office?"

"He'd never throw you out. I think if you went to him now he'd be the happiest man in New York."

"Don't say that if you don't mean it," Edward said sharply. "If he turns me down, I'll kill myself."

"Don't talk like that!"

"I mean it. Look at me. I'm a mess. But I don't give a damn what anyone thinks—anyone except Jan."

"He loves you," Marie Therese said quickly. "You're his cousin, his own flesh and blood."

Edward managed a weak smile. "Sometimes that's not

enough." The smile was replaced for a moment by a
haunted look. "I've always thought Jan would have sympathy . . . would care, no matter what I did. I used to tell
myself, don't worry, Jan will understand."

"He will."

The sardonic smile returned. "Will he?"

Marie Therese realized she would get nowhere if she
continued in this way with Edward. He had become so
accustomed to arguing with everyone that it was a natural
role for him to slip into. He had also become accustomed
to thinking of himself as an object of pity, and would expect pity as his due. She decided to deal otherwise with
him.

"Well, maybe you're right, maybe he won't forgive
you," she said. "But the only way you'll find out is if you
go and ask him."

"I'm serious about killing myself," Edward said, somewhat startled by her last words.

"That's your decision, Ned, and now if you'll excuse
me, I have a great deal of work to do." She rose from her
chair.

Edward came to his feet, his confusion written on his
face. He had expected anything but this. He would have
been ready if she insisted that Jan would forgive him. He
would have had ready answers if she had begged him not
to take his own life. He was prepared for arguments of
pity and compassion. But not for this sudden, impatient
coldness.

"I'm sorry if I . . . I . . ."

"That's quite all right. And now, since you're going to
see Jan, please remind him to be prompt for dinner, as
we have guests."

Marie Therese watched from the window as Edward
let himself out through the front door. Tears came to her
eyes as she watched him limping down Maiden Lane. In
her mind's eye she could see the Edward Goelet of former
years, a handsome man with a determined stride.

She went to her escritoire and sat down, hoping she
hadn't done the wrong thing in sending Edward to her
husband. She was fairly sure Jan would be understanding, but she also realized that Edward was one of the
great disappointments of his life. Jan's bitterness might be
deeper than she suspected.

Her speculation was interrupted by the arrival of another visitor, but this one was no surprise. Alice Livingston bustled into the room.

"It's a lovely day," she said. "Care to go for a drive with me?"

Marie Therese glanced out the window and saw the handsome coach at the iron gate. The driver stood beside the open door, waiting for the return of his mistress.

"Of course," Marie Therese said, knowing full well that Alice had already made up her mind. "Let me get my hat and coat."

The two women stepped into the open coach. The driver closed the door. He climbed up to his seat and snapped the reins, and the team started off at a lively trot. They went onto Cherry Street, passing some of the new buildings that were being built to extend the city's northern boundary. They drove with the East River on their right, and houses and farms on their left. By the time they passed the large Rutgers farm and came to Corlaer's Hook, they were in fairly open country, devoted mostly to fields and an occasional barn. As they drove, Marie Therese recounted the visit of Edward Goelet.

"It's a shame about that man," Alice said with a shake of her head. "With all his advantages, who would have expected him to turn sour? Having a father like Charlie Goelet, of course, didn't help. Charlie could put his finger in a bucket of fresh milk and make it curdle."

Marie Therese laughed. "Come on now, I've always enjoyed Uncle Charlie's cynicism. He's so predictable."

"It's all right if you don't have to live with it, I suppose, but in my opinion most of the blame for the way poor Ned's turned out can be laid at Charlie's doorstep."

"I'm not so sure Ned's wife has helped very much."

"She is a bit queer, isn't she?"

"Dora used to be quite normal," Marie Therese said. "And we were very good friends. But I haven't been able to talk to her—I mean really talk to her—for a long time."

"A bit dotty over religion, isn't she?"

Marie Therese nodded. "Far too much."

"If you let those grubs known as preachers get their hooks into you, you're in a lot of trouble. My motto has always been to keep them at a distance and treat them as you would a smelly goat. Most of them never wash, you know; they think being holy is enough."

Marie Therese smiled. "I don't think most people could get away with dispensing with the clergy quite the way you do."

"No doubt it wouldn't occur to most of them to even try," Alice said, and then she fixed her gaze on her riding companion. "But now I'd like to talk to you about something else, something to do with me."

Marie Therese became playful. "Don't tell me you're like Ned? Afraid to ask Jan for a favor?"

"I don't ask nephews for favors," Alice said testily. "I tell them what I want. No, it has to do with this Englishman they've sent over to be in charge of the army while it's stationed here in New York."

"Colonel Campbell," Marie Therese said, with a nod of recognition. "Yes, I've met him. A very distinguished man. He holds a title as well, doesn't he?"

"He's the fourth earl of Loudoun. Nice, I suppose, but nothing much as titles go," Alice said with a deprecatory wave of her hand.

"Isn't he a bit . . . well, a bit young for you?"

"It isn't him," Alice said, "it's his uncle."

Marie Therese nodded. "Yes, I've heard of him. He's here about something to do with trade, isn't that right?"

"His name is Francis Campbell—*Sir* Francis Campbell, if you please. He has a commission from the Crown. Something to do with supplying the army. Not that he needs it, the old fool's horribly rich, but anyway I met him at one of those silly parties Maggie de Peyster is always giving, and now I can't get rid of him."

The incredulous look on Marie Therese's face annoyed the other woman. "Well, do you think I'm *that* far gone that men still won't find me attractive?" And then she sighed. "Or at least the older men."

"No, good heavens. But you've always been more than able to handle your own affairs. I'm just surprised that you're asking me for advice."

"The old fool wants to marry me," Alice said.

"What do you want to do?"

"Lewis Morris kept asking me to marry him until the day he died," Alice said wistfully. "One of the finest men who ever lived. If I turned him down, why should I consider anyone else?"

"Then why *are* you?" Marie Therese asked bluntly.

Alice's chin lifted up and a sparkling smile came over her face. "Because he adores me and he'll pamper every vicious bone in my body."

"I never thought I'd live to see this happen," Marie Therese said, shaking her head in wonder.

"Two months ago I would have agreed with you," Alice said. "I guess I'm getting soft in the head, but I don't think I'll have the courage to turn him down the next time he asks. Which, by the way, will most certainly be this evening. He's coming to dinner with his stuffy nephew."

"Congratulations," Marie Therese said, and then she winked. "*Lady* Alice."

Alice laughed. "I don't think I'll ever get used to that." And then she became serious. "There is one thing that disturbs me. Francis is a substantial man back in England. His estates are there. His first wife is buried there. He has grown children and a host of grandchildren. And if all that weren't enough, he's one of the king's advisors and holds various Crown offices. He's not exactly an adventurer come to America to find a rich old lady who'll support him in his final years."

Marie Therese was suddenly aware of what Alice was leading up to, and it saddened her. "If you marry Sir Francis, you'll have to move to England."

"I can't ask him to move here," Alice said, and it was one of the few times in her life when she looked helpless. "Oh, he's said he would, and I love him all the more for saying it, but I know his heart's not in it. He's not a young man—good Lord, he's a year older than I am—and he's very comfortable with his life back home. If I forced him to come here I think the poor man would die in a year, and I won't have that on my conscience."

"And if you don't go back with him?"

"I think I'll be making the greatest mistake of my life. It may sound silly, because I seem to have most of the things everyone wants out of life, but now I feel I'm just another lonely old lady. My husband's been gone for more years than I care to remember. Jan was a big part of my life, but now he belongs to you . . . No, no, don't

try to shush me; it's true, he's yours and that's the way
it should be.

"For a time I was happy because of dear Lewis," Alice
continued, after a short pause to collect her breath, "but
then he passed away and suddenly there was nothing in
my life except library committees, park commissions, and
gatherings of silly old people prattling about their grandchildren—and these are the same fools I did my best to
avoid when they were young and good-looking! Why
should I want to spend my time with them now? When
they're fat and grouchy and senile?"

Marie Therese reached out and touched Alice's arm.
"Then go with Sir Francis. Marry him," she said with a
sudden fierceness. "Go and don't have a moment's doubt
or a moment's regret."

"I've already decided to go. But I'll miss you terribly,
Marie Therese, you and Jan and the children."

"And we'll miss you."

"It may sound strange, but although I've been here in
New York almost an entire lifetime, when I leave, there
are only four people I'll really miss."

"How about James?" Marie Therese said in surprise.

Alice smiled. "I love him, of course; he's my brother.
But we've never really been close. Even when we were
children there was something that set James at a distance
from me. I respect him more than I do anyone else in this
city, but I don't think I'll miss him. At least not in the
way I'll miss you and Jan. I guess that's because I realize
James doesn't need me. He never has needed me and
never will.

"Now don't ever repeat what I'm about to tell you, not
even to Jan, but I've come to a point in my life where I
want to be needed. Francis needs me. And I guess, if I
can stop lying to myself for a moment, I need him."

Alice put her arms around the woman she thought of
as her daughter-in-law and began to weep softly and quietly. It was the first time in her life Marie Therese had
seen the other woman shed tears. And they were the most
touching of all tears—tears of happiness mingled with
tears of loss.

Marie Therese couldn't stand it anymore, and she, too,
began to cry.

The driver heard the sniffling and, alarmed, turned

around to look. He quickly looked forward again, red-faced with embarrassment at having intruded on the women in a very private moment.

"Watch the road, you old fool," Alice cautioned him between sobs, taking a certain liberty with this man who had been in her employ for over thirty years.

"Yes, mum," the driver replied, pleased that whatever was bothering his employer wasn't bothering her enough to change her.

Edward Goelet was nervous, and he took his time getting to Jan's office. After leaving Maiden Lane, he walked alongside a row of newly planted trees in Park Row; stopped for a while to watch a group of boys playing ball; paused to observe four black men digging a ditch; then made his way over to Broad Way.

As he walked down the wide avenue, he approached the building that housed King's College. Two men were standing outside, and Edward recognized his father chatting with a large, rotund person who smiled a great deal and was constantly intertwining his fingers and bringing them to rest on his chest.

That would be Doctor Samuel Johnson of Stratford, Connecticut, Edward guessed; and the deferential way he spoke to Charles Goelet suggested the college was a recent recipient of the Goelet family's generosity.

Edward stepped into a doorway across from the college, and watched as the two men took their leave of one another. His father marched away down the street as if he owned it, the silver-headed cane digging into the ground with every other step. When he turned up a side street and disappeared, Edward stepped back onto Broad Way.

Doctor Johnson was still in front of the school building, and Edward crossed the street to get a better look at this man. He had to pause and wait as a cartman whirled past, furiously whipping his horse, shouting for pedestrians to get out of his way. The streets of New York were becoming a jungle, Edward reflected. It was only a few years ago that Broad Way had been a quiet street, as wide as now, but with far less traffic. The war, of course, had much to do with the change. There was a lot of money being spent, and men raced through the streets, delivering, supplying, filling orders, anxious to get their share of the loot.

As Edward walked past the door of the college, Doctor Johnson happened to look up at him. "Good morning," Edward said pleasantly.

The doctor took one look at this seedy individual and turned away with a sniff.

Normally Edward would have let it pass and gone on his way, but it suddenly occurred to him that it might help to get a little stimulation before meeting Jan. He had been thinking of going to a tavern for some liquid courage, but he knew that if he started drinking he would never finish the journey to his cousin's office.

"Excuse me, I said good morning," he repeated, going directly up to Doctor Johnson.

The doctor was startled, and also annoyed at being approached by such a common-looking man, but before he could gather his wits, the words were out of his mouth. "Yes, good morning."

"Now why couldn't you have said that in the first place," Edward said, "instead of pretending that I didn't exist?"

This was going too far. "See here," Doctor Johnson roared, "do you think I have time to waste on every tramp in the street?"

This was better than Edward hoped. His muscles tensed, and he could feel a surge of power flowing through his body, awakening him, sharpening his wits, making him more aggressive.

"What makes you think I'm a tramp?"

"One look's enough for that."

"Does one look also tell you I can read your thoughts?"

"What?"

"So you think you're going to make this school into another Harvard, do you?" Edward said, savoring every word.

Johnson backed up, his astonishment mirrored on his face. He was sure he had spoken of his ambitions only to a few select people.

"Isn't it true you made such a claim? Or was it only a boast?" Edward pressed, and clucked his tongue in mock sympathy.

"I do not boast."

"No? Then what did you tell Charlie Goelet?"

"What?"

"What did you tell him to pry him loose from some of his money?"

Johnson was now thoroughly confused. It had been only twenty minutes ago that Goelet had appeared in his office and generously donated two hundred pounds for the purpose of books. How did this—he forced himself not to even *think* the word *tramp* again—how did this person know about it already?

"What's this about Mister Goelet?" he asked weakly.

"Charlie asks my advice about everything," Edward lied. "Won't make a move without me."

"I . . ."

"Well," Edward said heartily, "I must be getting along. Good morning."

"Good morning!" the doctor fairly shouted at the departing figure. As he peered after Edward his fingers began knitting themselves together nervously.

Edward walked quickly now, with more spring in his step. He held his head higher and even had a smile on his face. It was a shame he wouldn't be around when the second act of this little farce would be played; when the doctor met his father again. The doctor would politely inquire about Charles's advisor, a request that would be met by a stony stare and incomprehension. The doctor would become uncomfortable and explain his confrontation in the street with a rather disreputable looking fellow. It would take a little while, but Charles would eventually figure out who had been playing a prank on the doctor, and then he would become livid and explode, no doubt taking out some of his rage on the duped Doctor Johnson.

Edward chuckled as he walked down Broad Way and arrived at the Battery, where he turned eastward and went toward his cousin's office. He passed a formation of troops drilling on the green, replicating the harsh, unending routine of soldiers everywhere in the world. The English generals thoroughly understood the mentality of soldiers: they must be kept busy from dawn to dusk or else they would get into mischief. Therefore, when they weren't fighting they were subjected to a constant series of drills, inspections, exercises, drills, and more drills. Discipline was merciless, and more than half the soldiers carried old scars from the cat on their backs.

He arrived at the office on Whitehall Street, took a deep breath, and entered the building. Recognizing him, an older clerk raised his eyebrows and inquired of the visitor's business.

In two minutes Edward crossed the threshold of Jan's private office. He met the inquisitive stare of his cousin, smiled, and said, "I hear you might be able to use another pair of hands."

"What do you mean?" Jan asked. His tone was flat, expressionless.

"There's a war on," Edward said dryly. "Or haven't you heard. You must have more work than you can handle. I'm here to tell you I'd like to help."

Jan's face showed surprise, then anger. "For years you've ignored me. You've turned your back on your wife and family. You've become a sot and a wharf rat. Now you say 'I'd like to help,' " he said in a fair imitation of Edward's voice. "What the hell can you do?"

"Anything you tell me," Edward said, surprising himself with his newfound determination and strength. "Give me the toughest job you can think of. When I finish, then ask me what the hell I can do."

"You can't do anything."

"Try me."

The friction between the two men was like a hot coal ready to burst into flames. Jan stood up and pointed to the door. "Get out of here! Go back to your whores!"

Edward shook his head. "The only way you're going to get me out of here is to throw me out."

"That can be arranged."

"Or give me a job. I should think you'd be glad to accept my offer. There's more work than men to do it."

"Men, yes," Jan said. "But who can count on you? Why can trust you? You're not a man anymore. Go back to your whores and your thieves and your bottles of rum. That's where you belong."

"Is that what's bothering you? That I consort with people who aren't acceptable to the high and mighty de-Kuypers?"

"No!" Jan was livid. "What's bothering me is what you've done to yourself," he said, walking over to the window and looking out. He did not want to see his cousin's face as he condemned him.

"Look at yourself. You could have been the best of us all, and you let yourself become the least; no, less than least—nothing. You took gold and turned it into garbage. And you did it all by yourself, without help from anyone else. That's what I hold against you, *cousin*, that you destroyed something I valued highly. You destroyed your*self*."

"It's my life, dammit, and I can do anything I want with it."

"I suppose you can," Jan said heatedly. "But why? What in God's name possessed you? I loved you like a brother, Ned, and you rejected me. In the name of God, why?"

Edward's jaw dropped and his shoulders resumed their accustomed hunch. He looked bleakly at his cousin for a moment, and then the tears began to run down his cheeks. He tried to speak, but the words were lost in a gurgling sound that came from deep within his throat.

Finally he took several deep breaths and then, without looking at his cousin, managed to speak. "I never rejected you. It was only that . . . how could I tell anyone about what . . . no one would understand . . ."

Jan was suddenly touched by the depth of the sorrow of this man he had once loved. He went across the room and put his arm around Edward's shoulders, but the man would not look back into his eyes.

"Ned, this is Jan. There's never been anything you couldn't talk to me about."

"Yes, there is . . . you must understand . . ."

"There is *nothing*," Jan said firmly, "nothing you couldn't talk to me about."

He led his cousin to the wooden bench that stood along one wall and helped him sit down. He then went to the sideboard and poured two glasses half full of rum. He returned and held one out.

"Are you trying to encourage my bad habits?" Edward asked, managing a smile even as the tears dripped down his cheeks.

"Drink. And then talk to me."

Edward took the glass in his shaking hand. He paused for a moment and looked at it, then downed the contents in several quick swallows. He sighed and sat back, allowing the fiery liquid to spread through his body, feeling the warmth settle his nerves and build his courage. "This isn't going to be easy," he said.

He squared his shoulders and looked across the room, his gaze on the minute bits of dust that floated slowly through the single ray of sunshine that filtered through the window.

"When I married Dora Van Cortlandt I was the happiest man in New York," he began almost inaudibly. "She was beautiful. Gentle and kind. She was fragile, and her skin . . . it was the softest skin in the world."

He sighed and wiped the traces of tears from his face. As difficult as it had been for him to begin speaking, now that he had started, the words poured from his lips. "It was about a year after we were married that things began to go wrong. The death of our child was a hard blow to her. She never really could accept it. And then that new minister came, you remember, the one who was all fire and brimstone—Turnbull. He use to single out the weaker people and threaten their souls by carping about sin and guilt. He convinced Dora the baby had died because . . . well, because she had gotten pregnant before she was married. It became an obsession with her, and when we . . . went to bed . . . it was like being there with a dead person. She would just lie there and endure it. It was awful. As if *both* of us were dead."

Jan sat silently on the bench while his cousin relived the nightmare.

"The best thing to do, of course, was for us to have stopped going to bed together, but Dora wouldn't hear of it. She claimed it was our duty to bring forth a child that was born of properly wed parents. It was that damned Turnbull's doing, of that I'm sure. He made her fanatical.

"No child came, and she began to claim it was because God was punishing us. Dear Jesus, Jan, it was a horror. She would insist we go to bed and then she'd lie there as rigid as a stick of wood, murmuring prayers while I was supposed to . . . supposed to go on with it and . . ."

It was a full minute before he could continue. The only sounds in the room were the ticking of the large clock on the far wall and Edward Goelet's own labored breathing.

"Finally the day came when we went to bed and . . . nothing happened. I mean, I just lay there and . . . couldn't get hard. I wasn't a man anymore. I remember lying on the bed, unable to be a man, crying. And there was Dora sitting beside me, her face flushed, telling me it was God's way of punishing the two of us for our sin, and all we could do was to keep on trying to have a child and maybe the Lord would relent."

He reached out and grabbed his cousin's arm. "Can you imagine what it was like? Jan, can you imagine what that did to me! It went on like that for months. Every night she'd insist we go to bed together and try to make a baby, but it was useless. So I began to drink. I drank enough every night so that I could pass out when she dragged me off to bed. No matter how much I drank she'd insist that we go to that damned bed. Nothing ever happened anymore; the idea of it was driving me mad.

"Then I began drinking during the day. I'd go to a tavern thinking I'd have one or two drinks to get rid of last night's hangover, but more often than not, I'd end up drinking a full bottle so I'd be able to face her when I went home.

"After a while the only time I was happy was when I was drunk in some tavern. And then one night there was a pretty girl at the next table. She was cheap and had a gutter mouth, but I found myself becoming aroused, so I talked with her, laughed with her. Paid her what she asked and went to her room."

Edward sat up straight on the bench, and there was a bright intensity to his eyes. "I don't expect you to understand what that night meant to me, how could any man who's led a normal life understand? When I found I could be a man again, nothing else mattered.

"Of course, the sensible thing at that point would have been to leave Dora. But I couldn't bring myself to do it. Our marriage had started off in scandal, and I didn't want to do any more to hurt her. So I stayed, and let myself drift into a life where at least for a few hours each day I could be happy. Dora eventually gave up trying to have a child—a God-given child as she puts it—and I . . . well, I guess I just let the years slip away.

"I should have come to you sooner, Jan, I understand that now. But I was ashamed. I didn't want anyone, even you, to know what had happened. It was too painful to even think about it, much less talk about it."

The last words were spoken in a whisper, and Jan reached out and took his cousin's hand in his own. "Will you forgive me for not trying to understand? I should have known something was terribly wrong, Ned, I should have known."

"You've got it wrong, I'm the one who's here asking to be forgiven."

"No!" Jan said, angry at himself. "I could have helped, Ned. But I was too busy being like the others—aloof, righteous, feeling superior. "I *could* have helped, and I didn't. But the least I can do is help now, find something for you to do."

"I'd like to make a suggestion," Edward said softly. "You might not think so, but I'm pretty much aware of what's going on right now."

Jan interrupted his cousin. "I need another drink. Then you can tell me what you have in mind."

He refilled his own glass, but Edward held his hand over the rim of the other. "Now's about as good a time as any for me to start cutting down on that," he said. He reached into his pocket and drew out a tattered piece of paper. He placed it on the bench beside him and smoothed it flat.

"That's the map we got from that Frenchman years ago!" Jan said.

Edward nodded. "A memento of our youth. And now it may be put to good use again."

"How so?"

"Look," Edward said, jabbing his finger at the map. "This is the route we followed south from Montreal. I remember most of it as if it were yesterday. All along here the French have been building up their forces. They expect us to attack Montreal from the direction of Albany. But why should we attack them where their strength is the greatest?"

His finger began to trace new directions of attack. "Why don't we send ships—privateers, most likely—up here to the mouth of the St. Lawrence? They could clean out any French ships and open the way to Quebec City.

Once Quebec falls, we'll control the St. Lawrence. Then, if we attack Montreal, we'll be able to come at her from two directions. We'll have caught the frogs in a trap— attack by both land and sea."

Jan studied the map and then disagreed. "We have a new garrison at Fort William Henry, here at the southern tip of Lake George. If this army moves north it can take Ticonderoga and Crown Point. That opens the way to Lake Champlain. If we can get that far, why do we have to bother with Quebec City?"

Edward was ready with his answer. "I hear a lot down along the waterfront. It seems to be common knowledge that the French will fight the battle of the lakes to the death. They don't want us to be in control of the lands directly beneath Montreal. Which brings me back to my first point—why attack the French at their strongest point?"

Jan was still skeptical. "I like your idea about using privateers to clear out the Gulf of St. Lawrence, but I doubt that our generals will agree to call off their plans to attack Montreal from the south by land."

"You know the Earl of Loudoun, don't you?"

"Yes, of course."

"The least you can do is talk to him about this."

"All right, but you must come with me. It's your idea and you'll be able to explain it better than I."

Edward looking down at his shabby clothes. "But first I must pay a call on a tailor. And a barber. We can't have the earl thinking he's talking to a tramp, can we?"

Jan smiled. "Fair enough. But there's one thing more we must settle right now."

"What's that?"

"Never again will either one of us be afraid to bring his problems to the other."

Edward held out his hand, and then the two men fell into one another's arms and were brothers again.

The recently wet-mopped steps of the city hall sparkled in the morning sun as Jan and Edward arrived to keep their appointment with Colonel Campbell, Earl of Loudoun.

The soldiers at the door barely glanced at the two gentlemen as they passed through the entrance to the house of government. Their job was to halt and question only those visitors who looked as if they had no business in these exalted chambers.

Edward Goelet was wearing a well-cut, dark blue coat of expensive cloth. His three-cornered hat was new and shiny, and his silver shoe buckles gleamed from recent polishing. There was a gauntness about his features, but it was no longer accentuated by a loose-fitting collar. A fresh lace scarf bounced jauntily beneath his chin. His eyes were clear.

The secretary who greeted Edward and Jan promptly escorted them into the earl's spacious private office. He greeted them warmly and introduced them to the two officers already in the room, General James Abercrombie and another, much younger, general, James Wolfe.

"Almost as if these men are family," the earl confided to the generals. "My uncle is taking their aunt back to Blighty as his wife."

General Abercrombie smiled politely, but General Wolfe's face was expressionless.

"Somewhat of a surprise, eh?" the earl said.

"The surprise of my life, Your Grace," Jan said. "I never thought my aunt would marry again."

"Well, I guess I thought the same about Sir Francis, but the sly old dog completely fooled me."

"I hope they'll be happy," Jan said, ill-at-ease to be talking about personal matters in front of two cold-eyed generals. "And now I think we'd better get down to business."

Looks of relief came over the faces of the generals, and Jan spoke briefly of their mission. He then turned to Edward and asked him to detail the thread of his argument. Edward spent ten minutes outlining his plan to defeat the French by using the sea.

"The idea is to seal off the French," he concluded. "If we take Fort Niagara in the west, and Quebec in the east, then our forces can converge on Montreal and win the war. The French won't be able to get reinforcements either from Europe or from their settlements to the southwest. We'll have them in a trap."

The earl looked at the map spread on the table, blinked his eyes, and then turned to General Abercrombie. "Well, General, what do you think?"

Abercrombie shook his head. "I disagree with this plan. I maintain the attack should begin here at the foot of Lake George," he said, pointing at the map. "Start here . . . go up the Champlain Valley and take Montreal directly."

"I've traveled over the country, sir," Edward said patiently. "It's heavily forested and very wild. The French, with their forest-wise Indians, will be difficult to defeat."

"But we have our own Indians," the general protested, looking toward the earl and asking for his assurance on this point.

"Yes, yes," the earl said. "We've been sending a fortune in supplies to these, what are they called . . ."

"Iroquois," Jan suggested.

"Yes, yes, those are the ones," the earl said. "Don't we expect them to neutralize the Indians of the French?"

"To an extent," Jan replied. "But the Iroquois are most effective in their own territory, which is farther to the south than the approaches to Montreal."

"How many men do you think will be needed to take Quebec?" General Wolfe asked. It was the first time he had spoken since the meeting had begun. He was a slight man, barely thirty years old, short and almost frail looking. But there was a determined thrust to his jaw, and his dark eyes were acute. James Wolfe was the youngest general in the service of the king, and, in the opinion of a number of knowledgeable men, the best.

"Ten thousand," Edward answered.

"Ten thousand!" Abercrombie was alarmed. "But if we're to advance north from Albany by land, we can't begin to spare that many."

"Within the year I believe the troops at our disposal will more than double," General Wolfe said. "The prime minister is committed to winning this war."

"Where's the money coming from?" Abercrombie snapped.

"When prime ministers want something, they usually manage to get it."

"You can't get blood from a stone, Wolfe. What do you think about this, Your Grace?" General Abercrombie said, dragging the unhappy earl back into the argument.

Above all, Colonel Campbell wanted to keep the peace between his generals. "It's true that Prime Minister Pitt is dedicated to winning this war," he said in a conciliatory tone. "However, since General Abercrombie's plans to attack Montreal have already been made, it would seem reckless to abandon them on the basis of what we have heard here this morning."

"You spoke of using privateers in the Gulf of St. Lawrence," General Wolfe said, addressing himself to Edward. "How many would you need?"

"Three to start with. More to come later on."

Wolfe turned to the older general. "At the very least we should adopt this part of Mister Goelet's plan."

"And my plans for attacking Montreal?"

"Continue with them. In the meantime Mister Goelet might rid us of some pesky French ships."

General Abercrombie considered this for a moment and then nodded his head, having decided it unwise to altogether oppose this young general, who had a reputation for stubbornness.

The earl breathed a sigh of relief. "Good, very good." He turned to Jan. "Mister de Kuyper, could you make arrangements for three vessels to be readied for this task?"

"Yes, Your Grace. And the money to do it?"

The earl coughed. "Well, I believe we'll have some money available, but I must warn you we seem to use it up as soon as we get it. Supplying all these thousands of regular troops . . . and then there are the provincials, not to mention what we spend on those bloody Indians. Well, I'm sure we'll find the money somewhere."

"Thank you, Your Grace," Jan answered, not believing for a moment that the commander had the slightest intention of providing more than token funds. "I'd best be seeing about the ships."

"Are you going to the docks, Mister de Kuyper?" General Wolfe asked.

"Yes. Two of our frigates are in port at the moment. I thought I'd look them over to see if they could fit our needs."

"Good," Wolfe said, and when Jan and Edward left City Hall, the general walked beside them.

As they made their way to the docks, Wolfe questioned Edward and Jan about the approaches to Quebec via the St. Lawrence seaway. They answered as best they could, and when they had reached the piers, the general said, "I'm convinced your plan is the correct one, Mister Goelet.

Our European troops know nothing about forest fighting."

"There's a good deal of open ground around Quebec."

"So you said. That would be a good place for us to force a battle."

"General Abercrombie plans to go up the Champlain Valley," Edward said. "He had better learn quickly about forest fighting."

"It's that bad?"

"The trees are so thick in places," Jan said, "that at midday it seems as dark as night."

General Wolfe was convinced. "Take your privateers and clear out the French ships. We'll be taking troopships up there one of these days."

They stopped and looked up at the sleek frigate that belonged to Jan de Kuyper. They went aboard, and General Wolfe's practiced eye quickly assessed the situation. "Add more cannon to the sides and mount a swivel gun on your poop deck, and you've a fair gunboat."

"May I count on your help in getting the cannon?" Jan asked.

Wolfe smiled. "I'll do what I can, but if you wait for the earl to give you everything you need, you'll be waiting forever."

"I thought the prime minister wanted to win the war."

"He does," Wolfe said thoughtfully. "But the mood in Parliament is that much of the cost must be borne by the colonies."

"Ah, so even in wartime, England insists on taking her profit from our labors."

An angry glint came into Wolfe's eyes. "The colonies are, after all, merely extensions of the motherland."

"That seems to be the standard excuse for one Englishman to rob the purse of another," Jan answered, refusing to back down.

"There may be truth in what you say, Mister de Kuyper. But the immediate task at this moment of any Englishman, whether he lives in London or New York, is the defeat of the French."

"I agree. But what happens after we defeat the French?"

"Let that question wait until after we have done just that."

They spoke no more on the subject as they inspected

the frigate from bow to stern. When they were done, Wolfe stood on the dock and took a last look at the ship. "Have you a man in mind to head this expedition?"

"I'm the man," Edward said immediately. "It's my idea, isn't it?"

"It's too dangerous," Jan protested.

Edward looked him straight in the eye. "I asked for the toughest job you had. I guess this is it."

Wolfe watched the two and sensed the undercurrent between them. The reason for it was none of his business, but this colonial, Goelet, had come up with a plan that was in accord with his own ideas, and he wanted to see it carried out.

"I think Mister Goelet would have the greatest interest in achieving success in this matter," he said. "Are there some doubts about that?"

Jan felt trapped. He wasn't sure Edward was ready for

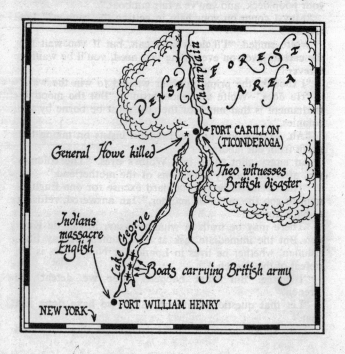

such a dangerous and risky job. On the other hand, he didn't want to belittle him in front of this English general. He saw the smile on Edward's face and knew he had lost.

"With three ships we need an admiral," he said. "I think my cousin is the perfect man for the job."

The Indians were accustomed to war, but to their way of thinking a war lasted one season; then everyone went home and picked up the threads of their normal lives.

But *this* war! It had dragged on into its fourth year and no one was winning, the chiefs agreed among themselves. More and more braves were abandoning the English and wandering back to their familiar hunting grounds. Theo Henry's job was to humor them into coming back.

He was now trekking in from the country of the Mohawk, leading two hundred of these formidable warriors, returning to the ruins of Fort William Henry. The fort, at the southern tip of Lake George, had been destroyed only ten months before by the forces of the French general Montcalm.

The army Theo joined, led by General Abercrombie, was the largest ever collected in North America. There were six thousand regular troops and nine thousand provincials. Their Indian allies numbered over a thousand.

As Theo made his way through the vast encampment toward the headquarters of the general, a tent on a small hill overlooking the lake, he counted at least a dozen different uniforms. Passing a platoon of Hessians drilling, he noticed with surprise that they were dressed in their heavy parade uniforms—uniforms that looked absurd here in the woods. Piles of equipment and supplies were everywhere. Large corrals had been constructed to contain over a thousand horses, and the carts and wagons numbered in the hundreds. There was a semblance of order, but hardly as much as was usually found in the encampment of a British army. Soldiers sat around in groups, talking and drinking crab apple cider and maple sugar beer.

"Here, you look thirsty," a soldier said to Theo as he passed, and handed him a large wooden cup. Theo accepted it, drank, and made a sour face.

The soldier laughed. "Home brewed," he said, and pointed to a group of soldiers preparing another batch.

The first step was to boil the tips and small branches

of spruce trees until they disintegrated. The pieces of tree were then strained out until all that remained in the pot was a murky broth. Now molasses was added to this liquid, which was then allowed to cool. Next, yeast was added; and in a few days hence, nature would have produced a brew that looked like beer, smelled like beer, and tasted like beer—not the best of beers, to be sure.

Theo managed to down the entire cupful. After the first few gulps it didn't taste all that bad. "Next time add a bit of rum," he said to the soldier as he handed back the cup and started to walk away.

"You provide it, mate, and I'll be glad to mix it in," the soldier said, and added a friendly wave of parting.

Theo walked on toward the general's tent, but stopped to look at the great flotilla that was collected at the southern end of the lake. There were canoes—more than he had ever seen in one place—and enough longboats to outfit a fleet. The major transport craft for the army, however, were the double-ended, flat-bottomed boats of lapstreak construction known as bateaux. They were twenty-five to thirty feet long and designed to be moved primarily by oars, although quite a few bateaux carried a single mast. Unfortunately there were no sails, so the inventive men adapted their blankets to this use in the hope that the wind could be harnessed to spare some of the punishment the heavy boats would give their backs. There were also a few flat-bottomed barges, over forty feet long, which were to be used to transport the cannons.

Reporting at last to Abercrombie, Theo not only informed the general of the arrival of the Mohawk warriors, but also registered a complaint about the uniforms of the Hessians.

"All our troops are wearing their regular uniforms," the general replied stiffly.

"But how can they fight?" Theo asked. "With all the equipment they carry, it's a wonder they can even walk around in this terrain."

"The regulations are quite clear about equipment and uniforms," the general said coldly. "I see no need to change them."

"Your regulations weren't made with our forests in mind," Theo reminded him.

General Abercrombie was a supercilious fellow, vain

and none too fond of colonials—especially ones who were suspiciously dark, like this Henry fellow. He pointed toward the water. "We do not *plan* to go through the forest, my good man. Don't you see the boats?"

"The boats will take the men to the northern shore of the lake, but what happens after that?"

"See here!" Abercrombie began, but he was interrupted by the mild voice of his second-in-command, Viscount George Howe.

"Do you know the country around Fort Carillon?" he asked Theo, using the French name for Ticonderoga.

"Yes, sir," Theo said, turning to face the tall, handsome Englishman. It was rumored he was supposed to have taken over this command, but Abercrombie had many well-connected friends in Parliament who had come to his defense. Rather than cause dissension by using his own influence, the gentlemanly Howe had accepted the secondary position.

"And you don't think our men are properly dressed?"

"You should hear what the Indians are saying about them," Theo replied. "They laugh at the 'white eyes' who go into the forest with those heavy coats and packs."

"What do you suggest?"

"Cut the longcoats down to jackets. Let them get rid of their breeches and wear leather leggings that will protect their legs from the brambles and thorns."

"What else?"

"We ought to leave most of the baggage in a camp when we reach the head of the lake. And I'd suggest we get rid of all these cook wagons. Let each man carry enough food for himself."

"*Soldiers* cook their own *meals?*" Abercrombie was scandalized.

"That's what the Indians do," Theo said. "And the French."

"Mister Henry makes sense, General," Viscount Howe said.

General Abercrombie looked at his lieutenant in annoyance and confusion. He was well aware he had retained his command over strong objections. He also knew that in the British peerage Howe held a rank far higher than his own. But to do what this . . . *colonial* wanted! English armies always traveled with a full train of sup-

plies—barrels of salt pork, salt beef and salt cod; kegs of
oatmeal, cornmeal, beans, peas, rice; tubs of butter and
cheese. Why, most armies of his experience always
brought along live cattle. A gentleman like himself could
enjoy a nice, tasty joint even while in the field. It was
damned foolish to change all this simply because a single
colonial was worried about some trees.

"Why don't we compromise," Howe said smoothly.
"We'll leave all our supplies and baggage at the head of
the lake. But we'll send for them as soon as it's feasible."

General Abercrombie clutched at the idea. "Excellent
suggestion, excellent. That should solve the problem."

"And cutting down the uniform?" Theo asked.

"Yes, yes, that too," Abercrombie agreed, anxious now
to terminate this disagreeable meeting.

Viscount General Howe left the tent with Theo. "I'll as-
semble the captains, and you can instruct them about the
changes to be made in the men's uniforms," he said when
they were out of the older general's earshot. "Bless me, I
thought the old man's teeth would fall out when you suggested the men see to their own meals," he added with a
laugh.

Theo found himself liking this understanding man. Unlike most of the other English commanders he had dealt
with, this one made you feel that he accepted you as an
equal. And Howe, as Theo knew, was a half cousin of
King George II himself. It seemed that this man, who
could have affected the greatest pretensions of them all,
affected none.

The viscount sent for his captains, and while they
waited he regarded Theo, liking what he saw in this serious, plain-talking man clad in buckskin. Theo was in the
prime of his life, with dark, intelligent eyes that could
hold another man's stare. His bronze coloring attested to
many hours in the open, as did his hard flat muscles.

"I understand you were here at the fort when it was destroyed ten months ago," the viscount said.

Theo nodded. "I was one of the few who managed to
escape. Slipped out through the back of the fort minutes
after it was surrendered."

"Why? Didn't you believe the French would act like
men of honor?"

"It wasn't the French who worried me. It was their allies, the Ojibways and the Ottawas. I know something of their customs."

"Julius Caesar liked to surround himself with men who knew the customs of the people he was fighting. He was a wise commander who knew it helped to understand the nature of his enemy."

"I tried to convince the commander of the garrison, but he wouldn't believe me," Theo said. "So he died."

The general looked at the poised man at his side. "At the very least, I think I'd listen whenever you spoke up."

"If you had been here at the fort, many lives might have been spared."

"Was it as terrible a massacre as they say?"

"Our commander surrendered after a long siege," Theo replied in flat tones. "Montcalm acted in a civilized manner, but while he was busy elsewhere, his Indians killed every man and woman in the fort."

"I didn't know there were any women with the garrison."

"Where you find soldiers, you'll always find some women," Theo said with a shrug.

"How did the people die?" the general asked, and when Theo was silent, he persisted. "Were they given easy deaths?"

"The Ojibway believe that if a prisoner takes a long time in dying, the strength of his spirit is passed along to the man who killed him. Also, when an Ojibway loses a kinsman in battle, he believes he can help the soul of the departed man by torturing an enemy. As he is using a red-hot knife or a tomahawk blade to burn the flesh, he speaks softly and affectionately to the tortured man—as if he was talking to the kinsman who'd been killed. Finally, after the man dies, his flesh is eaten.

"I hid in the woods for three days before I dared to start making my way back to Albany. I saw the cooking pots and smelled the boiling flesh."

The general's eyes had a glazed, faraway look, as if he was trying to visualize the scene.

"They did other things," Theo continued. "They dug up the fort's smallpox cemetery. There had been recent contagion. Who knows if it will begin to spread again."

"Dug up graves? Why?"

"To disturb the slumber of their enemies for eternity."

General Howe shuddered. "God Almighty! And Ambercrombie expects such savages to fight as if they were gentlemen."

"Our own allies—the Mohawk especially—have a tradition of eating human flesh," Theo said, almost apologetically. "In fact, it's a common custom among most Indian tribes."

Howe couldn't conceal his surprise. "They don't tell you this sort of thing before you come here," he said. "See here, Henry, they tell me you're part Indian yourself."

"Yes. My grandmother was a Wickquaskeek, an Algonkian tribe. Her father was Stone Eagle, the last chief of a tribe that made its home on Manhatan."

"And did your grandmother tell you . . ."

The general couldn't finish the sentence, but Theo shrugged and said, "I remember she kept a human skull in her bedroom. Grandmother claimed it belonged to a famous Mohawk chief my great-grandfather had killed and eaten. I suppose it was true."

"Do you still have the skull?"

"Oh, no," Theo said with a laugh, attempting to assuage the mounting horror reflected on the other man's face. "When Grandmother died my mother threw it away. She was a white woman, you understand, and wanted nothing like that in her house."

"I suppose I shouldn't be surprised," Howe said. "Five hundred years ago, when my own ancestors in England defeated an enemy, they'd cut off his head and carry it around on the end of a long pike until it rotted. I sometimes think we're all still savages at heart."

Their conversation was interrupted by the arrival of the captains for their briefing.

It had been the first of many discussions Theo would have with the general. He admired this nobleman who adapted so well to new situations. Howe became the first man in the army to wear a cut-down jacket and leather leggings, and the soldiers were quick to follow his lead.

Theo and the viscount became friends over the next weeks, as the barges and bateaux were loaded and made their way up Lake George to where it narrowed into a small stream leading north to Lake Champlain.

When they reached the head of the lake, the troops came ashore at the mouth of Wood Creek. Although General Abercrombie was the commander-in-chief, it was Viscount Howe who gave most of the orders.

"Take a force of colonials and Indians and scout ahead," he said to Theo. He looked with trepidation toward the dense forest that stretched as far as the eye could see in the direction of Ticonderoga.

What happened in the next few hours was something that would hang heavy on Theo's heart until the day he died.

While he and his men picked their way through the dense forest, Abercrombie took personal charge of stowing all the baggage and gear that was to be left behind under the protection of a rear-guard detachment. He insisted on supervising an item-by-item accounting.

Viscount Howe became impatient. "It's time to get the main column under way."

"See here, Howe, you're the one who wanted us to leave everything here. All right, we're doing it; but we'll not leave it a botched-up mess," Abercrombie replied indignantly.

Howe reflected that his superior had a pettiness about him. The man might reluctantly take your advice, but then he made you pay for your temerity in having offered it.

Howe paced for two hours while the commander-in-chief satisfied himself that there were 306 kegs of salted beef and 214 of salted pork, as indicated on the tally sheets. He was beginning his count of kegs of black powder for the artillery pieces when the viscount couldn't stand it any longer. "Dammit, sir, we can't allow the scouts to get too far ahead of us," he complained.

"You sent them out."

"Yes, but I didn't think the rest of the army would spend the day here, counting out knives and spoons."

"Then take a force of regulars and go on ahead," Abercrombie said curtly. "I must remain here until this work is finished."

"But it doesn't need to be done now," Howe protested.

General Abercrombie fixed the other man with his iciest stare. "You go on ahead, and when I'm finished here, I'll follow with the main force."

And so it happened that while Theo and his scouts ranged far ahead in the woods, Howe plunged into the undergrowth at the head of an English column. They marched easily, feeling secure from attack: if there were any dangers ahead, the advance scouts would alert them.

But the woods were thick—thicker than any the army had yet encountered—and Theo and his men had been allowed to range much too far ahead. Unknown to them, a roving band of over one hundred French soldiers and Indians had slipped in behind them. Indeed, the thick forest had prevented the Frenchmen from even being aware of the English scouts' presence. The two opposing forces had passed within three hundred yards of one another, and neither had detected the other.

But now the Frenchmen were positioned in the path of Howe's oncoming column. When they heard the sounds of the struggling soldiers, they waited quietly and prepared for a surprise attack—never dreaming they were actually caught between two English forces.

The Frenchmen waited until they could see the scarlet jackets of the British as they began to emerge from the green of the forest. When their targets were only twenty or thirty feet away, they opened fire. Characteristically, Viscount Howe was leading the column. He fell in the first volley, mortally wounded with a bullet in his chest.

The initial surprise gained by the Frenchmen was quickly counterbalanced by the superior numbers of the English. The French fought fiercely, but the heavier firepower from the English began to beat them back. The French captain soon realized he was facing a major force and ordered a retreat to the protection of the fortress at Ticonderoga.

Theo and his men heard the firing from the rear and realized that, somehow, they had passed a squadron of the enemy. They spread out in several lines through the trees and began to advance slowly back in the direction they had come from.

Theo was in the first rank. Something in front of him moved. It was the white shirtfront of a French soldier. He raised his musket to his shoulder and fired. There was a scream; then a babble of excited voices crying out in French. The voices were quickly drowned by a furious musket fusillade from the ranks of the English scouts.

The French now realized they were caught between two forces and began to seek escape routes to the sides.

But to no avail. Theo's men were spread out on either flank, and they blasted away as the French came into their sights. Some attempted to break through the forest back toward the river, but these were pounced upon and killed by the angered soldiers of Howe's column.

Although only a half dozen or so Frenchmen escaped the slaughter, over thirty Ottawas managed to elude their pursuers and melt into the forest.

Theo fired, loaded, and fired again. He was raising his musket for the twentieth time when he realized the man in his sights wore a scarlet jacket. He relaxed and called a greeting. The firing died down and, except for an occasional shot on the flanks, ceased. The main party and the scouts were united.

When Theo heard that General Howe had been shot, he raced through the woods until he reached the mournful group of soldiers milled in a circle around their fallen leader. Theo dropped to one knee at the side of the stricken general. A glance was enough to tell him there was no hope for this man. Tears formed in his eyes as he reached out and touched Howe's hand, which was now covered with his own blood.

The viscount opened his eyes at the touch. A weak smile crossed his lips. "My friend," he said in a whisper, and then he closed his eyes again and died.

Theo stayed at his side for a long time. In the few weeks he had known the viscount, he had come to value him as one of the better specimens of the human race. When such a man dies, he takes a little life away from all those who have known him, and it was this grief that Theo felt as he held the dead man's hand and watched his blood dry on the ground.

"Good-bye, friend," he finally said, and then proceeded to help dig a grave.

The soldiers paused to bury their thirty dead. It was a difficult task. The roots of the trees were thick, and to be found everywhere in the hard earth. The men had to chop through them in order to dig a hole large enough to hold the corpse of a full-grown man. By the time they were finished, it was getting dark. They spent the night in the forest, shifting their bodies in quest of a comfortable position and swatting at the bugs that kept sleep at bay.

The next morning the column continued on, finally emerging from the dense forest, halting on the plateau northwest of the fortress of Ticonderoga. Throughout the remainder of the day the army gathered until, just before dusk, General Abercrombie arrived on the plateau.

The general deeply regretted the loss of Viscount Howe, as he had become accustomed to relying on his intelligent advice. But he would not admit this to anyone. He began crackling out orders and refused to consider any alternatives to the first ideas that popped into his mind. It was as if he was trying to show everyone that he had been most decisive all along. He ordered Theo and his Indian scouts sent out to reconnoiter, and detailed the other officers to establish the camp.

"Double guards at all times," the general said.

The officers looked at one another. "Double guards, sir?" one of them asked.

"Can't have the French sneaking up on us."

"But, sir," the officer said, indicating the open plateau with his hand. "How could we be surprised out here?"

"Double guards, I said," Abercrombie snapped, and that was that.

"And dig a deep trench over there. Make it six feet deep."

The officers swore beneath their breath, and the men sweated and grumbled as they went to work digging a trench that not a man in the camp thought necessary.

By the end of the next day the camp was established and the officers were waiting impatiently for the scouts to return with their report.

As the sun was passing from the sky, Theo came back with discouraging news.

The French commander, Louis Joseph, Marquis de Montcalm, had fortified the ridge that lay in front of his fortress. He had felled trees and made a zigzag parapet. There was a platform on the inner side, and soldiers manned the wall behind the protection of its stout planks. But before an attacking force could reach even the parapet, they would be forced to penetrate a maze of twisted and sharpened branches and boughs. Clearly, any attempt at a frontal attack on Montcalm's fortress would be foolhardy.

General Abercrombie listened to all this with a patronizing expression on his face.

After realizing the disquieting news, Theo offered a solution to the problem. "Before we make an assault," he said, "we must bring up the artillery and destroy the parapet and maze."

The general stared with distaste at this man who had been one of Howe's favorites. "See here, Henry, you were the one who argued the army must travel light. You know what this forest is like. It would take a week to drag our cannon up here. We can't wait that long."

"The cannons could be placed on that hill over there, sir," a major volunteered. He pointed toward a hill whose elevation was slightly higher than the fort itself. "We could destroy the French at our leisure."

"And what if they came out to fight us in the open?" Abercrombie asked.

The major smiled. "I hardly think they'd do that, sir. We estimate they have no more than three thousand men."

The general became belligerent. "Three thousand men, you say? And you expect me to sit here for a week with our fifteen thousand while we wait for our cannon to arrive? What are we, sir? British soldiers, or cowards?"

The officers coughed, embarrassed, but not one of them offered to answer the general's question.

Only Theo refused to remain silent in the face of such stupidity. "General Abercrombie, I scouted the area to the north. If we send a thousand men about five miles along the road to Crown Point, we can bottle up the French. The hills crowd together up there, and the French would have to pass by through a narrow ravine. Put a battery of cannon there and Montcalm could never retreat. We'd have him in a trap."

Before Abercrombie could answer, the same major who had questioned the general before, spoke up again. "Holding that position would also insure that no reinforcements could reach Montcalm."

"Reinforcements," the general said in dismay. "Do you think there are reinforcements on the way?"

"Well, if I were the commander of three thousand men facing an army of fifteen thousand," the major said, "I'd certainly send for reinforcements."

The humor was lost on the general. At the instant he heard the word reinforcements, he became convinced that help was on the way to rescue the beleagered fortress. In his mind it now became essential to capture the enemy position before more French soldiers could arrive.

"Dammit, that's all the more reason to capture the fortress immediately," he said. "If we wait for our cannon to be brought up, we might find ourselves facing a vastly superior force."

Again none of the officers spoke, even though all were aware the general was speaking nonsense. Superior force? Where could the French find a force superior to the largest army ever collected on North American soil?

"We will attack tomorrow," the general announced. And then, taking note of the expressions on the faces of his officers, he laughed and tried to put them at their ease. "What are you all looking so sad about? One Englishman is easily the equal of three Frenchmen."

No one smiled. The officers stood silently until the general waved his hand in angry dismissal. They walked away without a word, and Theo returned to where the Mohawks had established their place in the camp.

The chief, Running Bear, asked him about the plans for the attack. Theo pointed toward the stout parapet. "The general plans to attack it directly from the front."

The chief squinted his eyes and surveyed the terrain. He looked again at Theo and then walked off without saying a word. Theo understood; Running Bear's contempt for Abercrombie's plans needed no words.

The next day, a half hour before noon, the army was drawn into battle position facing the parapet before the fortress. The order was given to fix bayonets. General Abercrombie raised his sword and then swiftly brought the point to the ground. The ranks of the general's soldiers—scarlet-clad regulars intermixed with colonials in their various uniforms—marched directly toward the waiting French. Drummers followed, their sticks beating a brave tattoo as they urged the men to greatness.

Theo had attached himself to a company of irregulars from Massachusetts. Ordinarily he would have been with the Mohawk allies, but he had awakened just after dawn to find there wasn't a Mohawk left with the army. Rather than fight what they considered a suicidal battle, Running Bear and his braves had slipped away in the night. There had been slightly over two hundred men with the chief, but so silently had they departed that not a white man in the camp had seen or heard them leave. If the other Indians knew anything, they kept it to themselves. There were eight hundred of them still with the army, but they stood on a knoll and watched as the ranks of white men marched toward the French. This was not their kind of warfare, and they refused to take part in it.

Theo's company, along with the other soldiers, found its bayonet charge broken up long before the soldiers reached the French. The charge required a mass of men, in ranks, presenting a solid wall to the enemy; but when the English came to Montcalm's first defense—the maze of sharpened stakes and branches—their ranks were split and scattered, and they were forced to pick their way slowly and carefully through the treacherous obstacle. When they were halfway through the outer tangle, the French opened fire from their protected positions behind the parapet. The ragged ranks of the English were met with a hailstorm of musket and grapeshot fired directly into their faces.

The maze and parapet became a bedlam of noise— shouts, screams, the blasting of guns. A thick, acrid smoke settled over the maze, blinding the English soldiers, causing them to blink their eyes and choke even as they were trying to aim their weapons at an enemy who was slaughtering them.

The man on Theo's immediate left seemed to explode as a lead ball smashed into his shoulder, knocking him to the ground, where he writhed and screamed. Theo raised his musket; but the smoke was causing his eyes to water, and he fired without even aiming, aware that the most damage he would cause would be to splinter a piece of the parapet.

"Help . . . for the love of God, help!" the wounded man to his left cried out in agony.

Theo bent down and winced when he saw the gaping hole and torn flesh that was covered in sticky red blood. There wasn't much Theo could do, but he tore off the end of his shirt and tried to stick it into the wound to stanch the flow of blood. But a heavy weight crashed into his back and pushed him down into the man's chest.

As he gurgled and choked, Theo wrestled the weight off his back and came to his feet as quickly as a cat. His knife appeared in his hand. And then he relaxed. The weight had been the falling body of a dead comrade. Half the man's head had been blown away by grapeshot, leaving strips of flesh, shattered sticks of bone, and half a ruptured brain.

The combined weight of Theo and the dead colonel falling on the wounded soldier had been enough to drive the man's broken bones through the flesh, and now his blood flowed from his body and made the ground slippery. There was a final gasp and he was freed forever from soldierly duties and battles. Theo said a silent prayer for him and was about to renew his efforts to reach the parapet when he noticed the other soldiers were retreating. There was nothing for him to do but stumble after them.

General Abercrombie was furious when he saw his men returning from the attack. Neither the number of wounded nor the number of dead strewn among the stakes of the maze could convince him he was making a mistake. He ordered the ranks re-formed for a second attack.

It was a long and bloody afternoon.

By nightfall Theo lay on a much-trodden sward, his hands and face black with gunpowder. Dirt and sweat were caked on his skin. He was exhausted, and his body ached down to his very bones. But the exhaustion did not bring numbness: he realized he had just witnessed a disaster.

Six times General Abercrombie had ordered the lines formed; six times the order to charge had been given; six times the men had marched forward to be slaughtered. Over two thousand brave soldiers were dead or wounded, and many of the wounded would never live to see the dawn of another day. The French, on the other hand, had stayed behind their stout parapet, and their casualties numbered less than fifty dead or wounded men. It was, by far, the most one-sided battle of the war.

Theo dragged his protesting body to the general's command post and listened to the officers as they argued among themselves about their next move against the enemy.

But the general was sitting on a camp stool, biting his nails and paying no attention to the talk going on about him.

"We must retreat," he said finally, in a voice that quivered with indecision.

"Retreat?" someone whispered, and the low voice was heard by every man in the circle.

The general looked up. "Of course," he said. "It's obvious we can't take the French position. They'll simply hold out until their reinforcements arrive."

"What reinforcements?" Theo asked in a hoarse voice.

The general turned a baleful eye on him. "By what authority do you speak in this gathering?"

"I represent the governor's council in New York."

The general leaped to his feet. "I want this man kept from my sight!" he shouted. He walked over to his tent and paused before he went inside. "We march back to Lake George in the morning."

The officers looked at one another in astonishment. Here was a British army—even with losses of over two thousand, still an army of thirteen thousand armed men— retreating from a French force of three thousand. It was mad. There wasn't an officer in the camp who believed that reinforcements were coming to rescue the enemy. And all of them knew that if the artillery were brought up, they could destroy Montcalm's defenses in an afternoon. But they were British officers, and they had been given an order by their general. There was no argument.

"If only General Howe hadn't been killed!" Theo said to the major who had been so outspoken at Abercrombie's councils.

"We lost this battle when he died," the major said. "I only hope it doesn't cost us the war."

"If they let this fool Abercrombie keep his command, it will."

The major nodded. "Howe and Wolfe were our best generals, and now one of them is gone. God help us."

Theo remained with the retreating army as it grumbled and complained its way back to the lake. He went south on a bateau, and on reaching the ruins of Fort William Henry, he left the others. On horseback he covered the sixty miles to Albany, and there took passage on the first boat leaving for the city to the south.

When he arrived in New York, the people of the city learned of the great disaster. There was a clamor of outrage, and Abercrombie was given a nickname that stuck —General Nambycrombie.

Never had the English prospects for winning the war looked so bleak. A vast army had been collected and sent north with the expectation that it would go all the way to Montreal. Now this army had fought one battle, lost, and retreated to Albany.

New Yorkers began to wonder if the time was not far off when a French army would advance on their city. Some men began to oil their muskets, and others made plans to leave the city altogether. The ninety-two cannons that bristled from the gunports of the fort were not as reassuring as they had been.

The disastrous defeat at Ticonderoga at least had the benefit of giving greater currency to the ideas of General Wolfe. A fleet was brought from England and made ready to sail north to capture the strategic French naval base of Louisbourg, on the northeast shore of Nova Scotia.

Word had come back to the city that Edward Goelet and his privateers were meeting with much success, but their string of small victories were hardly enough to reassure the townspeople. Wolfe contended that the work of the privateers and the planned capture of Louisbourg would mean little without a subsequent advance on Quebec and then Montreal.

"Your cousin has been doing splendidly for over a year now," General Wolfe said to Jan as they walked through the park at the Battery. "But of course he hasn't enough ships to do a complete job."

"The governor claims he has no more money for privateers," Jan replied. "He says he needs what he has for more important purposes."

The general swore beneath his breath. "God save us from our own leaders. Prime Minister Pitt keeps sending us more and more money, and we keep finding new ways to waste it. Fighting the French on many different fronts is foolish. We must concentrate on getting to the source of their power—the St. Lawrence River."

"When they begin to listen to you, maybe we'll begin to win this war."

"At least they're listening more than they did before. Perhaps Abercrombie's debacle at Ticonderoga was a blessing in disguise."

Jan realized a military leader looked at things quite differently than the average citizen; here was an extremely intelligent person talking about the slaughter of several thousand men as a *blessing!* He shook his head. I would have made a lousy general, he thought.

"The important thing," the general continued, "is that we get more privateers up in the gulf to harass the French. Do you have any ideas on this?"

Jan thought for a few moments and nodded. "It may be possible to finance new ships without any money from the governor. Give me a few days and I'll let you know where we stand."

"Three ships?"

"If you think three are required."

"I do," the general said vehemently. "Three is the absolute minimum. What I'd really like to do is send twenty, or even thirty."

Jan laughed. "You'll never be accused of thinking small."

"This is war, de Kuyper, and the idea is to win. I wish you luck with your ships."

"I'm pretty sure I can do it. Our family has certain resources."

"So I'm beginning to learn," the general said.

James de Kuyper stood in the visitors' gallery and applauded as the New York Assembly voted into law the resolution that had been introduced by David de Witt Sackett. Sackett, a member of the assembly, had his name attached to the bill, but the real author was James himself.

Henceforth, according to the new law, any black child born in the Province of New York would be free. It didn't matter even if both parents were slaves: the child was to be free.

"Well done, David," James said, slapping the stoutish young lawyer's back as they walked together from the city hall. Because the younger man was the grandson of the late Paul de Witt through his mother, Anne, he was James's second cousin, once removed.

"It's a good law, James, even if there's a bit of cynical talk going about."

"Cynical talk? What do you mean?"

"Some people are saying we passed the law because it's cheaper to hire a black man when you need him than to pay for his keep as a slave."

James smiled. "Let them say what they will. The important thing is we'll have no more slaves born here. Maybe in another thirty or forty years we won't have any slaves at all. I won't be around to see it, young fellow, but you will."

"Would you care to come back to our house for lunch?" David asked. "My mother complains it's been a year since she's seen you."

"I'd like to do that, David, but I'm afraid I have another engagement. Give your mother my regards. And tell her I'm planning to hold a family reunion up at the manor, but I'm waiting for this war to end. Somehow it doesn't seem right to hold a party when half our family is involved in the war in one way or another."

"I'll give her your best, sir."

"And give my regards to your dear wife," James said, remembering the plain, pleasant face of Mary Gansevoort Sackett.

They parted, and he walked casually toward his destination. Whenever he came to the city, he enjoyed his solitary walks. They took him past places he had known as a child. He walked down an alley and recalled that it was here he had been chased by a large and angry Goanese sailor he had pelted on the head with a snowball. It was so many years ago, he thought. We go through life and the years pass like leaves tossed on a high wind. Just when we seem to begin to understand it all, it's over.

He crossed King Street and shook his head as he counted ten taverns in one short block. We're becoming a city of saloon keepers, he grumbled to himself; and he was not far from the truth. There was one tavern for every twelve adult males living in the city. Of course a tavern owner couldn't make a living with only twelve customers: the heavy influx of sailors, soldiers, and traders helped to keep the rum moving briskly.

It had been a satisfying day's work. For months he had
been backing the passage of the new law. It was bad
enough that slavery existed, but to brand a newborn infant a slave was an abomination.

David had been most helpful, he thought. It was always
good to have a member of the family in government office; it was a tradition that went back to his own grandfather. Old Pieter had been on the Dutch board of
aldermen, and later, after the English had taken over, he
had served on Governor Nicolls's council. James's own father, Jacob Adam, had never held public office, but he had
always been there behind the scenes, manipulating, getting what he wanted. Paul de Witt and Charlie Goelet
had held various offices in their day. And now David de
Witt Sackett was carrying on.

It was a good arrangement, not only for the family,
but for the city itself. The de Kuypers had been committed to this place from the very beginning. Usually,
what was good for them was good for the town. Much
better, he thought, than allowing a lot of newcomers to
take over New York and run it for their own selfish interests.

Take the new law. How many newcomers would take
time out from making money to press for a resolution
like that? Not a single one of them, he decided. It's up to
people like us—the de Kuypers, de Witts, Goelets, and
Sacketts—people with family here over a hundred years
—to think ahead and do what's best for New York and
all its people.

Two men passed and tipped their hats. James returned
the greeting, although he didn't recognize the men. He
knew he was a well-known figure in town—a distinguished man, they said of him. He chuckled to himself.
If anyone ever asks me how to become distinguished,
I'll tell them the trick is simply to live long enough. Let
an old grayhead appear, and people assume they are
beholding someone possessed of great wisdom. I should
have had gray hair when I was twelve, he thought; *that*
would have confused them all.

And now, as he neared his destination, his thoughts
became more serious. These were dangerous years for
New York, and nothing was happening to brighten the
gloom. If the English lost the war in the north, it would

be certain to spread south, right here to the city. He shook his head. It was terrible to think of armies tramping over the town, killing and maiming with their muskets and artillery, destroying in a day what it had taken men a lifetime to build.

He knew the meeting he was going to now could have some bearing on the matter. His face was grim as he finally reached Maiden Lane and headed for the theater owned by his son. He stopped when he came to the building, looked around self-consciously, and then let himself in through the unlocked back door. He walked across the back of the stage and came to a door on the far side. He opened it and carefully made his way down the narrow, dimly lit stairs until he came to the dirt floor of the cellar. He went over to a bricked-off portion and stopped in front of a stout wooden door that was reinforced with bands of iron. Almost immediately the door opened to his knock, and he found his way blocked by the large form of Aaron Gerait.

Recognizing him, Aaron smiled and stepped aside. "Good day, Mister de Kuyper, and welcome to our humble treasure house."

James stepped into the room. Several oil lamps were burning, and he saw his son and Theo Henry—and, to his surprise, Marie Therese. He looked questioningly at his son.

"With Alice gone to live in England, I thought it would be a good idea to bring Marie Therese into our cozy circle," Jan said.

James nodded. "I've no argument with that." He turned to his daughter-in-law. "I'm not sure your husband did you a good service in allowing you to help us worry about all this wealth, my dear, but now that you're here, welcome."

Marie Therese smiled. "I'll try to do my share of the worrying."

Jan moved to a crudely made table and stood beside it. A piece of canvas cloth on the table covered a bulge. "I asked you to come here today," he said, "because a decision must be made about spending some of Kidd's treasure."

"The decision is yours," James said.

Jan shook his head. "I've never accepted the total responsibility as you did, Father. It belongs to everyone here."

"If that's the way you want it, I suppose we have no choice but to agree."

"It makes the most sense. What if I were to die tomorrow? My son is only a little boy, and if something happens to me, I expect the rest of you to take over."

James became impatient. "Let's get to the reason why we're here."

"As you all know, the war is going badly," Jan said. "General Wolfe believes we should have more ships up with Ned. But the governor says there's no money. I say we take some of our treasure and buy the ships needed. Three of them."

James nodded. "The money is to be used for the good of the city. I believe the ships would fit into that category."

Jan looked toward Aaron.

The black man shrugged. "Let's do it."

Marie Therese nodded her assent.

"We keep control of the ships ourselves?" Theo asked.

"Yes."

"Good. After watching the English generals, I'm not sure I'd want to trust their admirals."

"Then it's agreed," Jan said, removing the canvas from the table and exposing a pile of gleaming gold coins. "I figure this is enough to buy and outfit three ships. Aaron and I took this from one chest. It hardly made a dent."

Marie Therese's eyes widened. "Jan's told me about the treasure, but this is the first time I've seen any of it. Until now it seemed like a fairy tale."

"It's real enough," Jan said. "But now we have another problem. If we start spending these old coins, people are going to ask questions. If they even *think* we're sitting on pirates' treasure, there's going to be trouble."

"We could send it to London and deposit it with Twining Brothers," Theo suggested. "The bank could send us back an equal amount in less suspicious money."

Jan shook his head. "It's not a bad idea, but it would take too long. We've got to get the ships faster."

"What if I claimed it was an inheritance from my grandfather?" Marie Therese asked.

Jan smiled. "Would *you* believe that?"

Marie Therese blushed. "All right, it's a silly idea."

"What if we *found* it again?" James asked, speaking slowly, putting his thoughts into words as they came to him. "You understand . . . like we came across it as if it were a new discovery . . ."

Aaron slapped his thigh. "Mister de Kuyper, that's brilliant."

The others stared at him, not quite understanding what was being proposed.

Aaron turned to Jan. "You still own that empty lot over on Crown Street near the docks?"

Jan nodded.

"Well, tomorrow morning we're going to start digging on that lot. We'll say we're putting in a new dock. Nobody'll question that. Then, say about noon, after we've been digging for four hours or so . . ."

Aaron swung his pick and loosened another large chunk of dirt in the bottom of the growing hole. He glanced up at the sky; the position of the sun indicated it was almost midday.

Jan stood at the top of the hole and glanced over at another hole being dug by two hired laborers. They were going about their business and paying no attention to the activity on the other side of the lot.

He looked to the west and saw there was nothing between himself and the Hudson River. A packet was sailing south on a broad reach, directly opposite, but the ship was in the middle of the river. If any man aboard was interested in what was going on here—which was unlikely—he was too far away to make out any details.

Jan took out his watch and saw that it was almost noon. He glanced nervously up the street. There wasn't long to wait. A carriage came down Crown Street. Theo Henry was driving, and James sat beside him. They entered the empty lot and parked the carriage next to Aaron in a way that blocked off the view of the two laborers across the lot.

"Time for lunch," Jan called to them. They dropped their shovels and sat down to take a welcome rest.

There was no one watching as Theo shoved a scarred and weather-beaten wooden box to the edge of the carriage floor. With great nonchalance Aaron took the box and slid it down the side of the hole, using his knee to keep it from falling to the bottom. When the box rested on the loose dirt, he stamped on it so it would make an impression of itself there. Then he sprinkled dirt on the top.

Jan strolled over to the other hole and peered into it as if it held great interest for him.

"We'll have it down to eight feet by nightfall," one of the resting laborers said.

"Good," Jan replied. "These two holes will be where we'll place the main posts for the dock's anchorage."

He wandered back toward Aaron, who was resting and talking with James and Theo.

"I hope no one gets suspicious because it's you who's digging this hole," James said to Aaron.

"Don't worry about it. Most people will think I'm just another black man doing what black men are supposed to do—dig holes," Aaron said with a wide grin.

"Besides, when Aaron calls us over, we'll be the ones who open the box," Jan said. "Nobody will be looking at Aaron."

Thirty minutes later a cart with three men aboard pulled onto the lot. It was filled with heavy posts for dock construction. Jan had taken pains to make it look as if they really were planning to build a dock; also, he wanted the three lumbermen to be on the spot to authenticate Aaron's find.

As the men began to unload their cart, Aaron resumed his work in the hole. Now he was using a pick, taking care not to strike the box. Finally he hit it once on purpose, leaving a nasty looking gash on the top. He put down the pick and used his shovel to dig around the side of the box. When he was satisfied with the way things looked, he called out to the others, who had gone off to the side and were studying a roll of specifications for the allegedly planned dock. "Hey, Mister de Kuyper! You better come here," Aaron shouted. "There's something buried here in the ground."

Jan walked over without undue haste. "Well, well, what have you found? Buried treasure?"

"Could be," Aaron said, scratching his head. He turned toward the laborers at the other hole and called out, "Hey! One of you fellows give me a hand with this, will you?"

The two men came over and peered down into the hole at the box. "That's not very big," one of them said.

"Yeah, but it feels heavy," Aaron replied, pushing hard at the box with his foot.

One of the laborers dropped into the hole and took one side of the box while Aaron took the other. They lifted it up and placed it on the ground at the feet of James and Jan. The lumbermen came over, and Theo joined them. The group stood in a circle looking down at the box.

"Looks as if it's been in the ground for a long time," James said.

"Probably just some junk off an old ship," Theo offered.

"Probably," Jan agreed. "But we might as well open it anyway." He took Aaron's pick and pried up a corner of the box. The old, rusty nails that Aaron had used screeched in protest, and one of them broke in two.

"I wouldn't be surprised if this box has been here for a hundred years," James said, managing not to smile.

Jan pried open another corner and then grasped the lid with both hands, bending it back so everyone could see inside. A piece of mildewed canvas was stuffed in at the top, concealing what was below. Jan picked it up by an end and whisked it away.

Theo was first to react. "Good sweet Jesus!"

"Gold!" a lumberman exclaimed.

"*Buried treasure,*" said one of the laborers in an awed tone that was barely above a whisper.

Jan ran his hands through the gold. He looked up at the circle of faces. "I want you all to swear that you saw me discover this gold right here on my own land. I don't want another man claiming it belongs to him."

"Yes, sir, Mister de Kuyper," a laborer said. "We all saw it come out of the ground right here. No question."

The others all nodded their agreement.

"We'd better get this gold down to the office and put it into the vault," James said. "It isn't safe to keep it out in the open like this."

"Will you men come with us to help guard the gold?" Jan asked the lumbermen.

They quickly agreed, and all eight men joined Theo in the carriage. He snapped the reins and the horse moved off at a brisk trot.

James had to force himself not to smile as the laborers and lumbermen glared suspiciously at every person they passed. They did attract a lot of attention, because it was hardly usual to see a fine carriage filled nearly to overflowing with three men in gentlemanly dress, five burly white workmen, and a Negro.

The gold was safely deposited in the company vault, and Jan gave each of the workmen a gift of ten pounds for their help.

Word about the discovery spread like wildfire, and for the next two days people almost forgot about the war. All around the area of Crown Street men began to dig in their backyards, in vacant lots, and along the banks of the Hudson itself.

The lot belonging to Jan was dug up at night by men who hoped to find more treasure near the site of the original find. When Jan heard about it, he smiled. "Let them dig," he said. "When they're finished it will be easier for us to put in our dock."

"You're going ahead with that?" Theo asked.

"Of course. It would look suspicious if we didn't, and anyway, we could use another dock."

Nobody found any more buried treasure. A few people found bones, shells, old tools, and some discarded clothing. The bow of an old ship was uncovered, and a new furor of digging ensued. Everyone wanted to believe it was the treasure ship responsible for the de Kuypers' gold.

One lucky man found three ten-shilling pieces with the date 1705 stamped on them, and an old woman uncovered a William the Third tin ha'penny dated 1697; but these were as close to treasure as anything else that was turned up.

By the end of the week the excitement was over, and people grumbled as they went back to work. The spectre of the war once again hung heavily over their heads.

When Jan used the gold to buy three fast ships and outfit them as warships, no one questioned his seemingly endless supply of old gold coins. Everyone knew this had been just another example of the extraordinary de Kuyper luck.

"Let's get the train tackle a bit tighter on this gun," Jan said to a sailor, who nodded and moved forward to take up the slack on the heavy rope attached to the twelve-pounder. It was an iron cannon that had been placed in its gun port within the past hour, the last of the twenty-two cannons to be installed aboard the *Lord James.*

The frigate had the sleek lines of a racing dog. The three masts had a rakish tilt, and the complicated rigging toward the bow indicated the ship carried at least three foresails, plus provision for a large gollywobbler for use in light airs. The hull was painted black, and the long bowsprit seemed like the lance of a dark knight held in front of the ship to pierce the shield of an enemy.

"Make sure a gun ladle and a rammer and sponge are stored in this rack," Jan cautioned the sailor, who was stowing equipment that would be needed when the ship went into battle.

"Aye, aye, sir," the sailor replied as Jan began his inspection of the guns' breeching.

Theo Henry was checking off the stores manifest near the gangway when David de Witt Sackett came aboard. The lawyer wore a heavy bearskin coat and a long woolen muffler to ward off the coldness of the clear December morning.

"Morning, Theo," David said. "I've brought the final papers for the *Lord James.* She's all ours now."

Theo laid his manifest atop a covered barrel and stood next to David as he glanced through the papers. The physical contrast in the pair was striking—Theo trim and strong and his tight-fitting buckskin coat, the shorter David buried in his great bearskin. Theo had black hair and weathered skin; David was blond, and his fair cheeks were reddened by the crisp air. One thing they shared in common were eyes that missed little.

Theo folded the papers and put them in his pocket. "No problems getting these?"

"None. The governor accepted the status of the *Lord James* as a warship and waived all duties and taxes. May-

be the de Kuyper company could make the same arrangement for all its ships," David said, smiling.

"Good luck," Theo said. "Now there's a legal challenge that should make full use of your talents."

David leaned on the rail and watched the installa-
tion of the ominous looking cannons. This was unlike
Jan, he thought. Usually he would plan an operation and
then leave the details for someone else. But with the *Lord
James* and the two newly armed schooners at the de Kuyper dock, he was taking charge of everything.

"Why is Jan doing all this?" he asked.

Theo shrugged. "Can't you guess?"

The lawyer thought for a moment, and then a look of
sharp surprise came to his face. "It can't be that he plans
on—"

"You guessed it."

David whistled. "We need him here to run the company."

"His position is that if we don't win the war there won't
be any company to run."

David shook his head. "I'll bet the real reason is he
wants to be up there with Ned Goelet."

"The reports—and the ones we have are six months
old—tell us Ned has destroyed almost a dozen Frenchies.
Not bad for a man everyone thought was a bum."

David watched as Jan helped the sailors position the
gun carriages. They went about the task of securing the
heavy weapons in a workmanlike way. Jan had offered
wages that were twice the going rate, and from the large
number of applicants he had selected only the best—
hard-faced, clear-eyed sailors who had been in sea battles before. These men knew they were going to earn
their top wages. Sea battles at this time of year in the
freezing waters of the Gulf of St. Lawrence were not exactly a pastime for children. If past records were any
measurement, at least half these men would never see
New York again.

A carriage pulled up on the dock, and Marie Therese
stepped out. She wore a fur hat and a fur coat and kept
her hands warm inside a fur muff.

Theo helped her step over the raised part of the deck
at the head of the ramp. "What brings you here?"

"I've just received a letter from Alice and came to

show it to Jan," she said. "Would you and David like to hear what she has to say?"

They both nodded their heads, and Theo waved for Jan to còme join them.

Surprised by the sudden appearance of his wife, Jan wiped his oily hands on a rag and he walked across the deck.

"A letter from London—from Alice," Marie Therese explained, taking it out of her muff.

"What does our aunt have to say about her new life?"

"Oh, of course she goes on about her new home—excuse me, *homes*—Sir Francis must be horribly rich. Listen to what she says about his country place.

" 'The south wing has forty or fifty bedrooms, although I don't know why since no one ever seems to use them. Francis says his grandfather added the wing because King Charles gave him free use of the royal engineers for some favor or other.'

"Can you believe it? A house with that many bedrooms?" Marie Therese asked. "And I've always thought de Kuyper Manor was big." She returned to the letter.

" 'Our house in London is very lovely. I'm not sure but I think we have over twenty servants here. I know we don't need so many and Francis agrees, but he says all of them have been with his family for years and it wouldn't be fair play to let any of them go. There's one old man who does nothing but take care of the master's clothes. Not that Francis needs such a person, good Lord, if I didn't keep after him he'd wear the same clothes for weeks at a time. Do you suppose that comes from being without a wife for so many years?' "

Marie Therese looked up from the letter. "This next part might make you a bit angry. It's about the war."

"Go ahead and read it," Jan said. "I have an idea what it's going to be."

" 'I've met a great many people here in London through Francis—he knows everyone including the Prince of Wales, who I've heard is a ghastly person full of his own importance. Most of the people I've met—and these are people of influence, mind you—all agree that the war in America has been badly handled. But for some reason they believe the blame should be put on the colonials rather than their own inept generals. The costs have been very high and everyone says the king will expect the colonials to pay most of the bills—' "

"I knew it," Jan said. "This is what I've been saying all along."

"Does she give any details about how they intend to collect the money?" David asked.

"Yes," Marie Therese said. "Here, I was just getting to it.

" 'Francis took me to an elegant dinner party the other evening and I met the prime minister. Mister Pitt has all the charm of a coiled snake. A fat coiled snake. I asked him why the colonials should be expected to pay for the king's war. His reply was that since we lived under the king's protection, we had best be prepared to pay the price. I was my usual sweet self and I pointed out to Mister Pitt that his government seemed more anxious to protect its own profits than the lives of the colonials.

" 'Well, that brought on a long lecture, about the Glory of the Empire and how those places that lived under the British flag were the most civilized in the world. In the course of this lecture the PM let slip he's preparing a new tax stamp that will be required on certain goods. It seems to me it's a sneaky way to get us to pay for the cost of his war. It's also pretty obvious and I told him so, and now I doubt if I'll be invited to any of *his* dinners. I expected Francis to be angry, but to my surprise he was amused and told me it was a pleasure to see someone take the PM down a peg or two.' "

Marie Therese stopped reading. "There's more, but it's mostly woman-to-woman talk."

"A stamp tax," David Sackett said thoughtfully. "Well, there may be legal ways to fight that."

"Legal ways? When they have all the 'law' on their side?" Jan said.

"George is the king and we are his subjects," Theo said. "Whether we like it or not."

"Kings have fallen before," Jan said evenly.

"It's my guess Pitt won't try any stamp tax until after the war is over," David said.

Jan nodded. "Of course. First they'll get us to win their war for them, and then they'll tax the hell out of us for doing it."

"Cynic," Marie Therese said.

"Cynics often speak the truth," David said.

Marie Therese put the letter away. She looked at her husband. "I've never seen you spend so much time aboard a ship."

David, about to speak, suddenly realized that Marie Therese hadn't been told of Jan's plans. He politely looked away.

Marie Therese studied her husband's face. "Is there something you haven't told me about this particular voyage?" she asked shrewdly.

"Let's walk up to the bow," Jan said, and took his wife by the hand.

Theo stood at David's side and watched the couple. "She's not going to like it one bit."

"Can't say that I blame her. My wife would raise the roof if I told her I was going on a privateer to hunt French ships."

Jan and Marie Therese reached the farthest point of the front railing and stopped. Both looked down at the dark waters of the river.

"Why didn't you tell me you were planning to go?" Marie Therese asked. Her voice was tinged with anger.

"Because you'd have tried to talk me out of it."

"You're right. And I'll still try."

He shook his head. "This is something I must do. Everyone else has had a direct connection with the war —Theo, Ned. Aaron has gone on the ships when they took supplies north. Even my father once took a wagonload of rifles to Hartford. He put up the money to buy them, and he delivered them. But me? All I've done is sit behind my desk."

"Running the biggest supply operation anyone's ever seen. What's so bad about that?"

"Nothing. But I want to do as much as Ned."

"You are doing as much."

"There's no sense trying to talk me out of it," he said, and the depth of his stubbornness was obvious to her.

She sighed. "Then we'll drop the subject. You can count on my support and my prayers. I don't know how much good the first will do, but I'm pretty sure you'll need the second."

"Every little bit helps."

"When do you leave?"

"The ships will be ready in three days."

"Three days? But that means you won't be here for Christmas."

He nodded. "I'd like to wait, but I keep thinking of Ned. I want to get up there, because he may need me."

She reached out and held his hand. "Then we have only three more days. Let's not waste them."

He cupped her chin in his hand and tenderly brought her face close to his own. The moment before he kissed her, he said, "The sailors think it's bad luck to have a woman aboard a ship. I wonder what they'll think after they see this?"

Not everyone in New York was proud of Edward Goelet's success as a privateer commander.

Dora Goelet was sitting on a hard bench in the front parlor of Gideon Turnbull's house. The pastor's eyes had the sharp, pinpoint brightness of a fanatic. His pudgy head, set on an overweight torso, bobbed up and down. "Yes, yes, go on," he was saying.

"And I prayed all night to God, telling Him it was for the best if He punished Edward for what he has done . . . that it was best if he never returned to New York. That isn't wrong, is it?" she asked nervously.

"God makes it permissible for us to wish the death of incurable sinners," Pastor Turnbull said unctuously.

"And I prayed that everyone would realize that Edward's death was a sign from God, and then we would stop this fighting and killing, and everyone would come to their senses and return to fill the churches."

"Admirable, admirable . . ."

"And then I heard God speak!" Dora said shrilly, and her hands clutched the arm of the bench until her knuckles turned white. "He said it was our duty—those of us who truly believe His word—to go among the others and tell them we know the truth, that the sinners must change their ways or He will come down from His throne in Heaven and destroy us all!" Her voice cracked, and the last words were a mournful wail.

The pastor's head bobbed up and down. "God will punish the sinners, never fear. And we who understand the word must indeed pass it along to others. But it is a vast task, my sister, a vast task indeed," he said, and he threw both arms out to his sides as if to embrace the globe. "But who knows if we have the strength and means to accomplish it."

"I know. I know," Dora sniffled. She reached into the leather bag at her side and drew out a wad of pounds sterling in paper money. "Maybe this will help."

"Yes," the pastor said as he took the money. "It is not enough, but it will help us continue our sacred work."

She sniffled again, and patted at the edges of her eyes with a soft cloth. Gideon Turnbull looked greedily at the money in his hand. He wanted to count it, but dared not do so until this madwoman had left his house.

It was ten o'clock in the morning as David Sackett made his way up Broad Way. He came to Little Queen Street and turned toward the river. The wind cut through his heavy coat, and he pulled his hat tighter over his ears. Soon he was in the maze of narrow streets and alleys that were part of the dock area of the West Ward. He identified the alley he sought, entered it, and stopped in front of the fourth house. A scavenging cat halted and blinked at him.

David entered the shabby house and went down the sour smelling hallway to the last door at the back. He knocked. After a few moments he heard shuffling noises from behind the thin door. "Hold on, hold on," a voice called. The door opened. A woman rubbed her reddened eyes and looked at him with suspicion as she clutched her dirty robe closed with one hand. She appeared to be about thirty years old, and if she had washed the dirt from her face and combed her hair, she might even have been pretty.

"What d'you want?"

"Excuse me," David said politely, removing his hat. "I'm looking for Mrs. Richard Saxon."

"What'd you want her for?" the woman asked guardedly.

"Are you her?"

The woman ran her hand through her disarrayed hair. She looked more closely at her visitor and noted his expensive coat and the fine leather case. "Did that no-good Jenkins send you here at this time of day? I told the bastard I wanted no customers before the afternoon," she said angrily, and started to close the door.

"No, you misunderstand, I don't know anyone named Jenkins."

The door paused. "The prick who runs the tavern at the corner. Jenkins."

"I don't know him."

"Then who sent you?"

"I represent Mister Jan de Kuyper," David said quickly, keeping one eye on the door. "The matter concerns your husband, Richard."

"Richard!" she screeched. "I ain't heard nobody in years call him anything but Dickie. Except when they call him a dirty rotten bastard, like I'm calling him now. Who the hell *are* you?"

"That's what I'm trying to explain," David said. "Your husband was second mate aboard one of Mister de Kuyper's privateers. We've had word, unfortunately, that Mister Saxon died in battle."

"Old Dickie finally bought it, did he?" She opened the door. "Come on in. Get you a drink?"

"No, thank you," David said, stepping into the room.

The place was a jumble of furniture, clothes, plates, bottles. The curtains were drawn, and little light penetrated the gloom. A mussed bed was in one corner, and a table in the middle.

David tried not to look at the mess as he continued in a formal manner. "Mister Edward Goelet, who was there when your husband died, has informed us it was a most heroic death. Mister Goelet has asked Mister de Kuyper, for whom I am acting as agent, to provide something for his bereaved widow."

"Bereaved widow, am I?" she said, pouring a generous amount of rum into a cracked cup. "Doesn't bother *me* if I never see his ugly mug again."

"But he *was* your husband?"

"Husband? Shit! He never spent any time here, and never did a damn thing to take care of me. Little Rosie has to look out for herself, she does, and make her own living, poor as it is."

David opened his leather case and took out a little cloth bag. There was a clinking sound as he placed it on the table.

"That's for the bereaved widow?"

"There are twenty-five pounds here," David said. "Mister de Kuyper begs you accept it in the memory of your husband."

Her laugh was unattractive. "Twenty-five quid, you say? I'll accept it all right, but as far as Dickie Saxon's concerned, I hope he rots in hell."

David closed his leather case. "My job is to deliver the money, not pass judgment. And now I'll take my leave."

"What's your hurry? Maybe I'll break my rule about no morning business," she said, lowering her voice and brushing back the robe so he could see her shapely bare legs.

"My condolences on your husband's death."

Richard Saxon's wife laughed again. As David closed the door behind him, she was dumping the shining coins from the bag onto the table.

He hurried up the alley toward Little Queen Street, resolving that, if he could help it, he would never again set foot in this part of New York. And the next time such a situation required the company to extend its condolences, he'd bloody well send a clerk to do it.

The *Lord James*, together with the pair of two-masted schooners, waited in line at the dock. The three ships were fully manned, armed, and provisioned. In a few minutes the tide would shift and they would be off for the Gulf of St. Lawrence.

"The next time we meet, I hope to be aboard a troop ship sailing for Quebec," General Wolfe said to Jan as they stood on the main deck of the frigate. James de Kuyper was beside them.

"I'll try to make sure there are no French ships there to greet you."

The general smiled. "Good luck in finding your cousin, Mister de Kuyper."

"I'll just look for burning ships. French ones."

"Make sure it's not your own ship that burns," James said, and he reached out and grasped his son's arm.

"I'll take care," Jan said softly. "Don't worry."

General Wolfe added his own caution. "This isn't the best time of year to be going up there. The river itself will be frozen solid for thirty miles east of Quebec City."

"We plan on staying in open water off the coasts of Nova Scotia and Newfoundland. There's ice, but it's not solid. If the French can take their ships there at this time of year, so can we."

The general nodded. "Be careful all the same. Ice can kill a man as easily as a bullet," he said, and his companions soberly reflected that he spoke the truth. In normal times men rarely took ships into the northern gulf. There was ice to contend with, and fog; and if these dangers did not trap a man, he could freeze to death on the deck of his own ship. Add to these perils those of running gunfights with French ships and it could be easily understood that Jan was hardly sailing into a paradise.

Aaron Gerait came up the gangway ramp. "Tide's shifting," he called to Jan. "Time to get under way," he added as he swept forward toward the bow.

"Isn't Marie Therese coming to see you off?" James asked.

"We said our good-byes at the house. She dislikes watching me disappear over the horizon."

Theo came aboard and grasped Jan's hand. "Steady winds and fair seas, Jan."

"Thank you, Theo."

"I wish I could come with you."

"Someone's got to stay here and run the company. It's more urgent than ever that you keep the supplies moving."

"I hope to put your supplies to good use by next summer," General Wolfe said. "Now that we have Louisbourg, the next step is to take Quebec."

"To next summer," Jan said, holding out his hand to shake the general's. Then he took Theo's hand and wrung it between both of his.

Finally, James put his arms about his son. "May God take care of you," he said, and there was a hint of moisture in his eyes.

As the visitors departed, the crew went to work to move the ship out into the flow of the river's tide. The lines were shipped, and sailors ran up the ratlines to set the topsails. The men chanted as they went about their work.

Once the *Lord James* had drifted out into the channel,

the men used the wind to swing the bow so it was facing downriver. Sailors scampered up the lines, and more sails were set. The two schooners moved slowly away from the dock, following in the wake of the *Lord James*.

Jan stood at the railing with Aaron at his side. They waved at the men on the dock, who grew smaller and smaller as the ship picked up speed and moved toward the expanse of the Upper Bay.

There was a cold knife-edge to the wind, and Aaron pulled his collar tighter about his neck. Jan shivered and did the same.

The two men watched as the buildings and streets of New York passed in front of them. "I hope we live to see this place again," Jan said.

"That's up to us," Aaron said.

"Then we'll see it again."

6

Brave Men, Courageous Women

1759–1761

EDWARD GOELET STOOD AT THE STARBOARD rail and peered into the fog. The thick gray mist hung like a shroud all the way to the water. With the fog had come silence, and Edward strained to hear any sounds that would identify the presence of another ship. There was nothing.

The first mate stood at his side. "If we can't see him, at least you'd think we'd be able to hear him," he complained in a whisper.

"He's got to be out there, Mister Butler," Edward whispered back.

For two days they had been chasing a merchantman, but the canny French captain kept hiding in fog banks, one after the other. Every time Edward thought he had caught him, the Frenchman would find another fog bank and slip out of his grasp.

He walked across the quarterdeck to the port side of the ship. There was a briskness to his step despite his limp, and a healthy glow to his skin. His dark eyes were bright and aware, his hands steady and sure. The wind and sun had turned his skin brown even though it was the last week in March and the temperature rarely rose above freezing. The past months had brought great changes in Edward Goelet. The long days and nights at sea, the threat of ice floes, the running gun battles, the constant

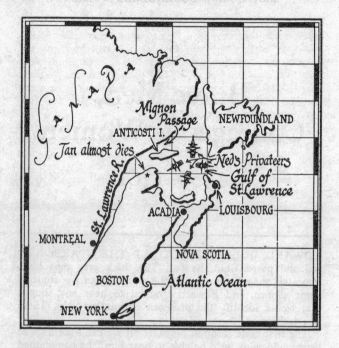

struggle with everything—it was a life that woke up the
senses and gave a man a sense of his own being.

Of Edward's original three ships, only two remained,
the frigates *Albany* and *Manchester*. The third had been
lost in a battle in Chaleur Bay, south of the Gaspé Peninsula.

The two ships were now in the Cabot Strait about
thirty miles northeast of Nova Scotia. These were good
waters for Edward's kind of hunting. Ships coming from
Europe at this time of year had to take this passage between Nova Scotia and Newfoundland, as the Strait of
Belle Isle, farther north, was choked with solid ice. In normal times there wouldn't be any ships coming into the Gulf
of St. Lawrence, because when they got to the river they
would find it filled with ice, blocking the way to Quebec
City. But these were hardly normal times. The French
ships had continued to come all year long, even in the

dead of winter, when the dense fogs and treacherous ice fields made the journey a hair-raising experience. Somehow they made their way through the gulf and into the head of the ice-jammed river. Thereafter most ships were forced to stop and put ashore the messengers and couriers from Paris, but a few managed to hug the northern shore and slip down to Quebec even during December and January. None made it during February.

Edward reckoned that his frigates had sunk or captured almost twenty enemy ships during the eighteen months they had been in these waters. Several French warships had been sent out to destroy the pesky enemy, but Edward had managed either to defeat his pursuers or to escape them.

The mate came to his side. "Fog seems to be lifting," he said. "Now maybe we'll be able to see the bugger."

Edward nodded and peered again into the fog. "Damn stuff," he said. "Makes you feel like a blind man." But the mate was right: the fog seemed less thick than before. The visibility began to increase with each passing minute. He looked down the length of his ship and saw his crew ready at their battle stations. They looked half-frozen as they stood in their heavy clothes, their heads bundled so that only their eyes were visible. They shifted from foot to foot to keep their blood moving, lest they become statues of ice.

That will change quickly, Edward thought. As soon as the ship went into battle, the heavy wraps would come off and the men would be sweating and cursing as they manned their cannons. When a man was engaged in a fight to the death, he quickly forgot everything but the enemy who was trying to kill him.

Now the wind began to pick up, and the banks of fog glowed brighter as the sun pierced through, burning the mist away, bringing a sparkle to the dark swells that rolled monotonously under the boats, comber after comber after comber; the deep voice of the ancestral sea.

"Over there!" the mate suddenly cried.

Edward peered into the evaporating fog and saw the French merchantman, now out in the open and vulnerable. She rode low in the water, an indication she carried a full cargo. Good, Edward thought: she'll be sluggish and easy to overtake. The loaded cargo ship was also a sign that the end of winter was at hand. In three weeks or so the ice in the St. Lawrence River would begin to break up. This ship had obviously planned its voyage so that by then it would be at the head of the river and able to sail down to Quebec with its much-needed supplies.

"Two points to port," Edward said to the helmsman. The wheel turned, and the *Albany* began to close on the Frenchman. "We'll pass to starboard and give her a broadside," he said to the mate. "Best get up more sail."

He looked back over his stern, but could see no sign of the *Manchester*. It would be nice if the fog cleared enough so the second ship could see what was happening and join the attack. Not that it really mattered: the *Albany* was more than a match for the Frenchman.

The captain of the French ship saw the approaching frigate and ordered that as much sail as possible be raised. He could tell from the swift lines of the enemy that he wouldn't be able to outrun him, but there wasn't much else to do but try. Besides, he might get lucky and find more fog.

The mist continued to lift, and Edward saw his second frigate emerge from a gray fog bank, half a mile astern. The *Manchester* had all its canvas aloft and was on a tack that would take it to the Frenchman.

The *Albany* closed on the plodding merchantman. Within ten minutes they would be in range to use their cannon. The French were preparing their own weapons, but they had only a few puny four-pounders. It wouldn't be much of a fight.

The fog was lifting more rapidly now. Chunks of ice could be seen floating in the water all the way to the horizon. As the fog diminished, the wind started to blow much more briskly and the ships began to slice faster through the water.

"Sail ho!" the lookout called from his perch three quarters of the way up the mainmast. Edward looked off into the distance and made out the masts of several ships. Edward took the mate's spyglass and peered through it.

"One . . . two . . . three . . . four . . . five . . . flying French flags! From their lines they appear to be frigates—all five of them!"

"*Five,* you say?" the mate exclaimed. "Best we break off and head back for the strait."

Edward looked again at the distant French squadron, and then toward the heavily laden cargo ship that was much closer. He made his decision quickly. "Continue with the attack, Mister Butler. Let's dispatch her with speed."

"Aye, aye, sir," the mate answered with resignation. In the past year he had grown accustomed to the almost mad daring this captain showed when it came to a battle.

"We'll not have time to wait for the *Manchester*," Edward said. "We'll attack at once."

"Aye, aye."

The sailors on the merchantman also saw the approaching squadron, and the sounds of their cheers came across the water to Edward's frigate.

"Let's see how long they'll keep cheering," he said grimly, carefully gauging the angle of his approach to the other ship. "Hold it a point higher," he growled at the helmsman.

When the French captain realized the Englishman did not intend to break off the engagement, he shifted his heading more to starboard. His hope was to delay the attack as long as possible. Surely the Englishman would not dare a prolonged attack—not with five French frigates on their way to the fight.

The captain's idea was a good one, but it didn't fool Edward Goelet. "So that's his plan," he said to the mate. "Let him think he's getting away with it for the moment."

He waited, his hand gripping the railing as he watched the merchantman slowly turn to the east.

"Now!" Edward cried. "Six points to starboard. We'll take him on the other side."

The frigate swung quickly onto its new course, and its speed brought it up on the other ship before the French captain could again alter his course.

The two ships closed. The bow of the *Albany* passed the stern of the merchantman, then inched forward until the forward cannons were pointed directly at the other ship. "Fire at will!" Edward shouted, and the first two guns on the port side opened up. The next two came into range and continued the barrage.

The loud booming of the cannon mingled with the shouts and screams of the men aboard the merchantman. The pungent odor of gunpowder filled the air. The heavy

iron balls crashed through the merchantman's planking,
carrying away everything in their path. The first salvo hit
the crew manning a four-pounder, butchering them where
they stood. One shot hit the mizzenmast, cracking it and
sending a shower of spars, rigging, and bits of broken
wood to the deck.

Now the English frigate was centered alongside the
length of the enemy, and the gunners fired, reloaded, and
fired again. Several of the cannons were loaded with
grapeshot, and the deadly pellets whizzed across the
French deck like swarms of angry bees. They were deadly
bees indeed, and men dropped to the deck in puddles of
their own blood.

The French captain, seeing his crew being slaughtered
by the overwhelming firepower of the frigate, adopted a
desperate measure. He changed his course, attempting to
close with the other ship and ram it with his bow.

Edward reacted instantly. "Hard astarboard!" he cried
to the helmsman. "Ship to wear—wear about!"

The mate shouted orders, and the sailors not manning
the cannons jumped to their positions and hauled on the
lines to bring the ship onto its new course. Half the men
didn't need any orders, having sailed with Edward long
enough to be able to read his mind.

The frigate veered away from the oncoming Frenchman, avoiding a collision and turning about in the other
direction. The cannoneers manning the stern swivel-gun
got off a shot that hit the French mainmast and snapped
off the upper half as if it had been a twig. The heavy
canvas, twisted and tangled with rigging and spars, bil-
lowed down on the deck, engulfing men, preventing them
from fighting, causing the maximum confusion. More important, from Edward's point of view, it ended the
Frenchman's maneuverability. The target was no longer
a sailing ship, only a floating hulk.

Edward's frigate came back around on its new course,
the sails filling as they took the wind, the bow leaping forward and churning up white water. And now the gunners
on the *Albany*'s starboard side began raking the Frenchman from stern to bow. One of their shots hit a keg of
powder. There was the screech of metal on metal, and
then sparks. There was a terrific explosion and a blinding
flash of light as a twenty-foot section of the merchant-

man's hull blew out into the water. A thick column of black smoke rose to the sky, and the fire began to spread as the frigate's guns continued to pound the stricken enemy until they passed out of range. The gunners reloaded and waited impatiently to ravage the enemy again; but they were to be denied this satisfaction.

Edward looked toward the horizon. He decided the squadron of five frigates was now only about three miles away and it was time for him to get out of this place.

"Break off attack!" he called to the mate. He turned to the helmsman. "Take a course due east. Straight out into the ocean."

The captain of the *Manchester* swore under his breath as he saw Edward breaking off from the battle. He too had wanted to get off a few shots at the Frenchman, but he also saw the approaching French ships and realized the wisdom of Edward's decision. The *Manchester* wore about and chased after the *Albany*.

Edward stood at the stern of his ship and watched the Frenchman burn and wallow in the water. There was much damage along the waterline, and it would be only a matter of time before it sank. The other French ships would not be able to save it, only rescue the sailors who were putting off in longboats.

Victory sat in Edward Goelet's stomach like a mellow wine. He went below to his cabin and took his log to make an entry about the battle. His version was a passionate view of what had happened, more a diary insert than a log entry, but Edward took each battle very personally. He wrote for twenty minutes and returned to the quarterdeck. The mate smiled when he saw him.

"Another fine day's work, sir."

"Yes," Edward admitted. He looked astern and saw that the five French frigates were in pursuit. "The frogs are after us."

"Aye, sir. What do you wish to do about it?"

"Head east until it gets dark. Then we'll head due north and lose them in the night."

"Aye, sir."

"They probably think we're going to stay down in these waters," Edward said. "We'll surprise them by sailing right up to the northern part of the gulf."

The mate looked troubled. "A lot of ice up there, Captain."

"It's starting to break up. Smile, Mister Butler, spring is right around the corner."

"But if we can go north, so can the Frenchies."

"Yes, but that's where they'll least expect us to go."

"Aye, sir," the mate answered. "And, begging your pardon, it's also where we can get into the most trouble."

"Nothing like a little trouble to spice up the day," Edward said, and he began humming a tune as he walked toward the bow, his keen eyes approving the way the sailors were cleaning up the ship and making her ready to fight again.

Two of the deckhands stopped their work and looked at their captain as he walked by humming.

"Bit barmy, that one;" the first sailor said in a low voice. "Likes all this 'ere fightin', 'e does."

"What about you? If you don't like fightin' why are you here?"

"For the extra pay, mate, the extra pay. And a share in all the prizes we take."

"So? Maybe that's why he's here, too."

The first sailor shook his head. "A rich man 'e is, very rich as I 'ear it told."

The second sailor's face showed his astonishment, and he looked at Goelet's jaunty back.

"You're right as rain, mate, he *is* barmy."

Five days after sinking the Frenchman, Edward came topside on the *Albany* and walked to the railing. He was bundled in a heavy bearskin coat, his arms crossed in front, his hands keeping warm under his armpits. If there's a colder place in the world than this, I'll believe it when I feel it, he speculated to himself. Every time he expelled air from his lungs, it came out as a cloud of vapor. He stamped his bad foot on the deck and ruefully thought that the cold didn't help his limp, either.

He squinted out at the bleak southern coast of Anticosti Island—a long rocky shore sitting out in the gulf, about fifty miles from the head of the St. Lawrence River. To Ned it looked like a giant cork stopper waiting to be used to plug up the river. A heavy mist cut off the tops of the hills on the island, the dreamy white blending with the heavy snowdrifts that tumbled down to the water's edge. The island was locked in the grip of an ice crust that extended offshore from a quarter mile to a half mile into the gulf. It was April, but winter did not die easily in this part of the world.

Chunks of ice floated in the water; and every few miles there was a majestic blue-white iceberg, cruising silently on an unknown course, causing ships' captains to sleep fitfully and men on watch to keep wide awake even though their fingers and feet felt frozen and the salt spray made their beards and eyelids icy and stiff. The bergs calved from glaciers that spilled into the gulf from the north; they were huge chunks of ice that would take all of the coming spring and summer to melt into harmlessness.

Edward looked down along the coast and blinked. Could his eyes be deceiving him, or had he actually seen the outline of a ship? He waited for a few moments and then was rewarded by another glimpse through a break in the mist. No doubt about it. A ship was out there. He called the mate, and the two of them waited tensely for another view of what was coming toward them. In less than a minute they saw not one ship, but three.

"The French squadron," the mate said.

"They must have figured out our plan," Edward said. "I'm surprised. They're usually not that bright."

Edward considered his choices. He could head south for the Gaspé Peninsula and hope to lose the French in open water. Or he could go up alongside Anticosti Island and sail around her northern shore into the Mingan Passage, a place where the fogs were always heavy at this time of year; but that might still be blocked solid with ice. There was still another choice, and this one had the most appeal: sail back and hug the coast of Anticosti. Let the French pass by. Let them remain unalarmed. If he could get behind them he might be able to attack by surprise in the heavy mist, cause some damage, and then disappear before they could counterattack.

He elected, naturally, to follow this last plan. His two frigates changed course and headed for a part of the shoreline that curved sharply inland. By staying just off the solid crust of ice, they might remain undetected by the French. The enemy would pass by and he could pounce on them like a wily dog harassing an unsuspecting horse.

This was the kind of game Edward enjoyed. It wasn't enough simply to beat the French; the real thrill was to make them look stupid. He stood at the rail, watching as the faint, ghostlike ships sailed through the mist farther out in the gulf. But his surprise attack was not to be. The leading enemy ship tacked onto a course that took it directly toward the island and the position of the two English frigates.

"They've seen us," Edward said to the mate. "Now our choices are narrowed—down to one."

Mister Butler nodded his head. "We fight."

The sailors had been interested observers of what was going on, and now assumed they were in for another battle. They moved to their stations and began preparing their cannons.

The three ships progressed slowly toward them, their sails filled with the gentle breezes. Anyhow, Edward said to himself, it would not be a good day to run away. Light winds meant slow sailing. He took the mate's spyglass and peered through it in order to get a closer look at the other ships. He suddenly dropped the glass away from his eye.

"That ship's flying an English flag," he said in surprise, handing back the glass.

"Aye, that she is," the mate replied, after taking a look for himself.

"Hove to, Mister Butler," Edward ordered. "And drop some sail."

Edward's frigate rocked easily in the gentle swells as the three ships drew closer. When they were within hailing distance, they too began to take down canvas. A deep voice boomed across the water. "What ships and masters?"

"*Albany* and *Manchester*, frigates out of New York. Edward Goelet at your service. Who are you?"

"Privateers out of New York. Might our captain be boarding your ship?"

"Come ahead."

All five warships now rocked close together in the swell, and a longboat was lowered from one of the newcomers. Several men climbed down into it. Within minutes it was bumping alongside the *Albany*, and Edward went to greet the occupants.

"Jan!" he yelled when he saw the face of his cousin staring up from the longboat.

Jan came aboard, and the two men embraced. "Jan, Jan," Edward said over and over again, pounding the other on his back until he winced. "What the hell are you doing up here?"

Jan's teeth were chattering from the exposure in the longboat, and he grabbed his cousin's arm. "Can't we go below and talk? I'm freezing."

"You'll get used to it after you've been up here for a while."

"We've been up here for two months," Jan said as he followed Edward toward the hatchway to the master's cabin. "I've been wondering when I'd find you."

When they were in the cabin, they took off their heavy coats. Jan warmed his hands on a steaming mug of coffee and studied his cousin, pleased with the changes. This was the Edward of old.

They spoke for over an hour, Edward describing in detail the engagements of his ships and how they had lost one of their number to the French. "We were down off the southern tip of Newfoundland engaged in a running battle with four Frenchmen who were trying to sneak past our blockade. I had my own three frigates and two others that had joined up with us for a time. We managed to turn them back, but they hit our frigate several times below the waterline. The ship was listing badly, and I still think we might have saved her, only we couldn't break off from the battle. We managed to capture two of the frogs, but by the time we came back it was too late to save our own ship. It sank, but that was in the summer and the water wasn't too cold, so we saved most of the men."

Impassioned, he told of other French ships and other battles. As Edward talked and Jan visualized what it must have been like in these frigid waters—howling winds, heavy snows falling on the men's heads, the constant threat of running into an iceberg, the endless fogs that gripped the ship, the iciness seeping deep to the bone—Jan's admiration for his cousin increased, and he felt ashamed that he had once questioned whether the man was equal to the task.

"When Jeff Amherst captured Louisbourg, it made life a lot easier," Edward continued. "Before that, we had to sail far to the south for supplies and powder. Besides, Louisbourg was always a safe refuge for French ships when we pursued them."

Jan nodded. The port of Louisbourg had been a French stronghold on Cape Breton Island in northeastern Nova Scotia. It had been General Wolfe's argument that before the attack could proceed on Quebec, Louisbourg must be taken. General Amherst and a strong force had wrested it from the French and made it the site of English operations for the north.

"We arrived in Louisbourg on February third," Jan said. "The commander said you'd been in for supplies and had left only two days earlier."

Edward smiled. "Only two days? It's too bad you didn't arrive earlier. We could have been sailing together."

"We were kept in port for two weeks," Jan said, somewhat defensively. "A heavy storm jammed the harbor with ice and it was impossible to leave."

"You get used to ice up here," Edward said dryly. "But now the ice is beginning to soften and become mushy. In another few weeks you'll be able to bring a ship right down to Quebec City."

"You still haven't told me why you're so far north."

"In good time," Edward said, with a cryptic smile. "Right now I want you to tell me what's happening in New York."

Jan, about to protest, suddenly realized all of Edward's old stubbornness was also back and there was no use trying to get him to talk about one thing when he was interested in another.

"All right, I'll let you win this one," he said with a laugh.

"Well, get on with it," Edward said impatiently.

Jan told him about the thousands of troops that were being prepared for Wolfe's assault on Quebec City. Edward had already heard about Loudoun's recall, and that his replacement was Sir Jeffrey Amherst. Loudoun should have been recalled in disgrace, in Jan's opinion; but the earl was one of only sixteen Scots peers, so the entire affair had been hushed up and Loudoun had returned to England with full honors.

Colonel Charles Lawrence also had been recalled to England, and Jan told his cousin of his disappointment in being unable to bait Lawrence into a duel. "I've been waiting to do that ever since he threw the Acadians out of their homes. But now he's gone, and I doubt that we'll ever meet again."

"Too bad," Edward observed. "I've heard he was a lousy shot."

Jan spoke of his own father, and also of Charles Goelet. Edward shook his head when he heard his father was as healthy as ever, griping and complaining all the time. He still swaggered about the city with his silver-headed cane, shooing beggars, dogs, and children out of his way. The old man called once a week at the de Kuyper house because he enjoyed seeing young Andrew. Charles maintained Jan's son would turn out to be the best of the family, and when Jan tried to defend himself and his contemporaries, the old man would shake his head and disagree. He claimed there hadn't been a real man at the head of the family since Paul de Witt had stepped down from the company.

"He thinks almost as much of you as he does of me." Edward said, grinning sardonically.

"At least he's never disowned me," Jan said.

"That's because he never had the chance. If you were his son, he'd have disowned you too."

Jan continued to detail the activities of other family members. Toward the end his recitation about Alice and her new life, Edward began to fidget.

"How's my wife?" he finally blurted out.

"I rarely see her," Jan said truthfully. "But from what I hear, she's unchanged. She spends a great deal of time at the church. I suppose the pastor is a close friend."

An angry glint came into Edward's eyes. "Still trying to buy her way into heaven, is she?" And then his voice became softer. "I guess it really isn't her fault, she's not very well. Being up here for over a year has helped me to understand a great many things."

"Such as?"

"I was weak and allowed Dora to ruin us both. If I had it to do over again, I'd handle it differently. But it's too late and nothing can be done."

There was a long silence. Edward suddenly said. "Well, there is one thing that should be done. And it will be."

Jan waited for his cousin to continue.

"That damned pastor," Edward said. "You know, the fat-faced one—Turnbull is his name. He's been stealing money from Dora for years. Takes advantage of her fears by offering eternal salvation. For a price."

This was news to Jan. "Are you serious?" he asked.

"She's always taking most of her money and handing it over to Turnbull," Edward said bitterly. "I did nothing about it because, at the time, I didn't give a damn. But now I do, and when I get back to New York I'm going to ask Mister Turnbull for an accounting."

"Can you prove anything?"

"Legally, probably not. Dora gave him the money, after all; he didn't actually steal it. But it's disgusting and immoral for a minister of God to prey on someone simply because she's not in her right mind."

"What do you plan on doing?"

"I don't know, but I'll think of something. I wouldn't be surprised if this Turnbull hasn't been extorting money from others as well."

Jan said nothing, but he swore a silent oath that when they returned to New York he would help his cousin punish this errant pastor. Mister Turnbull would be in for a surprise if he thought he could trifle with one of New York's most powerful families and get away with it.

"Enough of all this," Edward said, forcing himself not to dwell on the sad tale of his wife. "Now let's talk about what we're going to do next."

"Agreed."

"You asked why I was so far north," Edward said. "A good question. We sank a frog merchantman and were chased by a squadron of five ships."

"Ships of the line?"

"No, frigates. Now that you're here to help me, I think it's time we chased them."

Jan was thoughtful. The enemy had five frigates, and their forces consisted of three frigates and two schooners —five against five. But the enemy had the most frigates and therefore the greater firepower. "I'm not sure that's a good idea," he said cautiously.

"I know what you're thinking and you're wrong," Edward said quickly. "I don't want to take them head-on. What I had in mind was more of a surprise attack. You get a Frenchman thinking one way, and then turn around and do something else, he panics. Believe me, I've had enough experience with these frogs to know they lose their composure when they're surprised."

"All right, let's suppose what you say is true. Do you have a specific plan in mind?

Edward smiled enigmatically. "Of course."

"Is it a secret, or do you think I can be trusted?" Jan said sarcastically.

"The plan depends on two things. The first is that we must engage the frogs within the next two weeks. There must be a great deal of sluggish ice—not too hard, and yet still not really soft mush."

"What's the second thing?"

"That the French find us. That's important. They must think *they've* found *us,* and not the other way around. I want those frogs to think they've got one of our ships—and then we spring the trap on them."

"Interesting," Jan said. "Why don't you tell me more about it, Ned."

Edward smiled and pulled out several charts of the waters of the gulf. "Have another cup of coffee," he said. "This is going to take a bit of time."

When Jan returned to his own ship, he stood at the railing, oblivious of the cold, looking back at the *Albany* and thinking of his cousin. The man amazed him. How could anyone, even a man as clever as Ned, learn so much about ships and naval warfare in so short a time?

When Edward had unfolded his plans for defeating the French squadron, Jan was convinced they were worthy of a man who had spent his life analyzing battle tactics. As a New Yorker, Edward, had naturally been around ships, but never as a sailor. Indeed, he had rarely been known to go anyplace farther than Staten Island by ship. He had claimed ships smelled too much and their motion made his stomach feel queasy.

Jan shook his head as he realized what a waste it had been for Ned to have passed so many useless years, years that could have made him one of the greatest men in New York. Well, maybe he'll still become that. After all, many a man's fame has been made by the times he lives in, and from all wars come heroes.

A sudden gust of wind penetrated Jan to the bone, and he noticed the snow was beginning to fall again. The soft white flakes stuck on his coat and hat. He placed an un-gloved hand on his sleeve, and the snow immediately be-gan to melt. It seemed to be a softer form than the ice crystals of the past few months. Edward had said the rig-ors of winter were ending.

As Jan took a last look at the *Albany,* he could picture Ned in his cabin, poring over his charts and making his plans for the coming encounter with the French.

He went below to his cabin. Taking every blanket he could find, he burrowed under them to keep warm until it was time for the midday meal.

Marie Therese made her way through the mottled slush and snow piles that covered Pearl Street. She stepped over and around the icy puddles in a futile attempt to keep her feet dry. The snows had fallen only yesterday, but already they were melting and making the streets treacherous.

She passed a group of children at play, their faces barely visible under the heavy caps and scarfs inflicted on them by their mothers. Their noses and cheeks were bursting with color, and their eyes gleamed with pleasure. They had placed a wooden cage on top of a sled, and in-side it was a boy playing the part of a French prisoner. It took five of the children to move the heavy sled through the slush, and they jeered and taunted the prisoner. From the big smile on his face, however, it was clear he was thoroughly enjoying the game.

"Where are you taking him?" Marie Therese asked.

This caused momentary confusion, and the children looked to her for a suggestion.

"Take him to the governor's house," she said, and this appealed to the children. With a great deal of whooping and hollering they set off down the street, this time with a greater sense of purpose.

Children, Marie Therese thought; thank God for the children. Give them a war and a little snow and they'll figure out a way to make a game of it.

She came to the end of Pearl and walked into the broader expanse of Whitehall Street. She entered the mod-est structure housing the offices of the de Kuyper com-pany and stamped the slush from her feet as a solicitous clerk came to greet her. Within moments she was ushered into Theo Henry's office and offered a cup of tea.

"Put some gin in it," she ordered the clerk, who exited the room to do her bidding.

"You picked a wonderful day to pay a visit," Theo said, glancing out the window at the messy street. "Now, what can I do for you?"

Marie Therese removed her hat and gloves and went to the fireplace to warm her hands. "I hear a ship arrived this morning from Louisbourg."

"Yes, that's right. A brigantine owned by the Beekmans."

"Well?" she said impatiently. "Is there any news of Jan?"

Theo nodded. "He's been to Louisbourg and is now up in the gulf. I have no idea if he's found Ned. By the way, I planned on stopping at your house to tell you all this after the office closed."

"And what else?" she said, ignoring his feeble apology.

"There's not much else to tell. Ned lost a ship during the past year, but he's well. Wolfe is planning to bring his troops to Louisbourg this summer. Marie Therese, there's nothing to worry about. Jan will soon be coming home."

She sat down in a chair by the side of Theo's desk. "I feel so useless, staying here in New York while Jan . . ."

"*You* feel useless," Theo said after a moment's struggle with himself. "At least you're a woman. I'm stuck here, and I'm a man."

"What do you mean, 'You're a woman'?" Marie Therese said angrily. "Is that supposed to imply that women can't do their share? Now, you listen to me, Theophilus Henry—"

"Whoa!" Theo said, holding up his hands in surrender, knowing that the use of his full name was a sure sign of trouble. "I didn't mean that. It's just that I sit here shuffling papers and adding up numbers. Dammit, a year ago I was out in the field, fighting a war. Now, I'm just a glorified bookkeeper."

"All right, then you know how I feel. What are we going to do about it?"

Theo's eyes narrowed as he looked at his woman. His aunt was her father-in-law's second wife, but even though they weren't really related by blood, he thought of her as family, because their lives had been so closely connected for many years. He knew how stubborn she could be when she wanted something.

"I wasn't planning on doing anything," he said evenly.

"I am."

"Yes?"

"I'm going to Louisbourg," Marie Therese said, and when he started to protest, she stopped him. "Don't argue with me. I want to be there to see Jan. Now, what sort of boat do you have to take me there?"

"But your children—"

"Are already with their grandfather at his manor. Get back to Louisbourg."

"It's crazy," Theo protested. "Louisbourg is no place for a woman. The French may try to take it back at any time. Soon ships will begin taking the first of Wolfe's forces up there."

"Thank you for your concern, but what I'm asking about is the availability of a ship. If you don't help me, Theo, I'll find someone who will."

He looked at her and smiled ruefully. "I believe you would at that."

"Try to talk me out of it," she said, and glared at him.

"All right," he said finally. "We have a schooner in port right now. She's fast and dependable, and," he said, looking innocently at the ceiling, "as it turns out, she's being loaded with supplies for Louisbourg."

"Then it's settled. When do I leave?"

"On the morning tide. But I warn you, this schooner's not designed for comfort. She's a stripped ship—everything sacrificed for storage space."

Marie Therese ignored this statement; it was beneath her dignity to be concerned about something as trivial as passenger accommodations. The important thing was that she had found a ship to take her to her husband.

Theo began pacing back and forth across the polished pegged oak floor. He held his hands behind his back, muttering as if he was having an argument with himself. Finally he stopped in midstride and looked at Marie Therese. "I'm going with you."

"There's no need for that."

"For me there's a need."

"But the company—"

"Can run itself for a while. The hell with it."

"But—"

"Come on, "I'll take you home. You've got some packing to do."

"I'm already packed." she said. "I made up my mind before I set foot in this office."

The sail up the coast was uneventful.

Several ships flying British colors, heading south, passed them; and once the swift schooner overtook a lumbering brig that was wallowing its way north. Marie Therese tried to walk the decks to escape her cramped cabin, but the icy winds from Hudson's Bay drove her back inside. By the end of the tenth day she was chewing her fingernails with boredom. Fourteen days. Sixteen. When Theo told her the captain expected to arrive at Louisbourg the next day, she threw her arms about him and kissed him.

Marie Therese couldn't believe her eyes when she saw the former French port. She had been expecting a frozen little place with a few buildings and docks, but what she saw was a small army of men in frenzied activity. There were over two dozen tall-masted ships in the harbor, plus a few burned hulls that were remnants of the previous year's battle. One blackened and tattered wreck was *Le Prudent,* the sixty-four-gun ship that had been the pride of the French fleet in American waters. Now it was only a gutted hulk visited by rats and crustaceans making their home among the cracked timbers.

But it would prove to be only a temporary home. Hundreds of men were working to restore the harbor, readying it for the fleet that would bring General Wolfe and his troops. The hulks of destroyed ships were being torn apart, their timbers used to shore up damaged docks, their hardware stripped for other ships.

Even as these men built, others, British army sappers, were destroying the great fortress the French had erected. General Amherst had ordered this destruction in the hope of preventing the French from ever again establishing themselves on Cape Breton Island. The general knew that the balance of sea power rested with the English, and if Louisbourg had no fortress, but depended on ships for protection, it would remain in British hands.

Leaving the schooner as soon as it tied to a dock, Theo

and Marie Therese went to see the British military commandant, Colonel Fitzmaurice. A ruddy-faced man with a bushy mustache, he read their letter of introduction from General Wolfe, welcomed them, and offered his services. Marie Therese explained she was anxious to see her husband and asked whether the colonel knew his whereabouts.

"Ah, well, Mrs. de Kuyper, our privateers come and go as they please. Your husband was here, but left when the ice broke up in the harbor," the colonel said, and then added in a very proper, official voice, "I couldn't begin to speculate where he might be at the moment."

"I see," Marie Therese said coldly. "So presumably you wouldn't care to hazard a guess when he'll return."

The colonel shook his head. "When he needs more supplies and powder, he'll be back."

"And when will that be?"

"Most privateer captains don't stay out for more than six weeks at a time. Except, of course, for Mister Goelet."

"Ned?" she said quickly. "What about him?"

The colonel shook his head in wonder. "A brave man, ma'am. He stays out for as long as three months. The last time he was here he was down to his last barrel of powder. It's a marvel how he does it."

Marie Therese and Theo exchanged glances. Both were surprised by the colonel's description of Edward. "Mister Goelet is my husband's cousin," Marie Therese said.

"Yes, I am aware of that. Your husband took his ships out to look for Mister Goelet. I hope they've found one another," the colonel said. "And now, ma'am, what are your own plans?"

"I intend to wait here until my husband returns."

The colonel made a sour face and clucked his tongue on the roof of his mouth. He looked at this exquisitely dressed woman, recognizing in her the high-bred type he knew so well in London—good in salons and around hounds and foxes. But here? He pictured her amid the frenzy and shabbiness of the ruined town. "I'm not sure that's a good idea, Mrs. de Kuyper. This is a rough place."

"I'm not here on holiday."

"Just finding a place to stay is difficult, and—"

"I'm sure we'll find something," she replied. A hard

edge to her voice warned the colonel it was a waste of time to try to talk her out of it.

"I'm afraid I misjudged you, Mrs. de Kuyper. My apologies."

"Quite all right, Colonel," she said, and then put on her coyest smile. "You're forgiven."

"It's best you stay at the inn," the colonel said with new warmth. "Most of it was untouched by the fighting, and I'm using it as quarters for myself and my senior officers. That would be best for you too, sir," he added, looking at Theo.

Colonel Fitzmaurice ordered a soldier to accompany them to the inn, and although the walk was only a few dozen yards, Marie Therese was aware of being stared at by a hundred pairs of eyes. It wasn't only that she was a woman: there were others about, but none of them looked the way she did. The others were either camp followers or women who had elected to switch sides from the French to the English simply because they preferred to go with the side that seemed to be winning. Men were men, and a clever woman could make her living off them no matter what their nationality. In such company Marie Therese was decidedly out of place.

The dirt streets were frozen, but there had been so many carts and wagons moving about that they were scarred with deep ruts and potholes. When the snows began to melt, Louisbourg would turn into a swamp. The soldier led the way to the inn and presented them to the owner, Clément, an ebullient Frenchman who had decided to stay with his property and take his chances with the English.

He showed Marie Therese and Theo to their rooms and invited them to join him for a glass of wine in the tavern room, where he kept a great fire blazing. More for the fire than the wine, Marie Therese was happy to accept, and she sat on a hard bench close to the fireplace. The innkeeper told her that Jan had spent many evenings in this very room.

Theo had been looking around, and he could see that the only other people in the tavern were British officers. The patronage of ordinary soldiers and French civilians, it seemed, was not encouraged.

After Clément poured wine for his guests, he filled a

glass for himself and sat with them, warning them of the perils to be avoided in Louisbourg. There were many thieves and cutthroats roaming the streets, and it was dangerous to be abroad at night. The men drank and brawled a great deal.

"I tell you these things," he said, "because I can see you are a gentleman and a lady, not like these others who come here to Louisbourg."

"My husband, Monsieur Clément," Marie Therese said icily, "is one of 'these others.' "

"No, no, madame. You misunderstand me. Your husband is the captain of a privateer. I put him in the same class as the English officers. Gentlemen, all of them. They fight for a cause and with honor. The ones I refer to are all those who come looking for cheap land and easy loot. It is always thus in war."

"Do you plan on remaining in Louisbourg?" Theo asked, politely changing the subject.

"Of course," Clément said. "Everything I have is here. House. Business. Family. And if I left, where could I go? Quebec? Montreal? What's the use of going to those places? They will be English within the year."

Theo's eyebrows raised. "But until now the French have been winning the war. Why do you give them so little chance?"

Clément shrugged in Gallic fashion. "Until now the war has been fought on land; the French had a chance. Now the English have turned to the sea. Who can beat them on the sea? The war is as good as over."

"That's what General Wolfe has been saying all along," Theo said.

"He is a clever man, this Wolfe." Clément said, nodding his head slowly. "The English will take Quebec and Montreal and everything else. If one wishes to remain French, he will have to go back to France."

"I take it that isn't your wish?"

Clément smiled. "May I bore you with a story?"

Marie Therese smiled as she nodded. "Please tell us."

"I came to the New World as a cabin boy aboard a ship. I was ten years old," the innkeeper said. "You know the kind of foul slop they feed sailors? Well, that was the best food I had eaten in my life, and it was the first time I had ever eaten my fill. Until then, you see, I had been an urchin without mother or father, a beggar living on the streets of Marseille."

He sighed and looked closely at Marie Therese. "I have been to your New York, and I tell you, the worst places I saw there are nothing compared to what exists in Marseille.

"But that is not my point. When I came here—even though I was only a boy—I saw that one could build a good life for himself. So I stayed and built that life. I even took an Indian woman for a wife. Now the French have gone and the English have come. But I will stay, because this is my home. I will never go back to France."

The conversation was interrupted when the eldest of Clément's three daughters came and took him back to the kitchen to prepare the evening meal. She was a dark-eyed woman in her early twenties, with a slender figure and an enticing walk. She radiated sexuality in looks and manner, and stared with a saucy openness at Theo Henry. He was embarrassed by her undisguised interest, but found himself staring after her as she disappeared into the kitchen. It wasn't difficult to read his thoughts.

"Well, *she's* rather a surprise to find here, isn't she?" Marie Therese said in amusement.

"What are you talking about?"

"Man meets woman, Theo."

"Come on," he protested, embarrassed at having revealed his reaction to the girl. "She's half my age."

"Since when does that matter?" Marie Therese said, and then ceased her teasing as a young lieutenant came up to convey the colonel's respects and an invitation to dine with him that evening.

At the dinner hour the fire was stoked, and the tavern room filled with two dozen senior British officers. Aside from Madame Clément and her daughters, all three of whom served at table, the only woman in the room was Marie Therese. She sat at a table with Theo, the colonel, and three majors. "If I were twenty years younger, Colonel," she said with a smile, "I'd say the present company would be any girl's dream."

The colonel chuckled. His own wife was about the same age as this striking woman, and he couldn't help but make a comparison that, had his wife known of it, would have made that plain woman most unhappy.

"I doubt if any of my officers would consider your age a detraction from your appeal, Mrs. de Kuyper."

"You're most kind, Colonel, but then we must remember I have very little competition here in Louisbourg."

"Here, there, or anywhere, ma'am," the colonel asserted in his most gallant fashion.

At that moment Clément's eldest daughter entered the room with a platter of food. One look at those large eyes set above the tawny, high cheekbones told Marie Therese that there was, indeed, if anyone cared to notice, a good deal of competition—probably more than I could handle, if I'm to be honest with myself, she thought.

The talk at the dinner table, as always these days, turned quickly to the war. "From his letter of introduction, Mister Henry," the colonel said, addressing Theo, "I take it you are personally acquainted with General Wolfe?"

"Yes. It was through the offices of the general that our company sent six ships to these waters as privateers. We believed in helping him prove that his was the way to win this war."

"Six ships, Mister Henry? Yours is not a small business," the colonel said appreciatively. "And you are right about this war. It took Ticonderoga to make some people in London see things as they really are. Nasty bit of business that, losing Lord Howe and all."

A softness came into Theo's eyes as he thought of his long days with the general. "Lord Howe was a fine man."

"You knew him?"

"I held the viscount's hand as he died," Theo said.

There was an instant silence at the table as every man's eyes turned to Theo.

"You were there at Ticonderoga?" the colonel asked. "My dear Mister Henry, please, you must tell us about it."

For the next hour, as Clément's wife and daughters served a dinner consisting of a thick soup, crusty *habitant* bread, broiled venison steak, boiled cod, potatoes, green beans, and stewed turnips, Theo spoke of the great battle in the woods. Clément's eldest daughter brushed against him several times, but now he scarcely noticed her. The conversations at the nearby tables lapsed into silence as the British officers listened to Theo's account of the slaughter of the largest army ever put in the field in America. His story, quietly told, was yet vivid and explicit, and only such a group as this, an audience of military men, could have appreciated his extraordinary, professional eye. When he finished his account, there was a long silence in the room.

It was Colonel Fitzmaurice who finally spoke. "Damme, sir, but it was even worse than I had heard. Such stupidity. Such bloody waste. And to think no one was court-martialed."

At the beginning of the meal Theo had suspected a resentment among the officers at his presence, but now each one smiled and treated him with the greatest respect. He might be a civilian, but he had suddenly become a celebrity among them, a man who had fought in a bloody battle and survived.

After dinner Marie Therese bundled up in her furs, and Theo walked with her to the end of the harbor. She stood silent for a long time, the salt-tinged air whipping about her face. There was a three-quarters moon that tipped the water with silver as the waves marched to sea.

"I pray he's safe," she finally said, holding the image of Jan's features before her. "I pray to a God who must know and understand that no harm can come to him."

"Nothing will happen to Jan," Theo said.

"I never heard you talk of war before tonight, Theo," she said. "I didn't realize it could be so terrible."

"Most of the time it's just boring."

"No. I could see men dying as you spoke; it was that real to me."

"I was speaking of war on the land," he said, trying to spare her. "It's different at sea."

Marie Therese was not fooled. War was war. But if it made Theo happy to think he was keeping her from worrying, she was pleased to accommodate him.

The next day came.

And the evening.

And then days passed in quick succession, and suddenly they had been at Louisbourg a week; and every day and every night Marie Therese went down to the harbor and stared out to sea, to be met only by the same disappointment. Several times she watched anxiously as a frigate or schooner came into the harbor, but each was a ship with a strange woman's husband in command. The joy she wished for herself always belonged to another.

The fine lines about Marie Therese's eyes tightened, and her chin took on a firmer set. It became more difficult for her to smile.

One thought kept entering her mind even though she tried her best to keep it out. Could she already be a widow?

Jan paced back and forth on the quarterdeck, his eyes constantly darting to the top of the great rock. A man was on top of that cliff, waiting to give the signal that would tell him it was time to spring Edward's trap on the French ships. Aaron stood near the port railing, close to Jan, as he always was when trouble brewed.

The rock was a thousand yards long and five hundred wide, and it towered three hundred feet into the air. More an island than a nameless rock, it lay, in the waters of the gulf, about a mile off the northern shore of the Gaspé Peninsula. Beneath the snow and ice, the top and the ledges of the sides were covered with guano deposited by the thousands of auks, gannets, and gulls that used the rock as a rookery during the summer and fall months. Jan's fleet of three frigates and a schooner sailed back and forth along the northeastern end, carefully keeping themselves hidden from any ships approaching out of the east or southeast.

The fifth ship—the second schooner—was missing from the privateer fleet; it was off on the most daring part of the maneuver. Edward had insisted on being in command of the schooner, claiming it was his plan and no other man should have to take the risk. The regular captain of the schooner was now in command of Edward's frigate, the *Albany.*

The rock was shaped like a crooked L, its two arms creating a natural harbor. During the winter months it had been frozen solid with hard ice, but now, in April, the ice had softened and the little bay was filled with bits of solid ice amid a heavy slush. It was this slush that Edward planned on using to destroy the French ships.

The plan was simple in concept, but how simple it would be in execution remained to be seen. Today it would be tested, once and once only; and if it didn't work, there was a good chance that several English ships would be sent to the bottom of the gulf.

Edward had taken the swift schooner and gone looking for the French frigates. *He was the bait.* If he could get them to chase him, he would lead them back toward this rocky isle. He would come from the southeast and head right into the middle of the harbor, trapping himself in the slush and—if all went well—leading his single-minded pursuers into the goop as well. Jan's four ships would come sailing around from behind the cover of the rock at the very moment the French found their movements hindered, and the guns of his ships could leisurely pound the Frenchmen to bits.

The flaw in the plan had been uncovered quickly by Jan when Edward first told him of the idea. "But your schooner will be trapped in the harbor with the Frenchies. They'll blow *you* apart."

"If you get to the scene on time, you'll keep them too busy to pay any attention to me," Edward had replied.

"You can't be certain of that."

"You can't be certain of anything," Edward had snorted. "Just get there on time and I'll be all right."

"You're taking a big chance," Jan had warned.

Edward had winked. "That's what makes it so attractive."

"You're crazy."

"Only crazy men accomplish anything."

Now that the plan was nearing fruition, Jan was having more doubts. But it was too late to change anything: Edward's schooner was now probably in full flight from five enemy frigates. By Ned's reasoning, the French would have given up their search south of Newfoundland and returned to the gulf. All he had to do was sail out there until they saw him. Therefore he had gone off four days ago, promising to be back today.

"How can you know that for sure?" Jan had asked, perplexed at his cousin's blithe assurance.

"I told you, I've learned to think like a frog. I know where they'll be. It will take me two days to reach them and two to get back."

"You're positive?"

"I know my frogs."

And now Jan paced the deck. It was madness actually

to believe that five French frigates were going to show up today just because Ned had said they would. He shook his head in self-disgust. It was crazy—exactly the sort of thing that Ned was capable of doing. It made no sense if you thought about it logically. But it wasn't logic that Ned was using; it was gut instinct.

He glanced up at the top of the rock and froze in his tracks. The lookout was holding a white flag aloft. It was the signal that he had sighted a ship, or ships. Jan grabbed another white flag that had been placed next to the railing, and waved back. Now the moments of greater tension had arrived. Jan's orders were to wait for the second signal—a blue flag. That meant the sighted ships were Edward and his pursuers, not a false alarm. It also meant Edward's plan was going smoothly and Jan should move his ships into a position near the edge of the rock in preparation for the third signal—a red flag. The red one meant he was to come out of hiding and pounce on the Frenchmen from behind as they struggled in the harbor's slush.

The three frigates and lone schooner continued to sail in a tight pattern that would conceal them from ships approaching from the southeast. The minutes passed, and Jan despaired of ever seeing the second signal.

But then the man on the high cliff waved the blue flag. The oncoming ships belonged to Edward and the Frenchmen—there no longer was any doubt. Jan gave orders that sent the ships on a course to the jumping-off point behind the rock.

The crew swung into action. They opened the gun ports, uncovered the guns, unstopped the bores, brought more shot and powder from belowdecks, readied the flintlocks, and fussed over every detail. There was little talking; it was always the way before battle. Each man was too busy with his own thoughts, wondering whether today was the day God had decreed to be his last. This was the ultimate form of gambling: the stakes were the highest any man could bet.

Another ten minutes passed, and they seemed like hours. As Jan watched the cliff, his mind was filled with thoughts of his wife and his son and his daughter: Marie Therese, Andrew, and Celine—three names, three lives. They had always been precious to him, but now they seemed infinitely more so. Will I never speak to them or laugh with them or hold them again? The thought became unbearable, and he felt physical pain at the idea of not being able to kiss Marie Therese, or look at his pretty little Celine, or feel the growing muscles in young Andrew's arms.

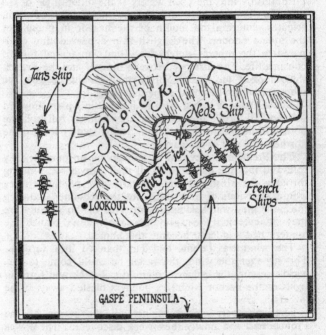

What men think of when they face the possibility of imminent death is the true measure of what they consider their wealth, Jan realized. While others aboard the *Lord James* might dream of piles of gold, mounds of silver, or casks of rum as they waited for the battle to begin, he thought of his family. They were the fundamental reason he enjoyed his life so much, the reason he looked forward as he did to each and every day.

The red flag was hoisted.

"Wear, wear about!" Jan shouted. The helmsman turned the wheel and the sailors pulled on the stout lines.

The flag had been seen by the captains of Jan's other ships, and they all began turning at once. It was a beautiful sight, this maneuvering of square-rigged ships in a precise ballet; it was the mind of man willing great wooden behemoths to behave.

The *Lord James* was in the lead as the privateers sailed purposefully into the open waters at the outer angle of the rock. Jan looked ahead and saw the enemy—five of them, frigates, entering the mouth of the harbor in pursuit of the lone schooner. The English ship appeared tiny compared to the others—defenseless—and Jan feared for his cousin's life. The distance between himself and the French ships looked too great. Surely they would destroy the schooner before he could come to her aid.

But if Jan was losing faith in his cousin's plan, Edward was not. He drove the schooner ahead under full sail, the bow churning through the slush, fleeing swiftly toward the northeastern end of the harbor.

The Frenchmen gave no sign of giving up pursuit; they followed into the harbor with all their canvas set, plowing through the slushy ice as Edward had predicted they would, oblivious of everything but the schooner, ignoring the peril they were placing themselves in. So intent were they on catching their prey that they didn't realize the hunters had suddenly become the hunted.

The wind was strong, and Jan thanked luck for this. The stronger the wind, the faster he could come to Edward's rescue, the quicker he could sail back and forth in front of the harbor while his gunners blasted away at the targets.

The privateers closed rapidly on the sterns of the Frenchmen, and finally they were discovered. There was a fury of activity aboard the French frigates as their captains ordered the ships to come about and face this new menace. But as they attempted to turn, the brilliance of Edward's plan became obvious.

It is one thing to drive a heavy wooden vessel straight ahead through slushy ice, but quite another, he had reminded Jan, to attempt to turn it in that same slush. The ice had built up enormous weight and resistance, slowing the ships down, impeding them, greatly hampering maneuverability. The ice had become the enemy. As the ships tried to turn, they lost way, just as Ned predicted,

and now the ice was an even more effective prison: the
French were proving that only when water is rushing past
a rudder can it be used to turn a ship. A grim smile came
to Jan's lips as he watched the cold logic of his cousin's
plan turn into death-dealing fact.

His own fleet was moving swiftly through blue, ice-free
water, fully under control and completely maneuverable.
The plan was to sail the ships in a line along the edge of
the slush pack. The gunners would pound the ships as
they passed, and when the line had reached the last ship,
it would turn and come back again, this time using the
cannon on the other side to rip the French—all in ice-free
water while the French floundered about with their half-
useless rudders.

As the line, led by the *Lord James,* came to the edge of
the slush, Jan veered to starboard and the ship continued
to pass through clear water, coming closer and closer to
the disorganized French.

And now, as the first of the enemy came within their
sights, the *Lord James* gunners began blasting away with
their eight-pounders and twelve-pounders. The *Albany,*
the *Manchester,* and the schooner followed, and soon
their guns added to the cacophony. The cannon blasts
boomed and echoed off the tall cliffs behind the little harbor; it sounded as if a hundred ships were fighting instead
of only a handful.

One of the Frenchmen fired back, but the captain had
little control of his ship's position, and his was a pitiful
resistance to offer against the effective gunnery of the
English cannoneers. By the time the privateers reached
the end of their first run, each French ship had taken
several hits and not one French gun had hit its mark.

Now the *Lord James* came about, and the line formed
to begin its second run. The results were even more devastating this time. The French were too busy trying to extricate their ships to fight back with any conviction, and
during this second run one frigate took half a dozen hits
and was already in serious trouble. Two masts were damaged, her deck was littered with spars and sails, and she
had lost way completely. As the other four frigates tried
to get out of the slush, they began to move away from
their sorely wounded companion.

The slush proved the greatest ally the privateers could

have wished for. While Jan made his third run, his fourth, his fifth, the Frenchmen were still fighting to get clear of the ice that held them fast in its oozy grip. Two of the frigates were now on fire, and a third was listing awkwardly to port.

Edward Goelet had not been idle while all this was going on. When the French realized they had been trapped by the privateers, they had quickly understood the schooner was a decoy sent to trap them and, worse luck, had succeeded. Their battle was no longer with the little ship, but with the ones whose guns were now breaking them to pieces.

Not without a struggle, Edward had managed to turn his schooner around in the slush. But his craft was lighter than the French frigates, and he was already gaining forward way.

As the schooner picked up speed, Edward spotted the frog that had lost two masts and was wallowing helplessly in the ice.

"Mister Butler," he called to the mate. "Have we sufficient way to attack?"

"Aye, sir."

"Bring us on a course so we can take that frog with our starboard battery."

"Aye, aye," the mate replied, his heart pounding with fear at the thought of his small boat attacking a heavily armed frigate.

Edward's schooner moved sluggishly through the churning ice, but in a few minutes he had drawn abeam of the stricken frigate.

"Drop sail, Mister Butler," he commanded. "Starboard battery, commence firing!"

The mate's mouth flew open in surprise, and it was several seconds before he regained enough composure to relay the order to drop sail. The schooner slowed in the water and then held position alongside the frigate as its guns blasted away.

The men aboard the frigate attempted to fight back, but Edward had directed his gunners to first destroy the enemy's cannon. This strategy paid off, and after a few minutes the frigate no longer returned Edward's fire. The French gunners had been slaughtered and their weapons rendered useless. Edward's men continued to pour shot after shot into the larger vessel. It had been a one-sided fight; but it was still an unfinished one.

"We've got the guns, now get the waterline," Edward ordered his gunners. There were only six cannons on the schooner's starboard side—seven, if one counted the swivel gun at the stern—but from such close range, and without the usual problems of shooting from a moving vessel, they proved to be more than enough for the task. The Frenchman listed and began riding lower and lower as her holds filled with slush and salty water.

Jan was on his eighth run when he saw the audacious task his cousin had now set for himself. But he also could plainly see that it was the frigate, and not Edward's schooner, that was in trouble. The schooner suddenly hoisted sail again, and Jan knew his cousin had put the frigate out of the fight for good. Edward's ship began to move through the ice as he attempted to free himself and join the others in the battle. He's totally mad, Jan thought, but at the same time he couldn't keep himself from smiling at his cousin's bravado.

"I'm seeing it, but I don't believe it," the first mate of the *Lord James* said to Jan. "A schooner dropping sail so it can stand abeam of a frigate and take her on!"

"It seems to have worked."

The mate shook his head. "I hope he has enough sense not to try it a second time."

"By the time he gets free of the ice, the battle will be over," Jan said, nodding his head toward the four other enemy ships.

Two of them had been on fire for over half an hour, and their crews, forced to keep the timbers of their ships from burning up beneath them, had all but given up fighting back. They were brave men, but theirs was a losing battle. As they worked to put out one fire, the English ships passed in line and bombarded them again. New fires broke out. Most of their masts and sails were down, and the only fate left for them was to die with honor.

A third frigate had been listing sharply to port for a long time, and the Englishmen pounded the hull until it could take no more. It was now almost over on its side.

"If it wasn't for the ice holding her up, she'd be on her way to the bottom," said the mate of the *Lord James*. And it was true. The crew of the ship was putting long-

boats into the water in an attempt to get away from their
doomed craft. But several of the longboats had been
damaged by cannonshot, and they began to sink. The men
scrambled back aboard the slanted deck of the frigate,
looking forlornly at the slushy ice, knowing their chances
of survival were nil; they could not swim in such water.
Their faces reflected the knowledge that they were looking
at their own grave.

There was only a single French ship left with any hope.
The captain of this lone survivor plowed his way through
the final bit of slush while the English line, hundreds of
yards away, was turning to come back for another deadly
pass.

Now the captain had his ship in clear water. It picked
up speed, beginning a dash eastward toward the safety of
the mouth of the St. Lawrence River.

Jan saw the enemy had reached ice-free water and immediately gave orders for pursuit. "We'll make it five out
of five!" he cried to the sailors, who struggled with the
lines and sails to bring their ship onto its new course.

The *Lord James* was faster than any of the other ships
except the schooner commanded by Edward, and that
small vessel was far to the rear. Jan narrowed the gap between himself and the Frenchman.

The French captain was sailing his ship close to the
shore of the peninsula and was now driving as fast as he
could, but he soon realized the pursuing English ship was
faster. Unless something happened to change the course of
events, the Englishman would overtake him. When that
happened, the French captain knew, he would be involved
in the classic test of the sea—warship against warship,
running side by side, guns blasting away at close range,
cutting and smashing one another to pieces; the classic
race of death.

The French captain smiled grimly as he gave orders to
prepare for the coming battle. He looked back and saw
the remains of his squadron: four once-proud frigates,
now reduced to burning and sinking hulks. There was one
chance for revenge—the frigate that was overtaking his
own ship. It would be his pleasure to take on this damned
Englishman.

The distance narrowed. The *Lord James* edged closer
to the enemy on the starboard side. The men stood ready

at their stations, tense, fully aware that this would be a true battle, not a massacre. The Frenchman was wounded, but obviously still full of fight.

"When we get abeam of her," the mate said to Jan, "we'll be about thirty yards off."

"Her mainmast is damaged," Jan observed. "Have the gunners give it special attention."

Now that he was coming close, he realized the *Lord James* would be outgunned in this fight. His frigate was small and swift, carrying twenty-three guns; the Frenchman looked as if it had thirty-eight or forty. But if he could take away some of the other's maneuverability, he reasoned, it could compensate for the lack of weaponry.

The mate seemed to be reading Jan's thoughts. "She's a big one for us to be taking on alone," he murmured.

Jan inwardly agreed. But his other ships were far behind, and if he waited for them to catch up, the Frenchman would escape into the St. Lawrence River, where he dared not follow. The ice was breaking up, and the river was certain to be patrolled by the French.

He shrugged. "Stand by to begin attack."

The bow of the *Lord James* pushed past the stern of the French ship. The gunners of both crews prepared to begin the cannonade; it was a moment of unbearable tension.

And then it began.

Smoke. Fire. Loud booms. Shouts.

The first shot from the *Lord James* crashed into the side of the other ship, smashing heavy timbers to splinters, an irresistible force careening across the deck, cutting a man in half before he knew it had happened.

The French guns fired back, and within five minutes both decks were covered with smashed equipment and dead men. The gunners of the *Lord James* blasted away at the masts, hoping to knock them down and disable the French ship, but success eluded them. A number of the English guns were silent, their gunners dead. The French were using grapeshot with devastating effect.

Jan had sent men up the ratlines with muskets, and now they began to fire down on the deck of the other ship, aiming at the gunners in hopes of silencing the cannons. But the French had been expecting this and had taken the same measure. As the ships ran side by side, the cannons boomed, and the great balls of iron and loads of grapeshot flew through the air, wounding and killing and bringing the battle that much closer to its end. And while the big guns did their work, the men in the shrouds and ratlines fought their opposite numbers, adding to the carnage with their smaller weapons.

Jan remained on his quarterdeck, firing his musket, reloading and firing again. Meanwhile the superior firepower of the Frenchman was destroying the Lord James. Most of the port railings were gone, and four guns out of commission. Hunks of iron junk littered the deck. It was hard for a man to walk from one side of the ship to the other without stepping on the bodies of fallen shipmates.

And then the French gunners had a bit of luck when a shot found the powder magazine of the Lord James. A great explosion rocked the ship. A column of flame shot up through the deck timbers, throwing debris in all directions, knocking men to the deck, hurling several of them through the air into the frigid water. Like an animal struck a terrible blow, the ship had jumped on sustaining the impact.

Sails came billowing down as the spars cracked. The mainmast quivered and then broke in two, the top half collapsing over the port side of the ship. The Lord James was stout and capable of taking terrible punishment, but the first explosion was followed by a second and a third and a fourth. The last two hits punched gaping holes in the hull, partly below the waterline, and the cold waters of the gulf began to pour into the bilges.

When the explosion blew skyward, Jan had been standing at the center of the quarterdeck, not more than a dozen feet away from the long deck planks that ruptured upward from the force of the detonated powder. Flung across the deck, he bounced off the bulkhead of the aft cabin. A chunk of splintered wood, flying through the air like a spear, hit Jan at an angle, penetrating deep into his left shoulder from behind. But it caused no pain—he was already unconscious. Aaron had been in the cabin getting more powder. He rushed through the cabin door, which had been partially blown off and was hanging at a crazy angle, and went to Jan's side. Seeing the piece of wood sticking from Jan's shoulder, he took hold of it and, as gently as he could, extracted it. Then he did what he could to stanch the flow of blood.

The *Lord James* was finished. The French captain, noticing that the other English ships were in pursuit, broke off the battle and headed for the distant mouth of the river. The men of the *Lord James* who were still whole now turned their attentions to helping their stricken shipmates and saving their vessel. The mate was uninjured, and, after one look at Jan's motionless figure on the deck, took command.

There was no doubt the *Lord James* was going to sink. This left the mate with three choices. The first was to wait and hope the other ships could reach them in time; but from the way the frigate was listing, he decided not to risk this course. The second was to lower the longboats and abandon ship, but a quick inspection convinced him most of the longboats were damaged and useless.

The third choice—and it had become apparent it was the only one he had—was to attempt to ground the ship on the shore, barely two hundred yards away. It was risky, but the ship still had a few sails aloft. They might be enough to give her way to reach the safety of the land.

The mate took the wheel—the helmsman lay dead beside it—and the *Lord James* responded sluggishly; but soon the bow was pointed at the Gaspé Peninsula and the ship began to move slowly toward the land.

Edward's schooner had caught up to the other English ships, and he watched in horror as his cousin's distant frigate seemed to blow apart. As he came within hailing distance, he shouted to the captain of the *Manchester* that the two frigates and the second schooner should chase the Frenchman while he went to the aid of the *Lord James*.

"I don't know if we can catch him," the captain of the *Manchester* shouted back.

"Dammit, you can try!"

As the three ships began to pursue the Frenchman, Edward's schooner veered off toward the afflicted *Lord James*.

The mate of the *Lord James* had brought his ship within a hundred yards of the shore when he spotted a little cove that would make an excellent landing place. He adjusted the wheel, and, almost reluctantly, the ship turned, her bow riding deeper and more mournfully in the water.

The distance between ship and shore narrowed, and the mate prayed the water would remain deep enough for the ship to poke its nose on land.

Ninety yards . . . eighty . . . seventy . . . "Ready the bowlines!" the mate shouted. "Prepare to take an anchor ashore."

Sixty . . . fifty . . . forty yards—and there was a sickening crunch as the ship passed over an underwater ridge; but then it was clear, and the cove almost at hand. Thirty . . . twenty . . . more scraping and bumping. But the deadweight of the *Lord James* kept the vessel moving until the bow punched through the ice crust and touched the frozen earth, carrying forward with enough force to crumple a few bow timbers as the ship shuddered to a sudden halt.

The sailors jumped off, and within moments the *Lord James* was held fast by a half dozen lines looped around the trunks of stout trees. An anchor was dragged ashore and one fluke dug into the frozen ground, and a foreshortened chain was wrapped about the samson post.

The ship continued to fill with water, and soon the hull was resting on the bottom. The cove was shallow, and the top decks remained dry.

But a storm was brewing, and if it proved to be a big one, it could easily tear the *Lord James* from this flimsy anchorage and push it back to deeper waters, where it would sink like a stone. The mate gave the order to abandon ship and turned his attentions to his stricken captain.

With Aaron's help he rigged a stretcher from a piece of torn sail, and the two carried Jan ashore. They found a flat spot of hard-packed snow under a stand of white pine trees and carefully placed the unconscious man there. Aaron peeled back the layers of clothing, and the mate grimaced when he saw the jagged, bloody wound. He said a silent prayer for the soul of Jan de Kuyper, fully expecting the man would meet his Maker before the day was over.

While the men took the dead and wounded off the ship, Edward arrived and anchored his schooner in the cove. He came ashore in a longboat and immediately made his way to Jan. The mate gave his opinion about Jan's chances, but Edward refused to accept it. He sent for one of his own crew members, Levi Seixas, the second mate.

Levi Seixas was the eldest son of Benjamin Seixas, the rabbi of Congregation Shearith Israel in New York. He was dark complexioned, tall, and almost too slender. His eyes were large and inquisitive, and he would have been handsome save for his ears, which stood out too far from his head. He had a mouthful of even white teeth, and a strong chin. He also had a quick tongue.

He was the black sheep of the Seixas clan, one of the leading families in the Jewish community. Its members, led by the rabbi, pursued honorable careers as merchants, shopkeepers, and professional men.

Levi had studied medicine, but found it too tame a life. He had made a career of shipping aboard privateers, enjoying the excitement of chasing other ships and fighting with them—and sharing the booty. Levi was probably worth more money than any other member of the Seixas family, but that didn't prevent them from refusing to have anything to do with him. Finally his father had sung kaddish—the prayer of the dead—for him. When Levi heard he was now officially dead to the Jewish congregation, he laughed, drank a bottle of rum, and shipped out on the next privateer going after Frenchmen. He always found it easy to get a second mate's berth, because he had two valued skills. He was an excellent sailor, and his knowledge of medicine made him a rare asset.

It was for this latter talent that Edward had sent for him. Levi took one look at Jan's wound, grunted, and opened his kit of medical instruments and potions.

Edward left him to his work and went among the other men. There was nothing to do for the dead except bury them; but the earth was frozen, so the decision was made to take the bodies out to the schooner and bury them in the cold waters of the gulf.

Many of the wounded men were beyond saving, and if they were conscious, were consoled with rum. But the men who were considered savable had another ordeal to endure. The little camp at the foot of the cove soon echoed with screams as hot tar was placed on open wounds and on stumps of arms and legs. Any severe compound fracture meant amputation. If the man could survive this torture, there was a chance he would live to end his days in more peaceful surroundings.

When Levi finished patching up Jan, he went among the other wounded, helping those who had a chance, shaking his head over the hopeless, and moving on to the next man. By the time he was finished, it was almost dark. He returned to Jan, whom Aaron had placed under a heavy canvas tent next to a blazing fire. Edward sat near by.

"How many will die?" he asked.

Levi shrugged. "Who knows? I've done what I could."

Edward pointed toward Jan's tent. "How about him?"

"I'll let you know in the morning after I take another look."

"Any opinion on his chances of making it?"

"I have my doubts."

Edward's head drooped, and he prayed to a God he half believed did not exist. He felt responsible for Jan's presence here in the northern waters, and if his cousin died, the death would be on his head.

He was interrupted in his thoughts as the other ships returned. The captains came ashore and reported they had not been able to catch the French frigate.

"Got away, did he, Mister Croffley?" he asked the man who had been captaining the *Albany*.

"Aye, that he did. Got to the river. We thought it prudent not to follow."

"Best we be away from here at dawn," the captain of the *Manchester* said. "We be like ducks in a pond if they catched us here in this cove."

Edward nodded. "We'll spend the night here. Get the wounded aboard the ships at first light. We'll head back to Louisbourg."

It hadn't been all that bad a day for the English: four French ships sunk, a fifth wounded and chased from the gulf. That was considerably more than their own loss of only a single ship. But Edward felt that if he lost Jan, he would have lost the battle.

Aaron came out of the little tent. Edward looked up. "He's breathing easily now," Aaron said. "The doc gave him something that keeps him asleep."

"How did it happen?" Edward asked, and he sat before the fire, ashen-faced, as Aaron recounted the story of the battle and what had happened to Jan.

When the black man was finished, Edward pulled a

blanket tighter about his neck. "Better get some sleep," he said quietly.

The dawn came, and men and ships were covered with an icy frost. Edward looked up at the sky. He could feel the wind on his face as it blew down the gulf.

Aaron, who had slept beside him, peered out from beneath a pile of canvas. "Storm," he said, sniffing the air.

Edward went over to the tent, stretching his arms and legs to work out the stiffness. He paused at the flap and realized that Levi Seixas was already inside, attending to Jan. He waited and watched as the sailors transported the wounded out to the ships. The dead had already been committed to the waters.

Levi finally came out of the tent. He snapped the top of his medical kit and went to the fire, where men were brewing coffee. He held the metal cup in his gloved hands and drank slowly, burning his lips, but happy to have the warmth.

Edward joined him. "Well?"

The doctor shook his head. "It's a bad wound. I closed it, but if it opens and starts to bleed again, he's a goner."

"Then you'll just have to keep it closed," Edward said determinedly.

The doctor looked at the other man and shook his head. "How do you expect me to do that?"

"What do you mean?"

"You're planning on leaving, aren't you?" Levi asked, gesturing toward the sailors, who were taking everything out to the ships by longboat.

"Yes."

"Butler says we're in for a storm today, a big one."

Edward looked up at the sky, dark and ominous despite the sun, now rising low over the gulf and decided his first mate was right.

"You put that man on a ship and send him out in a storm," Levi said, "and there's no chance of keeping the wound closed. When the ship starts pitching and rolling—and you know how fierce it gets in these storms up here—you're going to lose him."

"Can't you stay with him?" Edward asked in desperation. "Can't you watch his wound?"

Levi shook his head. "If I tried to work on him aboard a pitching ship, I'd probably kill him."

The two men stood by the fire in silence for a time, and then the captains and mates gathered. There wasn't much to discuss. The ships would leave their anchorages and head for Louisbourg by the fastest possible course. Their powder and shot supplies were low; it was dangerous to stay in waters where they might meet more Frenchmen. And they wanted to get the wounded to a place where something more might be done for them.

"The doctor says if we move Jan de Kuyper in this storm, he'll die," Edward said.

The captain of the *Manchester* shrugged. "We can't stay here," he said.

"And we can't leave him here," Mister Croffley added.

"We can."

The men turned to look at Aaron Gerait.

"He can be hidden in the forest," Aaron explained. "You send a ship back from Louisbourg to pick him up. Two or three weeks." He looked at Levi Seixas. "He should be able to be moved by then, right?"

"In two weeks he'll either be mostly healed, or dead," the doctor said.

"Then it's settled," Aaron said. "I'll stay with him. And you, too," he added, pointing at the doctor.

"Now wait a minute—"

"He needs the kind of help only you can give him. You stay and take care of him, and I'll take care of you both."

"I'll stay too," Edward said.

"No," Aaron said firmly. "Too many people makes it more dangerous. There's bound to be Indians around here. Three men will have a better chance of keeping out of their sight than half a dozen."

"But he's my cousin," Edward protested.

"Then do what's best for him," Aaron said. "Get to Louisbourg and then get back here as quickly as you can. By then he'll be ready to travel."

"All right," Edward agreed reluctantly. "You and Seixas stay."

"Thanks for volunteering me," the doctor grumbled.

Edward grew angry. "Are you saying you have objections to staying with my cousin?"

"No, only that if I'm to be a hero, I'd like to ask for the job myself."

"You're quite correct, Doctor," Edward said formally. "Tell us your pleasure."

"I think I'll stay around here and have a rest," Levi said, gazing around at the dense woods. "Looks like a nice quiet place."

The men stacked a small pile of supplies next to Jan's tent. As specifically requested by Aaron, it included a bow and a quiver of arrows. "I want to do my hunting quietly," he said. "In case any Indians happen to be listening."

Soon all the men were gone. A single longboat waited at the head of the cove for Edward, who stood with Levi and Aaron at the tent.

"The French are bound to see *Lord James*," Edward said. "They'll probably send men ashore, so you'll have to move inland."

Aaron nodded. "I'll find us a place as soon as you're gone."

"Maybe the storm will blow the ship back in the gulf and sink her," Levi said hopefully.

"If you're lucky," Edward said. "But I think she's stuck pretty solid in the ice."

"Doesn't matter," Aaron said, looking into the hills that swept up from the shoreline. There were dense stands of white pine, beech, yellow birch, and elm. All were heavily covered with snow and ice. "I plan on going way up there. Less chance of meeting Indians or Frenchmen. Can't see them climbing hills in the winter."

"Winter's almost over."

Aaron looked around at the packed ridges of snow and the crust of ice along the shoreline. "Kind of hard to tell, around here," he said dryly.

The longboat took Edward out to the *Albany*. The ships hauled their anchors aboard, raised sail, and began moving off to the east. Levi and Aaron stood quietly beside the tent and watched until the ships were out of sight, as if marking the disappearance of the last of the world they knew.

Aaron finally broke the spell. "You stay here with Jan while I find us a place to stay."

Levi's eyebrows went up. "A place to stay? What do you expect to find? A cozy French inn?"

"A cozy cave, if I'm lucky."

"What if there's a bear in the cave?"

Aaron smiled. "Don't bet on the bear," he said, picking up his musket, feeling the heft of it in his hand.

"I've heard about you," Levi said. "Jan de Kuyper's nigra shadow. I hope everything I've heard is true. We're going to need you."

"And I've heard about you," Aaron replied smoothly. "The Jew pirate. Jan's going to need you."

"A Jew and a nigra," Levi drawled, smiling and savoring the words. "Trust them to always give us the tough jobs."

"You got anything against nigras?"

"Only when they're anti-Semitic."

Aaron smiled and held out his hand.

Levi took it. "Partners," he said.

Aaron nodded, then turned and started walking toward a snow-filled ravine that led into the hills. "I'll be back, partner."

Levi went into the tent to assure himself that his patient had no immediate need of his services. Jan was asleep, seemingly at peace, each hour of such rest giving him that much greater a chance at remaining alive.

But even with rest and constant attention, Levi knew, it was going to be a close call. Jan's life was hanging by a thread, and if something happened in the next few days to disturb that thread, it would break and Jan would fall into the abyss. If he could only hold on for a few days, then the natural processes of his body would begin the true healing.

Levi went back outside the tent and walked down to the icy crust at the edge of the water. He turned and looked back at the hostile world that held him in its grip. He saw nothing but endless rows of trees, countless thousands of them soaring upwards for hundreds of feet, finally becoming lost in the swirling clouds of the storm that was about to break.

He knew life was all about him. Birds snuggled in their nests, aware of the coming storm and wise enough to wait it out. Squirrels, rabbits, otters, chipmunks, beavers and deer—all were out there, but not to be seen. Levi was also aware there were other animals in these woods, ones not so harmless and timid. There were the lumbering black bears and the fierce timber wolves. Most of the bears were probably in hibernation, but the wolves didn't sleep through the long night of winter. They roamed about in packs, desperately hunting food in the bleak months and afraid of neither man nor devil in their quest to fill their empty bellies.

And then, of course, Levi thought, there was the most dangerous animal of all—man. French fur trappers visited these parts; and, worst of all, there were the Indians. Levi shuddered to think what would happen to them if they fell into the hands of the savages. Death was never a pleasant subject to ponder; but there were ways to die, and ways to die.

His speculations were interrupted by a sudden rise of wind and the first flakes of snow. The sky grew heavy, and the heavens emptied themselves on the helpless land. Levi returned to the tent and huddled inside, hoping that his body heat would be of some use to the nearly dead man beside him.

James de Kuyper, in his nightshirt and nightcap, was standing by the window in his bedroom, staring out at the snow-covered fields. He was worried and, for once, looked his years. He had been having a dream that was so unpleasant it had wakened him. The dream had been about his son, and all he could remember was that Jan had been in trouble.

Was it a premonition?

James rubbed his hand against his chin, and his beard of whisker stubble made a scratching noise. Hope came from her bed to his side. She shivered in the early morning cold. "Is anything the matter?" she asked.

"Nothing. I just couldn't sleep."

"You look worried."

"I was thinking of Jan."

"But we've heard nothing about him."

"That's what worries me," he said, and then noticed that his wife's teeth were chattering. He took her by the hand and led her back to the bed. He tucked the heavy down coverlet under her chin and then went to the kitchen, where several servants were already busy with the chores of the new day. He stood near the cheery fire and accepted the mug of coffee offered him.

And he continued to worry about his son. If only there was a way to see him, talk to him, find out what could be done for him. Maybe Jan needed something as simple as this fire and this hot coffee, he thought. And I would bring them to you, my son, but I cannot. For all the talk about men being lords of the earth, we are more its servants. We pride ourselves on our power, boast of it, write about it, and yet we are powerless and inept for most of our days.

It was many days later, and Theo Henry was also having a dream. But his was most pleasant: he was gently running his hands over the smooth, silky skin of Louise Clément, and his hands kept finding new places to touch.

And then the dream changed. The smoothness disappeared, and he felt himself being shaken—roughly. He fought against the intrusion and tried to burrow more deeply under the heavy covers. But the hands would not desist.

Now a voice began to penetrate his mind, and it was not the husky voice of Louise urging him on, but a louder voice, a sterner one.

"Theo, wake up, for Godsakes, Theo . . ."

"What!" He now realized this intrusion was not part of his dream.

Marie Therese stood over him in the darkened room. He shook his sleepy head and blinked his eyes to clear the cobwebs. The weak gray light coming through the window told him it was that shadowy time just before dawn.

"Theo, you've got to get up," Marie Therese said, giving his arm another tug. "Ned's returned."

The news brought him awake instantly. Then he remembered the woman beside him in the bed. He turned with embarrassment toward Marie Therese. Louise was looking at both of them with inquisitive eyes that held not a trace of shame.

"Look, Marie Therese . . . Louise and I . . ."

"Stop apologizing, it doesn't matter," Marie Therese

snapped. "Get some clothes on and come downstairs." She turned on her heel and whisked out of the room.

"You'd better go," Louise said quietly.

"Yes," Theo mumbled, slipping out from under the covers and grabbing his clothes from the chair where he had dropped them in a heap. "Don't worry about this. I'll explain it all to Marie Therese."

"I'm not worried," she said. "But it might be amusing to hear you 'explain'."

Theo pulled on his trousers, buckled his belt, and began fumbling in the semidarkness for his boots. His liaison with Clément's daughter had started the first night he had spent at the inn. She had come to his room, ostensibly to bring him another candle, but when he saw the burning look in her eyes, there was no doubt in his mind about her true mission. Without a word he had put his hands to her face and drawn it close to his own. In minutes they were naked beneath the covers.

Theo had never been a ladies' man. He had always felt more at home in a business office or off in the woods than in the drawing rooms of New York. He had been married when he was very young, to a girl chosen by his father. She had been a white girl, without a drop of Indian blood, the daughter of a farmer who owned a small amount of land near the manor. She had been a good wife, and innocent, but even at the start they had generated a fair amount of heat in their lovemaking. All had gone well for three years, and then she was taken from him by one of the ravaging poxes that swept back and forth across the land with discouraging frequency. He had never remarried.

Not that he became a celibate. Even though some women scorned his one-quarter Indian blood, there had always been enough women who thought it a pleasant idea to bestow their favors on a handsome man like Theo.

But never in his life had he made love to anyone like Louise Clément. It was like being in battle. She bit and scratched, tossed and moaned; and when he was sated and spent, she would get on top of him and continue to arouse him and keep him hard until he thought he would die from the agony. But it was the kind of agony that he didn't mind enduring again and again.

What happened on the first night had occurred every night since, except that as they learned about one another's quirks and desires, the agony decreased, and was displaced by their ever-increasing ecstasy. They never spoke about it during the day; in fact they rarely spoke to each other at all, and Theo spent most of his time with Marie Therese. But occasionally in the tavern room, when they were taking their meals, Theo would catch Louise staring at him with unashamed desire. He fought hard to keep himself from responding visibly to her presence, and he had been certain that he was successful in keeping the affair from Marie Therese.

But now she had pulled him out of bed when Louise had been at his side. He knew that Marie Therese would be discreet, but even so, he was Theo Henry, an important partner in the de Kuyper company, a man of substance, and there were certain proprieties to be observed. As he left the room, Louise smiled and, silently laughing at Theo's embarrassment, turned over to lie on her stomach. He is a good man, she thought, and I will try to cause him no more trouble. Well, maybe just a little more trouble, she decided.

Theo hurried into the tavern room and went to the table nearest the fire. Marie Therese was there with Edward and several other seafarers.

Theo was astounded by Edward's fit appearance, but he managed to keep his reaction to himself. "H'lo, Ned, good to see you," he said.

Edward introduced the other man, his captains and first mates, and immediately got down to business.

He told Theo and Marie Therese about the battle and the sinking of Jan's ship. He described the remote coast on the Gaspé Peninsula, and told why it had been necessary to leave Jan. "If we had taken him with us, he would have died. With Aaron and Levi to care for him, he at least has a chance. Now we've got to get back there to take him out."

"He'll be well enough to move?" Theo asked.

Edward nodded. "That's what the doc says," he replied, without adding Levi's comment that if Jan wasn't well enough to move by the time they'd returned for him he'd be dead.

Edward went on to explain the threat of the French

coming back to investigate the wrecked ship. "And then, of course, there could be a problem with the Indians. Although we're not sure they'd bother white men."

"They're Micmacs," Theo said. "They wouldn't be friendly." He turned to Marie Therese. "I don't want to be an alarmist, but in this situation we have to be realistic."

"I understand," Marie Therese said. "So what do we do now?"

"The schooner is the fastest ship we have," Edward said. "We'll take on supplies and do some fast repair work. We sail tomorrow. When the *Albany* is ready, she'll follow. I figure the schooner will get there two or three days earlier, but the *Albany* will come in handy if there are any frogs roaming about."

"I'm coming with you," Theo said.

"So am I," Marie Therese added. Both men were about to protest, but Marie Therese raised her hand and they realized there would be no argument.

Edward dismissed his captains, and now the three members of the de Kuyper clan sat by themselves. For the first time Marie Therese allowed emotion to creep into her voice. "Tell me the truth, will Jan be alive when we get there?"

"I don't know," Edward said honestly. "Levi Seixas didn't seem very optimistic. But I think he'll make it through."

"Jan has two good men with him," Theo said, trying to find something bright in the situation. "I only wish I was there myself."

Marie Therese looked closely at him. "You're worried about the Indians, aren't you?"

"Yes," he admitted. "Seixas may be a good doctor, and we all know what Aaron can do, but when it comes to our Indian friends . . . well, certainly it's in my blood. I can smell them at a half mile."

"I get hunches," Edward said, "and one of them is that Jan will be alive when we get there."

He left to return to the dock, and Marie Therese and Theo sat quietly together. She drank coffee while he worked up his courage to explain what had happened in the room upstairs. But after a few minutes Marie

Therese realized they might well sit there all day before
he would find the right words.

"Don't worry," she said. "She's a pretty girl and I
don't blame you."

Theo was miserable. "It's nice of you to be understanding. It's just that I'm a man and, well, she *is* a pretty girl
and—well I don't want you to get the wrong idea."

"Wrong idea?"

"We came up here to find Jan and, well, I feel sort of
guilty about wasting my time with, well . . ."

"There was nothing you could do for Jan until now."

"I suppose you're right," he said, grateful for any excuse.

"Besides, it wasn't all that much of a waste of time,
was it?"

Theo's face grew two shades darker. "Let's go down
and see what's happening at the schooner," he said.

Louise watched from a window in the tavern room as
the pair walked down the snow-covered path to the
docks. She, in turn, was observed by her father. He was a
shrewd man, and little happened at his inn that he was
unaware of. He knew his eldest daughter well, and after
the first few days had guessed what was happening between her and the dark Englishman.

"It seems your friend will soon be leaving," he said.

Louise turned and gave him a black look. "What is it
to you, Father?"

He shrugged and went over to the sideboard and
poured himself a glass of wine. "He is English, and rich,
and from New York. What could a girl like you mean to
a man like that? A few nights of laughter and pleasure.
Don't get any exaggerated ideas."

"And what is wrong with a girl like me?" she asked,
her temper quick to flare.

"You're half Indian. You're half French. And you're
from a little place like this. You know nothing about
cities and city men. In New York he would be ashamed
of you," Clément said, purposely being brutal, hoping to
spare his daughter unnecessary trouble and hurt.

"He's part Indian himself," Louise said. "That's how
much you know."

This bit of news surprised Clément, but he was not to
be put off. "Is he? Yes, but he is still rich and from New

York. You're strong, my daughter, but I'm not sure you're that strong."

Louise turned on her heel and walked away in angry dignity. Damn her nosy father—always prying and interfering in her business. What would he have her do? Marry one of these *coureurs* who came into town stinking of their hides and furs? Men who didn't wash for months at a time? Men whose idea of pleasure was to get stupefied from drink and pass out on the floor? To hell with them! There was more to hope for from life than that. She ran into the hallway and took her coat from the peg. She left the inn and strode toward the docks.

Marie Therese was standing with Theo and Edward. They were watching men carrying stores aboard the schooner. Other men were up in the rigging—patching, repairing, replacing. Carpenters swarmed over the ship, repairing holes, shoring up weakened timbers, replacing broken railings. The sailors from the ship were busy at the task of sewing the sails and cutting new panels to replace the parts that were beyond fixing. Everyone moved swiftly; they all knew they had less than twenty-four hours to complete the work.

"I think you have a visitor," Marie Therese said to Theo, pointing in the direction of the inn. The two men saw Louise Clément, and Edward looked questioningly at the other two.

"A friend of Theo's," Marie Therese explained.

"She works at the inn," Theo said lamely.

The wind was blowing strongly across the harbor, and it kept lifting Louise's coat, revealing her lithe, slender figure. Edward looked at Theo and smiled.

"I must talk to you," Louise said to Theo when she reached the group. "Alone," she added.

Theo nodded and walked to the other side of the dock with Louise. They spoke for a few minutes, Louise doing most of the talking, moving her hands in an animated way, obviously argumentative at times. Whatever the argument was about, they came to an agreement and walked back across the dock to rejoin the others.

"Louise, ah, Miss Clement," Theo said, "wishes to go with us."

Edward's eyebrows raised, and he waited for an explanation.

Theo was obviously uncomfortable, but a stern look from Miss Clément forced him to go on. "Louise is part Micmac, you see, and she understands the language. She could be of great help."

"Those are tough woods up there," Edward said.

"I am at home in the woods," Louise said.

Marie Therese glanced meaningfully at Theo and then turned to the girl. "Of course you may come with us. If nothing else, you can keep me company."

Louise had expected more of an argument, and her features had a determined look about them. Now, however, they softened, and she smiled. "You won't regret it."

"No, I'm sure some of us won't," Marie Therese said, looking at Theo, who blushed.

Louise was quick. "But you must stop the insulting remarks."

Marie Therese was taken aback, but then realized she *had* been something of a cat. "Of course; we shall be friends."

"That's up to you," Louise said evenly, and her eyes held Marie Therese's.

Well, well, Marie Therese thought. Let's hope dear Theo isn't biting off more than he can chew.

Aaron Gerait moved cautiously among the trees, stopping every few steps to listen for sounds of pursuit. Not that he expected any. In the past two weeks he hadn't seen a single sign of other men. He regularly checked the flatlands near the shore, about a mile from their cave in the hills. With the snows melting rapidly now, the French trappers would be moving about in their pursuit of furs, and the first signs of their presence would be along the shores.

It puzzled Aaron that he had seen no signs of Indians. He concluded that luck had been on their side; maybe there were no Indians living on this particular part of the peninsula. He knew the northern shore was sparsely populated; there might not be any Indians for dozens of miles. However, he was taking no chances, and when he went out to hunt with his bow and arrows, he always took

every precaution he could think of. He was returning to
the cave with today's catch: a single rabbit.

He was about fifty yards from the cave when he came
to an opening in the trees. It was a flat place covered with
huge rocks and boulders, the thick spine of granite accounting for the lack of trees. By climbing to the top of a
boulder he was able to get a good view of the waters of
the gulf and the shoreline where the *Lord James* was
beached. For the first few days Aaron had hoped a storm
would drag the ship away from its resting place and bring
it out to deeper water, where it would sink out of sight.
The opposite had happened. The storm had thrown the
Lord James farther onto the shore, and it was now em-
bedded beyond rescue.

Several French ships had come to investigate. Men had
come ashore and snooped about, but they did not go up
into the hills, and Aaron had been careful to erase any
sign of their presence. Fortunately, the frequent storms
helped to obliterate any tracks they left.

He came to his boulder several times a day now, hoping to see vessels coming from the east, but once again he
was to be disappointed. Fourteen days had elapsed since
Edward had sailed off with his ships. Unless something
had gone wrong, surely he would be returning at almost
any hour. Aaron resolved to visit the boulder more fre-
quently.

He had to stoop as he entered the mouth of the cave.
It had proved to be the perfect place to hide. A small
cave that had been neglected by bears and other animals,
it was large enough so that an average sized man—but
not Aaron—could stretch to his full height. The solid
walls protected the men from the storms, allowing them
to remain dry and out of the wind.

"Any luck?" Jan asked when the black man entered
the cave.

Aaron held up the rabbit. "Dinner," he said. "Assuming we can have a fire."

It was one of their rules of survival: they burned a fire
only at night, and only during a storm. The chance of
anyone's seeing smoke on such a night was almost zero.
During these times they cooked whatever game they had
caught, and warmed themselves against the times when
there would be no fire.

Jan stood up and walked over to inspect the rabbit. He looked gaunt, but his step was firm and he no longer needed the walking stick that Aaron had whittled for him. Levi Seixas had done his work well. In two weeks he had brought a man back from the edge of death.

"Rabbit, eh," Levi said, peering out from under a heavy pile of blankets and sailcloth. "Does it look like we'll have another storm?"

"Maybe," Aaron replied. "Wind seems to be picking up, but I couldn't tell for sure."

"Damme!" Levi exclaimed. "I can't face another dinner of ship's biscuit and salt meat."

"We've had so much, I'm getting used to it," Jan said.

"Good," Levi said in disgust. "Because if there's no storm, that's what you're having."

He got up, stretched his arms, and came over to the other two. He reached out and inspected the bandages that covered Jan's left shoulder. "Another day and all this comes off for good," he said.

"That's the best news I've heard in weeks," Jan said. "I'm really sick of them. They're so damned tight."

"They're supposed to be tight," Levi said, and shrugged. He was quite pleased with the progress of his patient. The bandages were now removed at night, and replaced only for the hours of light, when Jan moved about. But even the need for this had passed, Levi decided, and when he removed the bandages tonight, they would stay off.

The fourteen days had been a test of the three men, and they had not been found wanting. Jan had survived. Levi had attended him with patience and skill. And Aaron had watched over the other two as if he slept with one eye open.

"I didn't see any ships," he said. "I'll wait an hour and take another look."

The others said nothing, but they were beginning to get nervous. Uppermost in their minds was what would happen if the ships didn't make it back from Louisbourg. For the three of them to make their way overland down to Cape Breton Island seemed an impossible task. The forests were vast and uncharted, and the Indians certain to be hostile. And yet if the ships failed to return, what other alternative did they have?

About an hour later Aaron returned to the boulder in the clearing. Still no ships. But he saw something else that interested him. Dark clouds were beginning to gather in the sky, and the wind was from the southwest. A storm was coming. And it was coming from a direction that could mean rain, not just more snow. The winter was truly ending, and a heavy downpour would help clear away much of the snow. Aaron breathed deeply. He couldn't tell if it was only his imagination, but the air seemed warmer.

He left the boulder, satisfied there was nothing more to be seen.

He was wrong.

A half mile away, in another clearing, a Micmac brave had also been looking around at his surroundings. He had only one eye, but it was keen, and he spotted the movements of the man on the other boulder. Hunching motionless, he waited until the man left the boulder and disappeared into the trees. When Aaron was gone, the brave stood up and silently set off into the forest. He was from a village miles away, forming a hunting party with three others. His intention was to find his companions and then investigate the appearance of this strange man.

Swift Fox had lost his left eye in a fight when he had scouted for the French against the English. The Micmacs were an Algonkian people whose intense hatred for the English went back over a hundred years—further, even, if one took into account that the Micmacs were probably the first Indians in North America to meet with Europeans. The Venetian John Cabot, sailing under an English flag, had visited them on his voyage of 1497, and the Micmacs still had not forgotten their claim that he had cheated them out of two canoefuls of beaver pelts.

Their experience of the white man went back even further—to 1000 A.D., when the Norsemen first came to these northern shores.

Swift Fox was only dimly aware of this history, but he was extremely aware that he had only one eye, and that the English were responsible for his loss. He hoped the newcomer was English. He wanted to capture him—alive.

It was late in the afternoon, and the storm was about to break.

It had been Aaron's habit after he returned from an excursion to take himself away from the cave for about a hundred yards, find a hiding place, and then watch the approaches. He spent several hours of every day doing this. Today his caution proved to be foresight.

He was looking down the ravine and suddenly saw movement among the trees. He wasn't alarmed; most likely it was only a deer or some other animal. But he gripped his musket more tightly and peered into the trees. And then he saw an Indian move silently from behind one tree to the next. There was more movement, and he was able to count four Indians. They were stealthily moving toward the mouth of the cave, their keen eyes picking out even the vaguest signs of the passage of men.

Aaron let them pass, waiting to make certain there were no more. Satisfied there were only four, he moved as quietly as possible through the ravine behind the red men, hoping their full attention would be concentrated on the cave.

He thought of shouting to warn his companions, but realized that would only draw attention to himself. He kept following the Indians. If he could surprise them, he would gain the advantage, especially since they carried no firearms.

Swift Fox, in the lead, came within fifty feet of the mouth of the cave. He held up his hand and the other braves stopped dead in their tracks. He listened. Low voices of men could be heard from inside the cave. He signaled, and one brave circled and took up a position on the left side of the mouth of the cave. Swift Fox then took up an identical position on the right, leaving the two remaining men in front of the mouth of the cave.

Aaron quickly decided on his tactics. He placed his pistol on the ground in front of him. Then he took his musket and aimed at the back of one of the men in the middle. While the Indians were getting ready to dash to the cave, he fired the musket. The Indian screamed and pitched forward on his face.

Aaron dropped the musket, picked up his pistol, and ran at top speed toward the remaining man in the middle. The Indians reacted quickly, but Aaron fired as he ran, ducking an arrow that whistled over his head. The second Indian took the lead ball in his chest and was thrown backward to the ground.

Swift Fox and the remaining Indian had been startled, but now they fought back. Two arrows flew through the air and would have hit their target had not Aaron thrown himself to the ground the instant he fired the pistol.

Suddenly there was the explosion of a musket from the mouth of the cave, and the Indian on the left fell to the ground as Levi emerged with a smoking weapon in his hands.

"On your left!" Aaron shouted, and Levi had the quickness of mind to drop to the ground, grab his second musket, and fire in the general direction indicated by Aaron.

Levi's shot missed, but Swift Fox realized that now the odds were too great. He ran a few steps, threw himself on the ground, rolled over several times, and was back on his feet and into the trees before anyone could shoot at him again.

Aaron stood up to go after him, but then dismissed the silly notion of chasing an Indian through the woods. One might as well chase a deer. Instead, he made a quick check to be certain the other braves were dead.

The fight was over almost before it had begun.

Jan emerged from the cave with a musket he carried in his good arm. "You better get this bandage off," he said to Levi. "I can't get my left arm up to fire this damned thing."

Levi nodded, but his attention was elsewhere. "Are there more of them?" he asked, looking around at the silent trees.

"Nope," Aaron said. "There were only four. We got three, and the other one ran off."

"There may be others around."

"I doubt if there are any close by," Aaron said. "But I'll wager the one that got away comes back later with more of his friends."

"What can we do?" Levi asked.

"For one thing, you can start taking off this bandage," Jan complained again.

As Levi worked on the bandage, Aaron retrieved his musket. He reloaded it as he talked. "We can't stay here.

This will be the first place they'll come. And if they trap us in that cave, we're finished."

"Let's go back to the ship," Jan said. "We can set up some sort of defense and hope Ned arrives before the Indians. Unless someone has a better idea?"

Levi and Aaron looked at one another. Both shrugged. "I can't think of anything else," Aaron said. "Maybe we'll get lucky and Ned will be waiting for us."

"Don't count on it," Levi said, removing the last of Jan's bandages. "Now take it easy with that arm. You haven't used it in two weeks."

Jan flexed his arm slowly and grimaced. "It seems all right, but I feel as weak as a woman."

"Just go easy," Levi cautioned again.

Aaron had walked into the cave and was surveying their stores. "We'll take only weapons, powder, and a little food. One way or another, we won't be needing all this stuff any longer."

There was a flash of lightning, followed in a few seconds by a tremendous clap of thunder. The rain began to fall, softly at first, then harder and harder. The wind began to moan through the trees.

"Dammit," Levi said, holding out his hand and allowing the large droplets to fall on it. "Tonight we would have eaten that rabbit."

"We've got a lot more than a rabbit to worry about," Aaron said.

"Worry about what you want, but my head will be filled with thoughts of a missed meal."

They collected their weapons, powder, and shot. Each man put a canvas blanket over his shoulders, and they began moving down the ravine toward the distant shoreline. The rain pelted down on them, soaking them and making them miserable.

It was turning out to be a storm of awesome proportions.

If the storm was causing discomfort to Jan and his companions, it was wreaking disaster on Edward's schooner.

It had been his misfortune to meet a French schooner earlier in the day. Ordinarily Edward would have welcomed the chance to do battle, but today his one interest was to rescue his cousin. The Frenchman, however, insisted on a fight.

It was difficult to say who won, because both ships took a terrific pounding. When the Frenchman finally broke off the engagement and moved away, he was in the same condition as his opponent. Both ships were almost disabled, their decks strewn with broken wood and torn sails.

"My God," Marie Therese said to Edward after the battle was over. "Is it always this way?"

"Sometimes it's worse," he answered gruffly, and then he softened. "But we lived through it, didn't we?"

The storm hit not long afterward, as the men were struggling to get the ship back in shape. Slashing rains drenched everything. The wind howled about the ship, buffeting it, slamming into it, making it impossible for the men to repair the broken spars and tangled rigging. It tore the sails from their hands, and if a man was foolish enough to keep holding them, he was blown over the side into the cold water. The wind drove the helpless ship toward the west.

Marie Therese and Louise huddled in Edward's cabin, trying to pretend they weren't afraid, but not quite succeeding. They could tell from the worried expressions on the men's faces that they were in serious trouble.

The cabin wasn't the driest of places, either, since one of the French cannonballs had torn open a jagged hole in the hull, smashing right through the inner bulkhead.

Marie Therese was cold and miserable, but she tried to make herself useful as she helped Louise bandage the jagged gash on a sailor's arm. The rolling and pitching of the ship, together with the sight of the open wound, made her feel nauseated. Louise didn't seem bothered, and she worked quickly and efficiently.

Two sailors carried another wounded man into the cabin and placed him on the deck. He was unconscious, his shirt torn and bloodied.

"We'll need more bandages," Marie Therese said, forced to raise her voice almost to a shout to be heard over the wind that howled in through the shattered bulkhead.

Louise grabbed a man's shirt that was hanging from a

wooden peg. "Tear this into strips," she said. "Use my knife."

Marie Therese took the vicious looking blade and began to cut the cloth into long, narrow pieces. "For a time I thought we were all going to die," she said as she worked. "It was like nothing I've ever seen."

"This is not a place for you to be."

"Nor for you, either," Marie Therese said. "You must think a great deal of Theo to be here."

Louise was wary. "Maybe," she said, pinning the last of the bandage to the man's arm.

"I think a great deal of him, too," Marie Therese said, and their eyes met and held for a long moment.

"Then he's a lucky man," Louise finally said, and she moved over to where the unconscious man lay on the deck. She began to undo the blood-soaked shirt.

As Marie Therese prepared more bandages, she realized she was beginning to like the other woman's straightforward manner. But the basic question remained: was she right for Theo? She hoped she wasn't acting like a busybody, but after all, it was almost as if Theo were her husband's younger brother. This thought brought her back to Jan, and she decided her husband was who she should be worried about, not Theo and this girl from the woods.

Louise folded the shirt back over the man's chest. "Nothing we can do for this one," she said. "He's dead."

And now a new menace appeared. The ship was being driven toward the northern shore of the Gaspé Peninsula. With no sails and with masts broken, the ship was little more than a piece of flotsam driven by the wind, leaving the sailors with no control over their own fate. They tried throwing out several sea anchors, but the fierce winds quickly snapped the lines. The anchors were lost and the ship continued on its berserk course.

"Mister Butler," Edward shouted to be heard above the screech of the wind. "We must have sail."

"Impossible," the mate shouted back. "It's sure death for a man to go up in the rigging."

"But dammit, man, we're going to run aground."

"Can't be helped, sir."

"Do you have any control over the rudder?"

"Aye, but only if we run with the wind."

Edward thought quickly. If nothing else, they could try

to pick the least threatening spot on the nearby shores. He scanned the coastline with his glass. There was one area to the west that appeared to have a long sandbar running close to the shore and parallel to it. Plowing a ship into a sandbar was not exactly without risk, but it was far better than running into the naked rocks farther to the east.

"Can you get us to that sandbar, Mister Butler?" Edward asked, handing the glass to the mate.

After a quick look, the mate nodded. "Aye, sir, I think I can do that."

Edward watched as the mate turned the wheel. Slowly. very slowly, the ship began to point for the sandbar. If the sandbar was studded with rocks, they were certain to rip the bottom off the schooner. They wouldn't know until it was too late to do anything about it, Edward realized; but he had no choice.

The schooner pitched and tossed, but was driven relentlessly toward the shore. The motion of the ship didn't seem to bother the sailors, but Theo wasn't used to the sea, and he was beginning to turn green. He fought desperately with his stomach to keep from getting sick. And then a particularly vicious series of movements proved too much for him and he was hanging over the lee rail, emptying his guts into the turbulent waters.

Edward ordered everyone up on deck. If the ship struck rocks, their chances would be better topside.

Marie Therese stood with Louise Clément, and both were wide-eyed as they looked at the shore they were approaching. They were now dressed in buckskins, having discarded their dresses for more practical clothing. Louise, with her dark skin, black eyes, and braided hair, looked like a full-blooded Indian. Her sheathed knife hung from her belt.

The ship came closer to the sandbar, and Edward stood at the bow and watched anxiously. The seconds ticked off. Then, as the bottom of the ship made contact, it lurched to the left, and then straightened out as the wind kept driving the hull forward. There were a few rocks in the sandbar; they scraped and banged at the hull, but the timbers resisted their punishment.

And then the ship stopped, caught fast in the grip of the hard-packed sand. They were only fifty feet from the shoreline, which was covered with cruelly sharp rocks that would have torn the bottom out of the schooner. Edward immediately ordered the longboats dropped, and the crew and passengers wasted no time in climbing down the rope ladders to the smaller craft.

In fifteen minutes the entire party was ashore, huddling under the trees to avoid suffering the brunt of the winds and rain. After several failed attempts, a fire was started, and Theo held council with the mate and Edward.

"In another few minutes it'll be dark," Edward said. "This wisest thing is to spend the night right here."

"And in the morning?" Theo asked.

"How long will it take to get the ship ready?" Edward asked the mate.

"Two or three days to straighten her out. And then we'll have to kedge her off that sandbar. No telling how long that'll take until we try."

"Too long," Edward said. "The ship is out."

"We continue on land?" Theo asked.

"Yes. We split into two parties. Mister Butler, you stay with the ship and some men. Patch her up as best you can. Theo and I will take the others and go overland to where we beached *Lord James*. It's probably no more than ten miles west of here. We'll find Jan and the other two and bring them all back here."

Marie Therese insisted on going with Edward and Theo. "I'm not going to sit here doing nothing while I wonder if my husband is dead or alive only ten miles away."

"This is rugged country," Theo said. "But I suppose you've made up your mind?"

"Yes."

They spent an uneasy night, huddled together under makeshift tents patched together with bits of sail brought from the ship. The storm continued unabated, and most of them slept only when they became too exhausted to remain awake. Several of the men who had been badly wounded in the battle died during the night, adding to the general misery.

At dawn Theo roused the survivors. They ate a very cold breakfast, and then the crew was divided. Edward chose twenty men, only the strongest and most fit. They selected weapons from the ship's armory and prepared for the overland march.

Theo took the lead, and soon his observation that it was rough country was proved an understatement, as they picked their way through land covered with rocks, boulders, and trees. The storm compounded the problems. The downpour created rivulets, which swelled as they were fed by the melting snow. Often they were forced to go out of their way to follow a stream until they came to a fordable place. It was time-consuming and nerve-wracking—especially to Marie Therese. Every delay in reaching Jan was like a knife in her heart.

Through it all Louise was proving to be almost as valuable as Theo. The two alternated as scouts, moving ahead of the main body, finding the safest and easiest routes. Louise was a slender wood nymph who never seemed to tire.

Marie Therese marveled at the other woman's ability. She herself was having a tough time, but was determined to keep up with the others. There were enough delays without her being the cause of more.

Seeing her struggle in a swift-moving stream, Theo took her arm and helped her across.

"I wish I could be as nimble in the woods as your friend," she said as she reached the safety of the far bank.

"It's the Indian blood," Theo said, half in jest and half believing it.

"You're really very fond of her, aren't you?"

"To tell you the truth, she's the most fascinating woman I've ever met."

"What are you planning to do?"

Theo helped Marie Therese over a fallen tree, and then looked straight at her. "I haven't thought it through yet."

"She might feel out of place in New York."

"Most of the time I feel out of place there."

"You know what I mean," she said, refusing to let him get away with a flip answer. "For her sake you've got to consider what might happen."

Theo accepted the rebuke and tried to picture Louise in New York—strolling the streets, having tea with other women, presiding over a formal dinner party.

Maybe Marie Therese was right; maybe he would be

hurting Louise if he forced her into a foreign way of life.

He drove these thoughts out of his mind and concentrated on the job at hand. There would be time later on, he lectured himself, to ponder his future and that of Louise Clément. But the thoughts would not stay banished, and they were making him an unhappy man.

The party continued to struggle through the woods toward the cove to the west.

The same dawn that saw Theo and his party begin their trek found Jan, Aaron, and Levi hard at work turning the *Lord James* into a fortress. The bow of the ship had dug itself into the shore and was immobile. Aaron's many ventures outside the cave had made him realize that the ship was by far the strongest and most easily defended place in the cove, and they proceeded to strengthen it further with loose boards and timbers.

Levi had inspected the four-pounder swivel gun at the stern and found it in working order. With the help of Aaron and a couple of makeshift pulleys, he had managed to drag the thousand-pound weight the length of the ship and set it up in the bow. They also found an undamaged keg of dry powder that had not been in the ship's magazine when it exploded. The keg was set near the cannon along with a supply of grapeshot and fusing material. Levi was, he assured his shipmates, also an excellent gunner.

They scoured the ship for all the muskets and pistols they could find and set up an arsenal in the bow; and now there remained nothing else they could do but wait and hope that Edward's ship arrived before the avenging Indians.

The three men each made a silent resolution not to be taken alive. If the savages won, they would find it a costly victory.

Aaron looked at the swivel gun and touched it gingerly. "You sure you know how to work this thing?"

"When I sailed with Amos O'Higgins, I always manned the swivel gun," Levi said.

"Sort of a strange hobby for a doctor."

"Anything to make life more interesting."

"Is that the reason the doctor is a privateer?" Jan asked.

Levi smiled. "When I was a little boy I used to go down

to the docks to watch the pirates. They were men who did as they pleased. They acted like they owned the world. By the time I'd grown up my family had made me into a doctor, but I still wanted to be like those pirates. So I became a privateer. It's about the same thing."

"I understand it didn't make you very popular with your father," Jan said.

Levi grimaced. "I know he's a friend of yours, so if you want to keep his goodwill, don't ever mention my name to him."

"I intend to tell him you saved my life. If he chooses to dislike me for it, that's his business."

"Oh, I suppose he'll forgive you, especially since you didn't have any choice. Actually, I like my father. Too bad he could never understand that I have a right to pick my own way of life."

"I understand that," Aaron said quietly. "My father kept telling me to keep quiet, stay out of people's way, don't cause trouble. That was the way he lived most of his life, and that was what he wanted for me." He looked about himself and laughed. "Good thing he's not alive to see me today."

"You haven't done badly," Levi said.

"No, but I'm always poking my nose where it don't belong."

Jan understood what Aaron was talking about. "More and more people are beginning to realize how badly we've treated Negroes," he said. "Things are changing."

"Yes," Aaron admitted, "but at this rate it will take five hundred years for anything significant to happen."

"My people have been saying the same thing for three thousand years," Levi said. "What's your hurry?"

"Sh!" Jan signaled, and his companions tensed. He pointed toward the ravine. The others saw him—an Indian. And then another and another, until the ravine was filled with about forty of them.

Swift Fox had led the war party to the cave. Finding nothing there, he had figured that the enemy had gone to the flatland. And here he had found them.

Levi had already loaded the swivel gun with powder, wadding, and grapeshot. Now he checked the lanyard that fired the flintlock mechanism.

"Let's save that as a surprise," Jan said. "Muskets and pistols in the beginning."

Levi nodded and took his hand off the lanyard. He picked a musket from the row set against the railing and took up a position behind a stout timber.

The three men waited, their weapons ready. They watched as the Indians approached, showing no fear, but keenly alert and cautious.

At Swift Fox's signal the warriors halted. They had no firearms, only bows and arrows and tomahawks, but their numbers made them a vastly superior force. And now they attacked.

Aaron was the first to fire. His musket roared and a flash of flame erupted from its muzzle. Two more muskets boomed. Arrows whizzed through the air, and the Indians shouted their blood-curdling cries as they charged.

Aaron, Levi, and Jan fired steadily, dropping the empty ones to pick up others and fire again. They did not rush their movements, but took the time to aim carefully.

The Indians ran forward, dodging and twisting as they came toward the thundering guns. Three were hit in the first volleys, and they fell; but rather than deterring the others, the loss of these comrades spurred them on. The first one reached the ship and tried to leap up to the gunwale, but Jan grabbed a pistol and coolly shot him in the face. Six more sprang for the bow of the ship.

"The cannon!" Jan shouted.

Levi aimed the swivel gun toward the Indians who were clambering aboard the ship, and pulled the lanyard. The black powder exploded and the grapeshot spat out in an angry roar, blowing the Indians away from the ship, killing several and maiming others. Bits of the railing were splintered, and these too flew out as deadly projectiles.

One of the red men who had been climbing aboard the ship escaped being hit by the powerful blast, and he managed to roll onto the deck. He raised his tomahawk, but Aaron was swifter. He fired his pistol even as the Indian's arm was coming forward. The bullet hit him in the chest and knocked him backward. The tomahawk flew harmlessly over Levi's head.

The cannon had startled the rest of the Indians. Thrown into confusion, they retreated back into the trees. But Swift Fox quickly started chanting a war cry, and they began to build up their courage for another charge.

Levi wasted no time in reloading the cannon, while Jan and Aaron worked feverishly to prepare the muskets and pistols.

"Your gun really gets the job done," Jan said to Levi.

"Gives them something to think about," Levi admitted.

"Quit talking and load," Aaron growled, and he rammed the rod down the barrel of a musket to pack the powder.

The Indians attacked again; and again, they were on the point of gaining the deck when the swivel gun roared and sent them back into the protection of the trees. Nine of their number did not rise and join them.

The third assault proved a greater test. The Indians had learned to respect the swivel gun and did not throw themselves headlong into its muzzle. While a group of them shot arrows from the fringe of the woods, others plunged into the cold water and attempted to come aboard by the sides of the ship.

Aaron exhausted his supply of loaded guns. He picked up a cutlass and jumped to the starboard railing as an Indian was pulling himself aboard. The cutlass flashed through the air and caught the Indian on the shoulder, plunging down through muscle and bone. The Indian shrieked and toppled back into the water. But another one had gotten aboard, and he threw himself toward Aaron with his tomahawk raised.

Aaron managed to grab the tomahawk arm, and then the Indian grabbed the black man's arm that held the cutlass. They stood toe to toe for an instant, straining, and then Aaron dropped the cutlass and pulled the Indian into his huge bear hug of a grip. His strength overwhelmed the Indian, and he bent the man backward until he heard the snap of his spine.

He dropped the dead man, retrieved his cutlass, and looked around for more Indians. He found none. For the third time the Indians had had enough, and melted away into the woods.

An hour passed. Two hours. Aaron, Levi, and Jan loaded all their weapons and waited. They had used a great deal of gunpowder and now had only enough for two, possibly three more attacks. They might hold out during these attacks, but what would happen after that? Clearly, to defeat the savages with only cutlasses and knives would be impossible.

The Indians adopted a new tactic. Rather than expose themselves to the guns of the enemy, they stayed in the protection of the trees and shot arrows toward the ship. The men on board stayed low and exposed as little of themselves as possible, but even so, there were times when each of them came within inches of being killed by a silent arrow.

The air turned more chill as night began to overtake them. The war cries of the Indians increased, and Jan realized they were preparing to attack again before it became too dark.

"This time hold your fire until they start climbing aboard," he said, thinking of a way to conserve powder. "Pick them off as their heads come over the gunwale."

The Indians charged, and this time they weren't met by gunfire. Swift Fox was in the lead, and the silence of the enemy guns surprised him. He stopped and waited to see if the enemy was planning some trick. Then the first of the red men started climbing aboard the ship, and the guns boomed again. But why had the white men waited? And then the memory of his days with the French gave Swift Fox the answer: they were running low on gunpowder! He shouted and urged his men on.

But before they could mount a full-scale attack, the sound of gunfire came from along the shoreline. Men were coming from the east, shouting and firing at the Indians.

Swift Fox saw there were many white men, and he ordered his braves to retreat to the woods. While the others vanished among the tree trunks, he took up a position that offered both concealment and a good view of the ship. He watched as the white men came, firing sporadically into the woods, but making no moves that showed they intended to pursue the red men. There were about twenty of them, Swift Fox estimated, and they were heavily armed.

He watched the rescue party hail the men on the ship and then climb aboard the craft.

Swift Fox waited and watched. No more white men

arrived. Satisfied that the twenty men constituted the entire force, Swift Fox made a decision. Returning to the braves who were waiting in the woods, he told them what he had seen and promised they would celebrate a great victory on the morrow. A runner was sent to the west to gather more men.

Swift Fox knew his forces would number over a hundred by morning. That would be enough to destroy the English. His heart beat faster at the thought of taking prisoners.

Jan stood on the deck of the wrecked *Lord James* and held his wife in his arms. For many minutes neither spoke. Tears ran down Marie Therese's cheeks.

"When I think of how close I came to losing you . . ."

"Everything's all right now," he said soothingly.

"You have Ned to thank," she said. "He was the one who drove everyone on."

"What happened to his ship?"

Marie Therese explained about the French warship, and the storm, and the overland journey. She also told him how she had badgered Theo into getting her a ship to the north country, and how he had insisted on coming along.

"Theo?" Jan said in surprise. "He's here, too?"

Marie Therese pointed, and Jan saw Theo talking with Edward. He strode across the deck, and all three men fell into each another's arms; Jan not even bothering to worry about his sore arm.

After the first moments of reunion, the business at hand claimed their attention, and Edward saw to it that his men took up positions of defense.

Then he sat on the deck and rested his back against a piece of the broken mast. The others gathered around.

"We have two choices," Edward said. "We can start back to the schooner in the morning, or we can stay here and wait until they patch up the ship and come to get us."

"I wouldn't wait here," Theo said quickly. "Those Indians will be back."

"We've got a lot more men now," Jan said.

"But we don't know how many *they* can get."

"You don't think we can hold them off?" Levi asked.

Theo shook his head. "Not indefinitely."

Edward nodded. "Then it's settled. We leave this place at dawn."

"And just when I was beginning to think of it as home," Levi said. "Too bad we can't take the cannon. I'm growing rather fond of it."

"You did a good job fixing up Jan," Edward said.

"He's almost as good as new," Levi said, and then he realized Jan was listening, and turned to him. "But remember I said *almost*, so don't try to be a hero."

"It's hard to be anything else around here," Jan said, smiling.

"You really turned this place into a fort," Edward said admiringly as he walked about the deck. His limp was more pronounced than ever, and Jan noticed.

"The foot bothering you?"

"A bit. Our little walk through the woods didn't do it any good."

"What happened?" Levi asked. "Is there anything I can do?"

"It happened long ago," Edward said. "I'll be all right."

"Any news about General Wolfe?" Jan asked.

"His troops are starting to arrive in Louisbourg," Edward said. "The summer campaign is on for sure."

"Maybe now we'll win the war."

The rain stopped, and several men went ashore and started a fire. After guards were posted to prevent a surprise attack by the Indians, the sailors heated strips of meat and boiled coffee. They devoured the warm food, and for a brief moment, at least, peace reigned in the cove.

The clouds cleared and the moon came out. All hands aboard the ruined *Lord James* huddled together under their blankets and pieces of canvas sail, shivering as they tried to forget the cold and sleep. Eventually, all but the guards drifted off into a fitful slumber.

Jan found himself waking every few minutes, but then the warmth of his wife's body against his side reassured him and he would drift back to sleep. He didn't notice that almost every time he stirred, Aaron's eyes opened. In the cave Aaron had become used to sleeping in fifteen-minute segments. As far as he was concerned, he was still Jan's protector.

The first light was coming into the sky, and a guard in the bow of the ship stood up, raised his hands over his head, and yawned. He screamed as the stone-tipped arrow buried itself in his side. He fell to the deck, writhing and crying out.

Everyone on the *Lord James* came instantly awake. Savage cries filled the air as the Indians attacked in force. This time there seemed to be hundreds of them. Arrows flew through the air, and several men aboard the ship were hit. But now the arrows were answered by a barrage of musket fire; the battle had begun.

The Indians were beaten off with surprising ease. Had they been testing the men aboard the ship to try their strength?

"Keep your heads down," Edward shouted.

Jan tried to get Marie Therese to go below.

"You fire and I'll load," she responded.

It proved to be a long day.

After the initial attack the Indians began using fire arrows. Buckets of water were used to extinguish the arrows, but it was harrowing work. The Indians tried to pick off the men as they put out the fires.

There was only one more attack during the day which the whites beat off. Then the sun began to dip lower in the sky, and they realized they would be forced to spend another miserable night aboard the wrecked ship.

"No chance of your schooner getting here today, is there?" Jan asked his cousin.

"No. Probably not for another two days—if we're lucky."

"And if we're not lucky?"

Edward shrugged. "We keep fighting."

"Or go back to our plan of trying to get to the schooner."

"Let's wait and see."

They ate a cold supper and then huddled under their blankets with their muskets beside them as the sun disappeared from the sky and the cold night air settled on their bodies.

In the middle of the night the Indians mounted another attack.

The men at the bow were almost overwhelmed as war-

rior after warrior pulled himself over the gunwale. The
fight might have been lost had it not been for Aaron.

He was on his feet at the first cry. Grabbing his cutlass,
he rushed foward and hacked and slashed at the shadowy
forms coming over the side. He had killed four red men
by the time the other sailors found their wits and came to
his aid.

Other Indians had managed to climb onto the ship, and
the fighting became ferocious. Theo Henry found himself
locked in mortal combat with a brave. Both men had
knives in their hands as they rolled across the deck.

The Indian suddenly slipped from Theo's grasp and
raised his arm to strike home with the knife. A pistol
erupted in his face, and the Indian was blown to the side
with half his head missing. Theo looked up and, in the
silver moonlight, saw that his savior had been Louise. But
there was no time for words, and Theo went after another
Indian who was trying to climb over the side.

Jan had remained near the stump of the mainmast, firing one musket as Marie Therese loaded another. Once an
Indian sprang at him while he had an unloaded weapon
in his hands, but Jan swung the heavy gun and knocked
the man to the deck. Aaron scooped up the fallen Indian
and threw him over the side.

When the Indians finally broke off the attack, everyone
on the ship was black with gunpowder, and all were exhausted. But no one could even think of trying to sleep
again that night. There were three dead sailors and four
wounded. Levi advised Edward that he was almost out of
medical supplies.

Theo took Louise to the relative safety of the stern.
With their backs resting against a broken deck timber,
they held each other.

"You saved my life," Theo said.

"You'd save mine."

"What's to become of us, Louise Clément?"

"Whatever you wish. I will go where you want me to
go," she said, with no attempt at guile.

He pulled her closer and felt the warmth of her cheek
on his own and knew that if he lived through this horror
he was taking her back to New York with him. He didn't
care what anyone would think or say. To hell with them
all.

Louise seemed to sense his thoughts. "I will try to be the kind of woman you want."

The moment was interrupted when Edward summoned Theo to a discussion of what the stranded party should do. He went over and joined the group.

"If we wait here for the schooner, we might be waiting for three days," Edward said.

"We haven't got three days' worth of powder," Jan said.

"Seems we haven't got much choice," Aaron said.

"We go back to our plan of going to the schooner."

Theo shook his head. "Going through the woods with all these Indians around . . . I don't give us much of a chance."

"But if we stay here, we have *no* chance," Jan said quietly.

"Then we must leave," Edward said. "It comes down to that."

Theo shrugged. "At least we'll die fighting."

There was nothing more to discuss, only the long wait to dawn. Jan went back to Marie Therese and kept her close to his side. There was a good chance this would be the last time he would ever hold her.

Word of the morning departure was passed among the men. The wounded thanked God they would be able to walk. If their legs had been hurt, they would have been too much of a burden to the others.

Edward waited for an hour after dawn in order to have enough light to see clearly. The order to depart was passed, and the men began to climb down from the ship. Not an Indian was to be seen anywhere.

The entire party of the remaining twenty-two people was now on shore. Each man and woman carried at least one musket and a pistol, but several had two muskets. They were divided into pairs. If one man of a pair fired his weapon, the other had to wait until his mate reloaded before firing his own weapon. In a dire emergency, of course, this rule was to be waived. It was a good plan that would enable them to keep up a steady fire, but not a man among them believed they would be able to keep to it. There would be too many Indians, and they would be coming fast.

Theo was in the lead, and Edward claimed the rear position as his own. He insisted the two women be placed in the middle of the column. In this order of march the group began the journey toward the west and the relative safety of the schooner.

If Edward and the others had not seen an Indian, it was because the Indians had chosen not to be seen.

Swift Fox had been up before dawn, his eye fixed on the ship and the hated English. He watched as they formed their line of march. When he understood what they were doing, he decided to let them think they were getting away. Once they put a quarter mile between themselves and their protective fortress, he would order an attack.

Theo led the group around the western bend of the cove and began following the shoreline, where the trees were the thinnest. He had gone several hundred yards when a loud war cry pierced the air and the Indians came out of the woods, tomahawks whirling, convinced that, at last, they had the advantage.

The sailors whirled about and saw more than a hundred savages descending on their slender file.

"First group, fire in volley!" Edward commanded. "Now!" And every second man pulled the trigger on his musket. The air filled with thunderclaps and smoke. Half a dozen Indians fell to the ground.

The men who had fired their muskets worked feverishly to reload. The others waited for the signal to fire; their hair began to stand on end as Edward took his time.

"Fire!"

The second volley blasted the Indians. Their charge wavered. On Edward's order the first group fired a second volley, and the Indians broke off their attack.

But the battle had not been completely one-sided. One of the sailors was dead and two others were on the ground, writhing in pain and plucking at the arrows sticking out of their bodies.

Theo noticed a group of Indians circling to the front of their line of march. He went immediately to Edward.

"We'll never make it," he said. "They're setting up an ambush up there. Do you think we can get through ten miles of that sort of thing?"

"We agreed if we stayed here we had no chance," Edward argued.

"*You* agreed," Theo said, "not me. If we go on, we won't last a mile."

Jan had come up to where the two men were arguing. He pointed to one of the wounded men. "If we go on, what do we do with the wounded, leave them?"

Edward surrendered. "All right, we go back to the *Lord James*."

The group began the short march back to the ship. The wounded were picked up and carried; one had fainted, but the other kept crying out in pain. The dead man was left where he had died.

Swift Fox realized the Englishmen had changed their plans. He ordered another attack to prevent them from reaching their fortress. The war cries were again raised as the red men poured out from behind the trees.

A half dozen braves pounced on the column in the middle, and before anyone could react, one of them grabbed Marie Therese and started to carry her off. Jan was near by, but as he tried to aim his pistol at the man holding his wife, another Indian swooped down on him and knocked him off his feet. Jan had enough presence of mind to hang on to his weapon. He looked up at the Indian who stood over him with raised tomahawk, and shot him between the eyes.

Marie Therese punched at her captor, but her efforts were useless against his strength. She would have been lost except for Louise: she sprang at the Indian and drove her knife deep into his back. The savage screamed and dropped Marie Therese. Louise plunged her knife into his back three more times. The two women were on the ground next to the dead Indian, and their eyes met and held for a moment. Louise reached out and helped Marie Therese to her feet. "Let's get to the ship," she said.

The sailors were still following Edward's rule of firing every other musket, and the steady barrage kept the savages at bay as the file made its way back to the *Lord James*. Finally the first man reached the bow and climbed aboard. Others followed. The Indians made a desperate charge to keep the enemy from regaining the protection of their fortress. But by now Levi Seixas had climbed aboard. He quickly loaded and fired the swivel gun. The grapeshot scattered the Indians, giving the rest of the English party time to climb aboard.

For the moment they were safe, but the attack had utterly frayed their nerves and exhausted their bodies. They rested on the deck, their eyes empty of hope.

Captain Angus McGhee drove the *Albany* as hard as possible westward along the shore of the Gaspé Peninsula. Only a few hours ago he had sighted the schooner, which was still beached on the sandbar. When he had come within hailing distance, the mate, Mister Butler, explained what had happened and said that Edward Goelet had gone ahead on land.

Captain McGhee had wasted no time in heading the *Albany* toward the cove where the *Lord James* rested. He cursed the luck that had brought the storm and put him so far behind the schooner. At the same time he was racing to get to the cove, he dreaded the moment of arrival. He wasn't sure what he would find—a group of Englishmen waiting to be rescued, or an open graveyard littered with corpses.

It was an hour after noon when Captain McGhee spotted the cove. He shouted orders, and sailors swarmed up the ratlines and began to take down the topsails. As the *Albany* came closer to the cove, the captain thought he heard the sound of gunfire. He listened intently and then heard the unmistakable boom of a four-pounder.

As the frigate hove into sight, a cheer went up among those aboard the *Lord James*.

"Thank God," Marie Therese said softly.

Jan put his arm about her shoulder. "We're going to make it."

"Save the cheers until we're on board that ship," Edward said, reminding everyone of their still-precarious position. A hundred or so Indians were a lot closer than the ship.

As if to reinforce his warning, the Indians began another attack. The sailors fought back with a furious barrage of musket fire. Levi fired his swivel gun, reloaded, and fired again.

McGhee analyzed the situation. He didn't dare take the *Albany* into the cove, because he didn't know how deep the water was. He also didn't want to put his ship within reach of the savages on the shore. The only solution was to drop sail and send longboats to pick up the beleaguered party.

As the longboats came toward the stern of the *Lord James,* Swift Fox saw there was a good chance the Englishmen might escape, and he urged his warriors on. The fighting at the bow of the ship became fierce, but the muskets and Levi's cannon managed to keep the red men from swarming aboard.

The first longboat reached the stern of the *Lord James,* and Theo took charge of getting the wounded men aboard. Marie Therese and Louise followed. Six sailors slid down the ropes after them, and the loaded longboat pulled away as the second boat arrived.

"Is that thing loaded?" Edward asked Levi as he pointed toward the swivel gun.

"Yes."

"Then get on board the longboat. I'll fire it for the last time."

"No, I—"

"Get the hell out of here!"

Two Indians came over the side, but Aaron met them with two swift hacks of his cutlass. The first man caught the blade in his side, and he fell, screaming, to the deck. The second was hit in the neck and went down without a sound.

Edward pointed to the longboat. "Get off, all of you!" he shouted, and then he aimed his musket and fired again.

Jan, Aaron, and Edward were the last left on deck. As Jan reached the stern, he turned. "Come on, Ned!"

Edward waved his hand and stepped up to the swivel gun. The Indians were beginning to climb aboard. He waited a few seconds until there were enough of them, and then pulled the lanyard. The grapeshot blew four Indians into the next world.

He turned and started limping toward the stern. Jan saw him coming and slid down the rope after Aaron.

But Edward had waited too long. His bad foot was slowing him down, and he managed to take only half a dozen steps when a tomahawk grazed the side of his head and sent him to the deck. He shook his head to clear his vision. He raised himself to his hands and knees, and then to his feet. His face was white with pain as he tried to hobble toward the stern. A second tomahawk crashed into his shoulder, drawing blood and knocking him down again. And then it was too late, as the Indians, led by Swift Fox, swarmed aboard the vessel.

A warrior was about to bury his tomahawk in Edward's skull, but Swift Fox grabbed his arm. He shook his head, and the warrior understood that Swift Fox wanted the man alive.

The Indians ran to the stern of the ship, and the men in the longboat fired up at them, driving them back from the railing. The men on the oars decided it was time to leave, and they pulled for all they were worth.

"No!" Jan shouted. "My cousin's still aboard!"

But the oarsman continued to row. Arrows whistled past them, urging them even more.

"We've got to go back for Ned," Jan shouted, and for a moment it looked as if he was going to jump out of the longboat and swim back.

Swift Fox realized he was to be robbed of the men escaping in the longboat, but he took solace in the fact that he had captured at least one of them. He swore a silent oath that he would make this one suffer as if he were a dozen men.

He grabbed the weakened Edward and dragged him to the stern. It was not enough to savor the many tortures he would inflict on this man; no, the other white men must be made to understand what was going to happen. He stood at the stern railing and held Edward so the men in the retreating longboat would have a good look.

"Jesus Christ," Jan said in a whisper. "He's still alive. We've *got* to go back."

But by this time there were thirty Indians at the stern of the ship. Every man in the longboat realized it would be suicide to return.

"We've got to go back!" Jan shouted. "Don't you understand! He's alive!"

Theo had been watching in horror as the Indian snatched Edward's head by the hair and held it so the face could be seen. Steadying himself against the side of the longboat, Theo raised his musket, took careful aim, and fired.

The bullet hit Edward in the chest and its impact

knocked him backward, out of the grasp of Swift Fox and onto the deck. He was dead before he hit the timbers.

Jan looked at Theo in disbelief. And then he went berserk. "You killed Ned, you bastard, you killed Ned!" he said, and began a lunge across the longboat. Aaron Gerait was too swift for him. He grabbed Jan and pushed him down to the floorboard of the longboat, and then used his weight to keep him there.

"I had to do it," Theo said. "We couldn't let them have him alive."

Jan's anger passed as quickly as it had come, and now he began to cry.

Aaron shifted his weight and helped Jan get up from the deck. He looked back at the stern of the *Lord James*. "Ned . . . I loved him," he finally said.

Theo put his face into his hands and was silently miserable.

With the longboat out of danger, Captain McGhee ordered his gunners to open fire on the hulk of the *Lord James*. More than a hundred savages were swarming over its deck when the first cannonballs ripped into them, smashing them, wounding them with flying slivers of shattered timbers, hurling bodies and bits of bodies into the air. Swift Fox's rage at being robbed of his prisoner was short lived. A cannonball created an empty space where his head had been only a fraction of a second earlier. The headless body stood there for a moment and then collapsed to the deck.

Jan and Theo went up the *Albany*'s rope ladder. They looked at one another and then embraced as they shed tears for the lost Edward Goelet. Afterward, Theo couldn't remember ever having cried before in his life.

There was no shame in his tears, only despair.

It was the last week of October 1760.

Jan sat in his office, awaiting the visitor who was due at any moment. The day of reckoning had finally come— another interesting day in a very interesting year.

The old king had died, and his grandson, George III, now sat on the throne of England. There were some men in New York who claimed his accession was only a vicious rumor, that there was nothing wrong with the old king and they were going ahead with their plans to celebrate his birthday. Jan thought they were wrong, but with communications from England being the way they were, who could be sure?

General Wolfe had taken Quebec the previous fall and died in the battle; the loss was a tragedy to all who had known and admired him. But even with the general dead, his army had proceeded down the St. Lawrence River and captured Montreal. Not long afterward the report reached New York that Canada had officially surrendered on September 6 of this year. For two days and nights New York had been the scene of one gigantic, uproarious party. Because the English and the French were still at each other's throats in the Old World, a treaty had yet to be signed in Europe; but peace had come to North America. The only people who weren't pleased were the war profiteers who had grown rich and would have liked to grow richer still.

The de Kuyper family hadn't made a penny from the war. On the contrary: they had spent enormous sums in the English cause. Now that peace had finally come, they were looking forward to recouping their losses through an increase in honest trade.

There had been a tragedy in the family. Dora Goelet, on hearing of Edward's death, had rushed to the house of Pastor Gideon Turnbull and thereafter had walked around with a new glow in her eyes. For the past year she had become a distinct embarrassment to her family, but no one could think of anything to do. And then, only a month ago, she had emerged from Turnbull's house shouting, "We are saved, we are saved!" She ran down the street and burst out into Broad Way, where she had the bad fortune to run in front of a speeding drayman's horse and cart. The horse knocked her down, and before the driver could do anything, the wheels of his loaded cart ran over her body and killed her.

The past year had also seen the establishing of Louise Clément in New York as Theo Henry's wife. There had been some problems, but not many. Although Louise was determined to be a proper wife for Theo, she had a quick temper, and when she thought she was being slighted or patronized, she let her feelings be known. The one thing she was never accused of was being dull.

Levi Seixas had gone back to sea with Amos O'Higgins, the privateer captain whom everyone knew was really a pirate. O'Higgins had cleverly used the war as an excuse for his maraudings, claiming he attacked only French ships. Because a good percentage of his victims *were* French, the English authorities chose to overlook his indiscretions; but now, with the war over, their tolerance was most likely to vanish. Jan had gone to Levi and warned him of the dangers he courted by staying with O'Higgins, but Levi had only laughed.

"I never feel as alive as I do when I'm on a quarter-deck with Amos," he said. "Better to spend one year with him and live like that than to spend thirty here on shore and die of boredom."

"The odds are against you," Jan cautioned.

"To *begin* with, my friend," Levi said, "the odds in life are eight to five against."

At first Jan was concerned, but then he stopped worrying. Levi was an intelligent man, and if this was the way he chose to live his life, who had the right to tell him otherwise? Jan was sure Levi would eventually end up on the gallows, but no doubt he would face the rope with a smile on his face. If a man had the right to choose his way of life, then most certainly he had the right to choose his way of death.

There was a knock at the door. It opened immediately, and Aaron Gerait entered. He nodded, and held the door open wide.

The Reverend Gideon Turnbull entered, forcing a smile to hide his uneasiness. "Ah, Mister de Kuyper," he said. "I understand you wanted to see me? Ah, a matter of some urgency, it was said."

Jan looked at the portly cleric from head to foot. He did not rise from his chair or do anything else to make his visitor feel welcome. Aaron closed the door, but remained in the room, leaning against the wall, his arms folded in front of him. The reverend looked nervously over his shoulder at the black man, and then back to the man behind the desk.

"I want to talk to you about Dora Goelet," Jan said quietly.

"Ah, yes, the poor woman," Turnbull said, raising his eyes to the ceiling. "A dreadful way to die. There ought to be laws about how fast these, ah, rowdies can drive their carts."

"It isn't her death that concerns me," Jan said. "It's what she did when she was alive."

"Indeed?"

"Indeed."

There was a long silence, and the reverend fidgeted. "Ah, anything in particular, Mister de Kuyper?"

Jan reached for a folder on his desk and opened it. It contained a thin sheaf of papers. He glanced at the first page and then looked up at the reverend. "She seems to have been a great believer in your ministry, or so the records would indicate."

"One of the most pious in my flock," Turnbull said. "If only there were more people like Mrs. Goelet."

"Yes, I'm sure you'd like that," Jan said dryly, looking down at the sheet of paper. "One hundred pounds in January . . . fifty pounds in March . . . seventy-five more in May . . . all that within a period of only six months. Mrs. Goelet appears to have been quite generous, wouldn't you say?"

Gideon Turnbull's face reddened. "Matters between a pastor and a member of his congregation are private affairs, sir. I can't see what business this can be of yours."

"Ah, but you see I am the executor of *Mister* Goelet's last will and testament," Jan said. "It seems he has made a provision that concerns you."

A look of relief passed across the minister's face. He had entered this office not quite knowing what to expect. Dora Goelet's death had caused him some sleepless nights. He didn't know if she had kept records of what she had given him—but if she had, it could mean some sort of scandal. His fears had heightened when the black man appeared at his door and requested this visit to the office of Jan de Kuyper. Pastor Turnbull was well aware of Dora's family connections, and aware too that these old Dutch families could be very close and—God forbid—very unforgiving.

But now, here was Jan de Kuyper telling him that he had been included in Edward Goelet's will. "This is most welcome news, sir, ah, most welcome," he said, sitting down at last. "Would it be possible for you to tell me in what way Mister Goelet has provided for my ministry?"

"That is the purpose of this meeting."

"Very good, ah, very good indeed." Gideon Turnbull's face burst into a big smile.

Jan picked up a set of papers, scanned them, flipped a few pages, then proceeded to read.

"And finally, I will unto the Reverend Gideon Turnbull his own death, in partial payment for his sins as accounted in a separate letter to my executor. Toward this end I have paid out five hundred pounds sterling to a second executor, whose identity is known to me alone . . ."

The smile had vanished and Turnbull came to his feet, knocking the chair to the floor with a crash. "What!"

"I understand the word of this offer is being disseminated on the docks and in the taverns of New York," Jan said calmly, ignoring his guest's disturbance. "I suspect there are many men in the city who would perform such a deed for a tenth of the sum."

"I'm to be *murdered?*"

"So it seems."

Reverend Turnbull smashed his fist down on Jan's desk. "This is an outrage! I'll have you in jail . . . we have laws . . . the governor himself will hear . . . you can't do this, de Kuyper!"

"*I'm* not doing anything, Reverend," Jan said mildly. "The matter has nothing to do with me. It's in the will of Edward Goelet."

"The impudence! The damned scoundrel can't do this to me!"

"What do you intend to do, put him in jail?" Jan asked, a flicker of amusement crossing his face.

"Don't be funny."

"If you could find the man with the five hundred pounds, you might be able to save yourself."

"Who is he?"

"I have no idea. That part has been kept a secret from me. Reverend, I'd say you have a nasty problem on your hands. By nightfall there will be fifty footpads and wharf rats out to win that money."

"They can't do this to me. I'll get protection. The governor will send troops . . . they'll stay with me . . ."

"For the rest of your life?"

Gideon Turnbull had a sudden vision of what his future would be like: hiding in his house in terror; going

out only when accompanied by armed guards; afraid to
stand up in his own pulpit for fear of being shot. Good
God! It would be a nightmare.

"There is a way out," Jan said, offering the first glim-
mer of hope.

"What's that?" Turnbull asked hoarsely.

"Get out of the city. Leave America and go back to
Europe. Assume another identity and another life."

"That means giving up everything I've worked for!"

"Then stay here," Jan said curtly, "and enjoy what
you've accumulated—for the few days you may have
left."

The minister leaned on the desk. Then he picked up
the fallen chair and sat down heavily on it. There was an
expression of hopelessness on his face.

"But even if I try to leave," he said, "they might get
me before I have time to get everything together. I have
so many wonderful possessions—"

"What are you talking about?" Jan said sarcastically.
"I'm discussing a way to save your life, and you're worrying about packing your furniture. Stay around long
enough to do that and you won't need any chairs and tables."

"Leave all of my things?" the minister asked, with almost as much horror as he had expressed when he
learned he was going to be murdered.

"Yes."

"But how do I leave?"

"Fortunately, I know of a way for you to save yourself.
I want you to know I'm not doing it out of compassion. I
think you're a greedy bloodsucker and a disgrace as a
man. But I'd prefer not to have your blood on my late
cousin's hands. Because of this I'm willing to give you the
solution to your problem."

"What is it?"

"There's a ship leaving New York within the hour. The
captain has been paid to take you and protect you. At
this moment it's the one place on God's earth where you'll
be safe. Now, do you accept the offer, or not?"

"But you must understand . . . this is so sudden . . . I
need time."

"You have exactly ten seconds to make up your mind."

There was a brief pause. "Yes, I accept; yes, I must . . ."

Jan stood up and came around the desk. "Mr. Gerait will take you direct to the ship," he said, gesturing toward Aaron, who had moved to the door.

"Can't I even stop at my house?"

"The ship leaves within the hour."

"But there are some things I need."

"Prayer books, no doubt."

"Yes, yes, prayer books. And some other things."

"Mister Gerait," Jan said. "Take the reverend to his house first. But only for a few minutes."

"This is the only way?" the minister said pleadingly.

"The only way."

Turnbull gave up. He shuffled toward the door, his shoulders hunched forward, his head down. Aaron let him exit first, then looked back at Jan and winked.

The door was closed and Gideon Turnbull was gone.

Jan went over to the sideboard and poured himself a drink. He held the goblet up and made a mock toast. "Good luck Reverend Turnbull, good luck to you and your new shipmates."

He went back to the desk and picked up the file that held the damning evidence. Well, he thought, Gideon Turnbull has had his fun, and now he's about to pay the price.

Once aboard Amos O'Higgins's ship, he would be taken below and hidden until the ship cleared the harbor.

O'Higgins was sailing down to the Caribbean—ostensibly to continue as a privateer, but the end of the war had greatly reduced the legitimate quarry for such a ship. Levi Seixas had assured Jan that O'Higgins would turn pirate.

"And you're still going with him?" Jan had asked.

"Of course."

"You're out of your mind."

"Of course," Levi had agreed again.

But this exchange had given Jan the idea of how to get revenge for Edward Goelet. Once Gideon Turnbull was aboard the ship and it turned pirate, the ports of civilized men everywhere would be closed to him. He would be considered a pirate—which, in Jan's estimation, was exactly what he was—and hanged if he ever showed up in New York, or in any other city in America or Europe where O'Higgins was known. Somewhere, someday, no doubt Turnbull *would* be captured along with his shipmates. Oh, the good reverend would fuss and fume and complain bitterly about what had happened; only no one would believe him. He would be dragged off to a gallows.

The best part of the plan was that Edward had left no last will and testament. There was no five-hundred-pound reward, and never had been. No one was out to murder Turnbull. All this had been Jan's invention. But the Reverend Gideon Turnbull didn't know that.

Jan raised the goblet again and silently toasted Edward Goelet.

It was late in November when the first snow fell on New York, and Jan was heading home with six-year-old Andrew. He had taken his son down to the docks to inspect the cargo of a ship newly arrived from Europe, and the little boy's mind was filled with the wonders he had seen.

They rounded the corner and came onto Maiden Lane. The soft white powder was falling heavily now; the short dusk was ending and the darkness of night enveloping the city. The lamplighters were out, and the wicks looked cheery and warm as they blazed amid the swirling white.

Two men of business passed, so intent in their conversation that they noticed neither the other people in the street nor the white mounds that were building up on their shoulders and on the tops of their hats.

A carriage drawn by a steaming horse rattled by, the wheels drawing straight lines through the snow. The edges of the lines were hard and brittle where the snow was tightly packed, but soon they would be filled with new snow and disappear.

The man walked with the boy's hand in his own, and they both enjoyed the silence that descended upon the city with the snow. They could hear noises, but the sounds were muffled and seemed to be coming from faraway places. A dog barked, but instead of the usual racket, it seemed a pleasant sound.

"Your mother isn't going to be happy that we're so late," Jan said. "We have guests for dinner."

Andrew made a sour face. Dinner guests meant he wouldn't eat dinner with his father tonight, nor would his mother tell him the usual bedtime story. But he pretended not to care. "Can I go down to the docks when the next ship comes in?"

"Maybe," Jan said. "As long as it doesn't interfere with your lessons."

"They're not as much fun."

"But right now they're more important. A man must learn many lessons well if he's to command a ship."

This was a new prospect for young Andrew to consider, but in a few moments his fertile mind had grasped what his father was saying. "If I study hard and learn to read and write, will you give *me* a ship? Can I be the captain?"

Jan laughed. "All in good time, but you may have to wait a few more years for that to happen," he said. Then he noticed the crestfallen look on his son's face. But if you study hard and do well at your lessons, I'll let you go on a short voyage in, let's say, two more years—when you're eight."

The boy squeezed the man's hand. "Oh, thank you, Father," he said, and then another question popped into his mind. "Where will the voyage be going?"

They had come to the iron railing in front of their house. Jan reached down and picked the boy up in his arms and held him out in front of him. "Let's keep it a surprise until the time comes."

A gleam of happiness came over the boy's face. "A surprise!" And then the smile was replaced by a frown. "But I want to know *now*."

Jan put the boy back on the ground and went to the door. Only six years old, and yet the little imp was learning to think for himself. In a few years he'll be nobody's fool.

They entered the house and stamped the snow from their boots as they unwound their scarfs and took off their heavy coats.

"You're late," sixteen-year-old Celine announced from the parlor door. She had her most aristocratic air about her; the transition from girl to woman was almost complete.

"Pooh on you," Andrew said, and stuck out his tongue at his sister.

"None of that," Jan said, giving him a playful slap on the side of the head.

"But she's always so bossy," Andrew protested, maintaining a hurt dignity as he looked up at his father.

"That's what big sisters are for," Jan said, realizing it was a specious argument, but one that a six-year-old boy would probably accept.

"Come along," Celine said. "Your dinner is waiting in the kitchen."

Andrew looked up at his father in a last appeal, but the stern face he saw informed him it would be a waste of time to argue. "Aw," he grumbled, and walked toward the kitchen, shrugging off his sister's hand as she tried to place it on his shoulder.

Celine turned her blond head. "Mother's upstairs getting dressed," she said, and pointedly looked down at the bottom of Jan's trousers, which were soaked from snow. "Perhaps you should do the same, Father."

Jan chuckled and went toward the main staircase. Celine was turning into a master-at-arms around the house. In another year she'd probably be running it. Thank God she was at an age when boys would become important to her; they would give her something else to think about.

Jan changed his clothes in his bedroom and listened for a few moments, while Marie Therese lectured him about how impolite it was to arrive home at the same time as the guests were expected.

"It's not very considerate," she concluded.

Jan finished putting on his boots. He stood up, grabbed his wife, and kissed her. His hands played with the naked skin of her shoulders, and when he stepped back he could see that she had enjoyed it.

"You're lucky I don't forget about the guests altogether and take you to bed, woman."

"There's only one reason I put up with your craziness."

"What's that?"

She smiled. "I love you."

He reached out and touched her chin. "Same here."

She moved her chin sensuously against the hand. "It hasn't been all that bad, has it."

His fingers began to press into the flesh of her shoulders, but she squirmed out of his grasp. "Save those ideas for later. Right now I've got to get to the kitchen to make sure dinner is ready."

She left the room, and Jan looked at himself in the mirror. Not bad for a fifty-five-year-old man, he thought. And then he pictured the slender form of his wife at his side. And she's had a lot to do with keeping me young. And making me happy, and giving me the best part of my life.

The first guests had already arrived when he came downstairs. Theo and Louise Henry were being offered drinks by a black manservant. He was a freeman, as were the other servants. The de Kuypers kept no slaves.

As Jan chatted with a guest about the recent events of the city, he found himself stealing glances at Louise Henry, who had just arrived with Theo. Louise was a beautiful woman. Her clothes were in the latest style, and not a hair on her sleek head was out of place. It was hard to imagine that only a year and a half ago she had been a half-breed serving girl at her father's inn in the wilds of Canada.

It was good to see Theo so happy, Jan thought. He had always been too serious, too involved in his work to take time for anything else. But now Louise had brought another dimension to his life. He was a better man for it.

David de Witt Sackett arrived with his wife, Mary. The lawyer was now thirty-four years old and a great asset to the family's interests in dealing with the bankers and shippers of London. As a young man he had been steered into the study of law by Jan; never had one of his hunches paid off better than that one.

James and Hope de Kuyper arrived. Both faces had turned a healthy red during the boat trip down the East River from the manor. The couple started out that morning and were planning to spend several days with Jan and his family.

"I was beginning to worry about you," Jan said, placing a goblet of warmed rum in his father's hands.

"Takes more than a little snow to stop a pair of farmers like Hope and myself," James said. Then he noticed Louise Henry talking with Mary Sackett. He excused himself and walked across the room.

"My dears," he said, and kissed the ladies' hands. "How lovely you both look this evening."

Louise's gracious smile suggested she had spent her whole life having her hand kissed.

Jan watched them and realized his father was always extremely courtly with Louise Henry. Very few men would understand that despite the coolness she affected, Louise was still not all that comfortable in this society. Having James de Kuyper treat her as he did bolstered her self-confidence.

A few minutes later the last guest arrived. He came alone and was the only person in the room who wasn't, in one way or another, a member of the de Kuyper family. He was Colonel George Washington, twenty-eight years old and dressed in a well-tailored uniform.

Jan introduced the colonel to the others, and the man's Virginia manners immediately began to win the ladies to his side. The soft southern accent, although not a great rarity in New York, was hardly the common speech of the street.

"I've been especially anxious for you two to meet," Jan said, as he brought the colonel and his father together.

"I have heard of you, sir," Colonel Washington said. "No man in this city has a wider reputation."

James chuckled. "Knowing what goes on in this city, I'm not sure that's a compliment."

"You'll get nowhere using flattery on my father," Jan said. "Only if you flatter his horses."

Colonel Washington's eyes seemed to light up. "You are interested in horses, sir?"

James nodded. "I've spent most of my life trying to breed stronger workhorses."

"That's the kind of idea I used to have myself," the colonel said, and then added a bit wistfully, "unfortunately, I've been involved in other matters for the past few years."

"The name George Washington—and his exploits— has not gone unnoticed in New York," James said. "But now perhaps you'll have more time for your horses."

Jan noticed that Washington's eyes were on the staircase, and he glanced up to see what had diverted his attention.

A beautiful young woman in a white dress, her long blond hair coiled becomingly atop her head, was daintily making her way downstairs, one slender arm tracing the curve of the banister as she descended.

Jan was startled. For a brief moment he hadn't realized it was his own daughter. And then he remembered that Celine had been given permission to attend this dinner; for the first time in her life she was being accorded full adult status.

God, she's beautiful, Jan thought; the reincarnation of Marie Therese. Another marker in my life, he thought. Now I am the father of a woman. And what a woman she was turning out to be!

He walked to the bottom of the staircase and held out his hand. Celine took it with an easy grace, smiled, and let her father lead her back to Colonel Washington. As he did so, he realized that everyone in the room was looking at the girl.

"Colonel Washington, may I present my daughter, Celine de Kuyper. Celine, this is Colonel George Washington."

The girl held out her hand. George Washington bowed and kissed it. "I'm delighted to meet you, Colonel Washington," she said. "Your fame precedes you."

Jan wondered what had happened to the giggling little creature of yesterday. Not too long ago, Celine would have asked the colonel if he had any candy in his pocket. He smiled, knowing those days were gone forever.

James's look, however, was stern. "Now don't try to tell me that you're Celine, young woman. Go find her and tell her that her old grandpa is here and would like to see her."

Celine blushed, and a trace of girlishness returned to her manner. "Oh, Grandfather, don't tease."

James leaned forward and kissed her on the cheek. "You are absolutely correct. A man should never tease a beautiful woman."

She blushed again, but this time she fluttered her eyelashes, as her gaze came up to meet Colonel Washington's.

There was a fascinated spectator to the proceedings. Andrew had left his bed and was crouched at the top of the staircase, peering down through the slats of the banister rail. From his semidarkened perch he could see a portion of the brilliantly lit parlor.

He had hoped to catch a glimpse of a sea captain, but to his disappointment the guests were the same old people he saw all the time. There was one strange man in a uniform with shiny buttons, but Andrew had seen enough such uniforms to know that the man was just a soldier. Not a sea captain was to be seen.

He wondered why his father didn't have any sea captains at his party. Maybe it was because they were too large and rough. His mother wouldn't like to have them in her house. And stinky Celine! He could just see her turning her nose up at them—like she did with everything else. There she was now, talking to that soldier, pretending she was grown up. He stuck his tongue out at his sister.

Andrew decided that when *he* grew up he was going to have lots of parties, and invite no one but sea captains. And Celine. He bubbled with joy at the thought of forcing her to spend an entire evening in a room full of the tough, gruff men. It was wonderful. He stuck his tongue out again.

And then his dream vanished. "And just what do you think you're doing, boy?" the voice of the Scots nanny asked. "You get back to bed," she commanded.

Andrew went to his bed and was asleep in a minute, his dreams filled with proud ships.

In the parlor a manservant announced that dinner was being served, and everyone moved into the dining room. Jan sat at one end of the table, Marie Therese at the other. Colonel Washington escorted Celine and sat beside her. Jan had been careful to place his father opposite the colonel.

After the dinner had progressed through a soup course and a delectable dish of pan-fried salmon, Jan took the opportunity to welcome Colonel Washington to his home. "You may notice," he said, "that you're the only nonfamily member here. I had hoped to hear your views about our present situation in an atmosphere that would allow you to speak your mind."

"*My* views?"

"Yes. I promise that anything you say will go no further than this table."

The colonel cleared his throat. "I'm not quite sure what you have in mind," he said. "I have views of many subjects, although, as I've been told many times, most of them are incorrect. Is it your plan, Mister de Kuyper, to force me to expose the wrong sides of the issues of our times?"

There was a smattering of polite laughter. "To be more specific, Colonel, I would like to hear what you, and my father, have to say about the future of our colony. I suspect your views will be quite different."

"I would say our future is quite bright," Colonel Washington said.

"Yes," James said. "So where do we differ?"

"Colonel Washington," Jan said, "you support the colonialist point of view. My father is a royalist. Not too many years ago those positions were almost identical. The goal of both was to build the provinces and amass wealth under a kind and benevolent king. But recent events, including the war with the French have created a gulf between the colonialist and the royalist."

The room was absolutely still as Jan defined the problem that everyone knew was becoming the burning issue of the day. "For example," he continued, "the British government expects the colonies to cover most of the expenses of the recent war. What do you think about that, Colonel?"

"Certainly we should do our share. After all, it was our war as well as theirs."

"Interesting that you make a distinction—ours and theirs. What do you say to that, Father?" Jan asked.

"I disagree that such a distinction should be made. We are one people."

"Granted we are members of the same family," Colonel Washington said. "But members of the same family should share the same rights."

"Are you suggesting there are differences?" James asked.

Jan sat back, resting his goblet of wine at the edge of the table. His eye caught the manservant's, and signaled that the serving of food should cease. He wanted to hear the debate without distraction.

His father had been born in an English colony. He thought of himself as English, of his country as an English possession, of the English king as his own sovereign. George Washington, on the other hand, was one of the new breed: an outspoken colonialist who considered the New World his home and believed that ties to Europe should be maintained only if they were beneficial to both parties.

"Yes, there are differences," Washington said. "The laws favor the people in England over the people in America."

"How so?"

"This recent war was not of our doing, but merely an extension of the one that's been going on in Europe—on and off for the past hundred years."

"But this time we ourselves had much to lose. Our homes and businesses, for starters."

"Perhaps," Washington said. "But now we are being asked to pay more than our share. The king treats us as if we were children in a small outpost, when, in truth, we are one and three quarters of a million people."

"We have our own bodies of lawmakers. Their words are heard in London," James said.

"When it pleases London. When they are being honest, they admit they don't consider us fit to chart our own destiny."

"You would have us break away and become independent?"

Washington shook his head. "We may not have to go that far. I simply want London to recognize the reality of the situation—that what should exist is an Atlantic Empire of equals."

"But we *are* equal," James protested. "If you moved to England tomorrow, you could do so with full English citizenship. You could start a business, get married, and do anything else that a man born in London could do. And so could I."

"True enough," the Colonel admitted. "But to gain that equality you would have to move to England. As long as you remain here, you are not equal. But how *can* you be when England's exports to us are worth over a million pounds sterling more than the goods we ship to them?"

"The dictates of the market, sir. They obviously need less of our goods than we do of theirs."

Colonel Washington smiled. "I doubt if you really believe that, sir. The truth is, they force us to buy their goods. But, for a moment, forget our exports to England. Tell me, why is it we are not allowed to sell our goods direct to the nations on the continent? Why must we, *by law*, pass them through English middlemen, who take a profit for doing nothing?"

"Those middlemen in London know the European markets better than we do."

"Yes, but only because we haven't been allowed to find out about them for ourselves. What justification can you make for the fact that a portion of our profits lines the pockets of men in England?"

It was a tough question, and everyone waited for James to give his answer. Instead, he asked a question. "Would you agree that a nation creates colonies to increase its own wealth and power?"

"Yes, I will agree to that."

"Philosophically then," James said, carefully choosing his words, "the raison d'être of a colony is to contribute to the economic well-being of the mother country."

"I concede the point," Washington replied. "And raise another one. When does a colony grow large enough to cease being a colony and become a sovereign nation in its own right?"

"Since it is a question that has rarely arisen before, I don't know if any man can answer it. But do you think it fair for a colony to accept help for a hundred years, to use this help to build its own wealth, and then, because it seems convenient at the time, to turn its back on the mother country that made it all possible?"

"No, I do not. But I'm not suggesting that we turn our backs on England. I *am* asking for fair treatment and equality in our economy."

"The economy of a colony must be complementary, not competitive with the mother country."

"Yes, and look at what happens under such conditions," Washington said. "We cannot export our wool or woolen goods, or beaver pelts and beaver hats except to England. Our fish and other provisions must go to English colonies in the West Indies even though we could sell

them at higher prices to the Spaniards, the Dutch, or almost anyone else. We must buy our sugar and molasses
from the same colonies, although the French would sell
us the same quality for less. We are, sir, a captive
market for English goods, and a second-class captive at
that. The mercantile laws of England are making the
mother country wealthy, and ourselves poor. It is an in-
tolerable situation."

"Poor?" James asked with a slight smile. "By what
standards are we poor? Our people are well fed and at
work. The trouble is, we are becoming too greedy to part
with even a small share of our wealth to help support the
Crown, which, no matter what you think, has been responsible for allowing us more liberty than any other
government in the history of mankind."

"Perhaps that is true when compared to the past, but
I am saying we must look to the future and turn our
backs on the ways of oppression."

"Are we oppressed?"

"Aren't the new laws the epitome of oppression? English
officials are now allowed to search our homes for
smuggled goods—without an order of the court, without
prior warning, and at any hour of the day or night. Do
you consider yourself a free man when you are forced to
live under such conditions?"

"Not particularly," James admitted. "But if they are
bad laws, they will be changed."

"Perhaps, but in the meantime honest people suffer.
Take your own family, Mister de Kuyper. You provided
ships during the war without cost."

"We were pleased to do so."

"Granted. But now that the war is over, why aren't
you permitted to recoup your losses by trading with countries where you can make the most profits? Why must
you deal only with England and English possessions in a
way that skims the cream off your profits?"

"Because it is the law for the common good, and it
must be respected."

"The only thing I respect is law by consent of the governed," Washington said testily.

"Who can say if we are really ready to govern ourselves, Colonel Washington? The few examples that have
occurred in our wilderness areas were attempts that

ended in anarchy. Is that what you propose as a substitute for our king?"

"There are workable forms of government other than those headed by a king."

"You spoke of an Atlantic Empire, and yet what is an empire without an emperor?"

"The word was only used as an expression. The empire I envision has no emperor, or king—and its future grandeur lies on this side of the ocean."

James smiled. "You argue your case well, Colonel. If I were a younger man I might become interested in your ideas. But you will, perhaps, forgive an old man who has had a good life under the present system, and who sees no cause to throw it all away. Changes and adaptations, yes—but to ignore hundreds of years of progress seems presumptuous."

The smile returned to Colonel Washington's face. "One of the functions of the young is to presume on their elders. Forgive me, sir, for acting my age."

Several people laughed, and the serious mood at the table was broken.

Jan gestured for the servants to resume serving the food. He had listened to both men and realized there was a certain amount of truth and justice on either side. One stood for the old ways, loyally, maybe even blindly; no doubt there was some prudence in adhering to what had been tested and found workable. The other stood for reforms that were probably more sweeping than any ever previously attempted—reforms that, untested as they were, might as easily bring disaster as success.

"Thank you, gentlemen," Jan said. "Perhaps we can continue the discussion at another time. I smell a good roast in the kitchen, and it would be a shame if we had to eat it cold."

James looked across the table at Colonel Washington. "I'm not saying there might not be truth in what you say, but it's one thing to ask a man to change his mind and another to ask him to change his life."

"It's not myself who's doing the asking," Colonel Washington replied. "It's the times themselves."

"Perhaps a man can fight back against another man, but it's damned impossible to fight the course of history."

"Impossible is the word," Washington said; and then,

in an attempt to lighten the mood in the room, he turned to Celine. "I suppose if we had any sense, we'd ask your opinion when we speak about the future. After all, you're the one who will inherit it."

"Yes, tell us, my dear," James said. "Do you agree with your old grandfather or the colonel?"

"I think I agree with the colonel," she said quickly.

"Yes? And why is that?"

"I overheard my father telling Uncle Theo that he had smuggled a shipload of French molasses. My father is a good man, and if he breaks the law, the law can't be very just, can it?"

Jan's face turned red, and he looked in helplessness at his daughter as both James and Colonel Washington burst into laughter.

"Caught in the act," Theo said, and joined the laughter.

Jan looked to David Sackett. "If this comes to court, can I depend on you for a sound defense?"

"I'll put Colonel Washington on the stand," the lawyer said. "He seems to have a good grasp of the arguments."

"Under the present laws, Mister Sackett," the colonel said, "what could we do to prevent Mister de Kuyper from being hauled off to jail for what he's done?"

"Nothing."

The colonel smiled and looked at James. "And that, sir, is my final argument. The defense rests."

It was many hours later that Jan finally climbed into his bed. Marie Therese was beside him. He lay quietly for a long time, his mind going over what had been said at the dinner table. While he could understand his father's position, he couldn't accept it. Colonel Washington was correct: sooner or later things would have to change. If George III understood what was happening, he would allow those changes that needed to be made. If, however, the young monarch proved not to be the open-minded king who was needed—well, things would get ugly. There were many men who thought as Washington did, and their number was increasing every day. If there was a closing of minds on both sides, it might lead to war.

War against the English king? What an unthinkable idea! And yet it was being pondered by more and more men. For a hundred years now, the English flag had flown over New York, and the city had prospered. But they were entering a new phase, and the crumbs from the king's table that had once delighted the colonists were proving to be not enough for men who wanted a feast.

"Stop thinking about all those troublesome ideas," Marie Therese said.

"They are troublesome," Jan admitted. "The more troublesome when you think of how far apart are men like my father and Colonel Washington. If either was a wild-eyed fanatic it would be easy to dismiss him. But both are very reasonable men."

She reached across under the heavy covers and found his hand. "And yourself?"

"The more reasonable I think I am, the less sure I become of myself."

"*I'm* sure of you," Marie Therese said. "You can always count on that."

He brought her hand to his lips and kissed each finger. Then he held it close to his cheek. No matter what happened in the world outside, there would always be the sanctuary of the love he shared with his wife.

They both understood this, and found no need to speak of it.

Aaron Gerait came up from the cellar of the theater on Maiden Lane. Once a month he satisfied himself that the hiding place of Captain Kidd's fortune was secure. It was buried deep in the ground, because there didn't seem to be any compelling need for it.

He wondered when it would be called upon again. Under what circumstances? And for what use? And would he even be alive then?

It amused him to think of all that wealth buried beneath the old theater. Everybody in this city running around trying to make money, he thought, and this fortune sits right there beneath their feet.

He stopped at a tavern he frequented. The bartender nodded in recognition and poured a tankard of ale. "What are you up to?" he asked as he placed the foaming brew before his customer.

"Just coming from inspecting my stash of buried treasure," Aaron said.

The bartender grinned. "Yeah, I have one of those, too," he said.

"Doesn't everybody?" Aaron said, and brought the tankard to his lips.

The new year of 1761 was four days old.

The early morning air was cold, the sky a heavy and forbidding gray. James de Kuyper and his grandson, Andrew, left the snug manor house and tramped across dazzling snow, leaving the imprints of their boots as they went down the road toward the shoreline bordering Long Island Sound.

The boy stopped to make a snowball; the man puffed on his pipe. Andrew packed the frozen crystals together, the warmth of his hands coming through his mittens to melt them slightly, the better to form a solid sphere. He spotted a crow standing on the leafless limb of a nearby tree. With all the strength he could muster, he cocked his arm and threw the snowball. It fell far short of the mark, but created enough disturbance to cause the crow to voice his disapproval as he took to the air.

"Missed," Andrew said, as if it had been a close thing. "I'll get him next time."

James solemnly agreed. He took the little boy's hand, and they continued along the road, their feet tramping down the snow, leaving a clear trail behind them.

"Father said I can be a sea captain when I grow up," Andrew announced proudly.

"And when will that be?"

The little boy's brow tightened into a frown. "When I'm eight," he finally said.

"Yes, eight is a good age to be a sea captain," James said. "I wasn't as smart as you, I guess, because I didn't go to sea until I was fifteen."

"You were a sea captain, Grandpa?" Andrew said, his eyes becoming wider.

James began telling his grandson about his days at sea, omitting that he had been aboard a pirate ship with the notorious Captain Kidd. He told of the vastness of the great oceans, and of the fabled lands that existed many thousands of miles away. He spoke of the world of a sailor, and to Andrew it all seemed like a wonderful fairy-land where dreams came true.

"The seas were splendid, shining seas, and every morning I'd watch the sun come up at the edge of the earth, a glorious red ball bringing light and heat back to the world," James said. "And the lands we visited had houses of gold and silver, and strange birds that could speak like men. There were huge gray animals, many times larger than horses, and small brown men rode on their backs, poking them with sticks to tell them where to go.

"There were women who wore bells on their toes and silver rings in their ears; and men with slippers that curved into circles at the ends, and they carried swords whose hilts were studded with diamonds, rubies, and emeralds.

"It was so long ago, and yet I can close my eyes and see it all as if it happened only yesterday. I was a young lad and the whole world was spread out before me like a giant carpet that went on and on as far as I could see."

"That's what I'm going to do," Andrew said firmly. "I'm going to sail around the world and be just like you, Grandpa."

James smiled and helped the boy climb over a fallen tree trunk as they came to the frozen shoreline. They saw the white sails of a ship far out in the middle of the sound. Was it the beginning of a voyage, or the end of one? James wondered.

He stopped by a large boulder and leaned his back against it as he took pleasure in his pipe, the blue smoke curling upward into the air. He looked at the smooth, rosy cheeks of his grandson and compared them to his own. The beginning of a voyage . . .

"Why aren't you a sea captain now, Grandpa?" the little boy asked.

"There were other things I had to do."

"What things?"

"Oh, lots of things, like starting a family and building the farm. As you grow older, you'll find out."

"When I'm a sea captain, I won't change for anything."

"That may be true, but you'll have to wait a few years to see what happens."

The boy's attention was diverted by a pair of squirrels. The two furry gray animals were scampering near the trees by the shoreline, chasing each other's tails, enjoying a romp in the snow as they made the rounds of their domain. They looked sleek and fat, having been prudent, in the way of squirrels, to store up a supply of food sufficient for the winter.

Andrew moved slowly toward the squirrels in boyish imitation of a hunter. and James watched with grandfatherly affection.

A sea captain. And what little boy didn't want to be a sea captain? To go off, away from adult restrictions; to be on one's own and free—the dream of every little boy in every age and every place.

And men are not so different, he knew. Since the evening he had spent at Jan's house with Colonel Washington, James had thought often and deeply about the future. Not his own future—he was wise enough to understand that a man his age would see no new horizons—no, not a personal future, but the future he would experience through the descendants he left in this beloved land.

To be free: wasn't that what Washington was talking about? Like a boy anxious to break away from his mother's apron strings, the men of America were pulling away from the tethers that bound them to England and the king. He couldn't bring himself to accept their beliefs, but he was beginning to understand something of the forces that were urging them on.

James had been born in New York when being English was a relative novelty. Jacob Adam, his own father, born in New York, had never thought of himself as English. *His* father, Pieter, was a Dutchman who had never accepted English sovereignty. But Jacob Adam had been, above all, a practical man. The flag that flew over the fort at the tip of the island had been of little concern to him as long as the ruling powers left him to pursue his business interests.

With James it had been different. He had been brought up to admire the king and respect him. He loved the king, even though he had never seen him, and never would. The king was *his* king, whether it was old George II, who had died last year, or his grandson, who now held sway over the Court of St. James. The man didn't matter; it was the idea.

But now there were other voices rising in the land, and

there was nothing one could do but accept them: the voices of men like George Washington, and Benjamin Franklin, and Sam Adams in Boston; and—yes, he must admit it to himself—the voice of his own son. Jan hadn't fooled him that night in November. He had used Colonel Washington to state his own position.

James looked at his grandson. Here was the inheritor of the new ideas. For the time being, he was a little boy whose head was empty of such thoughts. But in a few years, as the boy grew and his mind matured, he would set about changing the order of things.

And I will be gone and forgotten—an old painting on the wall, cracking and peeling, representing a way of life that no longer existed except in memories.

James had no regrets. Life had been kinder to him than to most. There had been the girl who had been the love of his youth, Jan's mother, now long in her grave. There had been his own mother. There was Jan, and his family. There was Hope, who had come to him late in life, and who had added a loving softness to his waning years. There were the friends he had come to cherish, the places he had come to love, and the things he had done to make New York a better place.

His days. His work. The times of happiness outweighed the times of sadness. God had placed him on the balance scales of life and had given him more than a fair share.

He remembered his mother telling him, as a little boy no older than Andrew, of the shooting star that had terrorized New York not long before his birth. And that shooting star—or comet, as it was now called—had returned to blaze across the sky only a little over a year ago. The English royal astronomer, Edmund Halley, had predicted its return, and so it had been named after him. But, James thought, smiling at his own vanity, it could just as easily have been named after me, since it heralded my arrival in the world, even as it predicts my departure.

Now his spirit would continue, represented in the flesh and blood of the little boy who was vainly trying to surprise the playing squirrels. Andrew was six years old. How many more years would he have to chase after things? Sixty? Seventy? And then will he be like me, an old man standing in the winter snows of his own life, puffing on his pipe, content to know that most of what he would be called upon to do had been done?

The years the little boy had before him! The years would be his and his alone—to use to the fullest or to throw away; to turn into gold or tramp into mud. James silently willed his grandson to look up and see the stars, to see the breath of God in the miracle of life.

The boy returned from his fruitless hunt. "Those squirrels are too fast," he complained. "But there will be more," he added optimistically.

James eyes misted over as he reached out and touched the slender shoulder. "Yes, young Andrew, there will be more. Many more."

The sky pressed down to the earth and the snow of a new storm began to drop gently to the ground.

The old man took his grandson's hand in his own, and they started back toward the manor and its warming fire. They walked up the snow-covered road as the white curtain thickened. From the boulder where James had rested, two figures could be seen for a time; then the snow swallowed them and they became silhouettes, ghosts, and were gone.

The earth was burying itself, resting in preparation for the time when it would be born again.

There was a stillness.

Two sets of footprints, one large and one small, marked a trail to infinity.

The snow continued to fall.

A Tale of Lovers and Dreamers,
Scoundrels and Rogues, Long Ago,
on an Island Called Manhattan . . .

FROM DISTANT SHORES

The Novel of New York 1613-1667

BRUCE NICOLAYSEN

Book I in a Five-Book Series
that throbs with all the passion,
danger and excitement of a mighty land . . .

The deKuypers were courageous Dutch settlers who came
from distant shores to carve a place for themselves in the
settlement called New Amsterdam. There was Pieter, ex-
plorer, builder and whaler; Christiana, his bride, brave because she had to be; Young Pieter and Anne, their eldest
children; and Jacob Adam, the bastard son who would
usher in a ruthless new breed of empire builders on the
long island . . .

75424 . . . $2.50

**Parted by war,
driven from their Highlands home,
they were reunited in the forging
of a great New World.**

KANATA

DENNIS ADAIR AND | BOOK I: THE STORY OF CANADA | JANET ROSENSTOCK

Janet Cameron and Mathew MacLeod, separated by Scotland's tragic Battle of Culloden in 1746, escape to the New World. Each will suffer bitter heartbreak . . . and survive the unforeseen dangers of a savage wilderness. And when Mathew and Janet finally find each other again, they pledge their hearts and future to the glorious dream that is Kanata.

The Story of Canada is the magnificent series of the lives, loves, births and deaths, of three immigrant families who dare to carve a nation out of a savage wilderness. Spanning ten generations, it follows these proud people from the fall of the Scottish throne to the triumph of Canada's industrial giants!

77826 . . . $2.95

Coming soon: BITTER SHIELD, Volume II in
The Story of Canada